THE PORTABLE

MALCOLM
COWLEY

THE PORTABLE

MALCOLM COWLEY

*Edited, with an
Introduction and Notes,
by Donald W. Faulkner*

VIKING

VIKING
Published by the Penguin Group
Viking Penguin, a division of Penguin Books USA Inc.,
40 West 23rd Street, New York, New York 10010, U.S.A.
Penguin Books Ltd, 27 Wrights Lane,
London W8 5TZ, England
Penguin Books Australia Ltd, Ringwood,
Victoria, Australia
Penguin Books Canada Ltd, 2801 John Street,
Markham, Ontario, Canada L3R 1B4
Penguin Books (N.Z.) Ltd, 182–190 Wairau Road,
Auckland 10, New Zealand

Penguin Books Ltd, Registered Offices:
Harmondsworth, Middlesex, England

First published in 1990 by Viking Penguin,
a division of Penguin Books USA Inc.

1 3 5 7 9 10 8 6 4 2

LIBRARY OF CONGRESS CATALOGING IN PUBLICATION DATA
Cowley, Malcolm, 1898–1989
The portable Malcolm Cowley / edited, with an introduction and
notes, by Donald W. Faulkner.
p.   cm.
Includes bibliographical references.
ISBN 0-670-82721-5
I. Faulkner, Donald W.   II. Title.
PS3505.O956A6   1990
811'.54—dc20   89-40319

Printed in the United States of America

CONTENTS

PART THREE: POETRY: SELECTIONS FROM
BLUE JUNIATA: A LIFE

PART FOUR: A BRIEF SELECTION OF
           CORRESPONDENCE (1917–1961)

PART FIVE: ON WRITERS AND WRITING

EDITOR'S INTRODUCTION

In March of 1989 Malcolm Cowley, age ninety, joined what he himself once called "the great dead." Cowley had spent seventy of those years in the writing trade as a critic, poet, editor, translator, teacher, memoirist, and literary historian. His accomplishments were great.

It was noted by eulogizers that he was America's last great "man of letters," a term which Cowley, while living, felt had embalmed him prematurely.

Others said the following:

—that he secured our sense of the "Lost Generation" writers in books such as *Exile's Return* and *A Second Flowering*.

—that he was one of the great memoirists of our time, and that his autobiography is itself a history of American letters in the twentieth century.

—that he, with his peer, Edmund Wilson, was the great "public critic" of American writing for our century.

—that he was a shaper of what has come to be called "the American canon."

—that he resurrected William Faulkner's reputation from the ash heap of history.

—that he launched the careers of many writers, among them John Cheever, Jack Kerouac, and Ken Kesey.

—that he was one of the best editors in American publishing.

—that he was a teacher of genius whose genius inspired his students to greatness.

—that as a letter writer he was a binding force that kept America's many literary fiefdoms part of a larger republic of letters.

—that he was one of the significant minor poets of the American twentieth century.

Cowley would have been reticent to claim any of these praises. "The mantle," he once said, "is too large." His aims, as he wrote, were simply "to celebrate American literature and to defend American writers as a community within a larger community."

2. A LIFE, IN PART

Malcolm Cowley was born in a thunderstorm, on 24 August 1898, in a farmhouse near Belsano, Pennsylvania, in Blacklick Township, Cambria County, where the family spent summers. A doctor was slow to arrive in birthing him. His mother was alone, save for a maiden aunt who hid in a closet through the course of the storm. Cowley was an only child, and though he spent long summers in Belsano often keeping his own company, he was raised largely in Pittsburgh, where he attended school. He was the son of William Cowley, a homeopathic physician who was also a Swedenborgian, a member of a religious sect not completely uncommon among the German-rooted settlers of western Pennsylvania. William Cowley attended to middle- and lower-class families in the East Liberty section of Pittsburgh and never made much money. The Cambria County farmhouse, some sixty miles east of Pittsburgh, was not a summer retreat for the wealthy. Cowley's mother, Josephine, raised chickens there for food and extra cash.

For Cowley Cambria County was a place where a boy could be as "free as a weaned colt in an unfenced pasture," a place without restrictions and not unlike those in the visions put forth by American writers of the nineteenth century. Cowley often wrote of that region with an elegiac sense in his poetry. Recalling his youth Cowley would later note of his involvement with Southern writers such as Allen Tate and Robert Penn Warren that the line between North and South was transected by another, more rigid, the line of the Allegheny Mountains, part of the Appalachian range. "People from the Alleghenies," Cowley said, "can understand Tennessee people better than they can understand Virginians." There was a different sense of culture and a more parochial sense of pride. "Where I grew up in western Pennsylvania," Cowley more figuratively added on another occasion, "was not too far from the Frenchman's Bend of William Faulkner's Yoknapatawpha County."

At the age of three Cowley met the son of one of his father's patients, Kenneth Burke, who was then age four. They became fast friends, enrolled in school together and in adolescence often discussed literature and issues of immediate concern on walks home from evenings spent studying at the Carnegie Library. The thought of those walks never really left Cowley or Burke; both, fledgling writers, carried their colloquy into a correspondence that was to last more than seventy years. Through the years Cowley grew as a writer and Burke as a philosopher. Though they shared nothing of the familial charge that unites the works of William and Henry James, they seemed to maintain a trust in the continuity of their independent efforts, as well as similar blind spots for each other's work.

The two attended Peabody High School in Pittsburgh, from which they took quite different tracks, Cowley to Harvard, Burke, after some college, to a retreat of self-teaching. At Harvard Cowley was a remarkable student. He studied French, wrote poetry, and generally basked in the light left by "the Harvard aesthetes," and people like Eliot, Cummings, Dos Passos, Robert Hillyer, and Conrad Aiken, who had all attended Harvard shortly before him. In Cambridge he attended Amy Lowell's soirees and, as would any undergraduate, was enthralled by her cigar smoking and her acerbic wit.

But the Harvard of Cowley's time rarely offered a course on American literature. Moreover, it seldom offered any perspective on the life and culture of the city and the nation that surrounded it. As Cowley wrote of those days in *Exile's Return*, "On Brattle Street, in Cambridge, Longfellow's house was open to the public, and I might have visited Brook Farm. All these things, Emerson, doorways, factory hands and fortunes . . . were bound together into one civilization, but of this I received no hint. I was studying Goethe's *Dichtung und Wahrheit* and the Elizabethan drama, and perhaps, on my way to classes in the morning, passing a Catholic church outside of which two Irish boys stood and looked at me with unfriendly eyes."

In 1917, like many of his classmates, he dropped out of college to head to France to drive an ambulance in the war. He ended up driving munitions trucks instead. But he saw Paris and was energized by it. He returned to America, went to Greenwich Village to live with a painter named Peggy Baird, and eventually married her. Cowley went back to Harvard to finish his degree in the fall of 1919 and then, with a small gift of money and a couple of letters of introduction from his English teacher, Charles Townsend Copeland, he returned to New York to write poetry and to lead a Grub Street existence as a journalist. He wrote for *The Dial*, but he also wrote for *Charm*, a women's magazine, and *Brentano's Book Chat*, an organ for a chain of bookstores. As did other budding writers of the time he lived in a cold-water flat and painted his floors black.

Although, as Cowley's work would later confirm, the time was a period of transition between literary generations, the sensibility of a "genteel tradition" in American literature held sway. One dimension of that genteel tradition was, as Cowley would later write, "an attempt to compensate for the pettiness and provincialism of American life by creating a literature that would be cosmopolitan, weary, witty, and aristocratic—a literature that would deal for the most part with other times or countries and would approach America only in a spirit of urbane mockery and carefully mannered style. It was the tendency represented by James Branch Cabell and Joseph Hergesheimer; by Elinor Wylie in her novels. . . . They wrote stories or essays that were bejeweled and very often bewildering. . . . They wanted to prove that even Americans could be as wicked and distinguished as the Continental ironists."

In Manhattan Cowley didn't fare very well at living by his new vocation as a writer and critic for a new order. Once, while walking through Sheridan Square, he was so faint with hunger he collapsed. On another occasion Lionel Moise, a reporter for the *New York American* and a barroom roust-about, rescued Cowley when he was delirious with influenza. "He cradled me in his arms as if I were a rag doll and carried me into the hospital," Cowley wrote.

Duly chastened by the experience, Cowley took a job working as a copywriter for *Sweet's Architectural Catalogue*, where one of his fellow workers was a struggling young poet named Hart Crane. The pay at *Sweet's* was at least regular and could afford Cowley dinner at John Squarcialupi's Italian restaurant from time to time with friends Allen Tate, William Slater Brown, and Matthew Josephson, among others.

Although New York in the early twenties was a place for writers, the prospect Paris held was even greater. There one could live cheaply and find the means to make art. It was a way to live in exile and to yet still be among Americans, for a sizeable postwar population of expatriates lived there. Indeed, one could even look back across the sea and win some perspective. In 1921, Cowley received an American Field Service grant to study literature in France for two years. His first wife Peggy wrote to a friend: "It will be wonderful for both of us. Malcolm hasn't had any time to write since we have been married, which has worried me considerably. Now he will have two whole years."

Cowley lived in Giverny, but he spent weekends in Paris, weekends which, he wrote his friend Burke, "often last years." Cowley wrote poetry, tried his hand at fiction, and passed critical pieces back to New York. He acted as an ad hoc editor for the little magazines *Secession* and *Broom*, met fellow American expatriates such as Hemingway and Ezra Pound, and he attended—until he came to feel she was more infatuated with herself than with literature—the Thursday afternoon salons at Gertrude Stein's. He also met the Dadaists, Tristan Tzara and Louis Aragon among them, and joined ranks with them for a while. Cowley also met and befriended Paul Valéry, whose critical awareness and artistic integrity influenced him deeply. In the course of two years he had an experience that would last him a lifetime. It was rich; it was new, and was different from anything Cowley had yet encountered.

It destroyed preconceptions he'd had about the making of art and literature back in Pittsburgh and at Harvard. There "art," if one wasn't talking of Elinor Wylie (and one seldom did), seemed an act of religious piety, an end in itself. The romantic images of Byron, Shelley, or Swinburne Cowley had been fed on, images of isolation, purity, and melancholy, were replaced by the vibrancy and vitality of a confraternity of writers, writers gathering in cafes, talking all night, writers sharing their work not hiding it, writers commonly committed to respect for the craft of writing, even if they weren't too sure what they were doing.

In Paris, Cowley found himself part of both a fellowship of writers and a new literary generation. He had written to Burke: "I thank God constantly that I have crossed the water.

Not that my soul has been transformed with wonder, but just
that I have been drawn out of my fixed orbit." In trying to
weave his way through the Dadaists, through the factions of
American writers, and through ways of giving measure to his
own voice, he wrote Burke of attempting to raise "a pluralist
aesthetic," one which could maintain an abiding openness for
the new, in literature, and in culture.

Upon returning to New York Cowley wrote essays,
sketches, and poems. He supplemented his income by translating works from French authors such as Gide, Valéry, and
Aragon. Although he rejoined *Sweet's*, he soon found more
openings for his reviews with *The New Republic,* among other
publications, and won a major cash prize for his poetry that
allowed him to buy a farmhouse outside of Manhattan. The
days of *Sweet's* were soon gone.

In October of 1929 Cowley took over the literary editorship
of *The New Republic* from Edmund Wilson, who had suffered
a nervous breakdown that year and had asked to be reassigned
as a roving reporter. Cowley began writing about his youth,
his time in Paris, and his time back in New York, as somehow
symbolic of the life of a generation. These pieces, originally
published as essays in *The New Republic,* made the backbone
of *Exile's Return,* which, when published in 1934, fell on the
deaf ears of a public caught in the Depression. It was not
until nearly twenty years later when the book was reissued
that it began to gain the standing it has today.

Exile's Return was, in a sense, Cowley's postwar novel. It
took its place among the many now forgotten memoirs of the
decade between the First World War and the Depression.
What makes it endure, though, is the depth of its insight, and
the breadth and clarity of its view. *Exile's Return* is an exciting
book. Like the first-person narrator of an autobiographical
novel Cowley takes his readers through a series of gyrations
that move from immediate experience to literary history and
back again. Of books about Paris in the twenties probably
only Hemingway's first and last novelistic efforts, *The Sun
Also Rises* and *A Moveable Feast,* stand in comparison. *Exile's
Return*'s pentultimate section, a brief chronicle of the life and
death of Harry Crosby, a writer and publisher of the time,
was originally intended to mark the brief transit of Cowley's
close friend Hart Crane. When it came time to complete the

book, Crane's suicide, coming on the heels of an odd tryst with Cowley's newly divorced wife, made the circumstance of writing about Crane too painful for Cowley. Crosby makes a good stand-in. His life, darkly devoted to the romantic sense of art which the book criticizes, and his times, a rapid rise and a quick decline, serve to complete Cowley's critique of a literary culture devoted more to dalliance than to the true end of writing.

In the thirties, the time of Cowley's divorce and Crane's suicide, Cowley threw himself into his work of reviewing at *The New Republic.* Although he soon remarried, this time happily, to Muriel Maurer, a beautiful New York fashion editor, and shortly thereafter had a son, Robert, he went through some hard times. "I got to know every late night coffee shop in Manhattan," he wrote of those days to a correspondent. "When you're in such a situation," he added strongly, "work is the palliative." For more than a decade Cowley wrote a weekly column for the magazine, often alternating his 800-to-1500-word pieces between the issues of politics and literature. Increasingly, they were one and the same. It was a time of social upheaval. In the early years of the thirties, as Cowley recounted in *The Dream of the Golden Mountains,* America was in economic collapse. A revolutionary sense was in the air, and Cowley, writing for one of the foremost organs of American opinion, was in the thick of it. He continued to write ever-more searching essays and reviews on American literature, and, as that literature came to be more critical of American culture and society, as in the cases of John Dos Passos, James T. Farrell, Edmund Wilson, and Richard Wright, Cowley responded. He also responded with work of his own on the political and economic front, much of which was later incorporated into *The Dream of the Golden Mountains.*

In the late thirties and early forties Cowley suffered mightily for positions that he had taken on international fronts regarding both the Spanish Revolution and the ongoing Russian Revolution. Cowley took leave of his *New Republic* position to work for the Roosevelt administration during the time of "The Emergency," the period that preceded America's entry into the Second World War. Because of his radical past he was hounded out of that position by journalists such as Westbrook Pegler and Whittaker Chambers, and a group of congressmen headed by Martin Dies. After that he felt burned, badly, about commenting on politics in any way.

What got him out of direct commentary on politics got him more straightforwardly into writing about literature. The leave he had taken from *The New Republic* allowed him to speak, once he had quit wartime government work, more directly to the issues that were important to him, namely, the growth and development of a national literature. Cowley would attend to both the important precursors of his time and to those people in his own generation who had something to contribute.

In 1943, at age forty-five, Cowley was at the halfway point of his life. That year, the Mary Mellon Foundation awarded him a grant to write as he chose. The grant more or less matched Cowley's previous yearly income, which he had now given up. It is at this point that the Cowley whom readers have come to call one of the shapers of American literature truly began to write with a grounded sense of an unfolding tradition.

3. A LIFE, CONCLUDED

The Mellon grant, which lasted for five years, allowed Cowley to do exactly what he had wanted to do since the time he took on *The New Republic* job: to cast his eyes across the range of American writing and to write about what he had seen as though he were the first to have read it. What resulted was remarkable. For the rest of his life Cowley never had to look back. His life as a free lance, which he had continued while writing at *The New Republic*, was essentially over. It wasn't that he made more money; it was simply that he finally had time to write in depth about his sense of literature.

With his independence, he first looked to the writers most immediate to him. He began a relationship with Viking Press which allowed him, in short order, to generate Viking Portable editions of Hemingway, William Faulkner, and Hawthorne. The Portables were initially designed for wartime soldiers. (Alexander Woolcott, whose idea the series was, had called the Portable "a jeep of a book.") After the war they became a staple of university education during the period of the GI Bill. Cowley then worked on Whitman, Fitzgerald, Sherwood Anderson, all the while contributing lengthy articles to *The New Republic* and lead reviews in the New York *Herald Tribune* and *Times* that put him at the forefront of what has come to be called "The American Studies Movement."

What Cowley was doing was not unique; but at the same time a national interest in a national literature had finally emerged, Cowley was reaching the full heat of his creative energy. In the forties, he contracted to write a general history of American literature; he never completed the book. In part, he was simply overwhelmed with what he was finding: unpublished notebooks and letters of Hawthorne; variorum editions of Whitman that had never been explored; the opportunity to write of the continuity of William Faulkner's novels, virtually all of which were out of print when Cowley took them up; the chance to provide a definitive edition of F. Scott Fitzgerald's *Tender Is the Night* from manuscripts that Fitzgerald had left at his death. All the while, he kept writing of the people he knew best, people whose work he often felt was misestimated: Hart Crane, or Hemingway, or Cummings, or Wilder, or Wolfe. He wrote too of the generation that preceded them, of James and Howells, of Frank Norris and Jack London, even of Horatio Alger and Lafcadio Hearn, writers not always regarded for their literary acumen. He read, and he wrote, and read, and wrote. Cowley spoke to his audience with the enthusiasm of an explorer, returning home only long enough to report his findings and then set out again.

This is the Cowley, a pathfinder, a shaper of American literature that we know. To say moreover that in the fifties and sixties he edited many books for Viking, translated extensively from the French, taught many of today's remarkable writers in lectures and writing seminars at universities, and, too, that he wrote much of his finest poetry, is only to confirm what the latter half of Cowley's life allowed him.

It was as though he had waited for half of his life to do what he really wanted. There are reasons why he didn't before: working on weekly deadlines, waiting for his past to catch up with the literary present; waiting for the cultural moment of acceptance to be right for his perspective. Ezra

Pound had once noted a twenty-year lag between the making of art and the acceptance of it. In 1951, *Exile's Return* was reissued with resounding success. Cowley was elected to the National Institute of Arts and Letters and in short order to the American Academy, of which he became a guiding force as chancellor in the nineteen sixties and seventies. Through these two decades Cowley lectured and taught frequently in American, and sometimes foreign, universities, but remained unhappy with the prospect of being taken for an academic. Being addressed as a professor, he once said, left him feeling "like the piano player in a whorehouse."

It should be noted that the bulk of Cowley's books did not appear until the last twenty years of his life. Ten books by Cowley appeared between 1967 and 1986. They weren't all brand new. Many of them were taken and reworked from essays and articles Cowley had written much earlier in his life. But after the mid-forties his pieces seemed less designed for weekly magazines and more as chapters in a history of American literature. Where before, in his *New Republic* days, Cowley had taken the short book review as his métier (he had called it "my sonnet sequence, my letter to distant friends"), the longer essay, and its opportunities to write at length about the making of American literature, now became his art form.

4. UNDERSTANDING COWLEY

"Dig me down to bedrock," Malcolm Cowley wrote to his fellow critic Edmund Wilson in 1940, "and you'd find there was just one thing I was really fanatical about—clear writing of the English language, that and saying exactly what I think when writing over my own signature." Malcolm Cowley was foremost a stylist. He used language as a watchman would use a lamp, to illuminate what was before him. When he wrote of his native soil in his poetry, it was "cool and sweet enough to sink the nostrils in and find the smell of home. . . ." Or of a moment in old age in which he dreamed about life as a log in a river: "The river was history and we were all involved in it as objects on its relentlessly moving surface. It would never turn back. Our only freedom was to become more conscious of the spectacle as it unrolled." Or about a fellow writer, Willa Cather, he would say, "She humanized the land itself, the wide, gently rolling, but savage land of her girlhood. . . . She celebrated the pioneers . . . giving them a place they deserved in her American gallery of heroes and wonders." When Cowley wrote, he revised, painstakingly, until a clarity and elegance of style matched his thought.

Cowley's writing style is simple and direct. Probably the only contemporary of Cowley's who had greater faith in the power of the American language simply used was E. B. White. Although Cowley used poetic turns of phrase and tropes in his critical essays, he had a distaste for ornate structure and jargon that bordered on obsession. He felt similarly about criticism and was often astonished at the extent to which the critical enterprise had become bogged down in theory. In part this was because Cowley was most concerned with explaining to his readers what made a good writer good. Cowley's criticism was also journalism, in the sense that it was reporting news. His work was historical, biographical, psychological, sociological, and ethical. Most of the time it was all of these at once. Cowley's idea was to relate an author's work to his or her life, to illuminate the work by shedding light on the circumstances of its creation and the aims of the writer. Often, he sought to place the writer's work by comparing it with other writing and with the literature of other times.

In reading Cowley one always has the feeling of being told a story. His senses of narrative and theme are basic components of his writing style. Thus a long essay on Hawthorne becomes a story of how one man used the dimensions of his own solitude to create a singular voice. The beginning of the piece reads like the beginning of a short story: "After four moderately happy, moderately social years at Bowdoin College, Hawthorne came back to Salem in 1825 and disappeared like a stone dropped into a well." A tale hangs upon that line, just as it does upon the opening paragraph of Cowley's essay on William Faulkner: "When the war was over—the other war—William Faulkner went back to Oxford, Mississippi. He had served in 1918 as a cadet in the Royal Canadian Air Force. Now he was home again and not at home, or at least not able to accept the postwar world. He was writing poems, most of them worthless, and dozens of immature but violent and effective stories, while at the same time he was brooding over his own situation and the decline of the South. Slowly the brooding thoughts arranged themselves into the whole inter- connected pattern that would form the substance of his novels." In each of these cases there's an element of urgency; a story is begging to be told. Indeed, most of Cowley's critical essays conform to the conventions of short stories; there is a clear beginning, middle, and end, and a "something hap- pened" which sets forth an irreversible movement such that a "something changed" is a clear result of what occurred.

When Cowley wrote about literature, he often wrote as much about the individuals who made the literature as the work itself. He was enthralled with personalities, but he often found the motivations of individuals questionable. Dreiser he presented following his muse "in his fumbling, incompetent fashion." Hart Crane, he said, "tried to charm his inspiration out of its hiding place with a Cuban rumba and a pitcher of hard cider." F. Scott Fitzgerald, Cowley noted, "liked to describe his vitality and his talent in pecuniary terms." That is, in terms of money. But Cowley most of his life had the freedom to pick his subjects, and backed his selection by saying, "no complete son of a bitch ever wrote a good sen- tence." That Cowley personally knew most of the people he wrote about undoubtedly both aided his efforts and colored his perspectives. Still, this wasn't always the case. Once a young reporter, expecting to hear some barroom stories, asked Cowley how he got to know William Faulkner. "By reading him," came Cowley's sharp reply.

Cowley's approach to literature, as a series of stories about a series of writers, becomes more convincing when those sto- ries are set side by side. They become part of a larger tale, the story of a national literature. When he wrote on this level Cowley was following leads he had found in Emerson's *Rep- resentative Men*, or in Walt Whitman's *Democratic Vistas*, where Whitman wrote, "the literature, songs, esthetics, &c., of a country are of importance principally because they furnish the materials and suggestions of personality for the women and men of that country and enforce them in a thousand effective ways." In short, Cowley made himself skald and scop to the saga of American writing.

Nonetheless, Cowley was not a systematic thinker. Certainly not in the way Cowley's lifelong friend, the philosopher Kenneth Burke, was. Cowley wrote of what he immediately knew. Even when he wrote at length about the history of American literature, of figures like Hawthorne or Whitman, it was from original texts and sources which allowed him to get underneath what critics had already said. When Cowley wrote of individual writers, he was following a common sense: it is writers who make literature, and their individual visions serve to make a communal culture, no matter how disparate those visions are. Cowley's thematic perspective, perhaps as close to a sense of system as he came, was to say of a work or author he especially cared about, this too is a part of American literature. Among his goals in doing so was to acknowledge the technical achievement of good authors in order to give direction to younger writers. He wrote: "It is not by imitating one or another that a younger writer can hope to surpass Hemingway or Faulkner. What he or she can learn from them is not a method of living or writing, but a way of going about work, a way of 'starting with the simplest things,' as Hemingway said, that leads to setting down a new world in a new fashion."

In distinction to what eulogizers have said about Cowley, among them, that he served to establish an American canon, Cowley's effort was to set standards which, he hoped, would make both writers and critics acknowledge a sense of literary tradition, the openness of that tradition to new views, and, finally, means to give new writers a sense of the possibility that exists in extending that tradition. Cowley said of forthcoming generations of American writers, "They will be as different from those of the 'Lost Generation' as Hemingway and Faulkner were different from every American author who preceded them, though without ceasing to be in the American tradition. The tradition grows and changes, but persists. Eventually it will include everything honest and new and written with patient rigor, like a good line of verse, so that it becomes unchangeable."

5. A LEGACY

Cowley, looking back upon the writers of his own generation late in his life, called them "lonely mastodons looming among herds of patient Guernseys and shorthorns." Although he remained active in writing until his death (he left a third book of memoirs incomplete), in editing and revising his own work, and in patiently answering the queries of academics trying to straighten out the crooked lines of their critical biographies of members of his generation, he felt sad that he could number the survivors of his literary generation on one hand.

But his sense of "the lonely mastodons" was not of those of his generation who had outlived their time. It came from his sense of the greatness of those who had written well. Cowley was looking at the legacy he himself had marked. Of those makers of American literature he noted, "For new writers they serve sometimes as models, sometimes as warnings, but always as enhancers of life and, in their own diverse fashions, as heroes of literature: the incorruptibles."

In the fifties Cowley planned to make a book of writings on these people, a book in two parts, one of which would include the writers of the "American Renaissance" of the nineteenth century and after, leading up to writers of his own generation. The second half of the idea emerged in 1973 as probably Cowley's single-most important book, *A Second Flowering*. It was as close as he ever came to the history of American literature he had intended to write. Outside of collections of his work, each of Cowley's later books was intended to be something more. Despite his numerous accomplishments, Cowley suffered from what he termed "the perfectionist syndrome." He felt this way even about *A Second Flowering*, but upon reading it one cannot imagine any sharper vision of the eight writers he profiles. It was as though he was consciously making a zodiac of literary types.

For Cowley, "the incorruptibles" were people of his own generation: Fitzgerald, Hemingway, Faulkner, and Crane. And others before, especially Hawthorne, Emerson, and Whitman. Writers who inflamed American literature with their writing. For Cowley, their fire came not from some delphic source, but from their bellies, their sheer desire to say what they had seen, and to become by that great, or monied, or, simply, heard. What they made, art, admitted to no venalities. They wrote because they had to, in some cases because there was no alternative, in other cases because they found no such pleasure in anything else.

In both their writing and lives they became part of what Cowley made into the story of American writing. Among them were "the Fitzgerald young man, handsome and full of promise, but harried to death by an obscure need for self-destruction." There was "the Hemingway young man, hard-drinking and impassive, who roamed through Europe as warily as an Ojibway in the Michigan woods." There was "the Thomas Wolfe young man, the boy from the North Carolina hills who was bent on reading everything and writing everything, so that he prowled through the stacks of the Widener Library seizing and devouring books like a tiger in the jungle." And there was also William Faulkner, "sitting at home in a little Mississippi town and constructing a whole imaginary world without ever thinking, so he said, that strangers might read what he had written."

These stories, Cowley felt, helped to make America culturally rich. They evince a theme in Cowley's own nonsystematic work that runs as deep and stands as fresh as the tale-chronicling efforts of Irving and Hawthorne, of Twain about the Mississippi or Faulkner about the South. Cowley was the storyteller who wrote about storytellers. He had gleaned his own estimation of this from writers of the American nineteenth century, writers like Irving, Poe, Hawthorne, Melville, and Whitman. Speaking of those authors, Cowley said, "Those writers knew what they were doing. When they wrote to their friends of literary problems, they often used words like 'legend,' 'mystery,' 'tradition,' 'picturesque,' and 'romance.'" For Cowley all those words were ones referring "to the same quality . . . one which they felt lacking in American life." These authors were trying to make something new, Cowley felt. "They were trying to arouse in Americans a sense of community and of common destinies on a deeper level than that of practical affairs."

For Cowley the deep reason that these writers, and writers such as Whitman, Crane, Dos Passos, Hemingway, and Cheever, are valuable to us today is because they, as Cowley said, "make it possible for us to believe in ourselves as characters in the drama of American history."

6. THE BOOK

Malcolm Cowley wrote across many forms, memoirs and literary history, criticism across the broad scope of American literature, poetry, letters, and essays on the nature of writing. This book is designed to reflect that breadth.

It begins with Cowley's reflections on his own experiences up until the time he began writing in earnest about American literature. For lack of a better term I call them memoirs. They are remembrances of a culture Cowley helped create.

After that comes the spine of this collection, Cowley's critical estimations of American literature and its makers. It is followed by three sections that present brief estimations of his poetry, correspondence, and expositions on the making of literature and on the writing trade.

ACKNOWLEDGMENTS

For guidance in assembling this book I thank Malcolm Cowley, for eight years of teaching and friendship. I should note at the outset that though work on this volume was begun while Malcolm Cowley was still alive, his illness precluded any consultation on selections or editing. For better or worse, the editing and selections are completely my own. I thank Muriel Cowley for her kindness, and Robert Cowley for his enthusiastic support. I want here to dedicate my effort in making this book to Muriel Cowley.

I also thank Gerald Howard, formerly senior editor of Viking Penguin, who came up with the idea for the book and shepherded it along the way; and Michael Millman, associate editor at Viking Penguin, who brought it to publication.

In addition I thank James M. Kempf, Henry Dan Piper, and Hans Bak, three Cowley scholars who freely shared their ideas with me; and Ruth Nuzum, patron saint of Cowley scholars.

I especially thank Carolyn Sheehy, former curator of the Cowley Collection at the Newberry Library, Chicago, for her wit, energy, and prescience across two visits to the Newberry during the fall of 1988. None of my work there would have been possible without a Research Fellowship granted through the offices of Richard Brown at the Newberry. I also especially thank the entire staff of the Newberry Manuscript Collection for their diligent work on my behalf.

Patricia Willis, curator of the Yale University Beinecke Library 20th Century American Literature Collection, and her staff helped a great deal in my work on Cowley letters, as did Lisa Middents, Megan Desnoyers, and the staff of the JFK Library in Boston.

Randy Lyanne Gellman helped with the preparation of the manuscript and presided over its final shape with excellent advice, hugs, and sandwiches.

If there be fault in what is provided, the sin be on my head, not theirs.

MALCOLM COWLEY
A CHRONOLOGY

1898	Born on a farm near Belsano, Pennsylvania, August 24, to Josephine, née Hutmacher, and William Cowley, a Pittsburgh homeopathic physician and practicing Swedenborgian. The farm is a summer home for the family. Cowley is an only child.
1902	Meets Kenneth Burke, a childhood schoolmate and lifelong friend.
1910	Mother adopts Ruth, unwanted child of a distant friend. Ruth dies of a childhood disease in 1919.
1911–15	Attends first Liberty School and then Peabody High in the East Liberty section of Pittsburgh. Publishes first poetry. Graduates second in his class.
1915	Enrolls in Harvard. Is on scholarship every term there. Meets E. E. Cummings, Conrad Aiken, among others. Studies with Charles Townsend Copeland. Attends Amy Lowell's "salons." Writes for *Harvard Advocate*.
1917	Withdraws from Harvard to drive munitions trucks for the Camion Corps of the American Field Service in France. Writes about experiences for *The Pittsburgh Gazette*.
1918	Returns to Harvard for spring semester and becomes editor-in-chief of the *Harvard Advocate*. In June withdraws again to join the U.S. Army (Field Artillery Officer's Training School at Camp Taylor, near Louisville). Honorably discharged in December (he never leaves the States).
1919	In January moves to Greenwich Village; in August marries the painter Marguerite Frances Baird (Peggy); returns to Harvard for the fall term and graduates in winter 1920 (is listed with the grad-

uating class of 1919). Graduates ninth in his class. Honors, Phi Beta Kappa.

1920–21 Alternates between free-lance book reviewing in Greenwich Village (*The Dial, Freeman, New York Evening Post*), and working for *Sweet's Architectural Catalogue* as an advertising copywriter. Publishes poetry in little magazines.

1921–23 Holds two continuous American Field Service Fellowships to study at University of Montpellier in France. Lives in Giverny with his wife, and travels frequently to Paris, where he meets, works with, and writes about poets such as Valéry, the Dadaists Tzara and Aragon, and American expatriates such as Gertrude Stein, Ernest Hemingway, and Ezra Pound, among many others. Takes trips to Germany and Vienna. Becomes an ad hoc editor for *Broom* and *Secession*, avant-garde "little magazines" of the period.

1923–24 Returns to Greenwich Village (August) to writing poetry, freelancing, and working again at *Sweet's*. Meets Hart Crane, fellow worker at *Sweet's*, and works with writers Allen Tate and Matthew Josephson. First book publications: "Racine," an essay, and "Eight More Harvard Poets," first appearance of poetry in an anthology.

1925–29 Resigns from *Sweet's Catalogue* and begins a career of freelance writing and reviewing. Moves to Staten Island, then to Connecticut, and then to a farm in upstate New York where his neighbors are Allen Tate, Caroline Gordon, Hart Crane, William Slater Brown, Matthew Josephson, Peter Blume, and Robert M. Coates. Translates seven books from the French, including Valéry's *Variety* (1927). Receives the Levinson Prize from *Poetry* (1927).

1929 Publishes *Blue Juniata*, first book of poems, and in October begins work for *The New Republic*, as literary editor, his predecessor, Edmund Wilson, having given up the position to become a roving reporter for the magazine. Cowley serves as literary editor for the next decade.

1931	Cowley and Peggy Baird separate (February). In late March Cowley meets Muriel Maurer at a gathering at the Josephsons' house in Connecticut. They soon fall in love. In April, Crane travels to Mexico. Peggy goes to Mexico in June to seek an amicable divorce.
1932	In February, Cowley travels to Kentucky with Waldo Frank and Edmund Wilson, among others, as a union-sanctioned observer of the miners' strikes there. In April Crane and Peggy, having professed their love for each other, return to the States. At noon on April 27 Crane jumps to his death from the decks of the *Orizaba*. In June Cowley marries Muriel Maurer, his wife for the remainder of his life.
1933	Spends spring in Tennessee with Tate, Gordon, and occasionally, Robert Penn Warren, while finishing manuscript of *Exile's Return*.
1934	Publication of *Exile's Return* with Norton (first-year sales, 800 copies); son Robert is born in December. Commutes to New York City three days a week to do office work for *The New Republic*. Writes his weekly book column on weekends, a routine he keeps until the early forties.
1935	Helps organize League of American Writers, and serves for a period as vice-president of the organization. The League holds congresses in 1935, 1937, and 1939.
1936	Buys old farmhouse with a drying barn and seven acres in Sherman, Connecticut, for about $1500. It is Cowley's home for the rest of his life.
1937	Travels to Madrid for the World Congress of Writers. Attends, and at times leads, numerous meetings in New York supporting the League of American Writers and Popular Front causes such as those for Spanish refugees. Edits and writes sections of *After the Genteel Tradition*.
1939	Edits, with Bernard Smith, and writes sections of *Books That Changed Our Minds*.
1940	Resigns from League of American Writers after trying to get organization to break its communist

ties. Publishes letter of resignation from League in *The New Republic*. Leaves editorial position at *The New Republic* in the fall, but remains as a book reviewer.

1941–42   Publishes second collection of poems, *The Dry Season*. Goes to Washington to work for The Office of Facts and Figures (OFF) as Chief Information Analyst, second to Director Archibald MacLeish. Is investigated for security clearance by FBI. (File is begun that researches and monitors his political activity. Monitoring continues into the mid-1950s). Journalists Whittaker Chambers and Westbrook Pegler castigate Cowley for former radical/communist ties. Congressman Martin Dies of Texas accuses Cowley on the floor of Congress of having "no fewer than 72 Communist connections" to communist or front organizations. Cowley resigns under fire in March 1942 vowing never again to write about politics.

1943–48   Becomes recipient of a Five-Year Mary Mellon Fellowship grant. Translates Gide's *Imaginary Interviews* (1944); translates and edits (with Hannah Josephson) *Aragon, Poet of the French Resistance* (1945). Begins writing in earnest about the American literary tradition. Publishes *The Portable Hemingway* (1944), *The Portable Faulkner* (1946), and *The Portable Hawthorne* (1948), while writing numerous independent essays about American writing. Writes profile of Ernest Hemingway for *Life* magazine (1949). Becomes literary adviser to the Viking Press, a position he holds for the rest of his life. Continues long-term relationship with Yaddo, the artists' colony in Saratoga Springs, New York, both as administrator and frequent guest. Resigns from *The New Republic* when it moves to Washington (1948).

1949–50   Testifies at the second Alger Hiss trial. Testimony impugns Whittaker Chambers. Is named Walker-Ames Lecturer at the University of Washington. Elected to National Institute of Arts and Letters.

1951–54   Publishes a revised edition of *Exile's Return* (1951). Edits revision of F. Scott Fitzgerald's

Tender Is the Night as well as a collection of Fitzgerald's short stories (both 1951). Edits an om-
nibus volume of three Fitzgerald novels (1953).
Publishes *The Literary Situation* (1954), a contemporary exploration of the state of American writing since 1945.

1956–66 Begins a series of teaching sojourns at Stanford,
University of Michigan, Yale, Berkeley, and elsewhere for the next decade. Often teaches a lecture
course on American literature and a seminar in
creative writing. Travels to France (1957). Translates Valéry's *Leonardo, Poe, Mallarmé*. Edits the
first edition of Whitman's *Leaves of Grass* (1959).
Edits Sherwood Anderson's *Winesburg, Ohio*
(1960). Serves as President of National Institute
of Arts and Letters (1956–59 and 1962–65). Publishes *Black Cargoes, A History of the Atlantic
Slave Trade*, with Daniel Mannix (1962), *Fitzgerald and the Jazz Age*, with Robert Cowley (1966),
and *The Faulkner-Cowley File*, a chronicle of his
work with William Faulkner (1966). Develops
works such as Jack Kerouac's *On the Road* (1956)
and Ken Kesey's *One Flew Over the Cuckoo's Nest*
(1962) for publication with Viking.

1966 Is named Chancellor of the American Academy
of Arts and Letters, a position he holds until 1976.

1967 Publishes *Think Back On Us . . . , A Contem-
porary Chronicle of the 1930s*, a collection of *New
Republic* writings from the 1930s, edited by H. D.
Piper.

1968 Travels to Oaxaca, Mexico, for a three-month sojourn and writes a number of new poems. A volume of collected poems entitled *Blue Juniata:
Collected Poems* is published.

1970 *A Many-Windowed House: Collected Essays on
American Writers and American Writing*, edited
by H. D. Piper, is published.

1971 Publishes *Lesson of the Masters: An Anthology of
the Novel from Cervantes to Hemingway*, edited
with Howard E. Hugo.

1973 Publishes *A Second Flowering: Works and Days
of the Lost Generation*, a collection of essays on

twentieth-century American writers; teaches at University of Warwick in the U.K.

1978   —*And I Worked at the Writer's Trade*, a collection of memoirs and critical essays, is published.

1979–80   Works with Carl Bode on a new *Portable Emerson* for Viking. Jointly makes selections and writes some editorial material. The book is published in 1980 under Bode's editorship.

1980   Publishes *The Dream of the Golden Mountains; Remembering the 1930s*, a memoir, and *The View from 80.*

1985   *The Flower and the Leaf, A Contemporary Record of American Writing Since 1941*, edited by Donald W. Faulkner, and *Blue Juniata: A Life; Collected and New Poems* are published.

1986   Cowley announces his retirement from writing.

1988   *The Selected Correspondence of Kenneth Burke and Malcolm Cowley, 1915–1981*, edited by Paul Jay, is published.

1989   Dies Tuesday, March 28, age ninety.

PART ONE

Memoirs

EDITOR'S NOTE

When Malcolm Cowley wrote his candid portrait of aging in *The View from 80* in 1980 (a brief selection from it opens this volume), he put the issue of writing about one's self into cogent perspective. To Cowley, autobiography is an attempt to find "a shape or pattern in our lives." He continued:

> There are such patterns, I believe, even if they are hard to discern. Our lives that seemed a random and monotonous series of incidents are something more than that; each of them has a plot. Life in general (or nature, or the history of our times) is a supremely inventive novelist or playwright, but he—she?—is also wasteful beyond belief and her designs are hidden under the . . . rubbish of the years. She needs our help as collaborators. . . .
>
> Those outlines, if we find them, will prove to be a story, one with a beginning, a development, a climax of sorts (or more than one climax), and an epilogue.

Cowley considered himself less an autobiographer or a memoirist than a literary historian, but he maintained a novelist's sense in writing of his own life. For Cowley, the novelist's first duty was to write honestly and truthfully about his time. He held to those dicta and framed his own autobiographical efforts much as he did his criticism: as a series of stories, each with a beginning, middle, end, and a narrative theme. Moreover, he wrote about his personal experiences as though he were speaking of the drama of an entire generation.

His two autobiographical books, *Exile's Return* and *The Dream of the Golden Mountains*, chronicles of the twenties and thirties respectively, were designed to be followed by a

third, taking up the forties. It was a work he left incomplete
upon his retirement from writing in 1986. There are, however,
plans for publishing it.

Exile's Return, originally published in 1934 and then revised
and reprinted in 1951, chronicles the literary odyssey of a
generation, the so-called "lost generation" of the twenties.
Its form has antecedents and progeny. In its antecedents it is
like a *bildungsroman*: a central narrative figure is taken
through a series of episodes that mark his education and ma-
turation. Its progeny is the nonfiction novel that came to
prominence in the sixties and seventies. At issue is Cowley's
progression through the romance of art and the sense of art
as religion. His debunking of these is followed by periods of
disillusionment, even nihilism, and results in an understanding
that the making of art has its beginning and end in the social
context of community.

The themes of exile and alienation dominate the book and
its characters' lives. But what is fascinating is the way in which
Cowley's experiences mirror these larger ideas. Even his
"dadaist" act of punching the proprietor of the Café Rotonde,
humorously recounted in "Significant Gesture," is put into
perspective:

> Years later I realized that by punching a café proprietor in the
> jaw I had performed an act to which all [my French acquain-
> tances'] catchwords could be applied. First of all, I had acted
> for reasons of public morality; bearing no private grudge against
> my victim, I had been *disinterested*. I had committed an *indis-
> cretion*, acted with *violence* and *disdain* for the law, performed
> an *arbitrary* and *significant gesture*, uttered a *manifesto*; in their
> opinion I had shown *courage*. . . . For the first time in my life
> I became a public character. I was entertained at dinners and
> cocktail parties, interviewed by the newspapers, asked to con-
> tribute to reviews published by the Dadaists in Amsterdam,
> Brussels, Lyon and Belgrade.

The selections from *Exile's Return* collected here cover
three distinct periods in Cowley's early life: his time at Harvard and subsequent enlistment in the ambulance service in
France during the First World War; his sojourn in Paris and
the people he met there; and his return to America, captured
in a cameo remembrance of Hart Crane. These pieces bracket
a much later essay, "—And I Worked at the Writer's Trade,"

which is a memoir of Cowley's "literary apprenticeship" in Greenwich Village and elsewhere in the early twenties. Written with a light hand but with an attention to biographical detail, the essay originally appeared as the introduction to a bibliography of his work. In it, for example, Cowley recalls being a starving book reviewer in Manhattan:

> One morning I was crossing Sheridan Square after no breakfast when the sidewalk suddenly came up and hit me in the face. I didn't lose consciousness for more than a moment. Less frightened than surprised, I picked myself up and walked carefully into a lunchroom to spend my last dime for a stale bun and a cup of coffee. As I sat at the counter feeling not at all hungry and more than usually clear headed, I surrendered, for a time, my pride in living on the underside of society and my dream of being a free artisan working at his typewriter as if it were a cottage loom.

The Dream of the Golden Mountains is more straightforwardly a memoir. It covers the first half of the 1930s, from the time that *Exile's Return* ended to about mid-decade and the first signals of the disillusionment of American radical politics. It was a tempestuous time in Cowley's life. Cowley had won a job at *The New Republic* replacing Edmund Wilson as its literary editor in October, 1929, just as the country had begun its economic collapse. By 1932 the distinctions between literary concerns and political or economic ones, especially at *The New Republic*, had begun to disappear. Cowley found himself at a gathering of politically committed literati at Theodore Dreiser's home and shortly thereafter as a union-sanctioned observer in Pineville, Kentucky, during the coal miners' strikes there. At the same time, his first wife, Peggy Baird, was seeking an amicable divorce in Mexico. She quickly met up there with Hart Crane, one of Cowley's best friends. Crane, avowedly homosexual, and Peggy, given to bohemian excess, developed a tryst, and even planned to be married.

Crane was suicidal, on a drunken decline since publication of *The Bridge*, but he seemed redeemed in Peggy's company. Cowley, though dejected, was happy for them both. They appeared to give each other hope for a new beginning. Peggy and Hart both wrote to Cowley with some frequency and Crane sent Cowley his last poem, "The Broken Tower." In April 1932, the couple began their return to the States on the steamer *Orizaba*. Crane jumped overboard to his death. Cowley met the disembarking in New York among a host of reporters not come, Cowley sadly learned, to find news of Crane, but to meet another ship on which the aged Alice Liddell, Charles Dodgson's model for *Alice in Wonderland*, had arrived.

This tragic tale is deftly interwoven with another in the selections from *The Dream of the Golden Mountains*. Together they make a small masterpiece of storytelling and autobiography. The other tale is of Cowley's journey with Edmund Wilson, Waldo Frank, Quincy Howe, and Mary Heaton Vorse to Harlan County, a place that has now become synonomous in American history with labor violence and political resistance. In February 1932 the Kentucky antilabor laws had teeth in them. Coal miners were on strike and were trying to gain recognition for their demands. The group came down to report on the situation for the national media. "This is another war," Cowley reports a coal operator saying. "I admire your nerve in coming here where you don't know anything about conditions or the feeling of the people. If you don't watch out, you'll find out how ugly we can be. . . ."

The group found out. Waldo Frank was badly beaten. The rest were taunted and harassed. In fear of their lives they were ushered out of the state by "local authorities." The selection ends with Cowley having returned to his birthplace in western Pennsylvania to visit his parents with his new wife, Muriel, in the summer of 1932. On the road outside of Johnstown they watch truckload after truckload of the dispersed "bonus army" pass by. World War One veterans, demanding their rights, had marched on Washington, set up camps, and were driven out by National Guard troops. In the place where Cowley had first felt his exiling from the norms of American culture he sat by the side of the road and watched that culture disintegrate.

The last piece in this section, "A Personal Record," only begins to record Cowley's late-thirties political disillusionment. The essay is framed around a fairly notorious letter that Edmund Wilson wrote to Cowley in 1938 and Cowley's response to it. Cowley had been an ardent supporter of the Soviet "experiment" and an equally ardent supporter of Stalin. Cowley parted company with the Soviet line a bit too late for Wilson's and others' comfort, and a pained effort to explain his actions unfortunately closes this section. I say un-fortunately, because the bulk of Cowley's last book of memoirs remains uncollected or unpublished. It demonstrates far more circumspection and integrity about these issues than has previously been acknowledged.*

Cowley ends "A Personal Record" with what makes a fine bridge to the next section of this book. Writing of his transition from a life in politics and literature to a life in literature alone in the forties he says:

> I was . . . deeply interested in authors: how they got started, how they kept going, how they pictured themselves, and the myths they embodied in their work. I was interested in their social backgrounds and in the question of whom they were think-ing about when they said "we." I liked to speculate on the relation between the author and his audience. Perhaps from the 1930s I had retained the stubborn belief that literature, while having its own laws, is also part of history.

Cowley had begun his literary work by making his life a story. He had sought patterns in series of incidents. He had generated a plot. After examining his own life he began ex-amining the patterns in the lives of others, writers, both those immediate and those long gone.

---

* Among those pieces are: "The Sense of Guilt," collected in —*And I Worked at the Writer's Trade*; "No Homage to Catalonia: A Memory of the Spanish Civil War," *Southern Review* XVIII (January 1982); "Echoes from Moscow: 1937–1938," *Southern Review* XX (January 1984); "Lament for the Abraham Lincoln Battalion," *Sewanee Review* XCCII (Summer 1984); and "A Time of Resignations," *Yale Review* LXXIV (Autumn 1984). With other unpublished pieces they make a book not reflected here.

REASONS FOR WRITING

(from *The View from 80*)

Among the truly great American writers, Emerson was the
only one who resigned himself to occupying [the] position [of
being old]. Though he had lost his memory, everyone admired
him for what he had written in his middle years. Everyone
who approached him worshiped as at a shrine. Walt Whitman
visited Concord in 1881, the year before Emerson died, and
recorded an evening there in *Specimen Days*. ". . . without
being rude, or anything of the kind," he says, "I could just
look squarely at E., which I did a good part of the two hours.
On entering, he had spoken very briefly and politely to several
of the company, then settled himself in his chair, a trifle push'd
back, and, though a listener and apparently an alert one,
remain'd silent throughout the whole talk and discussion.
. . . A good color in his face, eyes clear, with the well-known
expression of sweetness, and the old clear-peering aspect quite
the same. Whitman was reverently gazing on the effigy of the
Emerson that had been.

There have been writers high in the second rank who at-
tained a similar position, and without losing their faculties:
some names are Longfellow, Whittier, Julia Ward Howe,
Robert Frost, and more recently Edmund Wilson. William
Dean Howells had the position too, but was toppled from it
at 70 by a revolt against the genteel tradition. At 78 he wrote
to his friend Henry James, "I am a comparatively dead cult
with my statues cut down and the grass growing over them
in the pale moonlight." Each new generation elects its own
heroes, and nobody can be certain who they will be. Besides,
that Emersonian place as a revered idol is not a tempting goal
for those, however ambitious, who are not much concerned
with reputation. Those others don't want to be regarded as
a monument to themselves, or a seemly model for the young,

or a memory bank for scholars; they want to do their work—
but at 80, what shall it be? . . .

One project among many, one that tempts me and might
be tempting to others, is trying to find a shape or pattern in
our lives. There are such patterns, I believe, even if they are
hard to discern. Our lives that seemed a random and monotonous series of incidents are something more than that;
each of them has a plot. Life in general (or nature, or the
history of our times) is a supremely inventive novelist or playwright, but he—she?—is also wasteful beyond belief and her
designs are hidden under the . . . rubbish of the years. She
needs our help as collaborators. Can we clear away the bundles of old newspapers, evading the booby traps, and lay bare
the outlines of ourselves?

Those outlines, if we find them, will prove to be a story,
one with a beginning, a development, a climax of sorts (or
more than one climax), and an epilogue. John Cowper Powys
says in one of his vatic moments, ". . . in only one way can
our mortal and, it may be, our immortal life be bravely,
thoroughly, and absolutely justified, and that way is by *treating
it as a story*." He might better have said, ". . . as a drama
for each of us in which he or she has been the protagonist."
Not only that; we have been the audience too, and perhaps
the critic planning his report for a morning paper: "The leading character was played by _____" (insert your
name), "who was no more than adequate in his difficult role."
Or was he better than merely adequate, or worse, much
worse? In age we have the privilege—which sometimes becomes a torture on sleepless nights—of passing judgment on
our own performance. But before passing judgment, we have
to untangle the plot of the play.

A first step in the untanglement, if we choose to make that
effort, is gathering together the materials that composed our
lives (including even the rubbish, which may prove to be more
revealing than we had suspected). In other words, the first
step is simply remembering. That seems easy in the beginning,
since it always starts with our childhood, whose scenes are
more vividly printed on our minds. Some of them, though,
may reappear unexpectedly—for example, in my case, the
picture of Jim Overman taking off his work shoes and insisting

that I wear them on my bare feet before crossing the patch
of nettles that barred our way to the farm lane. Jim followed
me in heavy woolen socks that had been knitted for him by
his older sister Maggie, who flashes across my mind as an
image of blowsy kindness. What happened to dear Maggie?
What happened to Jim after he went to work in a steel mill?
Both of those orphans played their parts in my world.

Like many older persons, or so one suspects, I find myself
leaping forward from childhood to recent years. These too
are easy for most of us to remember, except in such matters
as names and faces and where we mislaid our glasses. ("Thank
goodness, you don't have to look for them anymore," a long-
time neighbor phoned my wife to say. "I found them in the
freezer compartment.") But the old, as Cicero said, end by
recalling whatever really concerns them in the recent past. It
is the middle years that prove hardest to recapture, so many
of the persons and incidents having grown dim, but we can
find the shape of these too, if we continue our efforts.

There are tangible aids to remembering, as notably letters,
old snapshots, daybooks, and mementos, if we have saved
them. Old tunes ring through our heads and some of them
bring back pictures; this one was "our" song, Doris said, and
you see the look on her face when she hummed the words.
What became of Doris after she married somebody else and
moved to California? And Mr. Wagner, the boss who used
to dance the gazotsky at office parties? Characters crowd in
on us, each making a contribution, and gradually our world
takes shape. We tell stories about it, perhaps only to ourselves, and then arrange the stories in sequence: this must
have been our second act and this was the third. All these
efforts, if continued, might lead to an absolutely candid book
of memoirs; old persons have nothing to lose by telling the
truth. For others it might lead to nothing more than notebook
jottings and advice to the young that might or might not be
remembered. No matter: it is a fascinating pursuit in itself,
and our efforts will not have been wasted if they help us to
possess our own identities as an artist possesses his work. At
least we can say to the world of the future, or to ourselves if
nobody else will listen, "I really *was*"—or even, with greater
self-confidence, "I was and am *this*."

[1980]

THE MAKING OF EXILES

(from *Exile's Return*)

AMERICAN COLLEGE, 1916

It often seems to me that our years in school and after school, in college and later in the army, might be regarded as a long process of deracination. Looking backward, I feel that our whole training was involuntarily directed toward destroying whatever roots we had in the soil, toward eradicating our local and regional peculiarities, toward making us homeless citizens of the world.

In school, unless we happened to be Southerners, we were divested of any local pride. We studied Ancient History and American History, but not, in my own case, the history of western Pennsylvania. We learned by name the rivers of Siberia—Obi, Yenisei, Lena, Amur—but not the Ohio with its navigable tributaries, or why most of them had ceased to be navigated, or why Pittsburgh was built at its forks. We had high-school courses in Latin, German, Chemistry, good courses all of them, and a class in Civics where we learned to list the amendments to the Constitution and name the members of the Supreme Court; but we never learned how Presidents were really chosen or how a law was put through Congress. If one of us had later come into contact with the practical side of government—that is, if he wished to get a street paved, an assessment reduced, a friend out of trouble with the police or a relative appointed to office—well, fortunately the ward boss wouldn't take much time to set him straight.

Of the English texts we studied, I can remember only one, "The Legend of Sleepy Hollow," that gave us any idea that an American valley could be as effectively clothed in romance as Ivanhoe's castle or the London of Henry Esmond. It seemed to us that America was beneath the level of great

fiction; it seemed that literature in general, and art and learning, were things existing at an infinite distance from our daily
lives. For those of us who read independently, this impression
became even stronger: the only authors to admire were foreign authors. We came to feel that wisdom was an attribute
of Greece and art of the Renaissance, that glamour belonged
only to Paris or Vienna and that glory was confined to the
dim past. If we tried, notwithstanding, to write about more
immediate subjects, we were forced to use a language not
properly our own. A definite effort was being made to destroy
all trace of local idiom or pronunciation and have us speak
"correctly"—that is, in a standardized Amerenglish as colorless as Esperanto. Some of our instructors had themselves
acquired this public-school dialect only by dint of practice,
and now set forth its rules with an iron pedantry, as if they
were teaching a dead language.

In college the process of deracination went on remorse-
lessly. We were not being prepared for citizenship in a town,
a state or a nation; we were not being trained for an industry
or profession essential to the common life; instead we were
being exhorted to enter that international republic of learning
whose traditions are those of Athens, Florence, Paris, Berlin
and Oxford. The immigrant into that high disembodied realm
is supposed to come with empty hands and naked mind, like
a recruit into the army. He is clothed and fed by his precep-
tors, who furnish him only with the best of intellectual supplies. Nothing must enter that world in its raw state;
everything must be refined by time and distance, by theory
and research, until it loses its own special qualities, its life,
and is transformed into the dead material of culture. The ideal
university is regarded as having no regional or economic ties.
With its faculty, students, classrooms and stadium, it exists
in a town as if by accident, its real existence being in the
immaterial world of scholarship—or such, at any rate, was
the idea to be gained in those years by any impressionable
student.

Take my own experience at Harvard. Here was a university
that had grown immediately out of a local situation, out of
the colonists' need for trained ministers of the Gospel. It had
transformed itself from generation to generation with the
transformations of New England culture. Farming money,
fishing money, trading money, privateering money, wool, cot-

ton, shoe and banking money, had all contributed to its vast endowment. It had grown with Boston, a city whose records were written on the face of its buildings. Sometimes on Sundays I used to wander through the old sections of Beacon Hill and the North End and admire the magnificent doorways, built in the chastest Puritan style with profits from the trade in China tea. Behind some of them Armenians now lived, or Jews; the Old North Church was in an Italian quarter, near the house of Paul Revere, a silversmith. Back Bay had been reclaimed from marshland and covered with mansions during the prosperous years after the Civil War (shoes, uniforms, railroads, speculation in government bonds). On Brattle Street, in Cambridge, Longfellow's house was open to the public, and I might have visited Brook Farm. All these things, Emerson, doorways, factory hands and fortunes, the Elective System, the Porcellian Club, were bound together in one civilization, but of this I received no hint. I was studying Goethe's *Dichtung und Wahrheit* and the Elizabethan drama, and perhaps, on my way to classes in the morning, passing a Catholic church outside of which two Irish boys stood and looked at me with unfriendly eyes. Why was Cambridge an Irish provincial city, almost like Cork or Limerick? What was the reason, in all the territory round Boston, for the hostility between "nice people" and "muckers"? When a development of houses for nice Cambridge people came out on the main street of Somerville (as one of them did), why did it turn its back on the street, build a brick wall against the sidewalk, and face on an interior lawn where nurses could watch nice children playing? I didn't know; I was hurrying off to a section meeting in European History and wondering whether I could give the dates of the German peasant wars.

I am not suggesting that we should have been encouraged to take more "practical" courses—Bookkeeping or Restaurant Management or Sewage Disposal or any of the hundreds that clutter the curriculum of a big university. These specialized techniques could wait till later, after we had chosen our life work. What we were seeking, as sophomores and juniors, was something vastly more general, a key to unlock the world, a picture to guide us in fitting its jigsaw parts together. It happened that our professors were eager to furnish us with such a key or guide; they were highly trained, earnest, devoted to their calling. Essentially the trouble was that the world they

pictured for our benefit was the special world of scholarship
—timeless, placeless, elaborate, incomplete and bearing only
the vaguest relationship to that other world in which fortunes
were made, universities endowed and city governments run
by muckers.

It lay at a distance, even, from the college world in which
we were doing our best to get ahead. The rigorous methods
and high doctrines taught by our professors applied only to
parts of our lives. We had to fill in the gaps as best we could,
usually by accepting the unspoken doctrines of those about
us. In practice the college standards were set, not by the
faculty, but by the leaders among the students, and particularly by the rich boys from half-English preparatory schools,
for whose benefit the system seemed to be run. The rest of
us, boys from public high schools, ran the risk of losing our
own culture, such as it was, in our bedazzlement with this
new puzzling world, and of receiving nothing real in exchange.

Young writers were especially tempted to regard their own
experience as something negligible, not worth the trouble of
recording in the sort of verse or prose they were taught to
imitate from the English masters. A Jewish boy from Brooklyn might win a scholarship by virtue of his literary talent.
Behind him there would lie whole generations of rabbis versed
in the Torah and the Talmud, representatives of the oldest
Western culture now surviving. Behind him, too, lay the memories of an exciting childhood: street gangs in Brownsville,
chants in a Chassidic synagogue, the struggle of his parents
against poverty, his cousin's struggle, perhaps, to build a labor
union and his uncle's fight against it—all the emotions, smells
and noises of the ghetto. Before him lay contact with another
great culture, and four years of leisure in which to study, write
and form a picture of himself. But what he would write in
those four years were Keatsian sonnets about English abbeys,
which he had never seen, and nightingales he had never
heard.

I remember a boy from my own city, in this case a gentile
and a graduate of Central High School, which then occupied
a group of antiquated buildings on the edge of the business
section. Southeast of it was a Jewish quarter; to the north,
across the railroad, was the Strip, home of steelworkers, saloons and small-time politicians; to the east lay the Hill, al-

ready inhabited by Negroes, with a small red-light district along the lower slopes of it, through which the boys occasionally wandered at lunchtime. The students themselves were drawn partly from these various slums, but chiefly from residential districts in East Liberty and on Squirrel Hill. They followed an out-of-date curriculum under the direction of teachers renowned for thoroughness and severity; they had every chance to combine four years of sound classical discipline with a personal observation of city morals and sociology and politics in action.

This particular student was brilliant in his classes, editor of the school paper, captain of the debating team; he had the sort of reputation that spreads to other high schools; everybody said he was sure to be famous some day. He entered Harvard two or three years before my time and became a fairly important figure. When I went out for the *Harvard Crimson* (incidentally, without making it) I was sent to get some news about an activity for which he was the spokesman. Maybe he would take an interest in a boy from the same city, who had debated and written for the school paper and won a scholarship like himself. I hurried to his room on Mt. Auburn Street. He was wearing—this was my first impression— a suit of clothes cut by a very good tailor, so well cut, indeed, that it made the features above it seem undistinguished. He eyed me carelessly—my own suit was bought in a department store—and began talking from a distance in a rich Oxford accent put on like his clothes. I went away without my news, feeling ashamed. The story wasn't printed.

Years later I saw him again when I was writing book reviews for a New York newspaper. He came into the office looking very English, like the boss's son. A friendly reporter told me that he was a second-string dramatic critic who would never become first-string. "He ought to get wise to himself," the reporter said. "He's got too much culture for this game."

In college we never grasped the idea that culture was the outgrowth of a situation—that an artisan knowing his tools and having the feel of his materials might be a cultured man; that a farmer among his animals and his fields, stopping his plow at the fence corner to meditate over death and life and next year's crop, might have culture without even reading a newspaper. Essentially we were taught to regard culture as a veneer, a badge of class distinction—as something assumed like an Oxford accent or a suit of English clothes.

Those salesrooms and fitting rooms of culture where we would spend four years were not ground-floor shops, open to the life of the street. They existed, as it were, at the top of very high buildings, looking down at a far panorama of boulevards and Georgian houses and Greek temples of banking—with people outside them the size of gnats—and, vague in the distance, the fields, mines, factories that labored unobtrusively to support us. We never glanced out at them. On the heights, while tailors transformed us into the semblance of cultured men, we exercised happily, studied in moderation, slept soundly and grumbled at our food. There was nothing else to do except pay the bills rendered semi-annually, and our parents attended to that.

College students, especially in the big Eastern universities, inhabit an easy world of their own. Except for very rich people and certain types of childless wives, they have been the only American class that could take leisure for granted. There have always been many among them who earned their board and tuition by tending furnaces, waiting on table or running back kickoffs for a touchdown; what I am about to say does not apply to them. The others—at most times the ruling clique of a big university, the students who set the tone for the rest—are supported practically without efforts of their own. They write a few begging letters; perhaps they study a little harder in order to win a scholarship; but usually they don't stop to think where the money comes from. Above them, the president knows the source of the hard cash that runs this great educational factory; he knows that the stream of donations can be stopped by a crash in the stock market or reduced in volume by newspaper reports of a professor gone bolshevik; he knows what he has to tell his trustees or the state legislators when he goes to them begging for funds. The scrubwomen in the library, the chambermaids and janitors, know how they earn their food; but the students themselves, and many of their professors, are blind to economic forces and they never think of society in concrete terms, as the source of food and football fields and professors' salaries.

The university itself forms a temporary society with standards of its own. In my time at Harvard the virtues instilled into students were good taste, good manners, cleanliness, chastity, gentlemanliness (or niceness), reticence and the spirit of competition in sports; they are virtues often prized by a leisure class. When a student failed to meet the leisure-class standards someone would say, "He talks too much," or more conclusively, "He needs a bath." Even boys from very good Back Bay families would fail to make a club if they paid too much attention to chorus girls. Years later, during the controversy over the New Humanism, I read several books by Professor Irving Babbitt, the founder of the school, and found myself carried back into the atmosphere of the class-room. Babbitt and his disciples liked to talk about poise, proportionateness, the imitation of great models, decorum and the Inner Check. Those too were leisure-class ideals and I decided that they were simply the student virtues rephrased in loftier language. The truth was that the New Humanism grew out of Eastern university life, where it flourished as in a penthouse garden.

Nor was it the only growth that adorned these high mansions of culture. There was also, for example, the college liberalism that always drew back from action. There was the missionary attitude of Phillips Brooks House and the college Y.M.C.A.'s, that of reaching down and helping others to climb not quite up to our level. There was later the life-is-a-circus type of cynicism rendered popular by the *American Mercury:* everything is rotten, people are fools; let's all get quietly drunk and laugh at them. Then, too, there was a type of aestheticism very popular during my own college years. The Harvard Aesthetes of 1916 were trying to create in Cambridge, Massachusetts, an after-image of Oxford in the 1890s. They read the *Yellow Book,* they read Casanova's memoirs and *Les Liaisons Dangereuses,* both in French, and Petronius in Latin; they gathered at teatime in one another's rooms, or at punches in the office of the *Harvard Monthly;* they drank, instead of weak punch, seidels of straight gin topped with a maraschino cherry; they discussed the harmonies of Pater, the rhythms of Aubrey Beardsley and, growing louder, the voluptuousness of the Church, the essential virtue of prostitution. They had crucifixes in their bedrooms, and ticket stubs from last Saturday's burlesque show at the Old Howard. They wrote, too; dozens of them were prematurely decayed poets, each with his invocation to Antinoüs, his mournful descriptions of Venetian lagoons, his sonnets to a chorus girl in which he addressed her as "little painted poem of God." In spite of these beginnings, a few of them became good writers.

They were apparently very different from the Humanists, who never wrote poems at all, and yet, in respect to their opinions, they were simply Humanists turned upside down. For each of the Humanist virtues they had an antithesis. Thus, for poise they substituted *ecstasy;* for proportionateness, the Golden Mean, a worship of *immoderation;* for imitating great models, the opposite virtue of following each impulse, of *living in the moment.* Instead of decorum, they mildly preached a *revolt* from middle-class standards, which led them toward a sentimental reverence for sordid things; instead of the Inner Check, they believed in the duty of *self-expression.* Yet the Humanist and the Aesthete were both products of the same milieu, one in which the productive forces of society were regarded as something alien to poetry and learning. And both of them, though they found different solutions, were obsessed by the same problem, that of their individual salvation or damnation, success or failure, in a world in which neither was at home.

Whatever the doctrines we adopted during our college years, whatever the illusions we had of growing toward culture and self-sufficiency, the same process of deracination was continuing for all of us. We were like so many tumbleweeds sprouting in the rich summer soil, our leaves spreading while our roots slowly dried and became brittle. Normally the deracination would have ended when we left college; outside in the practical world we should have been forced to acquire new roots in order to survive. But we weren't destined to have the fate of the usual college generation and, instead of ceasing, the process would be intensified. Soon the war would be upon us; soon the winds would tear us up and send us rolling and drifting over the wide land.

AMBULANCE SERVICE

During the winter of 1916–17 our professors stopped talking about the international republic of letters and began preaching patriotism. We ourselves prepared to change our uniforms of culture for military uniforms; but neither of these changes was so radical as it seemed. The patriotism urged upon us was not, like that of French peasants, a matter of saving one's own fields from an invader. It was an abstract patriotism that concerned world democracy and the right to self-determination of small nations, but apparently had nothing to do with our daily lives at home, nothing to do with better schools, lower taxes, higher pay for factory hands (and professors) or restocking Elk Run with trout. And the uniforms we assumed were not, in many cases, those of our own country.

When the war came the young writers then in college were attracted by the idea of enlisting in one of the ambulance corps attached to a foreign army—the American Ambulance Service or the Norton-Harjes, both serving under the French and receiving French army pay, or the Red Cross ambulance sections on the Italian front. Those were the organizations that promised to carry us abroad with the least delay. We were eager to get into action, as a character in one of Dos Passos's novels expressed it, "before the whole thing goes belly up."

In Paris we found that the demand for ambulance drivers had temporarily slackened. We were urged, and many of us consented, to join the French military transport, in which our work would be not vastly different: while driving munition trucks we would retain our status of gentleman volunteers. We drank to our new service in the *bistro* round the corner. Two weeks later, on our way to a training camp behind the lines, we passed in a green wheatfield the grave of an aviator *mort pour la patrie*, his wooden cross wreathed with the first lilies of the valley. A few miles north of us the guns were booming. Here was death among the flowers, danger in spring, the sweet wine of sentiment neither spiced with paradox nor yet insipid, the death being real, the danger near at hand.

We found on reaching the front that we were serving in what was perhaps the most literary branch of any army. My own section of thirty-six men will serve as an example. I have never attended a reunion of T.M.U. 526, if one was ever held, but at various times I have encountered several of my former comrades. One is an advertising man specializing in book publishers' copy. One is an architect, one a successful lecturer who has written a first novel, one an editor, one an unsuccessful dramatist. The war itself put an end to other careers. A Rhodes scholar with a distinguished record was killed in action. The member of the section who was generally believed to have the greatest promise was a boy of seventeen, a poet who had himself transferred into the Foreign Legion and died in an airplane accident. Yet T.M.U. 526 was in no way exceptional. My friends in other sections where there was a higher percentage of young writers often pitied me for having to serve with such a bunch of philistines.

It would be interesting to list the authors who were ambulance or camion drivers in 1917. Dos Passos, Hemingway, Julian Green, William Seabrook, E. E. Cummings, Slater Brown, Harry Crosby, John Howard Lawson, Sidney Howard, Louis Bromfield, Robert Hillyer, Dashiell Hammett . . . one might almost say that the ambulance corps and the French military transport were college-extension courses for a generation of writers. But what did these courses teach?

They carried us to a foreign country, the first that most of us had seen; they taught us to make love, stammer love, in a foreign language. They fed and lodged us at the expense of a government in which we had no share. They made us more irresponsible than before: livelihood was not a problem; we had a minimum of choices to make; we could let the future take care of itself, feeling certain that it would bear us into new adventures. They taught us courage, extravagance, fatalism, these being the virtues of men at war; they taught us to regard as vices the civilian virtues of thrift, caution and sobriety; they made us fear boredom more than death. All these lessons might have been learned in any branch of the army, but ambulance service had a lesson of its own: it instilled into us what might be called a *spectatorial* attitude.

. . . Sometimes for three days at a time, a column of men and guns wound through the village where we were quartered. Chasseurs slouching along in their dark-blue uniforms, canteens and helmets banging against their hips; a regiment of Senegalese, huge men with blue-black faces, pink eyeballs and white teeth; then a convoy of camions of first and second gear, keeping pace with the moving files. Behind them, dust rose from an interminable line of seventy-fives drawn by great bay horses, with very blond Flemish artillerymen riding the caissons; then came a supply train; then, in horizon blue, an infantry regiment from Provence, three thousand men with sullen features; then rolling kitchens and wagons heaped with bread the color of faded straw. The Annamites, little mud-colored men with the faces of perverted babies, watched from the ditches where they were breaking stone; the airplanes of three nations kept watch overhead, and we ourselves were watchers. It did not seem that we could ever be part of all this. The long parade of races was a spectacle which it was our privilege to survey, a special circus like the exhibition of Moroccan horsemen given for our benefit on the Fourth of July, before we all sat down at a long table to toast *la France héroïque* and *nos amis américains* in warm champagne. In the morning we should continue our work of carrying trench-mortar bombs from the railhead to the munition dumps just back of the Chemin des Dames—that too would be a spectacle.

Behind the scenes, that early summer, a great drama was being played. The Russians had had their February revolution, the French and British their April offensive; the second had been turned into ridicule when the Germans safely withdrew to stronger positions. There were grumblings in the armies round Verdun and in the Ile de France. Too many men were being killed. The battalion of chasseurs once stationed in our village—those dark stocky men who asked how much longer it would go on, and begged a little gasoline for their cigarette lighters, and got drunk with us while telling of their losses in the last attack—had mutinied the following week. A division from the Midi had refused to go into the trenches. Everywhere there was discontent; it was a question whether the troops would imitate the Russians or fight on patiently till the arrival from America of the help that everybody said would end the war. We ourselves, as representatives of America at the front, were being used to soften this discontent, were being displayed as first-tokens of victory, but we did not realize that we were serving a political purpose. We were treated well, that was all we knew. We were seeing a great show.

I remember a drizzling afternoon when our convoy grumbled into an artillery park with a consignment of 155-millimeter shells. Soldiers came to unload our camions, old dirty Territorials with gunny sacks over their heads. We watched them wearily, having driven and stopped and driven since four in the morning. A shell suddenly burst on the north side of the park. The Territorials disappeared into holes in the ground like so many woodchucks; we ourselves found shelter under an overhanging bank. The bombardment continued: shrapnel mixed with high explosive was bursting in the road every two minutes, regularly. Somebody found that by rushing into the center of the road after each explosion, he could gather warm fragments of steel and return to the shelter of the bank before the next shell burst in the same spot. The rest of us followed his example, fighting over our trophies. A tiny change in the elevation of the German guns and the whole park would be destroyed, ourselves along with it, but we knew that the guns wouldn't change: our lives were charmed. Spectators, we were collecting souvenirs of death, like guests bringing back a piece of wedding cake or a crushed flower from the bride's bouquet.

On a July evening, at dusk, I remember halting in the courtyard of a half-ruined château, through which zigzagged the trenches held by the Germans before their retreat two miles northward to stronger positions. Shells were harmlessly rumbling overhead: the German and the French heavy batteries, three miles behind their respective lines, were shelling each other like the Brushton gang throwing rocks at the Car Barn gang; here, in the empty courtyard between them, it was as if we were underneath a freight yard where heavy trains were being shunted back and forth. We looked indifferently at the lake, now empty of swans, and the formal statues chipped by machine-gun fire, and talked in quiet voices—about Mallarmé, the Russian ballet, the respective virtues of two college magazines. On the steps of the château, in the last dim sunlight, a red-faced boy from Harvard was studying Russian out of a French textbook. Four other gentlemen volunteers were rolling dice on an outspread blanket. A French artillery brigade on a hillside nearby—rapid-firing seventy-fives—was laying down a barrage; the guns flashed like fireflies among the trees. We talked about the Lafayette Escadrille with admiration, and about our own service bitterly.

Yet our service was, in its own fashion, almost ideal. It provided us with fairly good food, a congenial occupation, furloughs to Paris and uniforms that admitted us to the best hotels. It permitted us to enjoy the once-in-a-lifetime spectacle of the Western Front. Being attached to the French army, it freed us from the severe and stupid forms of discipline then imposed on American shavetails and buck privates. It confronted us with hardship, but not more of them than it was exhilarating for young men to endure, and with danger, but not too much of it: seldom were there more than two or three serious casualties in a section during the year—and that was really the burden of our complaint. We didn't want to be slackers, *embusqués*. The war created in young men a thirst for abstract danger, not suffered for a cause but courted for itself; if later they believed in the cause, it was partly in recognition of the danger it conferred on them. Danger was a relief from boredom, a stimulus to the emotions, a color mixed with all others to make them brighter. There were moments in France when the senses were immeasurably sharpened by the thought of dying next day, or possibly next week. The trees were green, not like ordinary trees, but like trees in the still moment before a hurricane; the sky was a special and ineffable blue; the grass smelled of life itself; the image of death at twenty, the image of love, mingled together into a keen, precarious delight. And this perhaps was the greatest of the lessons that the war taught to young writers. It revivified the subjects that had seemed forbidden because they were soiled by many hands and robbed of meaning: danger made it possible to write once more about love, adventure, death. Most of my friends were preparing to follow danger into other branches of the army—of any army—that were richer in fatalities.

They scattered a few months later: when the ambulance and camion services were taken over by the American Expeditionary Force, not many of them re-enlisted. Instead they entered the Lafayette Escadrille, the French or Canadian field artillery, the tanks, the British balloon service, the Foreign Legion, the Royal Air Force; a very few volunteered for the American infantry, doing a simple thing for paradoxical reasons. I had friends in distant sectors: one of them flew for the Belgians, another in Serbia, and several moved on to the Italian front, where John Dos Passos drove an ambulance. Ernest Hemingway was also an ambulance driver on that front, until the July night when an Austrian mortar bomb exploded in the observation post beyond the front lines where he was visiting at the time, like a spectator invited to gossip with the actors behind the scenes. E. E. Cummings was given no choice of service. Having mildly revolted against the discipline of the Norton-Harjes Ambulance Corps, and having become the friend of a boy from Columbia University who wrote letters to Emma Goldman, he was shipped off to a French military prison, where he had the adventures later described in *The Enormous Room*. . . . But even in prison threatened with scurvy, or lying wounded in hospitals, or flying combat planes above the trenches, these young Americans retained their curious attitude of non-participation, of being friendly visitors who, though they might be killed at any moment, still had no share in what was taking place.

Somewhere behind them was another country, a real country of barns, cornfields, hemlock woods and brooks tumbling across birch logs into pools where the big trout lay. Somewhere, at an incredible distance, was the country of their childhood, where they had once been part of the landscape and the life, part of a spectacle at which nobody looked on.

This spectatorial attitude, this monumental indifference toward the cause for which young Americans were risking their lives, is reflected in more than one of the books written by former ambulance drivers. Five of the principal characters in Dos Passos's *1919*—the Grenadine Guards, as he calls them—Dick Savage (a Harvard aesthete), Fred Summers, Ed Schuyler, Steve Warner (another Harvard man, but not of the same college set), and Ripley (a Columbia freshman) first enlist in the Norton-Harjes Ambulance Corps, and then, when the American army takes it over, go south to the Italian front. In February of the last wartime year, Steve Warner reads that the Empress Taitu of Abyssinia is dead, and the Grenadine Guards hold a wake for her:

> They drank all the rum they had and keened until the rest of the section thought they'd gone crazy. They sat in the dark round the open moonlit window wrapped in blankets and drinking warm zabaglione. Some Austrian planes that had been droning overhead suddenly cut off their motors and dumped a load of bombs right in front of them. The anti-aircraft guns had been barking for some time and shrapnel sparkling in the moonhazy sky overhead but they'd been too drunk to notice. One bomb fell geflump into the Brenta and the others filled the space in front of the window with red leaping glare and shook the villa

with three roaring snorts. Plaster fell from the ceiling. They could hear the tiles scuttering down off the roof overhead.

"Jesus, that was almost good night," said Summers. Steve started singing, *Come away from that window my light and my life,* but the rest of them drowned it out with an out of tune *Deutschland, Deutschland über Alles.* They suddenly all felt crazy drunk. . . .

"Fellers," Fred Summers kept saying, "this ain't a war, it's a goddam madhouse . . . it's a goddam Cook's tour." It remained, for many of us, a goddam crazy Cook's tour of Western Europe, but for those who served longer it became something else as well.

Ernest Hemingway's hero, in *A Farewell to Arms,* is an American acting as lieutenant of an Italian ambulance section. He likes the Italians, at least until Caporetto; he is contemptuous of the Austrians, fears and admires the Germans; of political conviction he has hardly a trace. When a friend tells him, "What has been done this summer cannot have been done in vain," he makes no answer:

> I was always embarrassed by the words sacred, glorious, and sacrifice, and the expression in vain. We had heard them, sometimes standing in the rain almost out of earshot, so that only the shouted words came through, and had read them, on proclamations that were slapped up by billposters over other proclamations, now for a long time, and I had seen nothing sacred, and the things that were glorious had no glory and the sacrifices were like the stockyards at Chicago if nothing was done with the meat except to bury it. . . . Abstract words such as glory, honor, courage, or hallow were obscene beside the concrete names of villages, the numbers of roads, the names of rivers, the numbers of regiments and the dates. Gino was a patriot, so he said things that separated us sometimes, but he was also a fine boy and I understood his being a patriot. He was born one. He left with Peduzzi in the car. . . .

Two days later the Germans broke through at Caporetto. The passage dealing with the Italian retreat from river to river, from the mountains beyond the Isonzo along rain-washed narrow roads to the plains of the Tagliamento, is one of the few great war stories in American literature: only *The Red Badge of Courage* and a few short pieces by Ambrose

Bierce can be compared with it. Hemingway describes not an army but a whole people in motion: guns nuzzling the heads of patient farm horses, munition trucks with their radiator caps an inch from the tailboard of wagons loaded with chairs, tables, sewing machines, farm implements; then behind them ambulances, mountain artillery, cattle and army trucks, all pointed south; and groups of scared peasants and interminable files of gray infantrymen moving in the rain past the miles of stalled vehicles. Lieutenant Frederick Henry is part of the retreat, commanding three motor ambulances and half a dozen men, losing his vehicles in muddy lanes, losing his men, too, by death and desertion, shooting an Italian sergeant who tries to run away—but in spirit he remains a non-participant. He had been studying architecture in Rome, had become a gentleman volunteer in order to see the war, had served two years, been wounded and decorated: now he is sick of the whole thing, eager only to get away.

As he moves southward, the southbound Germans go past him, marching on parallel roads, their helmets visible above the walls. Frightened Italians open fire on him. The rain falls endlessly, and the whole experience, Europe, Italy, the war, becomes a nightmare, with himself as helpless as a man among nightmare shapes. It is only in snatches of dream that he finds anything real—love being real, and the memories of his boyhood. "The hay smelled good and lying in a barn in the hay took away all the years in between. We had lain in hay and talked and shot sparrows with an air rifle when they perched in the triangle cut high up in the wall of the barn. The barn was gone now and one year they had cut the hemlock woods and there were only stumps, dried tree-tops, branches and fireweed where the woods had been. You could not go back"; the country of his boyhood was gone and he was attached to no other.

And that, I believe, was the final effect on us of the war; that was the honest emotion behind a pretentious phrase like "the lost generation." School and college had uprooted us in spirit; now we were physically uprooted, hundreds of us, millions, plucked from our own soil as if by a clamshell bucket and dumped, scattered among strange people. All our roots were dead now, even the Anglo-Saxon tradition of our literary ancestors, even the habits of slow thrift that characterized our social class. We were fed, lodged, clothed by strangers, com-

manded by strangers, infected with the poison of irrespon-
sibility—the poison of travel, too, for we had learned that
problems could be left behind us merely by moving elsewhere—and the poison of danger, excitement, that made our
old life seem intolerable. Then, as suddenly as it began for
us, the war ended.

When we first heard of the Armistice we felt a sense of
relief too deep to express, and we all got drunk. We had
come through, we were still alive, and nobody at all would
be killed tomorrow. The composite fatherland for which we
had fought and in which some of us still believed—France,
Italy, the Allies, our English homeland, democracy, the self-
determination of small nations—had triumphed. We danced
in the streets, embraced old women and pretty girls, swore
blood brotherhood with soldiers in little bars, drank with our
elbows locked in theirs, reeled through the streets with bottles
of champagne, fell asleep somewhere. On the next day, after
we got over our hangovers, we didn't know what to do, so
we got drunk. But slowly, as the days went by, the intoxication
passed, and the tears of joy: it appeared that our composite
fatherland was dissolving into quarreling statesmen and oil
and steel magnates. Our own nation had passed the Prohibition Amendment as if to publish a bill of separation between
itself and ourselves; it wasn't our country any longer. Nevertheless we returned to it: there was nowhere else to go. We
returned to New York, appropriately—to the homeland of
the uprooted, where everyone you met came from another
town and tried to forget it; where nobody seemed to have
parents, or a past more distant than last night's swell party,
or a future beyond the swell party this evening and the disillusioned book he would write tomorrow.

[1934, 1951]

—AND I WORKED
AT THE WRITER'S TRADE

Let me turn back to my own beginnings in the writer's trade. I got started in the trade strictly from hunger, as people used to say in excusing their delinquencies. In the spring of 1919 I was twenty years old, I was hungry in Greenwich Village, and I was living in sin without paying the rent for our room. One of the possibly helpful persons I went to see was a former boy friend of my girl friend. Clarence Britten was his name, and he was literary editor of *The Dial*, then a political fortnightly that had moved from Chicago to New York under the somewhat reluctant patronage of an eccentric millionaire. Britten looked at me curiously as he invited me into his office. He asked after Peggy, made one or two abrupt gestures, then pushed half a dozen novels across his desk. "Try reviewing these," he said, "but don't give them more than a hundred words apiece." If and when the reviews were published, they would each bring me a dollar.

Six times one dollar seemed a happy prospect for the following month, but meanwhile there was the problem of buying food for dinner that evening. Later I wrote in *Exile's Return*, with you's standing for I's,

> So you would carry the books to a bench in Union Square and page through them hastily, making notes—in two or three hours you would be finished with the whole armful and you would take them to a secondhand bookstore on Fourth Avenue, where the proprietor paid a flat rate of thirty-five cents for each review copy; you thought it was more than the novels were worth. With exactly $2.10 in your pocket you would buy bread and butter and lamb chops and Bull Durham for cigarettes and order a bag of coal; then at home you would broil the lamb chops over the grate because the landlady had neglected to pay her gas bill, just as you had neglected to pay the rent. You were all good friends and she would be invited to share the feast. Next morning

you would write the reviews, then start on the search for a few dollars more.

The search led me to other editorial offices, for I was now definitely apprenticed to the trade of putting words on paper. On reading Diane Eisenberg's checklist of my published writings* compiled after she had grubbed among back files with more patience than most of the writings deserve, I find that each of the early items helps to evoke a way of life now vanished together with the magazines that made it barely possible. Mrs. Eisenberg does not list those brief reviews in the fortnightly *Dial*—for how could she identify the deservedly anonymous?—but one of her entries for the summer of the same year records my first signed appearance in a magazine that paid for contributions:

F5 "Through Yellow Glasses." *New Republic* XIX (July 23, 1919): 401.
Victorious, by Reginald Wright Kauffman.

As I read those cabbalistic words, I can see myself walking in cracked shoes under the Ninth Avenue Elevated. It is a late-spring afternoon and the sun is projecting a pattern of crossties on the pavement. Under my arm I carry a square brown notebook in which the first dozen pages are filled with clippings of my published work: not only those first unsigned reviews in *The Dial* but earlier signed ones in *The Harvard Advocate* and a long poem that has just appeared in *The Little Review*. I am hurrying to the offices of *The New Republic*, where Francis Hackett, the literary editor, has agreed over the telephone to give me a few moments.

Hackett, a big, red-faced Irishman looking like Jupiter in pince-nez glasses, is seated behind a pile of books at a scarred enormous desk that will be my desk ten years later (though the possibility does not then enter my mind). He glances at my little collection of press clippings, reads the brief notices from *The Dial*, then calls to his assistant, "Miss Updike, perhaps you can find a book for this young man." Taking off his pince-nez, he gives me a lordly smile of dismissal. Miss Updike looks at my cracked shoes, then picks out a novel by Reginald

---

* *Malcolm Cowley: A Checklist of His Writings, 1916–1973*, by Diane U. Eisenberg (Carbondale, Ill.: Southern Illinois University Press, 1973).

Wright Kauffman that she thinks might be worth five hundred words—or ten dollars, I calculate, at *The New Republic*'s two cents a word. She gives me the book as if she were pouring a saucer of milk for a starved kitten.

End of the memory, and almost the end of my first attempt to keep two persons alive by free-lance book reviewing. It was yielding us hardly more than one meal a day, and the meals were usually deficient in proteins and carbohydrates. I dreamed about the hilltop cabin upstate where I had lived with Foster Damon and Kenneth Burke on trout and wild strawberries (with bread and milk, all we could eat). One morning I was crossing Sheridan Square after no breakfast when the sidewalk suddenly came up and hit me in the face. I didn't lose consciousness for more than a moment. Less frightened than surprised, I picked myself up and walked carefully into a lunchroom to spend my last dime for a stale bun and a cup of coffee. As I sat at the counter feeling not at all hungry and more than usually clearheaded, I surrendered, for a time, my pride in living on the underside of society and my dream of being a free artisan working at his typewriter as if it were a cottage loom.

> When I was a bachelor I lived by myself,
>   And I worked at the weaver's trade,
>   And the only, only thing I did that was wrong
>   Was to woo a fair young maid.

My fair maid was older than I and more experienced, with many good friends in the Village who were now tired of lending her money. I had shielded her from the foggy, foggy dew, but, though she never complained, I had been remiss in providing bread and cigarettes and pretties. For me there was always that exasperating wait between writing a review and getting paid for it. "Anything else?" the counterman asked in an ominous voice. I started home, still walking with care and knowing now that a job would have to be found. A few days later I found it, too, by answering want ads and accepting a miserable salary. At least there would be enough to keep the two of us fed.

In the fall I went back to college, where I had a scholarship of sorts and could borrow a little money from the dean's office (there was none from home). I planned to earn a degree by taking six courses in one semester, a heavier load than any

Harvard student is now permitted to stagger under. To make things more difficult, I was married by then and Peggy was in frail health. Nevertheless, in the intervals between studying and nursing, I managed to do some writing for publication, as I am reminded by other items in Mrs. Eisenberg's checklist. Mary Updike, God bless her, remembered the starved kitten and sent me at least two packages of books for review. I must have been the only undergraduate who was a fairly regular contributor to *The New Republic*.

Still another entry for the same period records the beginning of what was to be a long and close collaboration:

F9 "The Woman of Ihornden." *Dial* LXVIII (February 1920):
259–62.
A Challenge to Sirius and *The Four Roads*, by Sheila Kaye-Smith.

Clarence Britten, out of kindness to me or to Peggy, I don't know which, had decided that I ought to do a signed piece for *The Dial*. As an occasion for it, he sent me two novels by Sheila Kaye-Smith, an English novelist then held in some estimation. The review was accepted soon after I went back to college, but weeks passed and it did not appear. Meanwhile Britten had lost his job. *The Dial* had been sold by its eccentric angel and purchased by two other millionaires, Scofield Thayer and Sibley Watson, both recently out of Harvard. They planned to transform the fortnightly *Dial* into the most distinguished monthly magazine of the arts that had appeared in this country. For the purchase price of I don't know how much, they had acquired the name, a modest list of subscribers, and a barrel, so called—it was really a small box—full of accepted but unpublished manuscripts. Having read their way through the barrel, they decided that nothing in it was worthy to appear in a magazine of the highest literary standards—nothing, that is, except my piece on Sheila Kaye-Smith, which would serve as the only link between the old and the new. It appeared in the second or February issue of the monthly *Dial,* just as I was packing to leave Harvard with my precariously earned degree.

Leave I must, but I had no destination except, vaguely, New York. Two days before we planned to go, if I could pay for our railroad tickets, there were footsteps on the stairs and a knock at the door of our attic room. A young man, a stranger, gave me an envelope and said, "Mr. Copeland told me not to wait for an answer." Inside the envelope was a ten-dollar bill folded in a note from Charles Townsend Copeland—"Copey," as everyone called him—my favorite English instructor. "I thought you could use this," Copey had written in his big sloping hand. The ten dollars paid our fare to Grand Central, in those days of cheaper transportation, with enough left over for a taxi to the house in Greenwich Village where our former landlady had offered to put us up for a few days. We rode there holding hands through streets still heaped with grimy snow from a storm two weeks before.

Our prospects were as bleak as the Manhattan streets, but we felt more cheerful now that Peggy had partly recovered her health. She began to circulate once more among Village friends, and one of them found us three rooms on the top floor of a tenement, reached by climbing five flights of stairs that smelled of Italian cooking. A check arrived in the nick of time—like every other check that did arrive—and paid the first month's rent of sixteen dollars. Our bed was borrowed, our chairs were begged, and my writing table was bought for next to nothing at a Salvation Army store. Soon I was writing every day—poems mostly, but also any sort of prose for which a market could be found at a penny a word; only *The New Republic* and the monthly *Dial* were more generous. Mrs. Eisenberg's checklist testifies to many afternoons spent tramping from one editorial office to another.

As I look back on those years, it seems to me that I must have had a somewhat special cast of mind. I wanted to be a writer, but not a celebrated writer appearing in glossy magazines. I wanted to live obscurely, limit my needs, and preserve my freedom to write something new and perfect at some moment in the future; that was the dream of producing a masterpiece that obsessed the young writers of my age group. While waiting for the moment I was willing to do hackwork, a meager source of income, as I had learned, but one that I judged to be permissible if the work was honestly performed. Always I tried to make it better work than I was paid for doing, with the result that my little commissioned pieces had qualities not to be found in my life at the time: punctuality, for example, and neatness and logic. Editors liked them because they could be sent to the printer without revision.

Editors are sometimes excessively kind to very young writers, especially if these are talkative or show any sign of promise. With special gratitude I remember Henry Seidel Canby and his assistant Amy Loveman. I first dropped in on them when Dr. Canby was starting a new weekly supplement, *The Literary Review of the New York Evening Post;* workmen were still installing partitions in what were to be their offices. Miss Loveman listened through the din of hammers while I gave her a lecture on contemporary French poetry. Once or twice she smiled maternally, and she let me carry away two books for unsigned reviews. Later that spring Dr. Canby invited me into his by then completed sanctum; we talked about trout fishing and he reproved me for using worms. Then he suggested that I take, each week, half a dozen books that *The Literary Review* was planning to discard. I should page through them and, if I found that one or two deserved attention, I should write the reviews. For this I was to be paid ten dollars a week. I accepted the arrangement, which made me, at the time, the only salaried book reviewer in New York.

Of course I was writing for other journals as well and, in one way or another, I managed to get along. When checks were slow in arriving, I played penny ante on Saturday nights, cards held close to my chest, and could count on winning ten dollars if the game lasted till morning. For two weeks I was a stagehand at the Provincetown Players and earned twenty dollars a week. Why, I was prosperous, and independent too, and when I was offered a regular job by *Sweet's Architectural Catalogue* I came near turning it down. But finally I accepted it, and held it for a year, until I was given a fellowship to a French university by the American Field Service, with which I had served during the war. Peggy and I got ready to go abroad.

2.

Reading over this account of a literary apprenticeship, I find that it often mentions very small sums of money. There is good reason for the mention, considering that money is the central problem of a young writer's life, or of his staying alive. True as the statement is today, it was even more true in the 1920s, when there were fewer sources of literary livelihood. Universities didn't then invite young novelists or critics to join their English staffs or young poets to give paid readings. There were very few literary prizes; there were no subsidies by foundations. Fellowships to foreign universities, like the one I had lately been given, were scarce and meager and hard to come by. More dependence had to be placed on the small sums paid for contributions by magazines of limited circulation. The smaller one's gross income, the more important each little payment became and the more pride one took in earning it.

The poverty of young American writers during the prosperous 1920s was of course a central reason for their exodus to Europe. There were other reasons too, as notably Prohibition, puritanism, and the triumph of business over art in American society, from which young writers felt no less alienated than their successors fifty years later; but there was chiefly the promise of cheaper living in Europe. It was not a false promise, as can be seen from my own experience in the years 1921–23. My fellowship was for twelve thousand francs, or one thousand dollars at what was then the rate of exchange. It was renewed for the following year, but was worth a little less in dollars, since the franc had fallen. I also earned a little money by writing for American periodicals, but not more than five hundred dollars for each of the years. On a total income for the two-year period of less than three thousand dollars, I paid for our passage to France, lived there in rather more comfort than at home, traveled a little, and had just enough left for our return passage to New York. As regards the writing I did for American periodicals while in France, there are several examples in Mrs. Eisenberg's checklist, but I shall mention only one:

> G9 "Henri Barbusse." *Bookman* LVI (October 1922): 180–182.
> Barbusse became famous overnight with *Under Fire*, a literarily and politically provocative novel.

The story of that article begins like many other stories, at a sidewalk table outside the Café du Dôme. There one summer afternoon I found Ivan Opffer, a feckless Dane I had known in the Village. Ivan told me that *The Bookman* had commissioned him to draw portraits of the best-known French authors. "Why don't you come along and do an article to go with the next picture?" he said. His next scheduled visit was to Henri Barbusse, author of a famous antiwar novel, *Le Feu*.

We found that the roads around his little country house were patrolled by gendarmes in pairs, on bicycles; one pair stopped us and asked to see our passports. "That's how things go in France," Barbusse said as he offered each of us a long, emaciated hand; he had the visionary look of a John the Baptist. I asked him questions and took notes in two languages while Ivan made hasty sketches on big sheets of drawing paper. Ivan was wonderful at catching facial expressions, but he had never learned to draw hands. My little profile in words was of course written on spec, but it resulted in a commission to do six others, all with Ivan's handless figures as illustrations. Lectured at by one author after another, I learned something about French literary politics and was modestly paid for writing what amounted to classroom reports on my studies.

I also contributed to magazines published in Europe, sometimes rather obscure ones, as Mrs. Eisenberg's checklist shows. One item recalls a story:

M73 "Madrigals." *Mécano* (Leiden), numbers 4 and 5 (1923), n.p.
Three short, rather scabrous poems printed in a Dutch Dadaist magazine edited by Theo van Doesburg. Never reprinted.

Again the story starts at the Dôme, where, one spring at noon, I found my good friend Tristan Tzara, the founder of Dada. A Rumanian living in Switzerland, he had been brought to Paris in 1919 by Louis Aragon, also my friend, and André Breton. Now he was having quarrels with the French Dadaists, originally his disciples, but he was still held in reverence by Dadaist groups sprung up in Germany, Belgium, and Holland. That afternoon Tzara was sitting with an eager, rather innocent—so it seemed to me—Dutch Dadaist named Theo van Doesburg; later he was to become internationally known for I forget what. Tzara introduced me as a *poète Dada américain*. Van Doesburg asked whether I wouldn't contribute to a little magazine he was publishing in Leiden. Why, yes, *volontiers*, I said, thinking of some scabrous songs I had written for my own entertainment. It would be amusing to print them in a Dutch Dadaist paper when they couldn't appear, at the time, anywhere in the English-speaking world:

> *masochistic Mazie*
> *very nearly crazy*
> *almost*
> > *very nearly*
> > > *quite*
> *insane*
> *scratched her pretty asshole*
> *over broken glass*
> > > *coal*
> *cinders*
> > *Joy*
> > > *Sex*
> > > > *Pain*
> *WASn't she insane?*

That was the first of the "Madrigals." There was another about Sadic Sam from Alabam, there were two lines about fetishistic Fanny, who married Jack the Ripper, and they were duly printed in Joint Nos. 4 & 5 of *Mécano*. A year later Hemingway published other scabrous lyrics in a German semi-Dadaist magazine called *Der Querschnitt,* one which had the greater distinction of paying its contributors.

In the late spring of 1923 my fellowship expired, money ran short, and we started to think about going back to New York. We were then living in three rooms above the former blacksmith shop in Giverny, a Norman village fifty miles down the Seine from Paris. Bob Coates, our big red-headed friend, agreed to take over the rooms and we began to pack our few possessions into a wicker trunk. I felt that there ought to be something more ponderable as a memento of those two years in Europe. An essay on Racine, just finished, was a brief work in which I took pride. I carried the essay to a printer in Paris and received his estimate: for two hundred copies of a stapled pamphlet he would charge me less than thirty-five dollars at the current rate of exchange. That brings me to the very first item in the Malcolm Cowley checklist:

A1 *Racine*. Paris: Privately printed, 1923.
> Of the 200 original copies only 15 are known to survive.
> . . . Later appeared in the *Freeman* (see G15, G16).

Let me explain why the pamphlet is so rare. The two hundred copies, dedicated to Copey, "In default of a better gift," I said, went back with us to New York, and there I started mailing them out to friends. There too I made the humiliating discovery that I hadn't two hundred friends or bowing acquaintances who might be interested in Racine; at most I could stretch the list to forty or fifty names. The remaining copies of the pamphlet lay piled in various closets for several years, until I got tired of carrying them from one habitation to another; then I dropped them into a wastebasket except for a dozen or more copies that I saved. In 1960 or thereabouts I looked at the catalogue of a rare-book dealer and found that one copy of the pamphlet, "slightly foxed," was being offered for thirty-five dollars, or a little more than I had paid for the whole edition. The price ten years later had risen to seventy-five dollars. By that time, however, I had only two copies left and couldn't be tempted to sell them.

When we got back to New York in August 1923 I had only five dollars in my wallet, but this time my prospects were somewhat brighter than they had been in 1920. I paid a visit to my former boss at *Sweet's Architectural Catalogue* and was promptly hired back at a better salary. For a long time I was kept too busy to write anything for publication except a few reviews for *The Dial* and for Dr. Canby. But I dreamed of going deep into the country and living once again as a free-lance writer, and already I was moving in that direction, one step at a time. First I began to look for other periodical outlets, then I rented a little house on Staten Island that had a vegetable garden to practice in, then I bought a very old Model T Ford, and then, as a decisive step, I resigned from *Sweet's* to see whether I could live for a year by writing. After living out the year, which ended in the spring of 1926, I helped to load our three sticks of furniture and our four boxes of books on a wheezing Model T truck, and we set out for Sherman, Connecticut. Friends of mine—Hart Crane, Allen Tate, William Slater Brown, Matthew Josephson—lived in the neighborhood, and they had found us an old farmhouse with exterior nonplumbing that rented for ten dollars a month. The wheezing truck broke down at the top of Briggs Hill, half a mile from its destination, and our belongings arrived on a farm wagon.

I note some further entries that explain how we had kept ourselves going.

G19 "Parnassus-on-the-Seine." *Charm* I (July 1924): 19, 80, 83.
"Montparnasse, the art student quarter of Paris, is the rendezvous of the world."

Charm was a rather elaborate magazine that had just been started by Bamberger's department store in Newark, New Jersey, for distribution to its charge customers. Its first editor was Bessie Breuer, a friend of Peggy's; later she became a novelist, sound and perceptive but not widely perceived. Bessie tried to help us by dreaming up articles for me to write—outlandish articles, so it seemed to this serious literary person, but still I accepted the challenge, much as if I had been an engineer asked to design an outlandish bridge. When Bessie was succeeded by another able editor, Lucie Taussig, I began suggesting my own subjects, often drawn from New Jersey history. I also wrote a monthly book page for *Charm* and presented the literary scene in terms that I hoped would interest New Jersey housewives.

F51 "Mr. Moore's Golden Treasury." *New York Herald Tribune Books*, August 2, 1925, p. 5.
An Anthology of Pure Poetry, edited with an introduction by George Moore.

That must have been the first review I wrote for Irita Van Doren. I don't remember whether I asked her for the book or whether she suggested my reviewing it after her friend Harrison Smith had written a front-page article about my first translation from the French, *On Board the Morning Star*, a cycle of pirate stories by Pierre MacOrlan. In either case I was soon contributing regularly to Mrs. Van Doren's book section. Among the kindhearted editors I have known, she was by far the kindest. She had taken over *Herald Tribune Books* after the sudden death of Stuart Pratt Sherman, its first editor, and had directed it successfully from the beginning. Young ambitious people wanted to write for her. On Wednesday afternoons, I think it was, when she held a sort of open house for reviewers and would-be reviewers, they used to gather in her waiting room from their garrets and cellars. That year it always rained on Wednesday afternoon, or so it seems to me now. The picture that stays in my mind is of one young woman—I never learned her name—sitting with wet shoes and a dripping skirt, her lank hair framing a long-jawed, pale, moist, eager face, as she waited for a word or still better a book from Mrs. Van Doren.

Irita was an Alabama woman with a soft voice and an enchanting smile, but she could be firm at moments; she could even be ruthless when that was the kindest thing to be. Once she had accepted a reviewer, she kept him on her staff year after year—sometimes too long—and looked for interesting books for him to write about. It was partly owing to her loyal friendship that I was able to carry out my project of living deep in the country with nothing to sell but words.

We didn't live very well. There was always something to eat in the house, but sometimes there wasn't very much, and on those days I would wait for the mailman in hope of his bringing me a nick-of-time check. If the check arrived, I would drive over back roads to New Milford, Connecticut, and deposit it in what passed for my bank account. I didn't dare to cash the check in New Milford, since the account was seldom large enough to cover it. Instead I would drive sixteen miles to Pawling, New York, buy groceries, and pay for them with a check drawn on New Milford. It would have to pass through the New York clearinghouse and the Boston clearinghouse before it reached the bank, a process that would take three or four days. By that time my deposit would have been collected and credited to my account, and the check written in Pawling would be honored. It sounds complicated, but it was all part of the writers' trade, just as much as the proper use of semicolons.

3.

There is one more of Mrs. Eisenberg's entries to mention, the one that records publication of my first book and hence the end of a literary apprenticeship. Once again it recalls a story.

L2 *Blue Juniata.* New York: Jonathan Cape and Harrison Smith, 1929. 115 pp.
   56 poems in five parts: 1. Blue Juniata; 2. The Adolescent; 3. Valuta; 4. The City of Anger; 5. Old Melodies: Love and Death.

Hart Crane is the hero of the story. It begins in the summer of 1928, when Hart came back to the rooms he rented in Addie Turner's bleak house, five miles from Patterson, New York, after a disastrous winter in California. I had moved across the state line that spring after contracting to buy, if I could make the payments, sixty acres of abandoned farmland and a hungry-looking house half a mile from Mrs. Turner's. We saw Hart almost daily that summer. Like everyone else we noted that his bristly hair was turning gray and that his face was redder and puffier. Those were signs of a physiological change, from being a "heavy social drinker," as we had always known him, to being a "problem drinker," the first stage of true alcoholism. He was paying more and more visits to Wiley Varian, the cashiered army officer who ran a speakeasy on Birch Hill. "Sometimes Hart gave a party," and then, says Nathan Asch,* who was living in the same big house that summer, "we, the writers rejected by New York booming with the market of the twenties, consoled ourselves with the gaiety we could engender ourselves. We drank the liquor from either Varian's or one of the other bootleggers, and then we shouted and then we danced. . . . We did not speak to each other, but rather each of us howled out, and we did not dance with our wives or even with each other, but whirled around Hart's room, faster and faster, as if we were truly possessed." Yes, we did all that and more, with the phonograph blaring and Hart leading the revels, but we did it on only one occasion; I think it was on his birthday, July 21. Hart wasn't much of a party giver.

Instead he was a party goer. He distinguished himself, though I don't remember how, at the Fourth of July party given by Slater and Sue Brown, and he came back from New York for the party on Labor Day. Everybody speaks of that summer in terms of parties. What I remember with more pleasure are the long, intensely quiet mornings, the games of

* Nathan Asch, a tragic figure in retrospect, hated to be known as a son of the famous Yiddish novelist Sholem Asch. Still in his twenties when he lived in Addie Turner's house, Nathan had already published two novels and was working on a third (*Pay Day*, 1930). He thought he was a better writer than his father, and indeed he wrote more lyrically, sometimes with deeper feeling, but he lacked the father's simple vigor and breadth of conception. After World War II, in which he served with courage, he couldn't get his books published any longer, at a time when his father's books were selling more widely than ever. Nathan's death in 1964 went almost unnoticed. [M.C.]

croquet at the Browns', where we gathered on Sunday afternoons, the weekday afternoons spent fishing by myself or walking in the woods with Hart, and the talks about poets and poetry. Hart had a purely unselfish project that summer; he was going to prod me into collecting a book of poems. "I have it at least in mind," he wrote to Isidor and Helen Schneider in July, "to try my best to get his poems accepted by some publisher or other before a twelvemonth. He'll never do much about it himself, as you know, and his collection is really needed on the shelves these days."

Hart was right in thinking that I would have been slow to do anything about it myself. I had sixty-odd poems, all printed in magazines during the preceding ten years—there was an immediacy that I enjoyed in magazine publication—but I felt no urgent desire to make a book of them. Although the book would come in time, I rather preferred to be unknown for the moment, except to magazine readers, and therefore unclassified, free to move in any direction. But Hart kept prodding me. Early in July he had made me assemble a sheaf of poems; then we went over them together, rejecting some by mutual consent and discussing which of the others belonged together, in exactly what order. Hart believed that emotions, and the poems that expressed them, should follow one another in the right sequence. He thought naturally in terms of structure and of "the book," which, he insisted, should be more than a random selection of poems by one author. In the poems themselves he did not change a word—not even later, when he retyped the whole manuscript—since both of us felt that a poet should speak in his own voice.

When he left for New York early in August there was a book of sorts and one that might have been printed, but I still had only a vague notion of showing it to a publisher. Hart's notion was more definite. On October 24 he asked me—it wasn't the first time, since some of his letters have been lost—"to bring in all the mss material of your poems which I was in the process of editing last summer. I'll soon have plenty of time to give the matter, and I have a suspicion that something will come of it now." On November 20 he announced in a drunken early-morning letter that the poems had arrived the day before. "I'll be careful with the mss," he said, "and your book'll be out within 7 months," that is, within the "twelvemonth" he had mentioned in his letter to the

Schneiders. On December 1, a week before sailing for Europe, he wrote, "It has been a pleasure for me to spend part of the last two days in typing the mss of your book. . . . I now have two copies, one to turn over to the 'secret' arbiter here and one to take with me to England." He had omitted one poem that both of us had questions about and had changed the position in the manuscript of three others. "Really the book as we now have it," he said, "has astonishing structural sequence," thus ending the sentence with two of his favorite words. The original manuscript was being returned to me by registered mail.

A few weeks later, when Hart was in London or Paris, I heard from the "secret arbiter." He turned out to be Gorham Munson, then an editor of the George H. Doran Company (which later merged with Doubleday). Munson and I had been on opposite sides of the quarrels in 1923 that hastened the deaths of two little magazines, *Broom* and *Secession;* that was why Hart hadn't mentioned his name. Now Munson laid the quarrels aside. In the name of his company he offered me a contract for the book—it had by then acquired a title, *Blue Juniata*—together with a modest advance against royalties. Hart's project was bearing fruit, and in less than the twelve-month he had specified.

At this point, however, the project was interrupted by the stiff-necked character of the author. Grateful as I was to Hart, I had a Pennsylvania Dutch side that hated to be—as my forebears would have said—"beholden" to anyone for the structure and publication of my first book. I thanked Munson for the offer and said I would think about it. Then I showed the original manuscript to Harrison Smith, a friend of mine (of Hart's too, and of the Van Dorens'), who had started a publishing house in partnership with Jonathan Cape of London. Hal, as everyone called him, promptly accepted it and gave me a slightly larger advance than Doran had offered.

I took the manuscript home—we were spending the winter in a cramped apartment on Avenue B, south of the present East Village—and set to work on it. First I gave the poems a completely different sequence, not emotional or dialectical, as Hart had suggested (and as he himself had followed in *White Buildings*), but autobiographical. The new framework made it possible to use a few of the poems that Hart and I had earlier decided to omit; they were callow, as we agreed, but callowness was part of the story I was telling. Then I divided the book into five sections and furnished notes, in prose, to introduce three of these. I revised most of the poems once again, a task that continued through the winter (though it was interrupted when I had to do translations to pay the rent). Meanwhile Hart had carried his copy of the earlier manuscript to Paris and was trying to persuade his rich friend Harry Crosby to publish it at the Black Sun Press. I learn from John Unterecker's biography of Hart that he was on the point of succeeding when I wrote him late in January that the book was coming out in New York.

By the middle of June *Blue Juniata* was in type and I sent an extra set of galleys to Hart. I was a little afraid that his vanity would be wounded by my failure to accept his suggestions, but I need not have been, for Hart had almost no vanity of the sort. He was not interested in whether the book embodied his ideas, but only in whether it was put together effectively. "Since reading the proofs," he wrote me on July 3, 1929, "I'm certain that the book is even better . . . a much more solidified unit than it was before. I haven't had the original mss with me for comparison, but wherever I have noted changes they seem to be for the better. Really, Malcolm—if you will excuse me for the egoism—I'm just a little proud of the outcome of my agitations last summer." It had been exactly a twelvemonth since he started them.

So I end with this message of gratitude to a dead friend. As I piece together the story, I think again how different Hart was, on that wise and amiable side of him, from the drunken rioter he is often pictured as being. All this took place in the time of his noisiest riots, and yet he devoted sober weeks to editing and typing and peddling someone else's manuscript. He was absolutely lacking in professional jealousy—except toward T. S. Eliot, and that was a compliment to Eliot; otherwise Hart was jealous only of the great dead. The little victories gained by his friends delighted him more than his own victories. "You're a lucky boy!" he wrote me after reading some favorable reviews of *Blue Juniata*. "I'm very glad about it all"—and he truly was. He was the first person to whom I sent an inscribed copy of the book. "If it's bad," I wrote on the flyleaf, "the sin be on your head." He carried

the book with him when he went to Mexico in 1931. My first
wife was there too, getting a friendly divorce, and finally they
sailed for New York together. Peggy retrieved the book from
his stateroom on the *Orizaba* the day he jumped overboard.

[1975]

EXAMINATION PAPER

People who read books without writing them are likely to form a simple picture of any celebrated author. He is John X or Jonathan Y, the man who wrote such a fascinating novel about Paris, about divorce, about the Georgia Crackers—the man who drinks, who ran off with the doctor's wife—the bald-headed man who lectured to the Wednesday Club. But to writers, especially to young writers in search of guidance, the established author presents a much more complicated image.

Their impressions of the great author are assembled from many sources. It is true that his books are a principal source, but there must also be considered his career, the point from which it started, the direction in which it seems to be moving. There is his personality, as revealed in chance interviews or as caricatured in gossip; there are the values that he assigns to other writers; and there is the value placed on himself by his younger colleagues in those kitchen or barroom gatherings at which they pass judgment with the harsh finality of a Supreme Court—John X has got real stuff, they say, but Jonathan Y is terrible—and they bring forward evidence to support these verdicts. The evidence is mulled over, all the details are fitted together like the pieces of a jigsaw puzzle, until they begin to form a picture, vague and broken at first, then growing more distinct as the years pass by: the X or Y picture, the James Joyce, Ezra Pound or T. S. Eliot picture. But it is not so much a picture when completed: it is rather a map or diagram which the apprentice writer will use in planning his own career.

If he is called upon to review a book by Joyce or Eliot, he will say certain things he believes to be accurate: they are not the things lying closest to his heart. Secretly he is wondering whether he can, whether he should, ever be great in the Joyce or Eliot fashion. What path should he follow to reach this goal? The great living authors, in the eyes of any young man enticed to the Muse, are a series of questions, an examination paper compiled by and submitted to himself:

1. What problems do these authors suggest?

2. With what problems are they consciously dealing?

3. Are they my own problems? Or if not, shall I make them my own?

4. What is the Joyce solution to these problems (or the Eliot, the Pound, the Gertrude Stein, the Paul Valéry solution)?

5. Shall I adopt it? Reject it and seek another master? Or must I furnish a new solution myself?

And it is as if the examiner had written: *Take your time, young man. Consider all questions carefully; there is all the time in the world. Don't fake or cheat; you are making these answers for yourself. Nobody will grade them but posterity.*

READINGS FROM THE LIVES OF THE SAINTS

To American writers of my own age, or at any rate to those who went abroad in 1921, the author who seemed nearest to themselves was T. S. Eliot. Essentially the picture he presented was that of the local-boy-makes-good. He was born in St. Louis; he was in the class of 1910 at Harvard, where he took courses that any of us might have taken and belonged to three or four undistinguished clubs; he continued his studies at a French provincial university and got a job in London. Now, ten years after leaving Cambridge, he was winding himself in a slow cocoon of glory. But his glory, his making good, was not in the vulgar sense of making money, making a popular reputation: in 1921 the newspapers had never heard of this clerk in Barclay's Bank. His achievement was the writing of perfect poems, poems in which we could not find a line that betrayed immaturity, awkwardness, provincialism or platitude. Might a Midwestern boy become a flawless poet?— this was a question with which we could not fail to be preoccupied.

But it was not the only question that Eliot answered, or

the only door by which he entered our secret minds. His early critical writings were concerned in large part with the dispute between form and matter, and he aligned himself with what we had learned to call our side of it. He effectively defended the intellect as against the emotions, and the conscious mind as against the libido, the dark Freudian wish. His poems, from the first, were admirably constructed. He seemed to regard them, moreover, as intellectual problems—having solved one problem, he devoted himself to another. From his early sketches in free verse, he moved on to "Portrait of a Lady" and "Prufrock"; thence he moved on to his Sweeney poems, thence to "Gerontion"; and it was certain that his new ambitious work soon to be published in the *Dial* would mark another departure. For he never repeated himself and never, in those days, persisted in any attitude or technique: once having suggested its possibilities, he moved on.

Eliot, of course, did not originate the idea of "moving on." It was part of the general literary atmosphere, part of a long tradition—for example, it closely resembled the "theory of convolutions" that developed among my high-school friends.*

---

* Cowley's tongue-in-cheek theory of convolutions is itself so convoluted that it deserves to be presented in full. It originally appears in "Exile's Return," pp. 21–22.

"The theory of convolutions was evolved in Pittsburgh, at Peabody High School, but it might have appeared in any city during those years before the war. It was generally explained by reference to the game of Odd or Even. You have held an even number of beans or grains of corn in your hand; you have won; therefore you take an even number again. That is the simplest argument by analogy; it is no convolution at all. But if you say to yourself, "I had an even number before and won; my opponent will expect me to have an even number again; therefore I'll take an odd number," you have entered the First Convolution. If you say, "Since I won with an even number before, my opponent will expect me to try to fool him by having an odd number this time; therefore I'll be even," you are Second Convolution. The process seems capable of indefinite extension; it can be applied, moreover, to any form of art, so long as one is less interested in what one says than in one's ability to outwit an audience. We were not conscious of having anything special to say; we wanted merely to live in ourselves and be writers.

There is, however, a practical limit to the series of convolutions. If it leads at one moment to reading Oscar Wilde because other high-school pupils have never heard of him, it leads at the next to disparaging Wilde because you admired him once and because First Convolution people still admire him. You have entered the Second Convolution: you read Schnitzler and "go beyond him" without ever understanding what he has to say. In this manner we passed through a whole series of enthusiasms—Mencken, Huneker, Somerset Maugham, Laforgue (after we learned French)—till we encountered Dostoevski, who didn't fit into our scheme, and Flaubert, whose patience overawed us.

But Eliot's influence had the effect of making the idea vastly popular among young writers. They began to picture the ideal poet as an explorer, a buffalo hunter pressing westward toward new frontiers—from the Shenandoah he marches into unknown Tennessee, thence into the Blue Grass, thence into Missouri, always leaving the land untilled behind him, but who cares?—there will be disciples to follow the plow. No other American poet had so many disciples as Eliot, in so many stages of his career. Until 1925 his influence seemed omnipresent, and it continued to be important in the years that followed. But in 1922, at the moment when he was least known to the general public and most fervently worshiped by young poets, there was a sudden crisis. More than half of his disciples began slowly to drop away.

When *The Waste Land* first appeared, we were confronted with a dilemma. Here was a poem that agreed with all our recipes and prescriptions of what a great modern poem should be. Its form was not only perfect but was far richer musically and architecturally than that of Eliot's earlier verse. Its diction was superb. It employed in a magisterial fashion the technical discoveries made by the French writers who followed Baudelaire. Strangeness, abstractness, simplification, respect for literature as an art with traditions—it had all the qualities demanded in our slogans. We were prepared fervently to defend it against the attacks of the people who didn't understand what Eliot was trying to do—but we made private reservations. The poem had forced us into a false position, had brought our consciously adopted principles into conflict with our instincts. At heart—not intellectually, but in a purely emotional fashion—we didn't like it. We didn't agree with what we regarded as the principal idea that the poem set forth.

The idea was a simple one. Beneath the rich symbolism of *The Waste Land,* the wide learning expressed in seven languages, the actions conducted on three planes, the musical episodes, the geometrical structure—beneath and by means of all this, we felt the poet was saying that the present is inferior to the past. The past was dignified; the present is barren of emotion. The past was a landscape nourished by

---

The sense of paradox ends by having nothing left to feed upon; eventually it is self-devouring. The desire to surprise or deceive leads often to a final deception—which consists in being exactly like everybody else. This was the stage that several of us had reached by our eighteenth year." [ed.]

living fountains; now the fountains of spiritual grace are dry.
. . . Often in his earlier poems Eliot had suggested this idea;
he had used such symbols of dead glory as the Roman eagles
and trumpets or the Lion of St. Mark's to emphasize the
vulgarities of the present. In those early poems, however, the
present was his real subject. Even though he seemed to abhor
it, even though he thought "of all the hands that are raising
dingy shades in a thousand furnished rooms" and was continually "aware of the damp souls of housemaids sprouting
despondently at area gates," still he was writing about the
life that all of us knew—and more than that, he was endowing
our daily life with distinction by means of the same distinguished metaphors in which he decried and belittled it. *The
Waste Land* marked a real change. This time he not only
expressed the idea with all his mature resources but carried
it to a new extreme. He not only abused the present but
robbed it of vitality. It was as if he were saying, this time,
that our age was prematurely senile and could not even find
words of its own in which to bewail its impotence; that it was
forever condemned to borrow and patch together the songs
of dead poets.

The seven-page appendix to *The Waste Land,* in which Eliot
paraded his scholarship and explained the Elizabethan or Italian sources of what had seemed to be his most personal
phrases, was a painful dose for us to swallow. But the truth
was that the poet had not changed so much as his younger
readers. We were becoming less preoccupied with technique
and were looking for poems that portrayed our own picture
of the world. As for the question proposed to us by Eliot,
whether the values of past ages were superior or inferior to
present values, we could bring no objective evidence to bear
on it. Values are created by living men. If they believe—if
their manner of life induces them to believe—that greatness
died with Virgil or Dante or Napoleon, who can change their
opinion or teach them new values? It happened that we were
excited by the adventure of living in the present. The famous
"postwar mood of aristocratic disillusionment" was a mood
we had never really shared. It happened that Eliot's subjective
truth was not our own.

I say "it happened" although, as a matter of fact, our beliefs
grew out of the lives we had led. I say "we" although I can
refer only to a majority, perhaps two-thirds, of those already

influenced by Eliot's poems. When *The Waste Land* was published it revealed a social division among writers that was not a division between rich and poor or—in the Marxian terms that would later be popular—between capitalist and proletarian.* Not many of the younger writers belonged to either the top or the bottom layer of society. Some of them, it is true, were the children of factory workers or tenant farmers, but even those few had received the education of the middle class and had for the most part adopted its standards. The middle class had come to dominate the world of letters; the dominant educational background was that of the public high school and the big Midwestern university. And the writers of this class—roughly corresponding to Marx's petty bourgeoisie—were those who began to ask where Eliot was leading and whether they should follow.

But there were also many young writers who had been sent to good preparatory schools, usually Episcopalian, before they went on to Yale, Harvard, Princeton, Williams or Dartmouth. Whether rich or poor, they had received the training and acquired the standards of the small but powerful class in American society that might be described as the bourgeoisie proper. These, in general, were the "young poets old before their time" who not only admired *The Waste Land* but insisted on dwelling there in spirit; as Edmund Wilson said, they "took to inhabiting exclusively barren beaches, cactus-grown deserts and dusty attics overrun with rats." Their special education, their social environment and also, I think, their feeling of mingled privilege and insecurity had prepared them to follow Eliot in his desert pilgrimage toward the shrines of tradition and authority.

There were exceptions in both groups, and Eliot continued

---

* It seems to me now that the division was more a matter of temperament, and less a result of social background, than I believed in 1934. The division was real, however, and it reflected attitudes toward life in our own time. When *The Waste Land* appeared, complete with notes, E. E. Cummings asked me why Eliot couldn't write his own lines instead of borrowing from dead poets. In his remarks I sensed a feeling almost of betrayal. Hemingway said in the *Transatlantic Review*, "If I knew that by grinding Mr. Eliot into a fine dry powder and sprinkling that powder over Mr. Conrad's grave Mr. Conrad would shortly appear, looking very annoyed at the forced return, and commence writing, I would leave for London early tomorrow with a sausage grinder." On the other hand John Peale Bishop, of Princeton, who was also in Paris at the time, told me that he was studying Italian so that he could get the full force of the quotations from Dante identified in Eliot's notes. [M.C., 1951]

to be recited and praised behind the dingy shades of a thousand furnished rooms, but most of the struggling middle-class writers were beginning to look for other patterns of literary conduct. We were new men, without inherited traditions, and we were entering a new world of art that did not impress us as being a spiritual desert. Although we did not see our own path, we instinctively rejected Eliot's. In the future we should still honor his poems and the clearness and integrity of his prose, but the Eliot picture had ceased to be our guide.

James Joyce also presented us with a picture of the writer who never repeats himself. From *Chamber Music* through *Dubliners* and *A Portrait of the Artist as a Young Man*, each of his books had approached a new problem and had definitely ended a stage of his career. *Ulysses*, published in Paris in the winter of 1921–22, marked yet another stage. Although we had not time in the busy year that followed to read it carefully or digest more than a tenth of it, still we were certain of one thing: it was a book that without abusing the word could be called "great."

Thus we learned to couple Joyce and Eliot in a second fashion. Joyce, too, had become a success picture to fire the imagination of young writers, even though the success was on a different plane. He was another local-boy-makes-good, but not a St. Louis boy or a Harvard boy. His birthplace was the lower middle class; his home, above which he seemed to have soared, was the twentieth century. Can a writer of our own time produce a masterpiece fit to compare with those of other ages? Joyce was the first indication that there was another answer to this question than the one we were taught in school.

But—here were more difficult questions—what were the methods by and the motives for which he had written his indubitably great work? Had he set an example we should try to follow?

It seemed that from all his books three values disengaged themselves, three qualities of the man himself: his pride, his contempt for others, his ambition. Toward the end of *A Portrait of the Artist* they stood forth most clearly. The hero, Stephen Dedalus, was lonely and overweening in his pride; he despised the rabble of his richer schoolmates for being his inferiors in sensibility and intellect; and he set for himself the ambition, not of becoming a mere bishop, judge or general, but of pressing into his arms "the loveliness that has not yet come into the world." He would be the spiritual leader standing alone; he was leaving Ireland "to forge in the smithy of my soul the uncreated conscience of my race." Stephen Dedalus was obviously a more or less accurate picture of Joyce himself; but in life the author had chosen a still lonelier ambition. As he wandered through Italy, Austria, Switzerland and France, he continued to write about the Dublin of his youth and remembered the sound of Irish voices, but he half forgot that Irish race whose conscience was being forged in the smithy of revolution. He had chosen another destiny. Like Napoleon landing from Corsica, like Cortés or Pizarro marching into the highlands, he set himself a task of self-aggrandizement: he would be a genius!—he would carve out an empire, create a work of genius.

The intellectual resources at his command were not superhuman, and material resources were almost totally absent. He came of a family that had decayed with Ireland; all during his young manhood he was poor, desperately poor and unpopular. He was unusually sensitive, but no more so than half a dozen other Irish poets; he had a mind equaled in nimbleness by some of his Jesuit instructors; he had great learning of a type not impossible for any diligent student to acquire. But he was patient, obstinate—having chosen a goal he was willing to disregard all difficulties; he was a foreigner, penniless, in frail health; Europe was crumbling about his ears, thirteen million men died in the trenches, empires toppled over; he shut his window and worked on, sixteen hours a day, seven days a week, writing, polishing, elaborating. And it seemed to us that there was nothing mysterious in what he had accomplished. He had pride, contempt, ambition—and those were the qualities that continued to stand forth clearly from *Ulysses*. Here once more was the pride of Stephen Dedalus that raised itself above the Dublin public and especially above the Dublin intellectual public as represented by Buck Mulligan; here was the author's contempt for the world and for his readers—like a host being deliberately rude to his guests, he made no concession to their capacity for attention or their power of understanding; and here was an ambition willing to measure itself, not against any novelist of its age, not against any writer belonging to a modern national literature, but with the father of all the Western literatures, the archpoet of the European race.

And now this poor boy from the twentieth century had conquered his Peru and created his work of genius. We were not among the enthusiasts who placed him beside Homer, but this at least was certain: except possibly for Marcel Proust, there was no living author to be compared with him in depth, richness, complexity, or scope. His achievement was there to urge us ahead; his ambition dignified our lesser ambitions. But obviously he had written *Ulysses* at a price—just how much had he paid in terms of bread and laughter? How did a man live who had written a masterpiece?

We fitted together passages from his books with sometimes erroneous information collected from magazine articles about him, bits of café gossip and the remarks of people allowed to meet him. The resulting picture, the Joyce picture of 1923, was not wholly pleasant. The great man lived in a cheap hotel, not picturesquely sordid, but cluttered and depressing. He was threatened with Homeric blindness, and much of his meager income was spent on doctors, for the disease from which he suffered was aggravated by hypochondria. He had no companions of his own intellectual stature and associated either with family friends or else with admiring disciples. Except in matters concerning literature and the opera, his opinions were those of a fourth or fifth-rate mind. It was as if he had starved everything else in his life to feed his ambition. It was as if he had made an inverted Faust's bargain, selling youth, riches and part of his common humanity to advance his pride of soul.

Having been granted an interview, I went to his hotel. He was waiting for me in a room that looked sour and moldy, as if the red-plush furniture had fermented in the twilight behind closed shutters. I saw a tall, emaciated man with a very high white forehead and smoked glasses; on his thin mouth and at the puckered corners of his eyes was a look of suffering so plainly marked that I forgot the questions with which I had come prepared. I was simply a younger person meeting an older person who needed help.

"Is there anything I can do for you, Mr. Joyce?" I said.

Yes, there was something I could do: he had no stamps, he didn't feel well enough to go out and there was nobody to run errands for him. I went out to buy stamps, with a sense of relief as I stepped into the street. He had achieved genius, I thought, but there was something about the genius as cold as the touch at parting of his long, smooth, cold, wet-marble fingers.

Ezra Pound presented a less intimidating picture, since he was known not so much for his own creations as for his advocacy of other writers and his sallies against the stupid public. His function seemed to be that of a schoolmaster, in a double sense of the word. He schooled the public in scolding it; he was always presenting it with new authors to admire, new readings of the classics, new and stricter rules for judging poetry. It was Gertrude Stein who said that he was "a village explainer, excellent if you were a village, but if you were not, not." Miss Stein herself seldom bothered to explain, although she liked to have young men sit at her feet and was not above being jealous of Pound's influence on the younger writers. The influence was extensive and well earned. He not only gave the best of advice to writers but often tried to organize them into groups or schools, each with its own manifesto and its own magazine; that is the second sense in which he might have been called schoolmaster.

In London he had started the Imagiste school and then, after relinquishing the name to Amy Lowell (who had dropped the "e" from it, together with most of the principles on which the group was founded), had assembled the Vorticists, who survived as a group until most of the members were called into military service. Besides these formal groups that Pound inspired he also had a circle of friends that included some of the greatest poets of our time. They deferred to Pound because they felt that he had shown an unselfish devotion to literature. He had fought to win recognition for the work of other writers at a time when much of his own work was going unpublished, and he had obtained financial support for others that he could as easily have had for himself. During most of his career he had earned hardly more than the wages of an English day laborer. "If I accept more than I need," he used to say, "I at once become a sponger."

He was in somewhat better financial circumstances in 1921, when he left London for Paris. During the next two years I went to see him several times, but the visit I remember is the last, in the summer of 1923. Pound was then living in the *pavillon,* or summer house, that stood in the courtyard of 70*bis,* rue Notre-Dame-des-Champs, near the Luxembourg Gardens. A big young man with intent eyes and a toothbrush mustache was there when I arrived, and Pound introduced him as Ernest Hemingway; I said that I had heard about him. Hemingway gave a slow Midwestern grin. He was then working for the International News Service, but there were rumors that he had stories in manuscript and that Pound had spoken of them as being something new in American literature. He didn't talk about the stories that afternoon; he listened as if with his eyes while Pound discussed the literary world. Very soon he rose, made a date with Pound for tennis the following day and went out the door, walking on the balls of his feet like a boxer. Pound continued his monologue.

"I've found the lowdown on the Elizabethan drama," he said as he vanished beard-first into the rear of the pavilion; he was always finding the lowdown, the inside story and the simple reason why. A moment later he returned with a worm-eaten leather-bound folio. "It's all in here," he said, tapping the volume. "The whole business is cribbed from these Italian state papers."

The remark seemed so disproportionate that I let it go unchallenged, out of politeness. "What about your own work?" I asked.

Pound laid the book on a table piled with other books. "I try not to repeat myself," he said. He began walking back and forth in his red dressing gown, while his red beard jutted out like that of an archaic Greek soldier (or, as I afterward thought, like a fox's muzzle). There was no attempt to play the great man of letters. With an engaging lack of pretense to dignity he launched into the story of his writing life.

At the age of twenty-two he had written a poem, the "Ballad of the Goodly Fere," that had been widely discussed and had even been reprinted in the *International Sunday School.* It was the first of the masculine ballads in the genre that Masefield would afterward exploit, and Pound might have exploited it himself—"Having written this ballad about Christ," he said, "I had only to write similar ballads about James, Matthew, Mark, Luke and John and my fortune was made." If he had missed falling into the gulf of standardization it was partly because he didn't see it was there. Instead he had gone to England in 1908 and started a new career.

He was still convinced that he had been right to leave America. America was England thirty years before. America was England with the fifty most intelligent men. America didn't print his poems in magazines until they had been collected into books in England. Perhaps he had been misled by the early recognition he received there; perhaps it had made him willing for a time to write the sort of poems that friendly critics expected him to write. He had spent three years studying Oxford English before he learned that he was wasting his efforts; that English is not Latin and must be written as one speaks it.

He had lost many of his English readers when he published *Ripostes* in 1912. The public doesn't like to be surprised and the new poems had been surprising, even a little shocking; they had proved that Pound wasn't merely an author of masculine ballads or a new Browning who brought medieval characters to life in medieval phrases. Still more of his readers had dropped away when he published *Lustra* in 1916; they hadn't liked his use of colloquial language or the frankness with which he described the feelings of *l'homme moyen sensuel*. It was the same when he published the *Mauberley* poems and the first of the *Cantos:* with each successive book he lost old readers and, after a time, gained some new ones, who disappeared in their turn; he had always outdistanced his audience.

Pound talked about some of his associates. Gaudier-Brzeska, killed at the front in 1916, had been the most gifted of the new sculptors; Pound had helped to keep him alive when he was starving in London. Wyndham Lewis was the real Vorticist, a man of amazing intellectual force. Lewis had visited New York in the spring of 1917 and two weeks later— Pound paused for emphasis—the United States had declared war on the Central Powers. In earlier days Pound had worked to gain recognition for Lewis, just as he had worked for Joyce, Eliot and dozens of gifted writers. Now he was thirty-seven years old and it was time for him to stop doing so much for other men and for literature in general, stop trying to educate the public and simply write. It would take years for him to finish the *Cantos;* he wanted to write an opera and he had other plans. To carry them out it might be best for him to leave Paris and live on the Mediterranean, far from distractions, in a little town he had discovered when he was in *villeggiatura*. . . .

I went back to Giverny, the village about sixty miles from Paris where I was living that year (not in *villeggiatura*), and reread all of Pound's poems that I had been able to collect in their English editions. I liked them better than on first reading and was less irritated by their parade of eccentric scholarship. What impressed me now was their new phrases, new rhythms, new images, and their resolute omission of every word that he might have requisitioned from the stockroom of poetry. I could see how much Eliot had learned from them (although I didn't know at the time that he had sent the manuscript of *The Waste Land* to Pound for criticism and had accepted almost all the changes that Pound advised). I could also see that E. E. Cummings had used *Hugh Selwyn Mauberley* as a model in writing his own satirical poems and I could trace other derivations as well. Pound deserved the credit for discoveries which other poets were using, yet it seemed to me that some of the others—notably Eliot and Cummings—had a great deal more to say. For all his newness of phrase Pound kept making statements that were simply the commonplaces of the art-for-art's-sake tradition, when they did not belong to the older tradition of the tavern minstrel. He kept repeating that the public was stupid, that the poet was happier living in a garret, that he wrote to shock the public and that his songs would live when his readers were dead:

> Go, little naked and impudent songs,
> Go with a light foot!
> (Or with two light feet, if it please you!)
> Go and dance shamelessly!
> Go with an impertinent frolic!
>
> Ruffle the skirts of prudes,
>   speak of their knees and ankles.
> But, above all, go to practical people—
>   go! jangle their door-bells!
> Say that you do no work
>   and that you will live forever.

In poems like this he was affronting the conventions in a fashion that was badly needed at the time and he was writing a declaration of independence for poets—but how could the songs live forever when they had so little fresh blood in their arteries? There was, moreover, another weakness in Pound's poetry that had been impressed on me by his remark about outdistancing his readers. He kept moving ahead into unexplored territory, like Eliot and Joyce, but it seemed to me that his motive was different. From his early ballads to *Ripostes*, to *Lustra*, to *Mauberley*, his poetic career might be explained, not as a search for something, but rather as a frantic effort to escape. I pictured him as a red fox pursued by the pack of his admirers; he led them through brambles and into marshes; some of them gave up the chase but others joined in. At present, in the *Cantos*, he had fled into high and rocky ground where the scent was lost and the hounds would cut their feet if they tried to follow, yet I felt that they would eventually find him even there and would crowd around muzzle to muzzle, not for the kill, but merely for the privilege of baying his praises. Then, with his weakness for defying the crowd, for finding crazily simple explanations and for holding eccentric opinions, to what new corner would the fox escape?

In November 1922 we heard that Marcel Proust had died, and it seemed that his death was the completion of a symbol. He represented an entirely different ambition from that of Pound or Joyce, for he strove neither to outdistance the public nor to create a work of genius by force of will. In Joyce the will had developed immediately; in Proust it seemed almost to be atrophied. Not only his passions but his merest whims were stronger than his desire to control them, and he dispassionately watched himself doing silly things—it was almost as if the living Marcel Proust were an unpleasant but fascinating visitor in the house of his mind. Nevertheless, he had set himself a task and had carried it through. He had determined to take the living Marcel Proust that was weak and fickle and transform it, transform himself, into an enduring work of art.

Eager to execute this project while he still had strength for it, he shut himself off from friendships, public life, the world in general, spending most of his time in bed in a room hermetically sealed to prevent drafts—they say he would feel and suffer from a breath of fresh air three rooms away. Flowers, even, were prohibited, because they brought on his asthma. He rarely saw daylight. Sometimes very late in the evening, wrapped to the ears in a fur-lined overcoat, he attended a reception in the Faubourg St. Germain; but usually he spent his nights writing hurriedly in a study that was completely lined with cork in order to shut out the street noises. He was racing against time, his enemy. Here in seclusion he was trying to recapture and preserve his past in the moment before it vanished, like a mollusk making its shell before it dies. And his death, I wrote in an essay published at the time, "was only a process of externalization; he had turned himself inside out like an orange and sucked it dry, or inscribed himself on a monument; his observation, his sensibility, his affectations, everything about him that was weak or strong had passed into the created characters of his novel."

When I came to read the last section of his book, which was not published until the end of the decade, I found that Proust had expressed the same idea about himself in different words. "Let us allow our body to disintegrate, since each fresh particle that breaks off, now luminous and decipherable, comes and adds itself to our work to complete it at the cost of suffering superfluous to others more gifted, and to make it more and more substantial as emotions gradually chip away our life." The passage must have been written only a few weeks before his final illness. By then his life was almost wholly chipped away and all its luminous particles were added to his work, which, in the process, had become the longest novel that had been written. Dying at a moment when *Remembrance of Things Past* was practically completed (only two sections remained to be revised), Proust had become for us a symbol of fulfilled ambition. And yet the symbol was too cold and distant to touch us closely. We had neither the wish nor the financial nor yet the intellectual resources to shut ourselves in cork-lined chambers and examine our memories. And Proust, moreover, had closed a path to us merely by choosing it for himself. He had accomplished his task so thoroughly that it would never have to be done again.

In 1921 Paul Valéry was fifty years old and had recently entered his second literary career, which in a short time would carry him to the French Academy. His first career had begun some thirty years before; it had been brilliant and very brief. And it was his abandoning of that career, it was his deliberate, twenty-year-long refusal to write for publication, that impressed us even more than the high poems and the noble essays he had printed since consenting once more to become a writer like anybody else.

He had come to Paris in the autumn of 1892, a boy from the provinces with his road to make. Soon he attached himself to the circle of Symbolist poets surrounding Stéphane Mallarmé. Writing of that time he later said, "There was a certain austerity about the new generation of poets. . . . In the profound and scrupulous worship of all the arts, they thought to have found a discipline, and perhaps a truth, beyond the reach of doubt. A kind of religion was very nearly established." And again: "It was a time of theories, curiosity, glosses and passionate explanation. . . . More fervor, courage and learning, more researches into theory, more disputes and a more pious attention have rarely been devoted, in so short a time, to the problem of pure beauty. One might say that the problem was attacked from all sides."

Valéry himself chose the intellectual side. His ambition resembled that of T. S. Eliot's early days: he was obsessed by the idea of always moving through and "going beyond." Each poem could be translated into a problem capable of solution, capable of supplying a principle which could then be applied to the writing of other poems. But why bother to write them? "From the moment a principle has been recognized and grasped by someone," Valéry says that he said to himself, "it is quite useless to waste one's time applying it." Thus, he was always driven further, to attack new problems, discover new principles, until it became evident at a certain point in the process that literature itself was a problem capable of solution, and therefore was only an intermediate goal, a stage to be passed through and gone beyond. The poet was free to abandon poetry and devote himself to more essential aims.

For a young man of twenty-five, Valéry had won an enviable position; he had become a favorite disciple of Mallarmé and a leader among the younger Symbolists. His future seemed assured, and he abandoned it almost overnight. This deliberate choice, this apostasy, one might almost call it, exerted a powerful influence on the young French writers who followed him. Suddenly their highest value had been called into question, and not by the stupid public. Suddenly it seemed that the highest ambition might not be the writing of a great novel or poetic drama or the creation of any work of genius whatsoever. Apollo, after all, might be only a minor deity.

Valéry himself found his arguments so cogent that he had a hard time explaining, twenty years later, why he had once more begun writing essays and poems. He justified himself by saying on several occasions that literature was an *exercise,* a game worth playing for the same reasons that one plays tennis or chess or bridge. All these have difficult and arbitrary rules, but we observe them for the sake of the game; and the arbitrary and far more difficult conventions of classical poetry may be observed for the same reasons. One might even assert that these laws and constant requirements are the true object of the poem. "It is indeed an exercise—intended as such, and worked and reworked: a production entirely of deliberate effort; and then of a second deliberate effort, whose hard task is to conceal the first. He who knows how to read me will read an autobiography, in the form. The *matter* is of small importance."—His justification would have been more accurate, I think, if he had admitted from the first that the sport of writing was not altogether non-professional: that he derived pleasure from the praise his poems received, and wrote his essays for magazine editors who ordered and paid well for them. But always, in reading Valéry, one must learn to expect a certain high pretentiousness that accompanies and dilutes and sometimes conceals his real acuteness.

Whether the new essays that he began to publish after 1917 were written for sport or hire, they contained a valuable record of his thoughts during the years of silence.

It seems that the starting point of his researches, his first great problem outside the field of poetry, was to re-create the mind of "the universal man," to discover the *method* that unified the extremely varied accomplishments in science, warfare, mechanics and the arts of a genius like Leonardo da Vinci. His essay on Leonardo, written two or three years before the great renunciation, is a magnificent defense of the conscious mind, and of "the poet of the hypothesis" as against the specialized poet of quatrains or the patient accumulator of facts. It also proposes a new type of ambition. Might we not, by discovering his method, produce a new Leonardo, able to work freely with the infinitely rich materials of the present? But Valéry rejected the idea and seems to say that it would be useless to put the method into action. *To act,* for any individual of the first magnitude, is only an exercise, and one that may end by impoverishing the mind, since it is equivalent to choosing a single possibility and rejecting all the others with which the mind is teeming. Even "the universal man" becomes a problem capable of being reduced to a principle, to something that "it is quite useless to waste one's time applying."

Once more Valéry moved on, and this time to a problem he now regarded as the most far-reaching and difficult of all, "the study of the self for its own sake, the understanding of that attention itself, and the desire to trace clearly for oneself the nature of one's own existence." But it soon became evident that even this problem was capable of further refinement. Within the "self," what is the universal and changeless principle? It cannot be the body, which changes daily, or the senses, which tempt and deceive, or the mind, in which memories fade and ideas are dissipated; it cannot even be our *personality*, which we thoughtlessly mistake for our inmost characteristic—even the personality is only a *thing* that can be observed and reduced to tables and statistics. No, underneath all these is something else, the *I*, the naked ego, an essence that can finally be reduced to consciousness alone, to consciousness in its most abstract state. "This profound *tone* of our existence, as soon as it is heard, dominates all the complicated conditions and varieties of existence. To isolate this substantial attention from the strife of ordinary verities— is this not the ultimate and hidden task of the man with the greatest mind?"

Again he says:

> Everything yields before the pure universality, the insurmountable generality, that consciousness feels itself to be. . . . It dares to consider its "body" and its "world" as almost arbitrary restrictions imposed upon the extent of its functions . . . and this attention to its external circumstances cannot react upon itself, so far has it drawn aside from all things, so great are the pains it has taken *never to be a part of anything it might conceive or do.* It is reduced to a black mass that absorbs all light and gives nothing back.

And still again:

> Carried away by his ambition to be unique, guided by his ardor for omnipotence, the man of great mind has gone beyond all creations, all works, even his own lofty designs; while at the same time he has abandoned all tenderness for himself and all preference for his own wishes. In an instant he immolates his individuality. . . . To this point its pride has led the mind, and here pride is consumed. This directing pride abandons it, astonished, bare, infinitely simple, on the pole of its treasures.

This was the cheerless ambition, this was the path and the goal that Paul Valéry was proposing to the young writers who followed him after an interval of thirty years. They should regard poetry only as a beginning: from this they should move on to the methods of poetry, thence to methods in general (and in particular the methods of genius), thence to the universal self that determines all methods, and thence to mere consciousness, which is the only unchanging element in the self. Having reached this point, still undeterred by the bleakness of the way, they will discover that consciousness itself is a perpetual process of detachment from all things, from all emotions and sensations. Then, lest they still persist, Valéry paints an image to drive them back: "The man who is led by the demands of the indefatigable mind to this contact with living shadows and this extreme of pure presence, perceives himself as destitute and bare, reduced to the supreme poverty of being a force without an object. . . . He exists without instincts, almost without images; and he no longer has an aim. He resembles nothing. I say *man,* and I say *he,* by analogy and through lack of words." The supreme genius has ceased even to be human.

But the perfected consciousness, which "differs from nothingness by the smallest possible of margins," is not merely a goal and an abstraction. Like all ideals, it is something to be embodied in a man who eats, lives and suffers. In *An Evening with M. Teste*, almost the only work he wrote for publication during his long retirement, Valéry performs this labor of incarnation. M. Teste, "Mr. Head," is the thinking man, the modern Leonardo, and he is an almost wholly dehumanized creature. He does nothing, desires nothing, occupies no position, is almost completely cut off from society (which nevertheless continues to nourish him). He looks at people as if they did not exist. At night, when he retires to his chamber, he is left alone with three realities: thought, sleeplessness and migraine. He suffers from incurable headaches.—And why, we asked ourselves when reading the story, does genius lead to this inhuman state in which suffering is the only reality? Why does it seem to exist in the atmosphere of a closed room, a sickroom, where the blinds are always drawn to exclude the movement and sunlight of the streets and where there is nothing living, not even a red geranium in a pot? Everything seemed to point in the same direction, James Joyce's blindness, Proust's asthma (no less real for being half imaginary), even Eliot's reiterated complaint of being devitalized, "an old man in a dry season"—all these seemed to possess the same symbolic value, as if life were taking revenge on these men for being eliminated from their calculations. These were the great literary men of our age and they resembled one another in proposing a future as cold as the touch of cold hands.

Without losing our admiration for them, we turned aside to wonder what the writers of our own age were doing in France. They might have no genius, but they were younger certainly, and might be warmer and nearer to ourselves.

[1934, 1951]

SIGNIFICANT GESTURE

During the last three weeks before sailing for America, I wrote no letters. I was much too excited to write letters; I had never, in fact, spent prouder, busier or more amusing days. I was being arrested and tried for punching a café proprietor in the jaw.

He deserved to be punched, though not especially by me; I had no personal grudge against him. His café, the Rotonde, had long been patronized by revolutionists of every nation. Lenin used to sit there, I was told; and proletarian revolts were still being planned, over coffee in the evening, by quiet men who paid no attention to the hilarious arguments of Swedish and Rumanian artists at the surrounding tables. The proprietor—whose name I forget—used to listen unobtrusively. It was believed, on more or less convincing evidence, that he was a paid informer. It was said that he had betrayed several anarchists to the French police. Moreover, it was known that he had insulted American girls, treating them with the cold brutality that French café proprietors reserve for prostitutes. He was a thoroughly disagreeable character and should, we felt, be called to account.

We were at the Dôme, ten or twelve of us packed together at a table in the midst of the crowd that swirled in the Boulevard Montparnasse. It was July 14, 1923, the national holiday. Chinese lanterns hung in rows among the trees; bands played at every corner; everywhere people were dancing in the streets. Paris, deserted for the summer by its aristocrats, bankers and politicians, forgetting its hordes of tourists, was given over to a vast plebeian carnival, a general madness in which we had eagerly joined. Now, tired of dancing, we sipped our drinks and talked in loud voices to make ourselves heard above the music, the rattle of saucers, the shuffle of feet along the sidewalk. I was trying, with my two hands on the table, to imitate the ridiculous efforts of Tristan Tzara to hop a moving train. "Let's go over," said Laurence Vail, tossing back his long yellow hair from his forehead, "and assault the proprietor of the Rotonde."

"Let's," I said.

We crossed the street together, some of the girls in bright evening gowns and some in tweeds, Louis Aragon slim and dignified in a dinner jacket, Laurence bareheaded and wearing a raincoat which he never removed in the course of the hot starlit night, myself coatless, dressed in a workman's blue shirt, worn trousers and rope-soled shoes. Delayed and separated by the crowd on the pavement, we made our way singly into the bar, which I was the last to enter. Aragon, in periodic sentences pronounced in a beautifully modulated voice, was expressing his opinion of all stool pigeons—*mouchards*—and was asking why such a wholly contemptible character as the proprietor of the Rotonde presumed to solicit the patronage of respectable people. The waiters, smelling a fight, were forming a wall of shirt fronts around their employer. Laurence Vail pushed through the wall; he made an angry speech in such rapid French that I could catch only a few phrases, all of them insults. The proprietor backed away; his eyes shifted uneasily; his face was a dirty white behind his black mustache. Harold Loeb, looking on, was a pair of spectacles, a chin, a jutting pipe and an embarrassed smile.

I was angry at my friends, who were allowing the situation to resolve into a series of useless gestures; but even more I was seized with a physical revulsion for the proprietor, with his look of a dog caught stealing chickens and trying to sneak off. Pushing past the waiters, I struck him a glancing blow in the jaw. Then, before I could strike again, I was caught up in an excited crowd and forced to the door.

Five minutes later our band had once more assembled on the terrace of the Dôme. I had forgotten the affair already: nothing remained but a vague exhilaration and the desire for further activity. I was obsessed with the idea that we should *changer de quartier:* that instead of spending the rest of the night in Montparnasse, we should visit other sections of Paris. Though no one else seemed enthusiastic, I managed by force of argument to assemble five hesitant couples, and the ten of us went strolling southeastward along the Boulevard Montparnasse.

On reaching the first café we stopped for a drink of beer and a waltz under the chestnut trees. One couple decided to return to the Dôme. Eight of us walked on to another café, where, after a bock, two other couples became deserters. "Let's change our quarter," I said once more. At the next café, Bob Coates consulted his companion. "We're going back to the Dôme," he said. Two of us walked on sadly. We caught sight of Montrouge—more Chinese lanterns and wailing accordions and workmen dancing with shopgirls in the streets—then we too returned to Montparnasse.

It was long after midnight, but the streets were as crowded as before and I was eager for adventure. At the Dôme I met Tristan Tzara, seized him by the arm and insisted that we go for a stroll. We argued the question whether the Dada movement could be revived. Under the chestnut trees we met a high-brown woman dressed in barbaric clothes; she was thought to be a princess from Senegal. I addressed her extravagant compliments in English and French; Tzara added others in French, German and his three words of Rumanian. "Go 'way, white boys," she said in a Harlem voice. We turned back, passing the crowded terrace of the Rotonde. The proprietor was standing there with his arms folded. At the sight of him a fresh rage surged over me.

"Quel salaud!" I roared for the benefit of his six hundred customers. *"Ah, quel petit mouchard!"*

Then we crossed the street once more toward the Dôme, slowly. But when I reached the middle of the tracks I felt each of my arms seized by a little blue policeman. "Come along with us," they said. And they marched me toward the station house, while Tzara rushed off to get the identification papers left behind in my coat. The crowds disappeared behind us; we were alone—I and the two *flics* and the proprietor of the Rotonde.

One of the two policemen was determined to amuse himself. "You're lucky," he said, "to be arrested in Paris. If you were arrested by those brutal policemen of New York, they would cuff you on the ear—like this," he snarled, cuffing me on the ear, "but in Paris we pat you gently on the shoulder."

I knew I was in trouble. I said nothing and walked peacefully beside him.

"Ah, the police of Paris are incomparably gentle. If you were arrested in New York, they would crack you in the jaw—like this," he said, cracking me in the jaw, "but here we do nothing; we take you with us calmly."

He rubbed his hands, then thrust his face toward mine. His breath stank of brandy.

"You like the police of Paris, *hein?*"

"Assuredly," I answered. The proprietor of the Rotonde walked on beside us, letting his red tongue play over the ends of his mustache. The other *flic* said nothing.

"I won't punch you in the nose like the New York policemen," said the drunken man, punching me in the nose. "I will merely ask you to walk on in front of me. . . . Walk in front of me, pig!"

I walked in front of him, looking back suspiciously under my armpit. His hand was on his holster, loosening the flap. I had read about people shot "while trying to escape" and began walking so very slowly that he had to kick me in the heels to urge me up the steps of the police station. When we stood at the desk before the sergeant, he charged me with an unprovoked assault on the proprietor of the Rotonde—and also with forcibly resisting an officer. "Why," he said, "he kicked me in the shins, leaving a scar. Look here!"

He rolled up his trouser leg, showing a scratch half an inch long. It was useless for me to object that my rope-soled shoes wouldn't have scratched a baby. Police courts in France, like police courts everywhere, operate on the theory that a policeman's word is always to be taken against that of an accused criminal.

Things looked black for me until my friends arrived—Laurence and Louis and Jacques Rigaut and my wife—bearing with them my identification papers and a supply of money. Consulting together, we agreed that the drunken policeman must be bribed, and bribed he was: in the general confusion he was bribed twice over. He received in all a hundred and thirty francs, at least four times as much as was necessary. Standing pigeon-toed before the sergeant at the desk and wearing an air of bashful benevolence, he announced that I was a pretty good fellow after all, even though I had kicked him in the shins. He wished to withdraw the charge of resisting an officer.

My prospects brightened perceptibly. Everyone agreed that the false charge was the more serious of the two. For merely punching a stool-pigeon, the heaviest sentence I could receive would be a month in jail. Perhaps I would escape with a week.

A preliminary hearing was held on the following evening, after a night in jail and a day spent vainly trying to sleep between visits from the police and telephone calls from anxious friends. I stopped at the Dôme to collect my witnesses; fortunately there was a party that evening and they were easy to find. They consisted of nine young ladies in evening gowns. None of them had been present at the scene in the Rotonde the night before, but that didn't matter: all of them testified in halting French that I hadn't been present either; the whole affair was an imposition on a writer known for his serious character; it was a hoax invented by a café proprietor who was a pig and very impolite to American young women.

The examining magistrate was impressed. He confided later to André Salmon that the proprietor of the Rotonde had only his waiters to support the story he told, whereas I had nine witnesses, all of them very respectable people, *des gens très bien*. That helped Salmon to get me out of the scrape, although he also brought his own influence to bear. He was a poet and novelist who was also a star reporter and covered all the important murder trials for *Le Matin*. Since magistrates liked to be on good terms with him, he managed to have my trial postponed from day to day and finally abandoned.

But the most amusing feature of the affair, and my justification for dealing with it at length, was the effect it produced on my French acquaintances. They looked at me with an admiration I could not understand, even when I reflected that French writers rarely came to blows and that they placed a high value on my unusual action. Years later I realized that by punching a café proprietor in the jaw I had performed an act to which all their favorite catchwords could be applied. First of all, I had acted for reasons of public morality; bearing no private grudge against my victim, I had been *disinterested.* I had committed an *indiscretion,* acted with *violence* and *disdain* for the law, performed an *arbitrary* and *significant gesture,* uttered a *manifesto;* in their opinion I had shown *courage.* . . . For the first time in my life I became a public character. I was entertained at dinners and cocktail parties, interviewed for the newspapers, asked to contribute to reviews published by the Dadaists in Amsterdam, Brussels, Lyon and Belgrade. My stories were translated into Hungarian and German. A party of Russian writers then visiting Paris returned to Moscow with several of my poems, to be printed in their own magazines.

The poems were not at all revolutionary in tone, but they dealt with a subject that, in those briefly liberal days of the New Economic Policy in Russia, had been arousing the enthusiasm of Soviet writers. They were poems about America, poems that spoke of movies and skyscrapers and machines, dwelling upon them with all the nostalgia derived from two long years of exile. I, too, was enthusiastic over America; I had learned from a distance to admire its picturesque qualities. And I was returning to New York with a set of values that bore no relation to American life, with convictions that could not fail to be misunderstood in a country where Dada was hardly a name, and moral judgments on literary matters were thought to be in questionable taste—in a city where writers had only three justifications for their acts: they did them to make money, or to get their name in the papers, or because they were drunk.

[1934, 1951]

HART CRANE: THE ROARING BOY

(from *Exile's Return*)

From earlier days I remember how Hart Crane used to write his poems. There would be a Sunday-afternoon party on Tory Hill, near Patterson, New York, just across the state line from Sherman, Connecticut. Besides Hart there might be eight or ten of us present: the Tates, the Josephsons, the Cowleys, the Browns—or perhaps Bob Coates and Peter Blume, both curly redheads, the novelist Nathan Asch* and Jack Wheelwright with his white week-end shoes and kempt and ruly hair; at one time or another all of them lived in the neighborhood. The party would be held, like others, in the repaired but unpainted and unremodeled farmhouse that Bill Brown had bought shortly after his marriage. When Bill was making the repairs, with Hart as his carpenter's helper, they had received a visit from Uncle Charlie Jennings, the former owner, an old-fashioned, cider-drinking New Englander who lived across the line in Sherman. Uncle Charlie had the plans explained to him and said, "I'm glad to see you an't putting in one of those bathrooms. I always said they was a passing fad." That was one of the stories told on a Sunday afternoon. I can't remember the other stories or why we laughed at them so hard; I can remember only the general atmosphere of youth and poverty and good humor.

We would play croquet, wrangling, laughing, shouting over every wicket, with a pitcher of cider half hidden in the tall grass beside the court; or else we would sit beside the fireplace in the big, low-ceilinged kitchen, while a spring rain soaped the windowpanes. Hart—we sometimes called him the Roaring Boy—would laugh twice as hard as the rest of us and drink at least twice as much hard cider, while contributing more

---

* Asch wrote a cycle of stories about life in the Tory Hill neighborhood (*The Valley*, 1935), and Slater Brown wrote a novel about it (*The Burning Wheel*, 1942). [M.C.]

than his share of the crazy metaphors and overblown epithets. Gradually he would fall silent, and a little later he disappeared. In lulls that began to interrupt the laughter, now Hart was gone, we would hear a new hubbub through the walls of his room—the phonograph playing a Cuban rumba, the typewriter clacking simultaneously; then the phonograph would run down and the typewriter stop while Hart changed the record, perhaps to a torch song, perhaps to Ravel's *Bolero*. Sometimes he stamped across the room, declaiming to the four walls and the slow spring rain.

An hour later, after the rain had stopped, he would appear in the kitchen or on the croquet court, his face brick-red, his eyes burning, his already iron-gray hair bristling straight up from his skull. He would be chewing a five-cent cigar which he had forgotten to light. In his hands would be two or three sheets of typewritten manuscript, with words crossed out and new lines scrawled in. "R-read that," he would say. "Isn't that the grreatest poem ever written?"

We would read it dutifully, Allen Tate perhaps making a profound comment. The rest of us would get practically nothing out of it except the rhythm like that of a tom-tom and a few startling images. But we would all agree that it was absolutely superb. In Hart's state of exultation there was nothing else we could say without driving him to rage or tears.

But that it neither the beginning nor the real end of the story. Hart, as I later discovered, would have been meditating over that particular poem for months or even years, scribbling lines on pieces of paper that he carried in his pockets and meanwhile waiting for the moment of genuine inspiration when he could put it all together. In that respect he reminded me of another friend, Jim Butler, a painter and a famous killer of woodchucks, who instead of shooting at them from a distance with a high-powered rifle and probably missing them, used to frighten them into their holes and wait until they came out again. Sometimes, he said, when they were slow about it he used to charm them out by playing a mouth organ. In the same way Hart tried to charm his inspiration out of its hiding place with a Cuban rumba and a pitcher of hard cider.

As for the end of the story, it might be delayed for a week or a month. Painfully, persistently—and dead sober—Hart would revise his new poem, clarifying the images, correcting the meter and searching for the right word hour after hour. "The seal's wide spindrift gaze toward paradise," in the second of his "Voyages," was the result of a search that lasted for several days. At first he had written, "The seal's *findrinny* gaze toward paradise," but someone had objected that he was using a non-existent word. Hart and I worked in the same office that year, and I remember his frantic searches through *Webster's Unabridged* and the big *Standard,* his trips to the library—on office time—and his reports of consultations with old sailors in South Street speakeasies. "Findrinny" he could never find,* but after paging through the dictionary again he decided that "spindrift" was almost as good and he declaimed the new line exultantly. Even after one of his manuscripts had been sent to *Poetry* or the *Dial* and perhaps had been accepted, he would still have changes to make. There were many poets of the 1920s who worked hard to be obscure, veiling a simple idea in phrases that grew more labored and opaque with each revision of a poem. With Crane it was the original meaning that was complicated and difficult; his revisions brought it out more clearly. He said, making fun of himself, "I practice invention to the brink of intelligibility." The truth was that he had something to say and wanted to be understood, but not at the cost of weakening or simplifying his original vision.

Just what were these "meanings" and these "visions"? They were different, of course, in each new poem, but it seems to me that most of them expressed a purpose that was also revealed in his method of composition. Essentially Crane was a poet of ecstasy or frenzy or intoxication; you can choose your word depending on how much you like his work. Essentially he was using rhyme and meter and fantastic images to convey the emotional states that were induced in him by alcohol, jazz, machinery, laughter, intellectual stimulation, the shape and sound of words and the madness of New York in the late Coolidge era. At their worst his poems are ineffective unless read in something approximating the same atmosphere, with a drink at your elbow, the phonograph blaring and somebody shouting into your ear, "Isn't that grreat!" At their best, however, the poems do their work unaided except

* After Hart's death Bill Brown found the word in *Moby Dick,* where Hart must have seen it originally. [M.C.]

by their proper glitter and violence. At their very best, as in "The River," they have an emotional force that has not been equaled by any other American poet of our century.

Hart drank to write: he drank to invoke the visions that his poems are intended to convey. But the recipe could be followed for a few years at the most, and it was completely effective only for two periods of about a month each, in 1926 and 1927, when working at top speed he finished most of the poems included in *The Bridge*. After that more and more alcohol was needed, so much of it that when the visions came he was incapable of putting them on paper. He drank in Village speakeasies and Brooklyn waterfront dives; he insulted everyone within hearing or shouted that he was Christopher Marlowe; then waking after a night spent with a drunken sailor, he drank again to forget his sense of guilt. He really forgot it, for the moment. By the following afternoon all the outrageous things he had done at night became merely funny, became an epic misadventure to be embroidered—"And then I began throwing furniture out the window," he would say with an enormous chuckle. Everybody would laugh and Hart would pound the table, calling for another bottle of wine. At a certain stage in drunkenness he gave himself and others the illusion of completely painless brilliance; words poured out of him, puns, metaphors, epigrams, visions; but soon the high spirits would be mingled with obsessions—"See that man staring at us, I think he's a detective"—and then the violence would start all over again, to be followed next day by the repentance that became a form of boasting. In this repeated process there was no longer a free hour for writing down his poems, or a week or a month in which to revise them.

Even before his disastrous trips to Southern California—which he called "this Pollyanna greasepaint pinkpoodle paradise"—to France and to Mexico, Hart's adventures had become a many-chaptered saga. There was, for example, his quarrel with Bill and Sue Brown, when he swept out of their house at midnight, vowing never to come back. But the Browns lived alone on a hillside, and the path to Mrs. Addie Turner's gaunt barn of a house, where Hart was living, twisted through a second-growth woodland in which even a sober man might have lost his way. About three o'clock the Browns were wakened by the noise of Hart crashing through the bushes and them stamping on their front porch. Soon they heard him mutter, "Brrowns, Brrowns, you can't get away from them," as if he were penned and circumscribed by Browns. On another evening that started in much the same fashion, he had been talking excitedly about Mexico. He got home safely this time, and he began furiously typing a letter to the Mexican President in Spanish, of which he knew only a few words. He blamed his typewriter for not being a linguist and threw it out the window without bothering to open the sash. When we passed the house next morning we saw it lying in a tangle of black ribbon. In it was a sheet of paper on which we could read the words, *"Mi caro Presidente Calles"*— in Spanish that was all the typewriter could say.

I suppose that no other American poet, not even Poe, heaped so many troubles on his friends or had his transgressions so long endured. Scenes, shouts, obscenities, broken furniture were the commonplaces of an evening with Hart, and for a long time nobody did anything about it, except to complain in a humorous way. The 1920s had their moral principles, one of which was not to pass moral judgments on other people, especially if they were creative artists. We should have been violating the principle if we had condemned Hart for his dissipations on the waterfront or had even scolded him for his behavior in company. But the real reason he was forgiven was that he had an abounding warmth of affection for the people around him. To hear him roar with laughter, to receive his clumsy, kind attentions when ill, to hear his honest and discerning evaluations of other people's work, offered without a trace of malice, and to realize that he always praised his friends except to their faces was enough to cancel out his misdeeds, even though they were renewed weekly and at the end almost daily. It was Hart himself who took to avoiding his friends, largely, I think, through a sense of guilt. During the last three years of his life he was always seeking new companions, being spoiled by them for a time and then avoiding them in turn.

One of my last serious talks with him must have taken place in November 1929. Hart had come back from Paris early that summer after getting into a fight with the police and spending a week in prison; his rich friend Harry Crosby had hired a lawyer for him, paid his fine and given him money for the passage home. The Crosbys' little publishing house, the Black Sun Press, had undertaken to issue a limited edition of *The Bridge*, and Hart had spent the summer and fall trying to finish the group of poems he had started five years before. He had worked desperately in his sober weeks, although they had been interspersed with drinking bouts. One afternoon I arrived at the Turner house to find Peter Blume sitting on Hart's chest and Bill Brown sitting on his feet; he had been smashing the furniture and throwing his books out the window and there was no other way to stop him. Hart was gasping between his clenched teeth, "You can kill me—but you can't—destroy—*The Bridge*. It's finished—it's on the *Bremen*—on its way—to Paris."

For the rest of the week he was sober and busy cleaning up the wreckage of his room. I called one day to take him for a walk. Hart began telling me about the Crosbys: Caresse was beautiful and gay; Harry was mad in a genial fashion; he would do anything and everything that entered his mind. They were coming to New York in December and Hart was eager for me to meet them. . . . We stumbled in the frozen ruts of the road that led up Hardscrabble Hill. I had always refrained from interfering with Hart's life, but at last I was making the effort to give him good advice. I said, bringing the words out haltingly, that he had been devoting himself to the literature of ecstasy and that it involved more of a psychological strain than most writers could stand. Now, having finished *The Bridge*, perhaps he might shift over to the literature of experience, as Goethe had done (I was trying to persuade him by using great examples). It might be years before he was ready to undertake another group of poems as ambitious as those he had just completed. In the meantime he might cultivate his talent for writing quiet and thoughtful prose.

Hart cut me short. "Oh, you mean that I shouldn't drink so much."

Yes, I said after an uncomfortable pause, I had meant that partly and I had also meant that his drinking was, among other things, the result of a special attitude toward living and writing. If he changed the attitude and tried to write something different he would feel less need of intoxication. Hart looked at me sullenly and did not answer; he had gone so far on the path toward self-destruction that none of his friends could touch him any longer. He was more lost and driven than the others, and although he kept fleeing toward distant havens of refuge he felt in his heart that he could not escape himself. That night I dreamed of him and woke in the darkness feeling that he was already doomed, already dead.

[1934, 1951]

RADICAL IMAGES

(from *The Dream of the Golden Mountains*)

AN EVENING AT THEODORE DREISER'S

I first became involved in "the movement" after an evening in Theodore Dreiser's studio in April 1931. Not long before that evening there had been two events in my nonpolitical life that had helped to prepare me for new convictions. I had separated from my first wife, Peggy Baird Johns, after twelve years together, and I had said good-bye to Hart Crane.

The separation from Peggy was friendly, but painful to both of us. Our marriage had cracked in pieces during the late 1920s, like many others among our friends, but it had been held together for three years more by the frayed ends of an old affection. Suddenly the string broke, as many others did at the time; there was an epidemic of divorces in the literary world. Perhaps the depression had something to do with those crises in private lives. Many people felt that they were setting out on journeys, and that first they had to put their houses in order by cleaning out the breakage of the past.

It may be that the experience was more painful for me than for others. My Swedenborgian father had instilled into me a belief in the sacredness of marital or, to use the word that Swedenborg spelled in his own fashion, "conjugial" love. I hated the notion of divorce, but Peggy and I had tortured each other in many heedless fashions. As time went on she had casual affairs, and I had less casual ones. She was a heavy drinker, though not an alcoholic like Hart Crane. I felt responsible for Peggy, but after I went to work for *The New Republic* I could no longer lead the old bohemian life. Often when I came home from the office I found the apartment full of her boon companions; bottles galore, but nothing to eat. I worried. Night after night I lay in bed staring at the shadows

on the ceiling, then dressed to roam the streets or stand alone
at a crowded bar.

In those days the respectable speakeasies closed at three
o'clock, by order of Mayor Jimmy Walker, but there were
some tougher ones that stayed open till six after paying
extra-large bribes to the police. Sometimes they recouped the
bribes from customers by forcing them to sign personal
checks for extra-large sums and then holding them prisoners
until the checks were cashed. I never had that experience,
since I didn't look prosperous, but once I was forced to pay
double prices for a lot of drinks I hadn't ordered or consumed, while an extra-large man stood over me with a
blackjack. Afterward I complained to the policeman on the
beat. "You ought to close up that place," I said. "It's a
gyp joint."

The policeman put a fatherly hand on my shoulder. "Son,"
he said, "you shouldn't go *in* to places like that."

I went home sober and lay awake until it was time to get
dressed for the office. There was, I had learned, a special
world in New York for men who couldn't sleep; it consisted
of speakeasies, all-night lunchrooms, and the waiting room
of Grand Central Station, where one sat on snowy nights and
read the bulldog edition of the morning papers; but it wasn't
a world designed for permanent habitation. I began to feel
that my only choice was between getting a divorce, much as
I hated to do so, and going off to a sanitarium. Some time in
February, Peggy and I moved into separate lodgings.

As for Hart Crane, I saw him late in March; it was in
Sherman, Connecticut, not far from the Tory Hill neighborhood across the New York state line where Hart and I had
both lived. Peter and Ebie Blume, who were very poor that
year—pictures weren't selling—had been spending the winter
in Matthew Josephson's comfortable farmhouse. They had
asked me up for the weekend and had also asked their friend
Muriel Maurer, a fashion editor, who came out on the same
train. When we reached the Josephson house on Saturday
afternoon, I was surprised to find Hart waiting there. He had
left the neighborhood at the end of the previous summer,
after a riotous period during which he had been evicted from
the two rooms that were as close to being a fixed home for
him as anywhere he had lived since boyhood. He was in
Sherman for the weekend, but merely to collect some of his

possessions before sailing for France on a newly awarded
Guggenheim fellowship.

Elsewhere I have recalled that weekend at length,* but
there are features of it that bear repeating. There is, for
example, the sharing out of gifts. Having brought forth his
possessions, Hart found among them something for each of
us: a dress suit for Peter (handed down from Hart's father),
a pea jacket for Ebie, a broad red-flannel sash for Muriel,
and for me a woven leather belt embossed with a brass anchor,
the nautical touch that Hart loved. Everything was considerate, everything was warm, but still one had a feeling of last
things, as if we were Roman soldiers casting dice for his
garments.

There is my walk with Hart on Sunday morning, when he
wondered where he should spend the year of his fellowship.
France, he had said on his application, but now he was beginning to be doubtful, remembering the months he had
wasted there in 1929.

"What about Mexico?" I asked him.

I had spent October in Mexico, and I spoke with enthusiasm
about its somber landscapes, its baroque churches, and its
mixture of Spanish and Indian cultures. Life there was even
cheaper than in Europe. One heard of sexual customs not
unlike those of the Arabs.

Hart walked on in silence for a moment, on the frozen
road. Then he said, "Maybe I'll go to Mexico if the Guggenheim people don't mind." He suddenly began talking about
a project he had in mind, a long poem with Cortes and Mon-
tezuma as its heroes.

Finally there is the comic episode of the bottle containing
the only liquor in the house (and no more to be had for miles
around). At dinner on Saturday the Blumes poured one drink
for each of us, then put the bottle away. Hart watched it go,
knowing that it was being hidden to keep him sober. At lunch
on Sunday there was nothing to drink and Hart didn't complain; his face was red and he was chuckling at his own jokes
one after another. Ebie, usually attentive to her guests, made
only a pretense of listening. Once she went out to the pantry
and came back with a worried look. Hart had found the bottle
and had hidden it somewhere else.

* See *A Second Flowering*, pp. 211-15. [M.C.]

For the rest of us, sober and thirsty, the afternoon was like a theatrical performance that we had sat through often. Hart was repeating a series of inevitable phases. First came the outgoing phase in which he paid warm compliments to each of us and left all blushing. Then, after another visit to the bottle, came the phase of wild metaphors and brilliant monologues in which he listened only to his own voice. The bottle must have been empty by now and a third phase supervened, during which he sank into himself and muttered darkly about "betrayal." It was the phase that sometimes led to his smashing other people's furniture, but everything remained peaceful that late afternoon; I think he was a little afraid of Peter, who did not tolerate nonsense.

We were driven twenty miles to the station in Peter's open touring car, an old Stutz, while the lights picked out board fences and an occasional white farmhouse. Hart shivered all the way and tried to bury himself in Muriel's thick-piled coat. Sometimes he wailed, "Oh, the white fences . . . the interminable white Connecticut fences." He slept in the train, then roused himself as it crawled into Grand Central. In the concourse he said good-bye to us, warmly but decisively, before hurrying off with his two heavy bags to find a taxi. I surmised that a fourth phase was about to begin, though I had never seen more than the beginning of it: the phase in which he cruised the Brooklyn waterfront in search of compliant sailors and was often beaten up or jailed. Something in my own life had ended. Hart and I had been close friends for seven years, but now he was not so much a friend as something more distant, an object of care and apprehension. He was living now by the iron laws of another country than ours.

During the week that followed, Hart went to see Waldo Frank, whose advice he sometimes followed, and asked him about going to Mexico. Waldo approved the notion, though he warned Hart against drinking anything stronger than beer at the high altitude of Mexico City. Henry Allen Moe of the Guggenheim Foundation also gave him a warning, but otherwise made no difficulty about the changed destination. Hart bought passage on the *Orizaba,* which was sailing the first Saturday in April. I wasn't sorry to miss his uproarious farewell party.

About that time I received an invitation—it was almost a

royal command—to a meeting in Theodore Dreiser's studio. The address on West Fifty-seventh Street turned out to be a big apartment building, an ornate pile. When I arrived at the meeting not very late, a butler took my coat and gave me a drink of scotch from a row of bottles that looked impressive in those days when we were used to nothing better than Jersey lightning or bathtub gin. The big studio was already crowded. There were novelists, critics, liberal editors, crusading journalists, almost everyone in the literary world—except Red Lewis and Dorothy Thompson, I noted—who had expressed an interest in the fate of American society. Nobody but Dreiser could have assembled them.

Dreiser, then fifty-nine, had been fighting our battles since his first book, *Sister Carrie,* had been encouraged to die of neglect in 1900. The younger writers were proud of his later success, and most of them felt that he and not Lewis should have been the first American to be awarded the Nobel Prize; but they also felt that he groped and fumbled more than anyone had a right to do. His mind, it often seemed to us, was like an attic in an earthquake, full of big trunks that slithered about and popped open one after another, so that he spoke sometimes as a Social Darwinist, sometimes as a Marxist, sometimes as almost a fascist, and sometimes as a sentimental reformer. Always he spoke, though, with an uncalculating candor that gave him a large sort of bumbling dignity.

It was so that evening in the clatter of glasses and gossip. Dreiser stood behind a table and rapped on it with his knuckles. He unfolded a very large, very white linen handkerchief and began drawing it first through his left hand, then through his right hand, as if for reassurance of his worldly success. He mumbled something we couldn't catch and then launched into a prepared statement. Things were in a terrible state, he said, and what were we going to do about it? Nobody knew how many millions were unemployed, starving, hiding in their holes. The situation among the coal miners in Western Pennsylvania and in Harlan County, Kentucky, was a disgrace. The politicians from Hoover down and the big financiers had no idea of what was going on. As for the writers and artists—

Dreiser looked up shyly from his prepared text, revealing his scrubbed lobster-pink cheeks and his chins in retreating terraces. For a moment the handkerchief stopped moving.

"The time is ripe," he said, "for American intellectuals to render some service to the American worker." He wondered—as again he drew the big white handkerchief from one hand to the other—whether we shouldn't join a committee that was being organized to collaborate with the International Labor Defense in opposing political persecutions, lynchings, and the deportation of labor organizers; also in keeping the public informed and in helping workers to build their own unions. Then, after some inaudible remarks, he declared that he was through speaking and that we were now to have a discussion.

A meeting like this was strange to all of us under forty; there had been nothing like it since the hopeful days before the Great War. We felt that writers should do their part, but we had no suggestions to volunteer. Louis Adamic, a plain-spoken man who wrote an account of the evening, thought that Dreiser's great honesty and bewilderment had engulfed everyone present. At last Lincoln Steffens, who had just finished writing his *Autobiography*, rose in a quiet fashion and began telling us what he knew about labor warfare. Small, trim, with a little white chinbeard and a Windsor tie tucked loosely into his collar, Steffens looked like a cartoonist's notion of a dapper French artist, an Aristide Duval, but he spoke with a flat-toned Western reticence. "Then they took him to the police station and beat him to death," he said in an unemphatic voice. "After the other leaders were run out of town and a few children starved to death, the strike was broken. The newspapers didn't print a word about it, naturally." He had a theory that facts should speak for themselves—a good theory for journalists, but less good for speakers trying to hold the attention of a restless audience. Adamic said in his diary (from which he quotes in his book *My America,* 1938): "Lincoln Steffens got up and spoke; what about I don't know. He rambled about in his own past and tried to be sage. By-and-by the meeting closed and people began to leave."

But the evening had more of a sequel than Adamic expected. Many of the writers present agreed with Dreiser that it was their duty to "do something" about the depression, since the politicians and financiers had done nothing whatever. The Communist Party, under its new leaders, was planning to make use of their enthusiasm, and it had assigned one

of its organizers to the task of assembling a writers' committee. Joe Pass was the organizer, a young man with a flattened
boxer's nose and a crooked engaging smile. He had been
spending a good deal of time with Dreiser, and now he began
making calls on other writers to reinforce Dreiser's hesitant
plea. Partly as a result of his efforts, the new organization
took shape; it was to be called the National Committee for
the Defense of Political Prisoners. The committee was en-
dorsed by an alphabetical list of sponsors beginning with an
anthropologist, Franz Boas, and ending with a sculptor, William Zorach, but mostly consisting of literary men. Dreiser
was its first chairman and Lincoln Steffens its treasurer.

According to a statement of purpose, "The National Committee recognizes the right of workers to organize, strike and
picket, their right to freedom of speech, press and assembly,
and it will aid in combating any violation of those rights,
through legal means, and above all, by stimulating a wide
public interest and protest." It invited "writers, artists, scientists, teachers and professional people" from the United
States and other countries "to join its ranks and aid its work."
In effect, the committee was a writers' and artists' branch of
the International Labor Defense, which in turn was an aux-
iliary created by the Communist Party for legal work and
propaganda; there was no secret about the connection. The
NCDPP—to use its imposing row of initials in the manner of
the period—was I think the first among hundreds of "front
organizations" designed to enroll middle-class sympathizers.
For me it was the first organization of any sort (except three
or four editorial staffs) that I had joined since getting out of
college.

At first I was not a very active member. I was writing a
series of articles for *The New Republic*, and besides I had
family problems that kept me occupied. Late in June Peggy
sailed for Mexico to get a divorce. I wrote to Hart asking him
to help her in cashing checks and getting settled. When she
arrived in Mexico City, Hart had gone north to attend his
father's funeral. He left a note for her offering the use of his
house, staffed with servants, but instead she accepted another
invitation, from Katherine Anne Porter. The fact was, as she
wrote me, that she felt some trepidation about seeing Hart

again. He had fallen into the habit of reviling his friends in public; also he had been spending nights in Mexican jails, usually as a result of a drunken fight with a taxi driver. Peggy was a little relieved to find that he was temporarily absent.

Meanwhile Dreiser was going ahead with his effort "to render some service to the American worker." In July he made an expedition to the Western Pennsylvania coalfields, where the National Miners Union, organized by the Communists, was conducting a hopeless strike. He issued a violent and merited rebuke to the American Federation of Labor for neglecting the miners. Early in November, in his capacity as chairman of the NCDPP, he led a delegation of writers into Harlan County, Kentucky, another area that the Communist union was trying hard to organize.

Harlan was a classical example of labor warfare in a depressed industry. The market for coal had been shrinking, with the result that the operators had tried to protect their investments by cutting wages, and also—since the miners were paid for each ton they produced—by using crooked scales to weigh the coal. In 1931 very few of the eastern Kentucky miners were earning as much as $35 a month, after deductions. Even that miserable wage was paid, not in cash, but in scrip, good only at the company store and worth no more, in most cases, than fifty or sixty cents on the dollar. The United Mine Workers—John L. Lewis's union—had withdrawn from the field, apparently on the ground that the situation was hopeless and that the miners couldn't afford to pay their union dues. Then the Communists had stepped in, as they often did in hopeless situations, but their meetings were broken up by deputized thugs armed with Browning guns.

It was much the same story as in western Pennsylvania and in Gastonia, North Carolina, but Harlan had its special features too. All the miners there were of English or Scottish descent, tall, lean mountaineers whose faces, Dos Passos said, "were out of early American history." They had come down from the hills with their Elizabethan turns of speech and also with their hillmen's custom of settling disputes with rifles. Harlan County at the time had the highest incidence of death by gunshot wounds in the United States. Mountain feuds had been transformed into battles between striking miners and

gun thugs first hired by the coal operators, then deputized by
the high sheriff. During one such battle, at the town of Evarts
in May 1931, heavy firing lasted for half an hour. Three deputies and one miner were killed, according to the district
attorney, but the miners counted ten coffins shipped out of
town on the evening train. After that the deputies were hot
for revenge, and a union sympathizer who ventured into Harlan County was likely to have a shorter life than a federal
revenue agent in search of a corn-liquor still.

For a wonder the writers' delegation came into the county
and conducted a series of public hearings without so much as
a bullet wound or a broken head. Besides Dreiser and among
others, the writers included Charles Rumford Walker and his
wife Adelaide, the novelist Samuel Ornitz, and John Dos
Passos. They were saved from injury partly by their innocence
and partly by a major of the Kentucky National Guard, who
was assigned to accompany them after Dreiser telegraphed
to the governor of the state and requested military protection.
Dreiser, who presided over the hearings, had a massive presence—"like a goofy old senator," Dos Passos said—that compelled the respect of friends and enemies. The hearings were
stage-managed by Ornitz—later successful in Hollywood, until he was placed on the blacklist—and he gave them the
professional air of courtroom dramas.

Followed by carloads of gun thugs, the delegation moved
from Pineville, the county seat of Bell County, to Harlan
town, and then to mining camps back in the hills. Everywhere
it heard the same stories from witnesses: miserable wages (or
none at all, after the deductions had been made), only two
meals a day of only beans and bulldog gravy (flour and water
with a teaspoonful of lard), houses broken into and searched
without warrants, miners thrown into jail and held for weeks
without being arraigned, and a general terror of "the law."
Dreiser asked one witness, a Harlan miner's wife, what the
law meant to her. "The law," she said, "is a gun thug in a
big automobile." At Straight Creek a volunteer nurse, Aunt
Molly Jackson, sixty-five years old, testified that from three
to seven babies in the camp were dying each week from malnutrition and "the bloody flux." Then she sang a song of her
own composition, "The Kentucky Miner's Wife's Ragged
Hungry Blues":

> All the women in this coalcamp
> > are a-sittin' with bowed-down heads,
> Ragged and barefooted
> > and their children a-cryin' for bread.
> No food, no clothes for our children,
> > I'm sure this ain't no lie.
> If we can't get no more for our labor
> > we will starve to death and die.

After a final night in Pineville the writers went back to New York with their stenographic records of the hearings. "The law" and the coal operators, sometimes indistinguishable one from the other, let the delegation go in peace; perhaps they had been confounded by Dreiser's self-assurance, but they soon rallied their wits. All the writers were indicted for criminal syndicalism, and Dreiser was charged with the additional crime of misconduct in the Pineville hotel with an otherwise unidentified woman named Marie Pergain. The deputies who had been watching his room testified that they had seen the woman go into it and had then leaned toothpicks against the door; the toothpicks were still leaning there in the morning. Dreiser answered indignantly that it would have been impossible for him to commit the offense, because he was "at this writing completely and finally impotent." The Communists, who were looking hard for martyrs, urged Dreiser and Dos Passos to go back to Kentucky and stand trial (for criminal syndicalism, not adultery), but they both refused the crown of thorns. All the indictments were later dismissed. The stenographic records of the delegation appeared in a book edited by Dos Passos, *Harlan Miners Speak* (1932), and some of them were read into the minutes of a Senate hearing. But the war continued in Harlan and Bell counties, and the miners' wives that winter were as ragged, hungry, and barefoot as before.

CUMBERLAND GAP

Meanwhile Peggy was leading a busy life in Mexico City, where she was being squired about by a Mexican artist. So as not to abuse Katherine Anne Porter's hospitality, she had moved out of her house as soon as she found a furnished room. Late in August Katherine Anne sailed from Veracruz on the German boat that she used as a setting for her novel published thirty years later, *Ship of Fools*. Peggy's determinedly brave letters of the following months might have been another novel appearing serially, with Hart Crane as the central character. Here are some extracts that tell part of the story:

September 8.

. . . Hart tracked me down last night just before the meeting [of a library committee that Peggy was trying to organize]. Lord, it was good to see him, although I had only a moment. He thought I was out of town and hadn't even tried to look me up before. He was rather pathetic and very subdued. I told him you were hurt at not having been looked up while he was in New York, and he said he wasn't sure you would want to see him. . . . I did one of "My darling Hart" stunts and we flung ourselves into each other's arms. Jacobo [the Mexican artist], who didn't know of Hart's proclivities and who merely saw me making a terrific fuss over an extremely good looking man, snubbed me and acted sulky during most of the meeting.

September 12.

. . . Last night Hart came all the way in town to get me to go out to Mixcoac [the suburb where Hart had rented a house] with him for supper. We do enjoy each other so much. I am on the water wagon and Hart says I am taking it like some religious enthusiast.

October 1.

. . . I too may have trouble with Hart, perhaps in more ways than one. He is drinking again all too heavily, acting all right but talking very erratically. . . . He is more than a little in love with me and almost fiendishly jealous of you. He spent all yesterday afternoon trying to make me promise not to write you and looked over the letters on my table to see if I had. By being in love with me I don't mean he wants my body, but he does want to marry me, all of course because he is more than a bit lonely and desires a close companionship that he has never found in sex.

Undated, early in November.

. . . Z——'s party was all right as such things go. After it was over one of the men took me to the Broadway, where we sat until five in the morning talking art. Found out from him that Z—— was spreading the report that Hart was my lover and that it was a shame that a nice girl like myself was being led astray by a degenerate. He also seemed to think it was a shame and did his damnedest to make me change my status. Like all such fool rumors, I see no use in denying it. . . . Hart took me to dinner last night and I told him, at which he said: "You'd better marry me and make me a decent woman."

November 15.

. . . As for Hart, we are more or less all right now [he had sent her an insulting telegram]. He will not be allowed in the house when he is drunk. I told the porter and also told him. God, I hate to see that boy simply making a wreck of himself, how pitiful with his really great power.

About this time the Mexican artist disappeared from the story. Peggy had been ill, and she decided to seek relief at a lower altitude. Having rented a house in Taxco, she invited guests to a Christmas party. Her letters continued:

December 21.

. . . Just as I was starting dinner yesterday a little boy appeared carrying a suitcase, who said my señor was down in the place and would be right up. For a spinster like myself this was highly mystifying. It turned out to be Hart, who had decided that either I needed to be taken care of or he did.

December 26.

. . . Hart intends staying with me until after New Years. We are very close and companionable, strangely so, with him very thoughtful and sort of the head of the house. I just let him do everything and the more I put on his shoulders in the way of responsibilities the more he accepts. He carved chickens for dinner, moved tables, ordered servants [all this at the Christmas party], made guests feel at home, squeezed lemons for the rum punch, stayed sober and filled other glasses before his own, and this morning with the help of the maid replaced the whole household. I shall take all I can get of this mood while it lasts.

They were really lovers now, and Hart had begun to write an epithalamium, his first new poem in more than a year. Peggy copied out for me the first stanza in its original form:

> The bell-cord that gathers God at dawn
> Dispatches me—as though I climbed the knell
> Of a clear morn—I could walk the cathedral lawn
> Clear to the meridian—and back from hell.

Soon after New Year's, Hart went back to Mixcoac. "I presume he will wait," Peggy said on January 12, 1932, "until the house and the servants have become an albatross around his neck, go out on a binge and then rush to me for salvation." On January 16, "Hart arrived just as I expected." On January 25, "Hart has been with me ever since he wrote the letter to you. He is so lovely and thoughtful of me that I shall miss him terribly when he does leave." The story continued in rapid installments.

January 27.
. . . Hart finished the first draft of a poem yesterday [it was the same poem, later to be called "The Broken Tower"]. All prophecies to the contrary, he is by no means finished. It is a magnificent piece of lyric poetry that is built with the rhetorical splendor of a Dante in Hell. I'll send you a copy as soon as I'm sure he's finished working on it. The boy can commit any fool flamboyant act he wishes, or rot in jail, if he only gets something like this out of his system once in a while.

We went on a jag last night all by ourselves, drinking a terrific amount, but so excited about the poem that neither one of us got drunk.

January 31.
. . . Hart left day before yesterday after getting in a huff with Clinton King. Since that time I have been receiving two telegrams a day for the simple reason that he is lonesome for me. . . . The boy has a gay time with his histrionics. Strange to relate I don't really mind them.

February 3.
. . . It was impossible to stay in Taxco after Hart's last telegram. I wired him to meet me at the Broadway at seven-thirty and for

five hours in the bus wondered what in hell was in store for me
on my arrival. But Hart can always give you a surprise.

After this hot dusty ride I arrived at the Broadway to find
cocktails on the table, with Hart not having touched his—a
corsage of violets and sweet peas, a magnificent meal ordered
and two new records for me. We dashed out here immediately
after dinner and played the records. . . . The servants had spent
the whole day fixing wreaths all over the place for my reception
and the whole thing was very touching and sweet.

I too was touched, and delighted for both of them, especially since the next letter reported that Hart was sober and
back at work on his poem. It was hard to believe, however,
that his new life was anything more than a respite from his
private hell. And I was slow to answer Peggy, engrossed as
I was in preparations for another mission in Kentucky.

One day in January, Charles Rumford Walker had come
to see me at *The New Republic* and had stayed all afternoon.
He told me that, from the standpoint of the National Miners
Union, Dreiser's visit to Kentucky had been a grand success.
It had directed attention to Harlan County, it had forced "the
law" to be a little more legal, and it had encouraged the union
to call a strike in the Eastern Kentucky coalfields on January
1. According to Charlie, most of the miners had come out,
and they would stay out as long as their families had "maybe
not enough to eat," so they said, "but just enough to breathe."
Food was the central problem and the hardest one for the
union to solve, because its relief kitchens were being burned
or dynamited and its relief trucks ambushed and looted by
deputies. Having served as a member of Dreiser's committee,
Charlie thought that another such mission might "open up
the situation"—that was his phrase—help in raising money
for relief, and keep "the law" from interfering with the distribution of food.

Charlie had large, soft, bright eyes like a squirrel's, and his
enthusiasm was infectious as he talked about the miners, their
mountain speech, their ballads, and their courage. He wanted
me to join a committee that would go, not to Harlan this
time, but to Pineville, which was said to be less embattled.
He didn't think the trip would be dangerous, but I could guess
that the authorities would be better prepared to receive a

second group of visitors. I told him I would go along if *The New Republic* would give me time off to write an article. As I started for the train I was humming under my breath a miner's song that someone had been playing on the phonograph:

> Oh, Daddy, don't go to the mine today,
> For dreams have been known to come true.
> Oh, Daddy, dead Daddy, don't go to the mine,
> I never could live without you.

The strike was being directed from Knoxville, Tennessee, the nearest city to the mines that was safe for union organizers. When our committee assembled there, it included among other writers Edmund Wilson, Waldo Frank, Quincy Howe (then editor of *The Living Age*), and Mary Heaton Vorse. Except for Mrs. Vorse, a novelist with radical sympathies who had been reporting strikes for thirty years, we had no experience in labor disputes. Waldo Frank had published more books than the rest of us, and we made him our chairman. We decided to keep out of trouble, if we could, and follow our own policies instead of being guided by the Communist union, which we felt would be delighted if we were all thrown into jail: think of the national publicity.

Just before starting for Pineville on the morning of February 10, we heard that Harry Sims, a Young Communist serving as a union organizer, had been shot by a sheriff's deputy and was dying in a Knox County, Kentucky, hospital. We drove north in hired cars through the lovely Powell River valley, afterward flooded by the Norris Dam, and then past the monument to Daniel Boone in Cumberland Gap. Beyond the Gap I remembered driving north from a French railhead in 1917 toward the front lines; the fact was that I hadn't seen so many guns since the Great War. A crowd of thirty men with rifles and shotguns was standing outside a filling station at a junction where one road led to Harlan. "They're fixing to keep you out of Harlan County," the driver said. "It's a tough county and Harlan is a tough town. I went there once, but I didn't stay long. A man came up to me in the street and said, 'I'll give you ten dollars for your gun.' I said, 'But you've got a gun already.' He said, 'A man ain't safe here withouten he has two guns.' So I took his ten dollars and got out of town."

There was another armed force of deputies waiting to meet

us at the Pineville city line. There were deputies mingled with the crowd of miners that had gathered in the courthouse square. We stopped outside the office of W. J. Stone, the only local attorney who would plead for the miners, and went upstairs to consult with him. A miner was telling Stone the story of how he had been beaten, while only his lips moved in a grotesquely swollen face. "Don't stand near the window," someone said. "They've got needle guns pointed this way." I looked across the street. In the third-story windows of the courthouse I could see machine-gun muzzles commanding the crowd of miners below.

We did not know then that the union was scheming to make the most of our visit. Since calling the strike six weeks before, it had not been permitted to hold a meeting. Now, without warning us, it had summoned the miners into Pineville for a distribution of food and a "free-speech speaking," in order to raise their spirits. Revolution was in the air that year. When news of the union summons reached the respectable citizens, they decided that the miners intended to seize the town, loot the stores, and burn down the churches. They believed that they were fighting now to save their property, their God, and their daughters from the Red menace, and that any measure of defense was justified, even shooting men in cold blood. That explained the machine guns in the courthouse and the general air of tense waiting. Our committee, arriving innocently on the scene, was like a party of civilians wandering into no man's land to gather flowers.

Later that morning we were summoned to a meeting in the Pineville hotel, where Mayor Brooks had assembled some twenty-five of the leading merchants, professional men, and coal operators. Waldo Frank presented our requests, speaking reasonably (but his voice was high and he lacked Dreiser's imposing presence). We wished to take three truckloads of food to the relief warehouse established by the union (not knowing that it had been closed); we wished to distribute the food to the miners who had come into town to meet us; we wished to consult with the miners, hear their grievances, if any, and learn whether relief supplies had been prevented from reaching them. We had been advised that these requests were within our constitutional rights. . . . The mayor refused all of them.

Frank said that we were determined to obey not only the

laws of Kentucky but also the commands of local officials, even though we knew them to be illegal. A coal operator delivered a speech on bolshevism. Another operator asked *Mr.* Frank if he had registered for the draft in 1917. A third operator, his mouth set like a steel trap, said that the meeting was no good anyway, and everybody started to leave. At the door Mayor Brooks stopped us to announce that if we attempted to distribute any food in Pineville, we would all be arrested. He walked out into the lobby of the hotel, then hurried back to tell us that if we held any sort of meeting in Pineville, whether on the public highways or in a vacant lot rented by ourselves, we would be arrested. He continued his series of prohibitions, stepping out into the lobby after each of them, like an actor who has forgotten his lines and must be prompted in the wings. We must not talk with the miners or we would be arrested. We must not print or distribute any handbills or we would be arrested. We must not invite any miners to our rooms in the hotel or we would be arrested for holding a meeting. If we wished to distribute our food outside of town, we must first get the permission of the county attorney, and he, Mayor Brooks, doubted whether it would be granted.

The coal operator with a steel-trap mouth walked up to us. "This is another war," he said. "I admire your nerve in coming here where you don't know anything about conditions or the feeling of the people. If you don't watch out, you'll find out how ugly we can be, and I don't care if your stenographer takes that down." "That goes for me too," some of the others said.

I learned afterward, by talking to witnesses at a Senate hearing, that the leading citizens held another meeting that continued through the afternoon. Some of the coal operators, I heard, had suggested shooting us all, as a means of proving to the outside world that nobody could interfere with their affairs, but they were voted down. Meanwhile our committee had been kept busy. We had visited the county attorney and had received his permission to distribute the truckloads of food on a county road, provided there was no speaking. We had handed out the food to miners—except for the last two hundred pounds of salt pork, which was stolen at gunpoint by one of the sheriff's men. A young miner who tried to speak had been chased by Deputy Sheriff John Wilson with two drawn guns, but had escaped into the crowd. Another deputy had beaten a miner whom we later saw in Stone's law office, his arms blue-black and swollen like toy balloons.

Early in the evening, our baggage was searched in the police station. The most incriminating document discovered in anyone's possession was a bulletin of the Foreign Policy Association, over which four men puzzled a long time before filing it away as evidence of criminal syndicalism. We went back to the hotel and some of us went to bed. At ten-thirty we were all arrested, in my case by two rather considerate deputies. "You'd better take along your toothbrush and razor," one of them told me while I was dressing. "You might be in jail for a spell." But after waiting half an hour in a locked police court, and breaking into nervous laughter when a deputy's gun slipped out of his pocket and clattered to the floor, we were informed by the judge that the charge against us, whatever it was, had been dismissed "for lack of prosecution." We began to be uneasy now, and demanded protection, but the judge ordered us to go back to the hotel. There, in the lobby, we found an armed crowd of deputies, coal operators, and merchants—"night riders and citizens," as they called themselves. They told us that we were to be carried out of the state and that, if we ever returned, it would be at our own risk.

Two by two we were placed in the back seats of automobiles. I noticed that Waldo Frank and Allan Taub, a lawyer for the International Labor Defense, were ordered into the same car. As the procession moved off I felt like a patient being wheeled into the operating room. I was thinking, "If they beat me I'll scream. It's the only hope of stopping them." The line of headlights undulated with the road, sometimes revealing a leafless patch of mountainside.

"This is some motorcade," said the young coal operator at the wheel. "Motorcade" was a new word then, and he repeated it lovingly: "I wouldn't have missed this motorcade for ten years of my life."

Quincy Howe sat beside me, sometimes answering a question politely in his flat Boston voice. Deputy John Wilson guarded us, and there were two men and a girl in the front seat. The driver talked like a college boy coming home from the big game. "You sure would have plugged that miner today, John, if you got a fair shot at him," he said. "It's a pity he got away into the crowd."—"I'll fix him," John Wilson said, "next time I see him. I'll take him to jail or I'll kill him." In Washington one of the witnesses would tell me that Wilson had killed several men for "resisting arrest" or "trying to escape." Still later I heard that he had been found in the woods with a bullet in his back.

We stopped at a filling station and John Wilson bought us each a bottle of Coke, then finished his own bottle at a gulp and wiped the last drops from the drooping ends of his mustache. The car speeded up to rejoin the procession. "They shot one of those Bolsheviks up in Knox County this morning, Harry Sims his name was," the driver said. "That deputy knew his business. He didn't give the redneck a chance to talk, he just plugged him in the stomach. We need some shooting like that down here. Say," he burst out, "they're striking down at my place. They talk about having a picket line. Let me tell you, I've got eight men with rifles waiting on the hill, and if any redneck tries to picket my mine, he's going to be dead before he knows it." The cars ahead of us had begun to climb out of the Cumberland River valley. "Listen," the driver said, "I want to ask you a question. Do you two fellows believe in a Supreme Being?"

"Yes," I said truthfully, but after a pause; I didn't like to placate an enemy. The "yes" was more confusing to the young coal operator than a "no" would have been, and he fell silent as the procession wound into Cumberland Gap. At the Tennessee line, there was a broad paved semicircle where motorists could stop to enjoy the daytime view of three states, and here the procession halted. We sat there for a while, then John Wilson nudged Quincy and me and told us to get out of the car. As we stood beside our bags in the headlights I thought to myself, "This is the operating room." Somebody ordered, "Lights out." Ten yards away in the darkness I heard a piercing and continued scream. Then the lights were turned on again and somebody shouted in a Kentucky-mountain voice, "Frank and Taub they've been having a fight."

Frank as our spokesman and Allan Taub as an argumentative lawyer were the two men against whom the coal operators were most incensed. Several deputies, one of whom was armed with a jack handle, had attacked them both in the darkness. Taub had escaped serious injuries by shielding his head with his arms, but Frank had some deep head wounds.

"Now let lawyer Taub make a speech on constitutional liberties," one of the Pineville businessmen said.

They searched our luggage once more, this time for motion-picture films, and confiscated an unexposed reel from the cameraman, who had managed to get his pictures out of town before we were arrested. (His name was Ben Leider, and five years later he would be killed in Spain, flying a plane for the Loyalists.) Then they let us go and we stumbled down the highway into Tennessee. One of us turned a flashlight on the monument to Daniel Boone, dead a long time ago with all his world. When we reached the hotel in the town of Cumberland Gap, a mile below, we found that a newspaperman had notified the proprietor some hours before that he could expect a party of New York writers. But instead of stopping there, we managed to hire three cars and reached Knoxville in time for a few hours of sleep.

Next day we found that our real tasks were in front of us: publicity and money-raising. We had been helped with both by the "night riders and citizens." Waldo Frank was photographed time and again, his head swathed in bandages, and the pictures were printed all over the country. The rest of us were busy being interviewed and writing newspaper stories. We took the night train to Washington, a city which had suffered less than others from the depression, but which, it seemed to me, had a curious air of emptiness and waiting. On Capitol Hill we talked at length to Senator Bronson Cutting of New Mexico, an honest liberal and a great gentleman; I think the meeting had been arranged by Cutting's volunteer secretary, the poet Phelps Putnam. Cutting had heard about the hardships of the miners and promised that he would do his best to arrange a formal Senate hearing (which in fact was held three months later). Phelps Putnam kept rushing into and out of the conference room, always wearing a broad-brimmed black slouch hat which, with his clean, Yalie-from-a-good-prep-school face, made him look like a Bones man disguised as a decadent artist of the 1890s. I thought that his poems had the same double aspect, incongruous and appealing.

In New York there was of course a protest meeting, to raise funds and spirits. It was held in a big drafty auditorium near the Harlem River, and there must have been four thousand people in the audience. I spoke in public for the first time since dropping out of the Harvard freshman debating team. Coming first on the program, I started in a loud voice, but apprehensively, "We went into Kentucky because we were told that local authorities were interfering with relief to the striking miners." I paused, wondering if I could go on—and was the loudspeaker working? "We can't hear you," somebody called from the back rows. Others took up the cry. Much louder I repeated, "We went into Kentucky. Can you hear me?"—"We can't hear you," more of the audience chanted. So I roared as if through a megaphone, "WE WENT INTO KENTUCKY NOW CAN YOU HEAR ME?"—"Yes," the audience roared back, and my stage fright was gone. It wasn't a very good speech, in the end, but radical audiences were satisfied with hearing a stentorian voice and the proper sentiments. I was asked to make the speech again, in Philadelphia, and then to make other speeches, so that for me, as for some others, the trip to Kentucky had a long sequel.

That second mission to Kentucky was one of many that writers undertook during the 1930s. There had been or would be others to North Carolina, Alabama, Cuba, the Imperial Valley of California, and even to Vermont during a strike in the marble quarries. At some point in a hopeless struggle the Communist leaders would say, "Let's organize a writers' committee." The missions were widely reported and, though they did not win strikes in Kentucky or elsewhere, they helped to raise funds for the strikers (and for the party). Another series of effects was on the writers themselves. Some of these drew back when they found they were being used by the Communists, as Edmund Wilson did for one, but others resigned themselves to being used, since they thought it was for the common good. They committed themselves to a new life not merely by accepting opinions, which can change in a day, but more lastingly by their own actions. That was the effect on me of the Kentucky mission and its aftermath. I found myself committed to "the movement" by working and speaking for it (and in some measure, I suppose, by the sense of importance that comes from working and speaking). I was also committed by the hungry, ragged, but clear-eyed look of the miners' wives, by the talk of shooting men in cold blood, and by the machine guns pointing at me from the Pineville courthouse. This was another war, as the steel-mouthed coal operator had said, and I knew which side I was on.

THE BROKEN TOWER

The Hart Crane story continued in Peggy's letters, though I was too busy now to answer most of them. Peggy had moved to Mixcoac and was presiding over Hart's household, which included a drunken *mozo*, his wife, his babies, and a beautiful Communist girl seeking refuge from the police while she worked as second cook and housemaid. Peggy tried to keep her from attending meetings at which she might be arrested, and tried with some success to keep Hart and the *mozo* sober. Her letters seemed to be written in an Indian-summer haze of good feeling.

> *February 22.*
> Arrived here the other night and a delightful homecoming Hart achieved. There was good white Spanish wine, which we sat over dinner until all hours of the night, our tongues going at both ends and scarcely listening to each other. . . .
> P.S. By the way I want to congratulate you on making the trip to Kentucky, both Hart and I feel that it is one of the most important definite acts you have ever made. Too, I feel that one of the greatest compliments you have ever paid me was in saying I would have enjoyed the trip. . . . Hart wishes to include his love.

> *March 21.*
> . . . Bob Haberman made me sign the final papers [for the divorce], though they don't go through until your power of attorney comes. . . . I can't understand why I ever think of coming north. I am really happy here and Hart outside of everything else, is the grandest companion any human being could ask for. . . . Frankly it's a real joy to see Hart so happy, contented, and really in love for the first time in his life.

From Hart came a carbon copy of "The Broken Tower," the poem on which he had been working for the last three months. It ended with a triumphant invocation to love (and to Peggy, I thought):

The steep encroachments of my blood left me
No answer (could blood hold such a lofty tower
As flings the question true?)—or is it she
Whose sweet mortality stirs latent power?—
. . . .
The commodius, tall decorum of that sky
Unseals her earth, and lifts love in its shower.

Beneath the last stanza Hart had typed in a message to me.
It was dated "Easter," which that year fell on March 27.

Peggy and I think and talk a great deal about you. That means
in a very fond way, or it wouldn't be mentioned. I'm wondering
whether or not you'll like the above poem—about the 1st I've
written in two years . . . I'm getting too damned self-critical to
write at all any more. More than ever, however, I do implore
your honest appraisal of this verse, prose or nonsense—whatever
it may seem. Please let me know.

And because I congratulate you most vehemently on your
recent account of the Kentucky expedition—please don't tell me
anything you don't honestly mean. This has already been submitted to POETRY—so don't worry about that angle.

I miss seeing you a great deal. Peggy is writing you some sort
of account of the Easter celebrations here. We're very happy
together—and send lots of love!

Happy, happy . . . the word was repeated in all the March
letters, but then it disappeared from the correspondence. Hart
drank at the Easter celebrations and again was violently drunk
a few days later. On April 7 Peggy wrote me:

. . . To keep me here he has promised to give up tequila. I didn't
ask him to, but I am frankly admitting to you that should he
start drinking heavily again I shall wire immediately for money
home. I don't want you to let him know I wrote this, and as
you knew it already, it doesn't seem very disloyal. All in all,
with my own disillusions I have probably been a great deal
harder on him, than the other way around. Drinking only beer,
the poor child is steadily losing his waist-line and gaining the
healthy color of a Burgundian friar. I am so pampered that I
feel at times I am done up in some superior kind of cotton
wool. . . .

Though Hart was red-faced as a Burgundian friar, he had fallen into a black mood. He had been excited by the Kentucky mission and by the news that his friends were going left, but then he became resentful. "Waldo and Malcolm are just cutting paper dollies," he said. Hart's money was running out, and he had recently learned that he could expect nothing for years from his father's estate, which had been whittled away by the depression. He no longer felt capable of finding a job or of keeping it if found. Still worse, he was appalled by a suspicion that his talent—which he seemed to regard as a personality apart from his ordinary self—was leaving him and might never return. That was why he asked humbly for reassurance that "The Broken Tower" was not prose or nonsense, but a great poem. Unfortunately the copy he submitted to Morton Zabel, then editor of *Poetry,* went astray in the mail. I thought the poem was splendid, but I was so taken up with *The New Republic* and my after-hours work for the NCDPP that I put off writing Hart from day to day. It seems that he waited in Mixcoac for news while bewailing the state of the world. "What good are poets today!" he exclaimed more than once, by Peggy's report. "The world needs men of action."

One morning in the middle of April, full of tequila, he stared angrily at the fine portrait that Siqueiros had painted of him, then slashed it to pieces with an old-fashioned razor. Having killed himself symbolically, he tried to die in the flesh by swallowing a bottle of iodine, but he spilled most of it. Later in the day he seized and drained another bottle from the medicine cabinet, but that one contained Mercurochrome. Though it harmed nothing else, I suspect that it fatally wounded his self-respect: if he tried to die again, he must not fail. Peggy was terrified and wired me for money to come north. Hart, now sober most of the time, decided to take the same boat, the *Orizaba,* and they sailed from Veracruz on April 24. Three days later I received a telegram from Palm Beach:

MALCALM COWLEY, CARE NEW REPUBLIC
HART COMMITTED SUICIDE MEET ME
PEGGY

Next morning I read a brief account of the suicide in the morning papers, from which I also learned that the *Orizaba* would reach New York on the afternoon of Friday the twenty-ninth. After some official hesitation—for *The New Republic* had never before shown an interest in ship-news reporting—I obtained a newspaperman's pass on the Coast Guard cutter that met arriving vessels at Quarantine. The cutter was full of reporters that day; there must have been sixty on board. With horror I pictured them swarming over Peggy, asking her intimate questions, and I pictured the headlines over their stories: "Says Poet Died for Love," or, "Despaired of Fame, Courted Death." Then the cutter stopped beside another liner, the *Berengaria*, and all but two of the reporters went on board. One of them told me that they had all come down the Bay to meet Mrs. Reginald A. Hargreaves, then eighty years old, who was said to be the original Alice of *Alice's Adventures in Wonderland*.

Having struck up a conversation with the two reporters left on the cutter, I remarked that a poet named Hart Crane had committed suicide by jumping from the stern of the *Orizaba*. They didn't think the story was news any longer, and neither of them spoke to Peggy when we went on board. I saw that her left hand was deep in bandages. After a while she told me that the injured hand might have had something to do with Hart's death. Drunk in Havana, he had invaded the crew's quarters, where he had been beaten and robbed; then an officer had locked him in his cabin. Meanwhile a box of matches had exploded in Peggy's hand as she was lighting a cigarette. At twelve o'clock noon, after the wound had been dressed for a second time, a stewardess was helping Peggy into her clothes. Hart burst into the room wearing a topcoat over his pajamas. "Good-bye, dear," he said, and rushed out again. There was something in his tone that frightened her. If it hadn't been for the painfully burned hand, she would have jumped up, and perhaps she could have stopped him.

"Perhaps for that one time," I said.

At the dock I helped Peggy through customs with her collection of Mexican baskets and serapes. She was staying with friends whom I didn't want to see at the time, so I put her into a taxi and kissed her good-bye. Having mourned for Hart a year before he died, I now felt that his suicide and Peggy's decree of divorce were echoes of an era that had ended. It had been a good era in its fashion, full of high spirits and grand parties, but also, it seemed to me now, inexcusably wasteful of time and emotions. We had lived on the reckless margins of society and had spent our energies on our private lives, which had gone to pieces. Now I wanted to get married again and stay married, I knew to whom. I wanted to live as simply as possible and turn my energies toward the world outside. I wanted to write honestly, I wanted to do my share in building a just society, and it did not occur to me that those last two aims, both admirable in themselves, might come into conflict.

THE ROUT OF THE BONUS ARMY

On May 1, 1932, which was the Sunday after my trip down the Bay, I made a public confession of faith by marching in the May Day parade. It was a big parade that year, with thirty-five thousand marchers by the lowest estimate and a hundred thousand by the highest, which of course was *The Daily Worker*'s. Arriving early I ran into John Herrmann, one of the Paris crowd; he now looked pale, shabby, and, I thought, exalted. He invited me to join a delegation of writers from *The New Masses* and the John Reed Club.

After an interminable but high-humored wait in a side street, under a threatening sky, we formed eight abreast with our slogans red-lettered on cardboard and marched around Union Square, which was crowded with friendly spectators. Somewhere near us was a larger delegation of students from local universities. When the band stopped playing "The International," we could hear them chanting a sort of college yell: "We confess communism." The parade moved down Broadway toward Rutgers Square, its destination on the Lower East Side. At some point the rain began falling, gently at first, then in heavy gusts. The sidewalks were empty now, except for policemen in black-rubber raincoats, and the red paint dripped from our wilted placards. There was, however, one last outburst of high spirits. Far down on East Broadway, as the marchers passed the offices of *The Jewish Daily Forward,* a Socialist newspaper, each contingent in turn booed and shouted, "Down with the yellow press." It seemed that the Socialists, more than the capitalists, were the enemy to be defied.

Hundreds of policemen were waiting as we plodded into Rutgers Square. "It's all over," they said in businesslike voices, pushing into the crowd but not using their clubs. "Break it up. Go home." The policemen didn't want trouble that day, and neither did the marchers. "Cossacks," a few of them shouted back, but not belligerently. A May Day parade was intended to be a peaceful show of strength and of beliefs held in common, almost like a saint's-day procession in Naples, and besides it was raining too hard for a riot.

John Herrmann came home with me by subway. While his cracked shoes dried on the radiator, we were busy talking, but not about writing or Paris or what Hemingway might be doing next. We talked about John's trip to Russia two years before, when he had been fired with enthusiasm by attending a writers' congress in Kharkov. Also we must have talked about the prospects of revolution in the United States, as everyone seemed to be doing in that year of wild fears and wilder dreams of tomorrow.

A few weeks later there was more talk of revolution when the Bonus Expeditionary Force descended on Washington. The BEF was a tattered army consisting of veterans from every state in the Union; most of them were old-stock Americans from smaller industrial cities where relief had broken down. All unemployed in 1932, all living on the edge of hunger, they remembered that the government had made them a promise for the future. It was embodied in a law that Congress had passed some years before, providing "adjusted compensation certificates" for those who had served in the Great War; the certificates were to be redeemed in dollars, but not until 1945. Now the veterans were hitchhiking and stealing rides on freight cars to Washington, for the sole purpose, they declared, of petitioning Congress for immediate payment of the soldiers' bonus. They arrived by hundreds or thousands every day in June. Ten thousand were camped on marshy ground across the Anacostia River, and ten thousand others occupied a number of half-demolished buildings between the Capitol and the White House. They organized themselves by states and companies and chose a commander named Walter W. Waters, an ex-sergeant from Portland, Oregon, who promptly acquired an aide-de-camp and a pair of highly polished leather puttees. Meanwhile the veterans were listening to speakers of all political complexions, as the Russian soldiers had done in 1917. Many radicals and some conservatives thought that the Bonus Army was creating a revolutionary situation of an almost classical type.

Although the Communists had no share in starting the Bonus March—in fact it took them by surprise—they tried hard to seize control of it. Members of the Workers Ex-Servicemen's League, one of their so-called "mass" organizations, were urged to enroll in the BEF, and at one time there were more than two hundred Communist veterans in Washington. They lived by themselves in a dismantled building, having been jim-crowed by the other veterans, who were patriots to a man. Commander Waters had begun to nurse political ambitions, which would be frustrated if the Reds got into his army. He was known to have organized an intelligence force that was charged with keeping them under surveillance. Any Communist who ventured into the camp on Anacostia Flats was likely to be denounced and given fifteen lashes with an army belt. Still the Communists kept trying to make converts. They hoped that the veterans would yield to the logic of events, which must end by persuading them all that there was no hope for the unemployed under capitalism. Left-wing journalists by the score had been visiting Washington to report "the situation." When they got back to New York, some of them told me jubilantly that the Bonus Army newspaper was becoming more "militant," a friendly word in the Communists' vocabulary (their enemies were not militant but "ruthless" or "demagogic"). The journalists also said that although the rank-and-file (another friendly term) wouldn't listen to Communists, they were beginning to talk like Communists themselves.

But the marchers still put their hopes in medals worn on ragged shirts, in discharge papers carried in their wallets, and in making congressmen believe that they controlled thousands of votes. To many people over the country, the marchers seemed to be speaking in behalf of all the unemployed. Congress was not yet disposed to help the unemployed, though the Patman Bonus Bill squeaked through the House of Representatives on June 15. Two days later it was debated in the Senate. While eight thousand veterans picketed the Capitol, massing their American flags on the steps of the Senate wing, the bill went down to a crushing defeat. The veterans, however, were still in Washington, where they proposed to stay till they got their money. "If we have to," they said, "we can wait here till 1945." Many of them had nowhere else to go. In Washington they at least had shelter of a sort, and they were fed by public and private charity, even if they could never be sure what next would go into their big kettles of mulligan. Some of the veterans had been joined by their wives and children. The Bonus Army was beginning to develop its own style of life, its legends, its loyalties, and its defiant folksongs:

> Mellon pulled the whistle,
> Hoover rang the bell,
> Wall Street gave the signal,
> And the country went to hell.

The veterans liked to believe that Andrew Mellon was the engineer of the all-American business express, that Wall Street was the train dispatcher who had put it on the wrong track, and that Mr. Hoover was only the fireman. They did not intend to wreck the train, as they thought the Communists were trying to do. "Hell, we're not against the government," they said. "We're just against the guys that are running it." All sorts of amateur and professional politicians were scheming to make use of their mild rebellion. There was Father Cox of Pittsburgh, who had organized a Jobless Party and named himself as its candidate for president; he made a trip to Washington and pleaded with the veterans to endorse him. There was Father Coughlin, the radio priest of Royal Oak, Michigan, who also wanted their support and gave $5000 to their treasury. Jacob S. Coxey of Massillon, Ohio, had led his own army of protest in 1894. Now he was the presidential candidate of a new Farmer-Labor Party—not allied with the more practical Farmer-Laborites of Minnesota—and he asked Commander Waters to be his running mate. Waters had what he thought was a better scheme; he wanted to lead a national movement of the unemployed that would be organized on military lines. He must have been thinking of Hitler and Mussolini when he decided to call it the Khaki Shirts.

There is some evidence that high officials of the administration had their own scheme for profiting from the Bonus

March. First they would try to persuade the public that most of the marchers were Reds bent on overthrowing the government. Then, at the first excuse, they would use military force to disperse the BEF, with the result, so they hoped, that the country would rally to Mr. Hoover as its saviour. Some but not all of the higher military officers were eager to prove that they knew exactly how to deal with civil commotions. At military posts near Washington all leaves were canceled and men were being drilled in the use of bayonets and tear gas against civilians. One difficulty had appeared in carrying out the scheme. As Secretary of War Patrick J. Hurley, famous for his indiscretions, complained in a private discussion with Waters, the BEF had been too law-abiding. There had been no "incident" that would offer an excuse for declaring martial law. After Congress adjourned on July 16, the Bonus Army had begun to melt away, with eight thousand men leaving in a week, and it now looked as though the episode would end peaceably, to the disappointment of many radical and conservative politicians.

Late in July I went to visit my father and mother at their country house near the village of Belsano, Pennsylvania. I wanted them to meet my new wife, and I wanted Muriel to see the house where I was born. In Belsano, on Friday the twenty-eighth, I read about the battle of Washington and the rout of the remaining veterans. While some of them were being evicted from an abandoned government building on Pennsylvania Avenue, there had been just enough of a fracas to serve as the incident for which Hurley and others were waiting. Mr. Hoover had called in the soldiers, and they had appeared in an imposing column: four troops of cavalry, all in gas masks and with drawn sabers, then a mounted machine-gun squadron, six tanks, a battalion of infantry with fixed bayonets, and a convoy of trucks. In command of the column was General Douglas MacArthur, then the highest-ranking officer in the Army of the United States.

I read about the march up Pennsylvania Avenue and the tear-gas bombs lobbed into the crowd of spectators. In the afternoon papers I read about the battle of Anacostia Flats, where the soldiers set fire to the miserable shacks and the veterans with their families scuttled through the smoke and the tear-gas fumes like dry leaves in a bonfire. I read a proclamation by Mr. Hoover, who announced that "after months of patient indulgence, the government met overt lawlessness as it always must be met if the cherished processes of self-government are to be preserved." I read more news about the veterans: outlaws now, they were being herded into trucks, which would carry them north into Pennsylvania, then westward along the Lincoln Highway. Mayor McCloskey of Johnstown, a red-haired ex-pugilist, had invited them to his city, and thousands of them were planning to establish a new camp there, if they could escape from the trucks that were rushing them toward the Middle West. That brought the story close to home. Belsano is only eighteen miles northwest of Johnstown, and the Lincoln Highway is about the same distance south of the city. On Saturday morning we set out in the family Hupmobile to see what was happening.

Johnstown, which had been one of the grimiest small cities in the world, looked unexpectedly bright and clean with the steel mills closed down. I had heard that half the working force of the city was unemployed and that a fifth or a sixth of the population was in need of charity. At such a time the arrival of several thousand hungry strangers was a threat in itself, but the editor of *The Johnstown Tribune* had conjured up new terrors. He wrote in an editorial published that morning:

> Johnstown faces a crisis. It must prepare to protect itself from the Bonus Army concentrating here at the invitation of Mayor Eddie McCloskey. . . .
>
> In any group the size of the Bonus Army, made up of men gathered from all parts of the country, without effective leadership in a crisis, without any attempt on the part of those leaders to check up the previous records of the individuals who compose it, there is certain to be a mixture of undesirables—thieves, plug-uglies, degenerates. . . . The community must protect itself from the criminal fringe of the invaders.
>
> Booster clubs, community organizations of every sort, volunteer organizations if no sectional group is available, should get together in extraordinary sessions and organize to protect property, women and possibly life.
>
> It is no time for halfway measures. . . .

The heroes of 1918, now metamorphosed into "thieves, plug-uglies, degenerates," were about to gather in the south-

ern outskirts of the city, at a campsite that someone had
offered them. Meanwhile the leading citizens, aided by state
troopers, were planning to use "extraordinary measures" to
keep them from reaching it. I thought as we drove southward
that Mr. Hoover's proclamation had done its work.

At the village of Jennerstown, on the Lincoln Highway, we
found a barracks of the Pennsylvania State Police that looked
for all the world like a prosperous roadhouse. There was a
traffic light in front of the barracks, and that was where the
veterans would have to turn north if they went to Johnstown.
It was the task of the state troopers to keep them moving
west over the mountains, toward Ligonier and the Ohio border. In half an hour on Saturday morning I saw more than a
thousand veterans pass through Jennerstown—that is, more
than fifty open trucks bearing an average of twenty men each.
Later I was told that the convoys kept passing at longer intervals until Sunday evening. The troopers waited at the in-
tersection, twenty men on their motorcycles, like a school of
gray sharks, till they heard that a convoy was approaching;
then they darted off to meet it in a foam of dust and blue
gasoline smoke, with their stiff-brimmed hats cutting the air
like fins. One of the troopers stayed behind to manipulate
the traffic light. As the trucks came nearer, he would throw
a switch that changed it to a yellow blinker, so they could all
shoot past without slackening speed.

The men in the trucks were kneeling, standing with their
hands on each other's shoulders, or clinging unsteadily to the
sideboards; they had no room to sit down. Behind each truck
rode a trooper, and there were half a dozen others mingled
with the crowd of farmers in overalls that watched from the
front of a filling station. We stood not far away while my
mother, a simple woman of strong feelings, kept clenching
and unclenching her big hands. She was moved by the contrast
between the hatless, coatless, unshaven veterans, all looking
half-starved—most of them hadn't eaten or slept for thirty-
six hours—and the sleekly uniformed, well-nourished troopers who were herding them past their destination. "I hate
those troopers," she said loudly enough for some of the troopers to hear. The farmers looked down, and one of them gave
a ruminative nod.

"Hey, buddies," the farmers began to shout as the trucks

racketed past. "You turn right. Turn right. Johnstown"—swinging their arms northward—"Johnstown."

The hungry men smiled and waved at them uncomprehendingly. A few, however, had seen that they were being carried beyond their meeting place, and they tried to pass the word from truck to truck, above the roar of the motors. As they bowled through the level village street, there was no way to escape, but just beyond Jennerstown the road climbs steeply up Laurel Hill; the drivers shifted into second gear and promptly lost half their passengers. The others, those who received no warning or let themselves be cowed by the troopers, were carried westward. The following week I met a New York veteran who hadn't escaped from a convoy until it passed the Ohio line. A Negro from Washington, a resident of the city for thirty years—he wasn't a bonus marcher, but had made the mistake of walking through Anacostia in his shirt sleeves—was arrested, piled into a truck, and carried to Indianapolis before he managed to tell his story to a reporter.

As for the veterans who escaped at Jennerstown, they lay by the roadside utterly exhausted. Their leaders had been arrested or dispersed; their strength had been gnawed away by hunger and lack of sleep; they hoped to reunite and recuperate in a new camp, but how to reach it they did not know. For perhaps twenty minutes they dozed there helplessly. Then—I saw this happening—a new leader would stand out from the ranks. He would stop a motorist, ask for the road to Johnstown, call the men together, give them instructions—and the whole group would suddenly obey a self-imposed discipline. As they turned northward at the Jennerstown traffic light, one of them would shout, "We're going back!" and perhaps a half dozen would mumble in lower voices, "We're gonna get guns and go back to Washington."

Mile after mile we passed the ragged line as we drove toward the camp at Ideal Park. We were carrying two of the veterans, chosen from a group of three hundred by a quick informal vote. One was a man gassed in the Argonne and tear-gassed at Anacostia; he breathed with a noisy gasp. The other was a man with family troubles; he had lost his wife and six children when the camp was burned and he hoped to find them in Johnstown. He talked about his wartime service, his three medals, which he refused to wear, his wounds, and his five years in a government hospital. "If they gave me a job," he said, "I wouldn't care about the bonus."

The sick man, as we passed one group of veterans after another, some empty-handed, others stumbling under the weight of suitcases and blanket rolls, kept pointing north and calling in an almost inaudible voice, "This way, comrades, this way. Comrades, this way," till his head drooped forward and he lapsed into a wheezing sleep.

At Ideal Park, an abandoned picnic ground, the new camp was being pitched in an atmosphere of fatigue and hysteria. A tall man with a tear-streaked face marched back and forth. "I used to be a hundred-percenter," he said, "but now I'm a Red radical. I had an American flag, but the damn tin soldiers burned it. Now I don't ever want to see a flag again. Give me a gun and I'll go back to Washington."—"That's right, buddy," a woman said looking up from her two babies, who lay on a dirty quilt in the sun, under a cloud of flies. Two men sat at a picnic table reading the editorial page of *The Johnstown Tribune*. One of them shouted, "Let them come here and mow us down with machine guns. We won't move this time." The woman with the babies said, "That's right, buddy." A haggard face—eyes bloodshot, skin pasty white under a three days' beard—looked in through the car window like a halloween spook. "Hoover must die," the face said ominously. "You know what this means?" a man shouted from the other side. "This means revolution"—"You're damn right it means revolution, buddy," the woman said.

"But a thousand homeless veterans, or fifty thousand, don't make a revolution," was what I said in an article written the following week. "This threat would pass and be forgotten, like the other threat that was only half concealed in the *Tribune*'s editorial. Next day the bonus leaders would come, the slick guys in leather puttees; they would make a few speeches and everything would be smoothed over. They would talk of founding a new fascist order of Khaki Shirts, but this threat, too, can be disregarded; a fascist movement, to succeed in this country, must come from the middle classes and be respectable. No," I said, "if any revolution results from the flight of the Bonus Army, it will come from a different source, from the government itself. The Army in time of peace, at the national capital, has been used against unarmed citizens—

and this, with all it threatens for the future, is a revolution in itself."

Rereading those words more than forty years later, I seem to find in them an undertone of something close to hysteria. Its presence does not surprise me. Not only the bonus marchers but millions of other Americans, rich and poor, were beginning to be hysterical in that summer of 1932.

[1980]

A PERSONAL RECORD

After the preceding, something is needed in the way of personal narrative.

I had been less surprised than others by the Hitler-Stalin pact of August 1939. During the spring of that year there had been many indications that Russian policy was about to change once again, this time to the disadvantage of the West. I had noted already that the Russians seldom changed their policies just a little; more often they made an about-face (though without ever breaking ranks). Something drastic was to be expected, but still I was shocked by the pact with Hitler and shocked once more by the events that followed it. In the mythology of the 1930s there had been a "good" country and a "bad" country; now the two had linked arms. Hitler invaded Poland, then Stalin invaded Poland. Stalin invaded Finland, then a few months later Hitler invaded Denmark and Norway (with Stalin providing a tankerload of oil for the expedition). Those events had their repercussions in New York, where dismay, dissension, and that private sense of guilt were spreading on the literary left; it was the time of resignations. I too wanted to resign from everything, but quietly, without offering public indictments or apologies. I did, however, write many private letters in the effort to explain how I felt. From the longest, which was to Edmund Wilson, I quote the closing paragraphs.*

"As for my own attitude toward Russia, communism, and all the etceteras," I said, "it is a little hard to define as of February 4, 1940. We have a little time now for thinking, and I don't want to rush into any position that I shall have to

---

* I was answering a severe letter from Wilson, in which he had accused me of having "given hostages to the Stalinists in some terrible incomprehensible way." See his *Letters on Literature and Politics*, pp. 357–58. [M.C.]

desert in a few months. I am profoundly disturbed by what has happened in the Soviet Union—as who isn't? I think that the Communists here are tied to the apron strings of Russian foreign policy. They have ceased to play the vitalizing part in the American labor movement that they played in 1937, and they are at this moment willing to destroy the united-front organizations they founded rather than lose control of them. You think that I should now frankly discard my illusions—but granted for the sake of argument that they are illusions, what is the good of discarding them if I have to adopt another set of illusions to the effect that Krivitsky, for example, is really a sterling character and Ben Stolberg a pure-hearted defender of labor unions?"

Krivitsky was a high official of the Russian secret service who had defected to the West and had written his memoirs, a book that I reviewed unfavorably in *The New Republic*. Ben Stolberg was a witty labor journalist, formerly a radical, who later attacked labor unions and the New Deal. My letter to Wilson continued with other rhetorical questions. "And must I believe," it asked, "that Communists I saw working hard and sacrificing themselves are really, without a single exception, unprincipled careerists?

"What I believe as of February 4 is that the situation makes necessary a much more fundamental change in attitude than simply deciding that what used to be white is now black and vice versa. *Why* did the Russian revolution get into its present situation? Is it Stalinism or Leninism or Marxism that is essentially at fault? What is the essential element that was left out of all those directions for making a better society? Was it democracy that was omitted? That seems to me a rather simple-minded answer—since it involves the further question why democracy had to be omitted—and I am inclined to look for something else. The Marxist theories are based on history and economics, among the social studies. Would anthropology give us a clue to their misreading of the human animal? What are the faults of communism as a religion? That it has become a religion in fact, there isn't much doubt, considering that all those heresies and inquisitions and excommunications remind one of nothing so much as the history of the Christian church during the first three centuries.

"I am left standing pretty much alone, in the air, unsupported, a situation that is much more uncomfortable for me than it would be for you, since my normal instinct is toward cooperation. For the moment I want to get out of every God damned thing. These quarrels leave me with a sense of having touched something unclean. They remind me of a night a dozen years ago when I went on a bat with a lot of noisy and lecherous people I thoroughly despised, while realizing that I was one of them. We stayed a long time in a Harlem speak-easy, down in a cellar. When I came up the stairs at last, I saw the doorman standing in the light of morning with his hands the color of cold ashes, and that is how I felt I was inside. Sometimes I feel a little like that today. Getting involved in these feuds and vendettas of the intelligentsia is like being an unwilling participant in a Harlem orgy.

"It makes me wonder what the world would be like if it were ruled by the intellectuals. Some of them we know are admirable people, humble and conscientious, but intellectuals in the mass are not like that. A world run by them would be a very unpleasant place, considering all the naked egos that would be continually wounding and getting wounded, all the gossip, the spies at cocktail parties, the informers, the careerists, the turncoats. Remember too that the character assassinations now so much in vogue (and even you are succumbing to the fashion, with your open letters to the *NR*) are nothing less than symbolic murders. They would be real murders if the intellectuals controlled the state apparatus. Maybe that is part of the trouble in Russia.

"(Note that nothing I said about the intellectuals is to be construed as an attack on the *intelligence,* which remains our best and almost our only tool for making this country a better place to live in. I am thinking about the customs and folkways of the intellectuals as a class—which compare pretty unfavorably with the folkways of coal miners and dairy farmers.)

"Meanwhile I can't forget that all this business started with high purposes and dreams of a better society. Not many people, intellectuals or workers, go into the radical movement to make a career for themselves—some do, I suppose, but they are damned fools because there are much brighter and easier careers to be found elsewhere. No, the best of the radicals start out with a willingness to sacrifice themselves—and even when they betray their ideals I tend to forgive them in their bastardy. Once I wrote in a poem addressed to the people of tomorrow:

Think back on us, the martyrs and the cowards,
the traitors even, swept by the same flood
of passion toward the morning that is yours:
O children born from, nourished with our blood.

"Well, we're all in a pretty pickle now, and I wonder how it happened. As a sequel to your present book describing the evolution of an idea to the moment of Lenin's arrival in the Finland Station, you ought to write another describing the devolution of an idea from Marx to *The New Leader* and from Lenin to the latest editorial in *Pravda* on exterminating the Finnish bandits."

That letter to Edmund Wilson was a statement, as accurate as I could make it, of my bruised feelings in the winter of 1940. I was appalled by the march of Hitler's armies, disheartened by the short-visioned cynicism of Russian policy, and revolted by the bickering of the American left. I wanted to get out of "the movement," as it was vaguely called, and take no further part in public arguments until I had made peace with my inner convictions. I wanted to think things out, but for this there was to be little time. By the middle of June France had fallen, the country I loved next to my own, and Hitler was in command of Western Europe. I was certain by then that the United States would have to enter the war—the sooner the better if anything was to be salvaged—and this belief brought me into open conflict with the Communists, who were then shouting for peace at any price: "The Yanks aren't coming." Soon I was being excoriated in *The Daily Worker* and caricatured in *The New Masses* (as a soldier with a whisky flask in his hip pocket and a chamberpot on his head, offering a fascist salute to J. P. Morgan), and meanwhile I was still under fire from the Trotskyites and the Red-hunters. It was a new experience to be attacked simultaneously as a lackey of capitalism and a tool of Stalin. Cannonaded from the left, the right, and the center, "Storm'd at with shot and shell," I felt like a retreating soldier who had lost his weapons.

Weapons I never had except my typewriter, and I couldn't use it for self-defense without involving *The New Republic* in my personal difficulties. That was something I did not propose to do. Moreover, in the winter of 1940–41 there was a crisis at *The New Republic* that changed my situation there. After the crisis Bruce Bliven was in charge of the paper, Edmund

Wilson had severed connections with it, and George Soule (that friendly, intelligent, unaggressive man) and I had been given writing assignments without editorial responsibility. Ruminating at home in the country, I became more and more disturbed by the possible effects that war, when it surely came, would have on a still divided country. I wrote long letters on the subject to Archibald MacLeish and others close to the President. A week before Pearl Harbor MacLeish had me come to Washington and join his newly formed government agency, the Office of Facts and Figures.

That was to be an unhappy and enlightening experience. The OFF—sad acronym—was a short-lived agency soon to be absorbed into the Office of War Information. Staffed with writers and editors, all eager to play a part in the war effort, it was regarded by congressmen as a haven for impractical people with dangerous opinions. The Dies Committee went to work on it. Since I had once permitted my name to be used on the letterheads of a great many radical organizations, I was chosen from the staff as the most vulnerable target. For two months or more I was presented in almost every issue of *The Congressional Record* as a horrible example; then I resigned in order to stop the attacks and let the OFF get on with its work. That ended the worst two years of my life, and it also ended my direct participation in the war against Hitler, since I was by then too middle-aged and deaf for the armed services.

By the first of April I was back in Connecticut, writing book reviews for *The New Republic* and spading up my garden. I made a number of resolutions between spadefuls of cold brown earth. Not to join anything in the future. Not to write statements. Not to sign statements written by others. Not to let my name appear on letterheads. Not to attend meetings, much less take the chair as I had often done in the past. "Not," I grunted, stepping hard on the spade. "Not . . . Not." I remembered something that Whittaker Chambers had said to me in 1940: "The counterrevolutionary purge is still to come." After the months in Washington I was ready to believe him on that point. Vaguely I foresaw the inquisitions of the McCarthy years and was preparing to survive them in obscurity, as regards political issues, but with self-respect, not beating my breast or turning informer. I felt politically amputated, emasculated, but then I had never been happy among politicians. Now, with a sense of release and opportunity, I could get back to my proper field of interest.

That field was and had always been the contemporary history of American letters, though I also liked to trace lines of descent by making incursions into the literary past. It was not at all a crowded field at the time. In the academic world Melville, Hawthorne, and Whitman showed signs of becoming growth industries, but contemporary writing was still a disputed area in which discoveries could be made. It was the time when the New Critics were coming forward with their "close readings" of masterpieces. While admiring their acute interpretations, I was distressed by their ignorance of the writing profession. They insisted on brushing aside everything social, economic, historical, or biographical, including the hopes and plans of the author. I too believed that the work itself should be the focus of the critic's attention, but I was also deeply interested in authors: how they got started, how they kept going, how they pictured themselves, and the myths that they embodied in their work. I was interested in their social backgrounds and in the question of whom they were thinking about when they said "we." I liked to speculate on the relation between an author and his audience. Perhaps from the 1930s, I had retained the stubborn belief that literature, while having it own laws, is also part of history.

[1978]

PART TWO

American Writing 1840–1980

EDITOR'S NOTE

Throughout the course of his writing, Malcolm Cowley offered chapters of a history of American letters. Some appeared as essays in journals and magazines. Others appeared as introductions to collections by other authors. Those chapters, when culled and pulled together, begin to form a book, a book Cowley himself had always intended to gather. He wrote of such intentions in the foreword to —*And I Worked at the Writer's Trade* ("Once I set out to write, but never finished, a history of American letters . . . ," he said there) and echoed his thought in cover notes for *The Flower and the Leaf*. "My aims," he noted then late in his career, "have always been to celebrate American literature."

The heart of that celebration lay with writing about those authors he most believed in, or those authors he felt were misunderstood by the public, in large because of the misestimation of critics of the time. Cowley's concentration was always on the public, the reader. Never one to write for other critics, Cowley always wrote as though he were the first to have read the book at hand. He did so whether literally, as he looked on Thomas Wolfe's *Of Time and the River* (Cowley begins his review saying, "I have just read Thomas Wolfe's new novel, . . . almost every one of the 450,000 words, and, like a traveler returning safely from Outer Mongolia, I am eager to record what I saw during forty days in the wilderness. . . .") or figuratively, as he did looking on William Faulkner's corpus, calling Faulkner's broad-ranging stories about the mythical Yoknapatawpha County a saga:

It sometimes seems to me that every house or hovel has been described in one of Faulkner's novels; and that all the people of the imaginary county, black and white, townsmen, farmers, and housewives, have played their parts in one connected story.

Cowley's celebration of American writing, and the writers involved, also makes parts of one connected story, a story that makes sense as a book.

Here is a simulacrum of that book. Parts of it are shadows of what Cowley might have done had he put his full effort into the project. Other parts are sharply drawn, as vivid as anything American writers have written about American writing. Always, Cowley focused on the individual as artist. He tried to dig beneath preconceptions to ask, even naively, "What is this work?" "What sort of background did this work come out of?" and "Who is this man speaking for and whom is he speaking to?" The result, whether based on intimate friendship or historical exploration, is always compelling.

The selection begins with Cowley's work on Hawthorne. It introduced Cowley's edition of *The Portable Hawthorne* in 1948, and was one of a number of major pieces that Cowley wrote on the man.* There, Cowley cited Henry James's short critical biography of Hawthorne to compose his picture of Hawthorne's isolation in Salem:

> "The best things come, as a general thing, from the talents that are members of a group. Every man works best when he has companions working in the same line, and yielding the stimulus of suggestion, comparison, emulation."

"Hawthorne," Cowley adds, "never had such a stimulus, and for a long time after his work began to be printed he even lacked the feeling that it was being read; he wrote like a prisoner talking aloud in his cell."

Cowley had liked the James quote and its context enough that he repeated it from earlier use in *The Portable Faulkner*. As isolated artists Hawthorne and William Faulkner had a great deal in common for Cowley. Whitman did, too. In the selections presented here Cowley shows Whitman as an independent discoverer, not simply of an American poetics, but

---

* Among the others are: "The Hawthornes in Paradise," collected in *The Flower and the Leaf*, and "The Five Acts of the 'Scarlet Letter,' " which appears in *Twelve Original Essays on Great American Novels*, edited by Charles Shapiro. Detroit: Wayne State University Press, 1958.

also of Eastern ideas that had been rudely absorbed by the transcendentalist movement.*

When Cowley began to write in earnest of the American literary tradition, he took up the period immediately prior to his own generation's efforts. He wrote, for example, of James caught between visions of public success and literary integrity. He also wrote, in two long essays, excerpted here, of the movements of naturalists and revolt that served to shape his own literary generation.

For Cowley the transition from the time of what is now called "the American Renaissance" to the award, in 1930, of the Nobel Prize in Literature to Sinclair Lewis, the first American to receive the accolade, was one of immense fascination and one of great contrasts. It marked at once the height of what Cowley termed, after Santayana, "the genteel tradition," and the raging of American naturalism, that effort begun by Frank Norris and Jack London which came to fruition in Dreiser and in Lewis's *Main Street*. These views are recounted in "A Natural History of American Naturalism" and "The Revolt Against Gentility," excerpts of which are provided here.

As Cowley saw it, the American movement of naturalism lacked a sense of tragedy which undermined its greatness as literature. Cowley expressed the issue as the difference between the tree in the forest that grows tall but is crashed by lightning and the tree that, stunted, dies for want of sunlight. The former, Cowley held, is tragedy; the latter is mere pathos. He saw, for example, the later writings of Dos Passos as "a whole forest of stunted trees."

For Cowley the antecedents to American naturalism were French; their sources lay in Balzac, Zola, and especially Flaubert—for Cowley, the linchpin between tragedy and naturalism.

As Cowley wrote in an introduction to a new translation

---

* Cowley's efforts to establish Whitman's aesthetic on the basis of Whitman's homosexuality and intuition of Eastern thought were ground-breaking in the late forties and fifties, but Cowley later said his efforts on these fronts were first estimations. He assisted, and then deferred, to later critics. Still, Cowley's presentation of the "Calamus" poems and his comprehension of the Eastern thought parallels to "Song of Myself" are a benchmark of broadened critical perspective.

of *Madame Bovary* (the introduction is collected in Cowley's *The Flower and Leaf*), estimations of Flaubert's Emma became a force in American writing:

> In 1889 [Emma] crossed the Atlantic and appeared in New Orleans. That was in *The Awakening*, long a forgotten novel [this was 1959] by Kate Chopin that reveals an almost Flaubertian talent for structure and language. But the public was not prepared to read about an American Bovary. . . . Broken and harnessed like a livery horse she reappeared in 1920 as the heroine of *Main Street*, and this time she found a new public that could sympathize with her frustrations. In 1923 she played the part of Marian Forrester in what I think is the all-around best of Willa Cather's novels, *A Lost Lady*. In 1949 she was called Grace Tate, and her adulteries were the subject of John O'Hara's *A Rage to Live*. In 1957 she was Marjorie Penrose, once again *By Love Possessed*; and these are only the most brilliant of her American avatars. Starting as a village innocent, Emma had traveled farther and risen higher than in her wildest dreams. She had become one of those lasting archetypes that people the literary imagination.

When Cowley wrote about members of his own generation he tended to write of what they, in either work or their lives, had contributed to the "lasting archetypes that people the literary imagination." The two immediate antecedents he wrote of were Dreiser and Anderson. In pieces presented here ("Sister Carrie's Brother" and "Sherwood Anderson's Book of Moments") he shows them as deeply conflicted individuals who made art of their lives and observations. Cowley deeply respected Dreiser's unwitting efforts to establish a national literature, but he had little regard for the venality of his life. ("He looked" and acted, Cowley strongly implied, "like a fish.") Anderson was "a writer's writer," remarkable not so much for his own efforts as for his telling and abiding influence.

The "lasting archetypes" emerge in Cowley's writings on Fitzgerald, Crane, Wolfe, Hemingway, and William Faulkner. Here collected are broad views of the accomplishments and personalities of these writers. These pieces reflect what readers immediately know of Cowley and what they've come to read him for: There is Fitzgerald, the writer whose personal battle between lucre and art served to define the jazz age;

Hemingway, the writer whose personal style, larger than life, contributes to the misestimation of him as a writer; and William Faulkner, the archetypal Southern writer whose seeming random efforts display a saga of the American South. Crane, the poet of intoxicated vision, is reflected in two essays on his poem "The Bridge"; while Wolfe, the self-taught writer of passions, appears in an early review of *Of Time and the River* and an excerpt from Cowley's homage to Scribners editor Max Perkins.

These essays bracket contemporary estimations of Edmund Wilson, John Dos Passos, and Richard Wright at mid-career. Written for *The New Republic,* the pieces, as well as "Art Tomorrow," the epilogue to the 1934 edition of *Exile's Return*, demonstrate Cowley's tendency in the 1930s to combine literary and political views. For Cowley, Dos Passos's writings in *The 42nd Parallel, 1919,* and *The Big Money,* lead with the idea "that life is collective, that individuals are neither heroes nor villains, that their destiny is controlled by the drift of society as a whole." Given Cowley's estimations of earlier American writers it can be seen why he called Dos Passos a naturalist. For Cowley writing about life as dominated by a political situation *is* naturalism.

After these selections come a handful that reflect the summary tone of Cowley's later literary estimations. He reviews Willa Cather's life as an artist in a stinging review of an early biography of her, and reflects on the lives of Conrad Aiken and John Cheever, each abiding friends, in retrospections of their careers. In with these pieces is an essay on the importance of myth in American writing. For Cowley, the folktales turned to story by Hawthorne, or Irving, or Twain, reflect an ongoing establishing of a national literature. He echoes this in "Hemingway's Wound and Its Consequences for American Literature." It amounts to a castigation of later neoconservative critics, notably Kenneth S. Lynn, who in their work have missed the point, claims Cowley, of what writing is, and specifically, what Hemingway, as well as the effort to establish an American literary tradition, is about.

HAWTHORNE IN SOLITUDE

(Introduction to *The Portable Hawthorne*)

After four moderately happy, moderately social years at Bowdoin College, Hawthorne came back to Salem in 1825 and
disappeared like a stone dropped into a well. He used to say
that he doubted whether twenty people in the community so
much as knew of his existence. He had thought that while
writing his first books he might support himself by working
for his uncles, who were prosperous stage-coach proprietors;
then later he might travel into distant countries. But the books
didn't come out—except for a poor little romance called *Fan-
shawe* that was printed at his own expense—and meanwhile
the place in his uncles' counting house was deferred from
month to month, the travels from year to year. Day after day
he spent in his room; it was an owl's nest, he said, from which
he emerged only at dusk.

If he had lived in Boston he might have found others who
shared his ambitions or at least understood them. Boston in
1825 had the beginnings of a literary society, but Salem was
a little desert where it seemed impossible for any writer to
flourish. Salem was shipping and politics; it was the waterfront, the new Irish slums, and the big houses on Chestnut
Street where people asked, "Who are the Hawthornes?" Any
young man of Salem who tried to enter literature as others
entered business or the law was condemned to solitude; and
Hawthorne was double condemned, by his character as well
as by his interests. He was intensely shy and proud—shy *because* he was proud, with a high sense of personal merits, a
respect for his ancestors, and a fear of being rebuffed if he
went into society. The fear grew stronger as his clothes grew
shabbier and his manners more reserved. "I sat down by the
wayside of life," he was to say in his preface to *The Snow
Image*, "like a man under enchantment, and a shrubbery
sprung up around me, and the bushes grew to be saplings,

and the saplings became trees, until no exit appeared possible, through the tangling depths of my obscurity."

As the years passed he fell into a daily routine that seldom varied during autumn and winter. Each morning he wrote or read until it was time for the midday dinner; each afternoon he read or wrote or dreamed or merely stared at a sunbeam boring in through a hole in the blind and very slowly moving across the opposite wall. At sunset he went for a long walk, from which he returned late in the evening to eat a bowl of chocolate crumbed thick with bread and then talk about books with his two adoring sisters, Elizabeth and Louisa, both of whom were already marked for spinsterhood; these were almost the only household meetings. The younger Hawthornes were orphans; their father was a sea captain who had died of yellow fever at Surinam when Nathaniel was four years old. Madame Hawthorne, as his mother was called, had fallen into the widow's habit of eating in her room, and Elizabeth often missed dinner because of her daylong solitary rambles. There was an old aunt dressed in black who wandered through the house or, in summer, worked among the flowers like the ghost of a gardener.

In summer Hawthorne's routine was more varied; he went for an early-morning swim among the rocks and often spent the day wandering alone by the shore, so idly that he amused himself by standing on a cliff and throwing stones at his shadow. Once, apparently, he stationed himself on the long toll-bridge north of Salem and watched the procession of travelers from morning to night. He never went to church, but on Sunday mornings he liked to stand behind the curtains of his open window and watch the congregation assemble. At times he thought that the most desirable mode of existence "might be that of a spiritualized Paul Pry, hovering invisible round man and woman, witnessing their deeds, searching into their hearts, borrowing brightness from their felicity and shade from their sorrow, and retaining no emotion peculiar to himself." At other times—and oftener with the passing years—he was seized by a fierce impulse to throw himself into the midst of life. He came to feel there was no fate so horrible as that of the mere spectator, condemned to live in the world without any share in its joys or sorrows.

No man is a mere spectator, and even Hawthorne had a somewhat larger share in worldly events than he was afterwards willing to remember. Each summer he took a fairly long trip through New England, riding in his uncles' coaches, and once he traveled westward to Niagara and Detroit. During those trips he talked—or rather, listened—to everyone he met in coach or tavern and "enjoyed as much of life," so he said, "as other people do in the whole year's round." Even at home he was less of a hermit than he later portrayed himself as being; sometimes there was company in the evening and sometimes he paid visits to his three Salem friends. One of these, William B. Pike, was a carpenter and a small Democratic politician in that Whig stronghold. Hawthorne shared his political opinions and must have discussed with him the questions of party patronage that would play an important part in both their lives. He could sometimes be seen at a bookstore that stocked the latest novels and, as time went on, he began writing for *The Salem Gazette*. He must have had still other contacts with the world, but not enough of them—the point is important—to destroy his picture of himself as a man completely alone. He began to be obsessed by the notion of solitude, both as an emotional necessity for a person like himself and also as a ghostly punishment to which he was self-condemned. "By some witchcraft or other," he said in 1837 when he was trying to escape from his owl's nest and had started to correspond with his Bowdoin classmate Longfellow, ". . . I have been carried apart from the main current of life, and find it impossible to get back again. Since we last met, which, I remember, was in Sawtell's room, where you read a farewell poem to the relics of the class—ever since that time I have secluded myself from society; and yet I never meant any such thing, nor dreamed what sort of life I was going to lead. I have made a captive of myself, and put me into a dungeon, and now I cannot find the key to let myself out—and if the door were open, I should be almost afraid to come out."

Those years of self-imprisonment in Salem were the central fact in Hawthorne's career. They were his term of apprenticeship and his early travels, corresponding to the years that other American writers of his time spent traveling in Europe or making an overland expedition to Oregon or sailing round Cape Horn on a whaler. In modern terms they were his postgraduate studies, his year in Paris or Rome, his military service, everything that prepared him for his career. Left alone, he traveled into himself and worked or idled under his own supervision. It was the Salem years that deepened and individualized his talent.

Talent cannot be acquired or explained, and in Hawthorne's case we have to start with the fact that he possessed it from boyhood. Moreover, it was a sturdier sort of talent than is usually assigned to him by critics—at least by those with the habit of regarding him as a delicate plant that was incapable of bearing much fruit and would have withered in the sun. His Concord neighbors had a different picture of him. Emerson, for example, was convinced that he had greater resources than he ever displayed in his works, and Margaret Fuller said of him in the Brook Farm days, "We have had but a drop or two from that ocean." We never had more than a trickle and perhaps the inner ocean was not so vast as she believed; yet Hawthorne's hundred-odd stories were only a few of those foreshadowed in his notebooks. Besides his four published romances he once had five others fully outlined in his head. The wonder is not that he never wrote them, but rather that some of his projects were finished with perfect workmanship at a time when circumstances were hostile to Hawthorne's type of richly meditated fiction. His talent had to be robust in order to survive and had to be exceptionally fertile in order to produce, against obstacles, the few books he succeeded in writing.

We can merely wonder at the talent in itself, but we can try to explain a few of the factors in its development. At the age of nine he injured one foot in a game of bat-and-ball and the doctors judged that he might be permanently lame. The lameness disappeared after two years, but meanwhile it had kept him home from school and left him alone to read storybooks hour after hour. Almost all great writers have been great readers at some period of their lives, and Hawthorne, having acquired the habit early, continued reading till he died. The books he read, first and last, were not the right ones for a Romantic novelist trying to keep abreast of the movement to which he belonged. Apparently Hawthorne never became acquainted with the works of Balzac, Stendhal, Hugo, or with any of the German Romantics except Tieck, one or two of whose stories he read laboriously in the original. His favorite book—the only one mentioned frequently in his writings—was *Pilgrim's Progress*; but he was also fond of the eighteenth-century writers, from whom he acquired a Latinized vocabulary and a formal sentence structure not always appropriate to the misty emotions he was trying to express. In his boyhood he would read anything, no matter how difficult, so long as it told a story. He raced through the Waverley novels one after another, almost as fast as they reached Salem.

Besides reading stories as a boy, he also retold them to his sisters with wild variations of his own, and certainly he fell into the habit of telling stories to himself. All imaginative children do that, but Hawthorne did something more: he started an inner monologue that lasted for most of his waking hours and seems to have continued from youth to age. It was this shy man's substitute for spoken conversation; once he observed in his notebook that he doubted whether he had ever really talked with half a dozen persons in his life, either men or women. The inner monologue also served another purpose: it was the workshop where he forged his plots and tempered his style. He dreamed in words, while walking along the seashore or under the pines, till the words fitted themselves in his stride. The result was that his eighteenth-century English developed into a natural, a *walked,* style, with a phrase for every step and a comma after every phrase like a footprint in the sand. Sometimes the phrases hurry, sometimes they loiter, sometimes they march to drums. Although he had no ear for music and couldn't tell one melody from another, Hawthorne developed an exquisite sense of rhythm.

There is more to be said about the inner monologue which played such an important part in his life and work. In one sense it was a dialogue, since Hawthorne seems to have divided himself into two personalities while dreaming out his stories: one was the storyteller and the other the audience. The storyteller uttered his stream of silent words; the audience listened and applauded by a sort of inner glow, or criticized by means of an invisible frown that seemed to say, "But I don't understand." "Let me go over it again," the storyteller would answer, still soundlessly; and then he would repeat his tale in clearer language, with more details, and perhaps repeat the doubtful passages again and again, till he was sure the invisible listener would understand. This doubleness in Hawthorne, this division of himself into two persons conversing in solitude, explains one of the paradoxes in his literary character: that he was one of the loneliest authors who ever wrote, even in this country of lost souls, while at the same time his style was that of a social man eager to make himself clear and intensely conscious of his audience. For him the audience was always present, because it was part of his own mind.

Another paradox is also connected with his solitude and self-absorption. Hawthorne was reserved to the point of being secretive about his private life, and yet he spoke more about himself, with greater honesty, than any other American of his generation. Not only did he write prefaces to all his books, in which he explained his intentions and described his faults more accurately than any of his critics; not only did he keep journals in which he recorded his daily activities; but also most of his stories and even, in great part, his four romances are full of anguished confessions. One can set side by side two quotations from his work. In the preface to his *Mosses* he said, "So far as I am a man of really individual attributes I veil my face; nor am I, nor have I ever been, one of those supremely hospitable people who serve up their own hearts, delicately fried, with brain sauce, as a tidbit for their beloved public." But he also said at the end of *The Scarlet Letter*, when drawing a moral from Mr. Dimmesdale's tragic life, "Be true! Be true! Show freely to the world, if not your worst, yet some trait whereby the worst may be inferred." Divided between his two impulses, toward secrecy and toward complete self-revelation, he achieved a sort of compromise: he revealed himself, but usually under a veil of allegory and symbol.

2.

No other writer in this country or abroad ever filled his stories with such a shimmering wealth of mirrors. Poe detested mirrors; when he wrote an essay on interior decoration he admitted one of them—only one—to his ideally furnished apartment, but on condition that it be very small and "hung so that a reflection of the person can be obtained from it in none of the ordinary sitting places of the room." Hawthorne, on the other hand, adorned his imagined rooms and landscapes with mirrors of every size and nature—not only looking-glasses but burnished shields, copper pots, fountains, lakes, pools, anything that could reflect the human form. And

the mirrors in his stories had other functions as well: sometimes they were tombs from which could be summoned the
shapes of the past (as in "Old Esther Dudley"); sometimes
they prophesied the future (like Maule's Well, in *The House
of the Seven Gables*); often they revealed the truth behind a
delusion (as in "Feathertop," where the scarecrow impresses
people as a fine gentleman, until they look at his image in a
mirror); and always they served as "a kind of window or
doorway into the spiritual world." "I am half convinced that
the reflection is indeed the reality—the real thing which Nature imperfectly images to our grosser sense," Hawthorne
wrote in his notebook after describing a scene mirrored in
the little Assabet River. Once he wrote a story, "Monsieur
du Miroir," in which the hero was simply his own reflected
image.

"From my childhood I have loved to gaze into a spring,"
says the narrator of another Hawthorne story, "The Vision
of the Fountain." One day he sees his own eyes staring back
at him, as usual; but then he looks again—"and lo! another
face deeper in the fountain than my own image, more distinct
in all the features, yet faint as thought. The vision had the
aspect of a fair young girl with locks of paly gold." This
substitution of a girl's face for that of the youth bending over
the spring makes one think of Narcissus in love with his twin
sister—according to one version of the legend—and gazing
into a pool because he fancies that his own mirrored features
are hers. In Hawthorne's life as well as in his stories there
are curious suggestions of the Narcissus legend. He had been
a beautiful boy, petted by his relatives and admired by
strangers; I think it was one of his aunts who said of him that
he had "eyelashes a mile long and curled up at the end."
Always he loved to wander by the edge of little streams. One
characteristic he showed from the beginning was a physical
distaste for ugliness in women. "Take her away!" the little
boy said of one woman who tried to be kind to him. "She is
ugly and fat and has a loud voice." Forty years later he would
be roused to thoughts of homicide by looking at English dow-
agers. "The grim, red-faced monsters!" he said in his usually
even-tempered notebook. "Surely a man would be justified
in murdering them—in taking a sharp knife and cutting away
their mountainous flesh, until he had brought them into reasonable shape." At times he was almost like Thomas Bullfrog

in one of his own stories. "So painfully acute was my sense of female imperfection," Mr. Bullfrog said, "and such varied excellence did I require in the woman whom I could love, that there was an awful risk of my getting no wife at all, or of being driven to perpetrate matrimony with my own image in the looking-glass."

Mr. Bullfrog's predicament was like the one in which Hawthorne had involved himself during his Salem years: in a sense he *was* married to his own image, for which—if his tales are a trustworthy guide—he felt an attachment that was physical as well as moral. Moreover, this self-absorption had come to have a sinister meaning for him, as we can see by the development of his mirror symbols. Thus, Roderick Elliston, the hero of "The Bosom Serpent," is tormented by a snake that lives in his own breast. The snake has come from an innocent-looking fountain (another mirror), where it had lurked since the time of the first settlers. Elliston spends "whole miserable days before a looking-glass, with his mouth wide open, watching, in hope and horror, to catch a glimpse of the snake's head far down within his throat." "The Bosom Serpent" was written in 1843, when Hawthorne was happily married and living in the Old Manse. By that time he was able to look back almost tranquilly on his autoeroticism, to express it in allegorical terms and even to give the allegory a happy ending—for Elliston is freed from the snake by his wife's love. But some of the stories that Hawthorne wrote in his Salem days—I am thinking especially of "Young Goodman Brown" and "The Minister's Black Veil"—so testify to his sense of guilt that they might have been cries from a convocation of damned souls. Like Goodman Brown, he had wandered alone into the forest of his mind and had suddenly found himself in the midst of a witches' sabbath.

Hawthorne had descended into a sort of underworld, as many great artists do at some stage in their lives. For various reasons—sometimes a moral fault, sometimes a physical infirmity or a violation of accepted standards—they are cut off from other human beings, left face to face with themselves, and given an unbearable sense of their own separateness. In time they discover that they are not alone in their underworld, being tied by links of guilt or weakness to millions of comrades and even to the whole sinful race of man; but this discovery comes later and usually precedes their return to the world of everyday. It was partly by his own choice that Hawthorne made such a descent into the pit—or rather, into a prison that had no visible bars. The key was in the lock; at any moment he might have returned to normal society. What kept him self-confined was his feeling that year by year the world was becoming more unreal for him and, even worse, that he was becoming less real than the world; he was a shadow effectively walled in by shadows. Eventually he came to resemble one of his own characters, Gervayse Hastings of "The Christmas Banquet," who considered himself the unhappiest of men. "You will not understand it," Hastings told his rivals in misery. "None have understood it—not even those who experience the like. It is a chilliness—a want of earnestness—a feeling as if what should be my heart were a thing of vapor—a haunting perception of unreality! . . . Mine—mine is the wretchedness! This cold heart. . . ."

Ice, not fire, was the torment that Hawthorne suffered in his private hell. It is amazing how often images of coldness (and torpor from coldness) recur in his work. Among his favorite adjectives are "cold," "icy," "chill," "benumbed," "torpid," "sluggish," "feeble," "languid," "dull," "depressed." He spoke of having "ice in the blood" and sometimes thought of the heart as being congealed or turned to stone. He also expressed a longing, not for mere warmth, but for an all-consuming fire to melt the ice and calcify the stone. It is curious to note how he fell into the habit of burning his letters as soon as he returned home, how he burned all the available copies of his first novel, and how he burned a whole group of his early stories, which, from the reports of those who read them, were somber and fanciful works that the world would be glad to possess; it was as if he were trying to immolate himself. One of his few amusements in Salem was going to fires—but only after sending Elizabeth to the top of the house to report whether they were big enough to make them worth watching. "Come, deadly element of Fire, henceforth my familiar friend!" is the prayer of one of his heroes, Ethan Brand. With a final laugh, Brand leaps into the lime kiln, as into hell. When the fire in the kiln burns down, there is the outline of a skeleton on top of the lime; and within the ribs is the shape of a human heart, like calcified marble.

But these metaphors of fire and ice were not all that Hawthorne learned from his years alone in a mirrored chamber. The plots of his stories came from the same background: time after time he presented a proud man who had cut himself off from society and suffered the tortures of isolation. The stories reflected a conflict between his instincts and his reasoned convictions. He came to believe that living by and for oneself was a sin against nature, and yet by instinct he was more of a recluse than Thoreau in his hermitage. By instinct he was more of an individualist than Emerson, yet he did not preach the virtue of self-reliance; instead his moral in story after story was that every person is dependent on society. "The truly wise," he said in one of his early sketches—and often said again in different words—"after all their speculations, will be led into the common path, and, in homage to the human nature that pervades them, will gather gold, and till the earth, and set out trees, and build a house." This dweller among phantoms was, on one side of his nature, a harshly practical New Englander like the magistrates and sea captains from whom he was descended. Everywhere in his character one finds a sort of doubleness: thus, he was a proud man to the end of his life, but he also came to practice an extreme humility, never speaking of himself or his work without a self-deprecation that was altogether sincere. He was cold and sensuous, sluggish and active, radical and conservative, and a visionary with a hard sense of money values. These contradictions, these inner tensions, lend force to his stories and make their author an endless study.

Out of his inner struggles and his sense of guilt, Hawthorne evolved a sort of theology that was personal to himself, but was at the same time deeply Christian and on most points orthodox. He believed in original sin, which consisted, so he thought, in the self-centeredness of each individual. He believed in predestination, as the Calvinists did; but at the same time he had a faith in the value of confession and absolution that sometimes brought him close to Roman Catholicism. He believed in his own unworthiness and in the universal brotherhood of men, based on their weakness before God. He believed in Providence, to which he submitted himself humbly, and he believed in a future life where the guilty would be punished, if only by self-knowledge of their sins. All these articles of faith he expressed, not philosophically—for he did not think in abstractions—but in terms of symbols as powerfully simple as those in *Pilgrim's Progress*, and closer to the modern mind.

In his plots he laid more emphasis on sin and retribution than on reformation through divine grace; yet it is not true that he regarded all sinners as hopelessly damned. Some might, it is true, be led by gradual steps into what he regarded as the Unpardonable Sin; it was intellectual pride, he would say, carried to such an extreme that it permitted them to manipulate the souls of others in order to gratify their own cold curiosity and thirst for power; then they deserved the fate of Ethan Brand. Others, however, might be taught human brotherhood by their very crimes and, if they publicly confessed, might be taken back into the community. Still others might be redeemed simply by their love for one human being, and that was Hawthorne's salvation. When he fell in love with Sophia Peabody, it seemed to him that he had been drawn from the shadows and made real, together with the world around him, by the intensity of his passion. "Indeed, we are but shadows," he said in one of those letters to Sophia in which he poured out his feelings for the first time; "we are not endowed with real life, all that seems most real about us is but the thinnest substance of a dream—till the heart be touched. That touch creates us—then we begin to be."

Sophia made him an admirable wife, cheerful in their early hardships, respectful of his daily need for solitude, always regarding him as the sun around which she revolved. She was painfully high-minded and probably she acted as an unconscious censor of his work, as certainly she played the conscious censor when she edited his notebooks after his death; that is perhaps the reason why she has received too little credit from some of Hawthorne's recent biographers. The fact is that his life turned outwards after 1842 and that his public career as a writer, during which he published all four of his romances, was made possible by his happy marriage. In that respect his story is of a success in life; he cured himself of his self-centeredness, became active in the world, a highly respected citizen like his Salem ancestors, and the head of a family. He even lived out his fable of the Great Stone Face: orphaned and seeking for a father image year after year, he at last discovered in himself the benignant parent. But there was another side to his public career: the books he was now able to write still depended on his self-discoveries in the under-world where he had lived for such a painful season. Now he had roofed over the entrance to the abyss and built another life about it, and the result was that after 1860 he found it more and more difficult to work, partly because he was tired, partly because he kept setting higher and higher standards for himself, but chiefly because he had blocked off the source of his inspiration.

3.

"The best things come, as a general thing, from talents that are members of a group," said Henry James in his little book on Hawthorne; "every man works best when he has companions working in the same line, and yielding the stimulus of suggestion, comparison, emulation." Hawthorne had no such stimulus; working completely alone and even unable to talk with others, he had to look in himself for the answer to every problem. The wonder is that the answers he found were in almost all cases suited to his needs, and in so many cases fixed a pattern that later American novelists would follow.

During his years of solitude Hawthorne learned more than he afterwards realized. He learned, for example—this was perhaps the principal lesson—that the best things he wrote were spoken by a voice deep within himself and one whose speech he was unable to control. Often this inner voice seemed to him a spirit of which he was merely the instrument, and the spirit was more demon than angel. "When I get home, I will try to write a more genial book," he said while he was working on *The Marble Faun*; "but the Devil himself always seems to get into my inkstand, and I can only exorcise him by pensful at a time." Still, when the demon refused to speak, Hawthorne's writing impressed him as being without interest, and at such times he was likely to say, "I have an instinct that I had better keep quiet." He learned a wise patience that he sometimes explained as indolence. It was really watchfulness; he was lying in wait for his own thoughts like a hunter stalking game. There was, however, another side to the picture, and he also learned to be active in pursuit of his thoughts. He collected the largest possible number of impressions and concrete details, so that he could make full use of the inspiration when it came at last; and he learned to wrestle with it and force it from its obscurity. "This forenoon," he said in his notebook, "I began to write, and caught an idea by the tail, which I intend to hold fast, though it struggles to get free. As it was not ready to be put on paper, however, I took up the Dial, and finished the article on Mr. Alcott." *The Dial,* organ of the Concord intellectuals, was one of his trusted tools, but it served a different purpose from that intended by its editors; Hawthorne read it when he was tired and usually went to sleep.

Cat-naps over *The Dial* were part of his routine, for he had learned a system of working, resting, exercising, and returning to work with a fresh mind. In the summer—I am speaking of the first years after his marriage—he made entries in his notebook and hoed the garden, trying, as he said, to be "happy as a squash, and in much the same mode." "I am never good for anything in the literary way," he wrote to his friend and publisher James T. Fields, "till after the first autumnal frost, which has somewhat such an effect on my imagination that it does on the foliage here about me—multiplying and brightening its hues." All his four romances were finished during the winter, when he made a practice of writing from two to four hours each day—seldom longer than that, except when he was working excitedly on *The Scarlet Letter*, for he had found that the mood on which he depended was likely to vanish when he became too weary. Yet he wrote a great deal more than one would infer from his easy schedule or conclude from merely looking at the little shelf of books with "Hawthorne's Works" on their back. Not only were there the early stories he burned, but there was also the hackwork he did when trying to break away from Salem and later when he was earning a living for himself and Sophia. In 1836, for a salary of five hundred dollars a year (of which he received only twenty), he edited and wrote about the entire contents of *The American Magazine of Useful and Entertaining Knowledge*. After the magazine went bankrupt, through no fault of the editor's, he wrote for a fee of a hundred dollars (this time actually paid) a history of the world, which went through scores of editions and eventually had a sale of more than a million copies. In England during the four years of his consulship he wrote nothing for publication (except a preface to Delia Bacon's crazy book on Shakespeare), but he kept a journal that ran to three hundred thousand words, and it was more carefully expressed than most published novels. If Hawthorne in his later years had a better, more flexible style than any other American author of his time, the fact was easy to explain: he had learned to write, first by reading, then by talking to himelf, and most of all by writing a great deal.

But style and methods of writing weren't all he taught himself, in his Salem solitude and afterwards. Directing his words to an inner audience, he learned to make his intentions absolutely clear and to write his books so that every sentence "may be understood and felt," so he said, "by anybody who will give himself the trouble to read it." He also learned the value of concrete details. "There is nothing too trifling to write down," he said in a letter to his friend Horatio Bridge, "so it be in the least degree characteristic. You will be surprised to find on re-perusing your journal what an importance and graphic power these little particulars assume." Hawthorne had learned to observe "little particulars"; he was a good reporter as well as an artist. He was a good journalist or magazinist too, and one reads his occasional articles with wonder at all the original methods he found for presenting his rather tame material. In his stories he learned the effective use of symbols, like the birthmark (which was the token of mortal frailty and was in the shape of a hand), the bosom serpent, the poisoned flower, and the Unpardonable Sin; he learned to give everything a double meaning and sometimes a whole series of meanings, one within another, like the endless series of reflections in two mirrors standing face to face. In his novels he learned to divide the action into scenes or tableaus, each strikingly visualized and balanced one against another; it was the dramatic method that Henry James would rediscover in his final period. Hardest of all the self-taught lessons Hawthorne learned was that each work of art should be right by its own laws, which are never quite the same as those governing any other work of art, and that each should be complete within its frame. Besides being a series of balanced tableaus, the action of his novels consists of *interactions* among a few characters (usually four), so that each book becomes a system of relationships, a field of force as clearly defined and symmetrical as a magnetic field. He was the first American writer to develop this architectural conception of the novel; and even in France *Madame Bovary* wasn't published until seven years after *The Scarlet Letter* had appeared in Boston.

Flaubert and Hawthorne had not a little in common: the same search for perfection, the same mixture of realism and romanticism, the same feeling that each new novel was a totally new problem in mood and organization. Frederic Moreau of *Sentimental Education* was said to be a self-portrait of Flaubert; and one cannot fail to note his resemblance to Miles Coverdale of *The Blithedale Romance*, who was said to be a self-portrait of Hawthorne. The striking difference between the two authors was that Flaubert regarded himself as living and working at the center of the civilized world, whereas Hawthorne remained the complete provincial even when living in Europe. He was provincial in both the good and the bad sense of the word; in the good sense because he knew his province, accepted his part in it, and serenely judged everything else in the world by New England standards (so that he transferred the Greek legends to the Berkshires after purifying them, as he said, of all moral stains); and provincial in the bad sense because his localism made him misjudge the works of art he saw and the persons he met in foreign countries.

Sometimes he talked and wrote less like Flaubert than like the late George Apley—as when he refused to meet George Eliot because she was living with a man she couldn't marry and when he refused to believe that any sculptor or painter was a genius unless he could portray nobility in coat and breeches. "I do not altogether see the necessity of ever sculpturing another nakedness," he said in his notebook for 1858. "Man is no longer a naked animal; his clothes are as natural to him as his skin, and sculptors have no more right to undress than to flay him." Hawthorne had always been interested in clothes as symbols that revealed a man's nature while concealing it, and now his interest had become an obsession. Having dressed his thoughts in trousers, he no longer moved with the freedom of the naked mind.

Yet he was, for all his decorum, a man of strong passions who liked to write about women of strong passions. Two of his four novels deal with adultery and a third, *The Blithedale Romance,* is about a woman trying to escape from an undesirable husband who has reduced her sister to moral slavery. In the background of *The Marble Faun*, adultery is compounded with incest and fratricide. Miriam is married to a near relative—one would guess her half-brother—who is a mixture of saint and devil. When the devilish side comes uppermost and he tries to resume their relationship, she encourages Donatello to kill him; and one assumes that she and Donatello became lovers that same night. I cannot imagine that Howells, for example, would have dared to tell such a story even discreetly and by implication, as Hawthorne told it; in most of the New England writers passion was not only censored but expunged from the heart. It is only the surface that is censored in Hawthorne, and it is chiefly the surface that has aged; his central problem hasn't aged at all. He wrote about the isolated individual trying to regain a place in society, and after a hundred years the individual is still isolated and our serious novelists are still dealing with loneliness and alienation. He wrote about the inner world, and that is the theme our novels have continued to express, if seldom in Hawthorne's bold symbols or with his sense of artistic rightness.

[1948]

WALT WHITMAN

THE POET AND THE MASK
(excerpts)

I haven't always been an admirer of Whitman's poetry. In the past when I tried to read *Leaves of Grass* from beginning to end, I always stopped in the middle, overcome by the dislike that most of us feel for inventories and orations. Even today, after reading all the book as Whitman wished it to be preserved and after being won over by what I think is the best of it—till I am willing, if not for the usual reasons, to join the consensus that regards him as our most rewarding poet—I still feel that *Leaves of Grass* is an extraordinary mixture of greatness, false greatness, and mediocrity. Whitman designed it as his monument, but he made the book too large and pieced it out with faulty materials, including versified newspaper editorials, lists of names from the back pages of a school geography, commencement-day prophecies, chamber-of-commerce speeches, and sentimental ballads that might have been written by the Sweet Singer of Michigan, except that she would have rhymed them. The fire bells ring in his poems, the eagle screams and screams again, the brawny pioneers march into the forest (décor by Currier & Ives), and the lovely Italian singer gives a concert for the convicts at Sing Sing, her operatic voice

> *Pouring in floods of melody in tones so pensive sweet and strong the like whereof was never heard.*

In no other book of great poems does one find so much trash that the poet should have recognized as trash before he set the first line of it on paper. In no other book, great or small, does one find the same extremes of inspiration and bathos. It is as if Whitman the critic and editor of his own work had been so overawed by Whitman the poet that he preserved even the poet's maunderings as the authentic record of genius. He did not succeed—though he worked on the problem all his life—in giving an organic form to the book as a whole. It doesn't grow like a tree or take wing like a bird or correspond in its various sections to the stages of the poet's life; instead it starts with a series of twenty-four "inscriptions," or doctrinal pronouncements, almost like twenty-four theses nailed to a church door. It reaches an early climax, with the "Song of Myself." It continues through celebrations of "woman-love," as Whitman called it a little coldly, and passionate friendship for men. Then, after a series of set-pieces—some of them magnificent, like the "Song of the Open Road"—after the Civil War sketches and the big symphonies of his Washington years, it dwindles away in occasional verses and old-age echoes.

The poems are grouped by their ostensible themes rather than by their underlying moods. Thus, a section or, as Whitman would say, a "cluster" of poems called "Sea-Drift" starts with the two great meditations he wrote during his period of dejection in 1859–60 ("Out of the Cradle Endlessly Rocking" and "As I Ebb'd with the Ocean of Life"), but it ends with a collection of minor and chiefly optimistic pieces that happen also to mention the sea. Another cluster called "Autumn Rivulets" consists in large part of late and occasional poems, like Whitman's bread-and-butter letter to the Seventeenth Regimental Band ("Italian Music in Dakota"), yet it also contains the marvelous "There Was a Child Went Forth" and other examples of his earlier and freshest work. In such an arrangement the man is lost, with his organic development; and the best poems are likely to be overshadowed, like young pines in a thicket of big-leaf poplars.

Almost all the American critics of Whitman's poetry have failed in their task of separating the pines from the poplars, the lasting values from what is trivial or sententious or weedy. It is true that Tennyson, Swinburne, and William Michael Rossetti were among his early English readers, that they were good critics as well as poets, and that, in general, they admired his work for its literary qualities instead of approaching it as a political or religious text. In this country, however, the poets of his time were hostile to Whitman; almost the only exception was Emerson in the very beginning. The hostility has vanished, but without giving way to enthusiasm. As a group the poet-critics of our time pay less attention to Whitman than to any other American author of the first magnitude. More and more Whitman studies are crowding the library shelves, but they are chiefly the work of two other groups: the liberal or nationalistic historians and the teachers or graduate students of American literature.

These latter groups are interested not so much in the poetry as in the historical or mythical figure of the poet. They *need* that figure; they need an author to represent in himself the vastness and newness of the country and the unity it achieved; they need someone in literature to play the same role as Daniel Boone in the forests or Davy Crockett in the canebrakes or Lincoln saving the Union. Whitman is there, dressed and bearded for the part, and they cannot fail to accept him as the literary archetype of the pioneer. But other readers, a little more familiar with the ways of authors, find something ambiguous in Whitman's portrait of himself. When he talks too much about loving every created person, they feel that he is indiscriminate in his affections, and that it is only a step from loving to hating everyone. When he talks too much about comradeship, they suspect him—not without reason—of being self-centered and lonely. When he celebrates the life of trappers and woodsmen or cries, "O pioneers!" they read his biography and are not surprised to learn that he was chiefly a stroller through city streets. And if they come to value his work far, far above that of the other nineteenth-century American poets, it is because of the poems in which he did not boast or posture, but spoke with marvelous candor about himself and his immediate world.

To find those poems in the mass of his work is like wandering without a guidebook from room to room of a French provincial museum and searching for pictures to admire. After looking at scores of stiff portraits and dozens of landscapes rightly rejected (or hung, it doesn't matter) by the French Academy, one suddenly finds a Corot, a Courbet with its clean lines, or a fifteenth-century Virgin with the colors still as tender as the day they were painted. Whitman's best poems—and most of them are early poems—have that permanent quality of being freshly painted, of not being dulled by the varnish of the years. Reading them almost a century after their publication, one feels the same shock and wonder and delight that Emerson felt when opening his presentation copy of the first edition. They carry us into a new world that Whitman discovered as if this very morning, after it had been created overnight. "Why, who makes much of a miracle?" the poet keeps exclaiming. "As to me I know nothing else but miracles."

There is no other word but miracle to describe what happened to Whitman at the age of thirty-six. The local politician and printer, the hack writer who had trouble selling his pieces, the editor who couldn't keep a job, quite suddenly became a world poet. No long apprenticeship; no process of growth that we can trace from year to year in his published work; not even much early promise: the poet materializes like a shape from the depths. In 1848, when we almost lose sight of him, Whitman is an editorial writer on salary, repeating day after day the opinions held in common by the younger Jacksonian Democrats, praising the people and attacking the corporations (but always within reasonable limits); stroking the American eagle's feathers and pulling the lion's tail. Hardly a word he publishes gives the impression that only Whitman could have written it. In 1855 he reveals a new character that seems to be his own creation. He writes and prefaces and helps to print and distributes and, for good measure, anonymously reviews a first book of poems not only different from any others known at the time but also different from everything the poet himself had written in former years (and only faintly foreshadowed by three of his experiments in free verse that the New York *Tribune* had printed in 1850 because it liked their political sentiments). It is a short book, this first edition of *Leaves of Grass*; it contains only twelve poems, including the "Song of Myself"; but they summarize or suggest all his later achievements; and for other poets they are better than those achievements, because in his first book Whitman was a great explorer, whereas he later became a methodical exploiter and at worst an expounder by rote of his own discoveries.

At some point during the seven "lost years" Whitman had begun to utilize resources deep in himself that might have remained buried. He had mastered what Emerson calls "the secret which every intellectual man quickly learns"—but how few make use of it!—"that beyond the energy of his possessed and conscious intellect he is capable of a new energy (as of an intellect doubled on itself), by abandonment to the nature of things; that beside his privacy of power as an individual man, there is a great public power on which he can draw, by unlocking, at all risks, his human doors, and suffering the ethereal tides to roll and circulate through him; then he is caught up into the life of the Universe, his speech is thunder, his thought is law, and his words are universally intelligible as the plants and animals." Whitman himself found other words to describe what seems to have been essentially the same phenomenon. Long afterwards he told one of his disciples, Dr. Maurice Bucke: " 'Leaves of Grass' was there, though unformed, all the time, in whatever answers as the laboratory of the mind. . . . The *Democratic Review* essays and tales [those he published before 1848] came from the surface of the mind and had no connection with what lay below—a great deal of which, indeed, was below consciousness. At last the time came when the concealed growth had to come to light, and the first edition of 'Leaves of Grass' was published."

Whitman in those remarks was simplifying a phenomenon by which, it would seem, he continued to be puzzled and amazed till the end. The best efforts of his biographers will never fully explain it; and a critic can only point to certain events, or probable events, that must have contributed to his sudden discovery of his own resources. His trip to New Orleans in 1848 was certainly one of them. It lasted for only four months (and not for years, as Whitman later implied), but it was his first real glimpse of the American continent, and it gave him a stock of remembered sights and sounds and emotions over which his imagination would play for the rest of his life.

A second event was connected with his interest in the pseudoscience of phrenology. The originators of this doctrine believed that one's character is determined by the development of separate faculties (of which there were twenty-six according to Gall, thirty-five according to Spurzheim and forty-three according to the Fowler brothers in New York); that each of these faculties is localized in a definite portion of the brain; and that the strength or weakness of each faculty can be read in the contours of the skull. Whitman had the bumps on his head charted by L. N. Fowler in July 1849, a year after his return from the South. In these phrenological readings of character, each of the faculties was rated on a numerical scale running from one to seven or eight. Five was good; six was the most desirable figure; seven and eight indicated that the quality was dangerously overdeveloped. Among the ratings that Whitman received for his mental faculties (and note their curious names, which reappeared in his poems) were Amativeness 6, Adhesiveness 6, Philoprogenitiveness 6, Inhabitiveness 6, Alimentiveness 6, Cautiousness 6, Self-esteem 6 to 7, Benevolence 6 to 7, Sublimity 6 to 7, Ideality 5 to 6, Individuality 6, and Intuitiveness 6. It was, on the whole, a highly flattering report, and Whitman needed flattery in those days, for he hadn't made a success of his new daily, the Brooklyn *Freeman,* and there was a question whether he could find another good newspaper job. Apparently the phrenological reading gave him some of the courage he needed to follow an untried course. Seven years later he had Fowler's chart of his skull reproduced in the second or 1856 edition of *Leaves of Grass.*

Another event that inspired him was the reading of Emerson's essays. Later Whitman tried to hide this indebtedness, asserting several times that he had seen nothing of Emerson's until after his own first edition had been published. But aside from the Emersonian ideas in the twelve early poems (especially the "Song of Myself") there is, as evidence in the case, Whitman's prose introduction to the first edition, whch is written in a style that suggests Emerson's, with his characteristic rhythms, figures of speech, and turns of phrase. As for the ideas Whitman expressed in that style, they are largely developments of what Emerson had said in "The Poet" (first of the *Essays: Second Series*, published in 1844), combined with other notions from Emerson's "Compensation." In "The Poet" Emerson had said:

> I look in vain for the poet whom I describe. . . . We have yet had no genius in America, with tyrannous eye, which knew the value of our incomparable materials, and saw, in the barbarism and materialism of the times, another carnival of the same gods whose pictures he so much admires in Homer; then in the Middle Ages; then in Calvinism. . . . Our log-rolling, our stumps and their politics, our fisheries, our Negroes and Indians, our boasts and our repudiations, the wrath of rogues and the pusillanimity of honest men, the northern trade, the southern planting, the western clearing, Oregon and Texas, are yet unsung. Yet Amer-

ica is a poem in our eyes; its ample geography dazzles the imagination, and it will not wait long for meters.

. . . Doubt not, O poet, but persist. Say "It is in me, and shall out." Stand there, balked and dumb, stuttering and stammering, hissed and hooted, stand and strive, until at last rage draws out of thee that *dream*-power which every night shows thee is thine own; a power transcending all limit and privacy, and by virtue of which a man is the conductor of the whole river of electricity.

Whitman, it is clear today, determined to be the poet whom Emerson pictured; he determined to be the genius in America who recognized the value of our incomparable materials, the Northern trade, the Southern planting, and the Western clearing. "The United States themselves are the greatest poem," he wrote, he echoed, in his 1855 introduction, conceived as if in answer to Emerson's summons. He abandoned himself to the nature of things. At first balked and dumb, then later hissed and hooted, he stood there until he had drawn from himself the power he felt in his dreams.

There was, however, still another event that seems to have given Whitman a new conception of his mission as a poet: it was his reading of two novels by George Sand, *The Countess of Rudolstadt* and *The Journeyman Joiner*. Both books were written during their author's socialistic period, before the revolution of 1848, and both were translated from the French by one of the New England Transcendentalists. *The Countess of Rudolstadt* was the sequel to *Consuelo*, which Whitman had described as "the noblest work left by George Sand—the noblest in many respects, on its own field, in all literature." Apparently he gave *Consuelo* and its sequel to his mother when they first appeared in this country, in 1847; and after her death he kept the tattered volumes on his bedside table. It was in the epilogue to *The Countess of Rudolstadt* that Whitman discovered the figure of a wandering musician who might have been taken for a Bohemian peasant except for his fine white hands; who was not only a violinist but a bard and a prophet, expounding the new religion of Humanity; and who, falling into a trance, recited "the most magnificent poem that can be conceived," before traveling onward along the open road. *The Journeyman Joiner* was also listed by Whitman among his favorite books. It is the story—to quote from Esther Shephard, who wrote an interpretation of Whitman based on his debt to the two novels—"of a beautiful, Christlike young carpenter, a proletary philosopher, who dresses in a mechanic's costume but is scrupulously neat and clean. He works at carpentering with his father, but patiently takes time off whenever he wants to in order to read, or give advice on art, or share a friend's affection."

There is no doubt that both books helped to fix the direction of Whitman's thinking. They summarized the revolutionary current of ideas that prevailed in Europe before 1848, and his early poems would be part of that current. But the principal effect of the two novels was on Whitman's picture of himself. After reading them he slowly formed the project of becoming a wandering bard and prophet, like the musician in the epilogue to *The Countess of Rudolstadt*. He no longer planned to get ahead in the world by the means open to other young journalists: no more earning, saving, calculating, outshining. He stopped writing for the magazines and, according to his brother George, he refused some editorial positions that were offered him; instead he worked as a carpenter with his father, like the hero of *The Journeyman Joiner*.

About this time there is an apparent change or mutation in his personality. Whitman as a young editor had dressed correctly, even fastidiously; had trimmed his beard, had carried a light cane, had been rather retiring in his manners, had been on good but not at all intimate terms with his neighbors, and, whenever possible, had kept away from their children. Now suddenly he begins dressing like a Brooklyn mechanic, with his shirt open to reveal a red-flannel undershirt and part of a hairy chest, and with a big felt hat worn loosely over his tousled hair. He lets his beard grow shaggy, he makes his voice more assured, and, in his wanderings about the docks and ferries, he greets his friends with bear hugs and sometimes a kiss of comradeship. It is as if he has undertaken a double task: before creating his poems he has to create the hypothetical author of the poems. And the author bears a new name: not *Walter* Whitman, as he was always known to his family and till then had been called by his newspaper associates, but rather *Walt* Whitman,

. . . a kosmos, of Manhattan the son,
Turbulent, fleshy, sensual, eating, drinking and breeding.

    The world is his stage and Whitman has assumed a role that he will continue to play for the rest of his life. Reading his letters we can sometimes see him as in a dressing room, arranging his features to make the role convincing. In 1868, for example, he sent his London publisher a long series of directions about how his portrait should be engraved from a favorite photograph (he was always having his picture taken). "If a faithful presentation of that photograph can be given," he said, "it will satisfy me well—of course it should be reproduced with all its shaggy, dappled, rough-skinned character, and not attempted to be smoothed and prettified . . . let the costume be kept very simple and broad, and rather kept down too, little as there is of it—preserve the effect of the sweeping lines making all that fine free angle below the chin. . . . It is perhaps worth your taking special pains about, both to achieve a successful picture and likeness, something characteristic, and as certain to be a marked help to your edition of the book." There is more in the same vein, and it makes us feel that Whitman was like an actor-manager, first having his portrait painted in costume, then hanging it in the lobby to sell more tickets.

    He had more than a dash of the charlatanism that, according to Baudelaire, adds a spice to genius. But he had also his own sort of honesty, and he tried to live his part as well as acting it. The new character he assumed was more, far more, than a pose adopted to mislead the public. Partly it was a side of his nature that had always existed, but one that had been suppressed by social conventions, by life with a big family of brothers and sisters, and by the struggle to earn a living. Partly it represented a real change after 1850: the shy and self-centered young man was turning outwards, was trying to people his loneliness with living comrades. Partly it was an attempt to compensate for the absence in himself of qualities he admired in others; for Whitman had already revealed himself as anything but rough, virile, athletic, savage, or luxuriant, to quote a few of what were now his favorite adjectives. Partly his new personality was an ideal picture of himself that he tried to achieve in the flesh and came in time to approximate. You might call it a mask or, as Jung would say, a *persona* that soon had a life of its own, developing and changing with the years and almost superseding his other nature. At the end one could hardly say that a "real" Whitman existed beneath the public figure; the man had become confused with his myth.

2.

I am not trying to write a biographical sketch of Whitman, but merely to mention some of the events that marked or hastened his readjustment. The Civil War was the greatest of those events, in the poet's life as it was in American history. It put an end to which he could devote himself. At first he wrote newspaper articles and a long poem, "Beat! Beat! Drums!" which he hoped would encourage others to enlist; then he heard that his brother George was wounded and, in December 1862, he paid a visit to the Army of the Potomac. He found when he reached the front that George had recovered; but it was just after the slaughter at Fredericksburg and the hospital tents were crowded with other wounded soldiers lying on the frozen ground. Whitman did the little he could for them; "I cannot leave them," he wrote in his diary. Instead of going back to New York he decided to stay in Washington as a hospital visitor. He said of himself in the best of his Civil War poems, "The Wound-Dresser":

> *Arous'd and angry, I'd thought to beat the alarum, and*
> *   urge relentless war,*
> *But soon my fingers fail'd me, my face droop'd and I*
> *   resign'd myself*
> *To sit by the wounded and soothe them, or silently*
> *   watch the dead.*

Afterwards Whitman liked to imply that he had served among the soldiers during the whole war and that, besides nursing the wounded in Washington hospitals, he had been for long periods at the front. His actual war work was briefer—perhaps two years in all—and less official; it consisted of writing letters for the wounded, making them lemonade in summer, giving them newspapers and small sums of money collected from benevolent persons, and sitting for hours beside the dying. Perhaps his greatest service was simply to be *there,* with his look of large health, at a time when most of the wounded had no visitors and no feeling that their life or death mattered to others. Whitman tried consciously to give them the will to live; and he may have been right in thinking that he had kept scores or hundreds of men from giving up the fight. If they were beyond saving, their last moments were rendered a little less painful by the presence of the red-faced, gray-bearded stranger who looked like the spirit of Father-hood, but spoke to them as tenderly as their mothers.

Whitman had found a useful and socially recognized expres-sion for the impulses that set him apart from other men; and he found more than that in Washington during the war. At times he saw Lincoln almost daily as the President rode in a little procession from his summer lodgings to the White House, and they often exchanged bows and glances; so that Whitman felt there was a wordless sympathy between them. "I love the President personally," he wrote in his diary. He had never loved his father in that fashion and had always felt half-orphaned; but now he had found a spiritual father. That was a step in his readjustment; and so too was his friendship with the young horsecar conductor Peter Doyle, whom he met every day after work; for years they lived on terms of calm affection. It was as if, after the unhappy love affair hinted at in some of the "Calamus" poems, Whitman had entered into a sensible marriage.

"I give here a glimpse of him in Washington on a Navy Yard horse car, toward the close of the war, one summer day at sundown," John Burroughs says in *Birds and Poets*. "The car is crowded and suffocatingly hot, with many passengers on the rear platform, and among them a bearded, florid-faced man, elderly but agile, resting against the dash, by the side of the young conductor, and evidently his intimate friend. The man wears a broad-brim white hat," and is Whitman, of course, while the young conductor is probably Peter Doyle. As for Burroughs, the spectator, he describes the scene as if he were taking snapshots with a candid camera:

> Among the jam inside the door, a young Englishwoman, of the working class, with two children, has had trouble all the way with the youngest, a strong, fat, fretful, bright babe of fourteen or fifteen months, who bids fair to worry the mother completely out, besides becoming a howling nuisance to everybody. As the car tugs around Capitol Hill the young one is more demoniac than ever, and the flushed and perspiring mother is just ready to burst into tears with weariness and vexation. The car stops

at the top of the Hill to let off most of the rear platform passengers, and the white-hatted man reaches inside and gently but
firmly disengaging the babe from its stifling place in the mother's
arms, takes it in his own, and out in the air. The astonished and
excited child, partly in fear, partly in satisfaction at the change,
stops its screaming, and as the man adjusts it more securely to
his breast, plants its chubby hands against him, and pushing off
as far as it can, gives a good long look squarely in his face—
then as if satisfied snuggles down with its head on his neck, and
in less than a minute is sound and peacefully asleep without
another whimper, utterly fagged out. A square or so more and
the conductor, who has had an unusually hard and uninterrupted
day's work, gets off for the first meal and relief since morning.
And now the white-hatted man, holding the slumbering babe
also, acts as conductor the rest of the distance, keeping his eye
on the passengers inside, who have by this time thinned out
greatly. He makes a very good conductor, too, pulling the bell
to stop or go as needed, and seems to enjoy the occupation.
The babe meanwhile rests its fat cheeks close on his neck and
gray beard, one of his arms vigilantly surrounding it, while the
other signals, from time to time, with the strap; and the flushed
mother inside has a good half hour to breathe, and cool, and
recover herself.

That is Whitman seen as Proust's narrator saw the Baron
de Charlus crossing the courtyard and momentarily assuming
the features, expression, and smile of a woman. It is, however,
one of the last intimate glimpses we obtain; for another event
of his Washington years had made Whitman much more cautious about revealing himself. In January 1865 he had been
appointed to a clerkship in the Indian Bureau of the Department of the Interior, a sort of political sinecure. In June
of that year the Secretary of the Interior, a professional Meth-
odist named James Harlan, read a copy of *Leaves of Grass*
that he found in Whitman's desk, and discharged his clerk as
the author of an indecent book. Whitman's friends not only
wrote letters and published a pamphlet in his defense, but
found him another clerkship, in the Attorney General's office,
which he was to hold for the next eight years. Thus, he did
not suffer financially from the scandle and it helped in a way
to bring his work before the public; but Whitman was frightened, as many other government clerks and administrators

have been when they were discharged for their outside activities. After 1865 the prudent side of his nature was uppermost, and he no longer felt, or no longer indulged, his passion for public confession. He became more discreet in his dress, his actions, his language, and even the ideas expressed in his poems. He couldn't ever be a conventional bureaucrat, but nobody seemed to feel any more that he was out of place in a government office.

The stroke of paralysis that he suffered in January 1873 was the end of his active career. His "inexpressibly beloved" mother died four months later, and Whitman in his grief relapsed into a complication of diseases from which he never fully recovered, although he lived on for nineteen years. They were bitter years at first, when he was still hoping to regain his physical strength and his imaginative powers; but then he resigned himself to old age and indolence. He reread his favorite books, he rearranged his poems and wrote new ones on occasional themes; chiefly he occupied himself with the defense of his literary reputation. Camden, where he now lived, had a ferry like Brooklyn and he liked to ride back and forth on it. As his strength declined he assumed a new role, that of the seated Buddha, serene and large in the midst of his infirmities.

When we consider the fate of other poets like Poe, Baudelaire, Nerval, and Hölderlin who tried to explore the subconscious and dreamed immoderate dreams, Whitman in his last years seems amazingly well adjusted. He was now conscious at all times of the social limitations on human conduct. "Be radical, be radical, be not too damned radical," he said to his young friend Horace Traubel. He was shrewd about people, a little sharp in his financial dealings—like an old Long Island farmer—and strong in his family ties; he spent a great deal of time and other people's money in designing a tomb for all the Whitmans. And he enjoyed a sort of success: he lived on a mean street, but in a house he owned; he had money in the bank; his rich admirers sent him barrels of oysters in season and baskets of champagne (he was fond of both); and although his work was still not officially recognized in his own country, he was famous in Europe and had his American disciples to compare him with "a greater than Socrates." Speaking for the last time, I hope, from the clinical point of view, one can say that Whitman in his age had effected a cure of himself and had moved from his private world into a stable relation with society. He is a reassuring, even an inspiring figure: good and gray, but not so much a poet as the effigy on a poet's tomb.

[1947]

THE BURIED MASTERPIECE
(excerpts)

The first edition of *Leaves of Grass,* as placed on sale July 4, 1855, bears little outside or inside resemblance to any of the later editions, which kept growing larger as Whitman added new poems. The original work is a thin folio about the size and shape of a block of typewriting paper. The binding is of dark-green pebbled cloth, and the title is stamped in gold, with the rustic letters sending down roots and sprouting above into leaves. Inside the binding are ninety-five printed pages, numbered iv–xii and 14–95. A prose introduction is set in double columns on the roman-numeraled pages, and the remaining text consists of twelve poems, as compared with 383 in the final or "Deathbed" edition. The first poem, later called "Song of Myself," is longer than the other eleven together. There is no table of contents, and none of the poems has a title.

Another calculated feature of the first edition is that the names of the author and the publisher—actually the same person—are omitted from the title page. Instead the opposite page contains a portrait: the engraved daguerreotype of a bearded man in his middle thirties, slouching under a wide-brimmed and high-crowned black felt hat that has "a rakish kind of slant," as the engraver said later, "like the mast of a schooner." His right hand is resting nonchalantly on his hip; the left is hidden in the pocket of his coarse-woven trousers. He wears no coat or waistcoat, and his shirt is thrown wide open at the collar to reveal a burly neck and the top of what seems to be a red-flannel undershirt. It is the portrait of a devil-may-care American workingman, one who might be taken as a somewhat idealized figure in almost any crowd.

His full name, though missing on the title page, appears twice in the first edition, but in different forms. On the copyright page we read, "*Entered according to Act of Congress in the year 1855, by* WALTER WHITMAN. . . ." On page 29, almost in the middle of the long first poem, we are introduced to "Walt Whitman, an American, one of the roughs, a kosmos." When a law-abiding citizen, even one of the roughs, changes his name even slightly, it is often because he wishes to assume a new personality. A reader might infer that *Walter* Whitman is the journeyman printer who had become a hack journalist, then a newspaper editor, before being lost to sight; whereas *Walt* Whitman is the workingman of the portrait and the putative author—but actual hero—of this extraordinary book.

No other book in the history of American letters was so completely an individual or do-it-yourself project. Not only did Whitman choose his idealized or dramatized self as subject of the book; not only did he create the new style in which it was written (working hard and intelligently to perfect the style over a period of six or seven years), but he also created the new personality of the proletarian bard who was supposed to have done the writing. When a manuscript of the poems was ready in the spring of 1855, Whitman's work was only beginning. He designed the book and arranged to have it printed at a job-printing shop in Brooklyn. He set some of the type himself, not without making errors. He did his best to get the book distributed, with the lukewarm cooperation of his friends the Fowler brothers, whose specialty was not bookselling but water cures and phrenology. He was his own press agent and even volunteered as critic of the book, writing three—or a majority—of the favorable reviews it received.

In spite of his best efforts not many copies were sold, and the first edition has not been widely read, except in the special world of literary scholars. The author himself might have been forgotten, if it had not been for a single fortunate event. One copy—not in pebbly green cloth, but paperbound—had been sent to Emerson, who was the most widely respected American of letters and the man best qualified to understand what the new poet was saying. Emerson wrote a letter of heartfelt thanks. When the letter was printed in the New York *Tribune*—without the writer's permission—it amazed and horrified the little American republic of letters. Nobody agreed with Emerson except a few of the extreme Transcendentalists, notably Thoreau and Alcott. Whitman was almost universally condemned, at least for the next ten years, but he would never again be merely a call in the midst of the crowd.

Concord   21 July
Masstts 1855

Dear Sir,

    I am not blind to the worth of the wonderful gift of "Leaves of Grass." I find it the most extraordinary piece of wit & wisdom that America has yet contributed. I am very happy in reading it, as great power makes us happy. It meets the demand I am always making of what seemed the sterile & stingy Nature, as if too much handiwork or too much lymph in the temperament were making our western wits fat & mean. I give you joy of your free & brave thought. I have great joy in it. I find incomparable things said incomparably well, as they must be. I find the courage of treatment, which so delights us, & which large perception only can inspire. I greet you at the beginning of a great career, which yet must have have a long foreground somewhere, for such a start. I rubbed my eyes a little to see if this sunbeam were no illusion; but the solid sense of the book is a sober certainty. It has the best merits, namely, of fortifying & encouraging.

    I did not know until I, last night, saw the book advertised in a newspaper, that I could trust the name as real & available for a post-office. I wish to see my benefactor, & have felt much like striking my tasks, & visiting New York to pay you my respects.

R. W. Emerson

Mr. Walter Whitman.

Emerson was being impulsive for a Concord man, but he was also trying to make his phrases accurate. Later, disapproving of Whitman's conduct, he would change his mind about the "great career." He would not and could not feel that most of the poems written after 1855 contained "incomparable things said incomparably well." But his praise of the first edition was unqualified, and it tempts me to make some unqualified statements of my own, as of simple truths that should have been recognized long ago.

First statement: that the long opening poem, later miscalled "Song of Myself," is Whitman's greatest work, perhaps his one completely realized work, and one of the great poems of modern times. Second, that the other eleven poems of the first edition are not on the same level of realization, but nevertheless are examples of Whitman's freshest and boldest style. At least four of them—their titles in the Deathbed edition are "To Think of Time," "The Sleepers," "I Sing the Body Electric," and "There Was a Child Went Forth"—belong in any selection of his best poems. Third, that the text of the first edition is the purest text for "Song of Myself," since many of the later corrections were also corruptions of the style and concealments of the original meaning. Fourth, that it is likewise the best text for most of the other eleven poems, but especially for "The Sleepers"—that fantasia of the unconscious—and "I Sing the Body Electric." And a final statement: that the first edition is a unified work, unlike any later edition, that it gives us a different picture of Whitman's achievement, and that—considering its very small circulation through the years—it might be called the buried masterpiece of American writing.

All that remains is to document some of these statements, not point by point, but chiefly in relation to "Song of Myself."

2.

The poem is hardly at all concerned with American nationalism, political democracy, contemporary progress, or other social themes that are commonly associated with Whitman's work. The "incomparable things" that Emerson found in it are philosophical and religious principles. Its subject is a state of illumination induced by two (or three) separate moments of ecstasy. In more or less narrative sequence it describes those moments, their sequels in life, and the doctrines to which they give rise. The doctrines are not expounded by logical steps or supported by arguments; instead they are presented dramatically, that is, as the new convictions of a hero, and they are revealed by successive unfoldings of his states of mind.

The hero as pictured in the frontispiece—this hero named "I" or "Walt Whitman" in the text—should not be confused with the Whitman of daily life. He is, as I said, a dramatized or idealized figure, and he is put forward as a representative American workingman, but one who prefers to loaf and invite his soul. Thus, he is rough, sunburned, bearded; he cocks his hat as he pleases, indoors or out; but in the text of the first edition he has no local or family background, and he is deprived of strictly individual characteristics, with the exception of curiosity, boastfulness, and an abnormally developed sense of touch. His really distinguishing feature is that he has been granted a vision, as a result of which he has realized the potentialities latent in every American and indeed, he says, in every living person, even "the brutish koboo, called the ordure of humanity." This dramatization of the hero makes it possible for the living Whitman to exalt him—as he would not have ventured, at the time, to exalt himself—but also to poke mild fun at the hero for his gab and loitering, for his tall talk or "omnivorous words," and for sounding his barbaric yawp over the roofs of the world. The religious feeling in "Song of Myself" is counterpoised by a humor that takes the form of slangy and mischievous impudence or drawling Yankee self-ridicule.

There has been a good deal of discussion about the structure of the poem. In spite of revealing analyses made by a few Whitman scholars, notably Carl F. Strauch and James E. Miller, Jr., a feeling still seems to prevail that it has no structure properly speaking, that it is inspired but uneven, repetitive, and especially weak in its transitions from one theme to another. I suspect that much of this feeling may be due to Whitman's later changes in the text, including his arbitrary scheme, first introduced in the 1867 edition, of dividing the poem into fifty-two numbered paragraphs or chants. One is tempted to read the chants as if they were separate poems, thus overlooking the unity and flow of the work as a whole. It may also be, however, that most of the scholars have been looking for a geometrical pattern, such as can be found and diagramed in some of the later poems. If there is no such pattern in "Song of Myself," that is because the poem was written on a different principle, one much closer to the spirit of the Symbolists or even the Surrealists.

The true structure of the poem is not primarily logical but psychological, and is not a geometrical figure but a musical progression. As music "Song of Myself" is not a symphony with contrasting movements, nor is it an operatic work like "Out of the Cradle Endlessly Rocking," with an overture, arias, recitatives, and a finale. It comes closer to being a rhapsody or tone poem, one that modulates from theme to theme, often changing in key and tempo, falling into reveries and rising toward moments of climax, but always preserving its unity of feeling as it moves onward in a wavelike flow. It is a poem that bears the marks of having been conceived as a whole and written in one prolonged burst of inspiration, but its unity is also the result of conscious art, as can be seen from Whitman's corrections in the early manuscripts. He did not recognize all the bad lines, some of which survive in the printed text, but there is no line in the first edition that seems false to a single prevailing tone. There are passages weaker than others, but none without a place in the general scheme. The repetitions are always musical variations and amplifications. Some of the transitions seem abrupt when the poem is read as if it were an essay, but Whitman was not working in terms of "therefore" and "however." He preferred to let one image suggest another image, which in turn suggests a new statement of mood or doctrine. His themes modulate into one another by pure association, as in a waking dream, with the result that all his transitions seem instinctively right.

In spite of these oneiric elements, the form of the poem is something more than a forward movement in rising and subsiding waves of emotion. There is also a firm narrative structure, one that becomes easier to grasp when we start by dividing the poem into a number of parts or sequences. I think there are nine of these, but the exact number is not important; another critic might say there were seven (as Professor Miller does), or eight or ten. Some of the transitions are gradual, and in such cases it is hard to determine the exact line that ends one sequence and starts another. The essential point is that the parts, however defined, follow one another in irreversible order, like the beginning, middle, and end of any good narrative. My own outline, not necessarily final, would run as follows:

First sequence (chants 1–4): the poet or hero introduced to his audience. Learning and loafing at his ease, "observing a spear of summer grass," he presents himself as a man who lives outdoors and worships his own naked body, not the least part of which is vile. He is also in love with his deeper self or soul, but explains that it is not to be confused with his mere personality. His joyful contentment can be shared by you, the listener, "For every atom belonging to me as good belongs to you."

Second sequence (chant 5): the ecstasy. This consists in the rapt union of the poet and his soul, and it is described— figuratively, on the present occasion—in terms of sexual union. The poet now has a sense of loving brotherhood with God and with all mankind. His eyes being truly open for the first time, he sees that even the humblest objects contain the infinite universe—

And limitless are leaves stiff or drooping in the fields,
And brown ants in little wells beneath them,
And mossy scabs of the wormfence, and heaped stones,
   and elder and mullen and pokeweed.

Third sequence (chants 6–19): the grass. Chant 6 starts with one of Whitman's brilliant transitions. A child comes with both hands full of those same leaves from the fields. "What is the grass?" the child asks—and suddenly we are presented with the central image of the poem, that is, the grass as symbolizing the miracle of common things and the divinity (which implies both the equality and the immortality) of ordinary persons. During the remainder of the sequence, the poet observes men and women—and animals too—at their daily occupations. He is part of this life, he says, and even his thoughts are those of all men in all ages and lands. There are two things to be noted about the sequence, which contains some of Whitman's freshest lyrics. First, the people with a few exceptions (such as the trapper and his bride) are those whom Whitman has known all his life, while the scenes described at length are Manhattan streets and Long Island beaches or countryside. Second, the poet merely roams, watches, and listens, like a sort of Tiresias. The keynote of the sequence—as Professor Strauch was the first to explain—is the two words "I observe."

Fourth sequence (chants 20–25): the poet in person. "Hankering, gross, mystical, nude," he venerates himself as august and immortal, but so, he says, is everyone else. He is the poet of the body and of the soul, of night, earth, and sea, and of vice and feebleness as well as virtue, so that "many long dumb voices" speak through his lips, including those of slaves, prostitutes, even beetles rolling balls of dung. All life to him is such a miracle of beauty that the sunrise would kill him if he could not find expression for it—"If I could not now and always send sunrise out of me." The sequence ends with a dialogue between the poet and his power of speech, during which the poet insists that his deeper self—"the best I am"— is beyond expression.

Fifth sequence (chants 26–29): ecstasy through the senses. Beginning with chant 26, the poem sets out in a new direction. The poet decides to be completely passive: "I think I will do nothing for a long time but listen." What he hears at first are quiet familiar sounds like the gossip of flames on the hearth and the bustle of growing wheat; but the sounds rise quickly to a higher pitch, becoming the matchless voice of a trained soprano, and he is plunged into an ecstasy of hearing, or rather of Being. Then he starts over again, still passively, with the sense of touch, and finds himself rising to the ecstasy of sexual union. This time the union is actual, not figurative, as can be seen from the much longer version of chant 29 preserved in an early notebook.

Sixth sequence (chants 30–38): the power of identification. After his first ecstasy, as presented in chant 5, the poet had acquired a sort of microscopic vision that enabled him to find infinite wonders in the smallest and most familiar things. The second ecstasy (or pair of ecstasies) has an entirely different effect, conferring as it does a sort of vision that is both tel-escopic and spiritual. The poet sees far into space and time; "afoot with my vision" he ranges over the continent and goes speeding through the heavens among tailed meteors. His se-cret is the power of identification. Since everything emanates from the universal soul, and since his own soul is of the same essence, he can identify himself with every object and with every person living or dead, heroic or criminal. Thus, he is massacred with the Texans at Goliad, he fights on the *Bon-homme Richard,* he dies on the cross, and he rises again as "one of an average unending procession." Whereas the key-note of the third sequence was "I observe," here it becomes "I am"—"I am a free companion"—"My voice is the wife's voice, the screech by the rail of the stairs"—"I am the man. . . . I suffered. . . . I was there."

Seventh sequence (chants 39–41): the superman. When In-dian sages emerge from the state of samadhi or absorption, they often have the feeling of being omnipotent. It is so with the poet, who now feels gifted with superhuman powers. He is the universally beloved Answerer (chant 39), then the Healer, raising men from their deathbeds (40), and then the Prophet (41) of a new religion that outbids "the old cautious hucksters" by announcing that men are divine and will eventually be gods.

Eighth sequence (chants 42–50): the sermon. "A call in the midst of the crowd" is the poet's voice, "orotund sweeping and final." He is about to offer a statement of the doctrines implied by the narrative (but note that his statement comes at the right point psychologically and plays its part in the narrative sequence). As strangers listen, he proclaims that society is full of injustice, but that the reality beneath it is deathless persons (chant 42); that he accepts and practices all religions, but looks beyond them to "what is untried and afterward" (43); that he and his listeners are the fruit of ages, and the seed of untold ages to be (44); that our final goal is appointed: "God will be there and wait till we come" (45); that he tramps a perpetual journey and longs for companions, to whom he will reveal a new world by washing the gum from their eyes—but each must then continue the journey alone (46); that he is the teacher of men who work in the open air (47); that he is not curious about God, but sees God everywhere, at every moment (48); that we shall all be reborn in different forms ("No doubt I have died myself ten thousand times before"); and that the evil in the world is like moonlight, a mere reflection of the sun (49). The end of the sermon (chant 50) is the hardest passage to interpret in the whole poem. I think, though I cannot be certain, that the poet is harking back to the period after one of his ten thousand deaths, when he slept and slept long before his next awakening. He seems to remember vague shapes, and he beseeches these Outlines, as he calls them, to let him reveal the "word unsaid." Then turning back to his audience, "It is not chaos or death," he says. "It is form and union and plan. . . . it is eternal life. . . . it is happiness."

Ninth sequence (chants 51–52): the poet's farewell. Having finished his sermon, the poet gets ready to depart, that is, to die and wait for another incarnation or "fold of the future," while still inviting others to follow. At the beginning of the poem he had been leaning and loafing at ease in the summer grass. Now, having rounded the circle, he bequeaths himself to the dirt "to grow from the grass I love." I do not see how any careful reader, unless blinded with preconceptions, could overlook the unity of the poem in tone and image and direction.

3.

It is in the eighth sequence, which is a sermon, that Whitman gives us most of the doctrines suggested by his mystical experience, but they are also implied in the rest of the poem and indeed in the whole text of the first edition. Almost always he expresses them in the figurative and paradoxical language that prophets have used from the beginning. Now I should like to state them explicitly, even at the cost of some repetition.

Whitman believed when he was writing "Song of Myself" —and at later periods too, but with many changes in emphasis—that there is a distinction between one's mere personality and the deeper Self (or between ego and soul). He believed that the Self (or atman, to use a Sanskrit word) is of the same essence as the universal spirit (though he did not quite say it *is* the universal spirit, as Indian philosophers do in the phrase "Atman is Brahman"). He believed that true knowledge is to be acquired not through the senses or the intellect, but through union with the Self. At such moments of union (or "merge," as Whitman called it) the gum is washed from one's eyes (that is his own phrase), and one can read an infinite lesson in common things, discovering that a mouse, for example, "is miracle enough to stagger sextillions of infidels." This true knowledge is available to every man and woman, since each conceals a divine Self. Moreover, the divinity of all implies the perfect equality of all, the immortality of all, and the universal duty of loving one another.

Immortality for Whitman took the form of metempsychosis, and he believed that every individual will be reborn, usually but not always in a higher form. He had also worked out for himself something approaching the Indian notion of karma, which is the doctrine that actions performed during one incarnation determine the nature and fate of the individual during his next incarnation; the doctrine is emphatically if

somewhat unclearly stated in a passage of his prose introduction that was later rewritten as a poem, "Song of Pru-
dence." By means of metempsychosis and karma, we are all
involved in a process of spiritual evolution that might be compared to natural evolution. Even the latter process, however,
was not regarded by Whitman as strictly natural or material.
He believed that animals have a rudimentary sort of soul
("They bring me tokens of myself"), and he hinted or surmised, without directly saying, that rocks, trees, and plants
possess an identity, or "eidólon," that persists as they rise to
higher states of being. The double process of evolution, natural and spiritual, can be traced for ages into the past, and
he believed that it will continue for ages beyond ages. Still,
it is not an eternal process, since it has an ultimate goal, which
appears to be the reabsorption of all things into the Divine
Ground.

Most of Whitman's doctrines, though by no means all of
them, belong to the mainstream of Indian philosophy. In some
respects he went against the stream. Unlike most of the Indian
sages, for example, he was not a thoroughgoing idealist. He
did not believe that the whole world of the senses, of desires,
of birth and death, was only maya, illusion, nor did he hold
that it was a sort of purgatory; instead he praised the world
as real and joyful. He did not despise the body, but proclaimed
that it was as miraculous as the soul. He was too good a citizen
of the nineteenth century to surrender his faith in material
progress as the necessary counterpart of spiritual progress.
Although he yearned for ecstatic union with the soul or
Oversoul, he did not try to achieve it by subjugating the
senses, as advised by yogis and Buddhists alike; on the contrary, he thought the "merge" could also be achieved (as in
chants 26–29) by a total surrender to the senses. These are
important differences, but it must be remembered that Indian
philosophy or theology is not such a unified structure as it
appears to us from a distance. Whitman might have found
Indian sages or gurus and even whole sects that agreed with
one or another of his heterodoxies (perhaps excepting his
belief in material progress). One is tempted to say that instead
of being a Christian heretic, he was an Indian rebel and
sectarian.

Sometimes he seems to be a Mahayana Buddhist, promising
nirvana for all after countless reincarnations, and also sharing

the belief of some Mahayana sects that the sexual act can serve as one of the sacraments. At other times he might be an older brother of Sri Ramakrishna (1836–1886), the nineteenth-century apostle of Tantric Brahmanism and of joyous affirmation. Although this priest of Kali, the Mother Goddess, refused to learn English, one finds him delivering some of Whitman's messages in—what is more surprising—the same tone of voice. Read, for example, this fairly typical passage from *The Gospel of Sri Ramakrishna,* while remembering that "Consciousness" is to be taken here as a synonym for Divinity:

> The Divine Mother revealed to me in Kali temple that it was She who had become everything. She showed me that everything was full of Consciousness. The Image was Consciousness, the altar was Consciousness, the water-vessels were Consciousness, the door-sill was Consciousness, the marble floor was Consciousness—all was Consciousness. . . . I saw a wicked man in front of the Kali temple; but in him I saw the Power of the Divine Mother vibrating. That was why I fed a cat with the food that was to be offered to the Divine Mother.

Whitman expresses the same idea at the end of chant 48, and in the same half-playful fashion:

> Why should I wish to see God better than this day?
> I see something of God each hour of the twenty-four,
>   and each moment then,
> In the faces of men and women I see God, and in my
>   own face in the glass;
> I find letters from God dropped in the street, and every
>   one is signed by God's name,
> And I leave them where they are, for I know that others
>   will punctually come forever and ever.

Such parallels—and there are dozens that might be quoted—are more than accidental. They reveal a kinship in thinking and experience that can be of practical value to students of Whitman. Since the Indian mystical philosophies are elaborate structures, based on conceptions that have been shaped and defined by centuries of discussion, they help to explain Whitman's ideas at points in the first edition where he seems at first glance to be vague or self-contradictory. There is, for example, his unusual combination of realism—

sometimes brutal realism—and serene optimism. Today he is usually praised for the first, blamed for the second (optimism being out of fashion), and blamed still more for the inconsistency he showed in denying the existence of evil. The usual jibe is that Whitman thought the universe was perfect and was getting better every day.

It is obvious, however, that he never meant to deny the existence of evil in himself or his era or his nation. He knew that it existed in his own family, where one of his brothers was a congenital idiot, another was a drunkard married to a streetwalker, and still another, who had caught "the bad disorder," later died of general paresis in an insane asylum. Whitman's doctrine implied that each of them would have an opportunity to avoid those misfortunes or punishments in another incarnation, where each would be rewarded for his good actions. The universe was an eternal becoming for Whitman, a process not a structure, and it had to be judged from the standpoint of eternity. After his mystical experience, which seemed to offer a vision of eternity, he had become convinced that evil existed only as part of a universally perfect design. That explains his combination of realism and optimism, which seems unusual only in our Western world. In India, Heinrich Zimmer says, "Philosophic theory, religious belief, and intuitive experience support each other . . . in the basic insight that, fundamentally, all is well. A supreme optimism prevails everywhere, in spite of the unromantic recognition that the universe of man's affairs is in the most imperfect state imaginable, one amounting practically to chaos."

Another point explained by Indian conceptions is the sort of democracy Whitman was preaching in "Song of Myself." There is no doubt that he was always a democrat politically— which is to say a Jacksonian Democrat, a Barnburner writing editorials against the Hunkers, a Free Soiler in sympathy, and then a liberal but not a radical Republican. He remained faithful to what he called "the good old cause" of liberty, equality, and fraternity, and he wrote two moving elegies for the European rebels of 1848. In "Song of Myself," however, he is not advocating rebellion or even reform. "To a drudge of the cottonfields," he says, "or emptier of privies I lean. . . . on his right cheek I put the family kiss"; but he offers nothing more than a kiss and an implied promise. What he preaches throughout the poem is not political but religious democracy, such as was practiced by the early Christians. Today it is practiced, at least in theory, by the Tantric sect of Buddhism.

The promise that Whitman offers to the drudge of the cottonfields, the emptier of privies, and the prostitute draggling her shawl is that they too can set out with him on his perpetual journey—perhaps not in their present incarnations, but at least in some future life. And that leads to another footnote offered by the Indian philosophies: they explain what the poet meant by the Open Road. It starts as an actual road that winds through fields and cities, but Whitman is doing more than inviting us to shoulder our duds and go hiking along it.The real journey is toward spiritual vision, toward reunion with the Divine Ground; and thus the Open Road becomes Whitman's equivalent for all the other roads and paths and ways that appear in mystical teachings. It reminds us of the Noble Eightfold Path of the Buddhists, and the Taoist Way; it suggests both the *bhakti-marga* or "path of devotion" and the *karma-marga* or "path of sacrifice"; while it comes closer to being the "big ferry" of the Mahayana sect, in which there is room for every soul to cross to the farther shore. Whitman's conception, however, was even broader. He said one should know "the universe itself as a road, as many roads, as roads for traveling souls."

I am not pleading for the acceptance of Whitman's ideas or for any other form of mysticism, Eastern or Western. I am only suggesting that his ideas as expressed in "Song of Myself" were bolder and more coherent than is generally supposed, and philosophically a great deal more respectable.

[1959]

THE TWO HENRY JAMESES

There is a rough justice in the fate of literary reputations, if we follow them through a period of years. Most—not all—of the true ones survive, even when they have been buried and must be exhumed from a mountain of trash. The false and fabricated reputations are eventually winnowed out and blown away; often without a single hot blast from the critics, they crumble like very old newspapers. Do you remember the days when *Jurgen* was regarded as a profound and devilishly clever work, the lasting ornament of American letters? Or the days when Dreiser *and* Joseph Hergesheimer were described in the same breath as the two living masters of the novel? Or the somewhat later days when Hemingway *and* Louis Bromfield were coupled by the critics as the two giants of a new generation? A short time ago in the *New Yorker,* Edmund Wilson wrote an essay ridiculing Bromfield, and most people wondered why he devoted so much space to proving what even the little children and professors knew. Where are the debunking biographers now, who won such easy triumphs over the bearded New England worthies? Where are the proletarian geniuses flung upward from the working class like Venus from the waves, all garlanded with college degrees and Brooks Brothers ties? Some of them were honest talents and have been unjustly forgotten, but in that case they need not worry too much; the world that neglected them may end by overwhelming them with praise.

Emerson's law of compensation seems to operate in such matters. If an author is overvalued during his lifetime, he will be blamed and overblamed after his death. If a great author goes unread, like Blake or Melville, he will end by being raised above his contemporaries. That was the fate of Donne, who was seldom mentioned for two centuries after his death and whose work was at one time unobtainable except in the big libraries; by 1930 the wheel had turned and he was not only valued at his own great worth but exalted as a greater poet than Milton. Some reputations climb imperceptibly, reach what appears to be their proper level, and hold it through decades or even centuries. Others are thrown out of balance at the very beginning and never regain it; they come down through the years like a skier down a slope that frightens him, making wild sweeps from shadow into sun.

Henry James is the great example in our time of an author whose reputation fluctuated during his life, declined before his death, and has now reached a higher point than ever before. Out of all the books he wrote—and he was almost as prolific as Horatio Alger—there was only one short novel, *Daisy Miller,* that became what we should now call a best seller. Only two of his novels—*The Portrait of a Lady* in 1881 and *The Ambassadors* in 1903—were greeted, in publishers' cant, "with a chorus of critical approval." These two dates twenty years apart marked the high points of his career. James thought it had reached its lowest point in 1895, when he was hissed and hooted from the stage after the first performance of *Guy Domville.* He wrote to his old friend Howells: "I *have* felt, for a long time past, that I have fallen upon evil days— every sign or symbol of one's being in the least *wanted,* any- where or by anyone having so utterly failed." But a worse blow was to strike him twelve years later, with the publication of the New York Edition of his novels and tales, for which he had revised the style of his earlier work and had written a preface to each novel or volume of stories. The whole was intended to serve as "a sort of comprehensive manual or *vade- mecum*" for students of fiction, besides preserving his work in lasting form, and it didn't quite go unnoticed. The *Nation* and the *New York Times Book Review* faithfully and briefly mentioned each successive volume; but there was, says Rich- ard Nicholas Foley, who has written a thesis on the treatment of James's work by American periodicals, little or no serious discussion of the edition as a whole. It might as well have been buried in a vault in Kentucky, like the American stock of gold.

Today the New York Edition is out of print and practically unobtainable; when a book dealer manages to find a set, he can put almost any price on it that he has the courage to ask.*

---

* Much later the New York edition was reissued by Scribner's, the original publisher. [M.C.]

All of James's books in their original editions are collectors' items, even the critical works and the travel sketches. His work is more widely discussed and has more admirers than during his lifetime. It has become a commonplace remark to call him the greatest or even the only American novelist.

Of course there are other reasons for this posthumous glory besides the quality of his work and besides the law of literary compensation. The return of Henry James is also the almost mathematical result of two tendencies among American readers. The first is a literary nationalism that has been growing from year to year; one sign of it is the new courses in American literature that were being offered, before the war, in all our universities. After a century and a half of living in the future, we suddenly faced about and began the search for a "usable past"; and very soon we discovered that James, in spite of being an expatriate, was the most usable of all the dead American novelists. He was the only novelist (except for Cooper and Simms and Howells, all far beneath him in talent) who planned and executed his life work on the scale of the masters; he was the only one to achieve a continuous, unified, organic career.

The second tendency that contributes to James's reputation today is the general reaction against political or social standards in literature. It began simply as a reaction against proletarian novels and Marxian criticism, but by now it has developed much further, into a reaction against historical or genetic criticism of any type. Nothing satisfies its leaders except absolute, permanent, unchanging moral and esthetic values. Works of art are being judged in and for themselves, as if independent of any social background; and the works most likely to be praised are those most widely removed from any social movement and least contaminated with ideas. There seems to be no taint of them in James's novels. He never mentions social forces, although they figure in his work indirectly and almost secretly. He is the great example in his country of the "pure" novelist.

His working notebooks, as quoted by F. O. Matthiessen, abound in expressions of priestly or soldierly devotion to his craft. "A *mighty will*," he wrote for his own eyes while working on *The Bostonians*, "there is nothing but that! The integrity of one's will, purpose, faith!"—"Oh art, art," he wrote a few years later, "what difficulties are like thine; and, at the same time, what consolation and encouragements, also, are like thine? Without this, for me, the world would be, indeed a howling desert."—"But courage, courage, and forward, forward," he wrote before starting *The Tragic Muse*. "If one must generalize, that is the only generalization. There is an immensity to be done, and, without being presumptuous, I shall at the worst do part of it. But all one's manhood must be at one's side." His two younger brothers had served in the Civil War, and Henry apparently had felt a sense of inadequacy of even guilt at being physically unable to join them. It was in the act of writing that he discovered a moral equivalent for the hardships and dangers of the military life. And a new generation of brave but quite unwarlike soldiers has come to admire him as a hero of art.

2.

Nevertheless a debate continues among James's readers and critics, with those who admire or at least concede the virtues of his early stories, but hold that his later work shows a rootlessness, a snobbishness, an unreality that might well be explained by his divorce from American life, standing against the others who believe that the three long novels he wrote when he was turning sixty are the high and frosty summits of American fiction. The debate goes back to the first publication of *The Wings of the Dove* (1902), *The Ambassadors* (1903), and *The Golden Bowl* (1904). William Dean Howells tried hard to end it in 1903, when he wrote his dialogue on "Mr. Henry James's Later work"; he spoke of course for the devoted Jacobites. In 1905 William Crary Brownell answered Howells in a longer essay that expressed his adverse moral judgments and his distinguished lack of comprehension. Van Wyck Brooks succeeded Brownell as leader of the anti-Jacobite faction, the Whig gentry. The simple thesis he advanced in *The Pilgrimage of Henry James* (1925) and still more forcefully in *New England: Indian Summer* was that the later novels could not be so good as the early ones because James had lived too long in England. That was for some time the accepted opinion, in the years when James wasn't being read, although it was combated by Matthew Josephson in his *Portrait of the Artist as American* (1930) and was roundly denied by Stephen Spender, who seemed to be saying in *The De-structive Element* (1936) that James was the central writer of our time.

Henry James, the Major Phase, by F. O. Matthiessen, might be approached as merely another episode in these Jacobite wars, but it has one great advantage over the earlier forays and incursions. It is better armed; it is equipped with new evidence. Recently James's working notebooks from 1878 to 1914, in which he recorded his intimate thoughts and the slow growth of his novels, were presented by his nephew and name-sake to the Houghton Library at Harvard. Mr. Matthiessen, with Kenneth B. Murdock, is now preparing them for pub-lication.* He quotes from them extensively in the present volume; and they show that James regarded his later work as more ambitious than anything attempted in the past.

They also show that the year 1895 was the turning point in his career. Feeling that his novels would never be popular, he had been writing a succession of plays—to make money, as he flatly said, but also in the effort to overcome a sense of solitude. He seems to have resembled one of his characters—Mortimer Marshal in "The Papers"—to the extent of nursing a secret: "that to be inspired, to work with effect, he had to feel he was appreciated, to have it all somehow come back to him." Not much came back of the effort James put into his plays. One of them, a dramatized version of his early novel *The American,* had been indifferently received in London after a mild success in the English provinces. Four others had been printed without being produced. A sixth, *Guy Domville,* closed in London after thirty-one performances that earned eleven hundred dollars for the author, as he wrote to his brother William; there had been many worse failures on the stage. But the first night of the play—January 5, 1895—had been worse than a failure; it was an international scandal. Some of the well-dressed people in the stalls approved of the play and cried, "Author, author!" The crowd in the pit hated

---

* This volume, *The Notebooks of Henry James,* was published in New York, 1947, by the Oxford University Press, which had published *Henry James, the Major Phase* in 1944. Later the most extreme of the anti-Jacobite statements was to be Maxwell Geismar's *Henry James and the Jacobites* (Boston, 1963), which most critics condemned as intemperate. From the other side, the most persuasive defense of James is of course Leon Edel's many-volumed life of the Master. [M.C.]

it and bore a grudge against the producer on this and older counts. When the author appeared before the curtain, they greeted him with hoots and jeers and roars—James wrote to his brother—"like those of a cage of beasts at some infernal 'zoo.'" Newspapers in London and New York carried the story of how the uproar continued for fifteen minutes while the author stood there cowering under the storm.

Deeply humiliated, so that he could never bear to be reminded of that night, James abandoned for all practical purposes his attempt to win a larger public. It is true that he would later publish several stories described by him as "shameless potboilers"—including one great story, "The Turn of the Screw," but also including others that were genteelly romantic in the tone of the popular magazines and almost as mechanical in plot as if they had been signed by O. Henry. For the most part, however, his next years would be devoted to the sort of work he regarded simply as "the best." He wrote in his notebook just after the great fiasco:

> I take up my *own* old pen again—the pen of all my old unforgettable efforts and sacred struggles. To myself—today—I need say no more. Large and full and high the future still opens. It is now indeed that I may do the work of my life. And I will.

A month passed and he felt more confident:

> I have my head, thank God, full of visions. One has never too many—one has never enough. Ah, just to let oneself go—at last; to surrender oneself to what through all the long years one has (quite heroically, I think) hoped for and waited for—the mere potential and relative increase of quantity in the material act—act of appreciation and production. One has prayed and hoped and waited, in a word, to be able to work *more*. And now, toward the end, it seems, within its limits, to have come. That is all I ask. Nothing else in the world. I bow down to Fate, equally in submission and in gratitude.

That notebook entry of February 14, 1895, foreshadows James's later period, though there was still to be some fumbling before the major works of the period were under way. Of one thing James was already certain: those works would utilize "the divine principle of the Scenario" that he had learned from his costly experience in the theatre. They would follow the scenic method, in other words, and would be as tightly constructed as plays. As for the "potential and relative increase of quantity in the material act," it was not to be long delayed. During the first five years that James spent in the little town of Rye, from 1898 to 1903, he produced a volume of work that was unprecedented even in his own generally fruitful career. He wrote two short novels, *The Awkward Age* and *The Sacred Fount;* two collections of stories, *The Soft Side* and *The Better Sort;* and a two-volume life of the sculptor William Wetmore Story, besides his three most richly elaborated novels. Nobody should doubt after rereading them that they are his best novels too. Mr. Matthiessen has every right to describe that period in James's life as "the major phase."

In his criticial essay, each of the three great novels receives a chapter of outline and analysis, in the light of James's working notes, and each is assigned its rank. Mr. Matthiessen has many reservations about *The Golden Bowl* and a few about *The Ambassadors;* he believes that *The Wings of the Dove* is James's masterpiece, "that single work where his characteristic emotional vibration seems deepest." *The Ivory Tower,* which also receives a chapter, might possibly have been as good, he says, if James had lived to finish it. There is an introductory chapter, extremely interesting, on "the art of reflection" that James applied to all his work; and there is a long appendix analyzing the changes James made in *The Portrait of a Lady* twenty-five years after its first appearance, when he was preparing the New York Edition of his collected works. Simple in structure and temperate in expression, *Henry James: The Major Phase* is almost a model of the critical monograph.

There is, however, one fault or omission to be noted that does not greatly affect the quality of the book, but that does have a bearing on the debate about Henry James. Mr. Matthiessen has not so much answered the arguments of the anti-Jacobites as he has introduced totally different arguments. Almost everything he says about the later James is true, but it is not quite the whole story. A great deal that Van Wyck Brooks says about him is also essentially true, even though overstated at times and written in the style of a highly cultured prosecuting attorney. It is true, for example, that James's later novels are rather thin in subject matter, considering their length and enormous elaboration. It is true that they reveal an ignorance of America and, even more strikingly, an ignorance of European life outside the international set. And it is true that they are novels about adultery (or something close to it, in *The Wings of the Dove*) that show a curious want of passion, almost as if James had written *War and Peace* without the battle scenes.

James himself, in the little book on Hawthorne that he wrote in 1879, gave us a sort of license to prefer his early work. He praised *The Scarlet Letter* in terms that might be applied to the first version of *The Portrait of a Lady*. Coming first among Hawthorne's novels, he said, it was simpler and more complete than the others. "It achieves," he continued, "more perfectly what it attempts, and has about it that charm, very hard to express, which we find in an artist's work the first time he has touched his highest mark—a sort of straightness and naturalness of execution, an unconsciousness of his public, and freshness of interest in his theme." James also admired *The Scarlet Letter* for its style. "It is admirably written," he said. "Hawthorne afterwards polished his style to a still higher degree, but in his later productions—it is almost always the case in a writer's later productions—there is a touch of mannerism. In *The Scarlet Letter* there is a high degree of polish, and at the same time a charming freshness; his phrase is less conscious of itself."

James's phrase, in his later novels, is extremely conscious of itself, and that is by no means its only fault. With its endless sentences dotted thickly with commas, it gives the impression of being both long-winded and short-breathed, as if the author were panting while he climbed an interminable flight of steps. He says in one of his prefaces, "This, amusingly enough, is what, on the evidence before us, I seem critically, as I say, to gather," and we feel that his words are uttered in little gasps. Most of them, in the sentence just quoted, add hardly a shade to the meaning he is trying to convey. Sometimes his famous density is little more than verbosity, and the reader feels himself to be fumbling for ideas, with sticky fingers, in a tub of very old hen-feathers.

Mr. Matthiessen believes that James's revisions in the New York Edition were generally an improvement over his early style; but after reading the discussion carefully I am not so sure that I agree with him. Some of his retouches made the characters more vivid and others introduced effective figures of speech. There were many changes, however, that merely complicated the style. When Madame Merle faces her former lover, in the first version of *The Portrait of a Lady,* she says to him, "How do bad people end? You have made me bad." In the revised version she says, "How do bad people end?—especially as to their *common* crimes. You have made me as bad as yourself." That is more definite, if a little harder to grasp; but it lacks the classical finality of the original statement. In his revisions, James was proud of the way he handled the "he said—she said" problem. But why should it be a problem at all? Why not, like Hemingway, write "he said" and "she said" whenever they are necessary for the sense, instead of looking for elegant variations? The later James was obsessed with finding elegant variations: "she returned," "he just hung fire," "she gaily engaged," and it reminds one of reading a play with too many stage directions.

But the worst feature of James's later style is the inversions that are most noticeable in very short phrases. "Will that so much matter?" he says, instead of, "Will that matter so much?" Very often he forces the verb to the end of the sentence, as in German. He writes: "Maud a little more dryly said"—"Had he had time a little more to try his case"—"What in the world's that but what I shall be just *not* doing?"—"But what are they either, poor things, to do?"—"I suppose that's what I horribly mean"—"I'll go to him then now"—"He wonderfully smiled." English is becoming more and more an uninflected language like Chinese, in which the function of words is shown chiefly by their position in the phrase. To change that position arbitrarily; to write, "He wonderfully smiled," instead of "smiled wonderfully" (and what does "wonderfully" mean in that connection: "for a wonder"?—"wonderingly"?—"in a wonderfully pleasant fashion"?) is to violate the spirit of the language as shaped by all the living and dead millions who speak or have spoken it. Not only is it a symbol of James's separation from the public; it directly expresses and, in a real sense, it *is* that separation.

The anti-Jacobites are right to say that James's later work shows the bad results of exile and expatriation; but they explain his problem in much too simple terms. James was not merely, as they believe, expatriated in the sense of making his home in England. He was self-exiled from England too, until the First World War; he spent most of his life in the world of creation. He wrote in his notebook: "To live *in* the world of creation—to get into it and stay in it—to frequent it and haunt it—to *think* intensely and fruitfully—to woo combinations and inspirations into being by a depth and continuity of attention and meditation—this is the only thing." It was the only thing that James really desired; and it explains the great virtues of his later novels as well as their vices. The virtues and the vices were interrelated and intermingled. In order to become a great novelist, he made himself purely a spectator of life; he denied himself the luxury of holding opinions "even on the Dreyfus case," as he said; and thereby he lost his sense of participation in life and the sort of understanding gained by those who act on their opinions. In the pursuit of combinations and inspirations, he divorced himself from the public, and the divorce made him feel, "well, blighted to the root." At the same time, however, the liberty gained through being unpopular helped him to create independent and self-sustaining works of art. In his "major phase," to follow Matthiessen, or in his decadent period, to rephrase Brooks, there are not two Henry Jameses, one of them a hero in the world of creation, the other a fussy old snob in a fawn-colored vest. There is one Henry James who must be accepted in his strength and weakness.

If we accept him so, the strength far outweighs the weakness. What we remember in his later novels is not their narrowness or their awkward style, but rather their rare quality of self-dependent life. James said in his preface to *Roderick Hudson* that the novelist's subject was like the painter's: it consisted in "the related state, to each other, of certain figures and things." His emphasis falls on the word "related"; and we note that everything in his later novels exists, develops, declines, is extinguished or transformed, *in relation* to something else in the book—not in relation to something outside, to the reader's supposed knowledge of historical incidents or social forces. Everything is bathed in the same consciousness as in some transparent medium; the characters move like swimmers seen from below in utterly clear water. The whole pattern they form, in its complexity, possesses and keeps an inner balance like that of a painting or a symphony; and that explains the permanence of his novels. Their subject matter is not only limited, but in many cases it is fatally out of fashion: for example we feel that Lambert Strether's late discovery of life in Paris, in *The Ambassadors,* was not so much tragic as pathetic. There is no longer the contrast that James described at such length, between the innocent American and the sophisticated European. In these days, however, when innocent and direct Europeans are likely to be confronted with cynical Americans; when the moral standards of New York are more lax than those of Paris; when the millionaire and the nobleman have lost the high position that James assigned to them in his novels—even now, the best of those novels have an inner life that illuminates the life about us and will continue to illuminate our children's lives.

[1945, revised 1970]

A NATURAL HISTORY
OF AMERICAN NATURALISM
(excerpts)

Naturalism appeared thirty years later in American literature than it did in Europe and it was never quite the same movement. Like European Naturalism it was inspired by Darwin's theory of evolution and kept repeating the doctrine that men, being part of the animal kingdom, were subject to natural laws. But theories and doctrines were not the heart of it. The American Naturalists turned to Europe; they read—or read about—Darwin, they studied Spencer and borrowed methods from Zola because they were rebelling against an intolerable situation at home. What bound them together into a school or movement was this native rebellion and not the nature of the help that, like rebels in all ages, they summoned from abroad.

They began writing during the 1890s, when American literature was under the timid but tyrannical rule of what afterwards came to be known as the genteel tradition. It was also called Puritanism by its enemies, but that was a mistake on the part of writers with only a stereotyped notion of American history. The original Puritans were not in the least genteel. They believed in the real existence of evil, which they denounced in terms that would have shocked William Dean Howells and the polite readers of the *Century Magazine*. The great New England writers, descendants of the Puritans, were moralists overburdened with scruples; but they were never mealymouthed in the fashion of their successors. Gentility—or "ideality" or "decency," to mention two favorite words of the genteel writers—was something that developed chiefly in New York and the Middle West and had its flowering after the Civil War.

Essentially it was an effort to abolish the various evils and vulgarities in American society by never speaking about them.

It was a theory that divided the world into two parts, as Sunday was divided from the days of the week or the right side from the wrong side of the railroad tracks. On one side was religion; on the other, business. On one side was the divine in human beings; on the other, everything animal. On one side was art; on the other, life. On one side were women, clergymen, and university professors, all guardians of Art and the Ideal; on the other side were men in general, immersed in their practical affairs. On one side were the church and the school; on the other side were the saloon, the livery stable, and other low haunts where men gathered to talk politics, swap stories, and remember their wartime adventures with the yellow girls in New Orleans. In America during the late nineteenth century, culture was set against daily living, theory against practice, highbrow against lowbrow; and the same division could be found in the language itself—for one side spoke a sort of bloodless literary English, while the other had a speech that was not American but Amurrkn, ugly and businesslike, sometimes picturesque, but not yet a literary idiom.

The whole territory of literature was thought to lie on the right side of the railroad tracks, in the chiefly feminine realm of beauty, art, religion, culture, and the ideal. Novels had to be written with pure heroines and happy endings in order to flatter the self-esteem of female readers. Magazines were edited so as not to disturb the minds of young girls or call forth protests from angry mothers. Frank Norris said of American magazines in 1895: "They are safe as a graveyard, decorous as a church, as devoid of immorality as an epitaph. . . . They adorn the center table. They do not 'call a blush to the cheek of the young.' They can be placed—oh, crowning virtue, oh, supreme encomium—they can be 'safely' placed in the hands of any young girl the country over. . . . It is the 'young girl' and the family center table that determine the standard of the American short story." Meanwhile there were new men appearing year by year—Frank Norris was one of them—who would not write for the young girl or the center table and could not express themselves without breaking the rules of the genteel editors.

These new men, who would be the first American Naturalists, were all in some way disadvantaged when judged by the social and literary standards then prevailing. They were not of the Atlantic seaboard, or not of the old stock, or not educated in the right schools, or not members of the Protestant churches, or not sufficiently respectable in their persons or in their family backgrounds. They were in rebellion against the genteel tradition because, like writers from the beginning of time, they had an urgent need for telling the truth about themselves, and because there was no existing medium in which they were privileged to tell it. . . .

There are other qualities of American Naturalism that are derived not so much from historical conditions as from the example of the two novelists whom the younger men regarded as leaders or precursors. Norris first and Dreiser after him fixed the patterns that the others would follow.

Both men were romantic by taste and temperament. Although Norris was a disciple of Zola's, his other favorite authors belonged in one way or another to the romantic school; they included Froissart, Scott, Dickens, Dumas, Hugo, Kipling, and Stevenson. Zola was no stranger in that company, Norris said; on one occasion he called him "the very head of the Romanticists."—"Terrible things must happen," he wrote, "to the characters of the naturalistic tale. They must be twisted from the ordinary, wrenched from the quiet, uneventful round of everyday life and flung into the throes of a vast and terrible drama that works itself out in unleashed passions, in blood and sudden death. . . . Everything is extraordinary, imaginative, grotesque even, with a vague note of terror quivering throughout like the vibration of an ominous and low-pitched diapason." Norris himself wished to practice Naturalism as a form of romance, instead of taking up what he described as "the harsh, loveless, colorless, blunt tool called Realism." Dreiser in his autobiographical writings often refers to his own romantic temper. "For all my modest repute as a realist," he says, "I seem, to my self-analyzing eyes, somewhat more of a romanticist." He speaks of himself in his youth as "a creature of slow and uncertain response to anything practical, having an eye single to color, romance, beauty. I was but a half-baked poet, romancer, dreamer." The other American Naturalists were also romancers and dreamers in their fashion, groping among facts for the extraordinary and the grotesque. They believed that men were subject to natural forces, but they felt those forces were best displayed when they led to unlimited wealth, utter squalor, collective orgies, blood, and sudden death.

Among the romantic qualities they tried to achieve was "bigness" in its double reference to size and intensity. They wanted to display "big"—that is, intense—emotions against a physically large background. Bigness was the virtue that Norris most admired in Zola's novels. "The world of M. Zola," he said, "is a world of big things; the enormous, the formidable, the terrible, is what counts; no teacup tragedies here." In his own novels, Norris looked for big themes; after his trilogy on Wheat, he planned to write a still bigger trilogy on the three days' battle of Gettysburg, with one novel devoted to the events of each day. The whole notion of writing trilogies instead of separate novels came to be connected with the Naturalistic movement, although it was also adopted by the historical romancers. Before Norris there had been only one planned trilogy in serious American fiction: The *Littlepage Manuscripts*, written by James Fenimore Cooper a few years before his death; it traces the story of a New York State landowning family through a hundred years and three generations. After Norris there were dozens of trilogies, with a few tetralogies and pentalogies: to mention some of the better known, there were Dreiser's trilogy on the career of a financier, T. S. Stribling's trilogy on the rise of a poor-white family, Dos Passos's trilogy on the United States from 1900 to 1930, James T. Farrell's trilogy on Studs Lonigan, and Eugene O'Neill's trilogy of plays, *Mourning Becomes Electra*. Later O'Neill set to work on a trilogy of trilogies, a drama to be complete in nine full-length plays. Farrell wrote a pentalogy about the boyhood of Danny O'Neill and then attacked another theme that would require several volumes, the young manhood of Bernard Clare. Trilogies expanded into whole cycles of novels somehow related in theme. Thus, after the success of *The Jungle*, which had dealt with the meat-packing industry in Chicago, Upton Sinclair wrote novels on other cities (Denver, Boston) and other industries (oil, coal, whiskey, automobiles); finally he settled on a character, Lanny Budd, whose adventures were as endless as those of Tarzan or Superman. Sinclair Lewis dealt one after another with various trades and professions: real estate, medicine, divinity, social service, hotel management, and the stage; there was no limit to the subjects he could treat, so long as his readers' patience was equal to his own.

With their eyes continually on vast projects, the American

Naturalists were careless about the details of their work and indifferent to the materials they were using; often their trilogies resembled great steel-structural buildings faced with cinder blocks and covered with cracked stucco ornaments. Sometimes the buildings remained unfinished. Norris set this pattern, too, when he died before he could start his third novel on the Wheat. Dreiser worked for years on *The Stoic*, which was to be the sequel to *The Financier* and *The Titan*; but he was never satisfied with the various endings he tried, and the book had to be completed by others after his death. Lewis never wrote his novel on labor unions, although he spent months or years gathering material for it and spoke of it as his most ambitious work. In their effort to achieve bigness at any cost, the Naturalists were likely to undertake projects that went beyond their physical or imaginative powers, or in which they discovered too late that they weren't interested.

Meanwhile they worked ahead in a delirium of production, like factories trying to set new records. To understand their achievements in speed and bulk, one has to compare their output with that of an average novelist. There is of course no average novelist, but there are scores of men and women who earn their livings by writing novels, and many of them try to publish one book each year. If they spend four months planning and gathering material for the book, another four months writing the first draft (at the rate of about a thousand words a day) and the last four months in revision, they are at least not unusual. Very few of the Naturalists would have been satisfied with that modest rate of production. Harold Frederic wrote as much as four thousand words a day and often sent his manuscripts to the printer without corrections. At least he paused between novels to carry on his work as a foreign correspondent; but Jack London, who wrote only one thousand words a day, tried to meet that quota six days a week and fifty-two weeks a year; he allowed himself no extra time for planning or revision. He wrote fifty books in seventeen years and didn't pretend that all of them were his best writing. "I have no unfinished stories," he told an interviewer five years before his death. "Invariably I complete every one I start. If it's good, I sign it and send it out. If it isn't good, I sign it and send it out." David Graham Phillips finished his first novel in 1901 and published sixteen others before his death in 1911, in addition to the articles he wrote for muckraking magazines. He left behind him the manuscripts of six novels (including the two-volume *Susan Lenox*) that were published posthumously. Upton Sinclair set a record in the early days when he was writing half-dime novels for boys. He kept three secretaries busy; two of them would be transcribing their notes while the third was taking dictation. By this method he once wrote eighteen thousand words in a day. He gained a fluency that helped him later when he was writing serious books, but he also acquired a contempt for style that made the books painful to read, except in their French translations. Almost all the Naturalists read better in translation; that is one of the reasons for their international popularity as compared with the smaller audience that some of them found at home.

The Naturalistic writers of all countries preferred an objective or scientific approach to their material. As early as 1864 the brothers Goncourt had written in their journal, "The novel of today is made with documents narrated or selected from nature, just as history is based on written documents." A few years later Zola defined the novel as a scientific experiment; its purpose, he said in rather involved language, was to demonstrate the behavior of given characters in a given situation. Still later Norris advanced the doctrine "that no one could be a writer until he could regard life and people, and the world in general, from the objective point of view— until he could remain detached, outside, maintain the unswerving attitude of the observer." The Naturalists as a group not only based their work on current scientific theories but tried to copy scientific methods in planning their novels. They were writers who believed, or claimed to believe, that they could deliberately choose a subject for their work instead of being chosen by a subject; that they could go about collecting characters as a biologist collected specimens; and that their fictional account of such characters could be as accurate and true to the facts as the report of an experiment in the laboratory.

It was largely this faith in objectivity that led them to write about penniless people in the slums, whom they regarded as "outside" or alien subjects for observation. Some of them began with a feeling of contempt for the masses. Norris during his college years used to speak of "the canaille" and often wished for the day when all radicals would be "drowned on

one raft." Later this pure contempt developed into a contemptuous interest, and he began to spend his afternoons on
Polk Street, in San Francisco, observing with a detached eye
the actions of what he now called "the people." The minds
of the people, he thought, were simpler than those of persons
in his own world; essentially these human beings were animals, "the creatures of habit, the playthings of forces," and
therefore they were ideal subjects for a Naturalistic novel.
Some of the other Naturalists revealed the same rather godlike
attitude toward workingmen. Nevertheless they wrote about
them, a bold step at a time when most novels dealt only with
ladies, gentlemen, and faithful retainers; and often their contemptuous interest was gradually transformed into sympathy.

Their objective point of view toward their material was
sometimes a pretense that deceived themselves before it deceived others. From the outside world they chose the subjects
that mirrored their own conflicts and obsessions. Crane, we
remember, said his purpose in writing *Maggie* was to show
"that environment is a tremendous thing and often shapes
lives regardlessly." Yet, on the subjective level, the novel also
revealed an obsessive notion about the blamelessness of prostitutes that affected his career from beginning to end; it caused
a series of scandals, involved him in a feud with the vice squad
in Manhattan, and finally led him to marry the madam of a
bawdy house in Jacksonville. Norris's first novel, *Vandover
and the Brute*, is an apparently objective study of degenera-
tion, but it also mirrors the struggles of the author with his
intensely Puritan conscience; Vandover is Norris himself. He
had drifted into some mild dissipations and pictured them as
leading to failure and insanity. Dreiser in *Sister Carrie* was
telling a story that he felt compelled to write—"as if I were
being used, like a medium," he said—though it now seems
obvious that the story was suggested by the adventures of one
of his sisters. In a sense he was being used by his own memories, which had become subconscious. There was nothing
mystic to Upton Sinclair about his fierce emotion in writing
The Jungle; he knew from the beginning that he was telling
his own story. "I wrote with tears and anguish," he says in
his memoirs, "pouring into the pages all that pain which life
had meant to me. Externally, the story had to do with a family
of stockyards workers, but internally it was the story of my
own family. Did I wish to know how the poor suffered in

Chicago? I had only to recall the previous winter in a cabin, when we had only cotton blankets, and cowered shivering in our separate beds. . . . Our little boy was down with pneumonia that winter, and nearly died, and the grief of that went into the book." Indeed, there is personal grief and fury and bewilderment in all the most impressive Naturalistic novels. They are at their best, not when they are scientific or objective, in accordance with their own theories, but when they are least Naturalistic, most personal and lyrical.

If we follow William James and divide writers into the two categories of the tough and the tender-minded, then most of the Naturalists are tender-minded. The sense of moral fitness is strong in them; they believe in their hearts that nature *should* be kind, that virtue *should* be rewarded on earth, that men *should* control their own destinies. More than other writers, they are wounded by ugliness and injustice, but they will not close their eyes to either; indeed, they often give the impression of seeking out ugliness and injustice in order to be wounded again and again. They have hardly a trace of the cynicism that is often charged against them. It is the quietly realistic or classical writers who are likely to be cynics, in the sense of holding a low opinion of life and human beings; that low estimate is so deeply ingrained in them that they never bother to insist on it—for why should they try to make converts in such a hopeless world? The Naturalists are always trying to convert others and themselves, and sometimes they build up new illusions simply to enjoy the pain of stripping them away. It is their feeling of fascinated revulsion toward their subject matter that makes some of the Naturalists hard to read; they seem to be flogging themselves and their audience like a band of Penitentes.

So far I have been trying to present the positive characteristics of a movement in American letters, but Naturalism can also be defined in terms of what it is not. Thus, to begin a list of negations, it is not journalism in the bad sense, merely sensational or entertaining or written merely to sell. It has to be honest by definition, and honesty in literature is a hard quality to achieve, one that requires more courage and concentration than journalists can profitably devote to writing a novel. Even when an author holds all the Naturalistic doctrines, his books have to reach a certain level of observation and intensity before they deserve to be called Naturalistic. Jack London held the doctrines and wrote fifty books, but only three or four of them reached the required level. David Graham Phillips reached it only once, in *Susan Lenox*, if he reached it then.

Literary Naturalism is not the sort of doctrine that can be officially sponsored and taught in the public schools. It depends for too many of its effects on shocking the sensibilities of its readers and smashing their illusions. It always becomes a threat to the self-esteem of the propertied classes. *Babbitt*, for example, is Naturalistic in its hostile treatment of American businessmen. When Sinclair Lewis defended Babbittry in a later novel, *The Prodigal Parents*, his work had ceased to be Naturalistic.

For a third negative statement, Naturalism is not what we have learned to call literature "in depth." It is concerned with human behavior and with explanatins for that behavior in terms of heredity or environment. It presents the exterior world, often in striking visual images; but unlike the work of Henry James or Sherwood Anderson or William Faulkner—to mention only three writers in other traditions—it does not try to explore the world within. Faulkner's method is sometimes described as "subjective Naturalism," but the phrase is self-contradictory, almost as if one spoke of "subjective biology" or "subjective physics."

Naturalism does not deal primarily with individuals in themselves, but rather with social groups or settings or movements, or with individuals like Babbitt and Studs Lonigan who are regarded as being typical of a group. The Naturalistic writer tries not to identify himself with any of his characters, although he doesn't always succeed; in general his aim is to present them almost as if they were laboratory specimens. They are seldom depicted as being capable of moral decisions. This fact makes it easy to distinguish between the early Naturalists and some of their contemporaries like Robert Herrick and Edith Wharton who also tried to write without optimistic illusions. Herrick and Wharton, however, dealt with individuals who possessed some degree of moral freedom; and often the plots of their novels hinge on a conscious decision by one of the characters. Hemingway, another author whose work is wrongly described as Naturalistic, writes stories that reveal some moral quality, usually stoicism or the courage of a frightened man.

Many Naturalistic works are valuable historical documents, but the authors in general have little sense of history. They present each situation as if it had no historical antecedents, and their characters might be men and women created yesterday morning, so few signs do they show of having roots in the past. "Science" for Naturalistic writers usually means laboratory science, and not the study of human institutions or patterns of thought that persist through generations.

With a few exceptions they have no faith in reform, whether it be the reform of an individual by his own decision or the reform of society by reasoned courses of action. The changes they depict are the result of laws and forces and tendencies beyond human control. That is the great difference between the Naturalists and the proletarian or Marxian novelists of the 1930's. The proletarian writers—who were seldom proletarians in private life—believed that men acting together could make a new world. But they borrowed the objective and exterior technique of the Naturalists, which was unsuited to their essentially religious purpose. In the beginning of each book they portrayed a group of factory workers as the slaves of economic conditions, "the creatures of habit, the playthings of forces"; then later they portrayed the conversion of one or more workers to communism. But conversion is a psychological, not a biological, phenomenon, and it could not be explained purely in terms of conditions or forces. When the conversion took place, there was a shift from the outer to the inner world, and the novel broke in two.

It was not at all extraordinary for Naturalism to change into religious Marxism in the middle of a novel, since it has always shown a tendency to dissolve into something else. On the record, literary Naturalism does not seem to be a doctrine or attitude to which men are likely to cling through their whole lives. It is always being transformed into satire, symbolism, lyrical autobiography, utopian socialism, communism, Catholicism, Buddhism, Freudian psychology, hack journalism, or the mere assembling of facts. So far there is not in American literature a single instance in which a writer has remained a Naturalist from beginning to end of a long career; even Dreiser before his death became a strange mixture of Communist and mystic. There are, however, a great many works that are predominantly Naturalistic; and the time has come to list them in order to give the basis for my generalities.

I should say that those works, in fiction, were *Maggie* and *George's Mother*, by Stephen Crane, with many of his short stories; *The Damnation of Theron Ware*, by Harold Frederic; *Vandover*, *McTeague*, and *The Octopus* (but not *The Pit*), by Frank Norris; *The Call of the Wild*, which is a sort of Naturalistic Aesop's fable, besides *The Sea Wolf* and *Martin Eden*, by Jack London; *The Jungle*, by Upton Sinclair, as far as the page where Jurgis is converted to socialism; *Susan Lenox*, by David Graham Phillips; all of Dreiser's novels except *The Bulwark*, which has a religious ending written at the close of his life; all the serious novels of Sinclair Lewis between *Main Street* (1920) and *Dodsworth* (1929), but none he wrote afterwards; Dos Passos's *Manhattan Transfer* and *U.S.A.*; James T. Farrell's work in general, but especially *Studs Lonigan*; Richard Wright's *Native Son*; and most of John Steinbeck's early novels, including *In Dubious Battle* and all but the hortatory passages in *The Grapes of Wrath*. There are also autobiographies, and one of them is *The Education of Henry Adams*, which presents the author's life as determined by the conflict between unity and multiplicity and by the law of historical acceleration. The book can be read as a Naturalistic novel, and in fact its technique is more fictional, in the good sense, than Dreiser's technique in *The "Genius."* In poetry there is Robinson's early verse, as far as *Captain Craig*, and there is Edgar Lee Masters' *Spoon River Anthology*. In the drama there are the early plays of Eugene O'Neill, from *Beyond the Horizon* to *Desire under the Elms*. Among essays there are H. L. Mencken's *Prejudices* and Joseph Wood Krutch's *The Modern Temper*, which is the most coherent statement of the Naturalistic position. There are other Naturalists in all fields, especially fiction—as note F. Scott Fitzgerald's *The Beautiful and Damned*—and other Naturalistic books by several of the authors I have mentioned; but these are the works by which the school is likely to be remembered and judged.

And what shall we say in judgment?—since judge we must, after this long essay in definition. Is Naturalism true or false in its premises and good or bad in its effect on American literature? Its results have been good, I think, insofar as it has forced its adherents to stand in opposition to American orthodoxy. Honest writing in this country, the only sort worth bothering about, has almost always been the work of an opposition, chiefly because the leveling and unifying elements in our culture have been so strong that a man who accepts orthodox judgments is in danger of losing his literary personality. Catullus and Villon might be able to write their poems here; with their irregular lives they wouldn't run the risk of being corrupted by the standards of right-thinking people. But Virgil, the friend of Augustus, the official writer who shaped the myth of the Roman state—Virgil would be a dubious figure as an American poet. He would be tempted to soften his values in order to become a prophet for the masses. The American myth of universal cheap luxuries, tiled bathrooms, and service with a smile would not serve him as the basis for an epic poem.

The Naturalists, standing in opposition, have been writers of independent and strongly marked personalities. They have fought for the right to speak their minds and have won a measure of freedom for themselves and others. Yet it has to be charged against them that their opposition often takes the form of cheapening what they write about; of always looking for the lowdown or the payoff, that is, for the meanest explanation of everything they describe. There is a tendency in literary Naturalism—as distinguished from philosophical Naturalism, which is not my subject—always to explain the complex in terms of the simple: society in terms of self, man in terms of his animal inheritance, and the organic in terms of the inorganic. The result is that something is omitted at each stage in this process of reduction. To say that man is a beast of prey or a collection of chemical compounds omits most of man's special nature; it is a metaphor, not a scientific statement.

This scientific weakness of Naturalism involves a still greater literary weakness, for it leads to a conception of man that makes it impossible for Naturalistic authors to write in the tragic spirit. They can write about crimes, suicides, disasters, the terrifying, and the grotesque; but even the most powerful of their novels and plays are case histories rather than tragedies in the classical sense. Tragedy is an affirmation of man's importance; it is "the imitation of noble actions," in Aristotle's phrase; and the Naturalists are unable to believe in human nobility. "We write no tragedies today," says Joseph Wood Krutch in his early book, *The Modern Temper*, which might better have been called "The Naturalistic Temper." "If the plays and novels of today deal with littler people and less mighty emotions it is not because we have become interested in commonplace souls and their unglamorous adventures but because we have come, willy-nilly, to see the soul of man as commonplace and its emotions as mean." But Krutch was speaking only for those who shared the Naturalistic point of view. There are other doctrines held by modern writers that make it possible to endow their characters with human dignity. Tragic novels and plays have been written in these years by Christians, Communists, Humanists, and Existentialists, all of whom believe in different fashions and degrees that men can shape their own fates.

For the Naturalists, however, men are "human insects" whose brief lives are completely determined by society or nature. The individual is crushed in a moment if he resists; and his struggle, instead of being tragic, is merely pitiful or ironic, as if we had seen a mountain stir itself to overwhelm a fly. Irony is a literary effect used time and again by all the Naturalistic writers. For Stephen Crane it is the central effect on which almost all his plots depend: thus, in *The Red Badge of Courage*, the boy makes himself a hero by running away. In "A Mystery of Heroism," a soldier risks his life to bring a bucket of water to his comrades, and the water is spilled. In "The Monster," a Negro stableman is so badly burned in rescuing a child that he becomes a faceless horror; and the child's father, a physician, loses his practice as a reward for sheltering the stableman. The irony in Dreiser's novels depends on the contrast between conventional morality and the situations he describes: Carrie Meeber loses her virtue and succeeds in her career; Jennie Gerhardt is a kept woman with higher principles than any respectable wife. In Sinclair Lewis the irony is reduced to an obsessive and irritating trick of style; if he wants to say that a speech was dull and stupid, he has to call it "the culminating glory of the dinner" and then, to make sure that we catch the point, explain that it was delivered by Mrs. Adelaide Tarr Gimmitch, "known throughout the country as 'the Unkies' Girl.'" The reader, seeing the name of Gimmitch, is supposed to smile a superior smile. There is something superior and ultimately tiresome in the attitude of many Naturalists toward the events they describe. Irony—like pity, its companion—is a spectator's emotion, and it sets a space between ourselves and the characters in the novel. They suffer, but their cries reach us faintly, like those of dying strangers we cannot hope to save.

There is nothing in the fundamental principles of Naturalism that requires a novel to be written in hasty or hackneyed prose. Flaubert, the most careful stylist of his age, was the predecessor and guide of the French Naturalists. Among the Naturalistic writers of all countries who wrote with a feeling for language were the brothers Goncourt, Ibsen, Hardy, and Stephen Crane. But it was Norris, not Crane, who set the standards for Naturalistic fiction in the United States, and Norris had no respect for style. "What pleased me most in your review of 'McTeague,' " he said in a letter to Isaac Marcosson, "was 'disdaining all pretensions to style.' It is precisely what I try most to avoid. I detest 'fine writing,' 'rhetoric,' 'elegant English'—tommyrot. Who cares for fine style! Tell your yarn and let your style go to the devil. We don't want literature, we want life." Yet the truth was that Norris's novels were full of fine writing and lace-curtain English. "Untouched, unassailable, undefiled," he says of the Wheat, "that mighty world force, that nourisher of nations, wrapped in Nirvanic calm, indifferent to the human swarm, gigantic, resistless, moved onward in its appointed grooves." He never learned to present his ideas in their own clothes or none at all; it was easier to dress them in borrowed plush; easier to make all his calms Nirvanic and all his grooves appointed.

Yet Norris wrote better prose than most of his successors among the American Naturalists. With a few exceptions like Dos Passos and Steinbeck, they have all used language as a blunt instrument; they write as if they were swinging shillelaghs. O'Neill was a great dramatist, but he never had an ear for the speech of living persons. Lewis once had an ear, but in later life he listened only to himself. He kept being arch and ironical about his characters until we wanted to snarl at him, "Quit patronizing those people! Maybe they'd have something to say if you'd only let them talk." Farrell writes well when he is excited or angry, but most of the time he makes his readers trudge through vacant lots in a Chicago South Side smog. Dreiser is the worst writer of all, but in some ways the least objectionable; there is something native to himself in his misuse of the language, so that we come to cherish it as a sign of authenticity, like the tool marks on Shaker furniture. Most of the others simply use the oldest and easiest phrase.

But although the Naturalists as a group are men of defective hearing, they almost all have keen eyes for new material. Their interest in themes that others regarded as too unpleasant or ill-bred has immensely broadened the scope of American fiction. Moreover, they have had enough vitality and courage to be exhilarated by the American life of their own times. From the beginning they have exulted in the wealth and ugliness of American cities, the splendor of the mansions and the squalor of the tenements. They compared Pittsburgh to Paris and New York to imperial Rome. Frank Norris thought that his own San Francisco was the ideal city for storytellers; "Things happen in San Francisco," he said. Dreiser remarked of Chicago, "It is given to some cities, as to some lands, to suggest romance, and to me Chicago did that hourly . . . Florence in its best days must have been something like this to young Florentines, or Venice to the young Venetians." The Naturalists for all their faults were embarked on a bolder venture than those other writers whose imaginations can absorb nothing but legends already treated in other books, prepared and predigested food. They tried to seize the life around them, and at their best they transformed it into new archetypes of human experience. Just as Cooper had shaped the legend of the frontier and Mark Twain the legend of the Mississippi, so the Naturalists have shaped the harsher legends of an urban and industrial age.

[1947, revised 1970]

THE REVOLT AGAINST GENTILITY

December 10, 1930. At a meeting in Stockholm attended by the King of Sweden and the Swedish Academy, the Nobel Prize for Literature was presented to the author of *Main Street* and *Babbitt*. He was the first American to be measured and weighed and certified as an international giant of letters.

Judged from a purely literary point of view, he was neither the greatest nor the least of the Nobel prizemen. He was certainly not of the same stature as Kipling or Shaw or Thomas Mann (or, to add the names of American writers who died without getting the prize, as Mark Twain or Henry James). On the other hand, he was bigger by head and shoulders than many of the saga singers and little-problem playwrights whom the Swedish Academy had immortalized *pro tem*. When Sinclair Lewis won the prize, its literary value was neither enhanced nor diminished.

But I suppose that nobody is innocent enough to believe that the Nobel Prize is a purely literary event. Nobody imagines that the Swedish Academy confines its efforts to finding the very best living author, no matter what his nationality or the color of his opinions. Clearly there are diplomatic issues involved and questions of national honor. If a big country gets the prize one year, a small country is likely to get it the year after. If there is too much competition between Germany and France or France and England, the difficulty can be avoided by naming a Dane or a Swede; some years it seems that almost anyone will do if he comes from the right country. It would be Italy's turn in 1934. That year we heard a pretty well substantiated rumor that the Italian ambassador in Stockholm had to engage in vigorous intrigues to keep the prize from going to Benedetto Croce, who was not a friend of Mussolini's. The successful candidate was Luigi Pirandello, who was politically inoffensive.

There was no whisper of backstairs maneuvering when Sinclair Lewis got the prize, and yet the choice in 1930 was unusually significant from the standpoint of world politics. During the sixteen years that began with the Great War, the United States had become not only a world power but industrially the greatest of the powers. American men of letters were supposed to have lagged behind American bankers and manufacturers, yet they could no longer be overlooked in favor of minor poets and short-story writers from Sicily, Lapland or wherever. When the Swedish Academy gave its medal and its forty thousand dollars to a man from Minnesota, it was saying in effect that American literature had ceased to be a minor province of British literature and must now be recognized in its own right.

The permanent secretary of the Swedish Academy, Erik Axel Karlfeldt, gave a speech of welcome in which he emphasized the national and international meaning of the prize (while revealing some ignorance of American history). "Yes," he said, "Sinclair Lewis is an American. He writes the new language—American—as one of the representatives of a hundred and twenty million souls. He asks us to consider that this nation is not yet finished or melted down; that it is still in the turbulent years of adolescence. The new great American literature has started with national self-criticism. It is a sign of health."

Two days later, when Lewis made his acceptance speech, he answered Dr. Karlfeldt as a lover and critic of America, as a representative of a hundred and twenty million souls. "The American Fear of Literature" was his subject. His address was front-page news in the American papers, and it remains a historical document of considerable meaning.

It seems that Dr. Henry Van Dyke had taken umbrage. Speaking as a member of the American Academy of Arts and Letters, this retired Princeton professor and former Presbyterian minister declaimed that the award of the Nobel Prize to a man who had scoffed so much at American institutions was an insult to our country. Lewis, after reporting the incident, suggested to his Swedish audience that Dr. Van Dyke might call out the Marines and have them landed in Stockholm to protect American literary rights. But he also had more serious comments to offer. Dr. Van Dyke, he said, was an almost official representative of the "genteel tradition" that for half a century had been the persistent enemy and slow poisoner of good writing in America:

. . . most of us—not readers alone but even writers—are still afraid of any literature which is not a glorification of everything American, a glorification of our faults as well as our virtues. . . . We still more revere the writers for the popular magazines who in a hearty and edifying chorus chant that the America of a hundred and twenty million population is still as simple, as pastoral, as it was when he had but forty million . . . that, in fine, America has gone through the revolutionary change from rustic colony to world empire without having in the least altered the bucolic and Puritanic simplicity of Uncle Sam.

In the new American empire it was possible for a writer to make plenty of money: he could have his butler and his motor and his villa at Palm Beach, where he could mingle almost on terms of equality with the barons of banking. But still, if he took his profession seriously,

. . . he is oppressed by something worse than poverty—by the feeling that what he creates does not matter, that he is expected by his readers to be only a decorator or a clown, or that he is good-naturedly accepted as a scoffer whose bark is probably worse than his bite and who certainly does not count in a land that produces eighty-story buildings, motors by the million and wheat by the billions of bushels. And he has no institution, no group, to which he can turn for inspiration, whose criticism he can accept and whose praise will be precious to him.

Lewis began to call the roll of the groups or institutions that ought to be friendly to creative writing. The American Academy? It contains so very few of the first-rate writers that "it does not represent literary America of today—it represents only Henry Wadsworth Longfellow." The American universities? Four of them have shown some real interest in contemporary creative literature: "Rollins College in Florida, Middlebury College in Vermont, the University of Michigan, and the University of Chicago." But most of the others have exemplified "the divorce in America of intellectual life from all authentic standards of importance and reality. . . . To a true-blue professor of American literature in an American university, literature is not something that a plain human being, living today, painfully sits down to produce. No, it is something dead; it is something magically produced by su-perhuman beings who must, if they are to be regarded as artists at all, have died at least one hundred years before the diabolical invention of the typewriter." And what about our literary criticism? "Most of it," Lewis said, "has been a chill and insignificant activity pursued by jealous spinsters, ex-baseball reporters, and acid professors." There have been no valid standards because there has been nobody capable of setting them up. Worse still, there have been the false and life-denying standards of critics like William Dean Howells and Henry Van Dyke, who were "effusively seeking to guide America into becoming a pale edition of an English cathedral town."

Fortunately, Lewis continued, the younger generation has untied itself from their stepmotherly apron strings. A whole new literature has come of age, a literature that tries to express the sweep and strength and beauty-in-ugliness of the American empire as it is today. There are a dozen American writers worthy of receiving the Nobel Prize. But no matter which of them had been chosen, there would have been the same outcry from the academicians and from the New Humanists drily embattled in their college libraries.

2.

In the most significant part of his speech, Lewis enumerated the great men and great achievements of the 1920's. He imagined what the older and more genteel critics would have said to each possible choice of the Swedish Academy:

Suppose you had taken Theodore Dreiser.

Now to me, as to many other American writers, Dreiser more than any other man, marching alone, usually unappreciated, often hated, has cleared the trail from Victorian and Howellsian timidity and gentility in American fiction to honesty and bold-ness and passion of life. Without his pioneering, I doubt if any of us could, unless we liked to be sent to jail, express life and beauty and terror. . . .

Yet had you given the prize to Mr. Dreiser, you would have heard groans from America; you would have heard . . . that his style is cumbersome, that his choice of words is insensitive, that his books are interminable. And certainly respectable scholars would complain that in Mr. Dreiser's world, men and women are often sinful and tragic and despairing, instead of being forever sunny and full of song and virtue, as befits authentic Americans.

And had you chosen Mr. Eugene O'Neill, who has done nothing much in American drama save to transform it utterly, in ten or twelve years, from a false world of neat and competent trickery to a world of splendor and fear and greatness, you would have been reminded that he has done something far worse than scoffing—he has seen life as not to be neatly arranged in the study of a scholar but as a terrifying, magnificent and often quite horrible thing akin to the tornado, the earthquake, the devastating fire.

And had you given Mr. James Branch Cabell the prize, you would have been told that he is too fantastically malicious. So would you have been told that Miss Willa Cather, for all the homely virture of her novels concerning the peasants of Nebraska, has in her novel, "A Lost Lady," been so untrue to America's patent and perpetual and possibly tedious virtuousness as to picture an abandoned woman who remains, nevertheless, uncannily charming even to the virtuous, in a story without any moral; that Mr. Henry Mencken is the worst of all scoffers; that Mr. Sherwood Anderson viciously errs in considering sex as important a force in life as fishing; that Mr. Upton Sinclair, being a Socialist, sins against the perfectness of American capitalistic mass production; that Mr. Joseph Hergesheimer is un-American in regarding graciousness of manner and beauty of surface as of some importance in the endurance of daily life; and that Mr. Ernest Hemingway is not only too young but, far worse, uses language which should be unknown to gentlemen; that he acknowledges drunkenness as one of man's eternal ways to happiness. . . .

Dreiser and O'Neill, James Branch Cabell, Willa Cather, H. L. Mencken, Sherwood Anderson, Upton Sinclair, Joseph Hergesheimer and Ernest Hemingway: this list of distinguished writers needs a few emendations. The speaker himself should most certainly be added to it. So too should Van Wyck Brooks, the first critic to express many of the ideas that Lewis was presenting to the Swedish Academy. So too should Frost and Robinson, as well as "the really original and vital poets, Edna St. Vincent Millay and Carl Sandburg, Robinson Jeffers and Vachel Lindsay and Edgar Lee Masters," mentioned in another passage of the same address. On the other hand,

Hemingway might have been omitted here, since he belongs by age and spirit to another generation. But with a very few changes of this order, the list would be definitive. Sinclair Lewis, in his speech at Stockholm, had named the prominent figures of the era in American literature that was just then drawing to a close.

But he did more than merely catalogue the "great men and women in American literary life today." He also specified the reasons for their greatness (and in quoting what the academic critics would say against them he was praising them still more, by indirection). Thus, Dreiser had "cleared the way from Victorian and Howellsian timidity and gentility." O'Neill had seen life "as not to be neatly arranged in the study of a scholar." Willa Cather had been "so untrue to America's patent and perpetual and possibly tedious virtuousness as to picture an abandoned woman . . . in a story without any moral" (though the moral was so patently there that Lewis must have been trying not to find it). Mencken had offended the godly by scoffing at evangelism; Anderson had offended them by not scoffing at sex; and even Hemingway had fitted into the pattern of negation and defiance by using "language which should be unknown to a gentleman." It seemed to Lewis that all these authors were united into one crusading army by their revolt against the genteel tradition.

3.

But what was the nature of this tradition against which so many writers had rebelled?

In part it was an attempt to abolish the evils and vulgarities and sometimes the simple changes in American society by never talking about them. It had some connection with the English movement or manner that was later known as Victorianism, but it was even more stringent in its prohibitions, possibly because the evils in a younger society were harder not to mention. It also had a connection with the Civil War. The war has been so idealized by genteel novelists and historians that we find it hard to recognize a simple fact: it was a war like any other, with its normal share of pillage, drunkenness, filth, profiteering and disorder. Moreover, the wartime atmosphere was prolonged through the Reconstruction

years, which were the years of lawlessness in the South and
financial corruption in the North; the years when millions of
immigrants were crowding into the slums; the gaudy and vicious years when bribe-taking congressmen had to push their
way through a crowd of prostitutes as they climbed the steps
of the Capitol.

It is no wonder that there was a moral reaction, which
gained strength after the panic of 1873. The pity is that much
or most of the reaction was not directed toward the real evils
of American life at the time. Instead the chief effort of many
reformers was focused on the American middle-class home
and its presiding spirit, the pure young girl. The reformers
tried to keep them both unsullied by ignoring or denying the
brutalities of business life. Every cultural object that entered
the home was supposed to express the highest ideals and
aspirations. Every book or magazine intended to appear on
the center table in the parlor was kept as innocent as milk.
American women of all ages, especially the unmarried ones,
had suddenly become more than earthly creatures; they were
presented as milk-white angels of art and compassion and
culture. "It is the 'young girl' and the family center table,"
Frank Norris complained in the 1890's, "that determine the
standard of the American short story."

Scribner's, Harper's and the *Century* were the principal
voices of the genteel era. Their standard of fiction was fairly
high in a literary sense, and I suspect that better magazines
for a wide audience have never been published in this country;
but in matters of decorum the standard was that of a rather
strict girls' boarding school. Richard Watson Gilder, who edited the *Century* from 1881 to 1909, once refused to print a
war story that he had already accepted. His change of mind
was caused by a sentence he had missed on a first reading:
"The bullet had left a blue mark over the brown nipple."
Even William Dean Howells sometimes failed to meet his
schoolmistressly standards. When the *Century* was serializing
The Rise of Silas Lapham, Gilder had the presses stopped in
order to delete a reference to dynamite in labor disputes.
Roger Burlingame, the distinguished editor of *Scribner's,* rejected an early novel by Hamlin Garland on the comprehensive ground that it contained "slang, profanity, vulgarity,
agnosticism, and radicalism." *Harper's,* edited for fifty years
by Henry Mills Alden, was a little more worldly than its two

great rivals; it went so far as to accept Hardy's *Jude the Obscure*. But before printing the novel in monthly installments, it imposed two conditions on the author: the children of Jude and Sue, born out of wedlock, had to be presented as adopted orphans, and the title had to be changed to *Hearts Insurgent*.

No such conditions had been imposed in England. The greater stringency or prissiness of American editors might be explained by a change in the Victorian proprieties after they crossed the Atlantic. In Boston and New York they acquired some provincial or native characteristics, and notably they became intermingled with a late and debased form of New England puritanism. Of course the original Puritans were not in the least genteel. Believing in the real existence of evil, they denounced it in language that was not intended for the young girl or the family center table. But their doctrines had been transformed by the years, and the puritanism of their descendants was hardly more than a set of rules and a tendency to divide practical life from the life of the mind, just as Sunday was divided from the days of the week. In *America's Coming-of-Age* Van Wyck Brooks discusses the tendency with much acuteness. Practical life, he says, had become a hard, dirty scramble in which the only justifiable aim was to get ahead, be successful, make money, but meanwhile the life of the mind was supposed to be kept as spotless and fragrant with lavender as a white Sunday dress. The two sides of this later puritanism might be those of a single man: for example, Andrew Carnegie, who made a fortune by manufacturing armor plate and then spent it in promoting peace by impractical methods and in building libraries where the men in his rolling mills, who worked twelve hours a day and seven days a week, would never have time to read masterworks. Culture was something reserved and refined for the Sunday people: women, ministers, university professors and the readers of genteel magazines.

But the Victorian spirit in America was also intermingled with the defiant optimism that grew out of pioneering and land speculation. There were always better farms to the westward. Prices would always go up, and the mortgage would be paid at the last moment, while the sheriff was pounding at the door. . . . With this background of belief, many American books had the same innocently hopeful atmosphere as American real-estate developments; they were like cement sidewalks laid down in the wilderness with the absolute certainty that, some day, there would be a skyscraper on this corner lot now covered with sagebrush. To fail or simply to be discouraged in the midst of so many opportunities was not only a sign of weakness; it was a sin like adultery, and it could scarcely be mentioned in novels written for decent people.

Those two characteristics of the genteel tradition in America—I mean its absolute divorce from daily life (or its "ideality," in the language of genteel critics) and its high optimism—were part of what Marxists would call its ideological superstructure. It also possessed, however, a pretty firm base in American society. It could depend on popular support because, in many social conflicts of the time, the genteel writers all represented the side that was older and firmly entrenched.

Thus, in the conflict between city ideals and country ideals, they all took the rural side. The United States in 1890 was already becoming urbanized and industrialized, and most of the genteel writers had followed the times by moving to New York or Boston; but the ideals they defended in their writing were those of an earlier day. "In a hearty and edifying chorus," as Lewis said, they chanted that this was still a nation of villagers devoted to plain living and high thinking.

In the conflict between the Eastern seaboard and the Middle West, most of the genteel writers represented the seaboard— and particularly New York and New England—no matter where they had been born. They found some room in their company for Southern writers, mostly local colorists, and later they admitted a whole school of Indiana novelists who yearned for the days when knighthood was in flower. They did not believe, however, that the Middle West of their own time was a proper subject for fiction. Hamlin Garland once complained that so far as the literary magazines were concerned, "Wisconsin, Minnesota and Iowa did not exist. Not a picture, not a single poem or story, not even a reference to those states could I discover in ten thousand pages of print."

In the conflict of racial strains, always fiercer in this country than historians like to admit, the genteel writers all represented the older immigration. They were English by descent, except for a few whose forebears were Scottish or Knickerbocker or Huguenot, and they looked down in a kindly way on the Irish and the Germans. England for them was "our old home," to be regarded with a mixture of emulative jealousy and pride of kinship. Their literary models were English, with the result that much of their writing seemed less national than colonial.

In matters of religion they were almost all Protestant by training, and many of them were church-going Episcopalians or Presbyterians all their lives. Those who lost their faith became Protestant agnostics, a very different breed from Catholic or from Jewish agnostics. They could not imagine a time when the United States might be anything else than a Protestant nation.

In politics they were civil-service reformers, Mugwumps in 1884, Bull Moosers in 1912, and strongly pro-British in the Great War. But the conflict in which they played the longest part was the old one between the rich and the poor, or rather—since the truly poor had found no voice in American letters—between the old rich families and the lower middle class. They chose their side without much hesitation, as a rule, though Howells and Garland both had struggles of conscience. Many of the genteel writers were themselves poor devils living in furnished rooms, but the world presented in their stories was that of people who always dressed for dinner and never talked about money, being too well bred. Theodore Dreiser, who knew nothing of that world, wondered how he could possibly write for the leading magazines. He says at the end of *A Book about Myself:*

> In a kind of ferment or fever due to my necessities and desperation, I set to examining the current magazines and the fiction and articles to be found therein: *Century, Scribner's, Harper's.* I was never more confounded than by the discrepancy existing between my own observations and those displayed here, the beauty and peace and charm to be found in everything, the almost complete absence of any reference to the coarse and the vulgar. . . .
>
> Maybe such things were not the true province of fiction anyhow. I read and read, but all I could gather was that I had no such tales to tell, and, however much I tried, I could not think of any. The kind of thing I was witnessing no one would want as fiction. These writers seemed far above the world of which I was a part. Indeed I began to picture them as creatures of the greatest luxury and culture, gentlemen and ladies all, comfort-

ably housed, masters of servants, possessing estates, or at least bachelor quarters, having horses and carriages, and received here, there and everywhere with nods of recognition and smiles of approval.

That was a lonely young man's picture of the genteel writers, but it was not wholly false. A few of them were truly men of substance, the intimate friends of millionaires, and they were models of conduct for the others. Even the poor devils in furnished rooms might hope for invitations to one of the great dinners at which Andrew Carnegie entertained the literary world. And the genteel tradition not only had wealthy patrons; it also had powerful institutions of its own. Besides the three great magazines and their respectable poor relations, the *Atlantic* and the *North American Review*, there were also the established publishing houses, most of which were glad to instruct their authors in the rules for meeting the genteel taste, besides furnishing them with subjects and, on occasion, with readymade plots. There were the great Eastern universities, given over to the promotion of culture, football and ideality. I remember a Leyendecker lithograph of a blondely handsome football team running out on the field in clean blue jerseys. Under it was an inscription that revealed the feeling of the time:

> Go, lose or conquer as ye can:
> Be each, pray God, the gentleman!

In New York there were many clubs that welcomed young writers who were also gentlemen, praise God: there were the Century, the Authors', the Players', the Lotos, the Aldine, the National Arts, some of them endowed by millionaires, and there were also the Bohemians in San Francisco and the Cliff Dwellers in Chicago, this last founded by Hamlin Garland, who described himself as "a great carpenter and joiner of clubs." In New York again there was the National Institute of Arts and Letters, with its Department of Literature that was, until 1930, almost wholly confined to genteel writers. The American Academy, which Lewis attacked with such violence (and to which he would be proud of being elected in 1937), was the inner circle of the Institute.

All these institutions together provided an imposing display of literary power and status. A young author of talent, if he was sufficiently genteel, might appear in the *Century* or *Harper's,* might be offered a contract for a novel to be serialized in the same magazine before being published in hard covers, might lecture on the Chautauqua circuit, might be elected to one or more of the endowed clubs, then to the National Institute, and might look forward to having his works published in a collected edition, like those of Thomas Nelson Page and F. Hopkinson Smith—though he might become so entranced with club life and dinners at big houses that he had little time for written works. But if the young writer insisted on being pessimistic; if he portrayed women whose virtue was not laced in whalebone stays—or if he insisted on writing about "religion, love, politics, alcohol or fairies," as one great editor advised Edith Wharton not to do—then the doors of the institutions were closed to him. He might still achieve a career if he had some quite rare advantage, like Mrs. Wharton's wealth or Frank Norris's lion-cub friendliness and energy or Stephen Crane's genius, but there were a thousand chances of failure to one of success.

The wonder is that young writers had courage enough to rebel against all this entrenched power. We know that many lost heart and that some of the best—Crane, Norris, Trumbull Stickney—died in their early thirties as if worn out by the struggle. But other young writers succeeded them and, in the course of time, they set themselves against every feature of the genteel tradition. Instead of being Puritans in the cant sense of the word, many of them were frankly sensual, given to praising sexual freedom and to justifying drunkenness "as one of man's eternal ways to happiness." Instead of being optimistic, they painted a world in which "men and women are often sinful and tragic and despairing." Instead of belonging to the North Atlantic seaboard, most of them boasted of having roots in the Middle West or the South. Instead of being inspired by English models, they either tried to create an American myth, in the American language, with saints and folk heroes like Abe Lincoln and Johnny Appleseed, or else they followed theories like socialism and Freudianism that had originated on the continent of Europe. But most of all, the new literary movement was a revolt of the lower middle classes against conventions that did not fit their personal lives and that prevented them from telling the truth about their world. On this last point Lewis was as eloquent as Dreiser:

I had realized in reading Balzac and Dickens that it was possible to describe French and English common people as one
actually saw them. But it had never occurred to me that one
might without indecency write of the people of Sauk Centre,
Minnesota, as one felt about them. Our fictional tradition, you
see, was that all of us in Midwestern villages were altogether
noble and happy; that not one of us would exchange the neigh-
borly bliss of living on Main Street for the heathen gaudiness
of New York or Paris or Stockholm. But in Mr. Garland's
"Main-Traveled Roads" I discovered that Midwestern peasants
were sometimes bewildered and hungry and vile—and heroic.
And, given this vision, I was released; I could write of life as
living life.

Hamlin Garland, after writing two good books, Lewis said,
"had gone to Boston and become cultured and Howellsized";
but the somewhat younger writers whom Lewis was praising
had kept their vigor and honesty by resisting the genteel in-
fluences. They had in fact created a new literature that was
as broad and native as the prairies. "As a chauvinistic American," Lewis said, "—only, mind you, as an American of
1930 and not of 1880—I can rejoice that they are my countrymen, and that I can speak of them with pride, even in the
Europe of Thomas Mann, H. G. Wells, Galsworthy, Knut
Hamsun. . . ." He did not believe that they had yet affected
the public at home. "It is not today vastly more true than it
was twenty years ago that . . . novelists like Dreiser and Willa
Cather are authentically popular and influential in America."
He thought that they still had to fight their war of liberation.
But in this idea, so it seems to us today, he was at least ten
years behind the times.

The war was already under way in 1890, but the decisive
battles had been fought in the decade after 1910, when almost
every new writer was a recruit to the army against gentility,
and when older writers like Dreiser and Robinson were being
rescued from neglect and praised as leaders. In those days
Mabel Dodge's salon, the Provincetown Playhouse and, in
Chicago, the Dill Pickle Club were the rallying grounds of
the rebel forces. The *Masses* (1911), *Poetry* (1912), the *Smart
Set* (of which the best year was 1913) and the *Little Review*
(1914) were its propaganda organs.

For a time every honestly written book was a foray against

the conservatives, and some were resounding victories—as notably *Jennie Gerhardt* (1911), America's *Coming-of-Age* and *Spoon River Anthology* (1915), *Chicago Poems* (1916), *The Education of Henry Adams* (1918), *Winesburg, Ohio* and *Our America* (1919). The battle over *Jurgen,* beginning that same year, ended as a major triumph over the censors. In 1920 came the success of *Beyond the Horizon,* the first play by one of the rebels to be produced on Broadway, and the vastly greater success of *Main Street.* The novel was published by Harcourt, Brace and Howe, one of several new publishing houses that supported the new writers. The older houses— even Charles Scribner's Sons, which had been the most conservative—were beginning to take more chances. As for the genteel critics, by 1920 they were fighting rearguard actions to protect their line of retreat. When Lewis renewed the battle ten years later, he was vastly overestimating the strength of his surviving enemies, so that an element of farce was mingled with the drama of his Stockholm address. For the truth was that Dr. Henry Van Dyke had lost his influence except with elderly grade-school teachers and with low-church Episcopalian rectors in the suburbs. The truth was that the whole decade of the 1920's had been dominated by the nongenteel, non-Anglican, nonidealistic writers. And the Swedish Academy, by deciding to honor a member of the group, had raised it to the highest point it would ever reach, to a mild and general apotheosis.

4.

Lewis's address might have received still more attention in the press, but that month it had to compete for attention with events of a different sort. On December 11, 1930, the day after the ceremony in Stockholm, the Bank of United States closed its doors. It had fifty-nine branches, all in New York City, and four hundred thousand depositors, and its failure was the biggest so far in a series of bankruptcies that threatened the entire banking system. The country was entering the second year of the depression. The number of unemployed was not accurately known, but was rising from week to week; by December it must have been six or seven million. Nobody felt sure of his business or his farm or his pay envelope for

Saturday after next. In the midst of the general uneasiness new political currents were swirling; the Democrats had won their first majority in Congress since 1916; the Communists were attracting their first disciples since 1920. There were new literary currents too; people were revising their attitudes toward reading and writing along with everything else. Many established writers of the 1920's were about to lose their public and lapse into silence, or into the *Saturday Evening Post,* or else to deny their past and set out in a variety of new directions.

The years since then have given us perspective enough to revalue the whole school that Sinclair Lewis was representing and glorifying at Stockholm. It would be easy to condemn these writers as a group, and the fact is that they have already been sentenced and mass-executed a dozen times. But they have clearly done too much to merit that quick treatment. They established—or, if we remember Concord, they reëstablished—the profession of letters in America. They made it possible for young Americans to write without a side-glance at London or Oxford, to speak in their own language about everyday matters, to be accurate, coarse, even bawdy, without too much fear of having their books suppressed—or stored in a publisher's cellar like *Sister Carrie*—because they were thought to contain an objectionable situation.

[1937]

DREISER:
SISTER CARRIE'S BROTHER

When he finished *Sister Carrie*, his first novel, Theodore Dreiser was a big, shambling youngster of twenty-nine with an advancing nose, a retreating chin, and a nature full of discordancies. He was dreamy but practical, rash but timid, persistent in his aims but given to fits of elation or dejection. His manners must have been frightful, in spite of the hours he had spent in his boyhood poring over *Hill's Manual of Etiquette*. He was full of understanding and sympathy for the weakness of others, including drunkards, wastrels, and criminals, but often he failed to show generosity toward those he regarded as rivals, with the result that his career was full of sudden friendships and estrangements.

He was an appealing young man in many ways and yet, on the basis of what he afterwards wrote about himself, he could hardly be called an admirable character. He was possessed by cheap ambitions; his early picture of the good life was to own what he called "a lovely home," with cast-iron deer on the lawn; to drive behind "a pair of prancing bays," and to spend his evenings in "a truly swell saloon," with actors, song writers, and Tammany politicians, amid "the laughter, the jesting, the expectorating, and back-slapping geniality." His taste was worse than untrained; it was actively bad except in fiction, and when he was offered the choice between two words, two paintings, two songs, or two pieces of furniture, he took the one that looked or sounded more expensive. In his "affectional relations," as he called them, he was a "varietist," to use his expensive word for a woman-chaser; and he makes it clear that he treated some women abominably after he caught them. If the character of Eugene Witla in *The "Genius"* is a self-portrait, as it seems to be, then his neighbors must have said rightly that his first wife was a saint to put up with him.

Yet Dreiser painted the portrait knowing that it would be

recognized; and in other books he described his transgressions in the first person. Once in his life he stole money; he needed a new overcoat and held out twenty-five dollars from his weekly collections for a Chicago furniture house. That petty crime must have been the hardest to confess to his reader, but he told the story in all its details, including his terror and shame when the theft was discovered. In writing of himself or his background he had a massive honesty that was less a moral than a physiological quality. It was his whole organism, not his conscious mind or his moral code, that made him incapable of any but minor falsehoods. Several times he tried writing false stories for money, but the words wouldn't come; and later in his career he found it physically impossible to finish some of the novels he had started, if their plots took a turn that seemed alien to his experience. He wasn't satisfied with easy answers. "Chronically nebulous, doubting, uncertain," he says of himself, "I stared and stared at everything, only wondering, not solving." It would take him thirty years to find—in his own life—the right ending for his last novel, *The Bulwark*.

There were always persons who believed in him and came to his help at critical points in his career. There was his mother first of all, a woman who could read a little, but couldn't sign her name until Dorsch, as she called him, and his youngest sister learned to write in the second grade of a German-language parochial school; they taught her to form the letters. But the mother understood her Dorsch sympathetically; and later when he confided to her that he wanted to be a writer more than anything else in the world, she made her painful little sacrifices so that he could read and study. Then there was the teacher at the Warsaw, Indiana, high school who was so impressed by this earnest and fumbling student that later she rescued him from his underpaid work at the warehouse in Chicago where he was showing symptoms of tuberculosis; she arranged to have him admitted to the University of Indiana and paid most of his expenses for his one college year out of her slender purse.

There was a copyreader on the Chicago *Globe*, a quietly raging cynic who took a fancy to Dreiser, insisted that he be hired, and taught him to write signed stories. There were various newspaper editors, including Joseph B. McCullagh of the St. Louis *Globe-Democrat*, who trained him and pushed him ahead. There was Arthur Henry, formerly of the Toledo *Blade*, who encouraged him to write *Sister Carrie*; the writing faltered and stopped for two months when Henry went away, then started again when Henry returned, read the early chapters and said, yes, it was going fine. There was most of all his brother Paul, who helped him in his recurrent fits of depression; he would go searching for Theodore, find him hiding in a cheap lodging house, force money on him, and invent a job that he could fill. Then, in later years, there were all the publishers (including Horace Liveright) who offered him large sums in the form of advances against royalties on novels that in most cases were never written; who gave him the money as a business venture, partly, but also as a token of respect for the work he had done.

Largely as a result of the interventions that saved him time and again, Dreiser came to have a mystical faith in his star. What he said of Eugene Witla might have been applied to himself: "All his life he had fancied that he was leading a more or less fated life, principally more. He had thought that his art was a gift, that he had in a way been sent to revolutionize art in America, or carry it one step forward." It was, however, only during his periods of elation that Dreiser regarded himself as a favored ambassador of fate. When he became dejected, "he fancied," as Dreiser said of Witla and presumably of himself, that "he might be the sport or toy of untoward and malicious powers, such as those which surrounded and accomplished Macbeth's tragic end, and which might be intending to make an illustration of him." Hurstwood, in *Sister Carrie*, was such an "illustration"; his story was based on Dreiser's fancies of sinking into the depths. Cowperwood, the financier of a later trilogy, was Dreiser riding the storm and battling among the Titans.

Believing himself to be a marked man, he displayed a curious self-confidence. James Oppenheim wrote a poem about the time when he and Dreiser watched an amazing sunset over the Hudson. "Could you describe that, Dreiser?" he asked. "Yes, that or anything," was the answer. Dreiser could describe anything, from the stupid to the sublime, because in a sense he could describe nothing; he never learned to look for the exact phrase. One sometimes feels that he would have been a great philosopher if he had acquired the art of thinking systematically, instead of merely brooding over ideas, and a great writer if he had ever learned to write. Or might one call him a great inarticulate writer? There are moments when Dreiser's awkwardness in handling words contributes to the force of his novels, since he seems to be groping in them for something on a deeper level than language; there are crises when he stutters in trite phrases that are like incoherent cries.

His memoirs make it clear that what he respected in himself was the intensity of his emotions and his sense of what he calls, in another trite phrase, "the mystery and terror and wonder of life." He often heard voices. One of them—it was the voice of Chicago—spoke to him in his youth, and later he transcribed its words into a sort of elemental poetry. "I am the pulsing urge of the universe," it said to him. "All that life or hope is or can be or do, this I am, and it is here before you! Take of it! Live, live, satisfy your heart!"

A phrase often applied to Dreiser by others is "standing alone" or "marching alone." "It was Dreiser standing alone who won the battle against the censors," I heard a publisher say. In his Nobel Prize address, Sinclair Lewis told the Swedish Academy that Dreiser "more than any other man, marching alone, usually unappreciated, often hated, has cleared the trail from Victorian and Howellsian timidity and gentility in American fiction to honesty and boldness and passion of life." Although Dreiser deserved the tribute, its phrasing was inaccurate. He marched forward and at last won the battle, but he was seldom alone, except in the fits of dejection when he hid away from the world. Even then there was always someone who sought him out, gave him money or encouragement, and insisted that he go back to writing. Indeed, these helpers appeared so often at critical moments that one is tempted, like Dreiser himself, to regard them as emissaries of the powers that watched over him.

There were, however, less supernatural reasons for the support he received, and they also help to explain the abuse and hatred that made it necessary. In those days a new social class was appearing in the larger American cities. It consisted of young, ambitious, yearning, rootless men, chiefly from the Middle West, who were indifferent to the past and felt that their aspirations had never been portrayed in American literature. They knew that Dreiser was one of them, in his faults as well as his virtues, and they sensed that he would be loyal to his class. It was class loyalty that they expected of him, not personal gratitude. If he wrote great novels, they would not deal with foreigners and aristocrats, or with bygone days, and they would not be written politely for women and preachers. Instead the books would describe persons like those who helped him, like his brothers and sisters, his teachers, his newspaper friends, and his publishers, who would be appearing for the first time in serious fiction. It was the new men who recognized his integrity and chose him—elected him, one might say—to be their literary representative.

The post was dangerous. Later, when he fought their battles, Dreiser would be exposed to attacks from all those who disliked the vulgarity and what seemed to be the dubious moral standards of the new class from which he came. Instead of "marching alone," he would stand in a double relationship to American society: he would be the spokesman for one group and the scapegoat of others.

2.

In the summer of 1900 Dreiser joined forces with Frank Norris for a battle against the genteel tradition in American letters. Norris was then thirty years old, was newly married, and was working hard to finish his biggest novel, *The Octopus*. Meanwhile he was supporting himself by reading manuscripts for the new publishing house of Doubleday, Page and Company, which had issued his *McTeague* the year before. One of the manuscripts he carried home was that of a first novel called *Sister Carrie*. "I have found a masterpiece," he said to his first caller in the office one morning. "The man's name is Theodore Dreiser."

"I know him," the caller interrupted.

"Then tell him what I think of it. It's a wonder. I'm writing him to call."

A few weeks earlier Dreiser had found a masterpiece too. He had read *McTeague* and had been excited to learn that another novelist was trying to present an unretouched picture of American life. When he went to see Norris in the Doubleday office, he found that they were almost of an age—Norris was one year older—and that they shared the same literary convictions. There was, however, an essential difference between them. Norris had reached the convictions by an intellectual process, largely as a result of reading Zola and deciding that Zola's methods could be applied to American material. Dreiser insists that he hadn't read Zola when he wrote his first novel. He had become a Naturalist almost without premeditation, as a result of everything his life had been or had lacked. Unlike Norris he couldn't choose among different theories or move from the drably pitiful to the boisterous to the sentimental. He wrote what he did because he had to write only that or keep silent.

It was his friend Arthur Henry who first persuaded him to write fiction. They used to work at the same table, encouraging each other, and they each finished five or six stories. Dreiser's stories were accepted, not by genteel magazines like the *Century* and *Scribner's*, but by the new ten- and fifteen-cent monthlies that were less concerned with ideality and good manners. Henry then insisted that he write a novel. Dreiser protested that he couldn't afford the time, that he was too busy earning a living, that no novel of his would be published—and besides, he didn't have a plot; but still he kept pleasantly brooding over the notion. One day in October 1899, he found himself writing two words on a clean sheet of paper: "Sister Carrie."

"My mind was a blank except for the name," he told his first biographer, Dorothy Dudley. "I had no idea who or what she was to be." Then suddenly he pictured Carrie Meeber on the train to Chicago; it was a vision that came to him, he said, "as if out of a dream." But the dream was also a memory, for much of his own life went into the novel. In one sense Carrie was Dreiser himself, just as Flaubert once said that *he* was Mme. Bovary; the little Midwestern girl had Dreiser's mixture of passivity and ambition, as well as his romantic love for cities. More definitely she resembled one of his sisters, the one who ran off to Chicago, met a successful business man, the father of two or three grown children—like Hurstwood in the novel—and eloped with him to New York. Hurstwood's degradation after losing Carrie was another memory, connected with Dreiser's misfortunes in 1895, after he lost his job on the New York *World*. Unable to find other work, he had lived in cheap lodging houses and—before he was rescued by his brother Paul—had pictured himself as sinking toward squalor and suicide. But there was more of Dreiser in the book than simply the two chief characters: there was his obsessive fear of poverty, there was his passion for gaslight and glitter, and there was his hatred for the conventional standards by which his big family of brothers and sisters had been judged and condemned. Most of all there was his feeling for life, his wonder at the mysterious fall and rise of human fortunes.

Sister Carrie had the appearance of being a Naturalistic novel and would be used as a model for the work of later Naturalists. Yet it was, in a sense, Naturalistic by default, Naturalistic because Dreiser was writing about the life he knew best in the only style he had learned. There is a personal and compulsive quality in the novel that is not at all Naturalistic. The book is felt rather than observed from the outside, like *McTeague*; and it is based on dreams rather than documents. Where *McTeague* had been a conducted tour of the depths, *Sister Carrie* was a cry from the depths, as if McTeague had uttered it.

It was a more frightening book to genteel readers than *McTeague* had been. They were repelled not only by the cheapness of the characters but even more by the fact that the author admired them. They read that Hurstwood, for example, was the manager of "a gorgeous saloon . . . with rich screens, fancy wines and a line of bar goods unsurpassed in the country." They found him an unctuous and offensive person, yet they also found that Dreiser described him as "altogether a very acceptable individual of our great American upper class—the first grade below the luxuriously rich." Genteel readers didn't know whether to be more offended by the judgment or by the language in which it was expressed; and they felt, moreover, that Hurstwood and his creator belonged to a new class that threatened the older American culture. Most of all they resented Carrie Meeber. They had been taught that a woman's virtue is her only jewel, that the wages of sin are death; yet Carrie let herself be seduced without a struggle, yielding first to a traveling salesman, then to Hurstwood; and instead of dying in misery she became a famous actress. *McTeague* had offended the proprieties while respecting moral principles; every misdeed it mentioned had been punished in the end. *Sister Carrie*, on the other hand, was a direct affront to the standards by which respectable Americans had always claimed to live.

*   *   *

The battle over Carrie started even before the book was published. Dreiser had first given the manuscript to Henry Mills Alden, the editor of *Harper's Magazine*, who had already bought some of his articles. Alden said he liked the novel, but he doubted that any publisher would take it. He turned it over to the editorial readers for Harper and Brothers, who sent it back to the author without comment. Next the manuscript went to Doubleday, Page and Company, where it had the good fortune to be assigned to the man who could best appreciate what Dreiser was trying to do. "It *must* be published," Norris kept repeating to anyone who would listen. His enthusiasm for *Sister Carrie* won over two of the junior partners, Henry Lanier and Walter Hines Page; and with some misgiving they signed a contract to bring it out that fall. Then Frank Doubleday, the senior partner, came back from Europe and carried the proof sheets home with him to read over the weekend. Mrs. Doubleday read them too, and liked them not at all, but her part in the story is not essential. Her husband could and did form his own opinion of *Sister Carrie*. He detested the book and wanted nothing to do with it as a publisher.

There has been a prolonged argument over what happened afterwards, but chiefly it is an argument over words like "suppression"; most of the facts are on record. Doubleday spoke to his junior partners, who had great respect for his business judgment, and they summoned Dreiser to a conference. Norris managed to see him first. "Whatever happens," he said in effect, "make them publish *Sister Carrie*; it's your right." Dreiser then conferred with the junior partners, who tried to persuade him to surrender his contract. "Crushed and tragically pathetic," as Lanier remembers him, he kept insisting that the contract be observed.

It was a binding document and it *was* observed, to the letter. *Sister Carrie* was printed, if only in an edition of roughly a thousand copies. It was bound, if in cheap red cloth with dull black lettering. It was listed in the Doubleday catalogue. It was even submitted to the press for review, if only, in most cases, through the intervention of Frank Norris. When orders came in for it, they were filled. It wasn't "suppressed" or "buried away in a cellar," as Dreiser's friends afterwards complained, but neither was it displayed or advertised or urged on the booksellers. I think it was in the travels of Ibn Batuta that I read the account of some Buddhist fishermen whose religion forbade them to deprive any creature of life, even a sardine. Instead of killing fishes they merely caught them in nets and left them to live as best they could out of water. That is about what happened to *Sister Carrie*, which wasn't, incidentally, the first or the last book to receive such treatment from publishing houses that changed their collective minds. One couldn't quite say that it was killed; it was merely deprived of light and air and left to die.

Favorable reviews might have rescued it, but with two or three exceptions the reviews were violently adverse and even insulting. "The story leaves a very unpleasant impression," said the Minneapolis *Journal*. "You would never dream of recommending to another person to read it," said the *Post-Intelligencer* in Seattle. *Life*, the humorous weekly, was serious about Carrie and warned the girls who might think of following in her footsteps that they would "end their days on the Island or in the gutter." *Sister Carrie*, said the Chicago *Tribune*, "transgresses the literary morality of the average American novel to a point that is almost Zolaesque." The *Book Buyer* accused Dreiser of being "the chronicler of materialism in its basest forms. . . . But the leaven of the higher life remains," it added, "nowhere stronger than with us."

The book-buying public, most of which yearned for the leaven of the higher life, had no quarrel with the reviewers. The Doubleday records show that 1,008 copies of the book were bound, that 129 were sent out for review, and that only 465 were sold. After five years the other 423 copies, with the plates from which they had been printed, were turned over to a firm that specialized in publishers' remainders. That was the end of the story for Doubleday, but not for Dreiser. As soon as he could scrape together five hundred dollars, he bought the plates of his own novel. He succeeded in having it reprinted by the B. W. Dodge Company in 1907 and by Grosset and Dunlap in 1908. Later it would be reissued in successively larger editions by three other publishers—in 1911 by Harper and Brothers, the firm that had first rejected it, then in 1917 by Boni and Liveright, and in 1932 by the Modern Library—and it would also be translated into most of the European languages. For Dreiser the battle over *Sister Carrie* lasted for more than a quarter-century and ended with his triumph over the genteel critics.

Yet the first years were full of disasters, in spite of the help that Dreiser and his book received from Frank Norris. One English publisher remembered Norris as a man who was "more eager for Dreiser's *Carrie* to be read than for his own novels." Besides trying to get American reviews for the book, Norris kept writing about it to England. A London edition of *Sister Carrie* appeared in 1901 and was enthusiastically praised. "At last a really strong novel has come from America," exclaimed the *Daily Mail*; and there were echoes of the judgment in other English papers.

There was a different sort of echo in New York, a buzz of angry gossip about English critics and their fantastic notions of American fiction. Without the London edition, *Sister Carrie* might have been forgotten for years, but now it was arousing a quiet wave of condemnation among persons who had never seen a copy of the novel. Dreiser found that magazine editors were suddenly uninterested in his articles and stories, which had once been widely published; the new ones were coming back with rejection slips. One editor said, "You are a disgrace to America." The *Atlantic Monthly* wrote him that he was "morally bankrupt" and could not publish there. At the office of *Harper's Monthly* Dreiser happened to meet William Dean Howells, who had always been friendly since the day when Dreiser had interviewed him for another magazine. This time Howells was cold. "You know, I don't like *Sister Carrie*," he said as he hurried away. It was the first occasion on which he had failed to support a new work of honest American fiction.

In 1900 Howells had surrendered to the trend of the times. The great house of Harper, which had dominated American publishing, went bankrupt in that year, and Howells feared that he had lost his principal source of income. But the firm was soon reorganized, with new capital furnished through the elder J. P. Morgan and new editors for most of its magazines. Colonel Harvey, the new president, was determined to make the house yield dividends. He had an overnight conference with Howells, asked him to continue writing for *Harper's Magazine* on a yearly salary and told him, incidentally, that the battle for realism was lost.

Howells, who had been battling for realism since 1885, sadly agreed with Colonel Harvey. Whatever fire there had been in his critical writing was also lost after 1900, though perhaps that was merely because he was growing old. He still had his style, which was better than that of any other living American writer except Mark Twain. He had his almost official position as dean of American letters, but he was no longer the friend and patron of young writers in revolt.

The failure of *Sister Carrie* in its first edition was part of a general disaster that involved the whole literary movement of the 1890's. One after another the leaders of the movement had died young or else had surrendered to genteel conservatism. The first of them to go was the novelist H. H. Boyesen, a pioneer of social realism and once a famous figure, although his name is seldom mentioned now except in literature courses; Boyesen died in 1895. Next to go, in 1898, was Harold Frederic, the peppery rebel from upstate New York, who, in *The Damnation of Theron Ware*, had written the first American novel that questioned the virtue of the Protestant clergy. Stephen Crane, the one genius of the group, died in 1900, the victim of consumption, malaria, hard work, and hard living.

The dramatist James A. Herne had tried and failed to be the American Ibsen; but at least he had written the immensely popular *Shore Acres* and other plays that introduced daily American life to the American stage. He died in 1901, worn out and discouraged after the presidential campaign of the preceding year, in which he had fought for Bryan and against the annexation of the Philippines. Then Norris died in the autumn of 1902, at the beginning, so it seemed, of a grandly successful career; but he had already given signs, in *The Pit*, of abandoning his Naturalistic doctrines.

All these, except Herne, were comparatively young men and there were very few left to carry on the literary movement they had started. Hamlin Garland, after fulminating against the conservatives in art and politics, had gone over to the enemy by easy stages. Editors had taken him out to dinner and convinced him that his passion for reform was weakening his novels as works of art. Unfortunately Garland was no artist; when he lost his crusading passion he lost everything. Henry B. Fuller, the Chicago realist, remained faithful to his own standards; but his novels hadn't sold and he wrote very little for a dozen years after 1900. It was not only the rebel authors, almost all of them, who had died or fallen silent or surrendered. The little magazines that flourished in New York, Chicago, and San Francisco during the 1890's had also disappeared and the new publishing houses had become conventional or had gone out of business. Serious writing on American themes declined into a sort of subterranean existence. Speaking generally, the best American books of the following decade would either be privately printed, like *The Education of Henry Adams*, or else they would be written in Europe.

Meanwhile Dreiser himself had narrowly escaped the fate of his brothers in arms. After *Sister Carrie* was accepted, he had begun working simultaneously on two other novels, in a frenzy of production, but slowly he had been overcome by the feeling that he was unwanted and a failure. He had destroyed one of his two manuscripts, put the other aside, sent his wife to her family in Missouri, and retired to a furnished room in Brooklyn, where he sat day after day brooding over the aimlessness of life and trying to gather enough courage to commit suicide. This time again he was rescued by his brother Paul, who gave him new clothes and sent him to a sanitarium. After his recovery he became a magazine editor and climbed rapidly in his profession, until, as head of the Butterick publications, he was earning twenty-five thousand dollars a year. It was a long time, however, before he felt strength enough in himself to write another novel.

The story of *Sister Carrie* had a curious sequel. Imperceptibly the standards of the American public had been changing in the years after 1900 and Dreiser himself had been gaining a sort of underground reputation based on his one book. When his second novel, *Jennie Gerhardt*, appeared in 1911 it was a critical and even to some extent a popular success. The struggle for Naturalism came into the open again. Dreiser had new allies in the younger writers, and by 1920 they had ceased to be rebels; instead they were the dominant faction. It was a long and finally a triumphant chapter in the history of American letters that began with the lost battle over *Sister Carrie*.

[1947]

Rereading Sherwood Anderson after many years, one feels again that his work is desperately uneven, but one is gratified to find that the best of it is as new and springlike as ever. There are many authors younger in years—he was born in 1876—who made a great noise in their time, but whose books already belong among the horseless carriages in Henry Ford's museum at Greenfield Village. Anderson made a great noise too, when he published *Winesburg, Ohio* in 1919. The older critics scolded him, the younger ones praised him as a man of the changing hour, yet he managed in that early work and others to be relatively timeless. There are moments in American life to which he gave not only the first but the final expression.

He soon became a writer's writer, the only storyteller of his generation who left his mark on the style and vision of the generation that followed. Hemingway, Faulkner, Wolfe, Steinbeck, Caldwell, Saroyan, Henry Miller . . . each of these owes an unmistakable debt to Anderson, and their names might stand for dozens of others. Hemingway was regarded as his disciple in 1920, when both men were living on the Near North Side of Chicago. Faulkner says that he had written very little, "poems and just amateur things," before meeting Anderson in 1925 and becoming, for a time, his inseparable companion. Looking at Anderson he thought to himself, "Being a writer must be a wonderful life." He set to work on his first novel, *Soldier's Pay,* for which Anderson found a publisher after the two men had ceased to be friends. Thomas Wolfe proclaimed in 1936 that Anderson was "the only man in America who ever taught me anything"; but they quarreled a year later, and Wolfe shouted that Anderson had shot his bolt, that he was done as a writer. All the disciples left him sooner or later, so that his influence was chiefly on their early work; but still it was decisive. He opened doors for all of them and gave them faith in themselves. With Whitman he might have said:

> *I am the teacher of athletes,*
> *He that by me spreads a wider breast than my own proves*
>   *the width of my own,*
> *He most honors my style who learns under it to destroy*
>   *the teacher.*

As the disciples were doing, most of Anderson's readers deserted him during the 1930's. He had been a fairly popular writer for a few years after *Dark Laughter* (1925), but his last stories and sketches, including some of his best, had to appear in a strange collection of second-line magazines, pamphlets, and Sunday supplements. One marvelous story called "Daughters" remained in manuscript until six years after his death in 1941. I suspect that the public would have liked him better if he had been primarily a novelist, like Dreiser and Lewis. He did publish seven novels, from *Windy McPherson's Son* in 1916 to *Kit Brandon* in 1936, not to mention the others he started and laid aside. Among the seven *Dark Laughter* was his only best seller, and *Poor White* (1920), the best of the lot, is studied in colleges as a picture of the industrial revolution in a small Midwestern town. There is, however, not one of the seven that is truly effective as a novel; not one that has balance and sustained force; not one that doesn't break apart into episodes or nebulize into a vague emotion.

His three personal narratives—*A Story-Teller's Story* (1924), *Tar: A Midwest Childhood* (1926), and *Sherwood Anderson's Memoirs* (1942)—are entertainingly inaccurate; indeed, they are almost as fictional as the novels, and quite as deficient in structure. They reveal that an element was missing in his mature life, rich as this was in other respects. They do not give us—and I doubt whether Anderson himself possessed—the sense of moving ahead in a definite direction. All the drama of growth was confined to his early years. After finding his proper voice at the age of forty, Anderson didn't change as much as other serious writers; perhaps his steadfastness should make us thankful, considering that most Americans change for the worse. He had achieved a quality of emotional rather than factual truth and he preserved it to the end of his career, while doing little to refine, transform, or even understand it. Some of his last stories—by no means all of them—are richer and subtler than the early ones, but they are otherwise not much different or much better.

He was a writer who depended on inspiration, which is to say that he depended on feelings so deeply embedded in his personality that he was unable to direct them. He couldn't say to himself, "I shall produce such and such an effect in a book of such and such a length"; the book had to write or rather speak itself while Anderson listened as if to an inner voice. In his business life he showed a surprising talent for planning and manipulation. "One thing I've known always, instinctively," he told Floyd Dell, "—that's how to handle people, make them do as I please, be what I wanted them to be. I was in business for a long time and the truth is I was a smooth son of a bitch." He never learned to handle words in that smooth fashion. Writing was an activity he assigned to a different level of himself, the one on which he was emotional and unpractical. To reach that level sometimes required a sustained effort of the will. He might start a story like a man running hard to catch a train, but once it was caught he could settle back and let himself be carried—often to the wrong destination.

He knew instinctively whether one of his stories was right or wrong, but he didn't always know why. He could do what writers call "pencil work" on his manuscripts, changing a word here and there, but he couldn't tighten the plot, delete weak passages, sharpen the dialogue, or give a twist to the ending; if he wanted to improve his story, he had to wait for a return of the mood that had produced it, then write it over from beginning to end. There were stories like "Death in the Woods" that he rewrote a dozen times, at intervals of years, before he found what he thought was the right way of telling them. Sometimes, in different books, he published two or three versions of the same story, so that we can see how it grew in his subconscious mind. One characteristic of the subconscious is a defective sense of time: in dreams the old man sees himself as a boy, and the events of thirty or forty years may be jumbled together. Time as a logical succession of events was Anderson's greatest difficulty in writing novels or even long stories. He got his tenses confused and carried his heroes ten years forward or back in a single paragraph. His instinct was to present everything together, as in a dream.

When giving a lecture on "A Writer's Conception of Realism," he spoke of a half-dream that he had "over and over." "If I have been working intensely," he said, "I find myself unable to relax when I go to bed. Often I fall into a half-dream state and when I do, the faces of people begin to appear before me. They seem to snap into place before my eyes, stay there, sometimes for a short period, sometimes longer. There are smiling faces, leering ugly faces, tired faces, hopeful faces. . . . I have a kind of illusion about this matter," he continued. "It is, no doubt, due to a story-teller's point of view. I have the feeling that the faces that appear before me thus at night are those of people who want their stories told and whom I have neglected."

He would have liked to tell the stories of all the faces he had ever seen. He was essentially a storyteller, as he kept insisting, but his art was of a special type, belonging to an oral rather than a written tradition. It used to be the fashion to compare him with Chekhov and say that he had learned his art from the Russians. Anderson insisted that, except for Turgenev, he hadn't read any Russians when the comparisons were being made. Most of his literary masters were English or American: George Borrow, Walt Whitman, Mark Twain (more than he admitted), and Gertrude Stein. D. H. Lawrence was a less fortunate influence, but only on his later work. His earliest and perhaps his principal teacher was his father, "Irve" Anderson, who used to entertain whole barrooms with tales of his impossible adventures in the Civil War. A great many of the son's best stories, too, were told first in saloons. Later he would become what he called "an almighty scribbler" and would travel about the country with dozens of pencils and reams of paper, the tools of his trade. "I am one," he said, "who loves, like a drunkard his drink, the smell of ink, and the sight of a great pile of white paper that may be scrawled upon always gladdens me"; but his earlier impulse had been to speak, not write, his stories. The best of them retain the language, the pace, and one might even say the gestures of a man talking unhurriedly to his friends.

Within the oral tradition, Anderson had his own picture of what a story should be. He was not interested in telling conventional folk tales, those in which events are more important than emotions. American folk tales usually end with a "snapper"—that is, after starting with the plausible, they progress through the barely possible to the flatly incredible, then wait for a laugh. Magazine fiction used to follow—and much of it still does—a pattern leading to a different sort of snapper, one that calls for a gasp of surprise or relief instead of a guffaw. Anderson broke the pattern by writing stories that not only lacked snappers, in most cases, but even had no plots in the usual sense. The tales he told in his Midwestern drawl were not incidents or episodes, they were *moments,* each one of them so timeless that it contained a whole life.

The best of the moments in *Winesburg, Ohio* is called "The Untold Lie." The story, which I have to summarize at the risk of spoiling it, is about two farmhands husking corn in a field at dusk. Ray Pearson is small, serious, and middle-aged, the father of half a dozen thin-legged children; Hal Winters is big and young, with the reputation of being a bad one. Suddenly he says to the older man, "I've got Nell Gunther in trouble. I'm telling you, but keep your mouth shut." He puts his two hands on Ray's shoulders and looks down into his eyes. "Well, old daddy," he says, "come on, advise me. Perhaps you've been in the same fix yourself. I know what everyone would say is the right thing to do, but what do you say?" Then the author steps back to look at his characters. "There they stood," he tells us, "in the big empty field with the quiet corn shocks standing in rows behind them and the red and yellow hills in the distance, and from being just two indifferent workmen they had become all alive to each other."

That single moment of aliveness—that sudden reaching out of two characters through walls of inarticulateness and mis-understanding—is the effect that Anderson is trying to create for his readers or listeners. There is more to the story, of course, but it is chiefly designed to bring the moment into relief. Ray Pearson thinks of his own marriage, to a girl he got into trouble, and turns away from Hal without being able to say the expected words about duty. Later that evening he is seized by a sudden impulse to warn the younger man against being tricked into bondage. He runs awkwardly across the fields, crying out that children are only the accidents of life. Then he meets Hal and stops, unable to repeat the words that he had shouted into the wind. It is Hal who breaks the silence. "I've already made up my mind," he says, taking Ray by the coat and shaking him. "Nell ain't no fool. . . . I want to marry her. I want to settle down and have kids." Both men laugh, as if they had forgotten what happened in the cornfield. Ray walks away into the darkness, thinking pleasantly now of his children and muttering to himself, "It's just as well. Whatever I told him would have been a lie." There has been a moment in the lives of two men. The moment has passed and the briefly established communion has been broken, yet we feel that each man has revealed his essential being. It is as if a gulf had opened in the level Ohio cornfield and as if, for one moment, a light had shone from the depths, illuminating everything that happened or would ever happen to both of them.

That moment of revelation was the story Anderson told over and over, but without exhausting its freshness, for the story had as many variations as there were faces in his dreams. Behind one face was a moment of defiance; behind another, a moment of resignation (as when Alice Hindman forces herself "to face bravely the fact that many people must live and die alone, even in Winesburg"); behind a third face was a moment of self-discovery; behind a fourth was a moment of deliberate self-delusion. This fourth might have been the face of the author's sister, as he describes her in a chapter of *Sherwood Anderson's Memoirs*. Unlike the other girls she had no beau, and so she went walking with her brother Sherwood, pretending that he was someone else. "It's beautiful, isn't it, James?" she said, looking at the wind ripples that passed in the moonlight over a field of ripening wheat. Then she kissed him and whispered, "Do you love me, James?"—and all her loneliness and flight from reality were summed up in those words. Anderson had that gift for summing up, for pouring a lifetime into a moment.

There must have been many such moments of truth in his own life, and there was one in particular that has become an American legend. After serving as a volunteer in the Spanish-American War; after supplementing his one year in high school with a much later year at Wittenberg Academy; and after becoming a locally famous copywriter in a Chicago advertising agency, Anderson had launched into business for himself; by the age of thirty-six he had been for some years the chief owner and general manager of a paint factory in Elyria, Ohio. The factory had prospered for a time, chiefly because of Anderson's talent for writing persuasive circulars, and he sometimes had visions of becoming a paint baron or a duke of industry. He had other visions too, of being sentenced to serve out his life as a businessman. At the time he was already writing novels—in fact he had four of them under way—and he began to feel that his advertising circulars were insulting to the dignity of words. "The impression got abroad—I perhaps encouraged it," Anderson says, "—that I was overworking, was on the point of a nervous breakdown. . . . The thought occurred to me that if men thought me a little insane they would forgive me if I lit out, left the business in which they invested their money on their hands." Then came the moment to which he would always return in his memoirs and in his fiction. He was dictating a letter: "The goods about which you have inquired are the best of their kind made in the—" when suddenly he stopped without completing the phrase. He looked at his secretary for a long time, and she looked at him until they both grew pale. Then he said with the American laugh that covers all sorts of meanings, "I have been wading in a long river and my feet are wet." He went out of the office for the last time and started walking eastward toward Cleveland along a railroad track. "There were," he says, "five or six dollars in my pocket."

So far I have been paraphrasing Anderson's account—or two of his many accounts, for he kept changing them—of an incident that his biographers have reconstructed from other sources. Those others give a different picture of what happened at the paint factory on November 27, 1912. Anderson had been struggling under an accumulation of marital, artistic, and business worries. Instead of pretending to be a little crazy so that investors would forgive him for losing their money, he was actually—so the medical records show—on the brink of nervous collapse. Instead of making a conscious decision to abandon his wife, his three children, and his business career, he acted as if in a trance. There was truly a decision, but it was made by something deeper than his conscious will; one feels that his whole being, psyche and soma together, was rejecting the life of a harried businessman. He had made no plans, however, for leading a different life. After four days of aimless wandering, he was recognized in Cleveland and taken to a hospital, where he was found to be suffering from exhaustion and aphasia.

Much later, in telling the story time after time, Anderson forgot or concealed the painful details of his flight and presented it as a pattern of conduct for others to follow. What we need in America, he liked to say, is a new class of individuals who, "at any physical cost to themselves and others"—Anderson must have been thinking of his first wife—will "agree to quit working, to loaf, to refuse to be hurried or try to get on in the world." In the next generation there would be hundreds of young men, readers of Anderson, who rejected the dream of financial success and tried to live as artists and individuals. For them Anderson's flight from the paint factory became a heroic exploit, as memorable as the choice made by Ibsen's Nora when she walked out of her doll's house and slammed the door. For Anderson himself when writing his memoirs, it was the central moment of his career.

Yet the real effect of the moment on his personal life was less drastic or immediate than one would guess from the compulsive fashion in which he kept writing about it. He didn't continue wandering from city to city, trading his tales for bread and preaching against success. After being released from the hospital, he went back to Elyria, wound up his business affairs, then took the train for Chicago, where he talked himself into a job with the same advertising agency that had employed him before he went into business for himself. As soon as he had the job, he sent for his wife and children. He continued to write persuasive circulars—corrupting the language, as he said—and worked on his novels and stories chiefly at night, as he had done while running a factory. It would be nearly two years before he separated from his first wife. It would be ten years before he left the advertising business to support himself entirely by writing, and then the change would result from a gradual process of getting published and finding readers, instead of being the sequel to a moment of truth.

Those moments at the center of Anderson's often marvelous stories were moments, in general, without a sequel; they existed separately and timelessly. That explains why he couldn't write novels and why, with a single exception, he never even wrote a book in the strict sense of the word. A book should have a structure and a development, whereas for Anderson there was chiefly the blinding flash that revealed a life without changing it.

The one exception, of course, is *Winesburg, Ohio,* and that became a true book for several reasons: because it was conceived as a whole, because Anderson had found a subject that released his buried emotions, and because most of the book was written in what was almost a single burst of inspiration, so that it gathered force as it went along. It was started in the late autumn of 1915, when he was living alone in a rooming house at 735 Cass Street, on the Near North Side of Chicago, and working as always at the Critchfield Agency. Earlier that year he had read two books that impressed him deeply: *Spoon River Anthology,* by Edgar Lee Masters, and *Three Lives,* the early volume of stories by Gertrude Stein. The first may have suggested the possibility of writing about the buried selves of people in another Midwestern town, while the other pointed the way toward a simpler and more repetitive style, closer to the rhythms of American speech, than that of Anderson's first novels, *Windy McPherson's Son* and *Marching Men.* Both of these had recently been accepted for publication, but he did not feel that he had really expressed himself in either book. Then came another of those incandescent moments that seemed to reveal his inner self. Twenty years later he described the moment in a letter, probably changing the facts, as he had a weakness for doing, but remembering how he felt:

> I think the most absorbingly interesting and exciting moment in any writer's life must come at the moment when he, for the first time, knows that he is a real writer. . . . I remember mine. I walked along a city street in the snow. I was working at work I hated. Already I had written several long novels. They were not really mine. I was ill, discouraged, broke. I was living in a cheap rooming house. I remember that I went upstairs and into the room. It was very shabby. I had no relatives in the city and few enough friends. I remember how cold the room was. On that afternoon I had heard that I was to lose my job.
>
> . . . There was some paper on a small kitchen table I had bought and brought up into the room. I turned on a light and began to write. I wrote, without looking up—I never changed a word of it afterwards—a story called "Hands." It was and is a very beautiful story.
>
> I wrote the story and then got up from the table at which I had been sitting, I do not know how long, and went down into the city street. I thought that the snow had suddenly made the

city very beautiful. . . . It must have been several hours before I got the courage to return to my room and read my own story.

It was all right. It was sound. It was real. I went to sit by my desk. A great many others have had such moments. I wonder what they did. For the moment I thought the world was wonderful, and I thought also that there was a great deal of wonder in me.

"Hands" is still sound and real; as Henry James said of *The Scarlet Letter,* "it has about it that charm, very hard to express, which we find in an artist's work the first time he has touched his highest mark." It was, however, the second of the Winesburg stories to be written, since the first was "The Book of the Grotesque," which serves as a general prologue. "Paper Pills" was the third, and the others followed in roughly the same order in which they appear in the book. All the stories were written rapidly, often like "Hands" in a single night, each of them being, as Anderson said, "an idea grasped whole as one would pick an apple in an orchard." He was dealing with material that was both fresh and familiar. The town of Winesburg was based on his memories of Clyde, Ohio, where he had spent most of his boyhood and where his mother had died at the same age as Elizabeth Willard. The hero, George Willard, was the author in his late adolescence, and the other characters were either remembered from Clyde or else, in many cases, suggested by faces glimpsed in the Chicago streets. Each face revealed a moment, a mood, or a secret that lay deep in Anderson's life and for which he was finding the right words at last.

As the book went forward, more and more names and places were carried from one story or chapter to another, so that Winesburg itself acquired a sort of corporate being. Counting the four parts of "Godliness," each complete in itself, there would be twenty-five stories in all. None of them taken separately—not even "Hands" or "The Untold Lie"— is as effective as the best of Anderson's later work, but each of them contributes to all the others, as the stories in later volumes are not expected to do. There was a delay of some months before the last chapters—"Death," "Sophistication," and "Departure"—were written with the obvious intention of rounding out the book. It is a function they effectively perform: first George Willard is released from Winesburg by the death of his mother, then he learns how it feels to be a grown man, then he leaves for the city on the early-morning train, and everything recedes as into a framed picture. "When he aroused himself and looked out of the car window the town of Winesburg had disappeared and his life there had become but a background on which to paint the dreams of his manhood."

In structure the book lies midway between the novel proper and the mere collection of stories. Like several famous books by more recent authors, all early readers of Anderson—like Faulkner's *The Unvanquished* and *Go Down, Moses,* like Steinbeck's *The Postures of Heaven,* like Caldwell's *Georgia Boy*—it is a cycle of stories held together by their background, their prevailing mood, and their central character, but also by an underlying plot that is advanced or in some way enriched by each story. One might summarize the plot of *Winesburg* by saying that it deals with persons who have been distorted not, as Anderson tells us in his prologue, by their having seized upon a single truth, but rather by their inability to express themselves. Since they cannot truly communicate with others, they have become emotional cripples. Most of the grotesques are attracted one by one to George Willard; they feel that he might help them. In those moments of truth that Anderson loves to describe, they try to explain themselves to George, believing that he alone in Winesburg has an instinct for finding the right words and using them honestly. They urge him to preserve and develop his gifts. "You must not become a mere peddler of words," Kate Swift the teacher insists, taking hold of his shoulders. "The thing to learn is to know what people are thinking about, not what they say." Dr. Parcival tells him, "If something happens perhaps you will be able to write the book I may never get written." All the grotesques hope that George Willard will some day speak what is in their hearts and thus reestablish their connection with mankind. George is too young to understand them at the time, but the book ends with what seems to be the implied promise that he will become the voice of inarticulate men and women in all the forgotten towns. If that is what it truly implies, and if Anderson himself was fulfilling the promise, then *Winesburg, Ohio* is far from the pessimistic or morbidly sexual work it was once attacked for being. Instead it is a work of love, an attempt to break down the walls of loneliness, and, in its own fashion, a celebration of village life in the lost days of innocence.

[1960]

FITZGERALD:
THE ROMANCE OF MONEY

Those who were lucky enough to be born a little before the end of the last century, in any of the years from 1895 to 1900, went through much of their lives with a feeling that the new century was about to be placed in their charge; it was like a business in financial straits that could be rescued by a timely change in management. As Americans and optimists, they believed that the business was fundamentally sound. They identified themselves with the century; its teens were their teens, troubled but confident; its World War, not yet known as the First, was theirs to fight on the winning side; its reckless twenties were their twenties. As they launched into their careers, they looked about for spokesmen, and the first one they found—though soon they would have doubts about him—was F. Scott Fitzgerald.

Among his qualifications for the role was the sort of background that his generation regarded as typical. Scott was a Midwestern boy, born in St. Paul on September 24, 1896, to a family of Irish descent that had some social standing and a very small fortune inherited by the mother. The fortune kept diminishing year by year, and the Fitzgeralds, like all families in their situation, had to think a lot about money. When the only son was eleven they were living in Buffalo, where the father was working for Procter and Gamble. "One afternoon," Fitzgerald told a reporter thirty years later, ". . . the phone rang and my mother answered it. I didn't understand what she said, but I felt that disaster had come to us. My mother, a little while before, had given me a quarter to go swimming. I gave the money back to her. I knew something terrible had happened and I thought she couldn't spare the money now. 'Dear God,' I prayed, 'please don't let us go to the poorhouse.'

"A little later my father came home. I had been right. He had lost his job." More than that, as Fitzgerald said, "He had lost his essential drive, his immaculateness of purpose." The family moved back to St. Paul, where the father worked as a wholesale grocery salesman, earning hardly enough to pay for his desk space. It was help from a pious aunt that enabled Scott to fulfill his early ambition of going to an Eastern preparatory school, then going to Princeton.

In 1917 practically the whole student body went off to war. Fitzgerald went off in style, having received a provisional commission as second lieutenant in the regular army. Before leaving Princeton in November, he ordered his uniform at Brooks Brothers and gave the manuscript of a first novel to his faculty mentor, Christian Gauss, not yet dean of the college, but a most persuasive teacher of European literature. Gauss, honest as always, told him that it wasn't good enough to publish. Not at all discouraged, Fitzgerald reworked it completely, writing twelve hours a day during his weekends at training camp and his first furlough. When the second draft was finished, he sent it to Shane Leslie, the Irish man of letters, who had shown some interest in his work. Leslie spent ten days correcting and punctuating the script, then sent it to Scribners, his own publishers. "Really if Scribner takes it," Fitzgerald said in a letter to Edmund Wilson, "I know I'll wake some morning and find that the debutantes have made me famous overnight. I really believe that no one else could have written so searchingly the story of the youth of our generation."

Scribners sent back the novel, rightly called *The Romantic Egotist,* while expressing some regret, and Maxwell Perkins, who was still too young to be the senior editor, suggested revisions that might make it acceptable. Fitzgerald tried to follow the suggestions and resubmitted the manuscript that summer. In August it was definitely rejected, and Fitzgerald then asked Perkins as a favor to submit it to two other publishers, one radical and one conservative. His letter was dated from Camp Sheridan, in Alabama, where he was soon to be named aide-de-camp to Major General J. A. Ryan. It was at a dance in Montgomery that he fell in love with a judge's daughter, Zelda Sayre, whom he described to his friends as "the most beautiful girl in Alabama *and* Georgia"; one state wasn't big enough to encompass his admiration. "I didn't have the two top things: great animal magnetism or money," he wrote years afterward in his notebook. "I had the two second things, though: good looks and intelligence. So I always got the top girl."

He was engaged to the judge's daughter, but they couldn't marry until he was able to support her. After being discharged from the army—without getting overseas, as I noted—he went to New York and looked for a job. Neither the radical nor the conservative publisher had shown interest in his novel. All his stories were coming back from the magazines, and at one time he had 122 rejection slips pinned in a frieze around his cheap bedroom on Morningside Heights. The job he found was with an advertising agency and his pay started at $90 a month, with not much chance of rapid advancement; the only praise he received was for a slogan written for a steam laundry in Muscatine, Iowa: "We keep you clean in Muscatine." He was trying to save money, but the girl in Alabama saw that the effort was hopeless and broke off the engagement on the score of common sense. Fitzgerald borrowed from his classmates, stayed drunk for three weeks, and then went home to St. Paul to write the novel once again, this time with another ending and a new title, *This Side of Paradise*. Scribners accepted it on that third submission. The book was so different from other novels of the time, Max Perkins wrote him, "that it is hard to prophesy how it will sell, but we are all for taking a chance and supporting it with vigor."

This Side of Paradise, published at the end of March 1920, is a very young man's novel and memory book. The author put into it samples of everything he had written until that time—short stories, essays, poems, prose poems, sketches, and dialogues—and he also put himself into it, after taking a promotion in social rank. The hero, Amory Blaine, instead of being a poor relative has been reared as the heir of millions, but he looks and talks like Fitzgerald, besides reading the same books (listed in one passage after another) and falling in love with the same girls. The story told in the novel, with many digressions, is how Amory struggles for self-knowledge and for less provincial standards than those of the Princeton eating clubs. "I know myself," he says at the end, "but that is all." Fitzgerald passed a final judgment on the novel in 1938, when he said in a letter to Max Perkins, "I think it is now one of the funniest books since *Dorian Gray* in its utter spuriousness—and then, here and there, I find a page that is very real and living."

Some of the living pages are the ones that recount the eating-club elections, the quarrel between Amory and his first flame, Isabelle—Fitzgerald would always be good on quarrels—the courting of Rosalind Connage, and Amory's three-weeks drunk when Rosalind throws him over. Besides having a spurious and imitative side, the novel proved that Fitzgerald had started with gifts of his own, which included an easy narrative style rich with images, a sense of comedy, and a natural ear for dialogue. Its memorable feature, however, was that it announced a change in standards. "Here was a new generation," Fitzgerald or his hero, it isn't clear which, says in the last chapter, "shouting the old cries, learning the old creeds, through a revery of long days and nights; destined finally to go out into that dirty gray turmoil to follow love and pride; a new generation dedicated more than the last to the fear of poverty and the worship of success; grown up to find all gods dead, all wars fought, all faiths in man shaken." With energy, candor, and a sort of innocence, Fitzgerald (or the hero) was speaking for his contemporaries. They recognized the voice as their own, and his elders listened.

Suddenly the magazines were eager to print Fitzgerald's stories and willing to pay high prices for them. The result shows in his big ledger: in 1919 he earned $879 by his writing; in 1920 he earned $18,850—and managed to end the year in debt.* Early success and princely spending had been added to everything else that made him stand out as a representative of his generation; and Fitzgerald was beginning to believe in his representative quality. He was learning that when he wrote truly about his dreams and misadventures and discoveries, other people recognized themselves in the picture.

The point has to be made that Fitzgerald wasn't "typical" of his own period or any other. He lived harder than most people have ever lived and acted out his dreams with an extraordinary intensity of emotion. The dreams themselves were not at all unusual: in the beginning they were dreams of becoming a football star and a big man in college, of being a hero on the battlefield, of winning through to financial success, and of getting the top girl. They were the commonplace

---

* Those sums of money should be multiplied by three to give a notion of their equivalents half a century later. Income taxes were low in the 1920s. By the end of the decade Fitzgerald would be spending as much—but not for the same things—as the presidents of small corporations. [M.C., 1973]

visions shared by almost all the young men of his age and background, especially by those who were forging ahead in the business world; in many ways Fitzgerald was closer to them than he was to the other serious writers of his generation. It was the emotion he put into his dreams, and the honesty with which he expressed the emotion, that made them seem distinguished. By feeling intensely he made his readers believe in the unique value of the world in which they lived. He was to say later, writing in the third person, that he continued to feel grateful to the Jazz Age because "It bore him up, flattered him and gave him more money than he had dreamed of, simply for telling people that he felt as they did."

At the beginning of April 1920, Zelda came to New York and they were married in the rectory of St. Patrick's Cathedral—although Zelda's family was Episcopalian and Scott had ceased to be a good Catholic. They set up housekeeping at the Biltmore. To their bewilderment they found themselves adopted not as a Midwesterner and a Southerner respectively, not even as detached observers, but—Scott afterward wrote—"as the arch type of what New York wanted." A new age was beginning, and Scott and Zelda were venturing into it innocently, hand in hand. Zelda said, "It was always tea-time or late at night." Scott said, "We felt like children in a great bright unexplored barn."

2.

Scott also said, "America was going on the greatest, gaudiest spree in history and there was going to be plenty to tell about it." There is still plenty to tell about it, in the light of a new age that continues to be curious about the 1920s and usually misjudges them. The gaudiest spree in history was also a moral revolt, and beneath the revolt were social transformations. The 1920s were the age when puritanism was under attack, with the Protestant churches losing their dominant position. They were the age when the country ceased to be English and Scottish and when the children of later immigrations moved forward to take their places in the national life. Theodore Dreiser, whom Fitzgerald regarded as the greatest living American writer, was South German Catholic by descent, H. L. Mencken, the most influential critic, was North German

Protestant, and Fitzgerald did not forget for a moment that one side of his own family was "straight potato-famine Irish." Most of his heroes have Irish names and all except Gatsby are city-bred, thus reflecting another social change. The 1920s were the age when American culture became urban instead of rural and when New York set the social and intellectual standards of the country, while its own standards were being set by transplanted Southerners and Midwesterners like Zelda and Scott.

More essentially the 1920s were the age when a production ethic—of saving and self-denial in order to accumulate capital for new enterprises—gave way to a consumption ethic that was needed to provide markets for the new commodities that streamed from the production lines. Instead of being exhorted to save money, more and more of it, people were being exhorted in a thousand ways to buy, enjoy, use once and throw away, in order to buy a later and more expensive model. They followed the instructions, with the result that more goods were produced and consumed or wasted and money was easier to earn or borrow than ever in the past. Foresight went out of fashion. "The Jazz Age," Fitzgerald was to say, "now raced along under its own power, served by great filling stations full of money. . . . Even when you were broke you didn't worry about money, because it was in such profusion around you."

Young men and women in the 1920s had a sense of reckless confidence not only about money but about life in general. It was part of their background: they had grown up in the years when middle-class Americans read Herbert Spencer and believed in the doctrine of automatic social evolution. The early twentieth century seemed to confirm the doctrine. Things were getting better each year: more grain was reaped, more iron was smelted, more rails were laid, more profits earned, more records broken, as new cities were founded and all cities grew, as the country grew, as the world apparently grew in wealth and wisdom toward the goal of universal peace—and those magical results were obtained, so it seemed, by each man's seeking his private interest. After 1914 the notion of automatic progress lost most of its support in events, but retained its place in the public mind. Young men and women of Fitzgerald's time, no matter how rebellious and cynical they thought of themselves as being, still clung to their childhood notion that the world would improve without their help; that was one of the reasons why most of them felt excused from seeking the common good. Plunging into their personal adventures, they took risks that didn't impress them as being risks because, in their hearts, they believed in the happy ending.

They were truly rebellious, however, and were determined to make an absolute break with the standards of the prewar generation. The distinction between highbrow and lowbrow (or liberal and conservative) was not yet sharp enough to divide American society; the gulf was between the young and the old. The younger set paid few visits to their parents' homes and some of them hardly exchanged a social word with men or women over forty. The elders were straitlaced or stuffy, and besides they had made a mess of the world; they were discredited in younger eyes not only by the war and what followed it—especially Prohibition—but also, after 1923, by the scandals that clustered round Teapot Dome and the little green house on K Street, in Washington, where members of President Harding's Cabinet, and sometimes the President himself, played their cozy games of poker with the oil barons. So let the discredited elders keep to themselves; the youngsters would then have a free field in which to test their standards of the good life.

Those standards were elementary and close to being savage. Rejecting almost everything else, the spokesmen for the new generation celebrated the value of simple experiences such as love, foreign travel, good food, and drunkenness. "Immortal drunkenness!" Thomas Wolfe was to exclaim in a novel,* interrupting the adventures of his hero. "What tribute can we ever pay, what song can we ever sing, what swelling praise can ever be sufficient to express the joy, the gratefulness and love which we, who have known youth and hunger in America, have owed to alcohol? . . . You came to us with music, poetry, and wild joy when we were twenty, when we reeled home at night through the old moon-whitened streets of Boston and heard our friend, our comrade and our dead companion, shout through the silence of the moonwhite square: 'You are a poet and the world is yours.' " Others besides

* For the complete invocation to drunkenness, see *Of Time and the River*, pp. 281–82. The novel is in the third person, but here, in celebrating what he regarded as a generational experience, Wolfe shifts to the first person plural. [M.C., 1973]

Wolfe heard the voice repeating "You are a poet!" and they hastened to enjoy their birthday-present world by loving, traveling, eating, drinking, dancing all night, and writing truthfully about their mornings after. They all recognized the value of being truthful, even if it hurt their families or their friends and most of all if it hurt themselves; almost any action seemed excusable and even admirable in those days if one simply told the truth about it, without boasting, without shame.

They liked to say yes to every proposal that suggested excitement. Will you take a new job, throw up the job, go to Paris and starve, travel round the world in a freighter? Will you get married, leave your husband, spend a weekend for two in Biarritz? Will you ride through Manhattan on the roof of a taxi and then go bathing in the Plaza fountain? "W Y B M A D I I T Y?" read a sign on the mirror behind the bar of a popular speakeasy, the Dizzy Club. Late at night you asked the bartender what it meant, and he answered, "Will You Buy Me A Drink If I Tell You?" The answer was yes, always yes, and the fictional heroine of the 1920s was Serena Blandish, the girl who couldn't say no. Or the heroine was Joyce's Molly Bloom as she dreamed about the days when she was being courted: ". . . and I thought as well him as another and then I asked him with my eyes to ask again yes and then he asked me would I yes to say yes my mountain flower and first I put my arms around him yes and drew him down to me so he could feel my breasts all perfume yes and his heart was going like mad and yes I said yes I will Yes."

The masculine ideal of the 1920s was what Fitzgerald called "the old dream of being an entire man in the Goethe-Byron-Shaw tradition, with an opulent American touch, a sort of combination of J. P. Morgan, Topham Beauclerk and St. Francis of Assisi." The entire man would be one who "did everything," good and bad, who realized all the potentialities of his nature and thereby acquired wisdom. The entire man, in the 1920s, was one who followed the Rule of the Thelemites as revealed by Rabelais: *Fais ce que vouldras*, "Do what you will!" But that rule implied a second imperative like an echo: "Will!" To be admired by the 1920s young men had to will all sorts of actions and had to possess enough energy and boldness to carry out even momentary wishes. They lived in the moment with what they liked to call "an utter disregard of consequences." In spirit they all made pilgrimages to the abbey of the Thelemites, where they consulted the Oracle of the Divine Bottle and received for answer the one word *Trinc*. They obeyed the oracle and drank, in those days of the Volstead Act when drinking was a rite of comradeship and an act of rebellion. As Fitzgerald said at the time, they drank "cocktails before meals like Americans, wines and brandies like Frenchmen, beer like Germans, whiskey-and-soda like the English . . . this preposterous mélange that was like a gigantic cocktail in a nightmare."

But the 1920s were not so much a drinking as a dancing age—the Jazz Age, in the phrase that Fitzgerald made his own. In those days one heard jazz everywhere—from orchestras in ballrooms, from wind-up phonographs in the parlor, from loudspeakers blaring in variety stores, lunch wagons, even machine shops—and jazz wasn't regarded as something to listen to and be cool about, without even tapping one's feet; jazz was music with a purpose, *Gebrauchsmusik*; it was music to which you danced:

> *I met her in Chicago and she was married.*
> *   Dance all day,*
> *leave your man, Sweet Mamma, and come away;*
> *manicured smiles and kisses, to dance all day, all day.*
> *   How it was sad.*
>
> *Please, Mr. Orchestra, play us another tune.*
> My daddy went and left me and left the cupboard bare.
> Who will pay the butcher bill now Daddy isn't there?
> *   Shuffle your feet.*
> Found another daddy and he taught me not to care,
>   and how to care.
> Found another daddy that I'll follow anywhere.
> *   Shuffle your feet, dance,*
>
> *dance among the tables, dance across the floor,*
> *slip your arm around me, we'll go dancing out the door,*
> *Sweet Mamma, anywhere, through any door.*
> *Wherever the banjos play is Tennessee.*

Jazz carried with it a constant message of change, excitement, violent escape, with an undertone of sadness, but with a promise of enjoyment somewhere around the corner of next week, perhaps at midnight in a distant country. The young men heard the message and followed it anywhere, through any door, even the one that led into what was then, for Americans, the new world of difficult art. They danced too much, they drank too much, but they also worked, with something of the same desperation; they worked to rise, to earn social rank, to sell, to advertise, to organize, to invent gadgets, and to create enduring works of literature. In ten years, before losing their first vitality, they gave a new tempo to American life.

Fitzgerald not only represented the age but came to suspect that he had helped to create it, by setting forth a pattern of conduct that would be followed by persons a little younger than himself. That it was a dangerous pattern was something he recognized almost from the beginning. "If I had anything to do with creating the manners of the contemporary American girl I certainly made a botch of the job," he said in a 1925 letter. In a notebook he observed that one of his relatives was still a flapper in the 1930s. "There is no doubt," he added, "that she originally patterned herself upon certain immature and unfortunate writings of mine, so that I have a special fondness for _____ as for one who has lost an arm or a leg in one's service." When he was living at La Paix, a brown wooden late-Victorian lodge on a thirty-acre estate near Baltimore, a drunken young man teetered up to his door and said, "I had to see you. I feel I owe you more than I can say. I feel that you formed my life." It was not the young man— later a widely read novelist and an alcoholic—but Fitzgerald himself who became the principal victim of his capacity for creating fictional types in life. "Sometimes," he told another visitor to La Paix, late at night, "I don't know whether Zelda and I are real or whether we are characters in one of my novels."

That was in the spring of 1933, a few weeks after the banks had closed all over the country. It seemed then that the whole generation of the 1920s had been defeated by life, and yet, in their own defeat, Scott and Zelda were still its representative figures.

3.

Fitzgerald never lost a quality that very few writers are able to acquire: a sense of living in history. Manners and morals were changing all through his life and he set himself the task of recording the changes. These were revealed to him, not by statistics or news reports, but in terms of living characters, and the characters were revealed by gestures, each appropriate to a certain year. He wrote: "One day in 1926 we"—meaning the members of his generation—"looked down and found we had flabby arms and a fat pot and we couldn't say boop-boop-a-doop to a Sicilian. . . . By 1927 a widespread neurosis began to be evident, faintly signaled, like a nervous beating of the feet, by the popularity of cross-word puzzles. . . . By this time"—also in 1927—"contemporaries of mine had begun to disappear into the dark maw of violence. . . . By 1928 Paris had grown suffocating. With each new shipment of Americans spewed up by the boom the quality fell off, until towards the end there was something sinister about the crazy boatloads."

He tried to find the visible act that revealed the moral quality inherent in a certain moment of time. He was haunted by time, as if he wrote in a room full of clocks and calendars. He made lists by the hundred, including lists of the popular songs, the football players, the top debutantes (with the types of beauty they cultivated), the hobbies, and the slang expressions of a given year; he felt that all those names and phrases belonged to the year and helped to reveal its momentary color. "After all," he said in an otherwise undistinguished magazine story, "any given moment has its value; it can be questioned in the light of after-events, but the moment remains. The young prince in velvet gathered in lovely domesticity around the queen amid the hush of rich draperies may presently grow up to be Pedro the Cruel or Charles the Mad, but the moment of beauty was there."

Fitzgerald lived in his great moments, and lived in them again when he reproduced their drama, but he also stood apart from them and coldly reckoned their causes and consequences. That is his doubleness or irony, and it is one of his distinguishing marks as a writer. He took part in the ritual orgies of his time, but he kept a secretly detached position, regarding himself as a pauper living among millionaires, a Celt among Sassenachs, and a sullen peasant among the nobility; he said that his point of vantage "was the dividing line between two generations," prewar and postwar. Always he cultivated a double vision. In his novels and stories he was trying to intensify the glitter of life in the Princeton eating clubs, on the north shore of Long Island, in Hollywood, and on the Riviera; he surrounded his characters with a mist of admiration, and at the same time he kept driving the mist away. He liked to know "where the milk is watered and the sugar sanded, the rhinestone passed for the diamond and the stucco for stone." It was as if all his fiction described a big dance to which he had taken, as he once wrote, the prettiest girl:

> There was an orchestra—Bingo-Bango
> Playing for us to dance the tango
> And the people all clapped as we arose
> For her sweet face and my new clothes—

and as if he stood at the same time outside the ballroom, a little Midwestern boy with his nose to the glass, wondering how much the tickets cost and who paid for the music. But it was not a dance he was watching so much as it was a drama of conflicting manners and aspirations in which he was both the audience and the leading actor. As audience he kept a cold eye on the actor's performance. He wrote of himself when he was twenty, "I knew that at bottom I lacked the essentials. At the last crisis, I knew that I had no real courage, perseverance or self-respect." Sixteen years later he was just as critical, and he said to a visitor at La Paix, "I've got a very limited talent. I'm a workman of letters, a professional. I know when to write and when to stop writing." It was the maximum of critical detachment, but it was combined with the maximum of immersion in the drama. He said in his notebook, and without the least exaggeration, "Taking things hard, from Ginevra to Joe Mankiewicz," mentioning the names of his first unhappy love and of the Hollywood producer who, so he thought, had ruined one of his best scripts: "That's the stamp that goes into my books so that people read it blind like Braille."

The drama he watched and in which he overplayed a leading part was a moral drama leading to rewards and punishments. "Sometimes I wish I had gone along with that gang," he said in a letter that discussed musical comedies and mentioned Cole Porter and Rodgers and Hart; "but I guess I am too much a moralist at heart and want to preach at people in some acceptable form, rather than to entertain them." The morality he wanted to preach was a simple one, in the midst of the prevailing confusion. Its four cardinal virtues were Industry, Discipline, Responsibility (in the sense of meeting one's social and financial obligations), and Maturity (in the sense of learning to expect little from life while continuing to make one's best efforts). Thus, his stories had a way of becoming fables. For virtues they displayed or failed to display, the characters were rewarded or punished in the end.

The handle by which he took hold of the characters was their dreams. These, as I said, might be commonplace or even cheap, but usually Fitzgerald managed to surround them with an atmosphere of the mysterious and illimitable or of the pitifully doomed. His great scenes were, so to speak, played to music: sometimes the music from a distant ballroom, sometimes that of a phonograph braying out a German tango, sometimes the wind in the leaves, sometimes the stark music of the heart. When there was no music, at least there were pounding rhythms: "The city's quick metropolitan rhythm of love and birth and death that supplied dreams to the unimaginative"; "The rhythm of the week-end, with its birth, its planned gaieties and its announced end"; "New York's flashing, dynamic good looks, its tall man's quick-step." Fitzgerald's dream of his mature years, after he had outgrown the notion of becoming a big man in college, was also set to music, perhaps to the *Unfinished Symphony*; it was the dream of becoming a great writer, specifically a great novelist who would do for American society in his time what Turgenev, for example, had done for the old regime in Russia.

It was not his dream to be a poet, yet that was how he started and in some ways he remained a poet primarily. He noted, "The talent that matures early is usually of the poetic type, which mine was in large part." His favorite author was Keats, not Turgenev or Flaubert. "I suppose I've read it a hundred times," he said of the "Ode on a Grecian Urn." "About the tenth time I began to know what it was about, and caught the chime in it and the exquisite inner mechanics. Likewise with the 'Nightingale,' which I can never read without tears in my eyes; likewise 'The Pot of Basil,' with its great stanzas about the two brothers. . . . Knowing these things very young and granted an ear, one could scarcely ever afterwards be unable to distinguish between gold and dross in what one read." When his daughter was learning to be a writer he advised her to read Keats and Browning and try her hand at a sonnet. He added, "The only thing that will help you is poetry, which is the most concentrated form of style."

Fitzgerald himself was a poet who never learned some of the elementary rules for writing prose. His grammar was shaky and his spelling definitely bad: for example, he wrote "ect." more often than "etc." and misspelled the name of his friend Monsignor Fay on the dedication page of *This Side of Paradise*. In his letters he always misspelled the given names of his first and last loves. He was not a student, for all the books he read; not a theoretician and perhaps one should flatly say, not a thinker. He counted on his friends to do much of his thinking for him; at Princeton it was John Peale Bishop who, he said, "made me see, in the course of a couple of months, the difference between poetry and non-poetry." Twenty years later, at the time of his crack-up, he re-examined his scale of values and found thinking incredibly difficult; he compared it to "the moving about of great secret trunks." He was then forced to the conclusion "That I had done very little thinking, save within the problems of my craft. For twenty years a certain man had been my intellectual conscience. That man was Edmund Wilson." Another contemporary "had been an artistic conscience to me. I had not imitated his infectious style, because my own style, such as it is, was formed before he published anything, but there was an awful pull towards him when I was on the spot."

Fitzgerald was making the confession in order to keep straight with himself, not to forestall any revelation that might have been made by his critics. The critics would have said that there was little of Wilson's influence perceptible in his work and still less of Hemingway's, although he once wrote a story about two dogs, "Shaggy's Morning," that is a delicate and deliberate pastiche of the Hemingway manner. By listening hard one can overhear a few, a very few suggestions of Hemingway in the dialogue of other stories, especially the later ones, but Fitzgerald was faithful to his own vision of the world and his way of expressing it. His debt to Wilson and Hemingway is real, but hard to define. In essence they were two older-brother figures (though Hemingway was younger than Fitzgerald); two different models of literary conduct.

Though his style of life bore no resemblance to either of theirs, he used them to test and define his moral attitude toward the problems of his craft.

4.

There was one respect in which Fitzgerald, much as he regarded himself as a representative figure of the age, was completely different from most of its serious writers. In that respect he was, as I said, much closer to the men of his college year who were trying to get ahead in the business world; like them he was fascinated by the process of earning and spending money. The young businessmen of his time, much more than those of a later generation, had been taught to measure success, failure, and even virtue in pecuniary terms. They had learned in school and Sunday school that virtue was rewarded with money and vice punished by the loss of money; apparently their one aim should be to earn lots of it fast. Yet money was only a convenient and inadequate symbol for what they dreamed of earning. The best of them were like Jay Gatsby in having "some heightened sensitivity to the promise of life"; or they were like another Fitzgerald hero, Dexter Green of "Winter Dreams," who "wanted not association with glittering things and glittering people—he wanted the glittering things themselves." Their real dream was that of achieving a new status and a new essence, of rising to a loftier place in the mysterious hierarchy of human worth.

The serious writers also dreamed of rising to a loftier status, but—except for Fitzgerald—they felt that moneymaking was the wrong way to rise. They liked money if it reached them in the form of gifts or legacies or publishers' advances; they would have liked it in the form of prizes or fellowships, though there were few of these to be had in the 1920s; but they were afraid of high earned incomes because of what the incomes stood for: obligations, respectability, time lost from their essential work, expensive habits that would drive them to seek still higher incomes—in short, a series of involvements in the commercial culture that was hostile to art. "If you want to ruin a writer," I used to hear some of them saying, "just give him a big magazine contract or a job at ten thousand a year." Many of them tried to preserve their independence by earning only enough to keep them alive while writing; a few regarded themselves as heroes of poverty and failure. "Now I can write," Faulkner said when his third novel was turned down and he thought he would never be published again.

A disdainful attitude toward money went into the texture of Faulkner's work, as into that of many others. The work was non-commercial in the sense of being written in various new styles that the public was slow to accept. It was an age of literary experiment when young writers were moving in all directions simultaneously. They were showing the same spirit of adventure and exploration in fiction that their contemporaries were showing in the business world. That spirit made them part of the age, but at the same time they were trying to stand apart from it, and some of them looked back longingly to other ages when, so they liked to think, artists had wealthy patrons and hence were able to live outside the economic system.

Fitzgerald immersed himself in the age and always remained close to the business world which they were trying to evade. That world was the background of his stories, and these performed a business function in themselves, by supplying the narrative that readers followed like a thread through the labyrinth of advertising in the slick-paper magazines. He did not divorce himself from readers by writing experimental prose or refusing to tell a story. His very real originality was a matter of mood and subject and image rather than of structure, and it was more evident in his novels than in his stories, good as the stories often were. Although he despised the trade of writing for magazines—or despised it with part of his mind—he worked at it honestly. It yielded him a large income that he couldn't have earned in any other fashion, and the income was necessary to his self-respect.

Fitzgerald kept an accurate record of his earnings—in the big ledger in which he also kept a record of his deeds and misdeeds, as if to strike a bookkeeper's balance between them—but he was vague about his expenditures and usually vague about his possessions, including his balance in the bank. Once he asked a cashier, "How much money have I got?" The cashier looked in a big book and answered without even scowling, "None." Fitzgerald resolved to be more thrifty, knowing he would break the resolution. "All big men have spent money freely," he explained in a letter to his mother.

"I hate avarice or even caution." He had little interest in the physical objects that money could buy. On the other hand, he had a great interest in earning money, lots of it fast, because that was a gold medal offered with the blue ribbon for competitive achievement. Once the money was earned, he and Zelda liked to spend lots of it fast, usually for impermanent things: not for real estate, fine motorcars, or furniture, but for traveling expenses, the rent of furnished houses, the wages of nurses and servants; for parties, party dresses, and feather fans of five colors. Zelda was as proudly careless about money as an eighteenth-century nobleman's heir. Scott was more practical and had his penny-pinching moments, as if in memory of his childhood, but at other times he liked to spend without counting in order to enjoy a proud sense of potency.

In his attitude toward money he revealed the new spirit of an age when conspicuous accumulation was giving way to conspicuous earning and spending. It was an age when gold was melted down and became fluid, when wealth was no longer measured in possessions—land, houses, livestock, machinery—but rather in dollars per year, as a stream is measured by its flow; when for the first time the expenses of government were being met by income taxes more than by property and excise taxes; and when the new tax structure was making it somewhat more difficult to accumulate a stable and lasting fortune. Such fortunes still existed at the hardly accessible peak of the social system, which young men dreamed of reaching like Alpinists, but the romantic figures of the age were not capitalists properly speaking. They were salaried executives and advertising men, they were promoters, salesmen, stock gamblers, or racketeers, and they were millionaires in a new sense—not men each of whom owned a million dollars' worth of property, but men who lived in rented apartments and had nothing but stock certificates and insurance policies (or nothing but credit and the right connections), while spending more than the income of the old millionaires.

The change went deep into the texture of American society and deep into the feelings of Americans as individuals. Fitzgerald is its most faithful recorder, not only in the stories that earned him a place in the new high-income class, but also in his personal confessions. He liked to describe his vitality and his talent in pecuniary terms. When both of them temporarily disappeared, in his crack-up of the years 1935–36, he pictured the event as a sort of financial bankruptcy. He wrote (but without my italics), "I began to realize that for two years my life had been a *drawing on, resources* that I did not possess, that I had been *mortgaging myself* physically and spiritually up to the hilt." Again he wrote, "When a new sky cut off the sun last spring, I didn't at first relate it to what had happened fifteen or twenty years ago. Only gradually did a certain family resemblance come through—an over-extension of the flank, a burning of the candle at both ends; a call upon physical resources that I did not command, *like a man overdrawing at his bank.* . . . There were plenty of *counterfeit coins* around that I could pass off instead of these"—that is, in spite of the honest emotions he had lost—"and I knew where I could get them at *a nickel on the dollar.*"

"Where was the leak," Fitzgerald asked, "through which, unknown to myself, my enthusiasm and my vitality had been steadily and prematurely trickling away?" Vitality was something liquid and it was equated with money, which was also liquid. The attitude was different from that which prevailed before World War I, when people spoke of saving money as "piling up the rocks," instead of filling the reservoir, and when the millionaire in the funny papers was "Mr. Gotrocks." In Freud's great system, which is based on his observation of nineteenth-century types, money is something solid, gold or silver, and the bodily product it suggests is excrement. Thus, the pursuit of money for its own sake develops from anal eroticism, and Freud maintains that the miser is almost always a constipated man. I doubt whether recent analysts have observed how money is losing its old symbolic value and how, in the American subconscious, it tends to be identified with other bodily products such as urine ("I just pee'd it away"), blood, sperm, or milk.

Fitzgerald was more closely involved with contemporary values than most of the professional analysts. He uses the new imagery in much of his confessional writing, and it becomes especially clear in a free-verse poem, "Our April Letter," which he wrote during his crack-up. Three lines of the poem read:

I have asked a lot of my emotions—one hundred and twenty stories. The price was high, right up with Kipling, because there was one little drop of something—not blood, not a tear, not my seed, but me more intimately than these, in every story, it was the extra I had. Now it has gone and I am just like you now.

Once the phial was full—here is the bottle it came in.

Hold on, there's a drop left there. . . . No, it was just the way the light fell.

Note that the something more intimate than blood or tears or sperm—though suggested by all of these—had a monetary value and was being sold to the magazines at a price right up with what Kipling had been paid. Note also that in its absence Fitzgerald was no longer able to write salable stories, so that he came to identify emotional with financial bankruptcy. In that black year 1936 he was earning very little money and owed more than forty thousand dollars, but he kept a careful record of his debts and later paid off most of them, by living in a modest fashion even during the months when he was earning a big salary in Hollywood. He never became solvent, but his financial obligations were not so pressing at the end of his life, and he was doing some of his best work.

In writing about the romance of money, as he did in most of his earlier novels and stories, he was dealing not only with an intimate truth but also with what seemed to him the central truth of his American age. "Americans," he liked to say, "should be born with fins and perhaps they were—perhaps money was a form of fin."

5.

One of his remarks about himself has often puzzled his critics. "D. H. Lawrence's great attempt to synthesize animal and emotional—things he left out," Fitzgerald wrote in his notebook, then added the comment, "Essential pre-Marxian. Just as I am essentially Marxian." He was never Marxian in any sense of the word that Marxians of whatever school would be willing to accept. It is true that he finally read well into *Das Kapital* and was impressed by "the terrible chapter," as he called it, "on 'The Working Day' "; but it left in him no trace of Marx's belief in the mission of the proletariat.

His picture of proletarian life was of something alien to his own background, mysterious and even criminal. It seems to have been symbolized in some of his stories—notably in "Winter Dreams" and "A Short Trip Home"—by the riverfront strip in St. Paul that languished in the shadow of the big houses on Summit Avenue; he described the strip as a gridiron of mean streets where consumptive or pugilistic youths lounged in front of poolrooms, their skins turned livid by the neon lights. In *The Great Gatsby* he must have been thinking about the lower levels of American society when he described the valley of ashes between West Egg and New York—"A fantastic farm," he calls it, "where ashes grow like wheat into ridges and hills and grotesque gardens; where ashes take the forms of houses and chimneys and rising smoke and, finally, with a transcendent effort, of men who move dimly and always crumbling through the powdery air." One of his early titles for the novel was "Among Ash Heaps and Millionaires"—as if he were setting the two against each other while suggesting a vague affinity between them. Tom Buchanan, the brutalized millionaire, finds a mistress in the valley of ashes.

In Fitzgerald's stories there can be no real struggle between this dimly pictured ash-gray proletariat and the bourgeoisie. On the other hand, there can be a different struggle that the author must have regarded, for a time, as essentially Marxian. It is the struggle I have already suggested, between wealth as fluid income and wealth as an inherited and solid possession— or rather, since Fitzgerald is not an essayist but a storyteller, it is between a man and a woman as representatives of the new and the old moneyed classes.

We are not allowed to forget that they are representatives. The man comes from a family with little or no money, but he manages to attend an Eastern university—most often Yale, to set a distance between the hero and the Princeton author. He then sets out to earn a fortune equal to that of his wealthy classmates. Usually what he earns is not a fortune but an impressively large income, after he has risen to the top of his chosen profession—which may be engineering or architecture or advertising or the laundry business or bootlegging or real estate or even, in one story, frozen fish; the heroes are never novelists, although one of them is said to be a successful playwright. When the heroes are halfway to the top, they fall in love.

The woman—or rather the girl—in a Fitzgerald story is as alluring as the youngest princess in a fairy tale. "In children's books," he says when presenting one heroine, "forests are sometimes made out of all-day suckers, boulders out of peppermints and rivers out of gently flowing, rippling molasses taffy. Such . . . localities exist, and one day a girl, herself little more than a child, sat dejected in the middle of one. It was all hers, she owned it; she owned Candy Town." Another heroine "was a stalk of ripe corn, but bound not as cereals are but as a rare first edition, with all the binder's art. She was lovely and expensive and about nineteen." Of still another heroine Fitzgerald says when she first appears that "Her childish beauty was wistful and sad about being so rich and sixteen." Later, when her father loses his money, the hero pays her a visit in London. "All around her," Fitzgerald says, "he could feel the vast Mortmain fortune melting down, seeping back into the matrix whence it had come." The hero thinks she might marry him, now that she has fallen almost to his financial level; but he finds that the Mortmain (or dead-hand) fortune, even though lost, is still a barrier between them. Note that the man is not attracted by the fortune in itself. He is not seeking money so much as position at the peak of the social hierarchy, and the girl becomes the symbol of that position, the incarnation of its mysterious power. That is Daisy Buchanan's charm for the great Gatsby and the reason why he directs his whole life toward winning back her love.

"She's got an indiscreet voice," Nick Carraway says of her. "It's full of—" and he hesitates.

"Her voice is full of money," Gatsby says.

And Nick, the narrator, thinks to himself, "That was it. I'd never understood before. It was full of money—that was the inexhaustible charm that rose and fell in it, the cymbals' song of it. . . . High in a white palace the king's daughter, the golden girl."

In Fitzgerald's stories a love affair is like the secret negotiations between the diplomats of two countries which are not at peace and not quite at war. For a moment they forget their hostility, find it transformed into mutual inspection, attraction, even passion (though the passion is not physical); but the hostility will survive even in marriage, if marriage is to be their future. I called the lovers diplomats, ambassadors, and that is another way of saying that they are representatives. When they meet it as if they were leaning toward each other from separate high platforms—the man from a platform built up of his former poverty, his ambition, his competitive triumphs, his ability to earn and spend always more, more; the girl from another platform covered with cloth of gold and feather fans of many colors, but beneath them a sturdy pile of stock certificates testifying to the ownership of mines, forests, factories, villages—all of Candy Town.

She is ownership embodied, as can be seen in one of the best of Fitzgerald's early stories, "Winter Dreams." A rising young man named Dexter Green takes home the daughter of a millionaire for whom he used to be a caddy. She is Judy Jones, "a slender enamelled doll in cloth of gold: gold in a band at her head, gold in two slipper points at her dress's hem." The rising young man stops his coupé "in front of the great white bulk of the Mortimer Jones house, somnolent, gorgeous, drenched with the splendor of the damp moonlight. Its solidity startled him. The strong walls, the steel of the girders, the breadth and beam and pomp of it were there only to bring out the contrast with the young beauty beside him. It was sturdy to accentuate her slightness—as if to show what a breeze could be generated by a butterfly's wing." In legends butterflies are symbols of the soul. The inference is clear that, holding Judy in his arms, Dexter Green is embracing the spirit of a great fortune.

Nicole Warren, the heroine of *Tender Is the Night*, embodies the spirit of an even greater fortune. Fitzgerald says of her, in a familiar passage:

> Nicole was the product of much ingenuity and toil. For her sake trains began their run at Chicago and traversed the round belly of the continent to California; chicle factories fumed and link belts grew link by link in factories; men mixed toothpaste in vats and drew mouthwash out of copper hogs-heads; girls canned tomatoes quickly in August or worked rudely at the Five-and-Tens on Christmas Eve; half-breed Indians toiled on Brazilian coffee plantations and dreamers were muscled out of patent rights in new tractors—these were some of the people who gave a tithe to Nicole, and as the whole system swayed and thundered onward it lent a feverish bloom to such processes of hers as wholesale buying [of luxuries], like the flush of a fireman's face holding his post before a spreading blaze.

Sometimes Fitzgerald's heroines are candid, even brutal, about class relations. "Let's start right," Judy Jones says to

Dexter Green on the first evening they spend alone together. "Who are you?"

"I'm nobody," Dexter tells her, without adding that he had been her father's caddy. "My career is largely a matter of futures."

"Are you poor?"

"No," he says frankly, "I'm probably making more money than any man my age in the Northwest. I know that's an obnoxious remark, but you advised me to start right."

"There was a pause," Fitzgerald adds. "Then she smiled and the corners of her mouth drooped and an almost imperceptible sway brought her closer to him, looking up into his eyes." Money brings them together, but later they are separated by something undefined—a mere whim of Judy's, it would seem, though one comes to suspect that the whim was based on her feeling that she should marry a man of her own caste. Dexter, as he goes East to earn a still larger income, is filled with regret for "the country of illusions, of youth, of the richness of life, where his winter dreams had flourished." It seems likely that Judy Jones, like Josephine Perry in a series of later stories, was a character suggested by a Chicago debutante with whom Fitzgerald was desperately in love during his first years at Princeton; afterward she made a more sensible marriage. As for the general attitude toward the rich that began to be expressed in "Winter Dreams," it is perhaps connected with his experience in 1919, when he was not earning enough to support a wife and Zelda broke off their engagement. Later he said of the time:

> During a long summer of despair I wrote a novel instead of letters, so it came out all right; but it came out all right for a different person. The man with the jingle of money in his pocket who married the girl a year later would always cherish an abiding distrust, an animosity, toward the leisure class—not the conviction of a revolutionist but the smoldering hatred of a peasant.

His mixture of feelings toward the very rich, which included curiosity and admiration as well as distrust, is revealed in his treatment of a basic situation that reappears in many of his stories. Of course he presented other situations that were not directly concerned with the relation between social classes. He wrote about the problem of adjusting oneself to life, which he thought was especially difficult for self-indulgent American women. He wrote about the manners of flappers, slickers, and jelly beans. He wrote engagingly about his own boyhood. He wrote about the patching up of broken marriages, about the contrast between Northern and Southern life, about Americans going to pieces in Europe, about the self-tortures of gifted alcoholics, and in much of his later work—as notably in *The Last Tycoon*—he was expressing admiration for inspired technicians, such as brain surgeons and movie directors. But a great number of his stories, especially the early ones, start with the basic situation I have mentioned: a rising young man of the middle classes in love with the daughter of a very rich family. (Sometimes the family is Southern, in which case it needn't be so rich, since a high social status could still exist in the South without great wealth.)

From that beginning the story may take any one of several turns. The hero may marry the girl, but only after she loses her fortune or (as in "Presumption" and " 'The Sensible Thing' ") he gains an income greater than hers. He may lose the girl (as in "Winter Dreams") and always remember her with longing for his early aspirations. In "The Bridal Party" he resigns himself to the loss after being forced to recognize the moral superiority of the rich man she has married. In "More Than Just a House" he learns that the girl is empty and selfish and ends by marrying her good sister; in "The Rubber Check" he marries Ellen Mortmain's quiet cousin. There is, however, still another development out of the Fitzgerald situation that comes closer to revealing his ambiguous feelings toward the very rich. To state it simply—too simply—the rising young man wins the rich girl and then is destroyed by her wealth or her relatives.

It is the ballad of young Lochinvar come out of the West, but with a tragic ending—as if fair Ellen's kinsmen, armed and vengeful, had overtaken the pair or as if Ellen herself had betrayed the hero. Fitzgerald used it for the first time in a fantasy, "The Diamond As Big As the Ritz," which he wrote in St. Paul during the winter of 1921–22. In the fashion of many fantasies, it reveals the author's cast of mind more clearly than his realistic stories. It deals with the adventures of a boy named John T. Unger (we might read "Hunger"), who was born in a town on the Mississippi called Hades, though it also might be called St. Paul. He is sent away to St. Midas', which is "the most expensive and most exclusive

boys' preparatory school in the world," and there he meets
Percy Washington, who invites him to spend the summer at
his home in the West. On the train Percy confides to him that
his father is the richest man alive and owns a diamond bigger
than the Ritz-Carlton Hotel.

The description of the Washington mansion, in its hidden
valley that wasn't even shown on maps of the U.S. Geodetic
Survey, is fantasy mingled with burlesque, but then the familiar Fitzgerald note appears. John falls in love with Percy's
younger sister, Kismine. After an idyllic summer Kismine tells
him accidentally—she had meant to keep the secret—that he
will very soon be murdered, like all the former guests of the
Washingtons. "It was done very nicely," she explains to him.
"They were drugged while they were asleep—and their families were always told that they died of scarlet fever in Butte.
. . . I shall probably have visitors too—I'll harden up to it.
We can't let such an inevitable thing as death stand in the
way of enjoying life while we have it. Think how lonesome
it would be out here if we never had *any*one. Why, father
and mother have sacrificed some of their best friends just as
we have."

In *The Great Gatsby,* Tom and Daisy Buchanan would also
sacrifice some of their best friends. "They were careless people, Tom and Daisy—they smashed up things and creatures
and then retreated back into their money or their vast care-
lessness, or whatever it was that kept them together, and let
other people clean up the mess they had made." "The Diamond As Big As the Ritz" can have a happy ending for the
two lovers because it is a fantasy; but the same plot reappears
in *The Great Gatsby,* where for the first time it is surrounded
by the real world of the 1920s and for the first time is carried
through to what Fitzgerald regarded as its logical conclusion.*

There is a time in any true author's career when he suddenly
becomes capable of doing his best work. He has found a fable

* The plot appears for the last time in *Tender Is the Night.* "The novel should
do this," Fitzgerald said in a memorandum to himself written early in 1932,
after several false starts on the book and before setting to work on the published
version. "Show a man who is a natural idealist, a spoiled priest, giving in for
various causes to the ideas of the haute bourgeoisie"—that is, of the old moneyed class—"and in his rise to the top of the social world being his idealism,
his talent and turning to drink and dissipation." In the very simplest terms,
Dick Diver marries Nicole Warren and is destroyed by her money. [M.C.,
1973]

that expresses his central truth and everything falls into place around it, so that his whole experience of life is available for use in his fiction. Something like that happened to Fitzgerald when he invented the story of Jimmy Gatz, otherwise known as Jay Gatsby, and it explains the richness and scope of what is in fact a short novel.

To put facts on record, *The Great Gatsby* is a book of about fifty thousand words, a comparatively small structure built of nine chapters like big blocks. The fifth chapter—Gatsby's meeting after many years with Daisy Buchanan—is the center of the narrative, as is proper; the seventh chapter is its climax. Each chapter consists of one or more dramatic scenes, sometimes with intervening passages of narration. The scenic method is one that Fitzgerald possibly learned from Edith Wharton, who had learned it from Henry James; at any rate, the book is technically in the Jamesian tradition (and Daisy Buchanan is named for James's Daisy Miller).

Part of the tradition is the device of having events observed by a "central consciousness," often a character who stands somewhat apart from the action and whose vision frames it for the reader. In this instance the observer plays a special role. Although Nick Carraway does not save or ruin Gatsby, his personality in itself provides an essential comment on all the other characters. Nick stands for the older values that prevailed in the Midwest before the First World War. His family is not tremendously rich like the Buchanans, but it has a long-established and sufficient fortune, so that Nick is the only person in the book who has not been corrupted by seeking or spending money. He is so certain of his own values that he hesitates to criticize others, but when he does pass judgment—on Gatsby, on Jordan Baker, on the Buchanans—he speaks as for ages to come.

All the other characters belong to their own brief era of confused and dissolving standards, but they are affected by the era in different fashions. Each of them represents some particular variety of moral failure; Lionel Trilling says that they are "treated as if they were ideographs," a true observation; but the treatment does not detract from their reality as persons. Tom Buchanan is wealth brutalized by selfishness and arrogance; he looks for a mistress in the valley of ashes and finds an ignorant woman, Myrtle Wilson, whose raw vitality is like his own. Daisy Buchanan is the butterfly soul of wealth and offers a continual promise "that she had done gay, exciting things just a while since and that there were gay, exciting things hovering in the next hour"; but it is a false promise, since at heart she is as self-centered as Tom and even colder. Jordan Baker apparently lives by the old standards, but she uses them only as a subterfuge. Aware of her own cowardice and dishonesty, she feels "safer on a plane where any divergence from a code would be thought impossible."

All these except Myrtle Wilson are East Egg people, that is, they are part of a community where wealth takes the form of solid possessions. Set against them are the West Egg people, whose wealth is fluid income that might cease to flow. The West Egg people, with Gatsby as their tragic hero, have worked furiously to rise in the world, but they will never reach East Egg for all the money they spend; at most they can sit at the water's edge and look across the bay at the green light that shines and promises at the end of the Buchanans' dock. The symbolism of place plays a great part in *Gatsby,* as does that of motorcars. The characters are visibly represented by the cars they drive: Nick has a conservative old Dodge, the Buchanans, too rich for ostentation, have an "easy-going blue coupé," and Gatsby's car is "a rich cream color, bright with nickel, swollen here and there in its monstrous length with triumphant hat-boxes and supper-boxes and tool-boxes, and terraced with a labyrinth of wind-shields that mirrored a dozen suns"—it is West Egg on wheels. When Daisy drives the monster through the valley of ashes, she runs down and kills Myrtle Wilson; then, by concealing her guilt, she causes the death of Gatsby.

The symbols are not synthetic or contrived, as are many of those in more recent novels; they are images that Fitzgerald instinctively found to represent his characters and their destiny. When he says, "Daisy took her face in her hands as if feeling its lovely shape," he is watching her act the charade of her self-love. When he says, "Tom would drift on forever seeking, a little wistfully, for the dramatic turbulence of some irrecoverable football game," he suggests the one appealing side of Tom's nature. The author is so familiar with the characters and their background, so absorbed in their fate, that the book has an admirable unity of texture; we can open it to any page and find another of the details that illuminate the story. We end by feeling that *Gatsby* has a double value: it is the best picture we possess of the age in which it was written, and it also achieves a sort of moral permanence. Fitzgerald's story of the suitor betrayed by the princess and murdered in his innocence is a fable of the 1920s that has survived as a legend for other times.

[1953, revised 1973]

TWO VIEWS OF HART CRANE

A PREFACE TO HART CRANE

"The Poetry of Hart Crane is ambitious," said Allen Tate at the beginning of his valuable introduction to *White Buildings*. Four years later, in reviewing Crane's second book of poems, I can only make the statement again, but this time for a different reason. The ambitiousness of his earlier work was shown partly in tone, in its assumption of the grand manner, and partly in its attempt to crowd more images into each poem—more symbols, perceptions and implications—than any few stanzas could hold or convey. The result in some cases was a sort of poetic shorthand which even the most attentive readers could understand with difficulty. In this second volume, merely by making the poems longer, he has made them vastly more intelligible. His ambition, which has grown with his achievement, is now shown in his choice of subject.

The Bridge is a unified group of fifteen poems dealing primarily with Brooklyn Bridge. But the bridge itself is treated as a symbol: it is the bridge between past and future, between Europe and the Indies; it is the visible token of the American continent. And, although this book of poems—this one massive poem divided into eight sections and fifteen chants—begins with a modest apostrophe to a bridge over the East River, it ends bravely as an attempt to create the myth of America.

We might well conclude that such an attempt was foredoomed to failure. An ambitious subject is by definition a subject rich in platitudes; nor is this its only danger. A poet who chooses such a theme and who, by power of imagination or intensity of feeling, escapes the platitudinous, is tempted to assume the role of a messiah. Many ambitious poems are both messianic and commonplace, but *The Bridge*, I think, is neither. In its presumptuous effort the poem has succeeded—

not wholly, of course, for its faults are obvious; but still it has succeeded to an impressive degree.

The faults of *The Bridge* I shall leave to other reviewers. As for the causes of its artistic success, they are not mysterious; they are complicated. They depend on the structure of the volume as a whole, which in turn is too elaborate, too much a fabric of interwoven strands, to be explained in the present review. Instead of advancing a few vague statements, I prefer to suggest Crane's general method by describing in detail one of the fifteen poems. But which? . . . The poem that suggests itself is possibly his best; probably it is one of the important poems of our age, but it is not immeasurably better than others in the book—"Cutty Sark," for example, or "The Dance," or "Ave Maria"—and its method is neither too simple nor too complex to be typical of his work. Let us confine ourselves, then, to "The River."

It occurs in the second section of the book, a section bearing the name of Pocahontas, whom the poet has chosen as an earth-symbol to represent the body of the American continent. She also represents its Indian past. The section dedicated to her consists of five poems, each of which progresses farther into the continent and into the past, till the Indian tradition fuses, in the fifth poem, with that of the settlers. It should be noted, however, that the progression is not geographical or historical: it is a progressive exploration of the poet's mind. Thus, in the first poem of the series, he awakens to the dim sounds of the harbor at dawn; in the second he walks to the subway attended by the imaginary figure of Rip Van Winkle. In the fourth poem, he will picture a corn-dance held by the Indians before the first settlers landed on the marshy banks of the James. The third poem, with which we are dealing to the exclusion of the others, must serve as a link between the second and the fourth—between present and past, between New York City and the Appalachian tribes. Thus, it must have a movement both temporal and spatial, a movement like that of a river; and the subject Crane has chosen to perform this double function is the Mississippi.

His treatment of the subject is oblique; he does not proceed logically, but rather by associations of thought, by successive emotions. Since the preceding poem has ended in a subway, it seems emotionally fitting to begin the present one, not on the Mississippi itself, but on a train westbound from Manhattan into the heart of the continent. From the windows of the Twentieth Century Limited, the poet watches the billboards drifting past. And the first eighteen lines of this long poem are a phantasmagoria of pictures and slogans, an insane commentary on modern life, an unstable world as seen in glimpses by a moving observer.

Suddenly the angle of vision changes. The poet is no longer on the train; he is standing beside three ragged men "still hungry on the tracks . . . watching the taillights wizen." The rhythm of the poem changes at the same moment: it is no longer nervous and disconnected; it settles down to the steady pedestrian gait of hoboes plodding along a railroad. The next ninety-three lines, by far the longest section of the poem, will deal with the Odyssey of these unshaven men, "wifeless or runaway," of whom Crane once said in explaining his methods: "They are the leftovers of the pioneers. . . . Abstractly, their wanderings carry the reader through certain experiences roughly parallel to those of the traders and adventurers, Boone and others."

From the long passage that deals with these wanderings, I remember many lines, some for their vividness or wit, some for their music, and some for the imaginative quality that is poetry in the strictest sense:

> *"There's no place like Booneville though, Buddy,"*
> *One said, excising a last burr from his vest,*
> *"For early trouting. . . ."*
>
> *John, Jake or Charley, hopping the slow freight*
> *—Memphis to Tallahassee—riding the rods,*
> *Blind fists of nothing, humpty-dumpty clods.*
>
> *—They know a body under the wide rain;*
> *Youngsters with eyes like fjords, old reprobates*
> *With racetrack jargon—dotting immensity,*
> *They lurk across her, knowing her yonder breast*
> *Snow-silvered, sumac-stained or smoky blue—*

Lurking across immensity, they wander wherever the Mississippi "drinks the farthest dale." In Ohio, "behind my father's cannery works," they squat in a circle beside the tracks. They remember "the last bear, shot drinking in the Dakotas." Drifting through the Missouri highlands, they linger where—

Under the Ozarks, domed by Iron Mountain,
The old gods of the rain lie wrapped in pools—

and inevitably they gather at Cairo, where the waters gather. "For," says the poet addressing these belated pioneers—"For you, too, feed the River timelessly." The poem, after wandering over half the country, has found its proper subject. And at this point the rhythm changes once more; it becomes slower, more liquid; and finally, in a series of eight majestic quatrains, the river and the poem flow southward together, passing De Soto's burying place, passing "the City storied of three thrones," and mingling with the Gulf.

Even from this bare outline of one poem, one can glimpse the qualities by which the ambition of the volume is transformed into realization. Here is the conceptual imagination that resolves a general subject into an individual experience— one which it again dissolves into something universal and timeless. Here is the concrete imagination that reveals itself in terms of sound, color and movement. Here, lastly, is the constructive imagination that makes each separate poem play its part in a larger plan. As for the place of "The River" in this plan, I think I have shown that it succeeds in the two functions it was called upon to perform. At the same time, considered apart from the volume as a whole, it has a life of its own; and it has a separate structure also, one which might be compared to that of an ideal Chrysler Building. Just as the building stands broadly in a rubble of houses, narrows to a tower, rises implacably story after story, and finally soars upward in one clean shaft; so the poem, which began as a crazy jumble of prose and progressed by narrowing circles into the Great Valley, develops finally into a slow hymn to the river, a celebration of the Mississippi as it pours "down two more turns—"

> *And flows within itself, heaps itself free.*
> *All fades but one thin skyline round. . . . Ahead*
> *No embrace opens but the stinging sea.*
> *The River lifts itself from its long bed,*
>
> *Poised wholly on its dream, a mustard glow*
> *Tortured with history, its one will—flow!*
> *—The Passion spreads in wide tongues, choked and slow,*
> *Meeting the Gulf, hosannas silently below.*

[1930]

TWO VIEWS OF *THE BRIDGE*

Fifty years after the book was first published, little doubt remains that Hart Crane's *The Bridge* is a monument of American poetry. Among the longer poetic works I should place it below Whitman's "Song of Myself," but above almost everything else; and this is a judgment shared by many critics. The argument that continues to rage is about where its principal virtue lies. Should we reread it now as something unified, a special type of epic, or is it an aggregation of fifteen lyrics, most of them having a rather distant kinship with the others? Is the whole greater than the sum of its parts, or are a few of the parts greater than the whole?

In this argument the two opposing schools might be called the integrationists and the dispersionists. R. W. B. Lewis is an outstanding member of the first school. In *The Poetry of Hart Crane* he asserts that *The Bridge* has a unified plot, which is "the gradual permeation of an entire culture by the power of poetic vision." But is that a plot, strictly speaking, or is it something else, a theme with variations? In the other camp Brom Weber might be cited as an extreme dispersionist. "Nothing useful can be accomplished," he says in his *Hart Crane*, "by persisting in the consideration of *The Bridge* as a unified poem. . . . [It] is a collection of individual lyrics of varying quality." Its readers should "cease mourning the failure of *The Bridge* as a whole"—something that Weber takes for granted—"and begin acclaiming Crane for the poetic achievements which are lavishly strewn throughout its length."

Might it be that both sides are partly right in their opposite contentions? *The Bridge* does have a unity based on the poet's vision of the complete work; mark down a score for Lewis and his side. Each of the fifteen lyrics does embody parts of that vision, and each of them states or restates themes that are also sounded in other lyrics, thus creating a web of interconnections, as in a symphony. The vision is personal, however, and almost impossible to paraphrase. Sometimes it falters, with the result that the separate lyrics, or movements in the symphony, are of strikingly uneven value; Brom Weber was right about that, as almost everyone agrees. *The Bridge* might have seemed an even greater poem if two or three of them had been omitted.

Does it follow that the work as a whole is a failure? The answer must be a firm Yes and a firm No. Obviously *The Bridge* falls short of the author's sweeping conception. Crane, as he often explained, was undertaking to create a myth of America, a "mystical synthesis" of our past, present, and future. Success in such a venture is impossible; to fashion that myth of America will never be more than a Faustian dream. Crane was, if you will, a Faustian character, a heaven-stormer bent on rising above the human condition by magic and force of will, and if necessary by selling his soul. Even if his goal had been attainable, he was doomed to fall short of it by American realities, in which, as he often said, he was "caught like a rat in a trap."

He was also doomed by the strengths and failings of his character. He had vision, energy, obdurate patience—genius, in a word; he had a magnificent sense of rhythm; but also he had limited knowledge and something less than the immense stamina required for the completion of his task. Eventually he was worn out by his efforts (and of course by the debaucheries that he regarded as a necessary part of them). He abandoned the poem—that is the proper word here—a month before it was published in February 1930. But can one say that *The Bridge* was a failure except in his own Faustian terms? Hasn't the partially realized dream a grandeur of its own, like a crusader's castle that looms above a squalid village in Lebanon? Already *The Bridge* has survived its author by half a century. It will continue to live by virtue of its bold conception, the splendor of its language, and the almost complete rightness of some of its parts. As compared with other American poets of his time, Crane was an heroic success.

2.

How *The Bridge* was written is a story that has to be told again. It casts light on the extraordinary qualities of the work and on why they are absent from some passages.

The project was conceived in the first week of February 1923, when Crane was working for an advertising agency in

Cleveland. It was mentioned February 6 in letters he wrote to his friends Gorham Munson and Allen Tate. "I'm already started on a new poem, *The Bridge*," he said in the letter to Tate, "which continues the tendencies that are evident in 'Faustus and Helen,' but it's too vague and nebulous yet to talk about." Two weeks later he was ready to say more, in a letter to Munson:

> I am too much interested in this *Bridge* thing lately to write letters, ads, or anything. It is just beginning to take the least outline,—and the more outline the conception of the thing takes,—the more its final difficulties appal me. . . . Very roughly, it concerns a mystical synthesis of "America." History and fact, location, etc., all have to be transfigured into abstract form that would almost function independently of its subject matter. The initial impulses of "our people" will have to be gathered up toward the climax of the bridge, symbol of our constructive future, our unique identity, in which is included also our scientific hopes and achievements of the future. The mystic portent of all this is already flocking through my mind . . . but the actual statement of the thing, the marshalling of the forces, will take me months, at best, and I may have to give it up entirely before that; it may be too impossible an ambition. But if I do succeed, such a waving of banners, such an ascent of towers, such dancing, etc., will never before have been put down on paper!

Already he had started work on "Atlantis," which was to be the concluding section of the poem. But that waving of banners and ascent of towers had to be deferred when Crane lost his job in Cleveland and moved to New York. There, in the midst of distractions—looking for a job then finding it, sitting late in speakeasies, and roaming the city with exciting new friends—he had little time for the intense concentration that the poem required. He kept working on it, sometimes with a feeling of exaltation, but progress was slow. In the spring of 1924 it was halted altogether by his falling in love and writing his "Voyages" as a celebration. Again progress was halted when he decided to put together a book of shorter poems to precede *The Bridge*; he agonized over details. "I've spent all of today at one or two stubborn lines," he told a friend.

In December 1925 the financier Otto Kahn made him a

grant of (eventually) two thousand dollars, and Hart went to the country to spend the winter with Allen and Caroline Tate, in an old house near Patterson, New York. During the next four months he wrote another draft of "Atlantis" and made a good start on "Ave María"—jumping to the other end of his bridge—but more of his time was spent reading, and reading closely. Some of the authors were Melville, Prescott, Columbus (for the journals), and Alfred North Whitehead, each of whom would contribute something to his planned work. The plan itself was the principal achievement of those months. Now he saw more clearly what he hoped to write, if he could find the mood to write it.

The mood suddenly appeared in the last ten days of July 1926, when he was living in a house that his grandmother owned on the Isle of Pines. "Hail Brother!" he wrote on July 24 to his friend and mentor Waldo Frank. "I feel an absolute music in the air again and some tremendous rondure floating somewhere." He had just completed his Proem, "To Brooklyn Bridge," started earlier that summer, and was busy revising, once again, "Atlantis" and "Ave María." It was the beginning of the thirty-odd days that biographers call his *mensis mirabilis.* "I feel as though I were dancing on dynamite these days," he told Frank at the beginning of August, "—so absolute and elaborated has become the conception. All sections moving forward now at once!" Before the end of the month he had written something like two-thirds of *The Bridge* as it was finally published. Of course the materials had been patiently assembled, and he was chiefly waiting for the moment when they would put themselves together. But some productions of that miraculous month were completely new: "Cutty Sark" and "Three Songs"; and he had also written a number of lyrics that would be included in his posthumous sheaf of poems, *Key West.* Then, at the end of August, he had to rest, and he rewarded himself with a week in Havana that included an affair with a young Cuban sailor.

Those days on the Isle of Pines had been the climax of his creative life. Most of the symphony or cycle was completed by that time, but there were revisions to be made and there were missing sections that he regarded as essential. He worked on some of these after returning to the old house near Patterson. By the middle of July 1927 he had completed three of them, including "The River," which I think is the best of all. But it was to be the last of his greater poems—except for "The Broken Tower," written shortly before his death.

In September, before setting out to look for a job in the city, Hart wrote a very long letter to his benefactor Otto Kahn. The letter boasted of what he had so far accomplished and apologized for his delay in completing *The Bridge*. "It has taken a great deal of energy," he said, "—which has not been so difficult to summon as the necessary patience to wait, simply wait much of the time—until my instincts assured me that I had assembled my materials in proper order for a final welding into their natural form." Hart had always waited for those moments of confident inspiration and had tried to induce them by drinking, music, dancing, copulation, and anything else that might give him an overarching vision of his materials. It was all part of his system for producing masterpieces.

The letter continued: "Each section of the entire poem has presented its own unique problem of form, not alone in relation to the materials embodied within its separate confines, but also in relation to the other parts, *in series*, of the major design of the entire poem. Each is a separate canvas, as it were, yet none yields its entire significance when seen apart from the others." Hart himself was a resolute integrationist. He offered notes on several of the finished sections "as a comment on my architectural method," then went on to the still unwritten "Cape Hatteras." "It will be a kind of ode to Whitman," he said. "I am working on it as much as possible now. It presents very formidable problems, as, indeed, all the sections have." He was determined to complete not only "Hatteras" but the whole grand work as soon as possible. "If I could work in Mexico or Mallorca this winter," he said, "I could have *The Bridge* finished by next spring. But that is a speculation which depends entirely on your interest."

Kahn did show interest and offered a further loan, but *The Bridge* wasn't finished that winter, which Hart spent in California, or the following summer, when he returned to the old house near Patterson. His life was becoming more and more disordered, and his friends were disturbed by signs of physical deterioration. In December 1928 he received a legacy of five thousand dollars from his grandmother's estate and sailed for Europe. There he plunged into wilder revels, this time in the company of wealthy new friends, Harry and Ca-

resse Crosby, who admired his poems and applauded his follies. They gave him a room to write in, at the old mill they
had leased near Paris, and for a time he made some progress
on "Cape Hatteras." The Crosbys undertook to publish *The
Bridge* at their Black Sun Press, and finally Caresse, who could
lay down the law in her mild way, told him that she would
go ahead with the book, on schedule, whether or not Hart
supplied the missing sections. It would be a great poem, she
said, even without them. Hart was almost persuaded, but
then, begging for time, he insisted that three more sections
would be required to carry out his plan.

When he sailed home at the end of July, after spending a
week in jail as the sequel to a brawl outside a Montparnasse
café, Hart was determined to finish *The Bridge* at any cost.
It had become a test for himself and the supreme justification
he might offer to others for his apparently wasted years. He
could no longer afford to "wait, simply wait much of the time"
for the moment when his materials assembled themselves;
now he had to summon the moment by force of will. Drunk
or sober, but mostly sober, he reworked "Cape Hatteras"
and finished it by the middle of September. The other two
missing sections had been sketched out, and he told Caresse
in a letter that they might be ready the following week. Then
suddenly he found himself unable to write anything whatever,
and he began to drink heavily out of desperation.

The next three months were a series of battles with himself
in which he was usually but not always defeated. There were
nights when he telephoned wildly for help and a trusted friend,
usually Lorna Dietz or Peggy Robson, came to sit at his bedside while he threshed about in delirium tremens. There were
days and even weeks when he applied himself to the poems
in a sober frenzy. "Indiana" was finished after one of those
weeks. It went off to the Crosbys with apologies for the "let-
down" of its language—but, Hart added, "It does round out
the ["Powhatan's Daughter"] cycle, at least historically and
psychologically.

With only one more section to finish, Hart should have
been confident. Instead he fell into a period of despair and
sought refuge at his father's house in Ohio. He was cheerful
there until a threatened visit from his mother, with whom he
had bitterly quarreled, sent him scuttling back to Brooklyn.
Just as he was beginning to work seriously on the last section,

"Quaker Hill," the Crosbys appeared, bringing with them a round of parties. Hart was devoted to both the Crosbys, and he was deeply shaken by Harry's unexpected suicide, on the evening of December 10. Nevertheless he went back to work, by now in a dogged fashion. All of *The Bridge* was in type except for that last poem. Caresse, before sailing back to France alone, had promised to publish the book in February if she received a final manuscript of "Quaker Hill" by New Year's Day. Hart mailed it in time to catch the *Mauretania* on December 26. The great project had been completed in five weeks less than seven years.

Much as one admires Hart for having won that battle against his personal devils, one can't help asking whether those last two poems were worth the torments they inflicted on him. "Indiana" is flat and forced. It does provide a transition between two better sections, "The Dance" and "Cutty Sark," but not in the right manner. Lines such as "Lit with love shine" and "Will still endear her" belong in a music-hall ballad. "Quaker Hill" also has a function that it performs not too effectively. It deals with the decay of New England which, the poet felt, was involved with his own decay. On the whole it is better than "Indiana" and it has a very few memorable lines—among them "Shoulder the curse of sundered parentage," which applies so well to Hart—but most of the verse is tired. Only the last two stanzas rise to the level of his best work.

"Cape Hatteras," the section he finished in September of that year after struggling over it since 1927, has more to be said in its favor. It was part of his original conception; without it *The Bridge* would not have seemed to him complete. It embodies his complicated attitude toward American technology: first, admiration for its achievements and for the sheer beauty of machinery (including such items as ball bearings that revolve "In oilrinsed circles of blind ecstasy"); then, second, dismay at the dismal way of life that technology imposes on us, leading as it does to war in the skies; and finally the hope that technology will somehow be redeemed and spiritualized by a new race of poets, with Whitman, not Virgil, as their guide through the American inferno. "Cape Hatteras" has a sounder structure than most critics have been willing to admit, but it also has more ineptitudes of rhyme and image. Especially I am haunted by Hart's vision of a huge dirigible with landing decks, an aerial supership that would serve as mother vessel for whole squadrons of fighter planes. Hart was proud of that vision, and I remember his declaiming the passage, just after he had written it during a week spent at the old house near Patterson:

> While Cetus-like, O thou Dirigible, enormous Lounger
> Of pendulous auroral beaches,—satellited wide
> By convoy planes, moonferrets that rejoin thee
> On fleeing balconies as thou dost glide,
> —Hast splintered space!

Yes, we applauded the lines, but with a sense of uneasiness about his picture of wars to come. Of course he was writing in 1929, eight years before the *Hindenburg* burst into flames at Lakewood and ended the era of huge dirigibles. Hart was haunting himself as a futurist, a breed to whom the future is seldom kind. What seems less pardonable as one rereads the passage is the Elizabethan bombast, with all those capital letters and that high thee-thouing of a ballroom as if it were a divinity. "Cape Hatteras" is the section most often cited by those who insist that Hart's grand project was a failure. Still, the section had to be written. It sweeps along and—contrary to the judgment of some critics—almost reaches it goal. Continually it teeters on the edge of greatness, but at the risk of stumbling into absurdity.

3.

I don't like to align myself with the dispersionists, who are so often blind to implications and interconnections, but still I feel relief in passing from "Cape Hatteras" to the indubitably great sections of *The Bridge,* all finished by 1927. The great sections are "Ave Maria," "The River," "The Dance," "The Tunnel," and "Atlantis"; the nearly great are "To Brooklyn Bridge," "The Harbor Dawn," and "Cutty Sark." Each of these—including those I call "nearly great"—is not only successful in itself, having solved a special problem of form, but is also a contribution, as Hart rightly insisted, to "the major design of the entire poem." Each has the rich illogic of metaphor that marked his writing, as well as an extraordinary range of vocabulary. To put the revelations of modern music into words, Hart said in an early letter to Gorham Munson, "one needs to *ransack* the vocabularies of Shakespeare, Jonson, Webster (for theirs were the richest) and add on scientific, street and counter, and psychological terms, etc. Yet I claim such things can be done!" He had said in a still earlier letter: "One must be drenched in words, literally soaked with them to have the right ones form themselves into the proper pattern at the right moment."

One aspect of his vocabulary was the special effort he made to find concrete verbs of action that would vivify his images. There is a simple example early in the Proem, "To Brooklyn Bridge." The noonday sun *leaks* into the downtown canyons, where—in a noun so vigorous as to have the effect of a verb, it becomes "A rip-tooth of the sky's acetylene." Near the end of the same poem one admires the line "Already snow *submerges* an iron year." (The italics in these and later quotations are mine.) In the first stanza of "Van Winkle," a highway does not merely cross the continent; it *"Leaps* from Far Rockaway to Golden Gate." "And when the caribou *slant down* for salt," Hart writes in "The Dance," creating an image mostly with the one word *slant*. Another stanza in the same poem contains ten verbs, of which seven are in the imperative mood:

> *Dance,* Maquokeeta! snake that lives before,
> That casts his pelt and lives beyond! *Sprout,* horn!
> *Spark,* tooth! Medicine man, *relent, restore*—
> *Lie* to us,—*dance* us back the primal morn!

Of course Crane's magical use of language is not confined to verbs. Sometimes an adverb is the key to a phrase, as in two other lines from "The Dance": "Now lie *incorrigibly* what years between . . ." And "Fall, Sachem, *strictly* as the tamarack." *Strictly* is exactly the word for the fall of a conifer, just as *tamarack,* an Algonquian word, is a proper choice for the tree. Crane's adjectives are never wasted and are sometimes aptly new, as in "Preparing *penguin* flexions of the arms"—this in "The Tunnel," where "The subway yawns the quickest promise home." As for his nouns, when they are most abstract he likes to combine them with a concrete verb. Thus he says of his tramps in "The River" that *"dotting immensity/*They *lurk* across her, knowing her yonder breast."

Still it is the verbs that best reveal the intensity of his feelings or the simple accuracy of his perceptions. In the dementia of the subway he comes to suspect that love is only "a burnt match *skating* in a urinal"; it is the *skating* that makes the phrase unforgettable. In "The River" Crane is less agonized and more observing. Thus he notes that the tail-lights of an express train "wizen and converge, slip-/ ping gimleted and neatly out of sight." He says of the hoboes watching the Limited as they "ploddingly" follow the tracks:

> Caboose-like they go *ruminating* through
> Ohio, Indiana—blind baggage—
> To Cheyenne *tagging* . . . Maybe Kalamazoo.

Except for the rhyme that last word isn't quite right, having been abused by stand-up comics; but Crane is usually adept with place-names and their connotations. Far Rockaway, Golden Gate, Gravesend Manor (this last as a destination for people buried in the subway): each of these names serves one of his purposes. As for a town mentioned by the hoboes who used to follow the railroad tracks—

> "There's e like Boonville though, Buddy,"
> One said, excising a last burr from his vest,
> "—For early trouting."

Crane is trying to suggest a parallel between the hoboes and the American pioneers, and Booneville has the right echo for that. "Excising a last burr" is a modest but perfect phrase. When he comments on the hoboes as a group

> Each seemed a child, like me, on a loose perch,
> Holding to childhood like some termless play.
> John, Jake or Charley, hopping the slow freight
> —Memphis to Tallahassee—riding the rods,
> Blind fists of nothing, humpty-dumpty clods.

I could go on quoting from "The River," which is the section in which Crane best combined his accurate observation, his ear for idiom, and his broader vision of the American continent. It is also the longest section, except for "Cape Hatteras," and it is soundly constructed from the first to the last of its 144 lines; Crane had a gift for building with large blocks. The first of those blocks, in "The River," is the shortest; it is a passage of twenty-three lines. Hart described it in that famous letter to Otto Kahn, where he said that it is "an intentional burlesque on the cultural confusion of the present—a conglomeration of noises analogous to the strident impression of a fast express rushing by. The rhythm is jazz." In the second block, this one of forty-eight lines, "the rhythm settles down to a steady pedestrian gait, like that of wanderers plodding along. My tramps are psychological vessels, also. Their wanderings, as you will notice, carry the reader into interior and interior, finally to the great River." There follows a transitional passage of forty-one lines in a more elevated tone; it brings in suggestions of an earlier world, especially when "Trains sounding the long blizzards out" are transformed into "Papooses crying on the wind's long mane." The last block, in eight rhymed quatrains, is a solemn hymn in the River:

> You will not hear it as the sea; even stone
> Is not more hushed by gravity . . . But slow,
> As loth to take more tribute—sliding prone
> As one whose eyes were buried long ago. . . .

4.

I have always been stirred by those final quatrains, and the impression they made on me was deepened by a remembered circumstance. Early in October 1930, with Peggy, my first wife, I took passage on a freighter bound from New Orleans to Vera Cruz. We would be spending five or six hours on the Mississippi, I was told, before reaching the Gulf. I looked forward to those hours as I recalled Hart's poem. But the autumn day was ending without a sunset, and I could see little from the dock except a monotonous wall of forest to the westward and, if I walked to the bow, another wall to the east unbroken by villages or plantations. To soothe my disappointment I kept repeating lines from Hart's hymn:

> Down two more turns the Mississippi pours
> (Anon tall ironsides up from salt lagoons)
> And flows within itself, heaps itself free.
> All fades but one thin skyline 'round . . . Ahead
> No embrace opens but the stinging sea;
> The River lifts itself from its long bed. . . .

The last of these lines, in its marriage of image and sound impressed me as one of the greater lines in English poetry. I kept watching for the moment when the River would lift itself as if to embrace the Gulf, but it moved on in level silence. Gradually night fell. Then there was a light off the bow and I knew we were sliding out to sea, if only by the slap of little waves against the hull. I thought of Hart and his more poignant vision. I hadn't seen much of him the previous summer, though I heard that he was dejected after publication of *The Bridge* and unfavorable reviews by two or three of his respected friends. What would he do next?

Three years before, when he wrote "The River," he still hadn't seen the Mississippi except from transcontinental trains. In 1928, however, he had at last sailed from New Orleans on a steamer bound for New York. "The boat ride down the Delta," he reported in a letter to his father, "was one of the great days of my life. It was a place I had so often imagined and, as you know, written about in the River section of *The Bridge*. There is something tragically beautiful about the scene, the great, magnificent Father of Waters pouring itself at last into the oblivion of the Gulf." Hart had a gift that most of us lack, for first imagining a scene and then at last, when he beheld it, infusing the reality with his grand vision. I can picture him standing at the rail as he repeated his final majestic lines:

The River lifts itself from its long bed,

Poised wholly on its dream, a mustard glow
Tortured with history, its one will—flow!
—The Passion spreads in wide tongues, choked and slow
Meeting the Gulf, hosannas silently below.

My own disappointing voyage down the Mississippi and across the Gulf was to have its importance in his life. I enjoyed Mexico City more than I did the River, and in March of the following year, when Hart was awarded a Guggenheim fellowship, I suggested that he too might enjoy it instead of going to France as he had originally planned. It was dangerous advice in the circumstances, but Hart accepted it. Meanwhile my first marriage had broken up, and Peggy also went to Mexico, in June, to establish residence for a divorce. Hart lived wildly in Mexico City, and then in December he became Peggy's lover. To celebrate the change in his life, he wrote his last great poem, "The Broken Tower." On their return voyage to New York he committed suicide.

[1981]

ART TOMORROW: EPILOGUE TO THE 1934 EDITION OF *EXILE'S RETURN**

In the course of several articles recently printed in *The New Republic*, I criticized an attitude toward art and life that prevailed in the literary world of the 1920's. This attitude, which I called the religion of art, I tried to describe in terms of the books it produced and the unsatisfactory courses of action to which it led. I said that it now belonged to the past, that it died in theory with the Dada movement and in practice with the world crisis of capitalism, but I gave no more than a hint of the ideas or doctrines that I thought would take its place.

It is part of a critic's job to be honest with his readers, to state his own ideas and not to hide behind a mask of historical infallibility. What were the assumptions from which I wrote?

I might simply present them as the answers to an imaginary questionnaire. Let us suppose that you, the reader, have compiled a list of questions dealing with the problems of artists in the age now beginning. And let us suppose that I, the writer, have undertaken to answer them, not exhaustively, for that would require a book or a library of books, but informally and briefly.

Should artists devote themselves, you ask first of all, to art or propaganda?

In terms of an apparently simple distinction between two familiar words, this question conceals a type of metaphysical thinking that carries us back toward the beginning of German Romantic philosophy. It was Kant, in fact, who advanced the notion that esthetic activity and practical activity (in other words, art and life) are forever separate and that art has no goal outside itself, being "purposiveness without purpose"—

---

* This essay was used as the concluding section of *Exile's Return* in its first edition (New York: W. W. Norton and Company, 1934), but was omitted from later editions. [ed.]

Zweckmässigkeit ohne Zweck. This notion was elaborated by other German thinkers, and especially by Schopenhauer, who in turn exerted a great influence on the art-for-art's-sake movement in France. Eventually it took the shape of a whole series of things supposed to be in eternal opposition—form against matter, art against life, artists against philistines, poetry against science, emotion against reason, then vision or imagination against will or purpose, contemplation against action, and finally poetry or art against propaganda. In this last opposition, all the others are secretly contained. "Art" is vision, form, repose, truth and beauty, the eternal, everything that is "good" for the artist. "Propaganda" is effort, change, science, philistinism, falsity and ugliness, everything that is artistically "evil." Once we have accepted these definitions of art and propaganda, the question of choosing between them seems ridiculous.

But the definitions themselves are not to be accepted. They imply a special attitude toward life and, in particular, a metaphysical doctrine that Schopenhauer was the first to put forward. It was his idea that "the world" is evil and changing and animated by universal Will, and that the artist's duty and privilege is to escape from the world into the sphere of "art," of esthetic contemplation, of perfect will-lessness. One cannot say that any metaphysical notion of this sort is now "exploded" in the sense that a scientific theory may be exploded by the accumulated force of observed facts. It is certain, however, that Schopenhauer's metaphysic is sentimental and foreign to the scientific temper.

Today we know as a simple matter of record that the universe is actually changing in all its parts, from star galaxies down to species of microscopic plants, but we cannot say that this process of universal change is either "good" or "evil"; our adjectives aren't big enough to circumscribe the cosmos. Today we know by virtue of our personal experiences, our pains and pleasures, that human society is changing also. We know that men's ideas and ambitions, and the conflicts between them, are part of this changing world, as are also the works of art that men produce. There is no single type of human activity, whether it be painting pictures or smoking pipes or making money, that can be treated as if it existed separately from all the other types of activity. The whole series of oppositions—art against life, poetry against science, con-

templation against action—can safely be swept aside. The real
answer to the question whether writers and painters should
devote themselves to art or propaganda is that the question
is irrelevant: writers should devote themselves to writing and
painters to painting.

Yet there is a real distinction that partly takes the place of
the one supposed to exist between art and propaganda. The
real distinction is not metaphysical, but personal and practical,
and it depends very simply on the level of mind from which
one writes. If one writes only from the top level of consciousness, in the light of beliefs that have been recently acquired
and not assimilated, one is almost certain to write badly, to
neglect or distort the things that are hidden underneath, to
write in a way that is emotionally false and can be dismissed
as "propaganda." But if one has fully absorbed the same
beliefs, has felt and lived them, one may treat them in a way
that is emotionally effective—that is in other words "art."

And now you have another question. *What, you ask, is the
function of art? In other words, what will take the place of the
religion of art after it disappears?*

I don't know what is the function of art. Is it a "purging,"
a "refinement of gross experience," a "center of repose"; is
it amusement, escape, self-expression, or a useful means of
inciting people to good actions? I suspect that on occasion it
can be any or all of these. One thing I know for certain. There
is no single theory of the function of art that has not finally
confined and narrowed and impoverished art, whether the
theory be that of Plato, Aristotle, Kant, Schopenhauer, Mallarmé, Plekhanov or the Russian Association of Proletarian
Writers. Art is obviously richer, more varied in its purposes
and effects, than any of the theories that have tried to reduce
it to order and guide it in one direction. When the religion
of art disappears, let us hope that no other limiting doctrine
will take its place.

And yet—always this qualification creeps in—there is one
function of art I should like to see emphasized above the
others, and that is its humanizing function. I believe that all
good works of literary art have the same fundamental thesis.
All of them teach us that life is bigger than life; that life as
portrayed by the creative imagination is more intense, more
varied, more purposeful (or perhaps more futile), more tragic

or comic, more crowded with events and meanings and yet more harmoniously organized than is the life we have been leading day by day. Sometimes we are discouraged by the contrast and try to escape into a dream world that seems to be, but really is not, the world of the artist. Sometimes we merely contemplate the work of art, gratefully and with a feeling of relief from strain. Sometimes, however, we try to reinterpret our daily lives in the light of the artist's vision. The new values we derive from his work, when projected into our own experience, make it seem more poetic, dramatic or novelistic, more sharply distinguished from the world of nature, in a word, more human.

In addition to giving more humanity to our lives, art also has the function of humanizing nature, in the sense of making it more fit for human beings to live in. The prehistoric world must have seemed alien and terrible to the first tribes that wandered over the face of it. Vast portions of the world are alien to their descendants today. Before a man can feel at home in any surroundings, whether those of seaside or forest, metropolis or factory, he must first transform the objects about him by connecting them with human emotions, by finding their purpose and direction, by making them understandable. He repeats the same process in the world at large, by perceiving in it architectural and musical forms, unity and rhythm, by giving it a history, and chiefly by transfusing it with myth. This last phrase is a little pretentious, and yet it describes an essentially simple operation of the mind. It is what a sailor does by calling his vessel "she," and an engineer by giving a name and human attributes to his engine—"Old Ninety-Six is cranky" he says, reaching out to touch the iron side of it affectionately. A poet or a painter does the same thing in a richer and more communicable fashion; he gives things names and values; he makes them touchable.

At any rate this double humanizing function of art, as exercised on the world of nature and the world of society, is a task that is never finished; it has to be repeated with each succeeding age. Continually the natural environment is changing—is being changed by men whose relations with one another are also changing, together with the means by and the ends for which they live. Every age has its own myths to create, but some ages fail to create them. Often it happens that both the human and the natural worlds transform themselves so rapidly that they outrun men's ability to digest them. This undoubtedly is what has taken place since the Great War, with the rapid development of applied science, power machinery and mass production, the splendor and decay of capitalism and the growing self-awareness of the proletariat. What Shelley said of his own age can be applied more truly to ours: "We want the creative faculty to imagine that which we know; we want the generous impulse to act that which we imagine; we want the poetry of life: our calculations have outrun conception; we have eaten more than we can digest." Today we are entering a period when artists of Shelley's stature are more necessary than scientists or engineers.

And now you turn to the political questions that have been playing an always greater part in literary discussions. *Should artists*, you ask, *take part in the class struggle?*

There is no use adjuring them to take part in it or warning them to keep out of it; the adjurations and warnings are so much wasted breath. The artists will and do take part in it, because they are men before they are writers or painters, and because their human interests are involved, and because they can't stay out of the battle without deliberately blinding and benumbing themselves—and even then they are likely to find that they have been led into it without their knowledge and on a side they mightn't consciously have chosen.

And which side do you think the artists will choose?

I hope and trust that a great number of them will take the workers' side, and I think that doing so will make them better artists. On the other hand, I realize that it will be hard for many others not to take the side of the classes now in power.

On that side are most of their old friendships and childhood memories. On that side are all the institutions they have been depending on for a livelihood—the press, the stage, the movies, the radio and, in the background, business, the schools and universities, the Army, the Church, the State. On that side, too, there seems to be all the culture inherited from the past, and with it all the mellowness and tolerance of a class grown old in power, the glamor that surrounds men and women in the habit of being served and obeyed. On the other side are ordinary people who never heard of Chaucer, and dress without taste when they don't dress shabbily, and eat their food with smacking noises and pile cups and saucers on top of their plates to show that the meal is over. They are people without manners or distinction, Negroes, hill billies, poor whites, Jews, Wops and Hunkies. If they should win the struggle here as they have in Russia, there are likely to be years of privation and desperate inefficiency, and there are certain to be harshness, narrowness, fanaticism, the eternal vices of a class struggling to power.

Yet the capitalists can in reality promise less than they seem to promise. The audience they offer to works of art is always limited, not only in numbers but also in capacity for appreciation. Under capitalism only a few people can afford to buy books or pictures or attend plays or concerts, and many of them are snobs who don't come to see or hear, but merely to be *seen* in a good theatre, to be *heard* talking about the books they have read. The mellowness and liberalism of the present ruling class are merely the ornaments of its prosperous years; in times of danger they give way to brutality direct and unconcealed. Its cherishing of individual freedom gives way at critical moments to a call for unquestioning blind obedience to the State, and its fostering of science is replaced by dark myths of race and war and destiny. Eventually it threatens the complete destruction of culture, since its inevitable and insoluble self-contradictions are leading it toward wars in which, tomorrow, not only books will be destroyed, but the libraries that contain them, and not only museums, universities, theatres, picture galleries, but also the wealth by which they are supported and the living people for whom they exist.

These are the prospects really held out to the artist by those who rule under the profit system. As for the other side, that of the factory workers and poor farmers and people now looking for jobs, it can actually promise much more than it seems to promise. First of all, it can offer an end to the desperate feeling of solitude and uniqueness that has been oppressing artists for the last two centuries, the feeling that has reduced some of the best of them to silence or futility and the weaker ones to insanity or suicide. It can offer instead a sense of comradeship and participation in a historical process vastly bigger than the individual. It can offer an audience, not trained to appreciate the finer points of style or execution— that will come later—but larger and immeasurably more eager than the capitalist audience and quicker to grasp essentials.

And it can offer something else to the artist. Once he knows and feels the struggles of the oppressed classes all over the world, he has a way to get hold both of distant events and those near at hand, and a solid framework on which to arrange them. Two housewives gossiping on the back porch about their husbands' jobs and the price of groceries, a small merchant bankrupt in the next block, a love affair broken off, a mortgage foreclosed, a manufacturer's rise to power—all these incidents take their place in a historical pattern that is also illuminated by revolts in Spain, a new factory in the Urals, an obscure battle in the interior of China. Values exist again, after an age in which they seemed to be lost; good and evil are embodied in men who struggle. It is no longer possible to write, as did Joseph Wood Krutch only a few years ago, that "we have come, willy-nilly, to see the soul of man as commonplace and its emotions as mean," or to say that the tragic sense of life has been lost forever. Tragedy lives in the stories of the men now dying in Chinese streets or in German prisons for a cause by which their lives are given dignity and meaning. Artists used to think that the world outside had become colorless and dull in comparison with the bright inner world they tenderly nourished; now it is the inner world that has been enfeebled as a result of its isolation; it is the outer world that is strong and colorful and demands to be imaginatively portrayed. The subjects are waiting everywhere. There are great days ahead for artists if they can survive in the struggle and keep their honesty of vision and learn to measure themselves by the stature of their times.

[1934]

THE FORTY DAYS OF THOMAS WOLFE

I have just read Thomas Wolfe's new novel,* all of the 912 big, solidly printed pages, almost every one of the 450,000 words, and, like a traveler returning safely from Outer Mongolia, I am eager to record what I heard and saw during forty days in the wilderness. It isn't so much a book review I should like to write as a topographical description of the regions newly explored, with a list of deserts and oases.

I have to report that the good passages in the novel are, first of all, the picture of Uncle Bascom Pentland, originally published by itself and now partly deprived of its effectiveness through being sawed and mortised into another framework, but still grotesque and vastly appealing; then the description of the little people in Professor Hatcher's course in dramatic writing; then the burlesque adventures of Oswald Ten Eyck in search of food and fame; then the death of old Oliver Gant, a tremendous Dostoevskian scene; then the comedy of Abe Jones, the melodrama of the consumptive cuckold, the tragedy of the Coulson family at Oxford; then the disintegration of Francis Starwick, whom I knew at college under his own name, and whose story is long enough to form a good novel in itself; then finally the train ride to Orléans and the episode of the old humbug countess. Together these scenes compose at least a third of the book, and they are extraordinarily strong and living. Thomas Wolfe at his best is the only contemporary American writer who can be mentioned in the same breath with Dickens and Dostoevsky. But the trouble is that the best passages are scattered, that they occur without logic or pattern, except the biographical pattern of the hero's life, and that they lack the cumulative effect, the slow tightening of emotions to an intolerable pitch, that one finds in great novels like *The Possessed*.

I have to report that the bad passages are about as numerous

* *Of Time and the River.* [ed.]

and extensive in area as the good ones. There is the description of Eugene Gant's vast aloneness at Harvard, there are Eugene's reveries about time and death and the ever-flowing mysterious river of life, there is his drunken police-station brawl in South Carolina, there are his anxieties as a teacher and his European musings on the lonely American soul. In particular there are the beginning of the book, in which he flees like Orestes into the North, and the end, in which he returns to set his Antæus feet on native soil. And, just as the good parts of the novel are massively and overwhelmingly good, so too the bad parts are Brobdingnagianly bad, are possibly worse than anything that any other reputable American novelist has permitted himself to publish.

The good and the bad can both be expressed in a general statement. When Wolfe is writing about people that his hero loved or hated or merely observed with delighted curiosity, then he writes with real vigor and with an astonishing sense of character; he writes clear, swinging prose. But when he is dealing with the hero, Eugene Gant, he almost always overwrites; he repeats himself, grows dithyrambic, shouts and sings in blank verse, scatters his adjectives like a charge of rock-salt from a ten-gauge shotgun. He is prayerful and solemn; all his grand wild humor is hidden away. One could scarcely say that *Of Time and the River* becomes a bad novel whenever the hero appears on the scene, for he is always there; but the author's style goes flabby as soon as attention is taken away from the outside world and concentrated on the hero's yearning and hungering soul.

The truth is that although Eugene Gant has many individual and warmly human traits, they scarcely add up into a character. He is not anyone that we should immediately recognize in the street, like his father or his Uncle Bascom Pentland. Rather than being a person, he is a proud abstraction, "a legend of man's hunger in his youth," and his actions are magnified to such an extent that they cease to resemble those of ordinary young men. Never, in the course of this novel, does Eugene go for a walk: no, "like an insatiate and maddened animal he roamed the streets, trying to draw up mercy from the cobblestones." Never does he study a textbook: no, "he would prowl the stacks of the library at night, pulling books from a thousand shelves and reading them like a madman." If he receives a polite letter of rejection, he is not

merely downhearted: no, "he stood there in the hallway
. . . his face convulsed and livid, his limbs trembling with
rage, his bowels and his heart sick and trembling with a hideous gray nausea of hopelessness and despair, his throat chok-
ing with an intolerable anguish of resentment and wrong."
Then, when he begins to write once more, "the words were
wrung out of him in a kind of bloody sweat, they poured out
of his fingertips, spat out of his snarling throat like writhing
snakes: he wrote them with his heart, his brain, his sweat, his
guts." He is Goethe giving birth to Werther, he is Orestes in
flight before the Furies, he is Young Faustus, Telemachus,
Jason, he is Antæus seeking his own life-restoring soil—and
at the same time he is a tall young man from Asheville who
studied at the University of North Carolina and at Harvard,
taught at Washington Square College, spent two years abroad,
came back to Brooklyn—he is unmistakably Thomas Wolfe
himself, and there are at least two occasions, on pages 186
and 466, where the author refers to Eugene in the first person
singular.

Of Time and the River might have been a better book if
the author had spoken in the first person from beginning to
end. It seems to me that frank autobiography is a safer form
than the disguised autobiographical novel. When the writer
says "I felt this" and "I did that," he is forced, paradoxically,
to look at himself from the outside. There are common rules
of courtesy that compel him to moderate his boasts, to speak
as one person among others, even to invent a character for
himself. On the other hand, if he speaks of "me" under the
guise of "him," all his acts are made conveniently impersonal.
He is encouraged to regard himself, not as a character among
others, but rather as a unique and all-embracing principle—
in youth as the universal Boy, in manhood as the universal
Poet. He is tempted to exhibit and magnify and admire his
own adventures, till perhaps he reaches the point of wondering how he could ever "find a word to speak the joy, the
pain, the grandeur bursting in the great vine of his heart,
swelling like a huge grape in his throat—mad, sweet, wild,
intolerable with all the mystery, loneliness, wild secret joy,
and death, the ever returning and renewing fruitfulness of
earth." In other words, he reaches the point of writing like
a God-intoxicated ninny.

Such are the reports and ideas that I carried back from my

forty days in the wilderness. This book of Thomas Wolfe's is better and worse than I have dared to say—richer, shriller, more exasperating. Cut down by half, it would be twice as good. Strangely, in the midst of its gigantic faults, it gives you the idea that Wolfe might and could write a novel that was great beyond question. But he will not write it until he chooses some other theme and some other hero than a young Faustus and Orestes squeezing out his blood, his sweat, his guts and not enough of his brains to produce the fabulous great American novel.

[1935]

EDMUND WILSON IN RUSSIA

Four years ago Edmund Wilson wrote *The American Jitters*, possibly the most valuable and certainly among the least appreciated of all the books that have dealt with the depression. It contains a series of articles that appeared in *The New Republic*, but the book itself has to be read from beginning to end in order to get the cumulative effect of it. Ostensibly Wilson was reporting the state of the nation in 1931, after one of those transcontinental tours that so many journalists have made since then. But there was another story involved, the story of a traveler in search of a philosophy. At first Wilson was a progressive, mildly hopeful that older progressives like Senators Norris and Cutting would point out a path for him to follow; then step by step he became convinced that Marx was his real guide, that our whole society was bankrupt and would have to be reorganized. The book ends with a succession of powerful chapters, in one of which he expresses at some length his admiration for Soviet Russia.

Wilson has now fulfilled the promise half-made in those chapters: he has gone to Russia and has formed his own judgment of the new civilization there. But Wilson's new book, *Travels in Two Democracies*, also contains some further reports on America, and these I found definitely inferior to *The American Jitters*. The writing is just as good as ever, and there are two passages that are pretty nearly superb—a report on the Oxford Groups called "Saving the Right People and Their Butlers" and a fantasy called "What to Do till the Doctor Comes," full of tepid vice and people too passionless to be damned. But the section as a whole is composed of postscripts and codicils; it lacks the clear direction that Wilson's earlier pieces seem to derive from their sympathy for the working class.

The Russian half of the book, which was printed in part by *The New Republic*, has started an argument that shows no sign of stopping. It seems to me that most of those who have been abusing Wilson, and some of those praising him, have misunderstood what he was trying to do. In the first place, his account of Russia is more favorable to the Soviets than anyone would guess from the separately printed extracts (most of which dealt with Moscow, a city where he felt less at home than in Leningrad or Odessa). In the second place, his habit of relating trivial incidents does not reveal a trivial mind. It is part of a plan which consists in reducing socialism to the scale of daily life, and in writing an account of Russia based on what he saw with his own eyes and heard with his own ears. (The only time his method seems to betray him is in his passages on Stalin, where actually he departs from it to the extent of depending on hearsay.) And, in the third place, Wilson's narrative is valuable not only as a vivid impression of Russian life but also as a mental autobiography written with persistent candor.

In a sense it is a sequel to *The American Jitters*, but this time the stages in his thinking are more difficult to explain. The first stage, I think, was a puzzled disillusionment, never directly expressed but underlying whole chapters. Wilson in his earlier book had spoken of hoping to see "the whole world fairly and sensibly run, as Russia now is run, instead of by shabby politicians in the interests of acquisitive manufacturers, businessmen and bankers." He had condemned his fellow intellectuals for "their extreme skittishness about Russia," and had said that writers would be better off under socialism. But he found that Russian writers were either conforming to official standards at some cost to themselves or else were rebelling at a still heavier cost; and he decided that the intellectual world had an atmosphere of nervous tension that suggested New York. The politicians in Moscow were more honest but hardly more appealing than politicians elsewhere. As for the Russian masses, he was repelled by their inefficiency and vast inertia.

Soon his thinking entered a second stage. He became an American patriot, took pride in American initiative, the American standard of living, and partially forgot the ignorance and misery that he had chronicled in *The American Jitters*. It was unfortunate, he thought, that Russia had become the first socialist country. "The opponents of socialism can always put down to socialism anything they find objectionable in Russia. The advocates of socialism are betrayed into defending things which are really distasteful to them, and which they have no business defending." With its greater technical knowledge and its republican institutions, America would have an easier time developing a collective society.

A third stage in his thinking began on the homeward journey, even before he crossed the Polish border. He was suddenly sorry to be leaving Russia and began to think of all its friendly and human qualities. The sight of fat Polish businessmen, overbearing officers and whining beggars made him long to be back in a country where nobody seemed rude or servile or tried to sell you anything whatever. He reflected that the Soviet Union was "at the moral top of the world, where the light never really goes out." The Western capitals, Berlin, Paris, now seemed dead beyond hope of resurrection.

But Wilson had one other reaction to the Soviet Union. It is harder to explain, because partly it was an instinctive response to a new situation—almost a muscular reflex, as if he had touched a steam pipe and suddenly drawn back his hand. But the situation was permanent, and the response to it became fixed in his conscious thinking. . . . In Odessa, Wilson spent six weeks recovering from an attack of scarlet fever. The hospital where he was quarantined was not one of the new ones designed since the revolution: it was the old Odessa pesthouse, built in 1795 and practically never cleaned. It was understaffed, archaic, crowded with noisily convalescent children; the nurses were most of them incompetent, even though they were enormously friendly and obliging; only the few Communists were trying seriously to keep things in order. But the point of the episode was that Wilson was forced to be among other people, eat, talk, play, sleep among them day after day, with scarcely an hour to himself. For the first time since the War he had the experience of living collectively and, in a curious fashion, he liked it. He was for a short time very unhappy when he left the hospital and went to a hotel:

> Alone in the silence of the room, I suddenly dropped into a depression of a kind which I had never known all the time that I had been in the hospital. It was loneliness: I was missing the children and the nurses who had bothered me when I was trying to work and from whom I had looked forward to escaping. I walked back and forth across the room a few times, then began

declaiming aloud some old poems of my own composition. I
found that some need was relieved: my loneliness disappeared.
It was the assertion of my own personality against those weeks
of collective living.

To me this episode seemed to explain a good deal that had
gone before it. More than once Edmund Wilson in the Soviet
Union had been asserting his own personality against the
threat or the temptation of collective life—hence his discom-
fort in Moscow and his rather hostile attitude toward Russian
writers, especially toward those who lived at peace with the
new society. Back in Washington he had felt and expressed
the same dislike for the New Dealers; his logical reasons for
distrusting them were entirely different, but the emotional
background was the same. He had sheared away from all sorts
of political groups even when their ideas appeared to be similar to his own—first from the Progressives, then from the
Communists, then later, I think, from the American Workers'
Party; and I am not aware that he responded to the persistent
overtures of the Trotskyites and the Lovestonites. Fundamentally he was an individualist of the old school, without
even the need for blind and partial coöperation that is forced
on most of us by capitalism. As he explained at the end of
The American Jitters, his own family of doctors and lawyers
and professors had retained the traditions of a pre-capitalistic
era. They were descended from country squires; and Wilson
himself, in any large gathering, must have felt very much like
a country squire forced to go into town for a lawsuit and rub
elbows with greasy politicians.

Always, retiring into himself, he would declaim "some old
poems of my own composition"—that is, he would remind
himself of those defenses built by any sensitive man against
the risk of having his personality invaded by the anonymous
and colorless throng. But nobody in this age can live alone,
can live without help; and Wilson has begun lately to invoke
the great men of the age that is passing. He is developing a
cult of the genius and the hero that is evident in more than
one of his Russian notes—for example, in his tribute to Elinor
Wylie and in what he says about Borodin, the man who organized a Chinese army and nearly won the East for Communism. "I believe," Wilson wrote after seeing him at a

theatre, "that his moral stature and the attitude that people adopt toward him make him seem bigger and taller than he is. This is what the early race were like."

The attitude that Wilson half reveals—the mixture of distrust for the masses and admiration for the "early race" who tried to redeem them—is even clearer in a final passage, a magnificent tribute to Lenin in his tomb under the Kremlin wall:

> And here we come to gaze down at this shell of flesh, in its last thinness, its delicacy and fragility, before it crumbles and loses the mold—this skin and bone still keeping the stamp of that intellect, that passion, that will, whose emergence has stunned the world almost more with embarrassment at being made to extend its conception of what man, as man alone, can accomplish, than admiration at the achievements of genius. And these countrymen of his are amazed, with their formless and expressionless faces, when they look down on him and know that he was one of them, and that he invoked from their loose and sluggish plasm all those triumphs to which life must rise and to which he thought himself the casual signpost.

At first on reading a passage like this one feels an exhilaration compounded of pride and gratitude—pride that one of our human race could rise so high, and gratitude to the writer who was moved by Lenin's greatness and expressed it in such fine prose. But why did Wilson have to emphasize his admiration for Lenin by asserting a contempt for Lenin's countrymen? Is there not a purely subjective emotion mingled with and falsifying his judgment of history? Why does he forget to say that Lenin, in addition to creating the new revolutionary Russia, was himself shaped and forged by an older revolutionary Russia? For it is the simple fact that Lenin's triumphant career was made possible by hundreds of broken careers, including that of his own brother, who was executed for trying to kill the Tsar. It is the simple fact that his mind was sharpened by disputes with other minds almost as keen; that his revolutionary determination was strengthened by his determined comrades; that he could depend on the help of thousands not too humble to die for the cause which he represented; that in short he was the arm and voice of an idea, the symbol to a nation of that new age in which everything would be different. Lenin is the archetype of the modern hero, the man whose individual character is affirmed and enforced by his very sacrifice of individuality to a common cause. And it seems now that Wilson has studied his books, has worshiped at his tomb, has even shared in his heritage, without understanding the sources of his strength or the dream for which he lived.

[1936]

DOS PASSOS:
POET AGAINST THE WORLD

Sometimes in reading Dos Passos you feel that he is two novelists at war with each other. One of them is a late-Romantic, a tender individualist, an esthete traveling about the world in an ivory tower that is mounted on wheels and coupled to the last car of the Orient Express. The other is a hard-minded realist, a collectivist, a radical historian of the class struggle. The two authors have quarreled and collaborated in all his books, but the first had the larger share in *Three Soldiers* and *Manhattan Transfer*. The second, in his more convincing fashion, wrote most of *The 42nd Parallel, 1919* and *The Big Money*. Although the conflict between them seems to me rather less definite on reflection than it did at a first glance, nevertheless it is real; and it helps to explain several tendencies not only in the work of Dos Passos but in recent American fiction as a whole.

The late-Romantic element in his novels goes back to his years in college. After being graduated from Choate, a good New England preparatory school, Dos Passos entered Harvard in 1912, at the beginning of a period which was later known as that of the Harvard esthetes. The best fictional record of those years has been written by Dos Passos himself, in the section of *1919* that deals with the early life of Richard Ellsworth Savage. But Dos Passos does not discuss the ideas of the period that underlay its merely picturesque manifestations, its mixture of incense, patchouli and gin, its erudition displayed before barroom mirrors. The esthetes themselves were not philosophers; they did not seek to define their attitude except vaguely, in poems; but I think that most of them would have subscribed to the following propositions:

That the cultivation and expression of his own sensibility are the only justifiable aims for a poet;

That originality is his principal virtue;

That society is hostile, stupid and unmanageable; it is the

world of the philistines, from which it is the poet's duty and
privilege to remain aloof;

That the poet is always misunderstood by the world, and
should, in fact, deliberately make himself misunderstandable,
for the greater glory of art;

That he triumphs over the world, at moments, by mystically
including it within himself: these are his moments of *ecstasy,*
to be provoked by any means in his power—alcohol, drugs,
asceticism or debauchery, madness, suicide;

That art, the undying expression of such moments, exists
apart from the world; it is the poet's revenge on society.

There are a dozen other propositions that might be added
to this unwritten manifesto, but the ideas I have listed were
those most generally held. They are sufficient to explain the
intellectual atmosphere of the young men who read Pater and
Arthur Machen's *The Hill of Dreams,* who argued about St.
Thomas in sporting houses, and who wandered through the
slums of South Boston with dull eyes for "the long rain slant-
ing on black walls" and eager eyes for the face of an Italian
woman who, in the midst of this squalor, suggested the Virgin
in Botticelli's "Annunciation." As a matter of fact, it was not
Dos Passos who argued about St. Thomas, but he was the
one who found the Botticelli Virgin, and it is significant that
he found her in the slums. There was more realism even in
his early poems than in those of the other young men who
contributed to the *Harvard Monthly;* but there was no less
yearning after ecstasy and no less hatred of the stupid world
that never understands a poet until he is dead.

The attitude I have been describing was not confined to
one college and one magazine. It was often expressed in the
Dial, which for some years was almost a postgraduate edition
of the *Harvard Monthly;* it existed in earlier publications like
the *Yellow Book* and *La Revue Blanche;* it has a history, in
fact, almost as long as that of the upper middle class under
capitalism. For the last half-century it has furnished the intellectual background of poems and essays without number.
It would seem to preclude, in its adherents, the objectivity
that is generally associated with good fiction; yet the esthetes
themselves sometimes wrote novels, as did their predecessors
all over the world. Such novels are still being published, and
are often favorably criticized: "Mr. Zed has written the somber and absorbing story of a talented musician tortured by

the petty atmosphere of the society in which he is forced to live. His wife, whom the author portrays with witty malice, prevents him from breaking away. After an unhappy love affair and the failure of his artistic hopes, he commits suicide. . . ."

Such is the plot forever embroidered in the type of fiction that ought to be known as the Art Novel. There are two essential characters, two antagonists, the Poet and the World. The Poet—who may also be a painter, a violinist, an inventor, an architect or a centaur—is generally to be identified with the author of the novel, or at least with the novelist's ideal picture of himself. He tries to assert his individuality in despite of the World, which is stupid, unmanageable and usually victorious. Sometimes the Poet triumphs, but the art novelists seem to realize, as a class, that the sort of hero they describe is likely to be defeated in the sort of society he has to face. Sometimes, but not as a general rule, that society is seen with the accurate eyes of hatred. More often it is blurred in a fog of mere dislike; so little does it exist in its real outlines, so great is the author's solicitude for the Poet, that we are surprised to see him vanquished by such a shadowy opponent. It is as if we were watching motion pictures in the dark house of his mind. There are dream pictures, nightmare pictures; then suddenly the walls crash in and the Poet disappears without ever knowing why; he perishes by his hand, leaving behind him the memory of his ecstatic moments and the bitter story of his failure, now published as a revenge on the World.

Dos Passos's early books are by no means pure examples of the art novel. The world was always painfully real to him; it was never veiled with mysticism and his characters were rarely symbolic. From the very first he was full of pity for the underdogs and hope for the revolution. Yet consider the real plot of a novel like *Three Soldiers*. A talented young musician, during the War, finds that his sensibilities are being outraged, his aspirations crushed, by society as embodied in the American army. He deserts after the Armistice and begins to write a great orchestral poem. When the military police come to arrest them, the sheets of music flutter one by one into the spring breeze; and we are made to feel that this ecstatic song choked off and dispersed on the wind—like how many others—is the real tragedy of the War. Some years later, in writing *Manhattan Transfer,* Dos Passos seemed to be undertaking a different type of novel, one that tried with no little success to render the color and movement of a whole city. But as the book goes on, it comes to be more and more the story of Jimmy Herf (the Poet) and Ellen Thatcher (the Poet's wife), and the poet is once again frustrated by his wife and the World: after one last drink he leaves a Greenwich Village party and commits an act of symbolic suicide by walking out alone, bareheaded, into the dawn. It is obvious, however, that a new conflict has been superimposed on the older one: the social ideas of the novelist are, in *Manhattan Transfer,* at war with his personal emotions. The ideas are now those of a reformer or even a revolutionist; the emotions are still those of the *Yellow Book* and the *Harvard Monthly.*

Even in *The 42nd Parallel* and *1919* and *The Big Money,* that second conflict persists, but it has become less acute. The social ideas have invented a new form for themselves and have drawn much closer to the personal emotions. Considered together—as they have to be considered—the three novels belong to a new category of American fiction.

2.

In the trilogy ending with *The Big Money,* Dos Passos is trying to write a private history of the thirty years that began with the new century and ended with the crash in 1929. He continues to deal with the lives of individuals, but these are seen in the perspective of historical events. His real hero is society itself—American society as embodied in forty or fifty more or less typical characters who drift along with it, struggle to change its course, or merely to find a secure footing—perhaps they build a raft of wreckage and grow fat on the refuse floating about them; perhaps they go under in some obscure eddy—while always the current sweeps them onward toward new social horizons. In this sense, Dos Passos has written the first American collective novel.

The principal characters are brought forward one at a time; the story of each is told in bare, straightforward prose that describes what they do and see but rarely what they feel. Thus, Fainy McCreary, born in Connecticut, is a printer who joins the Wobblies and later goes to Mexico to fight in the revolution there, but runs a bookstore instead. J. Ward

Moorehouse, born in Wilmington, Delaware, begins his business career in a real-estate office. He writes songs, marries and divorces a rich woman, works for a newspaper in Pittsburgh—at the end of fifty-seven pages he is a successful public-relations counselor embarked on a campaign to reconcile capital and labor at the expense of labor. Joe and Janey Williams are the children of a tugboat captain from Washington, D. C.; Janey studies shorthand and gets a job as J. Ward Moorehouse's secretary; Joe plays baseball, enlists in the Navy, deserts after a brawl and becomes a merchant seaman. Eleanor Stoddard is a poor Chicago girl who works at Marshall Field's; she learns how to speak French to her customers and order waiters about "with a crisp little refined moneyed voice." Charley Anderson is a wild Swedish boy from the Red River Valley who drifts about the country from job to job and girl friend to girl friend, till at last he sails for France as the automobile mechanic of an ambulance section.

All these characters are introduced in *The 42nd Parallel* and, except for Fainy McCreary and Charley Anderson, they all reappear in *1919*. Now they are joined by others: Richard Ellsworth Savage, a Kent School boy who goes to Harvard and writes poetry; Daughter, a warm-hearted flapper from Dallas, Texas; Ben Compton, a spectacled Jew from Brooklyn who becomes a radical. Gradually their careers draw closer together, till all of them are caught up in the War. "This whole goddam war's a gold brick," says Joe Williams. "No matter how it comes out, fellows like us get the s—y end of the stick, see? Well, what I say is all bets is off . . . every man go to hell in his own way . . . and three strikes is out, see?" Three strikes is out for Joe, when his skull is cracked in a saloon brawl at Saint-Nazaire on Armistice night. Daughter is killed in an airplane accident; she provoked it herself in a fit of hysteria after becoming pregnant and then being jilted by Dick Savage—who for his part survives as the shell of a man, all the best of him having died when he decided to join the army and make a career for himself and let his pacifist sentiments go hang. Benny Compton gets ten years in Atlanta as a conscientious objector. Everybody in the novel suffers from the War and finds his own way of going to hell—everybody except the people without bowels, the empty people like Eleanor Stoddard and J. Ward Moorehouse, who stuff themselves with the right sentiments and make the proper contacts.

In *The Big Money* the principal character is Charley Anderson, the skirt-chasing automobile mechanic, who comes sailing back from France as a bemedaled aviator, hero and ace. He helps to start an airplane manufacturing company (like Eddie Rickenbacker); he marries a banker's daughter, plunges in the stock market, drinks, quarrels with the men under him, loses his grip and gets killed in an automobile accident. Dick Savage, the Harvard esthete of doubtful sex, is now an advertising man, first lieutenant of the famous J. Ward Moorehouse in his campaign to popularize patent medicines as an expression of the American spirit, as self-reliance in medication. Eveline Hutchins, who played a small part in both the earlier novels, is now an unhappy middle-aged nymphomaniac. Don Stevens, the radical newspaper man of *1919*, has become a Communist, a member of the Central Executive Committee after the dissenters and deviationists have been expelled (and among them poor Ben Compton, released from Atlanta). New people also appear: for example, Margo Dowling, a shanty-Irish girl who gets to be a movie actress by sleeping with the right people. Almost all the characters are now tied together by love or business, politics or pure hatred. And except for Mary French from Colorado, who half-kills herself working as the secretary of one radical relief organization after another—except for Mary French and her father and poor honest Joe Askew, Charley Anderson's friend, they have let themselves be caught in the race for easy money and tangible power; they have lost their personal values; they are like empty ships with their seams leaking, ready to go down in the first storm.

The trilogy has been getting better as it goes along, and *The Big Money* is the best of Dos Passos's novels, the sharpest and swiftest, the most unified in mood and story. Nobody has to refer to the earlier books in order to understand what is happening in this one. But after turning back to *The 42nd Parallel* and *1919*, one feels a new admiration for Dos Passos as an architect of plots and an interweaver of destinies. One learns much more about his problems and the original methods by which he has tried to solve them.

His central problem, of course, was that of writing a collective novel (defined simply as a novel without an individual hero, a novel of which the real protagonist is a social group). In this case, the social group is almost the largest possible: it is a whole nation during thirty years of its history. But a novelist is not a historian dealing with political tendencies or a sociologist reckoning statistical averages. If he undertakes to depict the national life, he has to do so in terms of individual lives, without slighting either one or the other. This double focus, on the social group and on the individual, explains the technical devices that Dos Passos has used in the course of his trilogy.

There are three of these devices, and it is clear enough that each of them has been invented with the purpose of gaining a definite effect, of supplying a quality absent from the simple narratives that form the body of the book. Take the Newsreels as an example. The principal narratives have dealt, necessarily, with shortsighted people pursuing their personal aims—and therefore the author intersperses them with brief passages consisting chiefly of newspaper headlines and snatches from popular songs. Thus, a chapter dealing with Eveline Hutchins' love affairs in Paris during the peace congress is interrupted by Newsreel XXXIV:

> *How are you goin' to keep 'em down on the farm*
> *After they've seen Paree*

If Wall Street needed the treaty, which means if the business interests of the country properly desired to know to what extent we are being concerned in affairs which do not concern us, why should it take the trouble to corrupt the tagrag and bobtail which forms Mr. Wilson's following in Paris?

ALLIES URGE MAGYAR PEOPLE TO UPSET BELA KUN REGIME

II WOMEN MISSING IN BLUEBEARD MYSTERY

Efin La France Achète les stocks Américains

> *How are you goin' to keep 'em away from Broadway*
> *Jazzin' around*
> *Paintin' the town*

Obviously the purpose here is to suggest the general or collective atmosphere of the given period. A slightly different end is served by a second technical invention, the brief biographies of prominent Americans (which incidentally contain some of the best writing in the trilogy). The principal narratives have dealt with people like Charley Anderson and Dick Savage, fairly typical citizens, figures that might have been chosen from a crowd—and so in order to balance them the author also gives us life sketches of Americans who were representative rather than typical, of men like Woodrow Wilson and J. P. Morgan and Jack Reed who were the leaders or rebels of their age.

The third of Dos Passos's technical devices, the Camera Eye, is something of a puzzle and one that I was a long time in solving to my own satisfaction. Obviously the Camera Eye passages are autobiographical, and obviously they are intended to represent the author's stream of consciousness (a fact that explains the lack of capitalization and punctuation). At first it seemed to me that they were completely out of tone with the hard and behavioristic style of the main narrative. It seemed to me that their softness and vagueness and impressionism belonged to the art novel rather than the collective novel; that they were in contrast and even in conflict with the main narrative. But this must have been exactly the reason why Dos Passos introduced them. The hard, behavioristic treatment of the characters has been tending to oversimplify them, to make it seem that they were being approached from the outside—and so the author tries to counterbalance this weakness (though not with complete success) by inserting passages that are written from the inside, passages full of warmth and color and hesitation and little intimate perceptions.

I have heard Dos Passos violently attacked on the ground that all these devices—Newsreels and biographies and the Camera Eye—were introduced arbitrarily, without relation to the rest of the novel. The attack is partly justified as regards *The 42nd Parallel,* though even in that first novel there is a clearer interrelation than most critics have noted. For instance, the Camera Eye describes the boyhood of a well-to-do lawyer's son and thereby points an artistically desirable contrast with the boyhood of tough little Fainy McCreary. Or again, the biography of Big Bill Haywood is inserted at the moment in the story when Fainy is leaving to help the Wobblies win their strike in Goldfield. Many other examples could be given. But when we come to *1919,* connections of this sort are so frequent and obvious that even a careless reader can hardly miss them; and in *The Big Money* all the technical devices are used to enforce the same mood, the same leading ideas.

Just what are these ideas that Dos Passos is trying to present? . . . The question sounds more portentous than it is in reality. If novels could be reduced each to a single thesis, there would be no reason for writing novels: a few convincing short essays would be all we needed. Obviously any novelist is trying to picture life as it was or is or as he would like it to be. But his ideas are important in so far as they help him to organize the picture (not to mention the important question of their effect on the reader).

In Dos Passos's case, the leading idea is the one implicit in his choice of subject and form: it is the idea that life is collective, that individuals are neither heroes nor villains, that their destiny is controlled by the drift of society as a whole. But in what direction does he believe that American society is drifting? That question is more difficult to answer, and the author doesn't give us much direct help. Still, a certain progress or decline can be deduced from the novel as a whole. At the beginning of *The 42nd Parallel* there was a general feeling of hope and restlessness and let's-take-a-chance. A journeyman printer like Fainy McCreary could wander almost anywhere and find a job. A goatish but not unlikable fraud like old Doc Bingham could dream of building a fortune and, what is more, could build it. But at the end of *The Big Money* all this has changed. Competitive capitalism has been transformed into monopoly capitalism; American society has become crystallized and stratified. "Vag"—the nameless young man described in the last three pages of the novel—is waiting at the edge of a concrete highway, his feet aching in broken shoes, his belly tight with hunger. Over his head flies a silver transcontinental plane filled with highly paid executives on their way to the Pacific Coast. The upper class has taken to the air, the lower class to the road; there is no longer any bond between them; they are two nations. And this idea—which is also an emotion of mingled pity, anger and revulsion—is the burden of a collective novel that was the first of its type to be written in this country, and is likely to remain for a long time the best.

3.

But the distinction I have been making in the course of this chapter could easily be carried too far. The truth is that the art novel and the collective novel as conceived by Dos Passos are in opposition but not in fundamental opposition: they are like the two sides of a coin. In the art novel, the emphasis is on the individual, in the collective novel it is on society as a whole; but in both we get the impression that society is stupid and all-powerful and fundamentally evil. Individuals ought to oppose it, but if they do so they are doomed. If, on the other hand, they reconcile themselves with society and try to get ahead in it, then they are damned forever, damned to be empty, shrill, destructive insects like Dick Savage and Eleanor Stoddard and J. Ward Moorehouse.

Long before, in *Manhattan Transfer*, Dos Passos had written a paragraph that states one of his basic perceptions. Ellen Herf, having divorced the Poet, decides to marry a rich politician whom she does not love:

> Through dinner she felt a gradual icy coldness stealing through her like novocaine. She had made up her mind. It seemed as if she had set the photograph of herself in her own place, forever frozen into a single gesture. . . . Ellen felt herself sitting with her ankles crossed, rigid as a porcelain figure under her clothes, everything about her seemed to be growing hard and enameled, the air blue-streaked with cigarette smoke was turning to glass.

She had made up her mind. . . . Sometimes in reading Dos Passos it seems that not the nature of the decision but the mere fact of having reaching it is the unforgivable offense. Dick Savage the ambulance driver decides not to be a pacifist, not to escape into neutral Spain, and from that moment he is forever frozen into a single gesture of selfishness and dissipation. Don Stevens the radical newspaper man decides to be a good Communist, to obey party orders, and immediately he is stricken with the same paralysis of the heart. We have come a long way from the strong-willed heroes of the early nineteenth century—the English heroes, sons of Dick Whittington, who admired the world of their day and climbed to the top of it implacably; the French heroes like Julien Sorel and Rastignac and Monte Cristo who despised their world and yet learned how to press its buttons and pull its levers. To Dos Passos the world seems so vicious that any compromise with its standards turns a hero into a villain. The only characters he seems to like instinctively are those who know they are beaten yet still grit their teeth and try to hold on. That is the story of Jimmy Herf in *Manhattan Transfer*; to some extent it is also the story of Mary French and her father and Joe Askew, almost the only admirable characters in *The Big Money*. And the same lesson of dogged, courageous impotence is pointed by the Camera Eye, especially in the admirable passage where the author remembers the execution of Sacco and Vanzetti:

> America our nation has been beaten by strangers who have turned our language inside out who have taken the clean words our fathers spoke and made them slimy and foul
>
> their hired men sit on the judge's bench they sit back with their feet on the tables under the dome of the State House they are ignorant of our beliefs they have the dollars the guns the armed forces the powerplants
>
> they have built the electric chair and hired the executioner to throw the switch
>
> all right we are two nations

In another passage Dos Passos describes his visit to a Kentucky sheriff at the time of the Harlan strike:

> the law stares across the desk out of angry eyes his face reddens in splotches like a gobbler's neck with the strut of the power of submachineguns sawedoffshotguns teargas and vomiting gas the power that can feed you or leave you to starve
>
> sits easy at his desk his back is covered he feels strong behind him he feels the prosecuting attorney the judge an owner himself the political boss the mine superintendent the board of directors the president of the utility the manipulator of the holding company
>
> his lifts his hand toward the telephone
>
> the deputies crowd in the door
>
> we have only words again

POWER SUPERPOWER

—And these words that serve as our only weapons against the machine guns and vomiting gas of the invaders, these words of the vanquished nation are only that America in developing from pioneer democracy into monopoly capitalism has followed a road that leads toward sterility and slavery. Our world is evil, and yet we are powerless to change or direct it. The sensitive individual should cling to his own standards, and yet he is certain to go under. Thus, the final message of Dos Passos's collective novels is similar to that of his earlier novels dealing with maladjusted artists. And thus, for all the vigor of *1919* and *The Big Money*, they leave us wondering whether the author hasn't overstated his case. They give us an extraordinarily diversified picture of contemporary life, but they fail to include at least one side of it—the will to struggle ahead, the comradeship in struggle, the consciousness of new men and new forces continually rising. Although we may seem to Dos Passos a beaten nation, the fight is not over.

[1936]

RICHARD WRIGHT:
THE CASE OF BIGGER THOMAS

Native Son is the most impressive American novel I have read since *The Grapes of Wrath*. In some ways the two books resemble each other: both deal with the dispossessed and both grew out of the radical movement of the 1930's. There is, however, a distinction to be drawn between the motives of the two authors. Steinbeck, more privileged than the characters in his novel, wrote out of deep pity for them, and the fault he had to avoid was sentimentality. Richard Wright, a Negro, was moved by wrongs he had suffered in his own person, and what he had to fear was a blind anger that might destroy the pity in him, making him hate any character whose skin was whiter than his own. His first book, *Uncle Tom's Children*, had not completely avoided that fault. It was a collection of stories all but one of which had the same pattern: a Negro was goaded into killing one or more white men and was killed in turn, without feeling regret for himself or his victims. Some of the stories I found physically painful to read, even though I admired them. So deep was the author's sense of the indignities heaped on his race that one felt he was revenging himself by a whole series of symbolic murders. In *Native Son* the pattern is the same, but the author's sympathies have broadened and his resentment, though quite as deep, is less painful and personal.

The hero, Bigger Thomas, is a Negro boy of twenty, a poolroom loafer, a bully, a liar and a petty thief. "Bigger, sometimes I wonder why I birthed you," his pious mother tells him. "Honest, you the most no-countest man I ever seen in all my life." A Chicago philanthropist tries to help the family by hiring him as chauffeur. That same night Bigger kills the philanthropist's daughter—out of fear of being discovered in her room—and stuffs her body into the furnace. This half-accidental crime leads to others. Bigger tries to cast the blame for the girl's disappearance on her lover, a Communist; he tries to collect a ransom from her parents; after the body is found he murders his Negro mistress to keep her from betraying him to the police. The next day he is captured on the snow-covered roof of a South Side tenement, while a mob howls in the street below.

In the last part of the book, which is also the best, we learn that the case of Bigger Thomas is not the author's deepest concern. Behind it is another, more complicated story he is trying hard to explain, though the words come painfully at first, and later come in a flood that almost sweeps him away. "Listen, you white folks," he seems to be saying over and over. "I want to tell you about all the Negroes in America. I want to tell you how they live and how they feel. I want you to change your minds about them before it is too late to prevent a worse disaster than any we have known. I speak for my own people, but I speak for America too." And because he does speak for and to the nation, without ceasing to be a Negro, his book has more force than any other American novel by a member of his race.

Bigger, he explains, had been trained from the beginning to be a bad citizen. He had been taught American ideals of life, in the schools, in the magazines, in the cheap movie houses, but had been denied any means of achieving them. Everything he wanted to have or do was reserved for the whites. "I just can't get used to it," he tells one of his poolroom buddies. "I swear to God I can't. . . . Every time I think about it I feel like somebody's poking a red-hot iron down my throat."

At the trial, his white-haired Jewish lawyer makes a final plea to the judge for mercy. "What Bigger Thomas did early that Sunday morning in the Dalton home and what he did that Sunday night in the empty building was but a tiny aspect of what he had been doing all his life long. He was *living*, only as he knew how, and as we have forced him to live. . . . The hate and fear which we have inspired in him, woven by our civilization into the very structure of his consciousness, into his blood and bones, into the hourly functioning of his personality, have become the justification of his existence. . . . Every thought he thinks is potential murder."

This long courtroom speech, which sums up the argument of the novel, is at once its strongest and its weakest point. It is strongest when Mr. Max is making a plea for the American

Negroes in general. "They are not simply twelve million people; in reality they constitute a separate nation, stunted, stripped and held captive *within* this nation." Many of them—and many white people too—are full of "balked longing for some kind of fulfilment and exultation"; and their existence is "what makes our future seem a looming image of violence." In this context, Mr. Max's talk of another civil war seems not so much a threat as an agonized warning. But his speech is weakest as a plea for the individual life of Bigger Thomas. It did not convince the judge, and I doubt that it will convince many readers.

It is not that I think Bigger "deserved" the death sentence for his two murders. Most certainly his guilt was shared by the society that condemned him. But when he killed Mary Dalton he was performing the first free action in his whole fear-tortured life; he was accepting his first moral responsibility. That is what he tried so hard to explain to his lawyer. "I ain't worried none about them women I killed. . . . I killed 'em 'cause I was scared and mad. But I been scared and mad all my life and after I killed that first woman, I wasn't scared no more for a little while." And when his lawyer asks him if he ever thought he would face the electric chair, "Now I come to think of it," he answers, "it seems like something like this just had to be." If Mr. Max had managed to win a life sentence for Bigger Thomas, he would have robbed him of his only claim to human courage and dignity. But that Richard Wright makes us feel this, while setting out to prove something else—that he makes Bigger Thomas a human rather than a racial symbol—shows that he wrote an even better novel than he had planned.

[1940]

MAXWELL PERKINS:
AUTHOR'S EDITOR
(excerpts)

Charles Scribner's Sons is not the oldest American publishing house—it was founded in 1846—but for a long time it had the reputation of being the most genteel and encrusted with traditions. No word unfit for a young girl's ear could be used in any book that Scribner's published. Because ladies were employed in the office, no gentleman could smoke there.

In 1920 the furniture looked—and some of it still does—as if it had been purchased from the estate of a very old country doctor. Most of the employees were even more elderly than their desks, and in publishing circles people said that nobody left Scribner's until he was carried out.

The second Charles Scribner, born in 1854, was not only president of the firm but also a sort of grandfather image; his wrath was feared like Jehovah's. His first assistant and the firm's chief editor, for a long period beginning in 1887, was William Crary Brownell, born in 1851. One of Scribner's young men, who went to work for the company in the nineteen-twenties, still remembers the first time he saw him. "Mr. Brownell was stretched out on a leather couch in his office, just beyond the room where we were having a sales conference," the young man recalls, "taking his afternoon nap, his white beard slowly rising and falling and one fly slowly circling about it. The scene made quite an impression on me." Another member of the staff, almost as old as Brownell, used to lunch by himself at the University Club, where he sometimes shouted and pounded on the table while arguing with an imaginary companion. The incumbent sales manager was reputed never to have read a book. When a new Scribner novel came out, he would take a copy home to his wife. She would read it over the weekend and the office force would gather on Monday morning to hear her verdict. "My wife cried over that book," he would sometimes say, and everybody knew it would be a best-seller.

There wasn't much chance for a book that even mildly disturbed the conventions. Scribner's had a distinguished list of British authors, including Meredith, Stevenson, Barrie, and G. A. Henty, who wrote eighty books for boys, an achievement surpassed only by Horatio Alger's record of a hundred and thirty (not all of them written by himself). Among the famous, and distinctly respectable, Americans Scribner's published were John Fox, Jr., Thomas Nelson Page, Dr. Henry van Dyke, Richard Harding Davis, F. Hopkinson Smith, Henry James (his last half-dozen books, at least), and Edith Wharton (up to *The Age of Innocence*). Theodore Roosevelt was a valuable publishing property, but most of the staff believed that as a politician he was too radical. Galsworthy represented the younger generation and was thought to be a little subversive, although sound at heart. Scribner's did not publish the realists who emerged during the so-called American Renaissance—Dreiser, Anderson, Sandburg, and so on. Instead, the firm took a sudden leap from the age of innocence into the middle of the lost generation.

That leap was the result of suggestions made by Maxwell Evarts Perkins, then one of the younger editors, but he offered them so quietly that hardly anyone noticed what was happening until the revolution was under way. It began in 1917 with an otherwise unimportant libel suit against one of Scribner's authors, Shane Leslie, an Anglo-Irish novelist and critic who was then teaching at Princeton. Leslie was a little contrite about the expense that Scribner's had been put to in defending the suit. Hoping to make amends, he came into the office with the manuscript of a novel written by a former student of his, F. Scott Fitzgerald. Perkins liked the novel, then called *The Romantic Egotist*, but he thought it needed some revision before it would be ready for publication. He said so in a letter to the author, who had meanwhile entered the Army. Fitzgerald asked him, as a favor, to submit it as it stood to two other publishers. Both of them rejected it with form letters. Just before going overseas, Fitzgerald came to New York, had a long talk with Perkins, and decided to revise the manuscript. As a matter of fact, he completely rewrote it twice and it wasn't published until 1920—under a new title, *This Side of Paradise*. In those days it seemed to be the terrifying voice of a new age and it made some of the older employees of Scribner's cringe. On the Monday after the first bound copies came into the office, everybody gathered to hear whether the sales manager's wife had cried. "That book? I wouldn't think of showing it to my wife," the sales manager said. "I picked it up with the fire tongs and dropped it in the fire."

This Side of Paradise sold fifty-two thousand copies, which was almost unprecedented, in those days, for a first novel. Fitzgerald then wrote *The Beautiful and Damned*, which sold forty-four thousand copies and, incidentally, was dedicated to Perkins. Full of enthusiasm for his editor, Fitzgerald told all his literary friends about him and told Perkins about the friends. One of them was Ernest Hemingway, who was a young newspaperman living in Paris. Perkins sent to Paris for a copy of his first volume of stories, *in our time*, which had just been brought out there by the Three Mountain Press. Then he wrote Hemingway and offered to publish his next book in America. But Horace Liveright had already sent a cable to Hemingway and signed him up for *in our time*, with options on his next two books.

The matter might have ended there, with an exchange of courtesies—Hemingway writing Perkins that he didn't even have a copy of his own book, Perkins sending him the copy he had ordered from Paris, Hemingway returning it to Perkins with an inscription—if it had not been for the fact that the public showed very little interest in the Liveright edition of *In Our Time*—with the words capitalized—which sold less than five hundred copies the first year. Liveright was dubious about making an advance payment for Hemingway's second book, and when he saw a reader's report on the manuscript, he was sure that he shouldn't make it. It was *The Torrents of Spring*, which not only looked unsalable to Liveright but also did a good deal of kidding of Sherwood Anderson, one of Liveright's most profitable authors. The manuscript was rejected and the contract between Hemingway and Liveright was thereby nullified. Hemingway came back to New York in 1925 and called on Perkins, who gave him an advance on the book of $1,500, which looked bigger to him, he has said, than the $150,000 he received from Paramount for the movie rights of *For Whom the Bell Tolls*.

By 1925 Ring Lardner, another member of the new literary generation, had been a Scribner author for about a year. Fitzgerald, who, like Lardner, lived in Great Neck, had persuaded him to collect some of his magazine pieces and give them to Perkins. It was quite an achievement, for Lardner didn't keep copies of his stories and had a hard time remembering where they had been published. "Maybe it was the *Saturday Evening Post*," he would say hopefully of some story. The manuscript which Lardner turned in to Scribner's consisted largely of photostats made from back issues of magazines in the Public Library. The book was published under the title of *How to Write Short Stories*. It was Lardner's seventh book, but it was the first to be seriously reviewed; the others hadn't been read except by the hammock trade. At Scribner's there had been an editorial meeting lasting all afternoon before the book had been accepted. The older Scribner employees felt that Lardner was merely a sportswriter and just one more of Perkins' roughneck authors. Perkins claimed that Lardner was literature. What eventually won the argument for Perkins' side was a letter from Sir James M. Barrie, who said that Lardner was the most exciting American story writer he had read, although it was a pity, he added, that Lardner hadn't written about cricket instead of baseball.

The older men at Scribner's continued to be outraged not only by Lardner but by all the indecorous authors whom Perkins had been introducing one after the other. One ex-Scribner man recently wrote to a friend, "I remember the old fellow in charge of the stockroom opening a book and with quivering fingers pointing to a word. He said, 'To think that Scribner's would publish a book with that word in it!' The book was *The Great Gatsby*, the word, or rather phrase, was 'son of a bitch.' " The letter continued, "There was a moment of crisis when the question was: would Scribner's publish Hemingway's *The Sun Also Rises*? Old Charles Scribner, Sr., ran the place then with a very firm hand and no two ways about it. We knew that Perkins had to go to bat for Hemingway, and it was reported with hushed voices one evening that Charles, Sr., had turned down the book and Perkins was going to resign. I don't believe that now, but I did then. Anyway, that was the lineup: van Dyke and Galsworthy or Hemingway and Fitzgerald, with Perkins representing the latter."

For his part, Perkins insists that Mr. Scribner was quick to recognize the talent of Perkins' new author, but it is known that the old man was worried about the moral standards of

Hemingway's heroines. He used to say fretfully, "I always felt that a woman at least ought to have some affection for a man." He wrote his friend Judge Robert Grant of Boston, asking for his comment on *The Sun Also Rises*. The judge, himself still a novelist at seventy-four, replied, "You *have* to publish the book, Charles, but I hope the young man will live to regret it."

In 1929, Scribner's published Thomas Wolfe's first novel, *Look Homeward, Angel*, which was a moderate financial success; it sold seventeen thousand copies in the trade edition before coming out in reprints. That year, too, Scribner's issued a biography, with nearly disastrous results: *Mrs. Eddy*, by Edwin Franden Dakin. The Christian Science Church made formal protests, but old Mr. Scribner refused to withdraw the book. One self-appointed champion of Mrs. Eddy appeared in the office and threatened to use malicious animal magnetism against the publishers. Charles Scribner, Sr., died in 1930, and his brother Arthur, who succeeded him as president, died in 1932. A number of impressionable people at Scribner's thought that malicious animal magnetism had something to do with it.

Old Brownell had died in 1928. His office was inherited by the poet John Hall Wheelock, who had been moved upstairs into an editorial post after fifteen years in the Scribner bookstore. Wheelock also inherited Brownell's leather couch. Young Charles Scribner, the new president, lived in Far Hills and belonged to the New Jersey foxhunting set. Like most Princeton men of his generation—he was class of '13—he had admired Fitzgerald and Hemingway from the beginning; also, he liked to smoke in the office. All these changes, combined with the changing character of the list of authors, meant that Scribner's was losing its mid-Victorian atmosphere. It became progressively less Victorian, reaching its low in the 1930s, when the office force, arriving in the morning, would find Thomas Wolfe, after a night on the town, asleep on the directors' table in the library.

The friendship between Wolfe and Perkins had been best described by Wolfe in his last novel, *You Can't Go Home Again*, in which Perkins is the editor called Foxhall Edwards and Wolfe is, of course, the hero, George Webber. "The older man," the novelist wrote, "was not merely friend but father to the younger. Webber, the hot-blooded Southerner . . . had lost his own father many years before and now had found a substitute in Edwards. And Edwards, the reserved New Englander, with his deep sense of family and inheritance, had always wanted a son but had had five daughters, and as time went on he made of George a kind of foster son."

For a whole year—1933—Wolfe worked ten to fourteen hours a day on *Of Time and the River*, and he began to acquire the disposition of a morose elephant. "People seem to expect a great deal of me in my next book," he wrote to his mother in Asheville, "and I am very nervous about it." He was also nervous about money, even though Scribner's had been taking good care of him. In the past three years, Wolfe had received more than $15,000, including an advance of $5,000 on his new book, paid in monthly installments of $250; a short-story prize of $2,500 from *Scribner's Magazine*; a Guggenheim fellowship, also of $2,500; and royalties from the American, English, Swedish, and German editions of *Look Homeward, Angel*. He was unmarried and hated to spend money on clothes or furniture, but he ate and drank on a scale commensurate with his six feet seven inches and his two hundred and fifty pounds. In February, 1933, he complained to his mother, "I have my back right up against the wall at the present time and have almost no money."

In his letters to his mother, he sounded as if he thought that everybody except Perkins—"the best friend I ever had"— was leagued in a conspiracy against him. These letters were full of phrases like "I have been hounded and driven crazy . . . beset and pressed on all sides . . . badgered, tormented, and almost driven mad at times by fool questions, fool letters from fool people, the tantrums of crazy women . . . cheap, slanderous, cheating, and canting swine—I see no reason why I should not tell them plainly what they are." Wolfe was not a man to keep his opinions to himself. Sometimes, at parties, he would begin to scowl and his face would go white; his friends would attempt to get him out of the room before he lowered his head and charged. Perkins told him, after one such scene, "You don't really hate those people. You hate yourself because your work is going badly." Wolfe promised he wouldn't act up again.

About half past eleven on the night of December 14, 1933, he came, late, to an appointment with Perkins in the editor's office and dropped a heavy bundle on his desk. It was two feet high, wrapped in brown paper, and tied with strong twine. When Perkins opened it, he found the manuscript of *Of Time and the River*, on several kinds of white and yellow paper. It totaled more than three thousand typewritten pages—nobody knows how many more, because the pages weren't numbered—but in any event it was too long to publish in one volume. "It was all disproportioned," Perkins has said. Wolfe wrote his mother, "God knows a lot of it is still fragmentary and broken up, but at any rate he can now look at it and give me an opinion on it." Perkins went through the manuscript carefully and told one of his associates, "This book has to be done."

It took Wolfe and Perkins, working together, more than a year to do it. The first step was for Perkins, in his own phrase, to "mark up" the manuscript. This meant pencilling brief notes in the margin, in his high, angular script—"Ought to be cut out," or "Repetition," or "Needs to be explained." At that time, Perkins was living in town, and the two men began meeting at eight o'clock five or six evenings a week in Perkins' office.

Perkins would glance at one of his marginal notes and say, "I think this section should be omitted."

Wolfe would answer, after a long, sulky pause, "I think it's good."

"I think it's good too," Perkins would say, and mean it, "but you have expressed the thing already."

The two men would argue for hours, while cigarette butts and sheets of paper piled up on the floor. Sometimes, in the midst of an argument, Wolfe would glance at a rattlesnake skin with seven rattles—a gift from Marjorie Rawlings—which hung from a coathook above Perkins' overcoat and under his hat. Wolfe, whose touch was seldom light, liked to call this collection of objects "The Portrait of an Editor," a joke that had an undertone of resentment. Usually he ended by doing as Perkins suggested, but passages cut out of the novel were never thrown away. Wolfe carried them home to Brooklyn Heights and put them in a big wooden packing case—eventually there were three such cases, the two largest being three feet high, three feet wide, and four feet long—in the centre of his parlor. In them he also kept cooking pots, old shoes, an electric flatiron, and bundles of receipted bills. He saved his discarded scenes as plumbers save lengths of pipe, and eventually fitted them into other novels. Thus the longest of the passages omitted from *Of Time and the River* became the second half of *The Web and the Rock*.

By February of 1934, work on *Of Time and the River* was going well. Sometimes, when the marginal note said "Needs transition," Wolfe pushed aside other manuscripts on a corner of Perkins' old-fashioned desk and wrote the necessary pages in his huge, sprawling, but legible hand, the words so widely spaced that five of them made a line and ninety filled a page. Wolfe had to have all his work copied; he never learned to type, because, he said, his hands were too big for the keyboard, just as his feet were too big for the pedals of an automobile. In April, the two men still hoped that the novel would be ready for fall publication, but Wolfe had developed a habit of writing new chapters, which he submitted at the evening sessions with a look of both penitence and pride. The book became like Penelope's web; whatever the two men unravelled by night, Wolfe rewove by day. One week he added a passage of some thirty thousand words, describing the death of the hero's father. Perkins thought that most of it was unnecessary, but he recently told an associate, "It was too good to let go."

In the middle of October, Perkins felt that the book was finished. "I don't think you should do anything more to it, Tom," he said, but Wolfe had been working on it so long that he couldn't stop. It wasn't until January 14, 1935, that the novel was in page proofs. Then Wolfe was forbidden to make any more changes. Suddenly he felt as if he had been released from bondage. He celebrated by eating an eight-pound porterhouse steak. Perkins took his first vacation in three years. He paid a visit to Hemingway in Key West and, with his help, he landed the first fish he had caught since he was a boy. Two weeks before anybody at Scribner's expected him, Perkins was back at his desk. When *Of Time and the River* was finally published, in March, 1935, it bore this dedication: "To Maxwell Evarts Perkins, a great editor and a brave and honest man, who stuck to the writer of this book through times of bitter hopelessness and doubt and would not let him give in to his own despair, a work to be known as 'Of Time and the River' is dedicated with the hope that all of it may be in some way worthy of the loyal devotion and the patient care which a dauntless and unshaken friend has given to each part of it, and without which none of it could have been written."

In the autumn of 1937, Wolfe transferred himself and his three packing cases of unpublished manuscript to another publisher. People often wonder how such a close relationship came to be broken. Perkins said nothing at the time it happened and has said very little since. In his last novel, Wolfe explained at great length that there was a fundamental difference in temperament. Foxhall Edwards (Perkins), he said, was as much a fatalist as the author of Ecclesiastes, whereas Wolfe believed that the world could be changed for the better. In simpler terms, Perkins had been an independent Democrat for fifty years but had turned against the New Deal at the moment when Wolfe, after a German friend had been persecuted by the Nazis, was beginning for the first time to think of himself as a radical. Both men, however, were much more interested in people than in politics. The principal reason for the separation—it was never a quarrel—seems to be that Wolfe's pride was touched. He had told everybody how much he owed to Perkins' editing, and everybody believed his story, which grew in the telling, until Wolfe began to feel that his own contribution was being slighted. Once, after this attitude had crystallized, he said to another Perkins author, "I'll show them that I can write my own books. I'll show them that I'm not a robot." One of his friends said that he was like a son who had risen rapidly in his father's factory and then resigned, just to prove that he could be as successful on his own. Wolfe chose Harper, in preference to two other publishers who were bidding for his work, after he found that Edward C. Aswell, Harper's editor, had been born in the same week of the same month of the same year as himself. This time there wouldn't be any question of foster parentage.

The separation weighed on Wolfe's conscience. The last, long section of *You Can't Go Home Again* takes the form of a letter to Foxhall Edwards. "Dear Fox, old friend," he concludes, "thus we have come to the end of the road that we were to go together. My tale is finished—and so farewell." A somewhat different version of the letter was actually mailed to Perkins; it was a leavetaking note of a hundred and thirty-two handwritten pages. On the day that his last illness took a fatal turn, Wolfe scrawled another letter to Perkins in pencil.

Perkins hurried to visit him at the Johns Hopkins Hospital in Baltimore, but by the time he reached the hospital, Wolfe was too near death to see him. Wolfe's will made Perkins executor of his involved estate. In this capacity, Perkins had to read the proofs of Wolfe's last three books, which were edited by Aswell. It was in these proofs that he saw for the first time Wolfe's portrait of Foxhall Edwards. The portrait was largely a caricature, but after publication people began to confuse it with Perkins' real personality. For example, Wolfe said that Edwards went to Groton, and now many people take for granted that Perkins went to Groton instead of St. Paul's. Perkins' first comment, made to Aswell, was simply, "That man he calls the Fox—I don't think Tom got him quite right." Then, a few days later, he added, "That man Tom calls the Fox—I took the passage home to show my wife and daughters, and they think he did get him right."

[1944]

HEMINGWAY AT MIDNIGHT

(Introduction to *The Portable Hemingway*)*

When Ernest Hemingway's first books appeared, they seemed to be a transcription of the real world, new because they were accurate and because the world in those days was also new. With his insistence on "presenting things truly," he seemed to be a writer in the naturalistic tradition (for all his technical experiments); and the professors of American literature, when they got round to mentioning his books in their surveys, treated him as if he were the Dreiser of the lost generation, or perhaps the fruit of a deplorable misalliance between Dreiser and Jack London. Going back to his work in 1944, you perceive his kinship with a wholly different group of novelists, let us say with Poe and Hawthorne and Melville: the haunted and nocturnal writers, the men who dealt in images that were symbols of an inner world.

On the face of it, his method is not in the least like theirs. He doesn't lead us into castles ready to collapse with age, or into very old New England houses, or embark with us on the search for a whale that is also the white spirit of evil; instead he tells the stories he has lived or heard, against the background of countries he has seen. But, you reflect on reading his books again, these are curious stories that he has chosen

---

* Since this introduction to *The Portable Hemingway* (1944) has become a subject of controversy, it is reprinted here without changes, except for the omission of one paragraph (at the beginning of Section 2). The paragraph summarized Hemingway's early life and it was based—it had to be based—on printed sources available at the time. One of these was *Who's Who*, which, in ten or more editions, gave his birth date as 1898 instead of 1899. There were gross errors in all the other printed sources. I learned in later years that most of the errors could be traced back to Hemingway, who liked to embroider stories about himself. He also was given to making honest and sometimes damaging confessions, not only in letters written late at night but in his fiction as well. "Complicated" is the one word for his character. He nursed grudges and could be, so people said of him, "as mean as cat piss," yet he was in many ways a vastly appealing person.   [M.C., 1984]

from his wider experience, and these countries are presented in a strangely mortuary light. In no other writer of our time can you find such a profusion of corpses: dead women in the rain; dead soldiers bloated in their uniforms and surrounded by torn papers; sunken liners full of bodies that float past the closed portholes. In no other writer can you find so many suffering animals: mules with their forelegs broken drowning in shallow water off the quai at Smyrna; gored horses in the bullring; wounded hyenas first snapping at their own entrails and then eating them with relish. And morally wounded people who also devour themselves: punch-drunk boxers, soldiers with battle fatigue, veterans crazy with "the old rale," lesbians, nymphomaniacs, bullfighters who have lost their nerve, men who lie awake all night while their brains get to racing "like a flywheel with the weight gone"—here are visions as terrifying as those of "The Pit and the Pendulum," even though most of them are copied from life; here are nightmares at noonday, accurately described, pictured without the romantic mist, but having the nature of obsessions or hypnagogic visions between sleep and waking.

And, going back to them, you find a waking-dreamlike quality even in stories that deal with pleasant or commonplace aspects of the world. Take for example "Big Two-Hearted River," printed in his first American collection of stories, *In Our Time*. Here the plot, or foreground of the plot, is simply a fishing trip in the northern peninsula of Michigan. Nick Adams, who is Hemingway's earliest and most personal hero, gets off the train at an abandoned sawmill town; he crosses burned-over land, makes camp, eats his supper and goes to sleep; in the morning he looks for bait, finds grasshoppers under a log, hooks a big trout and loses it, catches two other trout, then sits on the bank in the shadow and eats his lunch very slowly while watching the stream; he decides to do no more fishing that day. There is nothing else in the story, apparently; nothing but a collection of sharp sensory details, so that you smell or hear or touch or see everything that exists near Big Two-Hearted River; and you even taste Nick Adams' supper of beans and spaghetti. "All good books are alike," Hemingway later said, "in that they are truer than if they had really happened and after you are finished reading one you will feel that all that happened to you and afterwards it all belongs to you: the good and the bad, the ecstasy, the remorse and sorrow, the people and the places and how the weather was." This story belongs to the reader, but apparently it is lacking in ecstasy, remorse, and sorrow; there are no people in it except Nick Adams; apparently there is nothing but "the places and how the weather was."

But Hemingway's stories are most of them continued, in the sense that he has a habit of returning to the same themes, each time making them a little clearer—to himself, I think, as well as to others. His work has an emotional consistency, as if all of it moved on the same stream of experience. A few years after writing "Big Two-Hearted River," he wrote another story that casts a retrospective light on his fishing trip (much as *A Farewell to Arms* helps to explain the background of Jake Barnes and Lady Brett, in *The Sun Also Rises*). The second story, "Now I Lay Me," deals with an American volunteer in the Italian army who isn't named but who might easily be Nick Adams. He is afraid to sleep at night because, so he says, "I had been living for a long time with the knowledge that if I ever shut my eyes in the dark and let myself go, my soul would go out of my body. I had been that way for a long time, ever since I had been blown up at night and felt it go out of me and go off and then come back." And the soldier continues:

> I had different ways of occupying myself while I lay awake. I would think of a trout stream I had fished along when I was a boy and fish its whole length very carefully in my mind; fishing very carefully under all the logs, all the turns of the bank, the deep holes and the clear shallow stretches, sometimes catching trout and sometimes losing them. I would stop fishing at noon to eat my lunch; sometimes on a log over the stream; sometimes on a high bank under a tree, and I always ate my lunch very slowly and watched the stream below me while I ate. . . . Some nights too I made up streams, and some of them were very exciting, and it was like being awake and dreaming. Some of those streams I still remember and think that I have fished in them, and they are confused with streams I really know.

After reading this passage, we have a somewhat different attitude toward the earlier story. The river described in it remains completely real for us; but also—like those other streams the soldier invented during the night—it has the quality of a waking dream. Although the events in the foreground are described with superb accuracy, and for their own sake, we now perceive what we probably missed at a first reading: that there are shadows in the background and that part of the story takes place in an inner world. We notice that Nick Adams regards his fishing trip as an escape, either from a nightmare or from realities that have become a nightmare. Sometimes his mind starts to work, even here in the wilderness; but "he knew he could choke it because he was tired enough," and he can safely fall asleep. "Nick felt happy," the author says more than once. "He felt he had left everything behind, the need for thinking, the need to write, other needs. It was all back of him." He lives as if in an enchanted country. There is a faint suggestion of old legends: all the stories of boys with cruel stepmothers who wandered off into the forest, where the trees sheltered them and the birds brought them food. There is even a condition laid on Nick's happiness, just as in many fairy tales, where the hero must not wind a certain horn or open a certain door. Nick must not follow the river down into the swamp. "In the swamp the banks were bare, the big cedars came together overhead, the sun did not come through, except in patches; in the fast deep water, in the half light, the fishing would be tragic. In the swamp fishing was a tragic adventure. Nick did not want it. He did not want to go down the stream any further today."

Now, I question whether this shadowy background of "Big Two-Hearted River" was deliberately sketched in by the author, or whether it was more than half-consciously present in his mind. In those days Hemingway was trying to write with complete objectivity; he was trying, as he afterwards said, "to put down what really happened in action; what the actual things were which produced the emotion that you experienced." But the emotion was often more personal and more complicated than he suspected at the time (though he might afterwards define it more clearly); and the "actual things" were presented so vividly in his stories that they became, for the reader, something more than "what really happened in action"; they also became metaphors or symbols. Many poems have the same double effect; and Hemingway's stories are often close to poetry.

Years later he began to make a deliberate use of symbolism (as in "The Snows of Kilimanjaro"), together with other literary devices that he had avoided in his earlier work. He even began to talk about the possibility of writing what he called fourth-dimensional prose. "The reason everyone now tries to avoid it," he says in *Green Hills of Africa*, "to deny that it is important, to make it seem vain to try to do it, is because it is so difficult. Too many factors must combine to make it possible."

"What is this now?" asks Kandisky, the Austrian in leather breeches who likes to lead the life of the mind. And the author explains:

> "The kind of writing that can be done. How far prose can be carried if anyone is serious enough and has luck. There is a fourth and fifth dimension that can be gotten."
>
> "You believe it?"
>
> "I know it."
>
> "And if a writer can get this?"
>
> "Then nothing else matters. It is more important than anything else he can do. The chances are, of course, that he will fail. But there is a chance that he succeeds."
>
> "But that is poetry you are talking about."
>
> "No. It is much more difficult than poetry. It is a prose that has never been written. But it can be written, without tricks and without cheating. With nothing that will go bad afterwards."

Now, I don't know exactly what Hemingway means by prose with "a fourth and fifth dimension." It would seem to me that any good prose has four dimensions, in the sense of being a solid object that moves through time; whereas the fifth dimension is a mystical or meaningless figure of speech. But without understanding his choice of words, I do know that Hemingway's prose at its best gives a sense of depth and of moving forward on different levels that is lacking in even the best of his imitators, as it is in almost all the other novelists of our time. Moreover, I have at least a vague notion of how this quality in his work can be explained.

2.

Considering his laborious apprenticeship and the masters with whom he chose to study (including Pound and Gertrude Stein); considering his theories of writing, which he has often discussed, and how they have developed with the years; considering their subtle and increasingly conscious application, as well as the complicated personality they serve to express, it is a little surprising to find that Hemingway is almost always described as a primitive. Yet the word really applies to him, if it is used in what might be called its anthropological sense. The anthropologists tell us that many of the so-called primitive peoples have an extremely elaborate system of beliefs, calling for the almost continual performance of rites and ceremonies; even their drunken orgies are ruled by tradition. Some of the forest-dwelling tribes believe that every rock or tree or animal has an indwelling spirit. When they kill an animal or chop down a tree, they must beg its forgiveness, repeating a formula of propitiation; otherwise its spirit would haunt them. Living briefly in a world of hostile forces, they preserve themselves— so they believe—only by the exercise of magic lore.

There is something of the same atmosphere in Hemingway's work. His heroes live in a world that is like a hostile forest, full of unseen dangers, not to mention the nightmares that haunt their sleep. Death spies on them from behind every tree. Their only chance for safety lies in the faithful observance of customs they invent for themselves. In an early story like "Big Two-Hearted River," you notice that Nick Adams does everything very slowly, not wishing "to rush his sensations any"; and he pays so much attention to the meaning and rightness of each gesture that his life alone in the wilderness becomes a succession of little ceremonies. "Another hopper poked his face out of the bottle. His antennae wavered. Nick took him by the head and held him while he threaded the hook under his chin, down through his thorax and into the last segments of his abdomen. The grasshopper took hold of the hook with his front feet, spitting tobacco juice on it." The grasshopper is playing its own part in a ritual; so too is the trout that swallows it, then bends the rod in jerks as it pumps against the current. The whole fishing trip, instead of being a mere escape, might be regarded as an incantation, a spell to banish evil spirits. And there are other magical ceremonies in Hemingway's work, besides those connected with fishing and hunting and drinking. Without too much difficulty we can recognize rites of animal sacrifice (as in *Death in the Afternoon*), of sexual union (in *For Whom the Bell Tolls*), of self-immolation (in "The Snows of Kilimanjaro"), of conversion (in "To Have and Have Not"), and of symbolic death and rebirth (in the Caporetto passage of *A Farewell to Arms*). When one of Hemingway's characters violates his own standards or the just laws of the tribe (as Ole Andreson has done in "The Killers"), he waits for death as stolidly as an Indian.

Memories of the Indians he knew in his boyhood play an important part in Hemingway's work: they reappear in *The Torrents of Spring* and in several of his shorter stories. Robert Jordan, in *For Whom the Bell Tolls*, compares his own exploits to Indian warfare, and he strengthens himself during his last moments by thinking about his grandfather, an old Indian fighter. *In Our Time*, Hemingway's first book of stories, starts by telling how Nick Adams' father is called to attend an Indian woman who has been in labor for two days. The woman lies screaming in a bunkhouse, while her husband, with a badly injured foot, lies in the bunk above her smoking his pipe. Dr. Adams performs a Caesarean section without anesthetic, then sews up the wound with fishing leaders. When the operation is finished, he looks at the husband in the upper bunk and finds that he is dead; unable to bear his wife's pain, he has turned his face to the wall and cut his throat. A story Nick Adams later tells is of Trudy Gilby, the Indian girl with whom he used to go squirrel shooting and who, under the big hemlock trees, "did first what no one has ever done better." Most of Hemingway's heroines are in the image of Trudy; they have the obedience to their lovers and the sexual morals of Indian girls. His heroes suffer without complaining and, in one way or another, they destroy themselves like the Indian husband.

But Hemingway feels as even closer kinship with the Spaniards, because they retain a primitive dignity in giving and accepting death. Even when their dignity is transformed into a blind lust for killing, as sometimes happened during their civil war, they continue to hold his respect. Agustín, in *For Whom the Bell Tolls*, sees four of Franco's cavalrymen and breaks out into a sweat that is not the sweat of fear. "When I saw those four there," he says, "and thought that we might kill them I was like a mare in the corral waiting for the stallion." And Robert Jordan thinks to himself: "We do it coldly but they do not, nor ever have. It is their extra sacrament. Their old one that they had before the new religion came from the far end of the Mediterranean, the one they have never abandoned but only suppressed and hidden to bring it out again in wars and inquisitions." Hemingway himself seems to have a feeling for half-forgotten sacraments; his cast of mind is pre-Christian and pre-logical.

Sometimes his stories come close to being adaptations of ancient myths. His first novel, for example, deals in different terms with the same legend that T. S. Eliot was not so much presenting as concealing in *The Waste Land*. When we turn to Eliot's explanatory notes, then read the scholarly work to which they refer as a principal source—*From Ritual to Romance*, by Jessie L. Weston—we learn that his poem is largely based on the legend of the Fisher King. The legend tells how the king was wounded in the loins and how he lay wasting in his bed while his whole kingdom became unfruitful; there was thunder but no rain; the rivers dried up, the flocks had no increase, and the women bore no children. *The Sun Also Rises* presents the same situation in terms of Paris after the First World War. It is a less despairing book than critics like to think, with their moral conviction that drinkers and fornicators are necessarily unhappy; at times the story is gay, friendly, even exuberant; but the hero (who is also a fisherman) has been wounded like the Fisher King, and he lives in a world that is absolutely sterile. I don't mean to imply that Hemingway owes any debt to *The Waste Land*. He had read the poem, which he liked at first, and the notes that followed it, which he didn't like at all; I doubt very much that he bothered to look at Jessie L. Weston's book. He said in 1924, when he was writing about the death of Joseph Conrad: "If I knew that by grinding Mr. Eliot into a fine dry powder and sprinkling that powder over Mr. Conrad's grave, Mr. Conrad would shortly appear, looking very annoyed at the forced return, and commence writing, I would leave for London early tomorrow morning with a sausage grinder." And yet when he wrote his first novel, he dealt with the same legend that Eliot had discovered by scholarship; recovering it for himself, I think, by a sort of instinct for legendary situations.

And it is this instinct for legends, for sacraments, for rituals, for symbols appealing to buried hopes and fears, that helps to explain the power of Hemingway's work and his vast superiority over his imitators. The imitators have learned all his mannerisms as a writer, and in some cases they can tell a story even better than Hemingway himself; but they tell only the story; they communicate with the reader on only one level of experience. Hemingway does more than that. Most of us are also primitive in a sense, for all the machinery that surrounds our lives. We have our private rituals, our little superstitions, our symbols and fears and nightmares; and Hemingway reminds us unconsciously of the hidden worlds in which we live. Reading his best work, we are a little like Nick Adams looking down from the railroad bridge at the trout in "Big Two-Hearted River": "many trout in deep, fast-moving water, slightly distorted as he watched far down through the glassy convex surface of the pool, its surface pushing and swelling smooth against the resistance of the log-driven piles of the bridge. At the bottom of the pool were the big trout. Nick did not see them at first. Then he saw them at the bottom of the pool, big trout looking to hold themselves on the gravel bottom in a varying mist of gravel and sand."

3.

During the last few years it has become the fashion to reprimand Hemingway and to point out how much better his work would be (with its undoubted power) if only he were a little more virtuous or reasonable or optimistic, or if he revealed the proper attitude toward progress and democracy. Critics like Maurice Coindreau (in French) and Bernard DeVoto have abused him without bothering to understand what he plainly says, much less what he suggests or implies. Even Maxwell Geismar, who is one of the few professors with a natural feeling for literary values, would like to make him completely over. "What a marvelous teacher Hemingway is," he exclaims, "with all the restrictions of temperament and environment which so far define his work! What could he not show us of living as well as dying, of the positives in our being as well as the destroying forces, of 'grace under pressure' and the grace we need with no pressures, of ordinary life-giving actions along with those superb last gestures of doomed exiles!" Or, to put the matter more plainly, what a great writer Hemingway would be, in Geismar's opinion, if he combined his own work with equal parts of Trollope and Emerson.

And the critics have some justice on their side. It is true

that Hemingway has seldom been an affirmative writer; it is true that most of his work is narrow and violent and generally preoccupied with death. But the critics, although they might conceivably change him for the worse, are quite unable to change him for the better. He is one of the novelists who write, not as they should or would, but as they must. Like Poe and Hawthorne and Melville, he listens to his personal demon, which might also be called his intuition or his sense of life. If he listened to the critics instead, he might indeed come to resemble Trollope or Emerson, but the resemblance would be only on the surface and, as he sometimes says of writing that tried hard to meet public requirements, it would all go bad afterwards. Some of his own writing has gone bad, but surprisingly little of it. By now he has earned the right to be taken for what he is, with his great faults and greater virtues; with his narrowness, his power, his always open eyes, his stubborn, chip-on-the-shoulder honesty, his nightmares, his rituals for escaping them, and his sense of an inner and an outer world that for twenty years were moving together toward the same disaster.

[1944]

WILLIAM FAULKNER

HIS SAGA
(Introduction to *The Portable William Faulkner*)

When the war was over—the other war—William Faulkner went back to Oxford, Mississippi. He had served in 1918 as a cadet in the Royal Canadian Air Force. Now he was home again and not at home, or at least not able to accept the postwar world. He was writing poems, most of them worthless, and dozens of immature but violent and effective stories, while at the same time he was brooding over his own situation and the decline of the South. Slowly the brooding thoughts arranged themselves into the whole interconnected pattern that would form the substance of his novels.

The pattern was based on what he saw in Oxford or remembered from his childhood, on scraps of family tradition (the Falkners, as they spelled the name, had played their part in the history of the state), on kitchen dialogues between the black cook and her amiable husband, on Saturday-afternoon gossip in Courthouse Square, on stories told by men in overalls squatting on their heels while they passed around a fruit jar full of white corn liquor; on all the sources familiar to a small-town Mississippi boy—but the whole of it was elaborated, transformed, given convulsive life by his emotions; until by simple intensity of feeling the figures in it became a little more than human, became heroic or diabolical, became symbols of the old South, of war and reconstruction, of commerce and machinery destroying the standards of the past. There in Oxford, Faulkner performed a labor of imagination that has not been equaled in our time, and a double labor: first, to invent a Mississippi county that was like a mythical kingdom, but was complete and living in all its details; second, to make his story of Yoknapatawpha County stand as a parable or legend of all the Deep South.

For this double task, Faulkner was better equipped by talent and background than he was by schooling. He was born in

New Albany, Mississippi, September 25, 1897; he was the oldest of four brothers. Soon the Falkners moved to Ripley, in the adjoining county, then fifty miles southwestward to Oxford, where the novelist attended the public school, but without being graduated from high school. For a year or two after the war, he was a student at the University of Mississippi, where veterans could then matriculate without a high-school diploma, but he neglected his classroom work and left early in the second year. He had less of a formal education than any other good writer of his age group, except Hart Crane—less even than Hemingway, who never went to college, but who learned to speak several languages and studied writing in Paris with Ezra Pound and Gertrude Stein. Faulkner taught himself, largely, as he says, by "undirected and uncorrelated reading."*

Among the authors either mentioned or echoed in his early stories and poems are Keats, Balzac, Flaubert, Swinburne, Verlaine, Mallarmé, Wilde, Housman, Joyce, Eliot, Conrad Aiken, Sherwood Anderson, and E. E. Cummings, with fainter suggestions of Hemingway (looking at trout in a river), Dos Passos (in the spelling of compound words), and Scott Fitzgerald. The poems he wrote in those days were wholly derivative, but his prose from the beginning was a form of poetry, and in spite of the echoes it was wholly his own. He traveled less than any of his writing contemporaries. There was a lonely time in New York as salesclerk in a bookstore; there were six months in New Orleans, where he lived near Sherwood Anderson and met the literary crowd—he even satirized them in a bad early novel, *Mosquitoes*—then another six months in Italy and Paris, where he did not make friends on the Left Bank. Except for writing assignments in Hollywood and summers on the Gulf Coast, the rest of his life has been spent in the town where he grew up, less than forty miles from his birthplace.

Although Oxford, Mississippi, is the seat of a university, it

---

* The reading, though, was extensive. There was no public library in Oxford when Faulkner was a boy, but there were books in the house—a well-thumbed set of Dickens, for example. Also there was an older friend and neighbor, Phil Stone, who came back from Yale in 1914 apparently with trunkloads of books that were otherwise unavailable in Oxford. They included most of the authors, French, English, and American, who were read and prized by members of the literary generation. [M.C.]

is even less of a literary center than was Salem, Massachusetts, during Hawthorne's early years as a writer; and Faulkner himself has shown an even greater dislike than Hawthorne for literary society. His novels are the books of a man who broods about literature, but doesn't often discuss it with his friends; there is no ease about them, no feeling that they come from a background of taste refined by argument and of opinions held in common. They make me think of a passage from Henry James's little book on Hawthorne:

> The best things come, as a general thing, from the talents that are members of a group; every man works better when he has companions working in the same line, and yielding to the stimulus of suggestion, comparison, emulation. Great things of course have been done by solitary workers; but they have usually been done with double the pains they would have cost if they had been produced in more genial circumstances. The solitary worker loses the profit of example and discussion; he is apt to make awkward experiments; he is in the nature of the case more or less of an empiric. The empiric may, as I say, be treated by the world as an expert; but the drawbacks and discomforts of empiricism remain to him, and are in fact increased by the suspicion that is mingled with his gratitude, of a want in the public taste of a sense of the proportion of things.

Like Hawthorne, Faulkner is a solitary worker by choice, and he has done great things not only with double the pains to himself that they might have cost if produced in more genial circumstances, but sometimes also with double the pains to the reader. Two or three of his books as a whole and many of them in part are awkward experiments. All of them are full of overblown words like "imponderable," "immortal," "immutable," and "immemorial" that he would have used with more discretion, or not at all, if he had followed Hemingway's example and served an apprenticeship to an older writer. He is a most uncertain judge of his own work, and he has no reason to believe that the world's judgment of it is any more to be trusted; indeed, there is no American author who would be justified in feeling more suspicion of "a want in the public taste of a sense of the proportion of things." His early novels, when not condemned, were overpraised for the wrong reasons; his later and in many ways better novels have been ridiculed or simply neglected; and in 1945 all his seventeen books were effectively out of print, with some of them unobtainable in the second-hand bookshops.*

Even his warm admirers, of whom there are many—no author has a higher standing among his fellow novelists—have shown a rather vague idea of what he is trying to do; and Faulkner himself has never explained. He holds a curious attitude toward the public that appears to be lofty indifference (as in the one preface he wrote, for the Modern Library edition of *Sanctuary*), but really comes closer to being a mixture of skittery distrust and pure unconsciousness that the public exists. He doesn't furnish information or correct misstatements about himself (most of the biographical sketches that deal with him are full of preposterous errors). He doesn't care which way his name is spelled in the records, with or without the "u"—"Either way suits me," he says. Once he has finished a book, he is apparently not concerned with the question of how it will be presented, to what sort of audience, and sometimes he doesn't bother to keep a private copy of it. He said in a letter, "I think I have written a lot and sent it off to print before I actually realized strangers might read it." Others might say that Faulkner, at least in those early days, was not so much composing stories for the public as telling them to himself—like a lonely child in his imaginary world, but also like a writer of genius.

2.

Faulkner's mythical kingdom is a county in northern Mississippi, on the border between the sand hills covered with scrubby pine and the black earth of the river bottoms. Except for the storekeepers, mechanics, and professional men who live in Jefferson, the county seat, all the inhabitants are farmers or woodsmen. Except for a little lumber, their only commercial product is baled cotton for the Memphis market. A few of them live in big plantation houses, the relics of another age, and more of them in substantial wooden farmhouses; but still more of them are tenants, no better housed than slaves on good plantations before the Civil War. Yoknapatawpha

---

* I have let this paragraph stand, with the one that follows, as an accurate picture of Faulkner's reputation in 1945. [M.C., 1973]

County—"William Faulkner, sole owner and proprietor," as he inscribed on one of the maps he drew—has a population of 15,611 persons scattered over 2400 square miles. It sometimes seems to me that every house or hovel has been described in one of Faulkner's novels, and that all the people of the imaginary county, black and white, townsmen, farmers, and housewives, have played their parts in one connected story.

He has so far [1945] written nine books wholly concerned with Yoknapatawpha County and its people, who also appear in parts of three others and in thirty or more uncollected stories. *Sartoris* was the first book to be published, in the spring of 1929; it is a romantic and partly unconvincing novel, but with many fine scenes in it, such as the hero's visit to a family of independent pine-hill farmers; and it states most of the themes that the author would later develop at length. *The Sound and the Fury*, published six months later, recounts the going-to-pieces of the Compson family, and it was the first of Faulkner's novels to be widely discussed. The books that followed, in the Yoknapatawpha series, are *As I Lay Dying* (1930), about the death and burial of Addie Bundren; *Sanctuary* (1931), for a long time the most popular of his novels; *Light in August* (1932), in some ways the best; *Absalom, Absalom!* (1936), about Colonel Sutpen and his ambition to found a family; *The Unvanquished* (1938), a cycle of stories about the Sartoris dynasty; *The Wild Palms* (1939), half of which deals with a convict from back in the pine hills; *The Hamlet* (1940), a first novel about the Snopes clan, with others to follow; and *Go Down, Moses* (1942), in which Faulkner's principal theme is the relation between whites and Negroes. There are also many Yoknapatawpha stories in *These 13* (1931) and *Doctor Martino* (1934), besides other stories privately printed (like *Miss Zilphia Gant*, 1932) or published in magazines and still to be collected or used as episodes in novels.*

* That was the tally in 1945. With one exception, all the books that Faulkner published after that year are concerned with Yoknapatawpha County. The exception is *A Fable* (1954), about a reincarnated Christ in the First World War. The Yoknapatawpha books, eight in number, are *Intruder in the Dust* (1948), about a lynching that is averted by a seventy-year-old spinster and a pair of boys; *Knight's Gambit* (1949), recounting the adventures in detection of Gavin Stevens; *Collected Stories of William Faulkner* (1950), containing all the stories in *These 13* and *Doctor Martino* as well as several not previously

Just as Balzac, who may have inspired the series, divided his *Comédie Humaine* into "Scenes of Parisian Life," "Scenes of Provincial Life," "Scenes of Private Life," so Faulkner might divide his work into a number of cycles: one about the planters and their descendants, one about the townspeople of Jefferson, one about the poor whites, one about the Indians, and one about the Negroes. Or again, if he adopted a division by families, there would be the Compson-Sartoris saga, the continuing Snopes saga, the McCaslin saga, dealing with the white and black descendants of Carothers McCaslin, and the Ratliff-Bundren saga, devoted to the backwoods farmers of Frenchman's Bend. All the cycles or sagas are closely interconnected; it is as if each new book was a chord or segment of a total situation always existing in the author's mind. Sometimes a short story is the sequel to an earlier novel. For example, we read in *Sartoris* that Byron Snopes stole a packet of letters from Narcissa Benbow; and in "There Was a Queen," a story published five years later, we learn how Narcissa got the letters back again. Sometimes a novel contains the sequel to a story, and sometimes an episode reappears in several connections. Thus, in the first chapter of *Sanctuary*, we hear about the Old Frenchman place, a ruined mansion near which the people of the neighborhood had been "digging with secret and sporadic optimism for gold which the builder was reputed to have buried somewhere about the place when Grant came through the country on his Vicksburg campaign." Later this digging for gold served as the subject of a story printed in *The Saturday Evening Post:* "Lizards in Jamshyd's Courtyard." Still later the story was completely rewritten and became the last chapter of *The Hamlet.**

As one book leads into another, the author sometimes falls into inconsistencies of detail. There is a sewing-machine agent

---

collected; *Requiem for a Nun* (1951), a three-act drama, with narrative prologues to each act, about the later life of Temple Drake; *Big Woods* (1955), a cycle of hunting stories, some of them revised from chapters of *Go Down, Moses; The Town* (1957), second volume in the Snopes trilogy; *The Mansion* (1959), concluding the trilogy; and *The Reivers*, published a month before Faulkner's death on July 6, 1962. In all, sixteen of his books belong to the Yoknapatawpha cycle, as well as half of another book (*The Wild Palms*) and it is hard to count how many stories. [M.C., 1973]

* The Old Frenchman place was built in the 1830s by Louis Grenier, as Faulkner tells us in the prologue to the first act of *Requiem for a Nun* (1951). [M.C., 1973]

named V. K. Suratt who appears in *Sartoris* and some of the stories written at about the same time. When we reach *The Hamlet*, his name has changed to Ratliff, although his character remains the same (and his age, too, for all the twenty years that separate the backgrounds of the two novels). Henry Armstid is a likable figure in *As I Lay Dying* and *Light in August*; in *The Hamlet* he is mean and half-demented. His wife, whose character remains consistent, is called Lula in one book and Martha in another; in the third she is nameless. There is an Indian chief named Doom who appears in several stories; he starts as the father of Issetibeha (in "Red Leaves") and ends as his nephew (in "A Justice"). The mansion called Sutpen's Hundred was built of brick at the beginning of *Absalom, Absalom!*, but at the end of the novel it is all wood and inflammable except for the chimneys. But these errors are inconsequential, considering the scope of Faulkner's series, and I should judge that most of them are afterthoughts rather than oversights.

All his books in the Yoknapatawpha cycle are part of the same living pattern. It is the pattern, not the printed volumes in which part of it is recorded, that is Faulkner's real achievement. Its existence helps to explain one feature of his work: that each novel, each long or short story, seems to reveal more than it states explicitly and to have a subject bigger than itself. All the separate works are like blocks of marble from the same quarry: they show the veins and faults of the mother rock. Or else—to use a rather strained figure—they are like wooden planks that were cut, not from a log, but from a still-living tree. The planks are planed and chiseled into their final shapes, but the tree heals over the wound and continues to grow.

Faulkner is incapable of telling the same story twice without adding new details. In compiling *The Portable Faulkner* I wanted to use part of *The Sound and the Fury*, the novel about the fall of the Compson family. I thought that the last part of the book would be most effective as a separate episode, but still it depended too much on what had gone before. Faulkner offered to write a very brief introduction that would explain the relations of the characters. What he finally sent me was the much longer passage printed at the end of the *Portable*: a genealogy of the Compson family from their first arrival in America. Whereas the novel is confined (except for

memories) to a period of eighteen years ending on Easter
Sunday, 1928, the genealogy goes back to the battle of Cul-
loden in 1745, and forward to the year 1943, when Jason, last
of the Compson males, has sold the family mansion and Sister
Caddy has last been heard of as the mistress of a German
general. The novel that Faulkner wrote about the Compsons
had long before been given what appeared to be its final shape,
but the pattern or body of legend behind the novel—and
behind his other books—was still developing.

Although the pattern is presented in terms of a single Mississippi county, it can be extended to the Deep South as a
whole; and Faulkner always seems conscious of its wider application. He might have been thinking of his own novels when
he described the ledgers in the commissary of the McCaslin
plantation, in *Go Down, Moses*. They recorded, he says, "that
slow trickle of molasses and meal and meat, of shoes and
straw hats and overalls, of plowlines and collars and heelbolts
and clevises, which returned each fall as cotton"—in a sense
they were local and limited; but they were also "the continuation of that record which two hundred years had not been
enough to complete and another hundred would not be
enough to discharge; that chronicle which was a whole land
in miniature, which multiplied and compounded was the entire South."

3.

"Tell about the South," says Quentin Compson's roommate
at Harvard, a Canadian named Shreve McCannon who is
curious about the unknown region beyond the Ohio. "What's
it like there?" he asks. "What do they do there? Why do they
live there? Why do they live at all?" And Quentin, whose
background is a little like that of Faulkner himself and who
sometimes seems to speak for him—Quentin answers, "You
can't understand it. You would have to be born there." Nevertheless, he tells a long and violent story that reveals something
essential in the history of the Deep South, which is not so
much a region as it is, in Quentin's mind, an incomplete and
frustrated nation trying to relive its legendary past.

The story he tells—I am trying to summarize the plot of
Absalom, Absalom!—is that of a mountain boy named

Thomas Sutpen whose family drifted into the Virginia low-lands, where his father found odd jobs on a plantation. One day the father sent him with a message to the big house, but he was turned away at the door by a black man in livery. Puzzled and humiliated, the mountain boy was seized upon by the lifelong ambition to which he would afterward refer as "the design." He too would own a plantation with slaves and a liveried butler; he would build a mansion as big as any of those in the Tidewater; and he would have a son to inherit his wealth.

A dozen years later Sutpen appeared in the frontier town of Jefferson, where by some presumably dishonest means he managed to obtain a hundred square miles of land from the Chickasaws. With the help of twenty wild Negroes from the jungle and a French architect, he set about building the largest house in northern Mississippi, using timbers from the forest and bricks that his Negroes molded and baked on the spot; it was as if the mansion, Sutpen's Hundred, had been literally torn from the soil. Only one man in Jefferson—he was Quentin's grandfather, General Compson—ever learned how and where Sutpen had acquired his slaves. He had shipped to Haiti from Virginia, worked as an overseer on a sugar plantation, and married the rich planter's daughter, who had borne him a son. Then, finding that his wife had Negro blood, he had simply put her away, with her child and her fortune, while keeping the twenty slaves as a sort of indemnity. He explained to General Compson, in the stilted speech he had taught himself as appropriate to his new role of Southern gentleman, that she could not be "adjunctive to the forwarding of the design."

"Jesus, the South is fine, isn't it," Shreve McCannon says. "It's better than the theater, isn't it. It's better than Ben Hur, isn't it. No wonder you have to come away now and then, isn't it."

In Jefferson he married again, Quentin continues. This time Sutpen's wife belonged to a pious family of the neighborhood and she bore him two children, Henry and Judith. He became the biggest cotton planter in Yoknapatawpha County, and it seemed that his "design" had already been fulfilled. At this moment, however, Henry came home from the University of Mississippi with an older and worldlier new friend, Charles Bon, who was in reality Sutpen's son by his first marriage.

Charles became engaged to Judith. Sutpen learned his identity and, without making a sign of recognition, ordered him from the house. Henry, who refused to believe that Charles was his half-brother, renounced his birthright and followed him to New Orleans. In 1861 all the male Sutpens went off to war, and all survived four years of fighting. Then, in the spring of 1865, Charles suddenly decided to marry Judith, even though he was certain by now that she was his half-sister. Henry rode beside him all the way back to Sutpen's Hundred, but tried to stop him at the gate, killed him when he insisted on going ahead with his plan, told Judith what he had done, and disappeared.

"The South," Shreve McCannon says as he listens to the story. "The South. Jesus. No wonder you folks all outlive yourselves by years and years." And Quentin says, remembering his own sister with whom (or with a false notion of whom) he was in love—just as Charles Bon, and Henry too, were in love with Judith—"I am older at twenty than a lot of people who have died."

But Quentin's story of the Deep South does not end with the war. Colonel Sutpen came home, he says, to find his wife dead, his son a fugitive, his slaves dispersed (they had run away before they were freed by the Union Army), and most of his land about to be seized for debt. Still determined to carry out "the design," he did not pause for breath before undertaking to restore his house and plantation as nearly as possible to what they had been. The effort failed; Sutpen lost most of his land and was reduced to keeping a crossroads store. Now in his sixties, he tried again to beget a son; but his wife's younger sister, Miss Rosa Coldfield, was outraged by his proposal ("Let's try it," he seems to have said, though his words are not directly repeated—"and if it's a boy we'll get married"); and later poor Milly Jones, whom he seduced, gave birth to a girl. At that Sutpen abandoned hope and provoked Milly's grandfather into killing him. Judith survived her father for a time, as did the half-caste son of Charles Bon by a New Orleans octoroon. After the death of these two by yellow fever, the great house was haunted rather than inhabited by an ancient mulatto woman, Sutpen's daughter by one of his slaves. The fugitive Henry Sutpen came home to die; the townspeople heard of his illness and sent an ambulance after him; but old Clytie thought they were arresting him for murder and set fire to Sutpen's Hundred. The only survivor of the conflagration was Jim Bond, a half-witted, saddle-colored creature who was Charles Bon's grandson.

"Now I want you to tell me just one thing more," the Canadian roommate says after hearing the story. "Why do you hate the South?"—"I dont hate it," Quentin says quickly, at once. "I dont hate it," he repeats, apparently speaking for the author as well as himself. *I dont hate it,* he thinks, panting in the cold air, the iron New England dark; *I dont. I dont hate it! I dont hate it!*

The reader cannot help wondering why this somber and, at moments, plainly incredible story has so seized upon Quentin's mind that he trembles with excitement when telling it, and why Shreve McCannon felt that it revealed the essence of the Deep South. It seems to belong in the realm of Gothic romance, with Sutpen's Hundred taking the place of a haunted castle on the Rhine, with Colonel Sutpen as Faust and Charles Bon as Manfred. Then slowly, if you read it again, it dawns on you that most of the characters and incidents have a double meaning; that besides their place in the story they serve as symbols or metaphors with a general application. Sutpen's great design, the land he stole from the Indians, the French architect who built his mansion with the help of wild Negroes from the jungle, the woman of mixed blood whom he married and disowned, the unacknowledged son who ruined him, the poor white whom he robbed and who killed him in anger, and the final destruction of the mansion like the downfall of a social order . . . all these might belong to a tragic fable of Southern history. With a little cleverness, the whole novel might be explained as a connected and logical allegory, but this, I think, would be going far beyond the author's intention. First of all he was writing a story, and one that affected him deeply, but he was also brooding over a social situation. More or less unconsciously, the incidents in the story came to represent the forces and elements in the social situation, since the mind naturally works in terms of symbols and parallels. In Faulkner's case, this form of parallelism is not confined to *Absalom, Absalom!* It can be found in the whole fictional framework that he has been elaborating in novel after novel, until his work has become a myth or legend of the South.

I call it a legend because it is obviously no more intended as a historical account of the country south of the Ohio than

The Scarlet Letter was intended as a history of Massachusetts or *Paradise Lost* as a factual account of the Fall. Briefly stated, the legend might run something like this: The Deep South was ruled by planters some of whom were aristocrats like the Sartoris clan, while other were new men like Colonel Sutpen. Both types were determined to establish a lasting social order on the land they had seized from the Indians (that is, to leave sons behind them). They had the virtue of living single-mindedly by a fixed code; but there was also an inherent guilt in their "design," their way of life; it was slavery that put a curse on the land and brought about the Civil War. [I must add, in deference to Cleanth Brooks, that although Sutpen had more than his share of the guilt, he never pretended to follow the code of conduct that in some measure atoned for it. Temperamentally he was less of a Southerner than a Northern robber baron out of his time and place; or he might even stand for the blindly ambitious man of all ages. To the other planters, he was always an alien. Quentin Compson, their descendant, regarded him as "trash, originless"—so Faulkner told me in a letter—but Quentin also grieved the fact that a man like Sutpen "could not only have dreamed so high but have had the force and strength to have failed so grandly." Thus, it was not at all in his character, but rather in his fate, that Sutpen became emblematic of the South.]

After the war was lost, partly as a result of the Southerners' mad heroism (for who else but men as brave as Jackson and Stuart could have frightened the Yankees into standing together and fighting back?), the planters tried to restore their "design" by other methods. But they no longer had the strength to achieve more than a partial success, even after they had freed their land from the carpetbaggers who followed the Northern armies. As time passed, moreover, the men of the old order found that they had Southern enemies too; they had to fight against a new exploiting class descended from the landless whites of slavery days. In this struggle between the clan of Sartoris and the unscrupulous tribe of Snopes, the Sartorises were defeated in advance by a traditional code that kept them from using the weapons of the enemy. As a price of victory, however, the Snopeses had to serve the mechanized civilization of the North, which was morally impotent in itself, but which, with the aid of its Southern retainers, ended by corrupting the Southern nation. In a later time, the problems of the South are still unsolved, the racial conflict is becoming more acute, and Faulkner's characters in their despairing moments foresee or forebode some catastrophe of which Jim Bond and his like will be the only survivors.

4.

This legend of Faulkner's, if I have stated it correctly, is clearly not the plantation legend that has been embodied in hundreds of romantic novels. Faulkner presents the virtues of the old order as being moral rather than material. There is no baronial pomp in his novels; no profusion of silk and silver, mahogany and moonlight and champagne. The big house on Mr. Hubert Beauchamp's plantation (in "Was") had a rotted floorboard in the back gallery that Mr. Hubert never got round to having fixed. Visitors used to find him sitting in the springhouse with his boots off and his feet in the water while he sipped his morning toddy. Visitors to Sutpen's Hundred were offered champagne: it was the best, doubtless, yet it was "crudely dispensed out of the burlesqued pantomime elegance of Negro butlers who (and likewise the drinkers who gulped it down like neat whisky between flowery and unsubtle toasts) would have treated lemonade the same way." All the planters lived comfortably, with plenty of servants, but Faulkner never lets us forget that they were living on what had recently been the frontier. What he admires about them is not their wealth or their manners or their fine horses, but rather the unquestioning acceptance—by the best planters— of a moral code that taught them "courage and honor and pride, and pity and love of justice and of liberty." Living with single hearts they were, says Quentin Compson's father,

> . . . people too as we are, and victims too as we are, but victims of a different circumstance, simpler and therefore, integer for integer, larger, more heroic and the figures therefore more heroic too, not dwarfed and involved but distinct, uncomplex, who had the gift of living once or dying once instead of being diffused and scattered creatures drawn blindly limb from limb from a grab bag and assembled, author and victim too of a thousand homicides and a thousand copulations and divorcements.

The old order was a moral order: briefly that was its strength and the secret lost by its heirs. But also—and here is another respect in which it differs from the Southern story more commonly presented—it bore the moral burden of a guilt so great that the Civil War and even Reconstruction were in some sense a merited punishment. There is madness, but there is metaphorical meaning too, in Miss Rosa Coldfield's belief that Sutpen was a demon and that his sins were the real reason "why God let us lose the War: that only through the blood of our men and the tears of our women could He stay this demon and efface his name and lineage from the earth." Colonel Sutpen himself has a feeling not exactly of guilt, since he has never questioned the rightness of his design, but rather of amazement that so many misfortunes have fallen on him. Sitting in General Compson's office, he goes back over his career, trying to see where he had made his "mistake," for that is what he calls it. Sometimes the author seems to be implying that the sin for which Sutpen and his class are being punished is that of cohabiting with Negroes. But before the end of *Absalom, Absalom!* we learn that miscegenation is only part of it. When Charles Bon's curious actions are explained, we find that he was taking revenge on his father for having refused to recognize him by so much as a glance. Thus, heartlessness was the "mistake" that ruined Sutpen, not the taking of a partly Negro wife and Negro concubines.

The point becomes even clearer in the long fourth part of that tremendous story "The Bear." When the protagonist, Isaac McCaslin, is twenty-one he insists on relinquishing the big plantation that is his by inheritance; he thinks that the land is cursed. It is cursed in his eyes by the deeds of his grandfather: "that evil and unregenerate old man who could summon, because she was his property, a human being because she was old enough and female, to his widower's house and get a child on her and then dismiss her beause she was of an inferior race, and then bequeath a thousand dollars to the infant because he would be dead then and wouldn't have to pay it." At this point Faulkner seems to be speaking through Ike McCaslin. The lesson is that the land was cursed—and the Civil War was part of the curse—because its owners had treated human beings as instruments; in a word, it was cursed by slavery.

All through his boyhood, Faulkner must have dreamed of

fighting in the Civil War. It was a Sartoris war and not a Snopes war, like the later one in which he had enlisted for service in a foreign army. And yet his sympathies did not wholly lie with the slave-holding clan of Sartoris, even though it was his own clan. The men he most admired and must have pictured himself as resembling were the Southern soldiers—after all, they were the vast majority—who owned no slaves themselves and suffered from the institution of slavery. The men he would praise in his novels were those "who had fought for four years and lost . . . not because they were opposed to freedom as freedom, but for the old reasons for which man (not the generals and politicians but man) has always fought and died in wars: to preserve a status quo or establish a better future one to endure for his children." One might define the author's position as that of an antislavery Southern nationalist.

Faulkner's novels of contemporary Southern life [those written before 1945] continue the legend into a period that he regards as one of moral confusion and social decay. He is continually seeking in them for violent images to convey his sense of outrage. *Sanctuary* is the most violent of all his novels; it has been the most popular and is by no means the least important (in spite of Faulkner's comment that it was "a cheap idea . . . deliberately conceived to make money"). The story of Popeye and Temple Drake has more meaning than appears on a first hasty reading—the only reading that early critics were willing to grant it. Popeye himself is one of several characters in Faulkner's novels who represent the mechanical civilization that has invaded and conquered the South. He is always described in mechanical terms: his eyes "looked like rubber knobs"; his face "just went awry, like the face of a wax doll set too near a hot fire and forgotten"; his tight suit and stiff hat were "all angles, like a modernistic lampshade"; and in general he had "that vicious depthless quality of stamped tin." Popeye was the son of a professional strike-breaker, from whom he had inherited syphilis; he was the grandson of a pyromaniac, and he had spent most of his childhood in an institution. He was the man "who made money and had nothing he could do with it, spend it for, since he knew that alcohol would kill him like poison, who had no friends and had never known a woman"—in other words, he was a compendium of all the hateful qualities that Faulkner assigns to finance capitalism. *Sanctuary* is not a connected allegory, as George Marion O'Donnell condemned it for being—he was the first critic to approach it seriously—but neither is it a mere accumulation of pointless horrors. It is an example of the Freudian method turned backward, being full of sexual nightmares that are in reality social symbols. It is somehow connected in the author's mind with what he regards as the rape and corruption of the South.

In his novels dealing with the present Faulkner makes it clear that the descendants of the old ruling caste have the wish but not the courage or the strength to prevent this new disaster. They are defeated by Popeye (like Horace Benbow), or they run away from him (like Gowan Stevens, who had been to college at Virginia and learned how to drink like a gentleman, but not to fight for his principles), or they are robbed and replaced in their positions of influence by the Snopeses (like old Bayard Sartoris, the president of the bank), or they drug themselves with eloquence and alcohol (like Quentin Compson's father), or they retire into the illusion of being inviolable Southern ladies (like Mrs. Compson, who says, "It can't be simply to flout and hurt me. Whoever God is, he would not permit that. I'm a lady."), or they dwell so much on the past that they are incapable of facing the present (like Reverend Hightower of *Light in August*), or they run from danger to danger (like young Bayard Sartoris) frantically seeking their own destruction. Faulkner's novels are full of well-meaning and even admirable persons, not only the grandsons of the cotton aristocracy, but also pine-hill farmers and storekeepers and sewing-machine agents and Negro cooks and sharecroppers; but they are almost all of them defeated by circumstances and they carry with them a sense of their own doom.

They also carry, whether heroes or villains, a curious sense of submission to their fate. "There is not one of Faulkner's characters," says André Gide in his dialogue on "The New American Novelists," "who properly speaking has a soul"; and I think he means that not one of them exercises the faculty of conscious choice between good and evil. They are haunted, obsessed, driven forward by some inner necessity. Like Miss Rosa Coldfield in *Absalom, Absalom!* they exist in "that dream state in which you run without moving from a terror in which you cannot believe, toward a safety in which you have no faith." Or, like the slaves freed by General Sherman's army, in *The Unvanquished,* they blindly follow the road toward any river, believing that it will be their Jordan:

> They were singing, walking along the road singing, not even looking to either side. The dust didn't even settle for two days, because all that night they still passed; we sat up listening to them and the next morning every few yards along the road would be the old ones who couldn't keep up any more, sitting or lying down and even crawling along, calling to the others to help them; and the others—the young ones—not stopping, not even looking at them. "Going to Jordan," they told me. "Going to cross Jordan."

Most of Faulkner's characters, black and white, are a little like that. They dig for gold frenziedly after they have lost their hope of finding it (like Henry Armstid in *The Hamlet* and Lucas Beauchamp in *Go Down, Moses*); or they battle against and survive a Mississippi flood for the one privilege of returning to the state prison farm (like the tall convict in "Old Man"); or, a whole family together, they carry a body through flood and fire and corruption to bury it in the cemetery at Jefferson (like the Bundrens in *As I Lay Dying*); or they tramp the roads week after week in search of men who had promised but never intended to marry them (like Lena Grove, the pregnant woman of *Light in August*); or, pursued by a mob, they turn at the end to meet and accept death (like Joe Christmas in the same novel). Even when they seem to be guided by a conscious purpose, like Colonel Sutpen, it is not something they have chosen by an act of will, but something that has taken possession of them: Sutpen's great design was "not what he wanted to do but what he just had to do, had to do it whether he wanted to or not, because if he did not do it he knew he could never live with himself for the rest of his life." In the same way, Faulkner himself writes, not what he wants to, but what he just has to write whether he wants to or not.

5.

It had better be admitted that most of his novels have some obvious weakness in structure. Some of them combine two or more themes having little relation to each other, as *Light in August* does, while others, like *The Hamlet*, tend to resolve themselves into a series of episodes resembling beads on a string. In *The Sound and the Fury*, which is superb as a whole, we can't be sure that the four sections of the novel are presented in the most effective order; at any rate, we can't fully understand the first section until we have read the three that follow. *Absalom, Absalom!* though at first it strikes us as being pitched in too high a key, is structurally the soundest of all the novels in the Yoknapatawpha series—and it gains power in retrospect; but even here the author's attention seems to shift from the principal theme of Colonel Sutpen's design to the secondary theme of incest and miscegenation.

Faulkner seems best to me, and most nearly himself, either in long stories like "The Bear," in *Go Down, Moses*, and "Old Man," which was published as half of *The Wild Palms*, and "Spotted Horses," which was first printed separately, then greatly expanded and fitted into the loose framework of *The Hamlet*, or else in the Yoknapatawpha saga as a whole. That is, he has been most effective in dealing with the total situation always present in his mind as a pattern of the South, or else in shorter units which, though often subject to inspired revision, have still been shaped by a single conception. It is by his best that we should judge him, as every other author; and Faulkner at his best—even sometimes at his worst—has a power, a richness of life, an intensity to be found in no other American writer of our time. He has—once again I am quoting from Henry James's essay on Hawthorne—"the element of simple genius, the quality of imagination."

Moreover, he has a brooding love for the land where he was born and reared and where, unlike other writers of his generation, he has chosen to spend his life. It is ". . . this land, this South, for which God has done so much, with woods for game and streams for fish and deep rich soil for seed and lush springs to sprout it and long summers to mature it and serene falls to harvest it and short mild winters for men and animals." So far as Faulkner's country includes the Delta, it is also (in the words of old Ike McCaslin)

> . . . this land which man has deswamped and denuded and derivered in two generations so that white men can own plantations and commute every night to Memphis and black men

own plantations and ride in jimcrow cars to Chicago and live in millionaires' mansions on Lake Shore Drive, where white men rent farms and live like niggers and niggers crop on shares and live like animals, where cotton is planted and grows man-tall in the very cracks of the sidewalks, and usury and mortgage and bankruptcy and measureless wealth, Chinese and African and Aryan and Jew, all breed and spawn together.

Here are the two sides of Faulkner's feeling for the South: on the one side, an admiring and possessive love; on the other, a compulsive fear lest what he loves should be destroyed by the ignorance of its native serfs and the greed of traders and absentee landlords.

No other American writer takes such delight in the weather. He speaks in various novels of "the hot still pinewiney silence of the August afternoon"; of "the moonless September dust, the trees along the road not rising soaring as trees should but squatting like huge fowl"; of "the tranquil sunset of October mazy with windless woodsmoke"; of the "slow drizzle of November rain just above the ice point"; of "those windless Mississippi December days which are a sort of Indian summer's Indian summer"; of January and February when there is "no movement anywhere save the low constant smoke . . . and no sound save the chopping axes and the lonely whistle of the daily trains." Spring in Faulkner's country is a hurried season, "all coming at once, pell mell and disordered, fruit and bloom and leaf, pied meadow and blossoming wood and the long fields shearing dark out of winter's slumber, to the shearing plow." Summer is dust-choked and blazing, and it lasts far into what should be autumn. "That's the one trouble with this country," he says in *As I Lay Dying*. "Everything, weather, all, hangs on too long. Like, our rivers, our land: opaque, slow, violent; shaping and creating the life of man in its implacable and brooding image."

And Faulkner loves these people created in the image of the land. After a second reading of the novels, you continue to be impressed by his villains, Popeye and Jason and Flem Snopes; but this time you find more space in your memory for other figures standing a little in the background yet presented by the author with quiet affection: old ladies like Miss Jenny Du Pre, with their sharp-tongued benevolence; shrewd but affable traders like Ratliff, the sewing-machine agent, and Will Varner, with his cotton gin and general store; long-suffering farm wives like Mrs. Henry Armstid (whether her name is Lula or Martha); and backwoods patriarchs like Pappy MacCullum, with his six middle-aged but unmarried sons named after the generals of Lee's army. You remember the big plantation houses that collapse in flames as if a whole civilization were dying, but you also remember men in patched and faded but quite clean overalls sitting on the gallery—here in the North we should call it the porch—of a crossroads store that is covered with posters advertising soft drinks and patent medicines; and you remember the stories they tell while chewing tobacco until the suption is out of it (everything in their world is reduced to anecdote, and every anecdote is based on character). You remember Quentin Compson not in his despairing moments, but riding with his father behind the dogs as they quarter a sedge-grown hillside after quail; and not listening to his father's story, but still knowing every word of it because, as he thought to himself, "You had learned, absorbed it already without the medium of speech somehow from having been born and living beside it, with it, as children will and do; so that what your father was saying did not tell you anything so much as it struck, word by word, the resonant strings of remembering."

Faulkner's novels have the quality of being lived, absorbed, remembered rather than merely observed. And they have what is rare in the novels of our time, a warmth of family affection, brother for brother and sister, the father for his children—a love so warm and proud that it tries to shut out the rest of the world. Compared with that affection, married love is presented as something calculating, and illicit love as a consuming fire. And because the blood relationship is central in his novels, Faulkner finds it hard to create sympathetic characters between the ages of twenty and forty. He is better with children, Negro and white, and incomparably good with older people who preserve the standards that have come down to them "out of the old time, the old days."

In the group of novels beginning with *The Wild Palms* (1939), which attracted so little attention at the time of publication that they seemed to go unread, there is a quality not exactly new to Faulkner—it had appeared already in passages of *Sartoris* and *Sanctuary*—but now much stronger and no longer overshadowed by violence and horror. It is a sort of homely and sobersided frontier humor that is seldom achieved in contemporary writing (except sometimes by Erskine Caldwell, also a Southerner). The horse-trading episodes in *The Hamlet*, and especially the long story of the spotted ponies from Texas, might have been inspired by the Davy Crockett almanacs. "Old Man," the story of the convict who surmounted the greatest of the Mississippi floods, might almost be a continuation of *Huckleberry Finn*. It is as if some older friend of Huck's had taken the raft and drifted on from Aunt Sally Phelps's farm into wilder adventures, described in a wilder style, among Chinese and Cajuns and bayous crawling with alligators. In a curious way, Faulkner combines two of the principal traditions in American letters: the tradition of psychological horror, often close to symbolism, that begins with Charles Brockden Brown, our first professional novelist, and extends through Poe, Melville, Henry James (in his later stories), Stephen Crane, and Hemingway; and the other tradition of frontier humor and realism, beginning with Augustus Longstreet's *Georgia Scenes* and having Mark Twain as its best example.

But the American author he most resembles is Hawthorne, for all their polar differences. They stand to each other as July to December, as heat to cold, as swamp to mountain, as the luxuriant to the meager but perfect, as planter to Puritan; and yet Hawthorne had much the same attitude toward New England that Faulkner has to the South, together with a strong sense of regional particularity. The Civil War made Hawthorne feel that "the North and the South were two distinct nations in opinions and habits, and had better not try to live under the same institutions." In the spring of 1861 he wrote to his Bowdoin classmate Horatio Bridge, "We were never one people and never really had a country." "New England," he said a little later, "is quite as large a lump of earth as my heart can really take in." But it was more than a lump of earth for him; it was a lump of history and a permanent state of consciousness. Like Faulkner in the South, he applied himself to creating its moral fables and elaborating its legends, which existed, as it were, in his solitary heart. Pacing the hillside behind his house in Concord, he listened for a voice; one might say that he lay in wait for it, passively but expectantly, like a hunter behind a rock; then, when it had spoken, he transcribed its words—more cautiously than Faulkner, it is true; with more form and less fire, but with the same essential fidelity. "I have an instinct that I had better keep quiet," he said in a letter to his publisher. "Perhaps I shall have a new spirit of vigor if I wait quietly for it; perhaps not." Faulkner is another author who has to wait for the spirit and the voice. He is not so much a novelist, in the usual sense of being a writer who sets out to observe actions and characters, then fits them into the framework of a story, as he is an epic or bardic poet in prose, a creator of myths that he weaves together into a legend of the South.

[1946]

AN AFTERWORD

Long after the shock of Faulkner's death, I found myself looking back at him not only with the old admiration for his work but with respect for his character and also, it seems to me, with a degree of understanding. For all the differences between us, of which the enormous one was his genius, we were men of the same time, with many of the same standards, which were partly derived from our reading of the same authors, and we had the same instinctive love of the American land. His actions did not seem inexplicable to me, as they sometimes did to others. They were his own solutions, fresh and simple ones, as if he were acting without precedents, to problems that almost all the writers of our time had to face.

We were most of us countrymen, in one sense or another. There were exceptions and Scott Fitzgerald, for example, was less at home in the country, "up to my ass in daisies," than he was in a residential suburb. Most of the others lived in the country by choice, though preferably not too far from New York or Paris or, in Hemingway's case, Havana; or they found another compromise, as Cummings did by spending seven or eight months of the year in New York and the rest of it on a hilltop in New Hampshire. Perhaps we might be called a transitional generation, bent on enjoying the urban pleasures, but at the same time hunters and fishermen eager to feel the soil instead of asphalt underfoot. We were radicals in literature and sometimes in politics, but conservative in our other aspirations, looking back for ideals to the country we had known in childhood, where people led separate lives in widely scattered houses; where there were broad fields in which a boy could hunt without fear of No Trespass signs, and big woods, untouched by lumbermen, in which he could wander with a pocket compass. I suspect that we were the last generation in which those country tastes could be taken for granted. American fiction and poetry since our time have become increasingly urban or suburban.

Among us Faulkner was the only one who remained loyal to the neighborhood he had always known. The rest of us were uprooted and exiled from our native countrysides, as first by our schooling, then by the Great War, then by our travels; as one after another said, but Hemingway long before Wolfe, "You can't go home again." Faulkner seemed to be unaffected by that long deracination, as by the effort that followed it to put down new roots in middle age. He spent most of his life in Oxford, the country town where he grew up, which is thirty miles as the crow flies from New Albany, the other country town where he was born. He was nourished on local tradition and expressed it in his books: what was best in it as well as what was most violent and ominous. Yet there was another sense in which he too was uprooted; in which he lived as a foreigner among his neighbors and—to use a phrase that goes back to the Hitler era—an "internal émigré." For of course he lived almost from boyhood by another system of values—shared by many writers of his time—as well as by the local one; I mean the values of the artist in the Symbolist tradition.

The wonder is that he learned about that international tradition at such an early age, and in Oxford. He was introduced to it by a course of reading that started before his seventeenth birthday. In the summer of 1914 his neighbor Phil Stone came back from Yale. Faulkner "was painting some then," Stone said in a reminiscence printed in the Oxford weekly newspaper, the *Eagle,** "and was faintly interested in writing verse. I gave him books to read—Swinburne, Keats and a number of the moderns, such as Conrad Aiken and the Imagists in verse and Sherwood Anderson in prose." I doubt whether anyone else in Oxford had those books at the time, except

* In the issue of November 14, 1950, after the announcement that Faulkner had been awarded the Nobel Prize. [M.C.]

for Keats and Swinburne, but the list sounds familiar to me, since I was reading the same authors then or a little later, after the same sort of introduction by an older friend. And of course I went on, as Faulkner obviously did, to read others more definitely in the Symbolist tradition: Flaubert, Baudelaire, Verlaine, Rimbaud, Eliot, Joyce.

Faulkner was always a great reader, as one discovered in the course of time. Apparently he read poetry admired by the Symbolists, then fiction in the same tradition (though he would read almost any novel if it was recommended by people he respected or was written by one of his rivals), then Southern history and books about the Indians, and always Shakespeare and the Bible. He did not read the moral or social philosophers of our time, but there was in fact a great deal of disguised ethics, with a touch of metaphysics, in the Symbolist poets and novelists, who had founded what has often been called a religion of art. Faulkner seems to have found the religion congenial, for he was always a moralist, by one system of values or another.

In his later years the system was essentially Christian. In his early books, however—and to some extent in the later ones as well—he applied the Symbolist precepts, including the simple one that actions should be judged as art. Instead of being extolled or condemned for their social consequences, they should be observed and presented for their dramatic qualities. The most reprehensible actions, in social terms, might be precisely those which enhanced a work of art by virtue of their passion and singlemindedness, or "purity." That would explain why Faulkner showed something close to admiration for most of his villains, including Jason Compson, Joe Christmas (if he *is* a villain), and Mink Snopes, and why, if he returned to them in his later writing—as he returned to Jason in the Appendix on the Compson family and to Mink in the best chapters of *The Mansion*—he presented them almost with affection. Even Mink's rich cousin Flem, the type of everything that Faulkner detested, acquires a redeeming dignity at the end. It was as if the author felt that he owed a debt to those characters for lending strength to his work.

It was the work, not the author, that was important by the Symbolist system of values. The author should sacrifice himself to the work, producing it "in the agony and sweat of the human spirit," as Faulkner said, "not for glory and least of all for profit, but to create out of the materials of the human spirit something which did not exist before." Since he was sacrificing himself, he might claim the right to sacrifice others. "An artist," Faulkner told Jean Stein when she interviewed him for the *Paris Review*, ". . . is completely amoral in that he will rob, borrow, beg, or steal from anybody and everybody to get the work done. . . . Everything goes by the board: honor, pride, decency, security, happiness, all, to get the book written." To produce the work was the categorical imperative, and it was combined for many Symbolists—as it was for Faulkner—with the metaphysical notion of soaring in the work toward an unchanging realm of passions transmuted into art, a sort of heaven for good books where they dwell in timeless equality. One remembers the letter in which he said, "All the moving things are eternal in man's history and have been written before, and if a man writes hard enough, sincerely enough, humbly enough, and with the unalterable determination never never never to be quite satisfied with it, he will repeat them, because art like poverty takes care of its own."

The Symbolist movement was not only a religion with saints and martyrs; it was also a sort of international freemasonry (of the French or Grand Orient rather than the Scottish Rite). Many of its moral precepts proved somewhat confusing to the uninitiated. Note for example the general reaction to Faulkner's statement, in his introduction to the Modern Library edition of *Sanctuary*, that the book "was deliberately conceived to make money."

> I decided [he says] I might just as well make some of it myself. I took a little time out, and speculated what a person in Mississippi would believe to be current trends, chose what I thought was the right answer and invented the most horrific tale I could imagine and wrote it in about three weeks and sent it to [Harrison] Smith, who had done *The Sound and the Fury* and who wrote me immediately, "Good God, I can't publish this. We'd both be in jail." So I told Faulkner, "You're damned. You'll have to work now and then for the rest of your life."

That was enough to persuade most critics, at the time, that the book must be valueless and that Faulkner had degraded himself by committing an aesthetic crime. They scarcely bothered to read his qualifying statement that, after *Sanctuary* had at last been set into type, "I tore the galleys down and rewrote

the book. It had already been set up once, so I had to pay
for the privilege of rewriting it, trying to make out of it something which would not shame *The Sound and the Fury* and
As I Lay Dying too much and I made a fair job. . . ." But
Faulkner's writing contemporaries read the whole introduction, and most of them were more favorably impressed by it
than the critics had been (while noting its disastrous effect on
the public). They had learned by experience that the Muses
are capricious, and it seemed to them—even before reading
the book—that something written and revised in that fashion
might prove to be an accidental masterpiece (as is indeed the
case with *Sanctuary*). They did not feel that Faulkner had
transgressed the laws of their profession by writing a book at
top speed simply to make money. What he did was "all right,"
they said to themselves, provided that it was strictly an experiment and provided that his subsequent books were also
experiments, but of different natures. It was writing another
book by the same formula—something he never did—that
would have been a sin against the religion of art.

Moreover—I am trying to depict a state of mind that I more
or less shared at the time—there was something bold and
grandly disdainful in the whole project. To speculate about
current tastes; to meet them by inventing the most horrific
tale that could be imagined, then by writing it in three weeks;
to find after some delay that one's answer had been correct
and was to be rewarded with almost as much money as one
had dreamed of making; and later, when the book was reissued, to write an introduction that revealed the process off-
handedly—all that showed an admirable independence of
mind, as well as a vast indifference to what the public might
think. As if by sure instinct, Faulkner was obeying another
moral precept of the Symbolists: that the author should *épater
les bourgeois*—not "shock the bourgeois," as the phrase is
usually translated, but startle and affront respectable people,
quite literally, knock them off their pins. He should do so
with a negligent air, as if drawing on his gloves, and then,
never repeating himself, he should move on to some new
exploit or experiment.

Those were some rules of literary conduct, a few among
others, that we learned in our time and more or less tried to
follow. Because of our travels, most of us had the advantage
of learning them in Paris from the best instructors. Faulkner

stayed at home, except for his two or three years in New Orleans, and nevertheless he outdid the rest of us; he simply *was* what we vaguely thought of becoming. That is one reason—though his work is the principal reason—why he was admired by writers of his own generation at a time when his books as well as his actions confused the American public.

Even when his reputation was in eclipse, almost everyone was willing to grant that he had genius. Not so widely recognized then or later was that he also had talent. Here I am using the two words in one of their several pairings, one by which they are not measured on the same quantitative scale—with 180, for example, as a quotient for genius and 150 for talent—but instead are treated as sharply opposing qualities. "Genius" in that sense would stand for everything that is essentially the gift of the subconscious mind—inspiration, imagination, the creative vision—while "talent" would stand for conscious ingenuity, calculation, acquired skill, and the critical judgment that an author displays when revising his own work. "How many young geniuses we have known," Emerson said, "and none but ourselves will ever hear of them for want in them of a little talent."

Faulkner had talent in abundance, as is clear to anyone who examines the early draft of *Sanctuary*, for instance, or his three successive versions of "That Evening Sun." Each of his many changes reveals a sound critical judgment. The detective stories he collected in *Knight's Gambit* are examples of misapplied but impressive ingenuity. Again it was talent, not genius, that he revealed while working in Hollywood. He said in the *Paris Review* interview (1956), "I know now that I will never be a good motion-picture writer," but what he meant is that he wouldn't be a great one. He was good enough so that Warner Brothers made strenuous efforts to get him back to their studio, even in the years before they realized that he was a world-famous author. They wanted him because he could throw away the script and write new dialogue on the set, a technical achievement that few of their writers had mastered. But technique was never what excited him, and very often, I think, he sacrificed his talent to his genius.

The sacrifice is revealed not only in his books but in many casual remarks like those he made to me in Sherman. "I listen to the voices, and when I put down what the voices say, it's right. Sometimes I don't like what they say"—that is, their message might be in conflict with his conscious standards—"but I don't change it." Or that other remark, also quoted in an earlier chapter, "Get it down. Take chances," that is, give rein to the unconscious. "It may be bad, but that's the only way you can do anything really good. Wolfe took the most chances, though he didn't always know what he was doing. I come next and then Dos Passos. Hemingway doesn't take chances enough."

That was the argument at a distance between Faulkner and Hemingway, which sometimes became embittered on Hemingway's part. They had to differ, for the simple reason that they were rivals who—partly by the influence on both of them of their time—resembled each other in many fashions, great and small. Both of them had sharp eyes for landscape; both liked to go barefoot as boys and even as young men, as if they weren't satisfied with merely seeing the countryside but had to feel it as well; both were hunters by devoted avocation. Both loved the wilderness, lamented its passing, went searching for remains of it, and were proud of their ability to find their way in it without guides. Both returned in their work to many of the same themes: for example, the primitive mind, the mystical union of hunter and hunted, the obsessions of wounded men, and the praise of alcohol. There were even trivial resemblances, as in the British style of dress and the British officer's World War I mustache that Hemingway wore in his early years and Faulkner all his life. They differed radically, however, in their attitude toward the craft of writing.

Hemingway kept his inspiration in check, but he liked to know what he was doing at every moment. Quite the opposite of Hemingway in this respect, he sometimes sacrificed his genius to his talent. One thinks of his remark that I repeated in a letter: "Faulkner has the most talent of anybody"—here "talent" is being used in a different sense from mine—"but hard to depend on because he goes on writing after he is tired and seems as though he never threw away the worthless. I would have been happy just to have managed him." Hemingway was an excellent manager of others, and of himself until the last years, but it seems to me that he was wrong in this instance. The crucial problem with Faulkner was not that of managing his talent—let us say, of developing his skill and conserving his stamina as if he were a boxer training for the big fight—but rather that of keeping his genius alive through the years. To that problem he had to find his own solution.

All his life Faulkner was a problem solver. Obviously that was the way his mind worked: he regarded each new situation as a problem, which he usually reduced to a single question; then he tried to find his answer. It is of course a common procedure, but most of us make it easier by looking for precedents and then by responding to the problem with some action of which we hope the neighbors will say, "It's what any sensible person would have done in his case." Faulkner was not concerned with what his sensible neighbors might have done. He approached each problem as if nobody else had ever been faced with it and as if it required some radically new solution. In that respect he preserved a sort of innocence, a quality of mind or character that makes one think of the youngest son in fairy tales. Always the older brothers believe that the youngest is hopelessly stupid and ignorant of the world, but always he performs the right actions out of sheer simplicity.

So it is in the tale of "The Youth Who Went Forth to Learn What Fear Was." His quest leads him into a haunted castle where anyone who spends three nights will be rewarded with an immense treasure. Nobody else has come out alive after the first night, but the youth survives till morning by finding the proper answers. Then on the second night (I quote from the Brothers Grimm),

he again went up into the old castle, sat down by the fire, and once more began his old song: "If I could but shudder!" When midnight came, an uproar and noise of tumbling about was heard; at first it was low, but it grew louder and louder. Then it was quite for a while, and at length with a loud scream, half a man came down the chimney and fell before him.

"Hullo!" cried the youth [as Faulkner might have cried]. "Another half belongs to this. This is not enough."

Then the uproar began again, there was a roaring and howling, and the other half fell down likewise. "Wait," said he, "I will just stoke up the fire a little for you." When he had done that and looked round again, the two pieces were joined together and a hideous man was sitting in his place.

"That is no part of our bargain," said the youth. "The bench is mine." The man wanted to push him away. The youth, however, would not allow that, but thrust him off with all his strength, and seated himself again in his own place.

Problem: What do you do when two halves of a body fall down a chimney, when they join together into a hideous man, and when he takes your place by the fire? Why, nothing could be simpler: you push him off the bench. *Problem that follows:* What do you do when other men fall down the chimney, bringing with them two skulls and nine thighbones of dead men, then stand up the bones and start playing ninepins with the skulls? Why, nothing could be simpler, considering that you had the foresight to provide yourself with a turning lathe. You grind the skulls till they are round and then join happily in the game. *Problem* (this time in Faulkner's terms): What do you do when you find yourself at a grisly Hollywood party, with guests more fearsome to you than specters in a haunted castle, but when you don't want to embarrass the host by making public excuses for leaving? Why, nothing could be simpler. You go upstairs, open a window, and escape by climbing down a trellis (while probably thinking of Miss Quentin Compson and her escape down a rainspout—or was it a pear tree?).

And still another problem solved in Faulkner's terms: A motion-picture studio has put him on its payroll, but without telling him what to do. He simply waits in Oxford for instructions. Then a telegram arrives: WILLIAM FAULKNER, OXFORD, MISS. WHERE ARE YOU? MGM STUDIO. As he later told Jean Stein when being interviewed:

> I wrote out a telegram: MGM STUDIO, CULVER CITY, CALIF. WILLIAM FAULKNER.
> The young lady operator said, "Where is the message, Mr. Faulkner?" I said, "That's it." She said, "The rule book says that I can't sent it without a message, you have to say something." So we went through her samples and selected I forget which one—one of the canned anniversary messages. I sent that.

Those pleasant anecdotes reveal a pattern that Faulkner also followed, or tells us he followed, in writing his novels: always there was the problem reduced to a simple question, and always there was the simple but unprecedented answer.

In *Sanctuary,* as we have seen, the problem was chiefly that of making money, and the answer was to invent "the most horrific tale I could imagine." In *As I Lay Dying*, the problem was what an imagined group of people would do when subjected to "the simple universal natural catastrophes, which are flood and fire, with a simple natural motive to give direction to their progress." The answer in the writing of the novel "was not easy. No honest work is. It was simple in that all the material was already at hand. It took me just about six weeks in the spare time from a twelve-hour-a-day job at manual labor." The problem was never the same. In *The Sound and the Fury*—as Faulkner tells us in a passage already quoted—it was presented by an obsessive mental picture: "the muddy seat of a little girl's drawers in a pear tree, where she could see through a window where her grandmother's funeral was taking place and report what was happening to her brothers on the ground below." But who were the children, what were they doing, and why were her pants muddy? By the time those questions were answered in his mind, Faulkner "realized it would be impossible to get all of it into a short story and that it would have to be a book." *The Wild Palms*, though it ended as a novel with two plots told in alternating chapters, started, so he explains, as the simple story of two people "who sacrificed everything for love, and then lost that." The question was how to keep the story at a high pitch of intensity.

> When I reached the end of what is now the first section of *The Wild Palms* [he told Jean Stein], I realized suddenly that something was missing, it needed emphasis, something to lift it like counterpoint in music. So I wrote on the "Old Man" story until "The Wild Palms" story rose back to pitch. Then I stopped the "Old Man" story at what is now its first section, and took up "The Wild Palms" story until it began again to sag. Then I raised it to pitch again with another section of its antithesis, which is the story of a man who got his love and spent the rest of the book fleeing from it, even to the extent of voluntarily going back to jail where he would be safe.

As he explains the writing of each novel, he makes it sound as innocent as the behavior of the youth in the haunted castle. Faulkner too was exorcising demons and specters, but that seemed to be a trifling matter for a man who couldn't shudder. All he had to do, apparently, was to resolve each threatening

American Writing 1840-1980

situation into a question that could be answered in its own terms. We say once more, "Why, nothing could be simpler," and then with a start we realize that the questions were new and that the answers in each case were those of genius.

There were continuing problems in life to which he applied the same pattern of response. Of course the great problem of his early years was one that perplexes almost every young writer: how to live while getting his work done. Without reading Thoreau, it would seem, he instinctively chose Thoreau's answer: "Simplify, simplify!" He reduced his needs to the requisites of the writer's trade, which are, as he listed them to Jean Stein, "whatever peace, whatever solitude, and whatever pleasure he can get at not too high a cost," and beyond these, "Paper, tobacco, food, and a little whisky." The requisites could be supplied by any sort of odd job that was locally available, including house painting, rum running (from New Orleans), and shoveling coal in the University of Mississippi power station—always provided that the job didn't engross his attention and that he didn't hold it beyond the point of utter boredom.

That sort of barefoot heedlessness couldn't last after his marriage in 1929; his income as a family man had to be less intermittent. For a few years after *Sanctuary* (1931), his books and magazine stories produced enough to support the household. Then, in the later years of the depression, he found another expedient, which was to work in Hollywood for six months of the year and, by frugal living, to save enough from his never brilliant salary to carry him through the next six months in Oxford. Though not a happy answer, it was the best to be found.

But other problems remained, among them the one which I said was really crucial and which persisted from the years of obscurity into those of fame, that is, the problem of keeping his genius alive in a generally hostile environment. Faulkner's genius was essentially his sustained power of imagination. It could not be locked in a vault like precious stones; it needed space and air and especially solitude in which to breathe and grow. In my introduction to the Portable I had suggested that intellectual solitude was responsible for the faults in his writing (and Faulkner had agreed with me), but I should have seen even then that it was also a precondition of his writing. Only in solitude could he enter the inner kingdom—"William Faulkner, sole owner and proprietor"—that his genius was able to people and cultivate. Only by standing guard at the borders of the kingdom could he bar out invaders who might lay it waste. And that was only part of his guardianship, for he also had to be vigilant against tempters and corrupters who might destroy it from within.

His struggle against those two dangers was more precarious and his measure of victory over them was more admirable than is generally recognized. What we forget is that Faulkner was the first distinguished American man of letters who spent most of his life in a country town remote from any metropolitan center. Concord, of course, was also a country town, and the fact might help to explain some curious points of resemblance between Faulkner and the Concord sages, especially Hawthorne. There was also Emerson, who said in one of his journals—as Faulkner might have echoed—"Alone is wisdom. Alone is happiness. Society nowadays makes us low spirited, hopeless. Alone is heaven." But when Emerson got tired of being alone in heaven, he had literary neighbors for distraction, and Concord in his time was only an hour on the cars from Boston. For Thoreau it was a half-day's walk from the Harvard Library. So, Concord is no exception to my generality, and neither is the fact that a few gifted women had survived as writers in towns no larger than Oxford; one thinks first of Emily Dickinson, then of Mary Noailles Murfree and Elizabeth Madox Roberts. A gentlewoman's problem was slightly different in a country town, that is, if she didn't marry; she was permitted by public opinion, she might even be encouraged, to spend her leisure writing books instead of painting china. A man, however, was expected to follow some practical pursuit like farming or merchandising or legal counseling, at the cost, if he failed to do so, of being ridiculed as "Count No'count" by his former classmates. Perhaps that weight of public ridicule and incomprehension has been the greatest enemy of the arts in rural America. Faulkner was by no means the first man to resist it, but he was the first not to be warped by his resistance; the first simply to stand his ground and pursue a fruitful literary career.

To do so required pride, will power, and tough-hided indifference, in a measure of all three that is not generally associated with an imaginative writer. Moreover, he also had to display those qualities on another battlefield. When he emerged from his country town, as he did for as much as six months of the year, it was to work in Hollywood, which used to have a notorious fashion of embracing and destroying men of letters. After publishing an admired book, or two or three, the writer was offered a contract by movie studio; then he bought a house with a swimming pool and vanished from print. If he reappeared years later, it was usually with a novel designed to have the deceptive appeal of an uplift brassière. The process aroused Faulkner's scorn. "Nothing can injure a man's writing," he told Jean Stein, "if he's a first-rate writer. . . . The problem does not apply if he is not first rate, because he has already sold his soul for a swimming pool." Faulkner protected his soul, or rather his genius, by doing honest work for less than the usual Hollywood salary, by living in a cubbyhole where he had few visitors, and by staying away from parties. His only extravagance, except for buying conservative clothes, was a riding mare. Once the novelist Stephen Longstreet, then working in the same studio, found him sitting in a car at the curb, with the mare, swollen-bellied, behind him in a trailer.

"Hi, Bill, where you going?" Longstreet asked him.

Faulkner answered, "Home to Oxford. I don't want any mare of mine to throw a foal in California."

Faulkner himself was used to foaling his books in Oxford, but meanwhile the struggle against the Hollywood atmosphere must have been harder than he later made it appear. There is a note of triumph against odds in the letter that he sent me with the Compson genealogy: ". . . it took me about a week to get Hollywood out of my lungs, but I am still writing all right, I believe. . . . Maybe I am just happy that the damned west coast place has not cheapened my soul as much as I probably believed it was going to do."

But the problem of keeping alive his genius was still with him when he got back to Oxford; in fact it was becoming more difficult than ever. As his reputation spread, even the townspeople learned that he was a famous man, and some of them must have tried to invade his private life in the hope of being strengthened by his mana. There were also marauders from the outer world: "Last month two damned swedes, two days ago a confounded Chicago reporter, and now this one that cant even speak english. . . . I swear to christ being in hollywood was better than this where nobody knew me or cared a damn." He was faced with the beginning of the process by which an author is snatched from his private world and transformed into a public institution, a combined lecture hall, post office, and comfort station, all humming with strange voices and all surmounted with the effigy of the author as he had been.

Even at this early stage it must have been hard for him to maintain that "inner hush," as Fitzgerald calls it, in which the voices of his genius could be heard; there were always interruptions. One thinks of Coleridge and the dream he had that was "Kubla Khan." "On awaking," Coleridge said, speaking of the experience in the third person, "he appeared to himself to have a distinct recollection of the whole, and taking his pen, ink, and paper, instantly and eagerly wrote down the lines that are here preserved. At this moment he was unfortunately called out by a person on business from Porlock, and detained by him above an hour . . ." and that was the end of the vision. When Coleridge went back to his writing table, the rest of the poem "had passed away like the images on the surface of a stream into which a stone has been cast." Faulkner did not dream his stories (nor did Coleridge dream his poems, except for "Kubla Khan"). We shall never know how the stories first occurred to Faulkner, though it may be that the germ of more than one was the sort of "mental picture" that he mentioned as the beginning of *The Sound and the Fury*. It seems more certain, however, that they were consciously elaborated and revised in his mind, so that sometimes the process of setting them down was as simple as copying out a manuscript. At such times he could be interrupted by persons on business without damage to the text. The periods of solitude he required were the moments or hours when his imagination was at work and when intruders from Porlock might be fatal.

He stood at his threshold, as it were, to bar them out. He took measures against them, of which the simplest was not reading their letters, while in cases of threatened incursion he might flee to a cabin in the woods. Other measures failing, he was known to retreat behind an impenetrable wall of drunkenness; that too was in part a measure of self-protection. The intruders he feared were not the plain people of the town and countryside: hunters, carpenters, small farmers, black or white tenants, bootleggers, and deputy sheriffs; these offered no menace to his kingdom, and indeed they served to enrich its resources by the stories they told around campfires or sitting on the gallery of a crossroads store. There were many other people he was glad to see, for it is to be noted that one of his aims—besides that of protecting his imagined world—was living in the real world as a private person closely attached to family and friends. He was on cordial terms with his publishers and liked to work at Random House or at the Princeton residence of Saxe Commins. But that sort of private and professional life, with a degree of freedom and with days to be spent alone, could be preserved only by building walls against the world.

The strangers he feared were the infiltrators who tried to climb over or skirt around the walls—the correspondents, interviewers, would-be disciples, aspiring novelists, professors, literary ladies, and society people (unless they knew a lot about horses, in which case he enjoyed their company)—generally speaking, all those who were trying to use him or to make him over in their images. Sometimes he was rude to the wrong persons; I think of Ilya Ehrenburg, whom he would have found stimulating if they could have established communication, and there were many others. But the gifted people he snubbed might remember that, for all their gifts and good intentions, the part they might have played in Faulkner's days was that of persons from Porlock.

And Faulkner himself: did he find the right answers to his problems in life and in the continued production of his works? There are no completely right answers. It had better be said that his later books, in general, had not the freshness and power of the early ones. That is the common fate of imaginative writers (except for a few poets); some original force goes out of them. The books they write after the age of fifty most often lose in genius what they may possibly gain in talent. Faulkner lost substantially less than others did. Though none of his later books was on a level with *The Sound and the Fury* or *Go Down, Moses*, none of them made concessions to other people's tastes. One hears a person speaking in each of them, not an institution, and a person with reserves of power who may surprise us on any page. Some of Faulkner's best writing is in passages of *Requiem for a Nun* and *Intruder in the Dust* and especially—almost at the end—in the Mink Snopes chapters of *The Mansion*. In retrospect I should judge that he solved the problem of keeping alive his genius better than any other American novelist of our century.

Faulkner died almost exactly a year after Hemingway, eight months after James Thurber, and a few weeks before E. E. Cummings. Those were all great losses and, with earlier ones, they completely changed the literary landscape.

I think of their generation, which is also mine, as it started out many years ago. It was a generation like any other, I suppose, but it included what seems to be an extraordinary assortment of literary personalities. Of course the truth may be that the personalities, which might exist in any generation—which probably do exist there, by the law of averages—were given an extraordinary freedom to develop by the circumstances of the time. We started to publish in the postwar years, when our youth in itself was a moral asset. People seemed to feel that an older generation had let the world go to ruin, and they hoped that a new one might redeem it. The public was as grandly hospitable to young writers as it was to young movie actors and young financiers. Scott Fitzgerald was a best-selling novelist at twenty-four, and Glenway Wescott at twenty-seven. Hemingway, Dos Passos, Wilder, and Wolfe were all international figures at thirty. Even Faulkner, though slower to be recognized than the others, was a famous author in France while he was being neglected at home.

The generation had, like any other, a particular sense of life, which it was determined to express in books. Perhaps it felt more confidence than other generations have felt in its ability to make the books completely new. Everything in American literature seemed to be starting afresh. Every possibility seemed to be opening for the first time (since in those days we were splendidly ignorant of the American literary past), and almost any achievement seemed feasible. "I want to be one of the greatest writers who have ever lived, don't you?" Fitzgerald said to Edmund Wilson not long after they got out of Princeton. Wilson thought the remark was rather foolish, but he shared some of the feeling that lay behind it, as obviously Hemingway and Faulkner did. They all had a sense of being measured against the European past—against the future too—and of being called upon to do not only their best but something mysteriously better that could be done "without tricks and without cheating," as Hemingway said, if a writer was serious enough and had luck on his side.

Fortunate in the beginning, the generation was fortunate again after World War II. Most of the new writers who appeared in the 1950s were less adventurous than their predecessors had been in the realm of imaginative art, perhaps because their critical sense was more exacting and inhibiting. They were given to writing critical studies, and the subject of these, in many cases, was the books that Faulkner and other famous men of his time had written twenty or thirty years before. Thus, in middle age the generation had the privilege of basking in a warm critical afterglow. Even its less prominent members acquired a sense of reassurance from the presence of their great contemporaries. Their world was like a forest in which the smaller trees were overshadowed and yet in some measure protected by the giants.

Then came the autumn gales, and most of the tallest trees were among the first to be uprooted.

Now, from where the forest stood, we seem to look out at a different landscape. There are no broad fields like those where we ran barefoot, no briary fencerows for quail to shelter in, and no green line on the horizon like that which used to mark the edge of the big woods. Everywhere in the flatland, the best farming country, are chickencoop houses in rows, in squares and circles, each house with its carport, its TV antenna, and its lady's green cambric handkerchief of lawn. An immense concrete freeway gouges through the hills and soars on high embankments over the streams, now poisoned, where we fished for trout. It is lined equidistantly with toy-sized cars, all drawn by hidden wires to the shopping center, where they stand in equidistant rows. From a hillside we watch their passengers go streaming into the supermarket, not one by one, but cluster by tight cluster, and we wonder whether they are speaking in a strange language. There must be giants among them, but distance makes them all look smaller than the men and women we knew.

Among the great dead, I find myself thinking of Faulkner with more affection than of others I also admired and knew more intimately. Perhaps it is owing to his peculiar mixture of genius and talent, of dignity and impishness, with a fairy-book innocence of mind. Though almost lacking in vanity— except in such minor concerns as riding jackets—he was the proudest man I knew. The pride made him act by his own standards, which were always difficult ones. In his Nobel Prize address, when he spoke of work accomplished "in the agony and sweat of the human spirit," he had reason to think of his own work. When he invoked "the courage and honor and hope and pride and compassion and pity and sacrifice" that have been the glory of man's past, his big words precisely named the qualities that he demanded of himself and that he achieved more often than the rest of us did, if always in his own fashion.

[1966]

WILLA CATHER: AN ASSESSMENT

The Landscape and the Looking Glass is the longest book that is likely to be written about Willa Cather for many years, though not the most comprehensive. John H. Randall 3d, who teaches at Wellesley, is primarily concerned with only one aspect of his chosen author. He doesn't say much about her life story, since other writers have told as much as she wished to be known. More regrettably he fails to deal with Miss Cather's literary methods, except in a sidelong fashion. His real subject is her ideas—social, political, historical—and especially her moral philosophy, which he calls her "search for value."

In exploring this relatively narrow field, he shows a massive patience and a commendable zeal. He discusses each of her novels at length, retelling the plot and quoting what he regards as the significant passages. He passes all the characters in review. He examines the choice of incidents, the use of images, and tries to show what both imply in terms of ideology. Sometimes he ventures on shaky ground—for example, in his notion that *Sapphira and the Slave Girl* can be explained as a pious return to Protestantism—but most of his statements about Miss Cather's beliefs are documented and unassailable. To mention a few:

She was an unreconstructed individualist, a sister-in-art to the robber barons. Although she had a strong sense of duty, she felt no obligation to society as a whole. The only groups with which she sympathized were family units, and later the church as an extended family. She believed in the all-importance of the personal will: "The history of every country," she said in *O Pioneers!*, "begins in the heart of a man or a woman," and usually in a very young heart. Like an imperious child, she wanted this country to follow her desires. When the country went off in another direction, after World War I, she simply retired from the struggle, for she hated conflicts of any sort. In her later years she was always seeking a refuge—first in art, then in memories of her childhood, and finally in the distant past.

This is the picture of her mind that Mr. Randall presents at length, and he wants us to think it is damning. Indeed, he keeps scolding Miss Cather as if she were a Wellesley sophomore who had submitted a group of unwanted and unsatisfactory themes. He seems to feel they have wasted his time, and so he keeps making resentful comments in the margins. With some hesitation, he gives a B + to *O Pioneers!*, which is the first of her mature novels. He says it is the only one in which she sometimes approached what he regards as a properly tragic vision of the world. All the later novels, he thinks, "embody an outlook on life so distorted and falsified as to be practically worthless as an interpretation of human experience."

Thus, in *My Antonia*, Miss Cather is being "dishonest and evasive," while "willfully failing to see life steadily and as a whole." In *The Professor's House* she gives signs of "intellectual and artistic bankruptcy." Mr. Randall is determined to be candid, even at the cost of seeming to be a prig. In *Death Comes for the Archbishop*, he says: "The portrayal of her ecclesiastical heroes fails to take into account the fact that religious calling demands the continuous subordination of the lower self to the higher self. . . . Although religious in spots, the book is only intermittently Catholic at best." The fact is that Miss Cather never achieved "esthetic and emotional maturity." It was perfectly predictable that Willa Cather would hate the New Deal."

Mr. Randall is too young to have been a New Dealer, but he shows himself to be more civic-minded than Harry Hopkins in his prime. Wholly occupied with exposing malefactions against society, he seldom lets the defendant speak for herself, as she does admirably in her two critical volumes, *Not Under Forty* and the posthumous *Willa Cather on Writing*, and the rest of us might listen to what she said.

Miss Cather believed that the true author doesn't choose a subject, but merely accepts it, in accordance with his particular nature. A subject, she liked to say, quoting her older friend Sarah Orne Jewett, is "the thing that teases the mind over and over for years, and at last gets itself rightly put down on paper." If a writer is to achieve "anything noble, anything enduring, it must be by giving himself absolutely to his material."

That is a point she made time and again: the form of a novel grows out of the subject instead of being imposed on the subject. "It is a common fallacy," she said, "that a writer, if he is talented enough" can improve upon his subject-matter, by "using his 'imagination' upon it and twisting it to suit his purpose. The truth is that by such a process (which is not imaginative at all!) he can at best produce only a brilliant sham, which, like a badly built and pretentious house, looks poor and shabby in a few years."

The artist's real problem is not how to change his material but how to simplify it, "finding what conventions of form and what detail one can do without and yet preserve the spirit of the whole—so that all that one has suppressed and cut away is there to the reader's consciousness as much as if it were in type on the page."

Those were some of Miss Cather's literary principles, and she thought they were more important than the social and ethical and political ideas to which Mr. Randall devotes a long and overdocumented book. Her social ideas changed with the years, becoming always more conservative (and narrower and more regrettable). In literature, however, she was faithful to herself, to her ideal of good writing and to each of the subjects that teased her mind.

> The artist [she said] spends a lifetime in loving the things that haunt him, . . . in trying to get these conceptions down on paper exactly as they are to him and not in conventional poses supposed to reveal their character; trying this method and that, as a painter tries different lightings and different attitudes with his subject to catch the one that presents it more suggestively than any other. And at the end of a lifetime he emerges with much that is more or less happy experimenting, and comparatively little that is the very flower of himself and of his genius.

Miss Cather emerged with a number of books—nineteen, counting the two posthumous volumes—each of which is different from all the others and most of which, though written with her absolute integrity, might be classified as more or less happy experiments. But at least three books—*My Antonia*, *A Lost Lady*, and *Death Comes for the Archbishop*—are the very flower of her genius. There aren't many authors of whom we can say that three of their works are contributions to the small permanent body of American literature.

At this point I venture a remark about her writing that, with variations, might be applied to a few other talented authors. Those three masterpieces—and her remaining work as well, if in a lesser measure—did perform services to American society even if Miss Cather was seldom conscious of having social intentions. For one example, she humanized the land itself, the wide, gently rolling, but savage land of her girlhood, endowing it with folk memories and warm associations. She celebrated the pioneers, not so much the Anglos among them as the Central Europeans and especially the Czechs, giving them a place they deserved in her American gallery of heroes and wonders. Not a Catholic herself, she rendered the poetry of the Church, giving that too a place in her gallery. She made her readers feel that culture is all of a piece, depending almost as much on gardens and kitchens as on classrooms and concert halls. All these are social lessons, not painted on the text but woven into the fabric. Let us not forget that Miss Cather's integrity as an artist was also, in its way, a social lesson.

What if Mr. Randall—he wasn't born then, but what if some other civic-minded critic had managed to gain Miss Cather's ear in 1922 or thereabouts when she thought that the world broke in two? What if he had persuaded her, deaf as she usually was to arguments, that she was wrong about the world and wrong to trust her instincts?—that she should write stories full of dramatic conflicts, revealing the misery of the human condition as well as its splendor; that social relations were more important than individual relations; that she herself should become "adjusted" and "emotionally mature" by accepting the world as it is instead of dreaming about the past—what then?

She would have written different books, and Mr. Randall might have praised them for their ideology, but I doubt that he would have written about them at such great length. Although there is nothing in his own system of criticism by which to test the judgment, I think he would have felt obscurely that those other books were no longer true to her nature or her subjects and that they were all a brilliant sham, "which, like a badly built and pretentious house, looks poor and shabby in a few years."

Mr. Randall, who doesn't like Willa Cather, has chosen the

wrong subject, like many critics before him. He is like an overambitious marksman on the target range. He judges the distance; he tests the wind; he adjusts his sights; he tightens the strap; he aims with infinite patience; then, gently squeezing the trigger, he sends bullet after bullet into the bullseye— only to find, when he looks up for approbation, that he has been aiming all the time at the wrong target.

[1960]

CYCLES OF MYTH
IN AMERICAN WRITING

Even the Mississippi wasn't always a legendary river, famous in song and story. Early travelers described it as "a furious, rapid, desolating torrent," and some of them believed that the country through which it flowed would never be fit for human habitation. Captain Frederick Marryat, late of the Royal Navy and a justly famous novelist in his time, took passage up the river in 1837. "There are," he reported, "no pleasing associations connected with the great common sewer of the Western America, polluting the clear blue sea for many miles beyond its mouth. It is a river of desolation."

Today the Mississippi has been surrounded with all the "pleasing associations" that Marryat missed because he came too early. Mark Twain was to be the man who transformed the river into a legend. Of course he had thousands of collaborators, including his boyhood friends in Hannibal, Missouri, and the tall talkers he met when he was an apprentice pilot—not to mention all the novelists, poets, historians, playwrights, and jazz singers who have written or bellowed out their praises of Old Man River—but Mark Twain was the first to give shape and color to the story. In *Life on the Mississippi* and even more in *Huckleberry Finn,* he created a myth, one that will live as long as cotton grows behind the levees or schoolboys dream of drifting southward on a raft.

Older than Mark Twain's version of the Mississippi story were myths of rural New England, of the Southern plantations, of the Eastern forest, and of the always receding frontier. Very few nations so young as nineteenth-century America have developed such an extensive mythology or one so expressive of an age and people. But it changed with the times, as the nation was also changing, and now the question is what new myths will be created to mirror the new suburban or industrial landscapes, the new adventures and defeats beyond the oceans, the representative characters, the deep fears and uneasy aspirations of our day—and not only mirror all these but also make it possible for us to believe in ourselves as characters in the drama of American history.

Myths, for the present purpose, might be defined simply as familiar narratives that embody representative types of character and experience. Walt Whitman called them "national, original archetypes in literature" and said that they alone "put the nation in form, finally tell anything—prove, complete anything—perpetuate anything." Myths in this sense of the word can be recognized by their ability to live in the popular imagination quite independently of the incidents or books or ballads that gave birth to them. Myths are the wise Ulysses, the dutiful Aeneas, the fight at Roncesvalles, and—leaping over the centuries—they are Daniel Boone in the wilderness, the Texans at the Alamo, and Huck Finn drifting down the Mississippi.

Myths can be and often are false to history: for example, Skipper Floyd—or was it really Flood?—Ireson was a different figure in life from the protagonist of Whittier's poem. The real Flood Ireson never refused to rescue the crew of another fishing smack, and although he was tarred and feathered and carried in a cart, it wasn't by the women of Marblehead. Richard III of England lost the battle of Bosworth and his crown, but it wasn't "all for the lack of a horseshoe nail," as the old adage wanted us to believe. On the other hand, three hundred Spartans really defended the Pass of Thermopylae against the Persian hordes, and died to the last man, and their true exploit has also become a myth. Truth or falsity as judged by surviving records is not the test of a myth. The test is its ability to shape the popular mind, and hence we might say that the truth of a myth lies in the future.

One example should be familiar to every student of American history. During the 1830's the slave states of the American Union were quarreling with the free states and were becoming conscious of their separate identity. They tried—or, to be accurate, several of their novelists, poets, and journalists tried—to express that identity in the shape of a myth. They had been hearing from New England about the myth of the Puritans, and now they invented the counter myth of the Virginia Cavalier, the proud gentleman devoted to ideals of loyalty, honor, and personal courage. In order to find a historical basis for the myth, they claimed that Virginia had been settled by followers of King Charles I—the Cavaliers—whereas New England had been settled by his middle class enemies, the Roundheads.

It is still an unsettled question how many of the English cavaliers emigrated to Virginia after the defeat of the king to whom they were loyal. There may have been only scores of them; there may have been hundreds or a very few thousands. On the whole, the myth of the Southern cavalier rests on shaky historical foundations. We might say, however, that when the myth began to be popular, during the 1830's, the proof of it did not lie in the past, in the records of colonial Virginia, but rather in the future. The proof was in the contribution made by the myth to the feeling of separate Southern nationality that led to the Civil War. The proof was also in the loyalty, honor, and personal courage of Virginia cavaliers like Robert E. Lee, Stonewall Jackson, and J. E. B. Stuart.

Myths, as we see, may be good or bad in their effects, or a mixture of good and bad. Sometimes they lead to complacency, national arrogance, or tribal hatreds. Very often they are used by political leaders to delude the public, and yet they form an essential and generally helpful part of every culture, ancient and modern. A country without them would seem inhumanly bare and baleful, like Captain Marryat's vision of the Mississippi. A nation without myths would scarcely be a nation, but only a mass of separate persons living in the same territory and obeying the same laws because they were afraid of the police. The separate persons would have no common ideals of character and conduct unless these were enforced by some sort of mythology. Walt Whitman was thinking about this problem when he said, in *Democratic Vistas,* "The literature, songs, esthetics, &c., of a country are of importance principally because they furnish the materials and suggestions of personality for the women and men of that country, and enforce them in a thousand effective ways." Therefore he called for a race of myth-making poets, able to shape the nation "with unconditional uncompromising sway. Come forth," he cried, "sweet democratic despots of the west!" The democratic despots were slow to appear on this continent. America in the beginning had only the myths that the colonists carried with them from Europe. To the first settlers everything beyond their narrow clearings was not only strange but hostile and satanic. The New Englanders in particular regarded themselves as "a people of God settled in those which were once the Devil's territories; and it may easily be supposed," said the pious Cotton Mather, "that the Devil was exceeding disturbed when he perceived such a people here accomplishing the promise of old made unto our Blessed Jesus, that he should have the utmost parts of the earth for his possession." Cotton Mather and his friends believed that the forest, which they hated and feared—and destroyed as fast as the trees could be girdled, chopped down, and burned—was Satan's shadowy dominion. They believed that the Indian powwows or medicine men who lived in the forest were in league with Satan's other retainers, the witches and warlocks of northern Europe. Legends of witchcraft survived for a long time in New England, so that Nathaniel Hawthorne, who was born in 1804, remembered hearing them often by the kitchen fire. South of the Potomac feudal legends were more popular, especially those connected with courtly love, manor houses, and feuds between noble families. Yet both types of imported legends, Northern and Southern, slowly lost their hold on a new country which, as a whole, was neither feudal nor devil-fearing.

The colonists needed myths of their own, and, in the course of time, they created a fairly extensive native folklore. In a feeble but stubborn fashion, part of the lore has survived till our time, though chiefly in scattered regions like the Pennsylvania Dutch country, the Tennessee mountains, and the Ozarks, where it is still being tracked down and recorded by scholars. It must be added that the growth of folklore in the strict sense of an oral rather than a written tradition has been impeded in this country by the fact that Americans in the mass have been a literate people, with the habit of reading their stories instead of telling them by the fireside. Most of our mythology soon found its way into print; one might even say that most of it started there. More than in any other country it has been created by professional writers.

Those writers knew what they were doing, as anyone can learn for himself by studying their journals and correspondence. When they wrote to their friends about literary problems, they often used words like "legend," "mystery," "tradition," "picturesque," and "romance." All the words refer to the same quality, one that they felt was lacking in American life; Washington Irving defined it as "the color of romance and tradition." Hawthorne said that it was inconceivably difficult to write romances about a country "where there is no shadow, no antiquity, no mystery, no picturesque and gloomy wrong, nor anything but a commonplace prosperity, in broad and simple daylight, as is happily the case with my dear native land." Until the missing elements were supplied—if necessary by the private efforts of American writers—they doubted whether they could produce poems and stories equal to the best work of their English contemporaries.

That is one side of their effort to create myths—the selfish side, one might call it—but they also had other motives. Most of them were lonely men who felt themselves to be isolated from their practical-minded fellow citizens, and they were trying to arouse in Americans a sense of community and of common destinies on a deeper level than that of practical affairs. These writers loved their country—most of all when they were living in Europe—and they were trying to communicate a sense of its past trials and future greatness. With different motives working together, it is no wonder that our first successful authors, those who became widely known about 1820, were all professional mythopoeists.

Irving, for example, set out to people the Hudson Valley with ancestral ghosts and rather jovial demons. He invented some legends of the supernatural, heard others in Dutch villages along the river, and borrowed still others from European literature, as, for example, the plot of "Rip Van Winkle," which he found in a German book and moved to the Catskills. William Cullen Bryant devoted himself to the problem of putting American birds and flowers into poetry, where they had never been mentioned. He was the first poet to sing in honor of the bobolink and the fringed gentian. James Fenimore Cooper had a wooden style and no architectural talent, but his imagination was fired by the sea and the American wilderness. His great creation was the myth of the receding frontier. Some of his characters, including Long Tom Coffin in *The Pilot* and Natty Bumppo in the five Leatherstocking novels, were the first folk heroes in American fiction.

There would be many others before the nineteenth century had ended. One author after another contributed scenes and archetypical characters to American mythology. Hawthorne, for example, was a student of colonial times, bent on transforming the historical records into legends. Longfellow was fascinated by the same problem, and his work would bear a higher reputation today if we studied the substance of it as myth rather than sentiment or morality. Emerson turned away from the past to the present. His oration "The American Scholar" was a manifesto addressed to the new generation of writers. "I ask not for the great, the remote, the romantic; what is doing in Italy or Arabia; what is Greek art or Provençal minstrelsy," Emerson told them. "I embrace the common, I explore and sit at the feet of the familiar, the low. Give me insight into today, and you may have the antique and future worlds." One of his central problems was how to give a universal and eternal value to everyday experience. For him the meal in the firkin and the milk in the pan were the bread and wine of a new sacrament. Thoreau, who started as Emerson's disciple, wrote about his own township as if it were Athens in the time of Pericles. "I would fain set down something beside facts," he wrote in his journal. "Facts should be only as the frame to my picture; they should be material to the mythology which I am writing."

After the Civil War, Whitman complained that all the great literature of Europe was aristocratic or authoritarian. When he called for a new race of poets, in *Democratic Vistas,* he assumed that their principal function would be to furnish myths for a new continent and for democracy. The poets failed to come forth, but some of the myths were created in prose, as notably by Bret Harte in his stories about the California mining camps. Harte was followed by a school of local-color novelists, each romanticizing his own section of the country. Even William Dean Howells, the polite and rather timid realist, embodied in his work one famous American myth, that of the young girl or "tenderest society bud" who was distinguished, so it seems to us today, by her cast-iron innocence and inhuman refinement.

What we might call the first American mythology had taken a final shape by 1890. In retrospect it seems amazingly complete, including as it does a score of familiar backgrounds, each with its registered trademark. For New England the trademark was a low-roofed farmhouse with a well-sweep outside the kitchen door; for the tidewater South it was a high-porticoed mansion; for the Great Smokies it was a crazy-roofed cabin not far from a corn-liquor still. There were other trademarks as well, familiar to everyone who thumbed through the magazines or went to theatres: the Mississippi steamboat round the bend, the sod house on the prairie, the chuck wagon surrounded by cowboys squatting on their heels, the Indian village with dancing braves, and the gambling saloon near the California diggings. Against those familiar backgrounds moved a whole pantheon of mythological figures, at least twelve of which might be listed as the major gods of our first native Olympus. Here are the divine heroes and the one goddess who reigned over us like Zeus, Hermes, Artemis, and their kindred:

1. The sober-garbed and steeple-hatted Puritan, usually pictured on his way to the meeting house, with his Bible in one hand and his bell-mouthed musket in the other.

2. Contrasting with him, the plumed Virginia cavalier, spurring madly through the forest to defend his honor and rescue a damsel in distress.

3. The woods ranger in coonskin cap and fringed buckskin breeches, carrying a long rifle. Daniel Boone, Natty Bumppo, and Nick of the Woods are three of the many names to which he answered.

4. The backwoods boaster or Southwestern ring-tailed roarer, sometimes known as Davy Crockett. Half-horse, half-alligator, a little teched with the snapping turtle, he could grin the bark off'n a tree and hug a b'ar too close for comfort.

5. The Yankee to rhyme with lanky, a tall, loose-jointed figure with sallow cheeks, a sharp nose, and an eye to the main chance. First he was a schoolmaster called Ichabod Crane; then he changed his name to Sam Slick and peddled wooden nutmegs. It was his brother Jonathan, equally shrewd but kinder-hearted, who grew a long chin beard and was caricatured in the newspapers as Uncle Sam.

6. The Southern colonel with black slouch hat and shoestring tie, sitting behind tall white pillars in a rocking chair and calling, "Tom, you rascal, bring me another julep."

7. Uncle Tom, the faithful retainer, with his black head surrounded by a halo of white lamb's wool.

8. The slit-eyed, lean-jawed, soft-spoken gambler with two six-guns hidden beneath the frock coat made by the best Omaha tailor.

9. The bad man—Quantrill, Jesse James, Sam Bass—rid-

ing into town at the head of his outlaw band to rob a bank. He was whisky-eyed, unshaven, brutal, but he gave money to the poor and he never annoyed a woman.

10. The Indian chief in his bonnet of eagle feathers, his language consisting of "How" and "Ugh."

11. The Alger newsboy, doing and daring, rising by pluck and luck (and a willing smile) from rags to riches.

12. Finally the young girl who ruled over all the others by force of her unsullied innocence, so that the gambler blushed like a small boy when she spoke to him, the Southern colonel was ruled by her whims, the bad man fled, and the scarlet woman—on those few occasions when she appeared in American fiction—knelt to kiss the hem of her skirt.

Besides those major deities there were demigodlike figures not far behind them, including—to mention only a few—the Down East farmer who ordered his erring daughter into a snowstorm; the black-mustachioed villain with his city ways; the millionaire enslaved by his beautiful daughters; the bad boy that every American wished he could be once more; the widowed mother waiting for the mortgage to be foreclosed; the comic Irishman who outwitted the comic Dutchman and was in turn outwitted by the comic Jew; the abolitionist turned carpetbagger; the black mammy at her cabin door; the Eastern dude among cowboys; the half-witted old prospector; and—when some bolder author like Bret Harte dared to mention her—the dance-hall girl with a heart of twenty-four-karat gold.

In those days after the Civil War, it was the good women, wives and schoolmistresses, who bought the books and read the magazines; most men read only the newspapers. To be successful an author had to please a feminine audience. Women liked love stories and hence the magazines were full of them, while all the popular novels ended to the peal of a wedding march. On the other hand, romantic love was not a major theme either in American literature on its highest level or in familiar American folklore. After the first few chapters of our legendary novel, *Moby Dick,* it has no female characters except mother whales. There were not many women, either, in the great cycles of myth that dealt with the wilderness, the river, the cattle ranges, and the mining camps. All the cycles consisted of stories about men, working or wandering, hunting, fighting, enduring hardships, getting rich, or running away from civilization, but seldom or never passionately in love. Huck Finn was too young for love, but all the familiar heroes were boys at heart and old Leatherstocking died a bachelor.

Love was not the only topic that was seldom discussed in the American classical myths. As compared with the legendary epics of other nations, they treated a narrow range of subjects: for example, they were not much concerned with rivalries between countries or classes, with loyalty to rulers, or with the question of man's place in the universe, to mention themes that recur in epic poems from the *Iliad* to *Paradise Lost*. They did not express a strong sense of locality. Their heroes were lonely and often childless men who wandered farther than Ulysses, but always away from home.

Our myths were not tragic in the Greek sense of the word. The heroes were not punished for their pride, nor did they ever resign themselves to fate; when they found themselves in a tragic situation they pulled up stakes and moved farther west. Sometimes they couldn't move because they were surrounded by hostile Indians, but then they fought and triumphed over impossible odds by a mixture of courage, ingenuity, and blink luck. The U.S. Cavalry never failed to appear with gleaming sabers before the Redskins captured the wagon train. The heroes never lost hope, never smiled, and never stopped cracking jokes. Humor, dry or boisterous, was one quality of American myths and headlong action was another; but what they most admirably expressed was the buoyancy of a new nation, its faith in the individual, and its thirst for perpetual movement and improvement.

By 1890 the country had changed and the old American gods and heroes could no longer be followed as guides to daily living. There were no more Indians to fight on the frontier and in fact there was no frontier, in the sense of a continuous line beyond which there were no permanent settlements. The last big land rush had been the stampede across the Oklahoma border in 1889. The gold rush at Cripple Creek, Colorado, in 1890 was the last really big one south of Canada. The new pioneers would be the "back-trailers," as Hamlin Garland called them, from the Plains States to Chicago and Boston and New York. The new frontier was in the big cities.

Besides this movement from farms to factories and offices, there were other changes produced by expansion and immigration. The center of American life had shifted from the seaboard, with its colonial traditions, to the Mississippi Valley. English and Scottish were no longer regarded as the only true native strains. Eventually there would be a change in popular legends, to bring them closer to the new situation; but first came a long war in American literature, a battle of the books that began about 1885 and lasted for nearly half a century. Although it used to be described as a quarrel between the Idealists on one side and the Realists and Naturalists on the other, it was also a struggle between rival mythologies.

The Idealists, who included most of the established writers and the professors of literature, defended the older myths, those with a rural background and a message of optimism. The Naturalists were younger writers like Frank Norris, Theodore Dreiser, and their friends, who believed that the old mythology should be abandoned. Their favorite targets for ridicule were the Puritan, the Alger hero, and the young girl, but in general they regarded all the deities of the old pantheon as idols to be smashed. At the same time they were trying to create new myths that would embody scientific laws— for they were all disciples of Darwin and Herbert Spencer—besides expressing the aspirations of new racial groups and portraying the urban and industrial America of their own generation.

Strange things happened to the older American heroes during this civil war in the literary world and after the victory of the Naturalistic writers. Thus, the sharp-witted Yankee peddler disappeared from fiction after a final visit to King Arthur's court. The Puritan became a blue-nosed Prohibitionist and, in popular books, a generally mean fellow. Uncle Tom was rejected by his own people. Other traditional characters survived and prospered, but only by moving to the city. There the slit-eyed gambler ran a night club—hundreds of night clubs in one moving picture after another—and kept his six guns in the middle drawer of his executive-type desk. The bad man became a big-time mobster. Leatherstocking also moved to the city, where he wore a detective's badge and tracked down criminals as if they were hostile Indians. The young girl lost her innocence and, growing older, suffered a curious transformation. As the frigid, selfish wife and later as the possessive mother who kept her children tied to her silver-corded spoon, she became the familiar villainess of American fiction.

New characters, mostly city dwellers, came forward to join the earlier heroes of legend. Among those who now took hold of the popular imagination were the wise girl making her lonely way in the metropolis (like Dreiser's Sister Carrie and David Graham Phillips' Susan Lenox, who fell and rose again); the robber baron winning and losing fortunes without regard for the law (as in Dreiser's *The Financier*); the political boss who looked like Mark Hanna and met his cronies in a smoke-filled room; the blond beast, Jack London's favorite character, seeking gold in the Northland as recklessly as his Viking ancestors; the criminal not to blame for his bad ancestry (like Norris's McTeague); and the pawn of circumstances (like Dreiser's Clyde Griffiths) whose blind yearnings led him into an American tragedy.

After the First World War, still other characters found their places in mythology. The flapper rushed on the scene and then rushed off again with her friend the smoothie from Princeton; later she would reappear briefly in bobby socks. The intellectual small-town housewife, or Carol Kennicott, lived on Main Street and yearned for higher things. George F. Babbitt sold real estate, crowded his house with gadgets, and talked in gold-filled platitudes. The tough and cynical front-page reporter tried to conceal his soft-boiled heart. The girl in the green hat, copied from English life by Michael Arlen, went from one love affair to another with the same brave, broken-hearted smile. In Hemingway's first novel she kept her British passport, but she became an American in John O'Hara's *Butterfield 8*. Poor thing, she paid a heavy price for her trans-atlantic voyage. Soon she was dying a series of painful deaths in dozens of novels about New York, Beverly Hills, the San Francisco Bay Area, and Nashville, Tennessee. Some doctoral candidate for a degree in American literature should trace her whole unedifying story.

Still another figure in the new pantheon was the Hemingway young man, hard-drinking and impassive, who roamed through Europe with the wary look of an Ojibway in the Michigan woods. He had less time for reading than the Thomas Wolfe young man, who spent his nights in the stacks of the Widener Library, where he pounced on books and devoured them like a tiger in the jungle. The Fitzgerald young man was betrayed by a princess in a golden tower. Besides these individual figures, our second mythology also included many of the corporate or collective legends in which the hero is a group, a business enterprise, or a locality. Perhaps the first of these, since it flourished in the muckraking days from 1900 to 1910, was the legend of the trust or "octopus" that strangled little businesses in its widespreading tentacles. By 1920 we also had the legend of the small and mean Midwestern town, as presented by Edgar Lee Masters in *The Spoon River Anthology,* by Sherwood Anderson in *Winesburg, Ohio,* and by Sinclair Lewis in *Main Street.* Then in succession came T. S. Eliot's legend of the spiritual wasteland, Scott Fitzgerald's legend of the jazz age, the Hemingway legend of the lost generation, the Erskine Caldwell legend of Tobacco Road, the Steinbeck legend of dispossessed Oklahoma farmers jolting westward to California, and the Southern cavalier legend, which, though it went back for more than a century, was raised to a new dimension by William Faulkner. It was during this period, too, that Troy was burned again in the shape of Atlanta and that King Priam, reincarnated as a Southern planter, was murdered in the midst of his retainers. Hundreds of authors working in collaboration had given us another Iliad, of sorts.

Looking back on their work, we can see that the authors of the interwar years were skillful and bold in presenting characters that became archetypes of American life. Their books performed the function that Whitman assigned to the literature and songs of a country: they furnished, as he said, "the materials and suggestions of personality for the women and men of that country," and enforced them "in a thousand suggestive ways." By 1940 many young Americans were behaving like Hemingway or Thomas Wolfe characters, as later their tragic hero would be Scott Fitzgerald. Life once again had copied fiction—and this time had copied it all the more readily because movies and the radio, coming before universal television, were already making fiction omnipresent. When one of our novelists created a new figure, not only was it reproduced in bulk by less original writers, but it was dramatized for Broadway, adapted for Hollywood, and re-adapted for the national networks—so that sometimes the hero of a serious novel, having descended toward a wider audience step after giant step, was heard five times a week in a radio serial and was seen (or a figure dimly inspired by him was seen) daily and Sunday in a comic strip.

Continually enriched by novelists and poets, always more widely diffused by new methods of communication, American mythology had broadened through the years until it appeared to offer a complete image of American life. That appearance, of course, was an illusion even in 1940. Not all of American life, and especially not its average level, had been expressed in mythological terms—and this for the simple reason that novelists and poets have always been less attracted by the average than by the intense and extraordinary. A more serious weakness of the literary imagination, when measured against American realities, is that it tends to be retrospective. The world most effectively described by novelists and poets is that of their youth, not the world of their mature years. They change with the times, but never as fast as the times, and the result is that literary mythologies are always out of date. That was true even in 1940, and it is vastly more true of the 1960's, when we are waiting to descry the outlines of what should become a third American mythology.

For there have been three distinct periods in the life of this republic, or at least in our values for living. During the first, American values were predominantly rural and the standards of conduct were those of an ideal country town like Concord, Massachusetts. During the second, which lasted from 1890 till the end of World War II, the values became urban or metropolitan and the standards of conduct were those of New York and Chicago. There has been another shift in emphasis since 1945. The central cities are declining not only in population but in their power to set fashions, while factories are employing a smaller proportion of the labor force. In this new age the dominant values are suburban and the emerging standard of conduct is that of a sophisticated suburb like Westport, Connecticut, or Mill Valley, California.

In the first age the representative American was born on a farm and probably lived on another farm west of his birthplace. In the second age he worked in or managed or sold goods from a factory. In the third age he has become an organization man employed in an office or a laboratory or in one of the service industries—the Culligan man, the Fuller

Brush man—that is, unless he resigns from the organization and goes hitch-hiking over the country trying to recapture his own personality.

The American home in the first age was a log cabin or a farmhouse, in the second age it was a city apartment, and now—except for the poor and the rebels—it is a detached single dwelling in the suburbs, full of labor-saving machinery reduced to a family scale. Rivalry in producing things, as we often read, has given way to rivalry in consuming them. In the first age the conflict portrayed in American fiction was often that of the single man against nature; in the second age it was that of the single man against society, fighting to change it or simply to rise in it. Now, in the third age, the conflict is more likely to be that of group against group, of generation against generation, or of man against himself.

In order for us to feel at home in the new landscape where, old and young, we are all strangers; in order to form a new image of the nation, and chiefly in order for us to recognize ourselves as persons, we require, among other things, a new American mythology. "The experience of each age," as Emerson said, "requires a new confession and the world seems always waiting for its poet." This time the world has been waiting longer than it should, but there are signs in the fiction in the last few years that the new myths are beginning to appear. A few characters in postwar fiction have already become legends. That most of them are rebels is a fact in which I find no ground for complaint. The standards of an emerging society are revealed in its rebels as much as in its conformists, and the rebels are easier to remember. Who after all was the Man in the Gray Flannel Suit? The phrase survives, but the man himself has disappeared from our minds like gray flannel suits from Madison Avenue.

Some of the new figures we do remember are J. D. Salinger's troubled adolescent in a world where every adult is a phony, and Ralph Ellison's angry symbol of the American Negro as the *Invisible Man,* and Norman Mailer's hipster or "White Negro," and Saul Bellow's portrait, in *The Adventures of Augie March,* of a Jewish boy leaving the Chicago slums and wandering over three continents, not to win a fortune, but to find the answer to a simple question: Who am I? That question echoes through many other novels and helps to convey the puzzled spirit of the times, but it is still not enough.

There has to be something more than a few rebellious characters asking representative questions before the new mythology comes into being, as it is certain to do, and I keep reading the new novels to find what shapes it will assume.

[1962]

CONRAD AIKEN:
FROM SAVANNAH TO EMERSON

Rereading Conrad Aiken's work, one is impressed again by the unity that underlies its real mass and apparent diversity. He published some fifty books, all told, and they include novels, stories, criticism, a play, an autobiography, and thirty or more books of poems that were finally brought together in *Collected Poems: Second Edition*, a volume of more than a thousand closely printed pages. He was a poet essentially, but he was also the complete man of letters, distinguished for his work in many forms of verse and prose. The unity was there, however, and in every form he spoke with the same candid, scrupulous, self-deprecatory, yet reckless and fanciful New England voice. Yes, the voice was that of his ancestors, not of his birthplace. Aiken says of himself in his last poem, "Obituary in Bitcherel,"

> *Born in beautiful Savannah*
> *to which he daily sang hosanna*
> *yet not of southern blood was he*
> *he was in fact a damned Yankee.*

I remember first meeting him in 1918, when I was a junior at Harvard. Not long before I had read *The Jig of Forslin,* a long poem that impressed and a little frightened the apprentice poet by what it had done to achieve a symphonic form. I went to see its publisher, Edmund Brown, who ran a little bookstore near the Back Bay station, and he gave me the author's address. There was an exchange of letters and Aiken suggested that we meet in the lobby of the Hotel Touraine. I was to look for a man in an orange necktie who wasn't a fairy.

Aiken was then twenty-eight years old, was six years out of college, and was already the author of two red-haired children and four published volumes of post-Romantic poetry, besides two others waiting to appear. On that mild February evening I saw the necktie as he came in the door; it was brighter than his Valencia-orange hair. For the rest he wore the Harvard uniform of the period: white button-down oxford shirt and brown suit. His forehead was broad, his jaw was square, and his blue eyes were set wide apart. Short and solidly built, a block of a man, he had a look of mingled shyness and pugnacity.

I remember that our conversation was broken at first, but that later, over seidels of beer, we found many common interests in spite of my callowness and our nine years' difference in age. We both liked Boston in decay, we had notions about the French Symbolists, we spoke of achieving architectural and musical effects in verse (such as Aiken in fact had achieved), and we were fascinated by the political maneuvers of the poetry world without wishing to take part in them. Soon we were talking without pauses, talking with such excitement—at least on my part—that I didn't notice the streets through which we wandered before parting at the door of Aiken's lodging house, on the unfashionable side of Beacon Hill.

I was right to be excited, and elated too, since I found afterward that Aiken seldom opened himself to literary strangers. There were years when he stayed away from almost all writers and editors as a matter of principle, and I was lucky to be one of the few exceptions. He refused to attend literary dinners and could seldom be inveigled into cocktail parties. In some ways the shyest man I knew, he was also one of the best talkers. The shyness kept him from talking in company except for an occasional pun: thus, he would describe his friend Tom Eliot's notes to *The Waste Land* as a "verbiform appendix," or Frost's less successful poems as having "the artlessness that conceals artlessness"; but such phrases were spoken in a voice so low that most of the company missed them. Only quite late at night, or earlier over martinis with one or two friends, would he launch into one of those monologues that ought to be famous for their mixture of flagrant wit and complete unself-protective candor.

In the course of time I discovered that candor was close to being his central principle as a man and a writer, particularly as a poet. The principle evolved into a system of aesthetics and literary ethics that unified his work, a system based on the private and public value of self-revelation. No matter what sort of person the poet might be, healthy or neurotic, Aiken believed that his real business was "to give the lowdown on himself, and through himself on humanity." If he was sick in mind, candor might be his only means of curing himself. "Out of your sickness let your sickness speak," Aiken says in one of his Preludes—

> *the bile must have his way—the blood his froth—*
> *poison will come to the tongue. Is hell your kingdom?*
> *you know its privies and its purlieus? keep*
> *sad record of its filth? Why this is health.*

"Look within thyself to find the truth" might have been his Emersonian motto; and it had the corollary that inner truth corresponds to outer truth, as self or microcosm does to macrocosm. Aiken believed that the writer should be a surgeon performing an exploratory operation on himself, at whatever cost to his self-esteem, and penetrating as with a scalpel through layer after layer of the semiconscious. That process of achieving self-knowledge might well become a self-inflicted torture. At times the writer might feel—so Aiken reports from experience—"the shock of an enormous exposure: as if he had been placed on a cosmic table, *en plein soleil,* for a cosmic operation, a cosmic intrusion." Let him persist, however, and he will be rewarded by finding—here I quote from a letter— "what you think or feel that is secretly you—shamefully you— intoxicatingly you." Then, having laid bare this secret self, which is also a universal self, the writer must find words for it, accurate and honest words, but poured forth—Aiken says in a Prelude—without reckoning the consequences:

> *Let us be reckless of our words and worlds,*
> *And spend them freely as the tree his leaves.*

Here enters the public as opposed to the merely private value of complete self-revelation. By finding words for his inmost truth, the writer—especially the poet—has made it part of the world, part of human consciousness. He has become a soldier, so to speak, in the agelong war that mankind has been waging against the subliminal and the merely instinctive.

But service in that war involves much that lies beyond the simple process of discovering and revealing one's secret self. The writer must divide himself into two persons, one the observer, the other a subject to be observed, and the first must approach the second "with relentless and unsleeping objectivity." The observer-and-narrator must face what Aiken calls "That eternal problem of language, language extending consciousness and then consciousness extending language, in circular or spiral ascent"; and he must also face the many problems of architectural and sequential form. The words that depict the observed self must not only be honest; they must be "twisted around," in Aiken's phrase, until they have a shape and structure of their own; until they become an "artifact" (a favorite word of his) and if possible a masterpiece that will have a lasting echo in other minds. The "supreme task" performed by a masterpiece—as well as by lesser works and deeds in a more temporary fashion—is that of broadening, deepening, and subtilizing the human consciousness. Any man who devotes himself to that evolving task will find in it, Aiken says, "all that he could possibly require in the way of a religious credo."

His name for the credo was "the religion of consciousness."* It is a doctrine—no, more than that, a system of belief—to which he gave many refinements and ramifications. Some of these are set forth, with an impressive density of thought and feeling, in two long series of philosophical lyrics, *Preludes for Memnon* (1931) and *Time in the Rock* (1936); Aiken regarded these as his finest work. But the doctrine is a unifying theme in almost all the poetry of his middle years, say from 1925 to 1956, and in the prose as well. It is clearly exemplified in his novels, especially in *Blue Voyage* (1927), which brought young Malcolm Lowry from England to sit at the author's feet, and *Great Circle* (1933), which contains a brilliant, drunken, self-revealing monologue that Freud admired; he kept the book in his Vienna waiting room. Self-discovery is often the climax of Aiken's stories, and it is, moreover, the true theme of his autobiography, *Ushant* (1952). At the end of the book he says of his shipmates on a postwar voyage to England, "They were all heroes, every one

* The phrase "religion of consciousness" was I think first used in print by F. O. Matthiessen in *Henry James: The Major Phase* (New York: Oxford University Press, 1944); it serves as title for the last chapter. But the chapter has less to say about James's consciousness than one expects of such a fruitful critic as Matthiessen. Long after reading the book, I learned that he had discussed it with Aiken and had borrowed the phrase from him, after receiving Aiken's permission. [M.C.]

of them; they were all soldiers; as now, and always, all mankind were soldiers; all of them engaged in the endless and desperate war on the unconscious."

2.

Aiken's life had an intricate unity almost like that of his poetry and his fiction. Such is one's impression after reading *Ushant*, which deserves a place among the great autobiographies. In American literature there is nothing to compare with it except *The Education of Henry Adams*, which is equally well composed, equally an artifact—to use Aiken's word again—but which gives us only one side of the author. In *Ushant* the author writes in the third person, like Adams, and maintains the same objective tone, while recording not only his "education" but also his faults and obsessions, his infidelities, his recurrent dreams, his uproarious or shabby adventures: in short, while trying "to give the lowdown on himself, and through himself on humanity."

His pursuit of the essential self leads him back to his childhood in Savannah, spent in a house with a high front stoop and a chinaberry tree in the back yard. He tells of two experiences in the Savannah house that were to shape the rest of his life. One of these was lying on the carpeted floor of the nursery and reading the epigraph to the first chapter of *Tom Brown's School Days:*

I'm the poet of White Horse Vale, Sir,
With liberal notions under my cap.

Not understanding the word "poet," Conrad asked his father what it meant, and learned that the admired father had also written poems. From that moment the boy determined to be a poet himself, with liberal notions, and to live in England somewhere near White Horse Vale. Indeed he was to live there for many years, in a house with a big room in which he tried to re-create the parlor of the Savannah house. "The entire life," he says, "had thus in a sense annihilated time, and remained, as it were, in a capsule or in a phrase." It was the second experience, however, that confirmed the first and froze it into an enduring pattern. Since it was the last and grisliest scene of the poet's childhood in Savannah, it should be presented in his own words:

> ". . . after the desultory early-morning quarrel came the half-stifled scream, and then the sound of his father's voice counting three, and the two loud pistol shots; and he had tiptoed into the dark room, where the two bodies lay motionless, and apart, and, finding them dead, found himself possessed of them forever."

Perhaps it would be more accurate to say that the dead New England parents took possession of their son. Conrad was brought north to live with relatives in New Bedford, but still he was to spend the rest of his life coming to terms with his father and his mother. There was to be a third experience, however, that also helped to shape his career, though it was partly a sequel to what happened in Savannah. Conrad had spent happy years at Harvard and had made some lifelong friends, including Tom Eliot. When he was about to be graduated, in 1911, he was elected class poet. He refused the honor, resigned from college in something close to panic, and fled to Italy. "He had known, instantly," he says in *Ushant*, "that this kind of public appearance, and for such an occasion, was precisely what the flaw in his inheritance would not, in all likelihood, be strong enough to bear. . . . It was his decision that his life was to be lived *off-stage*, behind the scenes, out of view." In the next sixty years he did not change his mind. Aiken never, to my knowledge, gave a public lecture, read his poems to a women's club (or any other live audience), or appeared on a platform to accept an honorary degree.

Partly as a result of his obstinately remaining off-stage, he has been more neglected by the public than any other major American poet since Herman Melville, who was privately published, and Emily Dickinson, who didn't bother to put her poems into books. Aiken had those fifty published titles, but not one of them was a booksellers' choice. In 1934 I asked him for nominations to a list that was going to be printed in *The New Republic,* of "Good Books That Almost Nobody Has Read." He nominated Kafka's *The Castle*—that was long before the Kafka boom—then added in a postscript: "Might I also suggest for your list of Neglected Books a novel by c. aiken called Great Circle, of which the royalty report, to hand this morning, chronicles a sale of 26 copies in the second half year? and Preludes for Memnon, which I think is my best book, and which has sold about seven hundred copies in three years.

In 1946 I had the notion of trying to persuade some quarterly to publish a Conrad Aiken number. What should go into it? I asked him in a letter. He answered from England, making no suggestions whatever. "Appraisals of my work," he said, "have been rare or brief or nonexistent whether in periodicals or books on contemporary poetry: in me you behold an almost unique phenomenon, a poet who has acquired a Reputation, or a Position, or what have you, without ever having been caught in the act—as it were, by a process of auto-osmosis. At any given moment in the Pegasus Sweepstakes, in whatever Selling Plate or for whatever year, this dubious horse has always been the last in the list of the also-ran,—he never even placed, much less won, nor, I regret, have the offers to put him out to stud been either remunerative or very attractive. Odd. Very odd."

A few years later he began to receive a series of official honors,

> *And Awards and Prizes of various sizes*
> *among them a few quite delightful surprises. . . .*

as he said in his "Obituary in Bitcherel." He accepted the honors gladly, on condition that they didn't involve a public appearance. Thus, from 1950 to 1952 he served as Consultant in Poetry at the Library of Congress. He received the Bryher Award in 1952, a National Book Award in 1954, the Bollingen Award in 1956, the Fellowship of the National Academy of Poets in 1957, the Gold Medal for Poetry of the National Institute in 1958, and finally the National Medal for Literature in 1969. Meanwhile his position with the public (and with the booksellers) had improved scarcely at all; perhaps it had deteriorated. He reported in 1971 that his *Collected Poems: Second Edition,* containing the work of a lifetime, had a sale for its first half year of 430 copies.

It is hardly surprising that some developments in his later poems went unnoticed by poetry readers, and by critics too.

3.

Without in the least abandoning his religion of consciousness, Aiken's poems of the 1950s and 1960s introduced some new or partially new elements. One of these was a note of ancestral piety, with allusions to earlier Aikens, but more to his mother's connections, the Potters (who had started as New Bedford Quakers) and the Delanos. The note is already audible in "Mayflower," written in 1945. It is a poem partly about the ship (on which two of the poet's ancestors had been passengers), partly about the flower, and partly about the sandy shores of Cape Cod, where the Pilgrims had landed before sailing on to Plymouth. In other poems there is frequent mention of what might be called ancestral scenes: New Bedford and its whaling ships; the Quaker graveyard at South Yarmouth, on the Cape, where Cousin Abiel lies buried; Sheepfold Hill, also on the Cape; and Stony Brook, where the herring used to spawn by myriads. There is also talk of godfathers and tutelary spirits: among the poets Ben Jonson, Shakespeare, Li Po, and among historical figures Pythagoras and William Blackstone, the scholar and gentle heretic who built a house on the site of Boston before the Puritans came, then moved away from them into the wilderness. Blackstone becomes the hero of Aiken's cycle of poems about America, *The Kid* (1947). In "A Letter from Li Po" (1955), the Chinese maker of timeless artifacts is set beside the scoffing Quaker, Cousin Abiel:

> *In this small mute democracy of stones*
> *is it Abiel or Li Po who lies*
> *and lends us against death our speech?*

Another new or newly emphasized feature of the later poems is something very close to New England Transcendentalism. Its appearance should be no surprise, except to those who have fallen into the habit of regarding Transcendentalism as a purely historical phenomenon, a movement that flourished from 1830 to 1860, then disappeared at the beginning of the Civil War. On the contrary, it has been a durable property of New England thinking, a home place, one might say, to which some poets return as they grow older. In one or another of many aspects, the Transcendental mood is manifested in Robinson, in Frost, to some extent in Eliot, perhaps in Millay—see "Renascence" and some of the very late poems—then in Cummings, Wilder, S. Foster Damon, John Wheelwright, and most clearly in Conrad Aiken.

A complete definition of Transcendentalism would comprise most of Emerson's essays, beginning with *Nature*. As a shorter definition, the best I have found is a paragraph in the article "Transcendentalism" in *The Oxford Companion to American Literature*. One is grateful to the editor, James D. Hart, for bringing almost everything together in a few sentences. He says:

> . . . the belief had as its fundamental base a monism holding to the unity of the world and God and the immanence of God in the world. Because of this indwelling of divinity, everything in the world is a microcosm containing within itself all the laws and meaning of existence. Likewise the soul of each individual is identical with the soul of the world, and latently contains all that the world contains. Man may fulfill his divine potentialities either through a rapt mystical state, in which the divine is infused into the human, or through coming into contact with the truth, beauty, and goodness embodied in nature and originating in the Over-Soul. Thus occurs the doctrine of the correspondence between the tangible world and the human mind, and the identity of moral and physical laws. Through belief in the divine authority of the soul's intuitions and impulses, based on the identification of the individual soul with God, there developed the doctrine of self-reliance and individualism, the disregard of external authority, tradition, and logical demonstration, and the absolute optimism of the movement.

For a brief statement of Transcendental doctrines, James Hart's paragraph—from which I have omitted a few introductory phrases—seems to me almost complete. It does omit, however, two doctrines of some importance. One is the rejection of history—at least of history conceived as an irreversible process, a causally linked series of events in which the masses as well as the "representative men" play their part. For this rejection, see Emerson's essay "History" and also many of Cummings' later poems. Thornton Wilder, a New Englander by descent and residence—though born in Wisconsin—tells us that history is not a sequence but a tapestry or carpet in which various patterns are repeated at intervals.

Having spatialized time in this fashion, Wilder could never have become a social or a political historian, and the statement applies to others working in the same tradition.

One might say that Transcendentalists as a type—if such a type exists—are most at home in essays and poetry. If they turn to fiction, as Wilder did, they write novels dealing with morals rather than manners. Manners are the expression of standards prevailing in a group, and Transcendentalism denies the existence of groups except as arithmetical sums of separate persons: one plus one plus one. Only the individual is real and bears within himself a portion of the Over-Soul. That is the other doctrine omitted from Hart's admirable paragraph, and it explains why the Transcendental cast of mind is skeptical about political science and usually contemptuous of politicians. Aiken, for example, says of himself in *Ushant:* ". . . he had never found it possible to take more than a casual and superficial interest in practical politics, viewing it, as he did, as inevitably a passing phase, and probably a pretty primitive one, and something, again, that the evolution of consciousness would in its own good season take care of."

Is consciousness, for Aiken—the consciousness of mankind as shared by each individual—close to being an equivalent of the Over-Soul? That might be stretching a point, and indeed, I should be far from saying that, among twentieth-century New England writers, there is any complete Transcendentalist in a sense that might be accepted, for instance, by Margaret Fuller. It is clear, however, that there are several New England writers, most of them among the best, whose work embodies aspects of the Transcendental system (though seldom its "absolute optimism"). The aspects are usually different in each case, but two of them, at least, are shared by all the writers I mentioned. All are fiercely individual, in theory and practice, and all are moralists or ethicists, even or most of all when defying an accepted system of ethics.

Why this revival of the Transcendental spirit should be particularly evident in New England is hard to say. One is tempted to speak of something in the blood, or in the climate, or more realistically of a tradition handed down by a father or a favorite schoolteacher, rejected in the poet's youth, then reaccepted in middle age. Usually there is not much evidence of a literary derivation: for instance, Cummings and Millay were not at all interested in the earlier Transcendentalists.

Aiken might be an exception here. Boldest of all in his development of certain Transcendental notions, he also, rather late in life, found them confirmed by ancestral piety and especially by the writings and career of his maternal grandfather.

William James Porter was a birthright Quaker who became a Unitarian because he felt that the doctrines of the Friends were too confining. In 1859 he was called to the Unitarian church in New Bedford, where he soon began to feel that Unitarianism was confining too. In 1866 he refused to administer the rite of communion; following the example of Emerson, he told his congregation that he could no longer do so in good conscience. In 1867 he refused to call himself a Christian and was thereupon dropped from the roll of Unitarian ministers. He was so admired, however, for being upright and unselfish and a good preacher that his congregation gave him a unanimous vote of confidence. With Emerson, Colonel Higginson, and others, he then founded the Free Religious Association, which was intended to unite all the religions of the world by rejecting their dogmas and retaining from each faith only its ethical core. Dogmas were what he abhorred.

When the poet came to read Grandfather Potter's published sermons, he was impressed by their bold speculations about the divine element in men. He wrote an admiring poem about his grandfather, "Halloween," in which he quoted from the journal that Potter had kept during his early travels in Europe. A quoted phrase was ". . . so man may make the god finite and viable, make conscious god's power in action and being." That sounds the Transcendental note, and it is also close to phrases that Aiken himself had written: for example, in the 1949 preface to one of his Symphonies, where he says that man, in becoming completely aware of himself, "can, if he only will, become divine."

There is another point, apparently not connected with Grandfather Potter, at which Aiken comes even closer to Transcendentalism. Once more I quote from that convenient definition by James Hart: ". . . everything in the world is a microcosm containing within itself all the laws and meaning of existence. Likewise, the soul of each individual is identical with the soul of the world, and latently contains all that the world contains. . . . Thus occurs the doctrine of correspondence between the tangible world and the human mind."

Aiken, with his senses open to the tangible world, often speaks of this correspondence, which sometimes becomes for him an identity. Thus, he says in "A Letter from Li Po":

> *We are the tree, yet sit beneath the tree,*
> *among the leaves we are the hidden bird,*
> *we are the singer and are what is heard.*

Reading those lines, one can scarcely fail to think of Emerson's "Brahma":

> *They reckon ill who leave me out;*
> *When me they fly, I am the wings;*
> *I am the doubter and the doubt,*
> *And I the hymn the Brahmin sings.*

Aiken is still more clearly Emersonian, however, in what is almost the last of his poems, *THEE,* written when he was seventy-seven. Though comparatively short—only 250 lines, some consisting of a single word—it appeared as a handsome book, with lithographs by Leonard Baskin, and it is indeed one of his major works. First one notes that the poet has changed his style and that here—as, to a lesser extent, in some of the other late poems—he has abandoned the subtle variations and dying falls of his earlier work. *THEE* is written in short, galloping lines with rhymes like hoofbeats:

> *Who is that splendid THEE*
> *who makes a symphony*
> *of the one word*
> *be*
> *admitting us to see*
> *all things but THEE?*

Obviously THEE is being used here as the Quaker pronoun: "Thee makes," not "You make" or "Thou makest." Aiken may well have learned that usage from the Potter family. As for his question "Who?" it sends us back once more to Emerson. Just as Aiken's "consciousness" at times comes close to being the Emersonian Over-Soul, so THEE is the spirit of Nature as defined in Emerson's essay. "Strictly speaking," the essay says, ". . . all that is separate from us, all which Philosophy distinguishes as the NOT ME, that is, both nature and art, all other men and my own body, must be ranked under this name, NATURE." Aiken's name is THEE, but it has a different connotation. Whereas Emerson's Nature is admired for revealing in each of its parts the universal laws that wise men obey, Aiken's THEE is a pitiless force that nourishes and destroys with the divine indifference of the goddess Kali. Also and paradoxically, it is a force evolving with the human spirit—

> *as if perhaps in our slow growing*
> *and the beginnings of our knowing*
> *as if perhaps*
> *o could this be*
> *that we*
> *be*
> *THEE?*
> *THEE still learning*
> *or first learning*
> *through us*
> *to be*
> *THY THEE?*
> *Self-raise were then our praise of THEE*
> *unless we say divinity*
> *cries in us both as we draw breath*
> *cry death cry death*
> *and all our hate*
> *we must abate*
> *and THEE must with us meet and mate*
> *give birth give suck be sick and die*
> *and close the All-God-Giving-Eye*
> *for the last time to sky.*

When I first read *THEE*, it reminded me strongly of an untitled poem by Emerson, one that Aiken, so he told me, had never read—and no wonder he had missed it, since it does not appear in the *Complete Works*, even buried with other fragments in an appendix. One finds it in Volume II of the *Journals*, a volume including the period of spiritual crisis that followed the death of Emerson's beloved first wife, Ellen. She died February 8, 1831, and the poem was written July 6—at night? it must have been at night—immediately after a tribute to Ellen and thoughts of rejoining her in death. The poem, however, seems to announce the end of the crisis, since it is the entranced statement of a new faith. Here are two of the stanzas:

If thou canst bear
Strong meat of simple truth,
If thou durst my words compare
With what thou thinkest in the soul's free youth,
Then take this fact unto thy soul,—
God dwells in thee.
It is no metaphor nor parable,
It is unknown to thousands, and to thee;
Yet there is God.

. . .

Who approves thee doing right?
God in thee.
Who condemns thee doing wrong?
God in thee.
Who punishes thine evil deed?
God in thee.
What is thine evil need?
Thy worse mind, with error blind
And more prone to evil
That is, the greater hiding of the God within. . . .

Emerson never went back to polish or even finish the poem, so that it remains a broken rhapsody—rather than an artifact like THEE—and yet it states bluntly the seminal idea that he would develop in his essays of the dozen years that followed. What made me think of the poem when reading *THEE* is something in the style, in the irregular lines—not all of them rhymed—and in the message, too, with its identification of outer and inner worlds and its assertion that men are potentially divine. Of course where Emerson celebrates the power of the indwelling spirit, Aiken gives a twist to Transcendental doctrine by stressing, first, the indifferent power of THEE, and then the dependence of THEE on the individual consciousness—with which it must "meet and mate," from which it learns to become more truly itself, and with which, perhaps, it must die. The speculation seems more imaginative than philosophical, and yet one feels that—with the whole religion of consciousness—it finds a place in the Transcendental line.

In Aiken's beginnings, he had been poles apart from Emerson. He had been atheistic and pessimistic, not optimistic and Unitarian. He had never been impressed by the German Ro-

mantic philosophers or by the Neoplatonists, let alone by
Sufism and Brahmanism; instead his intellectual models had
been Poe first of all, then Santayana, Freud, and Henry
James. He would have been out of place in Emerson's Concord, since he continued all his life to be fond of women,
mischief, bawdy limericks, and martinis. Nevertheless, at the
end of his long career, he had worked round to a position
reminiscent of that which Emerson had reached in 1831, before he had published anything. That seems to me an intellectual event of some interest, especially since it was
announced in a memorable poem. But *THEE* aroused little
attention when it appeared in 1967, and later it seems to have
been almost forgotten.

In August 1972 I wrote Aiken to say that we had celebrated
his eighty-third birthday with a little party and that I had read
THEE to the guests. He answered wryly. My letter had arrived in the same mail as another announcing that the unsold
copies of *THEE*—most of the copies, that is—had been
remaindered.

4.

For the neglect of his work by the public, one can given several
explanations, though none of them seems adequate. In the
early days when he was writing a book-length poem every
year, Aiken's poetry was too modern and experimental for
him to share in what was then the enormous popularity of
Amy Lowell and Vachel Lindsay. Later, in the 1920s, it
seemed not experimental enough, or at least not eccentric
enough. In the 1930s it was condemned as having no social
or revolutionary meaning; in the 1940s it wasn't rich enough
in images (most of his work is musical rather than visual, and
music was becoming the lost side of poetry); in the 1950s it
was condemned again as not being "close enough in texture"
to suit the intensive reading methods of the new critics (but
what should one say of the *Preludes*?); and in the 1960s it was
disregarded as being written mostly in iambic pentameters, a
measure that had fallen out of fashion. Aiken followed his
own fashion, and his work developed by an inner logic which
was not that of the poetry-reading public.

But what about the admirable prose of his novels and stories and of his great autobiography? Two or three of the stories, including "Silent Snow, Secret Snow," have appeared in dozens of anthologies, but in general the prose, too, has failed to capture the public imagination.

I suspect that the long neglect of Aiken's work is due in large part to policies more or less deliberately adopted by the author. In his heart he didn't want to become a celebrity. Not only did he never appear on a public platform, but also he refused to cultivate the literary powers, if such persons exist; instead he went out of his way to offend them. Always for the best of reasons, he bickered with editors, jeered at anthologists, rejected his own disciples one after another, and made cruelly true remarks about fellow poets, who would soon take their revenge by reviewing his books. He must have expected those reviews, familiar as he was with literary folkways. They made him angry, they wounded his pride—but did they also give him a somehow comfortable assurance that he would continue to live "*off-stage,* behind the scenes, out of view"? Was it all part of the same pattern as his resigning from Harvard in preference to writing and publicly reading the class poem?

I last saw him in January 1972. By then he had made the great circle and was living in Savannah, only a few doors from the now gutted house where he had spent his childhood. Old Bonaventure Cemetery, where his parents lay buried, also was quite near. Conrad himself was suffering from the ills of human flesh, including some rare ones whose name I heard that day for the first time, but he still made puns while his beloved wife mixed martinis. We talked about the literary world, not so excitedly as at our first meeting half a century before and with more bitterness on Conrad's part. Still, he had done his work and knew it was good. He had proclaimed his religion of consciousness and had lived by its tenets. He had never compromised—as he was to say on his deathbed—and he could feel certain that, for all his hatred of intruders, the great world would some day come round to him.

[1975]

JOHN CHEEVER: THE NOVELIST'S
LIFE AS A DRAMA

Late in the fall of 1930, John Cheever appeared in my office
at *The New Republic*, where I was then a junior editor recently
assigned to the book department. John was eighteen and
looked younger.* He had a boyish smile, a low, Bay State
voice, and a determined chin. We had just printed the first
story he submitted to a magazine, a fictionized account of
why and how he got himself expelled from Thayer Academy,
in South Braintree. Promptly John had come to New York
to make his fortune as a writer.

The story—we called it "Expelled"—had come to us
marked for my attention. I had felt that I was hearing for the
first time the voice of a new generation. There were some
objections by the senior editors, who pointed out that we
didn't often print fiction. "It's awfully long," Bruce Bliven
said; he had the final voice on manuscripts. I undertook to
cut it down to *New Republic* size and it went to the printer.
When John appeared we talked about the story. I didn't tell
him that it had caused a mild dispute in the office. Instead I
invited him to an afternoon party, the first that the Cowleys
had dared to give in their bare apartment a few doors down
the street.

I had forgotten that party of Prohibition days, but John
remembered it fifty years later when he went to Chicago and
spoke at a dinner of the Newberry Library Associates. The
Library had acquired my papers and wanted to hold a celebration, with John as the principal speaker. "I was truly provincial," he said in evoking that long-ago afternoon.

---

* John always said "seventeen" in telling the story; he was inexact about his
age, since he was born May 27, 1912. He also said that his manuscript was
addressed to me because he had been reading my first book of poems, *Blue
Juniata*, and thought I might sympathize. [M.C.]

"Malcolm's first wife Peggy met me at the door and exclaimed, 'You must be John Cheever. Everyone else is here.' Things were never like this in Massachusetts. I was offered two kinds of drinks. One was greenish. The other was brown. They were both, I believe, made in a bathtub. I was told that one was a Manhattan and the other Pernod. My only intent was to appear terribly sophisticated and I ordered a Manhattan. Malcolm very kindly introduced me to his guests. I went on drinking Manhattans lest anyone think I came from a small town like Quincy, Massachusetts. Presently, after four or five Manhattans I realized that I was going to vomit. I rushed to Mrs. Cowley, thanked her for the party, and reached the apartment-house hallway, where I vomited all over the wallpaper. Malcolm never mentioned the damages."

John must have walked or staggered back to what he called "the squalid slum room on Hudson Street" that he had rented for $3 a week. At the time his only dependable income was a weekly allowance of $10 from his older brother Fred, who had kept his job during the Depression and believed in John's talent. His only capital was a typewriter for which he couldn't often buy a new ribbon. That first winter in New York he had lived—so he reported—mostly on stale bread and buttermilk. As time went on he found little assignments that augmented his diet; one of them was summarizing the plots of new novels for MGM, which was looking for books that would make popular movies. John was paid $5 for typing out his summary with I don't know how many carbons. *The New Republic* couldn't help him much except by giving him unreviewed books for sale; it was "a journal of opinion," mostly political, and John wasn't given to expressing opinions; by instinct he was a storyteller. He kept writing stories and they began to be printed, always in little magazines that didn't pay for contributions.

I told Elizabeth Ames about him. Elizabeth was the executive director and hostess of Yaddo, a working retreat for writers and artists in Saratoga Springs, and I had served on her admissions committee. She invited John for one summer, liked him immensely, and later renewed the invitation several times. John would never forget his indebtedness to Yaddo, which had fed and lodged him during some of his neediest periods.

In New York I sometimes gave him advice, not about his writing, which I had admired from the beginning, but about finding a market for it. Once I told him it was time for a novel that would speak for his new generation as Fitzgerald had spoken in *This Side of Paradise*. It turned out that John had already started a novel, and he showed me the first three or four chapters. They wouldn't do as the beginning of a book, I reported; each chapter was separate and came to a dead end. It might be that his present talent was for stories. . . . Then why wouldn't editors buy the stories? he asked me on another occasion. By that time I had been divorced from Peggy and had remarried, this time for good. It was a Friday evening and John had come for dinner in our new apartment. "Perhaps the stories have been too long," I said, "usually six or seven thousand words. Editors don't like to buy long stories from unknown writers." Then I had an inspiration. I suggested that he write four very short stories, each of not more than a thousand words, in the next four days. "Bring them to me at the office on Wednesday afternoon and," I said grandly, "we'll see whether I can't get you some money for them."

John carried out the assignment brilliantly. I doubt whether anyone else of his age—he was then twenty-two—could have invented four stories, each different from all the others, in only four days, but John already seemed to have an endless stock of characters and moods and situations. Although *The New Republic* seldom printed fiction, one of the four could be passed off as a "color piece" about a burlesque theater. "Yes. Short and lively," was Bruce Bliven's comment when I showed it to him. The other three ministories, plainly fictions, I sent along to Katharine White, then fiction editor of *The New Yorker*, and she accepted two of them. That event, which I have told about elsewhere, was the beginning of John's career as a professional writer. *The New Yorker* was his principal market for more than thirty years and it would end by printing 119 of his stories.

In the course of time John became impatient with the accurate reporting that was demanded of *New Yorker* writers, especially in the days when Harold Ross was editor. It set limitations on fiction, and John always wanted to go farther and deeper into life. "This table seems real," he later said in an interview, "the fruit basket belonged to my grandmother, but a madwoman could come in the door any moment." In the stories he wrote after World War II, the madwoman appeared more often. Once she was a vampire; that was in "Torch Song." Once she assumed the shape of an enormous radio that picked up conversations from anywhere in a big apartment building. That story, his first with a touch of the impossible, was also his first to be widely anthologized.

Some future critic should trace John's development as a writer by reading his work from the beginning in its exact chronological order. The work changes from year to year and from story to story. "Fiction is experimentation," he was later to say; "when it ceases to be that it ceases to be fiction. One never puts down a sentence without the feeling that it has never been put down before in exactly the same way, and that perhaps the substance of the sentence has never been felt. Every sentence is an innovation." That is too seldom true of fiction, but it is true of John's best work, in which the sentences, apparently simple, are always alive and unexpected. Reading them makes me think of a boyhood experience, that of groping beneath roots at the edge of a stream and finding a trout in my fingers.

There were times of crisis when his purposes changed rapidly. One of these must have been during his work on *The Wapshot Chronicle*, his first novel and still his most engaging book. Perhaps it isn't a novel so much as a series of episodes connected with the imaginary town of St. Botolphs, on the south or less fashionable shore of Massachusetts Bay, and with the fortunes of the Wapshot family; John was right to call it a chronicle. The characters are presented with a free-ranging candor that must have embarrassed the Cheevers, to whom the Wapshots bore a family resemblance, but also with an affection not often revealed in his New York or Westchester stories. John felt that he couldn't publish the book until after his mother died. It appeared in 1957 while the Cheevers were spending a year in Italy. John was happy about the *Chronicle*, and this without seeing the reviews, most of which were enthusiastic. Writing it seems to have given him a new sense of scope and freedom.

Nevertheless he was having trouble with his second novel, *The Wapshot Scandal*, which was to be seven years in the writing. While work on it progressed slowly, or not at all, he published two more collections of stories (there would finally be six of these in all). One of the new collections bore a title that suggested another change in direction: *Some People, Places, & Things That Will Not Appear in My Next Novel*. In the title story he was performing what almost seems a rite of exorcism: he was presenting in brief, and then dismissing with contempt, a number of episodes that, in his former days, he might have developed at length. Not one of them, he now believed, would help him "to celebrate a world that lies spread out around us like a bewildering and stupendous dream."

He tried to present that dream in *The Wapshot Scandal*, but in writing the book he found little to celebrate. He had to record how the Wapshots, with their traditional standards, faced the new world of aimlessness, supermarkets, and fusion bombs. They died or went to pieces—all of them except Coverly Wapshot, more solid and unattractive than the others, who found himself working in a secret missile base and lost his security clearance. The book is almost as episodic as the *Chronicle*, but with the episodes more tightly woven together. Each of them starts with a scene that is accurately observed—it might correspond to Cheever's real table and his grandmother's fruit basket—but then everything becomes grotesque, as if his madwoman had come in the door. On one occasion she is followed by a screaming crowd of madwomen in nightgowns with curlers in their hair. The book has an unflagging power of invention and was praised by critics when it finally appeared; also it had a fairly impressive sale. John himself "never much liked the book," as he was to say when he was interviewed much later for *The Paris Review*, "and when it was done I was in a bad way. I'd wake up in the night and I would hear Hemingway's voice—I've never actually heard Hemingway's voice, but it was conspicuously his—saying, 'This is the small agony. The great agony comes later.'"

But first would come another agony that was not the greatest, but was not a small one either. After thirty years of intimate relations, *The New Yorker* rejected one of his longer and more treasured stories, "The Jewels of the Cabots." John sold the story to *Playboy* for twice what *The New Yorker* would have paid, but still his pride had been hurt. There were other rejections, one or two of them inexcusable, and John stopped publishing in *The New Yorker*. If one were plotting his life as a theater piece, one might say the curtain had fallen on a second act.

A few years later John published a third novel, *Bullet Park* (1969), that was more tightly plotted than the second. It pleased him more than the *Scandal*. "The manuscript was received enthusiastically everywhere," he reported, "but when Benjamin DeMott dumped on it in the *Times*, everybody picked up their marbles and went home. I ruined my left leg in a skiing accident and ended up so broke that I took out working papers for my youngest son." John was exaggerating, as he liked to do with gullible reporters. The son, then twelve years old, never thought about working papers; in due time he went off to Andover and Stanford. But John, horrified at going into debt, wasn't making progress with his writing, and he confessed to himself that he had become an alcoholic. He had a heart attack, nearly fatal, in 1972. Having recovered, he accepted teaching assignments, first at the Iowa School of Writing and then at Boston University, where, so he said, "I behaved badly."

For the black years that might be called a third act in his life, I'm not sure about the sequence of events, and I have to depend on his later accounts. I was seeing less of John. In 1967 our only son, Robert, had been married to John's daughter Susan in a high-church ceremony at St. Mark's in the Bouwerie. The elder Cowleys played no part in the preparations for an expensive wedding. At the reception, under an outsize tent in the churchyard, the Cheever connection drank their champagne on one side of the tent, while the smaller Cowley contingent sat grouped on the other. That marked a growing difference in styles of life between the two families. For ten years after *The Wapshot Chronicle* and before *Bullet Park*, John had earned a substantial income: there were Hollywood contracts and what seemed to me huge advances from publishers. The Cheevers had bought and remodeled a big stone house in Westchester County, to the disapproval of some *New Yorker* editors, who felt that authors should defend their economic freedom by living on a modest scale. The Cowleys did live modestly, farther out in the country, and spent rather less than they took in. I came to suspect that the Cheevers, who traveled widely, always in first class, now regarded us as tourist-class country cousins. Then Rob and Susan were divorced, after eight years of marriage. It was an amicable divorce, with no children to argue about (only two golden retrievers) and with no hard feelings. Still it was the end of casual family visitings.

I was always overjoyed to see John, but was a little tongue-tied even when we met at Yaddo, where we were both on the board of directors, or at various committee meetings of the American Academy; there was never much time for confidences. Later John would tell the public about his misadventures. After Boston University he went home to the big stone house, where he fell into utter depression. He used to wash down several Valium tablets with a quart of whiskey. He was trying to abolish himself—but why? Clearly it was less a matter of his finances or his physical state than of his concern with the art of fiction; he felt that his life as a writer was at an end. He was also a sincerely religious man, though he wouldn't talk much about the subject, and he must have felt that he had fallen from grace forever. His family, deeply concerned, told him that alcohol would kill him, as it had already killed his loved and resented older brother. "So what?" he said, taking another drink. In 1975 he finally listened to the family and committed himself to Smithers, a rehabilitation center. He was to speak darkly, in later years, of going mad when deprived of liquor and of being wrapped in a straitjacket.* The treatment was prolonged, whatever it was, and it worked; after being released from Smithers, John never again took a drink. He experienced a new sense of redemption, elation, and release from bondage. Almost immediately he set to work on a novel, which he finished in less than a year.

The novel, of course, was *Falconer*, published in 1977; John was to call it "a very dark book that displayed radiance." It was the story of Ezekiel Farragut, a moderately distinguished professor who becomes a drug addict, who kills his brother with a poker, and who is sentenced to ten years in Falconer Prison. There he is redeemed, partly through a homosexual love affair, and loses his craving for Methadone. The book reads swiftly and displays John's gift for economical prose with not a misplaced word, beside his amazing and unflagging

---

* The treatment at Smithers did not include a straitjacket, but John had been confined briefly in another institution. [M.C.]

talent for invention. Some of the episodes have a touch of the miraculous. A cardinal descends from the skies in a helicopter and carries off Zeke's lover to freedom. A young priest appears in the cellblock and administers last rites to the hero. "Now who the hell was that?" Zeke shouts to the guard. "I didn't ask for a priest. He didn't do his thing for anybody else." Symbolically Zeke is about to die, be entombed, and rise again. In life his cellmate dies instead. Attendants come to put the corpse into a body bag. Farragut zips open the bag, removes the corpse, and takes its place; then he is carried out of the prison. Walking in the street a free man, his head high, his back straight, "Rejoice," he thought, "rejoice."

Those are the last words of Cheever's longest continuous fiction. Judged purely as a novel, *Falconer* has obvious faults. There are loose strings never tied up and events left unexplained. The reader is forced to wonder how Zeke Farragut will survive in his new life, considering that he has no money, no identity, and is still dressed in his prison clothes. Then one reflects that the faults don't matter much; that *Falconer* is not a novel bent on achieving verisimilitude, but rather a moving parable with biblical overtones of sin and redemption; it is Magdalen redeemed by divine grace and Lazarus raised from the dead. That is how it must have been read by thousands, and the book had an astoundingly wide sale, enough to pay off its author's debts for the first time in years.

And the fourth act in the drama?

The success of *Falconer* led to another change in John's character, as well as in his public image. He had always managed to keep from being a celebrity. When he was twelve years old his parents had given him their permission to earn his future living as a writer—if he could earn it—but only after he promised them that he had no idea of becoming famous or wealthy. In later years he had kept the promise, though with some latitude in the matter of income, since he liked to support the family on a generous scale. He had refused several offers that promised to make him rich, though he had always been shrewd in a Yankee fashion (and his agent was known for striking hard bargains). In the matter of fame, he had obdurately defended his privacy. Medals and honors he accepted when they came, if grudgingly, but he had done his best to avoid being interviewed—often by the simple device of getting drunk, or getting the interviewer drunk. But *Falconer* had made him a national figure as if by accident, and he found himself enjoying his new status.

For the first time in his life he gave interviews willingly—and brilliantly too, since he said without hesitation whatever was on his mind. Always the interviewers would mention his boyishness. I suppose the word was suggested by his lack of self-importance, his deprecatory smile, and his candor in speaking about intimate misadventures. In simple fact he was now an old man, wearied by the physical demands he had made on himself, so that he was older in body and spirit than his sixty-five years. He now had nothing to lose by telling the truth, so long as it made a good story. He was finding pleasure in addressing a new audience—as he explained more than once—but also he wanted to set things straight with himself and the world while there was still time.

His next book after *Falconer* would be a retrospective undertaking, *The Stories of John Cheever* (1978), collected at last in one big volume. He had chosen sixty-one stories for the book, after omitting all those printed before his army service in World War II (though some of that early work is worth preserving) as well as two or three stories written during his breakdown. Almost all the others he arranged in roughly chronological order. For the first time a wider public could note the changing spirit of his work over the years, not to mention its essential unity. John also had given the book a brief, illuminating Preface that has been widely quoted. "These stories," it says at one point, "seem at times to be stories of a long-lost world when the city of New York was still filled with a river light, when you heard the Benny Goodman quartets from a radio in the corner stationery store, and when almost everybody wore a hat. . . . The constants that I looked for in this sometimes dated paraphernalia are a love of light and a determination to trace some moral chain of being. Calvin played no part in my religious education, but his presence seemed to abide in the barns of my childhood and to have left me with some undue bitterness."

That moral element is always present, if concealed, in a Cheever story. At first the bad people, whose commonest sin is heartlessness, seem hard to distinguish from the good people, but they end by indicting themselves, and Cheever was an inexorable judge (especially when faced by women bent on expressing themselves at everybody's cost). He was not a tender judge of his own work, and there are only two sentences of the Preface that I think are in error as applied to himself. He says, "The parturition of a writer, I think, unlike that of a painter, does not display any interesting alliances to his masters. In the growth of a writer one finds nothing like the early Jackson Pollock copies of the Sistine Chapel paintings with their interesting cross-references to Thomas Hart Benton." That seems to me far from the truth. Among the important writers of this later time, Cheever reveals more alliances than others to three masters of the World War I generation.

Hemingway was his first master, as was evident in John's early and now forgotten stories. These copied many features of Hemingway's style, as notably the short sentences, the simple words, the paring away of adjectives, adverbs, conjunctions, and the effort to evoke feelings without directly expressing them, simply by presenting actions in sequence and objects seen accurately as if for the first time. I can testify that the novel John tried to write when he was twenty-one—and abandoned after three or four chapters—had as its obvious starting point a story by Hemingway, "Cross-Country Snow." It would have been the equivalent, in his case, of Jackson Pollock's attempts to copy the Sistine Chapel. Very soon Cheever developed a style of his own that became more effective than Hemingway's later style; he never parodied himself. Still, he retained what he had learned from that early master, including an enthusiasm for fishing and skiing. Hemingway as a father figure appeared in his dreams.

The resemblance to Fitzgerald was more often noted, especially during John's middle years. His characters, like Fitzgerald's, were mostly from the upper layers of American society (though Cheever didn't invest them with the glamour of great wealth). Like Fitzgerald he had the gift of double vision; he was both a participant in the revels and, at the same moment, a fresh and honest-eyed observer from a different social world. Both men were at heart romantics, even if they had different dreams. Cheever's was not the dream of early love and financial success; he was more obsessed with the middle-aged nightmare of moral or financial collapse. Sometimes, however, he wrote sentences that might grace a Fitzgerald story, as, for example, "The light was like a blow, and the air smelled as if many wonderful girls had just wandered across the lawn." Both men were time-conscious and tried to recapture the feeling, the smell, the essential truth of a moment in history. One can often guess the year when a Cheever story was written by internal evidence, without looking for the date of publication. It is the same with Fitzgerald, of whom Cheever was to say admiringly, "One always knows reading Fitzgerald what time it is, precisely where you are, the kind of country. No writer has ever been so true in placing the scene. I feel that this isn't pseudohistory, but the sense of being alive. All great men are scrupulously true to their times." It was one of the things that Cheever tried to be. His stories also imply moral constants that make them relatively timeless—but then Fitzgerald, too, was a moralist, "a spoiled priest."

And Faulkner? Here it is not at all a question of early influence or the relation between explorer and settler. I'm not sure that Cheever even read Faulkner during the 1930s, although he was an enormous reader. It is rather a question of natural resemblances in writing and in character as well. The two didn't look alike, but they were both short, handsome men attractive to women and blessed from childhood with enormous confidence in their genius. (The influence of mere stature on writers' careers is a subject that calls for more study. Often the Napoleons of literature—and the Balzacs—are short men determined not to be looked at from above.) Both Cheever and Faulkner were high-school dropouts and self-educated. Like Faulkner from the beginning, Cheever was a storyteller by instinct and kept turning description into narration. Note for examples the panoramic views of Bullet Park, at the beginning of the novel, and of St. Botolphs, in the first chapter of *The Wapshot Chronicle*. First we see the houses one by one, but each house recalls a family and each family suggests a story. That was how Faulkner proceeded too.

Like Faulkner again, Cheever depended at every moment on the force and richness of his imagination. Faulkner was preeminent in that gift, but Cheever had more of it than other writers of his own time, and he too created his "little postage stamp of native soil"; Westchester and St. Botolphs are in some respects his Yoknapatawpha. *Falconer*, the novel he liked best among his own works, was named for an imagined prison in Westchester County, but he usually pronounced the name in an English fashion: "Faulkner." Mightn't that be a form of tribute to the older novelist?

The two men had other points of resemblance, besides their common fondness for hard liquor. One trait of a different sort was their frequent use of symbols from the Bible, as if they were the last two Christians in a godless world. But I wanted to make the more general point about Cheever that he was carrying on a tradition. His age group or cohort has included many gifted novelists: Bellow, Welty, Updike, Malamud, to name only a few. I will never try to assign a rank to each of them like a schoolmaster noting down grades. Cheever may or may not be the best of them, but he is clearly the one who stands closest in spirit to the giants of the preceding era.

Most of the American authors admired in our time did their best work before they were forty-five. Many of them died before reaching that age. Most survived into their sixties, but their truly productive careers had been cut short by emotional exhaustion, alcoholism, or by mere repetition and drudgery. It was Scott Fitzgerald who said, "There are no second acts in American lives." We produced no Thomas Hardys or Thomas Manns (exception being made for Robert Frost) and no one who made a brilliant rebeginning after a crisis in middle life. More recently there have been other exceptions and Cheever is one of them. His career in literature not merely started over but had a last act as brilliant in a different way as the acts that preceded it.

After he published *The Stories of John Cheever*, honors came pouring down on him like an autumn shower. Among them was a doctorate from Harvard (1978), a Pulitzer prize for the stories, which also received the award for fiction of the Book Critics' Circle, both in 1979, the Edward MacDowell Medal in that same year, and finally, in 1982, the National Medal for Literature. He accepted the honors gladly, not with the indifference he had displayed toward the few that had been granted him in earlier years. Once he had acted like Faulkner, as if on the assumption that readers didn't exist; now he was delighted by their response. He gave public readings of his stories, most often of two favorites, "The Swimmer" and "The Death of Justina." His face and his Bay State voice became admiredly familiar on television. He was photographed on horseback, like Faulkner in his last years. Meanwhile, he had started a new novel for which he had signed, so we heard, a magnificent contract. To interviewers he said merely that it would be "another bulky book." There wasn't much time to work on it in the midst of distractions. After he had spent so many years in the shadows, even his New England conscience would have absolved him for basking a little in a transcontinental light.

There is often an essential change in writers as they grow older, something beyond a mere ripening of earlier qualities. (I am thinking here mostly of men and not of women, who are likely to follow a different pattern.) The writer, if he has something of his own to say, begins under the sign of the mother, which is also the sign and banner of rebellion—against tradition, against the existing order, against authority as represented by the father. The change comes after a middle-aged crisis, or even before it in many cases. The writer becomes reconciled with his father, indeed with all the Fathers who suffer from having wayward sons. (Here again women are different; they are likely to sign a truce with their mothers.) Cheever said more than once that the Wapshot books were "a posthumous attempt to make peace with my father's ghosts."

Whether men or women, writers find themselves going back in spirit to the regions where they spent their childhoods. For more than forty years Cheever had been a Yorker, not a Yankee; he had been mistakenly called a typical writer for *The New Yorker*. Now he rebecame a New Englander. One can be more specific: he became a Bay Stater, a native son of the Massachusetts seaboard, which has a different voice and different traditions from those of the Connecticut Valley. If Bay Staters are of Puritan descent, they trace their ancestral histories back to the founder of the family. In John's case the founder was Ezekial Cheever, a minister highly respected by Cotton Mather, who preached his funeral sermon. John quotes Mather as saying, "The welfare of the Commonwealth was always upon the conscience of Ezekial Cheever . . . and he abominated periwigs." The commonwealth of letters was always on John's conscience and he abominated all sorts of pretension, almost as much as he abominated pollution and superhighways.

While writing *Falconer* he had still smoked furiously; "I

need to have *some* vice," he explained. Now, after a struggle, he gave up smoking as well as drinking. In default of vices he practiced virtues, especially those native to the Bay State. That breed of Yankees are distinguished, and tormented as well, by having scruples; they keep asking themselves, "Was that the right thing for me to do?" John must have asked that question often in his prayers. Another Yankee precept is not to speak ill of people even if they are rivals. John, if he had grudges, now managed not to express them (except for a mild grudge against the fiction editor who had rejected "The Jewels of the Cabots"). He had become conservative in the Bay State fashion, that is, in manners though not always in politics, this last being a field that he continued to avoid. There was, however, one Yankee precept, "Be reticent about yourself!" that he now flagrantly violated. I suspect this was because he had come to regard himself as a fictional person, the leading character of a novel that he was composing not in written words, but in terms of remembered joys and tribulations.

The true Bay Stater discharges his obligations, and he sets high store by loyalty to his family, to a few old friends, and to chosen institutions. John became a devoted churchgoer, though he didn't often stay for the sermon. He worked for the institutions that had befriended him, as notably Yaddo and the American Academy, where he served for three years as chairman of the Awards Committee for Literature. In that post he had to read some two hundred novels a year; it was another of his unrecompensed services to the commonwealth of letters. He paid off his moral debts to friends; one example was his making a trip to Chicago in order to speak at a dinner held in my honor. He was like a man who puts his affairs in order before setting out on a journey.

The journey started, as always, sooner than was expected. In July 1981 John had an operation for the removal of a cancerous kidney. The operation appeared to be successful, but a few weeks later John was barely able to walk. The cancer had metastasized to the bones of his legs; then it appeared as a burning spot on his rib cage. There was no hope left except in chemotherapy and radiotherapy at Memorial Hospital. Once again John spoke of himself dispassionately, as if he were a character in fiction. He told an interviewer for *The Saturday Review*, "Suddenly to find yourself with thousands and thousands seeking some cure for this deadly thing is an extraordinary thing. It's not depressing, really, or exhilarating. It's quite plainly a critical part of living, or the aspiration to live."

Those were arduous months for John; I think one might call them heroic. Doggedly he prepared a manuscript for his publisher, though it was not the bulky novel he had planned. *Oh, What a Paradise It Seemed* was no more than a novella, but, like all the best of his work, it was accurate, beautifully written, and full of surprises. It appeared in the early spring of 1982. A few weeks later he wrote me, "I fully intend to recover both from the cancer, the treatment and the bills."

I last saw him in Carnegie Hall less than two months before his death. The occasion was the ceremony at which, among the recipients of lesser awards, he was presented with the National Medal for Literature. His face was gaunt after radiotherapy and almost all his hair had fallen out. I said that I admired him for having made the trip from Ossining and he answered, "When they give you fifteen thousand dollars you owe them an appearance." He hobbled out to the rostrum leaning on a cane—or was it two canes? From my folding chair in the wings I couldn't hear his little speech, but I heard the great rumble of applause; John had nothing but friends.

A few minutes later we met and embraced in an empty corridor; I remember feeling that the treatment at Memorial had altered his body. It was more than fifty years since John had first appeared in my office at *The New Republic*. We were two men who had grown old in the service of literature, but our roles had been transposed: John was now older than I and was leading the way.

[1983]

HEMINGWAY'S WOUND—
AND ITS CONSEQUENCES FOR
AMERICAN LITERATURE

Long ago I was asked to edit the Viking *Portable Hemingway,* one of the early volumes in a new series. I accepted the commission eagerly, though it promised nothing in the way of financial recompense beyond a fee of $500. On the other hand, it might further some larger purposes, one of which was to correct a general misestimation of Hemingway's work. He was, as I felt, not merely an international celebrity but also an important figure in the history of American literature, which was my field of study. Though he was not among my friends at the time, he was a member of my age group and had expressed, more clearly than others, our special sense of life.

I worked hard on the *Portable,* and especially on the introduction, during the early months of 1944. Here I repeat my opening paragraph, for two good reasons. The first is that the end of it, which had a discernible effect on later assessments of Hemingway, is now under attack by the critical revisionists, a contentious sect. The second is that what I wrote isn't widely available, the *Portable* having gone out of print in 1949.

> Going back to Hemingway's work after several years [I said] is like going back to a brook where you had often fished and finding that the woods are as deep and cool as they used to be. The trees are bigger, perhaps, but they are the same trees; the water comes down over the black stones as clear as always, with the same dull, steady roar where it plunges into the pool; and when the first trout takes hold of your line you can feel your heart beating against your fishing jacket. But something has changed, for this time there are shadows in the pool that you hadn't noticed before, and you have a sense that the woods are haunted. When Hemingway's stories first appeared, they seemed to be a

transcription of the real world, new because they were accurate and because the world in those days was also new. With his insistence on "presenting things truly," he seemed to be a writer in the naturalistic tradition (for all his technical innovations) and the professors of American literature, when they got around to mentioning his books in their surveys, treated him as if he were a Dreiser of the lost generation, or perhaps the fruit of a mis-alliance between Dreiser and Jack London. Going back to his work in 1944, you perceive his kinship with a wholly different group of novelists, let us say with Poe and Hawthorne and Melville: the haunted and nocturnal writers, the men who dealt in images that were symbols of an inner world.

Was there an explanation for the "haunted" quality that distinguished Hemingway's work and placed it in a lasting tradition of American literature? I looked for clues in his fiction, where they abounded, and also in his life as it was then known to readers. The first clue I found was clearer than others: it was the wound he had suffered in Italy. On the moonless night of 8–9 July 1918, near the ruined town of Fossalta di Piave, he had stood in a frontline trench talking in pidgin Italian with three soldiers. A little after midnight an Austrian mortar bomb had exploded in the trench. "I died then," Hemingway later told his friend Guy Hickok. "I felt my soul or something coming right out of my body, like you'd pull a silk handkerchief out of a pocket by one corner. It flew around and then came back and went in again and I wasn't dead any longer."

All three Italian soldiers had their legs blown off and two of them were dead. Hemingway's legs were full of steel fragments, 237 by the surgeons' later count; one fragment had penetrated his scrotum. Somehow he rose to his feet, heaved up the third soldier in a fireman's carry, and staggered up the road toward a forward command post. An Austrian search-light caught him in its beam and he was wounded twice again by slugs from a heavy machine gun. He didn't know how he reached the command post, where he collapsed. By then the man on his shoulder was dead.

Such is an account of his first great wound, or of those many first wounds, as it can be reconstructed by comparing several reports. Hemingway was never to forget the mortar bomb that exploded in the darkness "as when a blast-furnace door is swung open." It was a memory that returned obsessively in his fiction. The heroes of his first two novels were both of them wounded men. Consequences of the wound reappear in several of his stories and help to explain their preoccupation with dying and corpses. Often the hero tried "never to think about it," and that effort is mentioned or hinted at in unexpected places—for example in "Big Two-Hearted River," which seems to be only the beautifully accurate record of a fishing trip. But one notes that the fisherman has to control his emotions and that there are memories he is glad not to be thinking about. After rereading the story in connection with others, one suspects that his most perilous memory is of being blown up at night and of feeling the soul or something go out of his body. Perhaps—or so I conjectured—that might help us to understand the emotional power of the story, which is otherwise hard to explain.

The conjecture was taken up and amplified by other critics, as notably by Philip Young in his *Ernest Hemingway* (1952). This is, on the whole, an illuminating work, but I suspected on reading it that Young had gone too far toward presenting a complicated personality chiefly in terms of the wounds, moral and physical, that Hemingway had suffered during his early life. The late Mark Schorer, a venturesome critic, went farther in the same direction; he said that a wound was to become the central symbol of almost everything Hemingway wrote. More specialized critics devoted themselves to the symbols, mostly of fear, that they had unearthed with pick and shovel after digging through the text of "Big Two-Hearted River." The seach became popular in other countries, including Japan, where Keiji Nakajima wrote a compendious summary of the critical papers devoted to this one story.

After all this critical fabulation, some of it pretty hazardous, there was certain to be a reaction toward a more commonplace picture of Hemingway's work. The reaction was carried to an extreme by Kenneth S. Lynn in a very long review (*Commentary,* July 1981) of Hemingway's *Selected Letters.* It was reprinted in a collection of Lynn's writing (*The Air-Line to Seattle,* 1983), and I hear with trepidation that he has written a book on Hemingway, not yet published.* In the review I play the villain's role. One of its principal points is that I had

* The book when published in 1987, was simply titled *Hemingway.* [ed.]

been perversely mistaken in my picture of Hemingway's character and writing. I had presented him as a victim of capitalist society at war and had thereby led other critics astray. In particular I had sinned by what I said about "Big Two-Hearted River." The story is, in reality, "a sun-drenched, Cézannesque picture of a predominantly happy fishing trip," and I had transformed it into something as "spooky," to use Lynn's word, as anything by Poe or Hawthorne. The truth according to Lynn is that the story is not about a returned soldier and has nothing to do with a wound suffered in Italy. For proof of this reinterpretation Lynn cites the *Selected Letters*. Those written home from Italy are cheerful about the wound, and after his return Hemingway had nothing whatever to say about it. By the time he made his fishing trip to the upper Michigan peninsula in the summer of 1919, he had fully recovered from the fear of being blown up at night. Perhaps there are shadows in the background of his fishing narrative, but if so they depend on something else in his immature psyche, that is, his obsessive grudge against his mother.

Lynn attacks my motives for writing about Hemingway, which he asserts were wholly personal and political. "When, in 1940," he says, "Malcolm Cowley finally ceased apologizing for Stalinism, he, too [that is, like Edmund Wilson], began to cast about for non-Marxist modes of continuing his assault on the moral credentials of capitalist society. America's entrance into the war against Hitler made this problem particularly difficult for him, but Wilson's overinterpretation of Hemingway seems to have showed him how to solve it. In addition to shoveling much more war-victim material into 'Big Two-Hearted River' than Wilson had done, Cowley's introduction to the Viking *Portable Hemingway* (1944) went on to insist that a haunted, hypnagogic quality characterizes all of Hemingway's work." I hadn't read Wilson's essay at the time, but that is a personal note. I wasn't deeply interested in what some other critic, even one I admired, had said about Hemingway's work. I was rereading the work itself and was trying to suggest an underlying quality that helped to give it literary stature.

Lynn almost never discusses literature in its own terms. What he endeavors to find in it are psycho-political motives to excoriate. Why was it that the introduction to the *Portable Hemingway* "slew the minds of so many critics"? That general disaster came about, he says, because my discussion of Hemingway's wound appealed to the anti-American prejudice of intellectuals who automatically identified themselves with powerlessness. After the triumph of American power in World War II, that prejudice "became more virulent than ever before, and anti-American interpretations of American literature sprang up like poisonous weeds."

That is a pretty broad, vehement indictment and I shall come back to it later. But first I should like to consider Lynn's notion that "Big Two-Hearted River" has nothing at all to do with Hemingway's wound in Italy. Much of his case against me, and against American critics in general, depends on this one story, and there is substantive evidence about Hemingway's frame of mind when writing it.

Lynn takes for granted that such evidence, if it exists, can be found in the big volume of *Selected Letters* edited by Carlos Baker. He doesn't pause to consider that the letters in the book, nearly 600 of them, are *selected* from thousands of others. Baker was conscientious in the task of selection, but there is always the possibility that some letters he had to omit for one reason or another might cast a different light on various questions, including the consequences of Hemingway's wound. That happens to be one of many topics discussed with candor in his 43 long letters to me, some of which go deeply into his state of mind. Only two of those letters, not crucial ones, are printed in Baker's book.

The correspondence with me had begun with two letters that mentioned the Viking *Portable Hemingway*. In the first he reported that some GI's in Buck Lanham's regiment, then fighting in Hürtgen Forest, had read the book, which he still hadn't seen. They had teased him about being a haunted nocturnal writer and Hemingway had answered, "Well I'll be a haunted nocturnal son of a bitch." The second letter, this one included in Baker's selection, was written from Cuba in the fall of 1945. The first words are, "It was awfully good to hear from you [my letter has disappeared]. A few days after [ward] I got the book and liked the introduction very much. See what you mean about the nocturnal thing now."

In 1947 *Life* magazine asked me to write a full-scale profile of Hemingway. After some hesitation and an exchange of letters with the author, I undertook the project, which excited

American Writing 1840-1980

me; also it promised a visit to Cuba by myself and my little family. Hemingway had given his approval and letters became more frequent. I was finding that the profile was hard to put together, dealing as it did with a complicated person who had led many lives. I asked questions and Hemingway answered most of them, with candor; he liked to make confessions at night and was eager to have a confidant in the literary world. Our correspondence continued for some years after the pro-file—cut down by me from a much longer version—had appeared in the 10 January 1949 issue of *Life*. Arguments appeared in the letters, chiefly concerning the manuscripts of two books about Hemingway that had been sent to me by their prospective publishers; Ernest didn't like the suggestions I had made for improving them. I began to feel that the correspondence was taking too much out of me, since I had other pressing work. Late in 1952 I received a long, warm letter from Ernest and decided that it was a good point at which to stop. But we remained friends, if now distant ones, to the end of his life.

I treasured the correspondence in a thick folder, safe in my filing cabinet. The folder was shown to nobody, with a single exception. On one occasion I brought it out for Henry W. Wenning, a rare-book dealer in whom I had confidence, after telling him that I had no intention of selling it. Nevertheless, he described the folder to a wealthy collector in Hartford for whom he was acting as agent. The collector made me an offer of $15,000 for its contents, sight unseen. A condition of the sale was to be that I shouldn't copy the letters before letting them go.

The offer was tempting to a not-prosperous writer, even though accepting it would be against my standards of literary conduct. I consulted by mail with my friend Mary Hemingway, the author's widow and executor, and she consented to the sale. Wenning carried off the folder in April 1965, though first I had silently broken the agreement by copying one letter (25 August 1948) that seemed to me especially revealing. The story might have ended there, but it had a sequel. In 1977 the Hemingway-Cowley correspondence was put up for auction by Sotheby Parke Bernet (without my prior knowledge). A catalogue for that year devotes five double-columned pages to the collection. Two descriptive paragraphs read as follows:

Throughout this complete file of his correspondence to Cowley (a friend whom Hemingway refers to in one letter as the "critic who best understands my work"), Hemingway talks of his own writing in detail, gives revealing biographical information about himself (on subjects ranging from his difficult relationship with his parents to his controversial activities in World War II), and discusses literature and other writers (with lengthy critical passages on Faulkner and Fitzgerald in particular). At the time Cowley was doing several pieces of writing on Hemingway [no, only one] and many of the letters are in answer to specific questions.

This series of letters is so extensive (one 5-page letter running to 3000 words) and consistently of such high interest, that it is impossible to but suggest the remarkable quality of the contents.

The catalogue goes on to quote substantial passages from several letters. I didn't see it until long afterward, and of course I hadn't been present at the table. What I heard was that there had been competitive bidding and that the collection had gone to Maurice F. Neville, a Santa Barbara collector. His bid was $32,500. For me at the time that was water over the dam.

I now wish that the entire collection could appear in a book that would include my twenty-five surviving letters to Hemingway, printed from their carbon copies. (I didn't make carbons of the earlier letters, most of which have disappeared.) Such a book, besides telling a story that is of interest in itself, would cast new light on aspects of Hemingway's character and episodes in his career. Carlos Baker's big life of Hemingway is an admirable work, as complete as he could make it, but there are questions it leaves only partly answered, including the new ones raised by Kenneth Lynn. On several of those questions my correspondence with Ernest would provide definite evidence.

I couldn't reproduce any of the letters here except after delicate negotiations. Their present owner might reasonably feel that printing them would lessen their market value. Also there is the lawyer for the Hemingway estate, whose consent would have to be obtained and who keeps diligent guard against infringements. But in one of my notebooks is the revealing letter I copied, and this can be summarized. In the Sotheby 1977 catalogue are those extracts, including one from the same letter, and these, by being printed, have lost their so-called "natural copyright."

As for the letter, it was written at five o'clock in the morning of 25 August 1948, when the first light was showing. Ernest had just been rereading my introduction to what he called "the Portable, or potable, Hemingstein"; for him this was part of a refresher course and was also a pleasure. Since I was having a bad time writing another piece about him, he thought he would tell me a few things that were really true, things he had learned in the Royal Air Force to call "the true gen." (He had explained in an earlier letter, one of the two printed by Baker, that "The gen if RAF slang for intelligence, the hand out at the briefing. The true gen is what they know but don't tell you.") Now he was giving me the true gen as he saw it at five in the morning, the hour when he made the decisions that he would fight on.

The next paragraph of the letter is one of the excerpts printed in the Sotheby catalogue. This gives the wrong date for it, 19 August instead of 25 August, but otherwise I copy it faithfully:

> In the first war, I now see, I was hurt very badly; in the body, mind and spirit and also morally. . . . The true gen is I was hurt bad all the way through and I was really spooked at the end. Big Two-Hearted River is a story about a man who is home from the war. But the war is not mentioned. When I got off the train for the strip at Seney, which is a sort of whistle stop, I can remember the brakeman saying to the engineer, "Hold her up. There's a cripple and he needs time to get his stuff down." I had never thought of myself as a cripple. But since I heard I was I stopped being one that day and from then on I got my stuff down fast and asking favors from nobody. But I was still hurt very badly in that story.

That one paragraph demolishes Lynn's misreading of "Big Two-Hearted River" and with it the factual basis of his attack on American critics. If he should wish for additional evidence, easily available, he might turn to *A Moveable Feast* and read the passage (page 76) in which Hemingway tells how he wrote the story. It was at a café table in the Closerie des Lilas. "When I stopped writing," he says, "I did not want to leave the river where I could see the trout in the pool, its surface pushing and swelling smooth against the resistance of the log-driven piles of the bridge. The story was about coming back from the war but there was no mention of the war in it." The war and the wound, too, were present notwithstanding. In an earlier book, *Death in the Afternoon,* Hemingway had said, "If a writer of prose knows enough about what he is writing about he may omit things that he knows and the reader, if the writer is writing truly enough, will have a feeling of those things as clearly as though the writer had stated them. The dignity of an ice-berg is due to only one-eighth of it being above water." After rereading "Big Two-Hearted River" in connection with his other stories, I had sound reasons for feeling that the wound in Italy was the submerged seven-eighths.

The experience of being blown up at night had been a trauma—though Hemingway never used the word—and for a long time it had kept him from sleeping at night. His fishing trip had marked a stage in his recovery, but not a final stage, since he continued to be engaged in a struggle againt the fear of sudden death. A paradoxical result of the struggle was that he kept marching ahead into new dangers, as if proving to others—but chiefly, I think, to himself—that he was, after all, a brave man. Meanwhile, he kept telling the truth, or part of it, to his Corona Portable No. 3, which he called his psychoanalyst. The rest of the truth is that he was actually braver than those others who hadn't his lively imagination and had never felt the soul or something go out of their bodies.

That letter of 25 August 1948 goes on to describe some further stages in the battle against fear, his private war. He hadn't been afraid of big animals in Africa, it says, because they didn't carry guns. In Spain he had learned to fear only actual immediate danger: nothing in the future. The next step in his education was one that hasn't been recorded except in that single letter. It took place in China, 1941, during a thunderstorm, when his plane had to circle for a long time inside a range of steep hills; the ground was invisible. When the plane landed at last, and safely, Hemingway must have felt that a spell had been woven to protect him.

Later, when he was cruising in a heavily armed Q-boat off the north coast of Cuba, he and all his crew had believed that if they encountered a submarine they would all be killed, but first they would have destroyed the submarine. They were completely happy, the letter says, believing as they did that the adventure was worthwhile. In France with his guerrilla band, then later in Hürtgen Forest, he had been very little spooked—and he goes on to celebrate the joy of fighting for the first time in one's own language. He concludes by saying that everything in the letter is the True Gen.

He must have embroidered it at points, as always, but he was clearly trying to be honest about his long struggle with fear. This, as I said, had been reflected in much of his work and it had ended in victory, or so he felt in the summer of 1948. He would, however, return to the theme on one later occasion. Colonel Richard Cantwell, the last of his avatars (having been created later than Thomas Hudson of *Islands in the Stream*), finds the exact spot on the west bank of the River Piave where he had suffered his first wound. There he performs a private rite of defecation that closes out the experience. The rite is described in *Across the River* (1951), written more than thirty years after Hemingway himself was wounded.

So there is abundant evidence for the truth of what I wrote in the introduction to *The Portable Hemingway*. But had I any hidden political motives for writing it? Lynn makes that accusation, and at length, and it seems to me obstinately ill-informed.

I was writing early in 1944, before the Normandy landing, when the war against Hitler still hung in the balance. Two years before that time I had definitely withdrawn from political arguments, in which I felt out of place and out of character. If I was left with a political purpose, it was one I shared with most Americans, namely, to strengthen our country and win the war as soon as possible. On the literary front, to which my work was confined, I could put forward the real achievements of American writers, dead and living. It was not a time to assault "the moral credentials of capitalist society."

In the unlikely case that I had wished to assault them, Hemingway's wound in the First World War was the weakest possible occasion. It was not the bitter fruit of American or European capitalism. Hemingway had chosen to expose himself beyond the call of duty, as I could judge from my volunteer service in an outfit that greatly resembled his. "Volunteer" is a key word in his case. During the early spring of 1918 he was a cub reporter on *The Kansas City Star,* one who felt ashamed of not being in uniform. He had learned that he would probably be rejected by the armed forces because of defective vision in one eye. He had also learned that the American Red Cross was enrolling young men to drive ambulances and that it was willing to overlook minor physical defects. He volunteered for that service eagerly and was sent to the Italian front. "He seemed always to want to be where the action was," said his assistant city editor. His sector of the front was quiet at the time, which was the first two weeks of June, and he decided that there wasn't much action or danger in driving an ambulance. So he volunteered again, this time to distribute chocolate, cigarettes, and postcards to soldiers just behind the front lines. He wasn't supposed to endanger himself. There was no military reason, none whatever, for his presence in a frontline trench on the night of 8–9 July. He had joyously sought out the wound and would later be proud of it (though deeply shaken). He was in fact the first American volunteer to be wounded in Italy, and there would not be many others.

The wound was in many ways a personal disaster for Hemingway, but my introduction to the *Portable* implied that it was a literary blessing. (Elsewhere I broadened the statement to include many Americans of his age group who had served in World War I. The future writers among them had profited by the experience, unlike the English, the French, and the Germans, who had served much longer.) It was the wound, I thought, that gave much of the depth to his fiction, besides the "haunted" quality that I admired. Unwounded, completely happy men and women are seldom the best writers. If American society, in spite of every appearance, was somehow culpable in his case, a critic of literature is tempted to exclaim, with the authors of the Missal, *O felix culpa!*

The critic might continue the quotation, but now with an embarrassed stammer, "O happy fault, which has deserved to have such and so mighty a Redeemer." Hemingway did a great deal for American literature, but he was not a redeemer, even uncapitalized. As a young writer he was, if possible, more self-centered than the others and more bitterly competitive. His ambition was not merely to outdo his coevals, all of them, but to win a place among the giants of fiction: Mr. Maupassant, Mr. Turgenev, Mr. Stendhal he called them, as they stepped one after the other into an imaginary boxing ring. If he achieved that ambition in his limited fashion (and with many qualifications), his success was in part (and again with many qualifications when speaking of that complicated man) a fortunate consequence of his wound. Such was my conjecture at the time, and after forty years of accumulated evidence I can see no reason for changing it.

Since my political reasons for writing about the wound are under attack, it is time for me to break a self-imposed political silence and state my position bluntly. I am a Little American. I am and have always been a patriotic native of some American neighborhood: at first it was Blacklick Township in Cambria County, Pennsylvania, then later—and for fifty years— it has been Sherman, Connecticut (present population about 2300, which I think is too many). There were intervening years in Pittsburgh, in Cambridge, Massachusetts, in Paris, and in Manhattan, but as a country boy I have never felt quite at home in cities. The United States as a whole is quite simply my own nation. It is also one nation among others, with very great comparative virtues and with faults, too, which I should be dishonest and disloyal if I tried to conceal. Many of them are my own faults. Some of the broader ones can be remedied; indeed, they must be remedied if we are to survive as a nation. Other faults are among the irreparable defects of human societies.

I have never dreamed of spending my life in any other country (except France long ago, and China in the days when it was being invaded). I like and love America, but not in any abstract fashion, having learned to distrust abstractions. I like the people, or most of them, I like the landscapes when they aren't defaced, and I feel at home in almost any of the small communities in which Americans flock together. I like the sense of living securely on my seven acres of American soil (at least until the state decides to license a pipeline or build another superhighway). At the same time I like the feeling of being footloose that most of us enjoy: we are citizens free to try our luck elsewhere and let our tongues wag in abuse of the administration. I speak the American language. I like and love the American literature of this century, even while feeling that its past is still in process of creation, not to mention its future.

I don't like everything about us and, in particular, I detest superhighways, shopping malls, Standard Metropolitan Areas, chemical pollution, and international struggles for power. I wish I had a bumper sticker like one of those formerly seen in California: STAMP OUT PROGRESS. With the seeping away of earlier idealisms, I have become increasingly conservative (not neoconservative, a term that belongs with the jingo-jargon of the Cold War). Perhaps the America I love best is the country of my boyhood, with open fields to run barefoot in and never a chainlink fence in days of travel over dirt roads. I do not identify the America I love with any political or economic theory, whether it be the Free Market, Business Enterprise, or the Welfare State. Human beings have led tolerable lives under many systems, ranging from tribalism and primitive communism through absolute or limited monarchies and free republics to something approaching anarchism, provided only that people in the mass—and their leaders, too—were reasonably honest, aspired to justice, and felt a sense of loyalty to the earth and their fellow creatures. Let them go their separate ways.

And Soviet Russia (since it always comes into the argument)? It is not a country I ever visited, or strongly wished to visit even in the days when I regarded myself as a Marxist. Later the mere notion of living in Russia was one that filled me with horror. In historical terms the USSR now seems the greatest of failed experiments, since it had tried to effectuate the grandest of social theories. But was that social failure inevitable, given the nature of the theory, or was it partly the result of Stalin's character as a leader? That question is still being argued by historians, and meanwhile Russia has achieved a military strength that makes it one of the two great powers. It is still not a threat to Americans in their daily lives unless we choose to make it so. If we insist on living with the Russians in mortal rivalry, we run the risk of becoming like Russia in many respects, just as fascism and communism ended by copying each other. They were obeying an ancient law of social dynamics, namely, that polar opposites tend to assume the same structures. As a Little American I hate the notion of a world divided into spheres of influence by two

430 / American Writing 1840–1980

superpowers. Sometimes I have a nightmare in which the US and the USSR loom up as giants locked in a deadly contest. The aim of the contest is to see which will be first and do most to destroy this pleasant earth—and Blacklick Township, and Sherman, Connecticut.

Kenneth S. Lynn is not a Little American. On the literary front he has been making himself a spokesman for the neo-conservatives, the hard liners, the jingoes, as I would call them, who believe that the central reality of the contemporary world is a struggle for supremacy between American capitalism and Russian communism. They think in abstractions. For them America is not people, or landscapes and cityscapes, or human neighborhoods; it is a system based on business enterprise and the free market. That notion applied to literature gives them a simplified standard of judgment. Any piece of writing is "good," they seem to say, if it strengthens American self-confidence and American power. Everything else is malevolent or puerile.

From this standpoint Lynn has every right—so long as he bears the facts in mind—to attack my position as being moralistic, old-fashioned, lacking in realism, and—to use a word I detest—belletristic. He asserts that my misinterpretation, as he calls it, of "Big Two-Hearted River" helped to corrupt a whole generation of American critics, and he comes close to presenting it as a traitorous episode in a worldwide struggle for power. The critics, he says, were easy to corrupt since they "automatically identified themselves with powerlessness." The result—and I quote his words again—was that "anti-American interpretations of American literature sprang up like poisonous weeds." At this point, when he uses me as a club to beat down American critics in general, his picture of our critical history becomes not only mistaken but preposterous.

Let us look briefly at the facts in the case. Perhaps they will fit together into a picture that is exactly the opposite of his.

When I was in college, 1915–1920, American literature was at one of its low points in critical and scholarly estimation (after a brief period of literary boasting during the 1890's). In academic circles here and abroad it was still a question whether the body of prose and verse produced by Americans truly constituted a national literature or whether it was no more than a provincial branch of English writing. I can't remember that so much as a single course in American literature was offered to Harvard undergraduates. The authors to be emulated by young Americans were Shaw, Wells, and perhaps Compton Mackenzie. But already a group of rebel critics inspired by Van Wyck Brooks had engaged in the search for a "usable past"—usable, that is, as an American tradition and a basis for future writing.

The situation changed after World War I, slowly at first, then more rapidly during the Depression. In 1930 Sinclair Lewis became the first American author to win the Nobel Prize, which had not been awarded to Mark Twain or Henry James; that was a political as well as a literary event. At home a considerable number of younger writers seized upon the dream of helping to create a new America ruled democratically by the working classes, but the dream faded step by step. Other writers, appalled by domestic and foreign dangers, had been delving into the American past as a hidden source of strength in perilous times. Historical novels and plays became widely popular, as witness *Abraham Lincoln in Illinois*. In the critical field Van Wyck Brooks projected his five-volume history of American literary life, which began grandly with *The Flowering of New England* (1936). At Harvard, F. O. Matthiessen was slaving over *The American Renaissance*, which, on its appearance in 1941, would be saluted as ". . . perhaps the most profound work of literary criticism on historical principles by any modern American."

I have been hurrying through a quarter-century of critical and academic history without even mentioning some of the crucial events. The earliest of these was the discovery about 1920 of a great American novel—of course it was *Moby-Dick*—that had gone almost unread for sixty years. Step by step this led to the establishment of Melville scholarship as a campus industry. Another event, one that followed after an interval, was the second coming of Henry James. Courses in American literature were by then being offered in all our colleges, even the smallest and most provincial; it had become the flourishing field of study. A big cooperative venture was the three-volume *Literary History of the United States* (1948). Written and edited over a period of five years by a staff that included four editors, three associates, and forty-eight other contributors (all university men except Carl Sandburg and

H. L. Mencken), it was not only a monumental work but also, in one neglected aspect, a mass demonstration of pride in American writing, as if the fifty-five scholarly contributors had marched down Fifth Avenue behind a brass band.

During those same years, 1943–1948, there was a vast change in the international standing of American writers. Partly it began with the discovery by respected French men of letters—Malraux, Sartre, and Gide, among others—that there was a vital new generation of American novelists. Sartre announced that his own novels were based on fictional methods invented by Dos Passos. In one of his *Imaginary Interviews* (1944), André Gide remembered what the German statesman Rathenau had told him in 1921. "America has no soul," Rathenau had said, "and will not have until it consents to plunge into the abyss of human sin and suffering." Gide praised our new novelists, especially Faulkner and Hemingway, for drawing their readers out of the soulless complacency that Rathenau abhorred. Gide was offering a literary, not a political, judgment, but his words had their effect in the international republic of letters.

His interview praising the new American novelists had been written from exile in Tunis, shortly after the city had been liberated by American forces. Here in the United States a series of victories in Africa and Europe and the Pacific was calling forth a surge of pride in American power, a feeling that affected every field of culture, criticism not excluded. Almost all the intellectuals, even those who had been rebels during the Depression years, were by now reconciled with American society; some had become imperialists in a bumptious fashion. We were witnessing the rebirth of American nationalism, if now on a grander scale. The whole world, so Henry Luce had proclaimed, was entering the American Century.

I too was drawn into the movement, if peripherally and with strong reluctances that tempered my enthusiasm. The reluctances had several causes, one of which was misgiving about the notion of an American Century: wasn't the century big enough to accommodate many countries? At the same time I deeply admired American writing and my enthusiasm, such as it was, for the new movement was based on my conviction that many American authors—indeed, our literature as a whole—had long been misjudged and underappreciated.

In my small way I might do something to raise its standing both at home and abroad. That purpose, I can see today, made me part of the movement in spite of my reluctances. I even helped to supply a component of the movement that had seemed to be missing.

At the end of the war students came flocking into our universities under the GI Bill of Rights. Many of them were eager to study American literature, and by now there were hundreds of scholars trained in the field and eager to teach them. The difficulty was that most of the scholars had specialized in some figure or group of figures from the American past. They knew less about the present, as I found to my dismay at meetings of contributors to *Literary History of the United States*. If our literature was to play its part in that American Century, it had to offer something more than imposing tombs; there had to be living authors worthy of standing beside the great Europeans.

That widely felt need gave an unexpected importance to *The Portable Hemingway* and later still more importance to *The Portable Faulkner* (1946). I had portrayed both authors as representing an American tradition, as weaving American legends, as writing a prose that was rich in symbols, and as plunging into the human depths. By speaking in literary terms, I had helped to make them *teachable* (of course with many collaborators in the task). Soon they were being taught: Faulkner more than Hemingway, as seemed proper, but Hemingway, too, as well as Fitzgerald, Hart Crane, and one or two of their coevals whom I also admired. It would not be long before the actual work of those authors was buried in a snowbank of doctoral dissertations.

During the 1950's and 1960's there was a high tide in American studies and in the world reputation of American literature. It often seems that our culture, instead of moving in one direction, has surged forward and backward in waves of fashion. During those postwar decades the wave of literary nationalism engulfed our universities and spread to those of Europe, where programs or professorships of American Studies were being established almost everywhere. In England by 1968, American subjects were being taught at all thirty-six of the universities and university schools, with thirty of these offering courses in American literature. The United States hadn't fallen behind. At least two of our recent classics, *The*

Great Gatsby and *A Farewell to Arms,* had reached a quarter-million copies each year in classroom adoptions. I couldn't help being heartened by this very wide academic attention to authors whose work I had cherished for a long time. But still I drew back a little and wasn't the only one to be disturbed by the neglect of other literary and historical fields. Edmund Wilson reported wryly in 1968 that Harvard had six professors occupied with American history, as compared with two in modern European history.

Wilson himself had won distinction as an Americanist, a word he never used. His monumental study of Civil War writers and statesmen, *Patriotic Gore,* had appeared in 1962, but he had then moved on to other branches of study, including Russian literature and Hebrew. In 1968 Kenneth Lynn was preparing to resign as chairman of the Harvard program in American Civilization. I don't think he reflected that the existence of his post, as well as of a later one to which he was named at Johns Hopkins, was due in large part to the efforts of critic-scholars whose opinions he was soon to deride as "poisonous weeds."

Now that the high tide of American Studies has somewhat receded—having been followed by other tides of academic fashion, Black Studies, Women's Studies, and now Computer Science—we can see that it left behind it many solid achievements; not everything was wreckage on the shore. As its greatest achievement, the body of writing produced by Americans has been raised to its proper position among world literatures (and even beyond that position, for a time). The federal government has created endowments for the arts and the humanities; together they come close to serving the function of something we had always lacked, a ministry of culture. Scholarly studies have been published in multitudes and not all of them have been trivial or pedantic; some have greatly added to our national self-knowledge. Among other achievements, a recent undertaking should be celebrated. Beginning in 1982 the American classics are at last being republished in a uniform edition, the Library of America, which consists of handsome and readable volumes not priced beyond our reach. This admirable series is the realization of a project first dreamed of and preached by Edmund Wilson, most prominent of the critics whom Lynn excoriates for being un-American.

All those achievements and others are lasting monuments to the national movement in literature. In my sceptical fashion I have long since drawn apart from the movement to play the part of a simple observer. Still I continue to ponder happily on the complete change in the standing of American literature and in our attitude toward the writing profession that it has helped to produce since the First World War. For me the change began a long time ago, perhaps when I read Scott Fitzgerald's first novel or sat on the hard benches of the Provincetown Playhouse during an early performance of *The Emperor Jones;* I was hearing new voices in our American world. But the change was intensified in my case by rereading Faulkner after 1940 and by reflecting at length on the literary consequences, often distant, of Hemingway's wound.

[1984]

PART THREE

Poetry: Selections from
Blue Juniata: A Life

EDITOR'S NOTE

Much of what Cowley did not express of his life in formal
writing as a memoirist, critic, and literary historian he expressed through his poetry. It could easily have been the other
way around. Cowley made his first writing mark as a poet in
the 'teens and twenties with publications in *The Harvard Advocate*, *The Little Review*, *Poetry*, *The Dial*, *Secession*, and
Broom. It was as a poet that he became known to literary
circles in Paris and New York—circles that included such
diverse members as Paul Valéry and Louis Aragon, Allen
Tate and Hart Crane.

Arguably, Cowley was better known as a poet in America
in the early twenties than either Tate or Crane. He had made
a broad name for himself as a translator of French poetry
and, by 1927, had won a significant prize from *Poetry* magazine, enough to allow him to lay a down payment on a
farmhouse in upstate New York.

But Cowley was terribly shy with his own creative work.
Although his first book publication of poetry, part of an anthology entitled *Eight More Harvard Poets* (1923), gave him
something of a platform, it was not until his friend Hart Crane
helped him both select poems for a book and championed his
cause that Cowley published his first complete book effort:
Blue Juniata (1929). Crane had suggested an order of presentation which Cowley pulled back from in favor of a "more
organic" device: a book that would become an autobiography
in verse.

Tate reviewed the book saying, ". . . as a document of the
first postwar generation it is unique." Cowley's presentation

copy to Crane read: "If it's bad, the sin be on your head."
But it was Cowley's book all the way through. He had shaped
the book's design just as he had created his poetic autobiography. Although he only published one other independent
book of verse (*The Dry Season* with New Directions in 1941,
a book more famous for its reviews than for its content—
Whittaker Chambers had reviewed it in the national affairs
section of *Time* to claim that Cowley was unfit for a government post), Cowley incorporated his second book into collected editions that appeared in both 1968 and 1985, each
bearing the title *Blue Juniata*.

Cowley was right to ignore Crane's suggestions and assume
his own autobiographical form for the book. Crane, at the
time assembling his own *White Buildings*, wanted Cowley to
make a book of poems each of which could stand independently. Such an idea may have worked for Crane, but Cowley's sensibility was, frankly, less subtle. He wanted to write
what he saw both of himself and the world in his poetry. He
wanted it to be a record, not only of his life inspired by muses,
but also of his life as he lived it.

He began quite simply. From the beginning. His best poems
were both lyric and narrative, full of sharp descriptive language that reflected the things he knew most: farmhouses,
troutfishing, hawks screeching. In urban settings, his poetry
reflected the songs in the air: folk songs, popular I'll-be-down-
to-meet-you-in-a-taxi-honey songs. He had spent his time
trying to write like Swinburne, and then like LaForgue, and
even like Tzara, but he found his touchstone in his own experience. He took it as a titling device, *Blue Juniata*, at once
a river in his native state and a "sentimental ballad." "When
I was a boy," Cowley writes, "very old people in our neighborhood still hummed the tune, but they had forgotten the
words except for the first four lines:

> Wild roved an Indian girl,
>   Bright Alfarata,
> Where sweep the waters
>   Of the Blue Juniata."

Cowley's shaping of his ongoing book of poetry was brought
home in the 1968 edition, wherein he divided the book into
seven sections, incorporating *The Dry Season* fully into his
original effort. He wrote header notes which organized and

reflected his movement from western Pennsylvania to New York City, from New York City to Paris, and back again. The 1985 edition incorporated one more section of six poems which reflected his thoughts on old age and amounted to his poetic valedictory. The title also changed. Instead of *Blue Juniata: Collected Poems*, as the 1968 version was called, the 1985 edition became *Blue Juniata: A Life*.

Thus *Blue Juniata* became as oddly an organic book as did Whitman's *Leaves of Grass*; the book grew as the author grew. To be certain, the scope of the effort does not compare with Whitman's. Whitman painted a panorama; Cowley worked on discrete scenes. There are no echoes of political prescription save what the circumstances of Depression-era radicalism generated, no visions of ecstasy greater than what an upbringing in western Pennsylvania farm country could provide. I state the comparison between Cowley and Whitman for emphasis. Cowley's poetic efforts end up bearing even more similarity to those of Conrad Aiken's, the poet whom Cowley felt was one of America's great unacknowledged writers, a poet who put his life in verse with narrative clarity.

Although it's unfortunate that Cowley's critical efforts have eclipsed awareness of his poetry, he remains one of the great minor American poets of the twentieth century. Hemingway maintained that Cowley was a great critic precisely because Cowley had written poetry. To Hemingway, Cowley knew how to talk about writing because he knew how to make words work.

Among this brief selection of twenty-two poems there are a number of enduring quality. Poems such as "The Urn" and "The Long Voyage" only seem to deepen with time. Often, poems echo folk or popular songs of Cowley's youth as is the case with "Blue Juniata," "Variations on a Cosmical Air," or "Three Songs for Leonora," for, as Cowley writes,

> . . . sometimes a familiar music hammers
> like blood against the eardrums, paints a mist
> across the eyes, as if the smell of lilacs,
> moss roses, and the past became a music
> made visible, a monument of air.

More frequently, the poems are elegiac, reflecting a sense of lost simplicity, often tied with the poet's youth. Cowley's adopted sister, Ruth, who died of a childhood disease at age nine, appears in poems such as "The Pyre" and "The Red Wagon," Cowley's chilling version of the ages of man. She even haunts his beautiful elegy of remorse for his mother, "Prayer on All Saints' Day."

Other poems—"Commemorative Bronze," "Tomorrow Morning" (with its evocation, "think back on us," a call to commitment), and "Eight Melons"—reflect the despairing politics of the thirties. "The Dry Season" and "William Wilson," which echoes Poe's famous doppelgänger, are painful self-estimations at mid-career, while "Château de Soupir: 1917" remains as evocative a poem of World War One's diremption of an old order as has been written by an American.

There are pieces, too, that reflect Cowley's literary contacts. His "Ezra Pound at the Hôtel Jacob" is a fine miniature, while "The Flower and the Leaf" seems to create a Christless lost-generation last supper around a table at John Squarcialupi's Greenwich Village restaurant. "I knew them all," Cowley says. Variously presented are John Dos Passos, Matthew Josephson, Allen Tate, F. Scott Fitzgerald, Hart Crane, and Ernest Hemingway, among others.

Cowley's poetry is nothing if not direct, a depiction of his ability to chronicle his world. "I am a witness only," Cowley says in "The Log in the Current," one of his last poems. His final poem, "Horse Out to Pasture," is a far cry from earlier optimism. In it, he is already moving on.

The poems here presented are each dated not at time of composition, but at time of publication. I've tried to keep the sequence Cowley established in the last edition of *Blue Juniata* (1985). There's only one poem I regret not including, and its absence, due to space restrictions, compels my quoting its close. It's a Whitman-like piece written in 1968 during Cowley's sojourn in Mexico where he wrote many of his fine later poems. Cowley's friend Allen Tate suggested the Whitman-like title, "Here with the Long Grass Rippling." In part it's an antiwar poem of the Vietnam era. It ends with the humility of prayer:

I pray for this:
to walk as humbly on the earth as my father and mother did;
to greatly love a few;
to love the earth, to be sparing of what it yields,

and not to leave it poorer for my long presence;
to speak some words in patterns that will be remembered,
and again the voice be heard to exult or mourn—
all this, and in some corner where nettles grew in the black
    soil,
to plant and hoe a dozen hills of corn.

Boy in Sunlight

The boy having fished alone
down Empfield Run from where it started on stony ground,
in oak and chestnut timber,
then crossed the Nicktown Road into a stand
of bare-trunked beeches ghostly white in the noon twilight—

having reached a place of sunlight
that used to be hemlock woods on the slope of a broad valley,
the woods cut twenty years ago for tanbark
and then burned over, so the great charred trunks
lay crisscross, wreathed in briars, gray in the sunlight,
black in the shadow of saplings grown
scarcely to fishing-pole size: black birch and yellow birch,
black cherry and fire cherry—

having caught four little trout that float, white bellies up,
in a lard bucket half-full of lukewarm water—
having unwrapped a sweat-damp cloth from a slab of pone
to eat with dewberries picked from the heavy vines—
now sprawls above the brook on a high stone,
his bare scratched knees in the sun, his fishing pole beside
    him,
not sleeping but dozing awake like a snake on the stone.

Waterskaters dance on the pool beneath the stone.
A bullfrog goes silently back to his post among the weeds.
A dragonfly hovers and darts above the water.
The boy does not glance down at them
or up at the hawk now standing still in the pale-blue mountain
    sky,
and yet he feels them, insect, hawk, and sky,
much as he feels warm sandstone under his back,

or smells the punk-dry hemlock wood,
or hears the secret voice of water trickling under stone.

The land absorbs him into itself,
as he absorbs the land, the ravaged woods, the pale sky,
not to be seen, but as a way of seeing;
not to be judged, but as a way of judgment;
not even to remember, but stamped in the bone.
"Mine," screams the hawk, "Mine," hums the dragonfly,
and "Mine," the boy whispers to the empty land
that folds him in, half-animal, half-grown,
still as the sunlight, still as a hawk in the sky,
still and relaxed and watchful as a trout under the stone.

[1968]

Blue Juniata

Farmhouses curl like horns of plenty, hide
scrawny bare shanks against a barn, or crouch
empty in the shadow of a mountain. Here
there is no house at all—

only the bones of a house,
lilacs growing beside them,
roses in clumps between them,
honeysuckle over;
a gap for a door, a chimney
mud-chinked, an immense fireplace,
the skeleton of a pine,

and gandy dancers working on the rails
that run not thirty yards from the once door.

I heard a gandy dancer playing on a jew's harp
Where is now that merry party I remember long ago?
Nelly was a lady . . . twice . . . *Old Black Joe,*
as if he laid his right hand on my shoulder,
saying, "Your father lived here long ago,

your father's father built the house, lies buried
under the pine—"
                    Sing *Nelly was a lady*
. . . *Blue Juniata . . . Old Black Joe:*

for sometimes a familiar music hammers
like blood against the eardrums, paints a mist
across the eyes, as if the smells of lilacs,
moss roses, and the past became a music
made visible, a monument of air.

                                                    [1926]

The Chestnut Woods

While nobody's million eyes are blinking, come!

    It is too late now.

Come far, and find a place where orchard grass,
blue grass and fescue, white and yellow clover
tangle an orchard slope, and juneberries
ripen and fall at the edge of the deep woods.

    Highways and areaways,
    eyes, numbers, unremembered days;
    it is too late now.

Since unremembered days the ferns have grown
knee deep, and moss under the chestnut trees
hiding the footprints of small deer. You ran
and I ran after, till we reached the spring
that flows from underneath the chestnut roots
in a bright stream, we traced it through the laurel,
crossing burned ground where briars clawed us back,
then headlong crashing down a hill to find—

    and lose again and now it is too late.
    We have lived a long time under sheet-iron skies

in neon-haggard dreams where no moons rise;
the juneberries will be withered on the branches;
the chestnut woods are dead.

[1923]

The Pyre

Strangers were buying the house,
"Our summer home," his mother called it,
but always it was their real home.
Now everything in it had to be sold—

the barrels and trunks in the attic,
the stone crocks in the cellar,
the treasures in his mother's china closet
and the closet too, with one cracked side;
the bearskin rug with big jaws that scared his little sister,
the blackberry preserve that his mother had ranged in jars on
     the pantry shelves,
and the bed where she died.

Everything had to be sold,
but it wouldn't be fair to take the first offer;
that wouldn't be playing the game.
"Yes, Mrs. Powers, I was born in this room.
I had my first bath in that big china washbowl
there, with the blue flowers.
No, I don't think a quarter would be enough.
Fifty cents, with all the memories thrown in
and a cake of soap, Mrs. Powers."

Everything had to be sold at a fair price.
It was his duty to joke and wheedle,
to say, "Mrs. Altemus, I know you want only the best,"
or even, to Milt Bracken who was ailing,
and the beds were hard to sell,
"That was my mother's bed, with two good mattresses,
Milt, you can sleep there well."

It was what they expected,
and they were his own hard-worked, hard-minded people,
shapes of his childhood, patterns of his growth.

He would play the part they wanted him to play,
while feeling it was sin and penance both,
torture and solace both.

And still,
one thing he would not sell:
a little dropleaf desk in the upstairs hall
that belonged to his sister Ruth, dead long ago
when he was away at school.
Here in the desk he found her pencil box,
a doll with one squint eye and frizzly hair,
a set of building blocks,
and a red satin ribbon, the last she wore:
tokens of Ruth that his mother had saved.
It was no use saving them any more.

Two girls in pigtails came giggling up the stairs.
He didn't know their names,
but one of them was nine, Ruth's age, and he gave her the
    desk,
then gave the building blocks to her little sister.
Everything else he carried into the yard
and burned, even the frizzly-headed doll,
on a pyre of twenty-year-old newspapers.

The pale flames turned red.
He heard Milt Bracken shouting to his sons
as two of them carried out the bed.

"Ruth," he said, "Ruth,
you have died three times,
once in the flesh, once when your mother died,
and now again with your last treasures.
The black-haired squalling baby I detested,
the child I was sent to wheel in her gocart,
walking behind it shamefaced, yet in pride,
the schoolgirl racing home
to her blocks and her books and her doll with a squint eye—
all these and my own boyhood,
the big frame house under the locust tree,
the land itself, the woods in chestnut season,
the spring plowing, the hayfields in July—

all these and your mother's grief
consumed with the pencil box and the satin hair ribbon,
drifting in smoke into the pale sky."

[1968]

Variations on a Cosmical Air

Love is the flower of a day,
love is a rosebud—anyway,

when we propound its every feature,
we make it sound like horticulture,
and even in our puberty
we drown love in philosophy.

> *But I'm coming around in a taxi, honey,*
> *tomorrow night with a roll of money.*
> *You wanna be ready 'bout ha-past eight.*

As celibates we cerebrate
tonight, we stutter and perplex
our minds with Death and Time and Sex;
we dream of star-sent, heaven-bent
plans for perpetual betterment;
tomorrow morning we shall curse
to find the self-same universe.

> *Frankie and Johnny were lovers—*
> *Lordy, how those two could love!*
> *They swore to be true to each other,*
> *just as true as the stars above.*

The stars above my attic chamber
are old acquaintances of mine
and closer now than I remember;
the moon, a last year's valentine,
coquets with me, though growing fusty;
the Milky Way is pale and dusty.
"Freud is my shepherd, there are no sins,"
whispers the Virgin to the Twins.

> *Even the best of friends must part;*
> *put your money on the dresser before you start.*

Before I start let planets break
and suns turn black before I wake
alone tomorrow in this room;
I want a cosmic sort of broom
to reach the Bear and Sirius even,
annihilate our ancient heaven,
or rearrange in other pairs
those interstellar love affairs,
finding a mate for everyone
and me, and me, before I'm done.

>   *Ashes to ashes and dust to dust,*
>   *stars for love and love for money;*
>   *if the whisky don't get you the cocaine must,*
>   *and I'm coming around in a taxi, honey.*

                                              [1963]

Winter Tenement

When everything but love was spent
we climbed five flights above the street
and wintered in a tenement.
It had no bathroom and no heat
except a coal fire in the grate
that we kept burning night and day
until the fire went out in May.

There in a morning ritual,
clasping our chilblained hands, we joked
about the cobwebs on the wall,
the toilet in the public hall,
    the fire that always smoked.
We shivered as we breakfasted,
then to get warm went back to bed.

In the black snows of February
that rickety bed an arm's-length wide
became our daylong sanctuary,
our Garden of Eden, till we spied
one spring morning at our bedside,

          resting on his dull sword,
the rancorous angel of the bored.

"We raised this cockroach shrine to love,"
I said; "here let his coffin lie.
Get up, put coffee on the stove
to drink in memory of love,
then take the uptown train, while I
sit here alone to speculate
and poke the ashes in the grate."

[1966]

Château de Soupir: 1917

Jean tells me that the Senator
came here to see his mistresses.
With a commotion at the door
the servants ushered him, Jean says,
through velvets and mahoganies
to where the odalisque was set,
the queen pro tempore, Yvette.

An eighteenth-century château
remodeled to his Lydian taste,
painted and gilt fortissimo:
the Germans, grown sardonical,
had used a bust of Cicero
as shield for a machine-gun nest
at one end of the banquet hall.

The trenches run diagonally
across the gardens and the lawns,
and jagged wire from tree to tree.
The lake is desolate of swans.
In tortured immobility
the deities of stone or bronze
abide each new catastrophe.

Phantasmagorical at nights,
yellow and white and amethyst,
the star-shells flare, the Verey lights

hiss upward, brighten, and persist
until a tidal wave of mist
rolls over us and makes us seem
the drowned creatures of a dream,

ghosts among earlier ghosts. Yvette,
the tight skirt raised above her knees,
beckons her lover *en fillette,*
then nymphlike flits among the trees,
while he, beard streaming in the breeze,
pants after her, a portly satyr,
his goat feet shod in patent leather.

The mist creeps riverward. A fox
barks underneath a blasted tree.
An enemy machine gun mocks
this ante-bellum coquetry
and then falls silent, while a bronze
Silenus, patron of these lawns,
lies riddled like a pepper box.

[1922]

Ezra Pound at the Hôtel Jacob

Condemned to a red-plush room
    in a middle-class hotel
        in the decay of summer,

here prowls the polylingual,
    refractory, irrepressible
        archenemy of convention—

red fox-muzzle beard, red dressing gown—
    and growls at his guest while affably
        scratching himself.

"London," he ruminates, "New York,
    can't thinkably live in 'em.
        Provence might do.

"When I was in villeggiatura . . ."

The afternoon droops like a hot candle.
Sweat beads on spectacles
slither like melted tallow.

Only, from the couch where he sprawls back,
indomitable that obelisk of beard
admonishes the heavens.

[1922]

Three Songs for Leonora

[*And for Peggy Baird*]

1. Circus in Town

Allaga*zam*,
the princess with bobbed hair who rides
the rump of the bay mare.
Allagazam, the gilded charioteers,
the pink hyena, and also a little girl
making water behind the lilac bushes.

Allagazam,
the princess said and opened
her arms. Her eyes said, "Take me."
But I am in love, Madame,
with three eccentric dancers.
The steam calliope
played Annie Laurie.

Allagazam,
Allallagazam,
see the fat lady,
see the bearded lady,
see the lady with two heads,
only twenty-five cents,
only the fourth part
of allagazam.

allagazam. Either our world
outmeasures us or we have grown

too epical for the day.
Who is your tailor?
What is the time, Mr. Cowley,
by last year's calendar?

2. *Dumbwaiter Song*

Leonora, I have rented an apartment,
bath, kitchenette, electric, telephone.
Come hang your best pajamas in the closet,
Leonora, I am lording there alone.

I will show you in an album, Leonora,
my relatives departed long ago,
also a genuine oleograph of Jesus
blessing communion bread by radio.

In the morning I will make you toast and coffee,
Leonora, I will do the shopping later.
I will bring you back asparagus in a taxi,
    my heart on the dumbwaiter.

Leonora O'Mara, my bowels yearn after you.
I will carry you my kidneys in a toaster,
    my brains in a chafing dish,
    my hand on a wicker tray,
Leonora la mina, O nora malina.
But Leonora wailed and went away.

3. *Tennessee Blues*

I met her in Chicago and she was married.
    Dance all day,
leave your man, Sweet Mamma, and come away;
manicured smiles and kisses, to dance all day, all day.
    How it was sad.
Please, Mr. Orchestra, play us another tune.

My daddy went and left me and left the cupboard bare.
Who will pay the butcher bill now Daddy isn't there?
    Shuffle your feet.
Found another daddy and he taught me not to care,
    and how to care.

Found another daddy that I'll follow anywhere.
    Shuffle your feet, dance,

dance among the tables, dance across the floor,
slip your arm around me, we'll go dancing out the door,
Sweet Mamma, anywhere, through any door.
Wherever the banjos play is Tennessee.

[1927]

Commemorative Bronze
1928

EVERY MAN HIS OWN ROBESPIERRE ** IT WAS THE
FIRST DAY OF THE YEAR ONE ** LEGISLATIVE POWER
HAD BEEN SEIZED BY ACTORS EQUITY ** JUDICIARY
POWER BY THE ADVERTISING MENS POST OF THE AMERI-
CAN LEGION ** WHICH BECAME A COMMITTEE OF PUBLIC
SAFETY ** DEATH TO THE WOWSERS DEATH ** THE
MAYOR DIED UNDER THE WHEELS OF THE LEXINGTON
AVENUE EXPRESS ** THE POLICE WERE JAILED TO THE
LAST MAN ** THE COMMISSIONER OF THE PORT WAS
DROWNED ** POETS WERE HANGED IN CLUSTERS FROM
THE LAMPPOSTS ** UNDER THE SMALL BRIGHT LEMON
COLORED STARS ** ALL AVENUES DURING THE EXECU-
TIONS ** WERE LUMINOUS WITH RED ORANGE YELLOW
GREEN BLUE INDIGO AND DAYLIGHT BULBS ** FURNISHED
BY COURTESY OF THE NEW YORK EDISON COMPANY **
BROADWAY WAS CLOSED TO TRAFFIC ** THERE WERE
JAZZ BANDS AT THE CORNERS OF EVEN NUMBERED
STREETS ** OFTEN WE DANCED NAKED AT THE BURNING
OF A CHURCH ** UNDER CRIMSON SKIES ** IN THE
GUTTERS THAT OVERFLOWED ** WITH URINE ** BLOOD
** AND WINE

[1928]

The Flower in the Sea

[For Hart Crane]

Jesus I saw, crossing Times Square
with John the Beloved, and they bade me stop;
my hand touched theirs.

Visions from the belly of a bottle.

The sea, white, white,
the flower in the sea,
the white fire glowing in the flower;
and sea and fire and flower one,
the world is one, falsehood and truth
one, morning and midnight, flesh and vision
one.

I fled along the boulevards of night
interminably and One pursued
—my bruised arms in His arms nursed,
my breast against His wounded breast,
my head limp against His shoulder.

[1926]

The Dry Season

I climbed the mountain, to its inmost crags
    I climbed and found no rain,
only the steady dry southwester there,
beating and bending the sea-green hemlock boughs.

    No squirrel sang there,
nor fawn's foot rustled the early-fallen leaves,
nor partridge boasting in the underbrush
    drummed on a log.

    The springs were dry,
the stream bed stony there, its pools half-stagnant,
with snakes beside them dozing and the trout
gasping and dying at the water's brim.

    A man was there
who prayed for rain, who danced for rain, who sang,
aiyee, the lightning splits the skies apart
and rain pours out of them, *aiyee,* the meadow
dances with corn, the mountain sings with rain.

His voice died out
there in the wind, among the sun-bleached stones
    and the sun-dried air.

Sing if you must, old friend, dance if you will;
this month will bring no answer to your prayer.
It is August, the dry season of your life.
Take out your heart and wring it between your hands;
no pain will dart, no blood will drip from it.
    No blood is there.

[1938]

The Long Voyage

Not that the pines were darker there,
nor mid-May dogwood brighter there,
nor swifts more swift in summer air;
    it was my own country,

having its thunderclap of spring,
its long midsummer ripening,
its corn hoar-stiff at harvesting,
    almost like any country,

yet being mine; its face, its speech,
its hills bent low within my reach,
its river birch and upland beech
    were mine, of my own country.

Now the dark waters at the bow
fold back, like earth against the plow;
foam brightens like the dogwood now
    at home, in my own country.

[1941]

Tomorrow Morning

Tomorrow, walking in the dew-bright fields
or singing with your voices pitched above
the blackbird's chuckle, tomorrow when you scheme
to break new records, raise production, then

think back on us. Mechanics of the morning,
you of the blunt hands, the sensitive fingers,
think back on us, remember these dry bones,
earth-yellow, not a word of us in the textbooks
—our graves, even, marked by no white stones.

Think back on us who argued through the night
in a closed and crowded room, our voices low,
and spies who listened through the thin partitions
and traitors in the midst of us. Think back
on us who quarreled there, hating each other
more than the enemy, our cigarettes
burned down to the last half-inch, our faces gray
under the stubble. Then the lights went out.
We heard machine guns tapping yesterday.

Think back on us who poured into the streets
cold in the dawn twilight, peopled with
mechanical voices screeching out their lies
into the mist, and airplanes overhead:
confusion, rumor spreading from the skies.
A corpse was sprawled on the cathedral steps
—ours, for I knew his features in the beam
of a pocket torch. And now their riflemen
came slinking like the creatures of a dream,

crouching in doorways, always nearer. We
must rouse the labor unions, we must warn
the Central Committee. But the wires are down,
the streets are barricaded, the doors bolted
against us in a suddenly hostile town.
Too late to cry for help, too late to scurry
into safe hiding now. Across the broad
dim plaza, from the bull-ring by the river,
rises the rattle of the firing squad.

Think back on us, mechanics of tomorrow,
breakers of records, riders of the spray,
swimmers of air, think back on us who died
at Badajoz, like beasts in the arena,
in Canton, cornered in an alleyway.

Think back on us, the martyrs and the cowards,
the traitors even, swept by the same flood
of passion toward the morning that is yours:

O children born from, nourished with our blood.

[1937]

Eight Melons

August. On the vine eight melons sleeping,
drinking the sunlight, sleeping, while below,
their roots obscurely work in the dark loam;

motionless center of the living garden,
eight belly-shaped, eight woman-colored melons
swelling and feeding the seeds within them. Guns

west of the river at the Frenchman's Bridge;
they are fighting now at the cold river, they
are dying for tomorrow. While the melons

sleep, smile in sleeping, in their bellies hoard
September sweetness, life to outlast the snow.

[1937]

William Wilson

A man there is of fire and straw
consumed with fire, whom first I saw
once at a dance, when nearer and nearer
there swirled a mist, and lights grew dim,
and I came face to face with him
outlined against me in a mirror.

As red as wine, as white as wine,
his face which is not and is mine
and apes my face's pantomime.
    It makes a threatening movement, halts,
and orchestras in perfect time
continue the Blue Danube Waltz.

He makes a movement and retires,
this man of straw and many fires,
Iago doubled with Othello.
    Often I startle up in bed
to find him lying there, my fellow.
    Often I wish that he were dead,
and hack him often, skin and bone,
and dreaming often, hear my own
life's blood drip on the crumpled pillow,

where once, immortal as a stone,
true love lay strangled by Othello.

[1923]

The Flower and the Leaf

All of an age, all heretics,
all rich in promise, but poor in rupees,
I knew them all at twenty-six,
when to a sound of scraping shovels,
emerging from whatever dream,
by night they left their separate hovels
as if with an exultant scream,
stamped off the snow and gathered round
a table at John Squarcialupi's,
happy as jaybirds, loud as puppies.

They were an omnicolored crew,
Midwesterner and Southerner,
New Yorker and New Englander,
immigrant, Brahman, Irish, Jew,
all innocent in their pride because
not one of them had grown a paunch
or lost faith in himself, or was
deformed by any strict belief.
I saw the flower and the leaf,
the fruit, or none, and the bare branch.

This man strains forward in his chair
to argue for his principles,
then stops to wipe his spectacles,

blink like a daylight owl, and shake
his janitor's mop of blue-black hair.
He can outquibble and outcavil,
laugh at himself, then speak once more
with wild illogic for the sake
of logic pure and medieval;
but all that night he will lie awake
to argue with his personal devil.

This man is studiously polite.
Good manners are an armor which
preserves for him an inner hush,
also, I think, a harbor light
that steers young ladies to his bed.
There was no hush that winter night
when flown with Squarcialupi's wine,
he made a funnel, then adopted
the look of a greedy child and said
in a five-beat iambic line,
having flung back his enormous head,
"All contributions gratefully accepted."

And this man, who has spent his day
wrestling with words, to make them mean
impossibly more than words convey,
now pours them out like a machine
for coining metaphors. He stalks
between the tables. His brown eyes
gleam like a leopard's as he talks
with effortless brilliance, then grow smaller
and veiled, the eyes of a caged fox.
Our money counted, dollar by dollar,
we taxi to Small's Paradise,
but Hart storms out to roam the docks
in search of some compliant sailor.

I think of the tangled reasons why
this man should flourish, this one die
obscurely of some minor hurt;
why this one sought his death by sea,
and this one drank himself to death,
and this one, not of our company,

but born on the same day as Hart,
should harvest all the world can give,
then put a gun between his teeth;
or why, among the friends who live,
this one misled by his good heart,
and this forsaken by a wench,
should each crawl off to nurse his grief.
I saw the flower and the leaf,
the fruit, or none, and the bare branch.

The famous and the forgotten dead,
the living, still without a wound,
I see them now at a sudden glance,
the possibly great, the grandly failed,
the doomed to modest eminence,
gathered once more, but not around
that table stained with dago red.
For some inconsequential reason,
I see them now in a hilltop field
on the first day of hunting season
and wonder if, on such a day
of misty, mild October weather,
they would be friend and equal still.
A sound of guns drifts up the hill,
a wind drives off the mist, and they,
brothers again, break bread together,
empty a pocket flask together.

[1968]

The Urn

Wanderers outside the gates, in hollow
landscapes without memory, we carry
each of us an urn of native soil,
of not impalpable dust a double handful,

why kept, how gathered?—was it garden mould
or wood soil fresh with hemlock needles, pine,
and princess pine, this little earth we bore
in secret, blindly, over the frontier?

—a parcel of the soil not wide enough
or firm enough to build a dwelling on
or deep enough to dig a grave, but cool
and sweet enough to sink the nostrils in
and find the smell of home, or in the ears
rumors of home like oceans in a shell.

[1926]

The Red Wagon

Once for his birthday they gave him a red express wagon
with a driver's high seat and a handle that steered.
His mother pulled him around the yard.
"Giddyap," he said, but she laughed and went off
to wash the breakfast dishes.

"I wanta ride too," his sister said,
and he pulled her to the edge of a hill.
"Now, sister, go home and wait for me,
but first give a push to the wagon."

He climbed again to the high seat,
this time grasping the handle-that-steered.
The red wagon rolled slowly down the slope,
then faster as it passed the schoolhouse
and faster as it passed the store,
the road still dropping away.
Oh, it was fun.

But would it ever stop?
Would the road always go downhill?

The red wagon rolled faster.
Now it was in strange country.
It passed a white house he must have dreamed about,
deep woods he had never seen,
a graveyard where, something told him, his sister was
  buried.

Far below
the sun was sinking into a broad plain.

The red wagon rolled faster.
Now he was clutching the seat, not even trying to steer.
Sweat clouded his heavy spectacles.
His white hair streamed in the wind.

[1976]

Log in the Current

He stood alone on the east bank of the great river,
having wandered that day from where his grandmother
    lived.
He was fourteen, he was wearing his first long pants.
It was during his first journey far from home.

The current held and frightened him,
solid, implacable, it moved past,
a mile wide from bank to bank.
Not far from shore a watersoaked log,
worn smooth and more than half submerged,
moved with the stream.

In his grandmother's almost empty house
he dreamed of it that night and other nights.
His world had changed.

In the dream he was the watersoaked log,
but with eyes to see what happened on the shore,
mile after mile, day after day,
also with memories to be interpreted
and a voice even, though one that nobody heard.
Arms he had none.

Years later the dream came back.
The river came back and the log in the current.
"I am a witness only," he muttered on waking,
"a boat without oars, a prisoner for life of the stream."

[1985]

Prayer on All Saints' Day

Mother,
lying there in the old Allegheny Cemetery,
last in the family plot—
I went there on that overcast November day.
I have never gone back.
Graves played no part in our Swedenborgian family,
with my father's trust in celestial reunions
and my oblivious selfishness.
Now after thirty-eight years I go back in spirit,
I kneel at the graveside, I offer my testimony:
this I have done, Mother, with your gift,
this I have failed to do.

Your hope, all that was left, you placed in me:
I should outshine the neighbors' children,
grow up to be admired,
have worldly possessions too.
Those were modest aims you gave me, Mother.
I have achieved them all.

A wife you might have chosen for me,
but I chose her first;
a son to bear my father's name;
an unmortgaged house and a mowed lawn.
The banker squeezes my hand,
the neighbors beam at me, each knowing
I will not wound his self-esteem.
You would have liked that, Mother.
"Oh, Doctor," you might have said,
"we have a good son."

Good, good. There was a time
I called myself a bad son, but a poet.
"My world has deeper colors than yours,"
I boasted, "and the words will come
to match the colors."
Words were like horses loose in the back pasture;
I bridled and saddled them,
rode off with a tight rein at a steady trot,

came back and paid my debts one day,
survived.

Now I am older than you were ever to be,
deaf as a gravestone,
incipient cataracts in both eyes,
weak knees, a faltering walk;
at night lying awake with borborygmus,
by day farting and fiddling among papers.
I have outlived most of my great coevals;
now I write epitaphs for the dead lions.
Does that make me a jackal?

Sometimes lying awake I think of Ora Newton,
an orphan, yellow skinned, always looking half-grown,
who served our family for how many years
and was paid three dollars a week and saved all three.
She loved me in a tolerant, half-resentful fashion.
Once, long after she was married,
she wrote that the mortgage was being foreclosed,
but her little farm might still be saved.
She needed money, but I didn't have it then
and I told her so, if warmly and at length.
She didn't answer my letter.
I don't know when Ora died.
I think of that equivocating letter.
It is what I haven't done that tortures me at night
—rumbles of gas, rumbles of guilt.

Stephen, that just man who helped me often
—we sat together mornings in the smoking car;
he listened, gave sound advice, then turned to his
    crossword puzzle—
Stephen dying of cancer forty miles away;
I went to his house when it was too late.
Is there a circle of thorns around the dying?
a circle of ice around the aged,
ice at the center too?

I can be kind at easier moments.
"Don't be unfair to yourself," I say.

"Don't forget the unpaid days, the uncredited work
for the craft, for brilliant youngsters, for the town,
or the yearlong struggle to make the words come right."
Yes, I remember the good things too.
Trust me to be here, not complaining,
not making excuses, not letting my envy speak,
not ever slipping a knife in the back.
In other things don't trust me too far.

There in the last grave
in that unvisited family plot,
smile up at me through the earth, Mother,
be jubilant for what you achieved in me.
Forgive my absences.

[1978]

Horse Out to Pasture

The old horse tethered to a stake
dreams of galloping free.

There is greener grass in the fencerow
always farther away.

Week after week the tether shortens
and has more knots that nobody untangles.

The grass in his reach is nibbled always closer
with spreading patches of brown clay.

Where are the stablemates that nuzzled him
or rested their heads on his mane?

Those are strangers who give him lumps of sugar
sometimes, then leave him standing there

to dream that the stake will be pulled up,
the tether unloosed one day.

[1985]

PART FOUR

A Brief Selection
of Correspondence
(1917–1961)

EDITOR'S NOTE

As a writer, as a participant in literary culture, Cowley was most relaxed as a correspondent. The time of his letter writing covers about seventy years and the incomplete files of his letters at the Newberry Library in Chicago (which maintains an archive of his work) cover some thirty-two shelf feet. My sampling from those files and elsewhere can hardly be said to be representative. "Sampling" is the operative word.

When Cowley found new and compelling ideas for his writing, for his thoughts about the times, for his criticism of literature, he wrote to friends about them. Most steadily he wrote to Kenneth Burke, his lifelong friend. (That correspondence, provisionally gathered in *The Selected Correspondence of Kenneth Burke and Malcolm Cowley, 1915–1981*, is tangentially reflected here.) Like a naturalist explorer in a distant climate Cowley wrote to Burke of time spent in the camion corps in France during the First World War; or again, during his twenties sojourn near Paris, he wrote to Burke: "I can't imagine people living in Paris. It is a town where one spends weekends which occasionally last a lifetime." Later, when the two were in their sixties, Cowley wrote Burke in assessment of their early literary dreams:

> I had an instinct or impulse or urge or drive, all the words are unsatisfactory, NOT to become a celebrity, but that was partly a conscious decision too. I'd seen too many talents ruined by an early success: what a price they pay for it in this country!

Doubtless Cowley was thinking of Fitzgerald and Hemingway, among many others. Cowley wrote to Hemingway frequently about Fitzgerald during the late forties and early fifties, a time when Cowley was working on Fitzgerald and completing essays on Hemingway. In a 1951 letter (uncollected here), he writes to Hemingway:

> Every time a young professor . . . goes to work on a writer of our generation it seems to me that he doesn't know what it was all about. I've always had a feeling of loyalty to all the writers of our generation. . . . We started out from the same place, even if we had very different experiences since we drove ambulances or camions in that other war that's so far away now. I think that as a generation of writers we have done a good job, one of the best, and if each man has had his individual failings that's something we can talk about among ourselves and let the twerps find out for themselves—but it seems to me that they always pick up the wrong things as failings. They're shouting up Scott Fitzgerald now, but they don't know why he was good, let alone why he was bad. And there's your immense work for them to attack with their poisoned spitballs. . . .

Cowley's disparagement of other critics wasn't limited in time frame, though. He despaired of the fifties New Critics "teeth-grating prose" and during his tenure at *The New Republic* he mentioned often the sadness he felt about the lack of "independent thought."

Though much of Cowley's correspondence from his time at *The New Republic* would make fascinating reading, little of it has survived. Most of it was lost when the magazine's business manager, Dan Mebane, decided in the late thirties that *The New Republic*'s letter files were taking up too much space. They were burned; it was an act Cowley once compared, jokingly but bitterly, to the destruction of the library at Alexandria.

What does survive of Cowley's correspondence are his many efforts on behalf of younger writers like John Cheever and Jack Kerouac. To Cheever he writes: "What is becoming evident in your work is a sort of apocalyptic poetry, as if you were carrying well observed suburban life into some new dimension where everything is a little cockeyed and on the point of being exploded into a mushroom cloud." He writes to Kerouac during the time he was "conspiring," as Cowley put it, with Pascal Covici of Viking to get *On the Road* published: "What your system ought to be is to get the whole thing out in a burst of creative effort, then later go back, put yourself in the reader's place. . . . If you'd do that job of revision too, then most of your things would be published, instead of kicking around publishers' offices for years." (In January 1955 Cowley wrote to Kenneth Burke of Kerouac and William Burroughs: "Kerouac is a natural writer like a natural spitball pitcher but [has] no sense and no control. Burroughs has every manifestation of genius except the genius.")

There are numerous ongoing correspondences such as those with Robert Penn Warren and Edmund Wilson, which are merely touched on here. An important letter to Wilson becomes the basis for an essay, "A Personal Record," reprinted in the first section of this book. Equally significant is Cowley's response to Wilson's cranky letter accusing Cowley of ignorance in politics. Cowley dissents. Others, with Allen Tate and Granville Hicks, are, sadly for lack of space, not reflected at all.

It seems to me useful to include correspondence with people perhaps less well known, as Cowley often wrote about projects, his own self-estimation, or views of literature and the literary trade with candor and ease to individuals who merely asked his assistance. Thus Cowley wrote in 1955 with a self-estimation in response to a query from John G. Cawelti, then finishing a doctoral dissertation: "Writing about an author, I try to understand his life, and I also try hard to understand the actual nature of his achievement. . . . Great is language, but it is great because it is the medium and almost the basis of human society—so that I try never to lose sight of the connection between books and life." He also wrote to Harriet Arnow, a novelist active in the fifties, about the state and condition of editing in American publishing houses, a situation which has not necessarily improved. His letters to Norman Holmes Pearson and to Howard Mumford Jones, scholars at Yale and Harvard, respectively, effectively mark prospects or summations of Cowley's studies of the American literary tradition.

I've also included two reader's reports prepared for Viking to show some semblance of Cowley's work as an editor. One is on Marianne Moore's translation of La Fontaine's *Fables*, the other on Ken Kesey's *One Flew Over the Cuckoo's Nest*, each report written for Pascal Covici, Cowley's colleague at Viking. The report on Moore is fascinating because it both demonstrates Cowley's lifelong concern with the proper translation of French writing and his respect for Moore, a writer he encountered in his first dealings with *The Dial* at the beginning of his career. Moore's translation was eventually published, but not until after a remarkable and lengthy exchange of manuscripts and corrections that remained at all times friendly.

When Cowley taught at Stanford in 1960, one of three teaching sojourns there, he encountered Ken Kesey in his graduate creative writing class. As he reported of Kesey to Pascal Covici in a letter: "He hasn't ever learned how to spell, and didn't even begin reading for pleasure until he was an upperclassman . . . He went to school in Oregon on a football scholarship. . . . Last year Kesey nearly made the Olympic wrestling team—he has a 19-inch neck, like wrestlers. He's married, 1½ children, works in a state loony bin in this vicinity. . . . [his] manuscript might just turn out to be something that would HAVE to be published." The manuscript was *One Flew Over the Cuckoo's Nest*, which, when completed, Cowley took no credit for aiding, but wrote about ebulliently.

Of this brief selection, it is the series of letters to Hemingway that most stand out. In the late forties and early fifties Hemingway, living in Cuba, was well out of the contemporary mainstream of American letters. Cowley wrote him frequently in a sense of comradeship about the contemporary literary situation. Thus his letters to Hemingway allow Cowley to talk of immediate issues with a candor and completeness that Cowley couldn't have shared with any of his other contemporaries. Remarkable in this exchange are Cowley's missives about the "Agnes Smedley affair" at Yaddo and the creeping tide of McCarthyism; Cowley's feelings about the new standards of fiction set by then young writers such as Bellow, Capote, and Trilling; as well as Cowley's estimations of the burgeoning and waning public interest in Fitzgerald and William Faulkner.

Section-Groupe Américaine
TM526 Peloton B
October 9, 1917.

[to Kenneth Burke]
Dear K:

I shall try to write you a letter this evening; a hard job with a crowd at the end of the barracks . . .

. . . Section 133 went up to a little advanced park some 300 meters from the lines, and underwent a severe bombardment, during the course of which one man had his hand shot off, and another was wounded in the body and the leg. A French ambulance section refused to bring back the wounded on account of the shelling, so the section chief got them in his Torok. For this, the first deed approaching heroism in the service, there was a meeting. Also a couple of our French captains received the Legion of Honor . . .

Your letter of the 14–20 September reached me last night. You complained of my indifference to your mental states. It's just part of my indifference to everything. You can't imagine with what a feeling of absolute negation I play cards . . . But I have climbed a little out of the depths. For those weeks I read nothing, wrote not even letters, confined myself, in fact, exclusively to eating, sleeping, rolling, and seven and a half.

In your letter you also asked for local color. I can give you that, and plenty. Zum beispiel, we leave camp at four o'clock on a rainy, windy afternoon, and go to the immense park at [B?] to have our camions loaded. The bearings are loose on the fan, and the steering gear doesn't work well, but then it is much too cold to leave the seat, so we smoke cigarettes and wonder what is going to happen in the night. The trip is for O—another of the depots avancés—some 1,500 meters from the lines.

That night we left the park at six. One of the other camions broke down after a two-kilometer ride, and that caused us a two-hour wait. When we finally climbed the hill above Veste, the night was so black that I was reminded of G. A. Henty and the mythical nights through which his trappers and Indians used to crawl toward Fort George and Fort William. I rode on the dashboard and called out whenever Root ran too near the ditch. Once I didn't call out in time, but we crawled out on first.

After that I had a great poetic emotion and lines kept running through my head like

"The jolly star shells rioted"
and
"And in the valley a river of mist"
or
"While a cold cynical moon looked down"

The cold cynical moon actually crept in at just that point, for in the battle of the cold wind and the cold rain, the cold wind proved the stronger.

How conventionalized the night seems now to me, after reading thousands of war diaries. At S occurred the conventional road shelling, during the course of which Root, who is scary, ran a zigzag down the road, and bumped into the next camion. At our destination we encountered the conventional Franco-American who knew Root's friends in Hartford, Connecticut. We drove home past the conventional mule convoys. The only fresh note about it all, I think, was the barracks when we got home. From the outside these are plain wooden buildings, but inside at night, their shadowy length makes them as mysterious as ancient caves. Side by side a dozen lives—individual lives—go on. Some sleep, some sing, some read, some play cards. After five months of such life, they all become at home in it, so that the requests to shut up or to shade a candle are merely perfunctory. In a way everyone has become a stoic, believing that no one else can harm him. And that night at two as we came in exhausted to drop into bed, one man was just getting up to go on guard while those others were still playing cards.

M.

Giverny par Vernon,
Eure
February 8, 1923.

[to Kenneth Burke]
Dear Kenneth:

Paris is a town I enter with joy and leave without regret: I repeat that experience weekly and have repeated it since November 1917. I can't imagine people living in Paris. It is a town where one spends weekends which occasionally last a lifetime.

My last voyage was spent chiefly with Dadas. The crowd is trying to recreate itself. Tzara, . . . Breton, . . . Aragon, Picabia were assembled together for the first time in eighteen months. They fought but finally decided to stage a joint manifestation. About twenty of us signed a paper. I suppose I am now officially a Dada, although none of them greet me with great warmth except Aragon and Tzara. . . . At the same time I lunch with the hated enemies of the Dada group: Salmon and MacOrlan, and interview in the most fraternal manner the enemies of Salmon, MacOrlan, and the Dada group, like Vildrac and Duhamel. . . . I am being received into the complex life of Paris. To become a true citizen of that fantastic and unlivable city, I should only have to steal the mistress of, let us say, Vitrac, and to hand on Peggy to, let us say, Tzara. I have no wish to be a citizen of Paris.

Dada c'est le jemenfoutisme absolu. It is negation of all motives for writing, such as the Desire for Expression, the Will to Create, the Wish to Aid. A Dada has only one legitimate excuse for writing: because he wants to, because it amuses him. Therefore the movement becomes a series of practical jokes. Dada c'est le seul état d'esprit vraiment logique.

But not entirely logical. A writer who was truly dada would disdain collective action as he would disdain any other attempt to influence the mind of the public. The actual Dadas, on the contrary, try to accomplish things which are sometimes serious. They try to work together.

Their love of literature is surprisingly disinterested. At their memorable meeting it was proposed that none of them should write for any except dada publications during the next three months. No dada publication is widely read or pays. The proposal would have been carried except for the objection of one man out of twenty.

Their commerce is tiring and stimulating. I left Paris with fifty new ideas and hating the groupe dada. They are a form of cocaine and personally take no stimulants except their own company. . . .

Talent. We have as much as they, perhaps more, but less vitality, less courage. Because we write for other aims we achieve less fun out of our writing, which is often equally true of our readers.

They live in Paris. That is my final criticism. They are over-stimulated, living in a perpetual week-end. I like to meet them on weekends. . . .

M.

The New Republic
April 21, 1933.

[to Robert Penn Warren]
Dear Red:

There happens to be a fair chance—it is by no means a certainty—that I'll be able to spend six or eight weeks near Allen in Trenton, Kentucky. He writes me about a marvellous place there where a poverty stricken writer can live for twenty-five berries or seeds per month and finish a book—which is what I crave most in this world. In that case I shall certainly look forward to seeing you, either when you visit Allen or when I drive down to Nashville before the end of my visit. But I won't contribute much fresh blood or hot air to arguments. There is nothing I like better than a good argument—between two other people. I'm going down (A) to work, (x) to fish, (z) to rediscover what golden corn tastes like. That is, I'm going to do all these things if I get away. . . .

As ever,
[Malcolm]

The New Republic
April 1, 1937.

[to Fred B. Millet]*
Dear Mr. Millet:
At present I am interested particularly in one critical problem, that of bringing together esthetic and social criticism. An error made by most of the critics who are politically radical has been to put the two into separate bins. They will say that such and such an author is admirable for his "form" or his "expression," but that his social ideas are deplorable. For my own part, I believe that form and matter can't be separated in this fashion, and that the really good authors are likely to be good from whichever point of view you approach them— whereas many authors whose social ideas are apparently quite virtuous are in reality bad and harmful both to literature and society because they lack any sense of living people. In other words, there must be some unifying principle that comprehends both esthetic and social criticism, and my present interest lies in finding and stating it. But I should also like to get back to writing poetry and get a rest from reviewing books. . . .

Sincerely,
[Malcolm Cowley]

RFD Gaylordsville, Conn.,
October 31, 1938.

[to Edmund Wilson]
Dear Edmund:
I hate letters and would much rather do my explaining or berating face to face—that's why I wrote a couple of months ago that I was anxious to talk things out with you. But once I set out to write a letter, it will have to be a long one. . . .
I agree with you that I ought to get out of politics and

* Probably for an article in *Contemporary American Authors*, of which Millet was editor. [ed.]

back to literature. We ought to all do that—and it's a course I want to urge on you very seriously. I don't lay claim to much political talent. But yours—my God—is a minus quantity, for the simple reason that politics is based on the activities of groups, and you have always congenitally mistrusted and at times completely misunderstood group activities. And when political convictions lead you to accusing me of being bribed or blackmailed by the C[ommunist] P[arty]—well, it's time to stop and think whether the whole business shouldn't be chucked overboard.

Did you read the piece I wrote about "To Have and Have Not" or did you read Margaret Marshall's attack on the piece in "The Nation"? I'm asking because I don't think you'd disagree with most of what I said. The piece began with a general tribute to Hemingway, written because I heard that he thought I had always treated him unfairly, and because I wanted to set the record straight. For God's sake, if I had wanted to praise him for helping the revolution, I'd have done it when he wrote "Green Hills of Africa," because I knew then that he was doing a lot for the revolutionists in both Spain and Cuba. But after this general tribute, I said that "To Have and Have Not" sounded, with all its faults, as if he were about to begin a new career. It's still too early to decide whether I was wrong. He may crack up after all—there are dangerous signs of self-loathing and self-pity in "The Snows of Kilimanjaro," written about the same time. And his new play is only fair. . . .

And one other point, this time about your Marx series. I had the feeling that although the biographical chapters will be very effective in your book, they weren't much good in or for the magazine. You seemed to be trying a good stunt—to bring the discussion of Marx down to earth, to write about him without awe or fireworks, as if he were a great literary figure—but the result in the magazine sounded like a combination of Mehring and Ruhle, with the good points of both but without much added to either. The new piece, the long summary chapter on Marx's ideas, is vastly better because it carries you into new ground. But George has written you about that. Meanwhile your two long essays in Partisan Review—on

Flaubert and James—would have been fine for the N[ew] R[epublic], because we are terribly in need of good literary material. I don't think that any arrangement with the paper will be satisfactory unless you can talk or write to us in advance and tell us what you are planning to do. . . .

Let's actually forget this political stuff, Stalin hiding under your bed and Trotsky in my hair, and talk about books for a change. There are three young poets, no four, who I think are pretty good. One is Winfield Townley Scott, who works on the Providence Journal. One is Howard Nutt of Peoria, Illinois; we're printing some of his stuff. One is Nelson Algren of Chicago, author of a proletarian novel; he is now writing a series of free-verse rhapsodic poems on the destruction of Mayor Kelly's Chicago at twenty minutes to two in the morning. One is an ex-Objectivist named Kenneth Rexroth, of San Francisco; he does very nice pedestrian poems, like translations from the Chinese, on his girl and his boyhood. Be watching out for all of them. The last three are or were on WPA. Another WPAyer named Sterling Brown, a Negro, is also very good, though I think you've heard about him.

I find it harder and harder to read novels. And I still want a chance to talk things out with you.

As ever,
Malcolm

RFD Gaylordsville, Conn.,
November 22, 1944.

[to F. O. Matthiessen]
[After querying Mattheissen about Henry James's letters, and James's last visit to America, Cowley follows with some remarks about W. H. Auden.—ed.]

. . . One idea has been on my mind, about the general subject of literature in the colleges. Why, for God's sake, doesn't some big university give a chair of prosody, or at least a year's professorship of prosody, to W. H. Auden? I know the arguments that would be brought against such a proposal. But the facts are that Auden is one of the few great living poets; that his coming to this country was an important event, like Eliot's going to England; that he is now writing some of his best work, but meanwhile wasting his great talent for teaching on freshman English students at Swarthmore; that he knows more about the forms of English verse, and of verse in general, than anybody else since Saintsbury (and unlike Saintsbury knows how to write them too); that one of his last long poems, the commentary on "The Tempest," is almost a specimen book of verse forms—and that young poets learning to write ought to have the benefit of his knowledge. It's just possible that something might be done at Harvard, if Bob Hillyer is going to be out for another year; I can imagine Auden teaching a course like the one Hillyer was supposed to give, and really effecting a revolution. The educated public in this country is so damned ignorant about the rules and conventions of English verse that it is hard even to write about them. The criticism of verse has no firm foundation because you can't refer to the rules, except at the risk of befuddling your ignorant readers. The poets themselves, in most cases, are so ignorant that they don't even know when they're being conventional, let alone when they're being experimental. Auden with a good course to give, and good students, might change a lot of that. Of course he's Christian, homosexual, and has been seen to blow his nose on his dirty socks—but he keeps his sexual proclivities under cover and is probably trying to change them; he'd buy handkerchiefs if he had a housekeeper, and the real professorial objection to him would probably be his Christianity.

Cordially,
[Malcolm Cowley]

·August 9, 1945.

[to William Faulkner]
Dear Faulkner:

It's gone through, there will be a Viking Portable Faulkner, and it seems a very good piece of news to me. . . . It won't be a very big transaction from the financial point of view. The Viking Portables have only a moderate sale—the Hemingway I edited sold about 30,000 copies [in the first year] and they thought that was extra good. But the reason the book pleases me is that it gives me a chance to present your work as a whole, at a time when every one of your books except "Sanctuary"—and I'm not even sure about that—is out of print. The result should be a better sale for your new books and a bayonet prick in the ass of Random House to reprint the others.

And now comes the big question, what to include in the book. It will be 600 pages, or a shade more than 200,000 words. The introduction won't be hard; it will be based on what I have written already (bearing your comments in mind)—but what about the text?

I have an idea for that, and I don't know what you'll think about it. Instead of trying to collect the "best of Faulkner" in 600 pages, I thought of selecting the short and long stories, and passages from novels that are really separate stories, that form part of your Mississippi series—so that the reader will have a picture of Yocknapatawpha [sic]* county from Indian times down to World War II. That would mean starting with "Red Leaves" or "A Justice" from "These Thirteen"—then on to "Was" for plantation days—then one or two of the chapters from "The Unvanquished" for the Civil War, and maybe "Wash" for Reconstruction—you can see the general idea.

I'd like to include "Spotted Horses" (is there much difference between the magazine version and the chapter in "The Hamlet"?), "The Bear" certainly, "All the Dead Pilots" (that being part of the Sartoris cycle), "That Evening Sun" (anthologized till its bones are picked, like Nancy's in the ditch, but still part of the Compson story), "Old Man (from "The Wild Palms"—it's not Yocknapatawpha, but it's Mississippi), "Delta Autumn" and a lot more.

The big objection to this scheme is that it has nothing from "The Sound and the Fury," which is a unit in itself, and too big a unit for a 600-page book that tries to present your work as a whole; and nothing from "Absalom, Absalom" (except "Wash," a story with the same characters). If I include any complete novel it would have to

* Cowley misspells the word consistently through the letter. [ed.]

be "As I Lay Dying," because it is the shortest of them all; it's not my favorite. But in spite of this objection, I think that a better picture of your work as a whole could be given in this fashion. You know my theory, expressed somewhere in the essay—that you are at your best on two levels, either in long stories that can be written in one burst of energy, like "The Bear" and "Spotted Horses" and "Old Man," or (and) in the Yocknapatawpha cycle as a whole. The advantage of a book on the system I have in mind is that it would give you at both these levels, in the stories and in the big cycle.

I wish I could see you and talk over the whole business. Not as a matter of idle curiosity, but for my guidance, I'd like to know, for example, which pieces in some of your books ("The Hamlet," for instance) were originally written as separate stories and later fitted into the longer novel. I wish you had time to go back over your earlier work and fix up a few factual discrepancies (I called attention to some of them in my NY Times piece . . .). For example, the Indians started out being Choctaws (in "A Justice") and ended up as Chickasaws, which I think is right. (And compare "A Justice" with "The Bear.") But what to hell, those inconsistencies aren't important— the chief thing is that your Mississippi work hangs together beautifully as a whole—as an entire creation there is nothing like it in American literature.

For God's sake, send me an answer to this, because it will soon be time for me to get to work on the book, and I don't want to plan it in a way that would meet with fundamental objections from you.

Did I tell you what Jean-Paul Sartre said about your work? He's a little man with bad teeth, absolutely the best talker I ever met, not the most eloquent but the most understanding. He's the best of the new French dramatists: one of his plays has been running in Paris for more than a year, and he says that his work is based on qualities he learned from American literature. What he said about you was, "Pour les jeunes en France, Faulkner c'est un dieu." Roll that over on your tongue.

Cordially,
Cowley

RFD Gaylordsville, Conn.,
July 24, 1946.

[to Robert Penn Warren]
Dear Red:
  I like very much the idea of a special number of Kenyon
[Review] devoted to Faulkner, and I should like to contribute to it. Unfortunately I find myself in the state of
being written out, practically, about Faulkner. There is
just one point that I had to make and didn't develop in
my series of pieces about him (really one long essay, of
which parts were printed in three magazines, then the
whole thing boiled down for the introduction to the
book). The one point was about Faulkner (and others,
too, but I'd confine myself to him) as a Southern nationalist, and the South itself as a sort of incomplete or
frustrated nation, belonging somewhere in a scale of
more or less realized nations that might include, say,
Scotland, Brittany, Provence, Catalonia, Croatia,
Ukrainia, God knows how many other countries that
aren't shown on most political maps. I sometimes think
that the Southern attitude toward Negroes, which to
Northerners is of something that is fundamentally quite
other. . . . Language is another flag or emblem which
Southerners, in this case, have chosen not to wave, although they would have more justification for doing so
than Norwegians or Croatians or Slovakians, each of
which peoples has *invented* a language, simply by writing
literary works in the dialect of a given district. (With the
Croatians, it was simpler; they simply wrote Serbian in
the Latin instead of the Cyrillic alphabet.) If the South
ever wanted a language, it could choose the popular
speech and pronunciation of some given city—say Montgomery, Alabama—as the standard Southern speech, and
spell it phonetically so that it looked much different from
standard Anglo-American. . . . And what is the other-
ness that these flags are subconsciously intended to represent? I can't quite phrase it, but it is the sense that
certain persons form an independent group with its own
patterns of life; and any gifted poet or novelist, Faulkner more than others, becomes the voice of the group
spirit. . . .

. . . I read your novel* and was enthusiastic. Wrote a letter to Lambert Davis about it, which he wanted to use as a blurb—now he tells me that he lost the letter and won't I do it over again. It's been a little driven out of my mind by a long trip that the Cowley family has just taken, up into French Canada (another frustrated nation), but the gist of my remarks was that one felt from the first page that here was a picture of how things were—that one was held from the first page—that your work as a novelist, always brilliant but sometimes dispersed, had this time come together, taken shape. . . . For your own ear, let me add that the Huey Long figure is more interesting than the hero, that I think the structure does get a little loose beyond the middle of the book (until the drama of the end) through this divided focus; that the women are fine, especially the Governor's wife and Sadie Burke; that all together it's a damned impressive job, the best novel I have read since God knows when. . . .

As ever,
[Malcolm]

June 27, 1947.

[to Mrs. Shiela Cudahy Pellegrini
President, Pellegrini & Cudahy, Publishers]
Dear Mrs. Pellegrini:
. . . Because of the production problems involved in the American Classics series, I think we ought to go slow for the present.** But I think we ought to bring out one and better two volumes in the spring or summer of 1948 to hold our franchise. One of the volumes, obviously, is a Whitman, because the copyright on Whitman's Deathbed Edition is expiring—actually it expired on May 19

---

* *All the King's Men* [ed.]
** Cowley was acting informally as an advisory editor to Pellegrini & Cudahy. A two-volume set, *The Complete Poetry and Prose of Walt Whitman,* edited by Cowley, was published by the company in 1948. [ed.]

of this year—and if we don't bring out the book somebody else will do a Complete Poetry and Prose in one
volume. I've been working on Whitman all this month.
I don't know what the other book should be, but maybe
a Thoreau Complete would be as good as anything.

I have a lot of new things to say about Whitman—
good Lord, I could write a book about him instead of a
simple essay. I used to hate his poetry for its inflatedness
and catalogues of names and damp, sticky quality; he
wrote more bad verse than any other American except
Ella Wheeler Wilcox; but when he was good he was, oh,
so good, so full of fresh sights, sounds, phrases, as if he
had waked at five in the morning in a totally new summer
world. If you remember that he lied about his family—
that actually it was poor, that one brother, a sailor, died
of paresis, that another married a drunken prostitute and
still another was a congenital idiot, then you understand
what he meant when he said in one place that he spoke
for inarticulate generations:

Through me many long dumb voices,
Voices of the interminable generations of prisoners and
     slaves,
Voices of the diseas'd and despairing and of thieves and
     dwarfs,
Voices of cycles of preparation and accretion,
And of the threads that connect the stars, and of wombs
     and of
          the father-stuff,
And of the rights of them the others are down upon,
Of the deform'd, trivial, flat, foolish, despised,
Fog in the air, beetles rolling balls of dung.

There—and elsewhere in his earliest poems—he struck
down to something grand and elemental. "Song of Myself" is his longest poem, and his best, and it's more like
Rimbaud's "A Season in Hell" than like anything written
in America, and it comes before Rimbaud, and is actually
better, and it has always been read by the wrong people.
Whitman has to be taken away from the professors and
the politicians; he's too good a poet to belong to them.

But sometime we can talk more about him; and if it's all right with you I'll go ahead with my introduction.

As ever,
[Malcolm Cowley]

February 3, 1948.

[to Le Baron Barker, Doubleday & Doran]
Dear Lee:

. . . I think I have found the angle from which I can write a short history of American literature without merely summarizing the other historians and without doing what I've found has taken so much time on Hawthorne and Whitman—I mean digging away until I got underneath most of the other historians. The angle is to write about the American legend as created in American literature—Franklin and the legend of the wise citizen, Irving and the Knickerbocker legend, Cooper and the legend of the lonely woodsman, Hawthorne and the legend of the Unpardonable Sin, Whitman and his own legend . . . [Cowley's ellipses] and so on down to Hemingway and the lost generation, Faulkner and the decaying mansion, Wolfe and his legend of man's hunger in his youth— all these myths that have contributed to our picture of man in America. A country without legends is a naked country, and our authors from the beginning set out rather consciously to create the legends that would clothe it; they did the work here that anonymous ballad singers did in the Middle Ages to create the European tradition. . . .

As ever,
[Malcolm Cowley]

RFD Gaylordsville, Conn.,
July 11, 1948.

[to Ernest Hemingway]
Dear Ernest:

. . . For me the problem is to get over the buck fever that I feel so often when sitting down at the typewriter.

Trouble is that I always want to do better work than I'm capable of doing, with the result that often I don't do any work at all. I suspect that a great many serious authors suffer from that same complaint. I hear that Mark Twain had whole trunkfuls of unfinished books, and he wrote easily—comparatively speaking—whereas most of us write hard, and it keeps getting harder all the time. But it has to be done, and without shortcuts. I've known a lot of authors who were psychoanalyzed and cured, both of the complaints they wanted to have cured and also of that other complaint known as good writing. Maybe our faults are all we have to depend on. . . .

As ever,
Malcolm

RFD Gaylordsville, Conn.,
October 21, 1948.

[to Norman Holmes Pearson]
Dear Norman:

I got back from Yaddo yesterday, by way of New York, where Muriel and I attended a small but lavish dinner for Wm Faulkner. . . .

Faulkner, whom I hadn't ever met, is a small man, low forehead, eagle beak, looking somewhat like Poe and, also like Poe, extremely dignified. A wonderful story teller when anyone gives him a chance; but that night everyone else was also talking. He seemed most at ease when the ladies withdrew from the dinner table—it was that kind of dinner—and the gentlemen discoursed over cigars and cognac. I'm going in tomorrow to have lunch with him; he's staying at the Algonquin, he says until October [November?] 1. He didn't say whether he was going to pay you a visit at Yale, but apparently thinks of doing so. Having sold this book to the movies for $50,000, he figures that he won't have to work any more in Hollywood, or at least not for five years.

I was, as you might have guessed, somewhat disappointed in Stewart's Hawthorne.* He's wonderful on facts, as I expected; the only possible error I found was the statement that H had a salary of $1,200 a year at the Salem custom house. My suspicion is that there were perquisites attached to the job, so that his real income in Salem was more than $1,200. He wouldn't have fought so hard to keep a $1,200 job—not Hawthorne, when he had surrendered a $1,200 (Stewart says $1,500 and may be right) job in Boston without a single argument, months before the Whig politicians would have forced him out of it. But the disappointment I felt was in the interpretation, with its tendency to emphasize the ordinary side of Hawthorne and also to miss the crisis in his life in 1835–38, when he had to get out of Salem or, he thought, perish. His Salem solitude was real, and frightened him, and that is the key to what happened afterwards. The chief error made not only by Stewart but by most biographers is that they don't realize that most people change in the course of their lives, that Hawthorne (or Poe) in 1830 is not the same as Hawthorne (or Poe) in 1840—he's the same ship, perhaps, but he's sailing on another tack and toward a different port, with a different cargo. . . .

As ever,
Malcolm

RFD Gaylordsville, Conn.,
December 9, 1948.

[to Kenneth Burke]
Dear Kenneth:

Here I am faced with the problem of writing a piece on Myths in American Literature and the piece refuses to write itself and so I'm thinking aloud in a letter as if I were walking east along Ellsworth Avenue after the library had closed and telling you what I was vaguely planning to do.

Myths, I want to say, are permanent archetypes of

---

* *Nathaniel Hawthorne: A Biography,* by Randall Stewart, a classic in the field. [ed.]

human character and experience. Myths are the wise Ulysses, the dutiful Aeneas (is that the best reading for *pius?*), the courtly Lancelot and—leaping over a few centuries—Daniel Boone in the forest, Huckleberry Finn on the river and Buffalo Bill on the prairies. Myths provide a pattern for our emotions; they are variously shaped windows through which we look at the world.

A country without myths is a country naked of human associations in which we are intruders, not residents. A central concern of American writers from the very beginning has been to create or give a final form to myths that would make this new country our home. Many of them (Irving, Hawthorne, Poe) started by writing ghost stories. They were acting on the sound instinct that a house has to be a little haunted before we can feel at home in it.

In older countries the myths had a basis in folklore; they were repeated time after time at the fireside on winter evenings before they were copied into manuscripts. But this country was the first to be settled by men and women who were, in the majority, literate, so that they worked with printed words from the beginning. Oral traditions have played a great part in our myths, but they were quickly seized upon by professional writers, so that a figure like Paul Bunyan, for example, is one-tenth an invention of the lumbermen and nine-tenths a literary elaboration. Sometimes, yes, often, a figure invented by a man of letters—like Peter Rugg, invented by an obscure New England man of letters named William Austin—has passed into folklore and has been taken from folklore by other professional writers, as a subject for their poems. And when one thinks of the heroes of the American myth, it seems to me that more of them—Leatherstocking, Evangeline, Captain Ahab, Huck Finn, the Connecticut Yankee, Babbitt, Daisy Miller and the Hemingway hero among others—come from literature than come from history (Washington, Boone, Crockett, Lincoln) or from folklore like Mike Fink and Paul Bunyan. Indeed, it is the folklore heroes who have the dust of scholarship. Skipper Ireson (literature) is vivid where Captain Stormalong (folklore) seems academic.

Whitman was writing about the importance of myths in Democratic Vistas. He said, "The central point in any nation, and that whence it is itself really sway'd the most, and when it sways others, is its national literature, especially its archetypal poems. . . . Few are aware how the great literature penetrates all, gives hue to all, shapes, aggregates and individuals, and, after subtle ways, with irresistible power, constructs, sustains, demolishes at will."—"The literature, songs, esthetics, &c., of a country are of importance principally because they furnish the materials and suggestions of personality for the women and men of that country and enforce them in a thousand effective ways."—"All else in the contributions of a nation or age . . . remains crude . . . until vitalized by national, original archetypes in literature. They only put the nation in form, finally tell anything—prove, complete anything—perpetuate anything." And Whitman wrote the essay, not only to justify his own career, but to summon other "orbic bards, with unconditional, uncompromising sway," to create new myths for the nation.

I have a lot to say on the subject, and some fears that I might fall into nationalistic hurrah. I don't think most people realize how consciously our nineteenth-century writers set about the task of creating or transcribing American myths. They had found what they called romance in Europe and wanted to transport it to the American scene, so that it too would "serve to make our country dearer and more interesting to us," as Hawthorne said, "and afford fit soil for poetry to root itself in." By 1890 they had actually created a unified tissue of nationality—but then the country began changing from agricultural to industrial, rural to urban, and the new generation required new myths. The battle between idealism and realism that raged from 1886 to 1910 and after (to be revived in the Humanist controversy) was also a battle between two mythologies. Now the country has changed again and we are looking for new myths to express a new time.

And more and more to be said—but still I don't know how to begin or how to phrase my remarks, and I'm writing this letter chiefly in the effort to clarify my own muddy mind. But so far the mud refuses to settle. . . .

As ever,
Malcolm

Sherman, Conn.,
May 3, 1949.

[to Ernest Hemingway]
Dear Ernest:

Note that we have a new address. As the result of a campaign run by our little mimeographed fortnightly newspaper, the Sherman Sentinel, our little town now has its own post office, and aren't we sorry. The chief result is that the mails are slower and packages sometimes get mislaid for a week. The town snoop is postmistress. I haven't written you for an age, or damned near ten weeks. Just after writing you the last long letter—the one which I sent off the same day as the letter to Mary, and which it appears from your letter that you never received—just then I got involved in a hell of a troublesome situation that kept me busy for a long time. It was about Yaddo, an old Robber Baron estate in Saratoga Springs endowed as a foundation to give free board and lodging to writers, artists and composers. I'm on the board of directors, worse luck. One of the writers who had spent a long time at Yaddo, more than four years, was Agnes Smedley. She is and has always been an enthusiastic supporter of the Chinese Communists. A year ago it began to look as if her political activities would make trouble for Yaddo, and Mrs. Elizabeth Ames, who runs the place, asked Agnes either to moderate those activities or else to leave. She left. On February 10 of this year General MacArthur's headquarters issued a big statement that accused Smedley of being a Russian spy. She isn't, of course, and Smedley forced the Army to apologize. But meanwhile the effbiyai had descended on Yaddo to ask questions of Mrs. Ames and the writer guests.

Does this sound complicated? It's only the beginning of a story that belongs in the history books. The guests, as it happened, were all of the type now described as "passionate anti-Stalinists." They became so disturbed at being questioned by the effbiyai that they got together, added two and two, squared the result, multiplied by pi squared, and reached the conclusion that Mrs. Ames was, in their words, "somehow deeply and mysteriously involved" in subversive activities. A meeting of the directors was called in Saratoga, and it turned out to be one of the grisliest days through which I have ever lived. All sorts of suspicions, dislikes, malice came to the surface. Charges were made, evidence was offered, and in the course of seven or eight hours the evidence slowly dissolved into nothing but unfounded gossip. The meeting was adjourned for a month to allow the directors to make further investigations.

The end was, as you might say, happy for these times. At a second meeting in New York Mrs. Ames was formally cleared of the charges. But then the guest who had been most active in bringing the charges, Robert Lowell—who is incidentally a very fine poet—suddenly went out of his head, not at the meeting, but a few days later in Chicago, and had to be put into handcuffs by four sweating policemen and carried off for treatment. Paranoid psychosis was the doctors' verdict. What we had really been living through and sitting in grave judgment over was paranoia that had passed from mind to mind like measles running through a school. Not so long afterwards Drew Pearson gave his famous broadcast about Forrestal and how he had been carried off to the loony bin shouting, "The Russians are after me." This great nation had been adopting its policies on the advice of a paranoiac as Secretary of Defense. Maybe this is the age of paranoia, of international delusions of persecution and grandeur. Maybe persons like Forrestal and Robert Lowell are the chosen representatives and suffering Christs of an era. . . .

As ever,
Malcolm

260 Cumberland St.,
Brooklyn 5
[August (?) 1949]

[to Pascal Covici, Viking Press]
[A Memo]
[Pascal Covici]

This Marianne Moorescript saddens me.* So much talent, toil, application—and so much dullness as the end product. She goes wrong by enormous effort, by the painstaking application of the wrong principles, when by doing half as much work she could go right. The two principles that led her astray are (1) that the rhythm of the English should resemble that of the French—whereas the truth is that rhythm is comparatively unimportant in French poetry, many lines having only two accents, one before the cesura and the other at the end of the line; and (2) that she should use rhymes resembling the *sound* of the French rhymes—so she gets the sound and loses the sense. This is especially apparent at the ends of the fables, where La Fontaine points his morals in an easy aphoristic way.

Compare, for example:

> —Nuit et jour à tout venant
> Je chantais, ne vous déplaise.
> —Vous chantiez? j'en suis fort aise:
> Eh bien! dansez maintentant.

("Night and day" (said the grasshopper) "I sang, if it please you, for everyone who passed by."—"You sang?" (said the ant). "I am very glad to hear it. Now dance.")

Compare those simple lines with Miss Moore's version:

> "—Night and day, trilled for perchance
> Errant ears, offending yours.

* Marianne Moore was translating *La Fontaine's Fables*, a project that was finally completed in 1954. Cowley worked extensively with Moore and their relationship remained friendly. [ed.]

—Not care for chirrs? Sweet sound allures.
Rather than shiver better dance."

What the hell does that mean, and who's saying what? Or again, take the last line of the fable of the wolf and the dog:

Cela dit, maître loup s'enfuit et court encor.

(At which Master Wolf ran off and is running still.)

But Miss Moore writes:

"Fleeing his undoing and still going—ears a-roar."

"Ears a-roar" is inserted simply to preserve the *or* sound of La Fontaine's rhyme in *Encor*. And it spoils the line and doesn't make sense.

I could go on. And go on. I still think we should publish the book. Miss Moore is a very distinguished author and it is fine to have her on the Viking list. The book might sell on her reputation, as an engineless Ford is said to run. An introduction by Miss Moore would help, and so would illustrations. At present I think it might be just as well to let her go ahead with the job without bothering her too much. Anyhow I'd hate to butt in. But it might be a good idea for me to write her and say that with Monroe Engel in Italy I would be glad to answer any questions as they come along; and in the same letter I might argue with her gently about her final lines. If she could just make them sharp and simple and aphoristic, a good many of the fables would be redeemed.

MC

Sherman, Conn.,
October 7, 1949.

[to Ernest Hemingway]
Dear Ernest:

. . . Just now I'm doing a pretty hard critical job. I've got stacked in front of me ten novels by authors who appeared during or since the war—novels that have been favorably reviewed by the highbrow critics—and I'm trying to see whether they reveal any new standards in fiction. To some extent they do. Especially they reveal negative tendencies: they aren't naturalistic, aren't experimental, aren't rebellious, aren't social, aren't behavioristic. On the positive side, they are concerned with the moral problems of individuals. About their most striking feature, outside of the conscious efforts at symbolism, is how they are preoccupied with evil—how they personify or objectify evil as an old fairy, a little girl, a professor, a hired man or a mountain lion.

I'm talking about authors like Lionel Trilling, Saul Bellow, Eudora Welty, Truman Capote, Jean Stafford, Robert Lowry. They write good prose, sometimes very good prose. They can tell you the shades of meaning conveyed by a look; you might say that was their specialty. But, God, how most of them flinch away from a big scene. And if they happen to run into a big theme (like Mary McCarthy in "The Oasis"), how they do insist on avoiding its implications and sticking to their fine jewelry work, as if they were carving cameos on the side of Stone Mountain. . . . [Cowley's ellipses] Thought I would contrast them with Nelson Algren, who, as far as subject goes, might still be writing in 1935, but who has recklessness and a real feeling for the language as it is not spoken at Vassar. Outside of writers like Algren, and there aren't many of them, we're getting back into an era of books by old maids . . . the membrane over their minds has never been broken. . . .

As ever,
Malcolm

Sherman, Conn.,
November 3, 1951.

[to Ernest Hemingway]
Dear Ernest:
I almost wrote "November 3, 1851," and that gives a picture of how a man can live in the past. I had been reading a big collection of documents called "The Mel-

ville Log," in which Melville's life is recorded from day to day, so far as the records survive. His daughter Fanny hated him and burned most of the family papers, so that people thought for a long time for the last twenty years and now they've collected so many documents that merely to quote the pertinent passages from them makes up a two-volume work of 933 pages. In November 1851 Melville had finished "Moby Dick"; he had written it in a little more than a year, written it twice, in a high state of elation, but after he finished it he was dead-tired, morose, suicidal. Then, without giving himself a chance for rest he plunged into "Pierre," worked on it from eight o'clock to dark each day in a cold room in Pittsfield, didn't eat till he staggered out of the room in the dusk. It was a crazy book when he finished it, and was such a complete failure (362 copies sold in twenty years) that he was never again able to earn a living as a writer. He had himself a long breakdown, stopped seeing his friends, tried to earn a living as a magazine writer but failed at it, tried to earn a living as a lecturer but failed at it, finally gave up the writing game completely (he was trying to learn to be a poet and some of his poems were very good, but he regarded that as a private matter), got a job in the customs house at $5 a day and lived in retirement for thirty years. When other writers who admired him—there were a few—looked him up in his retirement, he gave them the brush-off and apparently most of his family came to regard him as a mean old man.

He had no education beyond age 12—or no education but the very best, the sort to be had by shipping before the mast. He read enormously. He couldn't spell and his grammar was shaky, but his sisters used to copy his mss for him in those days before the typewriter and they peppered the text with commas and changed "don't" to "doesn't." He accepted that for a time. But later when his wife copied his mss he taught her not to use any punctuation whatever and put it all in himself on the final revision.

So we're back at that big question, how much should an editor do? I think it all depends whose ms he is working on. When a writer knows what he wants to do, then the editor should keep his hands off the ms, strictly, and the copyreader and the proofreader should confine themselves to queries and questions of spelling. When a writer is worth publishing like our late friend L'il Abner,* but doesn't know when to stop, then an editor like Max Perkins can certainly help him (and help the public more, by saving them the trouble of reading whole packing-boxes full of tripe). Scott's a different matter. Generally speaking he knew what he wanted in a big way, and in small ways too, but he was always running into trouble about questions of spelling (especially proper names; he called you "Hemminway" and always misspelled the name of Ginevra King, with whom he had been in love for three years desperately; he called her "Genevra"), punctuation, grammar, geography, chronology (as when a man named McKibben, in *Tender*, "unscrewed two blooded wire-hairs from a near-by table and departed." On the next page he was still there, still talking.) He hadn't any theory about those details; he just wanted them to be conventionally right and hadn't the sort of eye that caught them on the page. For some damned reason Max never put the book through Scribner's copy-editing department, where those matters would have been caught and queried; he simply turned it over to Miss What's-her-name, his nice secretary, to handle. Scott himself got a Frenchman to fix up the French quotations (though a couple must have slipped past the Frenchman), but had no help on the Italian. What I did to the book was just what Scribner's proofreading department would have done if the manuscript had passed through their hands. I thought it was the only fair thing to do for Scott, because otherwise people were privileged to think that he was the only illiterate author in the United States. They ought to see some other manuscripts.

People like you who work over every detail of their mss are rare as hell in the country these days. They are the last individual handicraftsmen. Most of our so-called writers just do part of their work, as if they had only one job on the production line, before the ms moves on into the varnish room. . . .

As ever,
Malcolm

* Hemingway's name for Thomas Wolfe [ed.]

Sherman, Conn.,
January 28, 1952.

[to Ernest Hemingway]
Dear Ernest,

. . . What's Dos* been converted to? Pelmanism? I
haven't read his last novel about the Chosen Country,
but the reviews made it sound as exciting as cornmeal
mush. Still, it seemed to have a lot about his family and
early life in it, so that I'll have to pour milk on it and
lick the bowl, sooner or later, but not in this dismal
weather. Right now I couldn't stand his bracing sentiments. Dos did something truly remarkable in his early
novels, especially Manhattan Transfer and USA. Here
for a hundred years the world has been getting more and
more crowded and collective, so that the real heroes of
an action story are likely to be not a man (where are men
these days?) but a squad, a platoon, a company, an army
or a city or a nation. Dos discovered and evolved a technique for treating these collective heroes in a unified
novel. That was something for the age, and hundreds of
younger writers have been adapting his technique to their
own subjects. Most of the World War II novelists did so
(Mailer, Burns, for example), besides Sartre and many
other Frenchmen—in fact the French still think that Dos
is one of the world classics. After a man has done that
sort of job it's a pity to see him conked or sapped or
sandburged [sic.] into conformity and hurrah for the
American way of canned life. I love my country when
it's in trouble but not when it's a chosen country throwing
its platitudes around. . . .

As ever,
[Malcolm]

* John Dos Passos [ed.]

Sherman, Conn.,
May 24, 1952.

[to Ernest Hemingway]
Dear Ernest:
   . . . I didn't know Charlie Scribner very well, but he
had character and I liked what I knew of him. His death
coming not so long after Max Perkins' was tough for the
house and for the literary world. I hear that young Charlie
is taking hold of things in a good fashion. In general the
publishing trade is in a pretty chaotic condition—readers
are showing more hesitation about paying $3 or $4 for
novels when they can wait and buy them for 25 or 35
cents. Brentano's took the books out of its gallery and
is replacing them with a line of sea shells—I'm not making
a joke, that's what they're doing. Maybe we should try
inscribing little poems on sea shells. The great purge*
hasn't really hit the publishing trade (except at Little,
Brown), but there are signs that the purgers are working
in this direction and the publishers are scared enough so
that they don't bring out some books that would probably
have a large sale. Hollywood has just made the big surrender to the American Legion, which henceforth will
decide who is to be hired and fired. The motto everywhere is Play It Safe, and that explains why publishers'
lists are so full of the trivial and inconsequential. Last
year the movies tried to break over, since they were
suffering from malnutrition in the box office; they produced several good films (Streetcar, Place in the Sun,
Death of a Salesman, Born Yesterday, The Marrying
Kind) and most of the good films were picketed by the
American Legion and the Catholic War Veterans, so that
the error is unlikely to be repeated.
   The Fitzgerald boom is over. The Faulkner boom is
still running strong, and it's encouraged by the fact that
Faulkner is getting holy. These days nothing succeeds
like a strong dose of piety. I don't blame Faulkner at all,
since he doesn't give a damn for the public, but the Faulkner critics are becoming gloriously silly. The young novelists are just crazy about symbols, symbol, symbol, who's

* The McCarthyite loyalty and morality crusade. [ed.]

got the symbol. They think that a good symbol takes the place of a story—lucky for them if it does, because most of them can't tell stories. Their characters are so damned symbolic you don't know what they mean. The two mottoes of the young novelists are, "Mother was to blame" and "Evil is in the human heart." . . .

Love to Mary in this time of personal and public trouble.

As ever,
[Malcolm]

Sherman, Conn.,
January 22, 1953.

[to John Cheever]
Dear John,

I enclose a little statement that you can send to your publishers and they can use it if they think it's worth using. I tried to express what I think has been the central virtue of your stories, or at any rate of your best stories—that of giving moments in which the Victim Tells All, or in which the narrator has a sudden feeling of heightened life (as at the end of "Goodbye, My Brother"). The best of all the moments—Joyce called them "epiphanies"—is the end of "Torch Song," which reminds me always of the end of "The Raven":

"Take thy beak from out my heart and thy form from off my door."

Criticisms: for what they are worth. "Goodbye, my Brother" is finally ambiguous. The boys, meaning the critics, talk about the virtues of irony, and it is ironical that the narrator is as bad as Lawrence in his different way, but it is also troublingly uncertain, so that one wishes you had made your own point of view clearer. On the other hand, the emotional quality of the story is wonderful and the characters are solid. It is a story that you could expand into a novel, and my theory is that you'll have to write a novel that way, by starting with one short story and expanding it backward (into the past of the characters) instead of by looking for a "novel" plot, whatever that may be. When you start by looking for a novelistic plot, you'll always break it into complete and separate episodes, out of habit.

Every once in a while you try to buy your epiphanies too cheaply, without paying for them in advance. Two examples: the husband's accusations in "The Enormous Radio," which are unforeshadowed by anything he has said or the wife has thought earlier in the story, and the mother's Ophelia-nutty passage in "The Sutton Place Story," also unforeshadowed by anything in her character as already presented. In "The Pot of Gold" the epiphany approaches on somewhat too noisy feet. But these are all very fine stories.

What next? Go abroad, for Christ's sake. Go abroad and write a novel or a play about these people. If you keep on writing short stories about them you'll reveal your irritation more and more. . . .

As ever,
[Malcolm Cowley]

November 30, 1953.

Mr. Howard Mumford Jones
Widener 115
Harvard University
Cambridge 38, Massachusetts

Dear Howard:
I do have some ideas about the 1890s, and at one time I thought of writing a little book about the period, but that idea has long since been abandoned along with others. Your knowledge of the period is so much broader than mine that I hesitate to bring forth my story—thinking as I do that you'd mark it down from A− to B+ or even lower if you found it in a blue book. But maybe it does have the advantage of being based on a special point of view, that of the student of serious or avant-garde writing. I ought to make some more apologies too, but any how here goes—

In literature the 1890s were an abortive renaissance, a sort of false spring in February. They were a renaissance—or close to being one—because our literature was fructified, or let us say inseminated—it stood to stud, but the operation didn't take—by the new literature of Europe, Tolstoy, Zola, Ibsen—only Herbert Spencer left a really wide imprint (or foal). The renaissance was abortive because the new authors never found a public to support them.

For me the period opens in 1887, I think it was, when young Hamlin Garland went to see Howells at a residence hotel in the Boston suburbs. That was a real laying on of hands, with Howells' influence passing over to the new generation, whether they called themselves Realists or Veritists or naturalists, or whether they were trying to write perfectly balanced novels in the French fashion.

The battle between the Realists and the Idealists—climaxed at the Chicago Fair in 1893 (all the principal figures were there)—was lost by the Realists in 1895, for the illogical reason that Oscar Wilde was convicted of pederasty. Everybody opposed to the new literature tried to bury it under Wilde's infamy—while setting against it the pure idealism, so they called it, of Stevenson. No market for realistic books, or not much.

(Note that international copyright law in 1893 had shut off the free translation of naughty European books, though the earlier ones were still available at fifteen to twenty-five cents. When I was a boy you could still find *Germinal* and the *Kreuzer Sonata*, paperbacked, in second-hand stores.)

Howells was still the center of the battle and he didn't give up the fight in 1895. As a matter of fact, he was still doing very well financially—he needed a lot of money—and he was still encouraging young authors. Another scene in the drama was Frank Norris' visit to Howells shortly before he published *McTeague* and Howells' praise of the novel in *The Reviewer* (or was it *The Critic*? I'm dictating without notes). Another laying on of hands, another passing of *mana* from one generation to another. But when *Sister Carrie* appeared in 1900 that was too much for Howells. On his one meeting with Dreiser he said, "You know I didn't like *Sister Carrie*."

Until that time Howells had been encouraging the new group of Naturalists, who had gone much further than the Realists. But the mood of the country had changed, for political and social reasons, about which you know vastly more than I. There was also a professional accident that helped to defeat the avant-garde writers and I hope you don't overlook it in your story. It was the bankruptcy of the great house of Harper, which had occupied the same position in relation to the new American writer that the NRF did in France before World War II. Howells' entire income came from Harper's. He was relieved when J. P. Morgan put money into the firm and worry began when Morgan had it taken over by Colonel Harvey. There was another quietly dramatic scene when Harvey had Howells out for the weekend. Harvey told Howells that he should go on writing for Harper's at the same salary, but I think he took him off books at that time. Also he said, "The battle for realism is lost." Howells agreed sadly that the battle for realism was lost and quit defending the avant-garde writers.

Dreiser might have gotten off practically unscathed—except for having his first novel effectively if not technically suppressed—if the novel hadn't been published in England and very highly praised by English reviewers. That was the cause of resentment and scandal here, and the magazines—Dreiser had lived by writing for them—quit publishing his work, almost by common consent. Dreiser was on the manic depressive side and might have gone into a depressed period in any case, but the closing off of his magazine career certainly made the depression worse and he would have committed suicide if Brother Paul hadn't rescued him.

That was in 1902 and by that time almost all the leading figures of the abortive renaissance were dead or silenced. You can go over the list for yourself—Harold Frederic, James A. Herne, Crane, Norris, Kate Chopin (although I think she lived until 1904, but in silence), and without my notes I forget the others. Trumbull Stickney, of course. Almost the only survivors were Dreiser (after the years out of the literary picture), John J. Chapman (after a nervous breakdown), and E. A. Robinson, and practically speaking these didn't reappear until after 1910.

That is my specialized story of the period and if you think it has any value or illumination, do what you will with it—and my apologies for setting it down so briefly and dogmatically. . . .

As ever,
Malcolm Cowley

Sherman, Conn.,
October 12, 1954.

[to Harriet Arnow]
Dear Mrs. Arnow:

I won't try to justify your publishers, because what they did with your manuscript was indefensible, but maybe (not perhaps) I can explain the situation that led them to attack your novel with pencils and pickaxes. Actually it's explained in the last part of your letter, when you talk about the sort of education your children are getting. They aren't learning to read for pleasure or take a joy in language. They're learning to read for facts and read fast, because they're bright children, but most of their schoolmates aren't even learning that.

Little reading for pleasure, hence little good writing. You'd be surprised to learn how badly a lot of professional American writers write. They know how to select a subject that is in the public eye. They know how to present sympathetic characters in taut situations, but they don't know how to write. If their books are grammatical and correctly punctuated and spelled, that's because a copy editor has worked on them.

The publishers who take their work seriously (like Macmillan) have style books and copy editors who know them by heart. They may have editors (as distinguished from copy editors) with a thwarted creative instinct that makes them suggest changes and more changes to authors, so as to strengthen their own egos and give them a feeling of creative achievement. You seem to have run into one of those people. When dealing with journalists and scholars and fiction wrights—I was thinking of those good souls who go at fiction like millwrights—these editors and copy editors actually do a lot of good. American popular literature would seem less professional and entertaining without their help. The trouble is that they don't always realize when they are dealing with writers proper, who know how their characters must act and know where every word should fall in a sentence. And the trouble is also that there aren't enough writers proper in America today, so that you can't always blame the editors for failing to recognize them and for treating them as they do the fiction wrights. That's partly the fault of our secondary education, though I don't want to blame the schools for everything. Still the fact remains that average Englishmen write better prose than average Americans.

I'd better turn this off, because I'm beginning to sound like Cassandra. . . .

Cordially,
Malcolm Cowley

Sherman, Conn.,
February 20, 1955.

[to Mr. John G. Cawelti]*
Dear Mr. Cawelti:
    Thoughts on your project.
    . . . I've often wondered what sort of critic I was. Primarily I have been a contemporary historian of letters rather than a critic. When, as often, I wrote essays that were primarily critical, they were likely to be biographical criticism—in this sense, that I feel strongly that an author changes, that Hawthorne in 1837, for example, was not the same author as Hawthorne in 1860—and that most generalities about an author, when made on the basis of his life work, without allowing for the changes in that work, are meaningless. I am impressed by the effect on authors, not of broad social changes, but of social changes, sometimes much narrower, that directly affect his life—for example, Whitman was apparently not af-

* Cawelti was then a graduate student working on a thesis that involved Cowley. [ed.]

fected greatly by the panic of 1855, but he was greatly affected by losing his job on the Brooklyn Eagle in 1848. Writing about an author, I try to understand his life, and I also try hard to understand the actual nature of his achievement (at which point I do a good deal of *explication de texte,* but without carrying the procedure to the extreme of the New Critics.) Great is language, but it is great because it is the medium and almost the basis of human society—so that I try never to lose sight of the connection between books and life. I feel that a critic who doesn't prove by his own style that he understands the art of using language is incompetent to discuss language as an art.—And why does all this make me? An eclectic?

Sincerely,
Malcolm Cowley

Sherman, Conn.,
September 16, 1955.

[to Jack Kerouac]
Dear Jack,
On the Road—I think that's the right title for the book, not *The Beat Generation*—is now being very seriously considered, or reconsidered, by Viking, and there is quite a good chance that we will publish it, depending on three *ifs: if* we can figure out what the right changes will be (cuts and rearrangements); *if* we can be sure that the book won't be suppressed for immorality; and *if* it won't get us into libel suits. The libel question is important, because I take it that you're dealing with actual persons. Most of them won't mind what you said about them—Dean Moriarty, for example—and Bill Burroughs for another example—but you run a risk when writing about anyone with a position of respectability to maintain, like the character you call Denver D. Doll; I wish you'd tell me more about him, so that I'd know whether the portrait had to be changed. . . .
Are you sure that you haven't used any actual names?

I've promised to do a short introduction if the book is published.

. . . It's good news that you're writing again, and writing a lot on big projects. Also I think that the proper system for you is to write all in a breath, pouring out what you feel. But there are those two sides of writing, the unconscious and the conscious, the creation and the self-criticism, the expression and the communication, the speed and the control. What your system ought to be is to get the whole thing written down fast, in a burst of creative effort, than later go back, put yourself in the reader's place, ask whether and how the first expression ought to be changed to make it more effective. If you'd do that job of revision too, then most of your things would be published, instead of kicking around publishers' offices for years. And being published is what you need right now.

Give my regards to Allen Ginsberg and tell him I'm hoping to write him next week. And I'll write you again about *On the Road* when I've had time to go through the manuscript carefully, carefully.

As ever,
[Malcolm Cowley]

Sherman, Conn.,
September 16, 1960.

[to Betty Cox]*
Dear Mrs. Cox,

That's a very long story you're asking for. No, I'm not any longer sore or sensitive about it, and in fact I've been planning to set it all down, perhaps in a book that would continue *Exile's Return*. There's no time to write about it this week, when we're packing for the trip to Stanford while a stream of visitors pours in to say goodbye. But I'll set down some hasty notes.

I was pretty Red in the early 1930s, up to the time

---

* Betty Cox wrote a master's thesis on Cowley in 1960. [ed.]

when I wrote the first version of *ER*. It was the time, now forgotten, when the economic structure was going to pieces, and when nobody seemed to have the answer except Marx. The turning point for me was the expedition to Pineville, Kentucky, with Waldo Frank, Edmund Wilson, Mary Heaton Vorse, and Quincy Howe, in the early months of 1932. Then I was one of fifty-two writers who signed the pamphlet called *Culture and the Crisis,* calling for Communist votes in the election of that year. Later I helped to organize the League of American Writers, with its congresses in—wasn't it?—1935, 1937, and 1939. There was another congress in 1941, but by that time I had resigned from the League, of which I had been a vice president from the beginning. (There were books published about each of the congresses. The one I remember is *Fighting Words,* edited by Donald Ogden Stewart. I think they all included speeches of mine.)

I began to have a lot of doubts about the Communists, especially after attending the World Congress of Revolutionary Writers in Madrid in the summer of 1937 (you must have read my account of it). But the world situation, in which Russia was following a better policy than any of the Western nations, kept me from making any public complaints until after the Russo-German pact in the summer of '39. Then I tried to get the League of American Writers, which was about 97 percent nonCommunist in membership, to cut loose from the Communists. The efforts were unsuccessful, and I resigned from the League in the spring of 1940, finally publishing my letter of resignation in the New Republic.

At that time the great debate in this country was between the isolationists and the interventionists. The debate raged on the staff of the New Republic. I was the interventionist, and junior, editor. Bruce Bliven and George Soule, the senior editors, were both of them isolationist, and the paper followed an isolationist policy, even though it was owned and financed by Dorothy and Leonard Elmhurst, who were British subjects. In the fall of 1940 I took a leave of absence. While I was gone Leonard Elmhurst came to New York and decreed that the paper should be reorganized and should become interventionist. Bliven became editor in chief (and changed all his beliefs); George Soule and I were removed from management and became, in effect, merely contributing editors. I thought the position was very uncomfortable.

All that year I had been corresponding with Archie MacLeish about policies for this country. We were pretty well agreed on them. When Archie was asked to organize an information service for this country—the Office of Facts and Figures—he invited me to join his staff, and I went to Washington, in December, for a salary of $8000, considered large at the time. Then the storm broke in Congress. I saw a lot of people, collected a lot of good advice, and finally, in February, decided to resign, though I stayed on for a month to finish some work I had undertaken. (I wrote one speech for the Boss, of about 250 words, his Christmas message in 1941. I also wrote part of another speech defending the surviving New Deal agencies, but he didn't use what I wrote, and I knew the Deal was ended.)

It was a grisly experience in Washington, always feeling that I was being watched, talking with security officers, giving depositions to the FBI; and it left me with the feeling that the less I had to do with government agencies in the future the happier I would be. I got out of politics, but strictly out (except for a little participation in local affairs). I'd been attacked and reviled by the Communists, attacked and reviled by Congressman Dies, and it was a great relief to get back to the garden in Sherman, where everything was peaceful in wartime. I didn't suffer much during the McCarthy era—there was one brush with the American Legion when I was Walker Ames lecturer at the University of Washington in 1950, but the Legion decided that I wasn't a threat to the nation and called off the dogs. I testified at the two trials of Alger Hiss—I hadn't ever met Hiss, but I had known Whittaker Chambers, and he had told me some stories that were diametrically opposed to his later testimony. That did make some trouble for me, but amazingly little, considering what some other people suffered. I was sort of proud about never beating my breast in public or rushing to accuse other people of deadly sins, but also my self-imposed silence gave me an uncomfortable feeling of political impotence. I do have some pretty strong political convictions, as you would guess. I think the one great and overriding question is whether the human race will survive on this planet or whether it is going to commit suicide. Atomic suicide is quite possible, and of course I'm for peace—but even if we avoid an atomic war there is the great possibility that the human race will exhaust all the natural resources of the planet, minerals first, then soil, air, pure water, and that the teeming billions will have to live like Indian peasants. I suppose I want a world like Cambria County when I was a boy—thinly settled, full of big woods and trout in little streams. I'm not a radical now or a conservative, but a conservationist, a radical conservationist. . . .

Cordially yours,
[Malcolm Cowley]

490 Oregon Avenue,
Palo Alto, Calif.,
February 10, 1961.

[to John Cheever]
Dear John,

I just this minute finished reading *Some People, etc.,* with a feeling that it is as good writing as I've run into for a long time. After *Justina,* with that wonderful scene of the interview with the mayor about burying the poor woman from a residential zone where death is forbidden, the story I like best and that sticks in my mind (I first read it on a plane coming back from Salt Lake City) is "The Scarlet Moving Van," with Peaches and Gee Gee and the hill towns where sorrow is forbidden like death in Justina's neighborhood. In the other story where the man bakes cakes secretly, the wife dreams of the H-bomb falling in the suburbs. John, I fear that *you're* the H-bomb of suburban neighborhoods. . . .

. . . what is becoming evident in your work is a sort of apocalyptic poetry, as if you were carrying well observed suburban life into some new dimension where everything is a little cockeyed and on the point of being exploded into a mushroom cloud. . . .

As ever,
[Malcolm Cowley]

[Winter 1961?]
[From Mac*]

[to Pascal Covici, Viking Press, A reader's report]

ONE FLEW OVER THE CUCKOO'S NEST

By Ken Kesey

Here's the loony-bin novel I've been talking about. I think that for all its obvious faults, the book and the author are worth working with, and publishing.

It's hard to get into. The story is told by a schizophrenic—I'd say that the diagnosis was catatonic dementia—who is also half Indian, the son of the chief of a dispossessed salmon-fishing tribe. His delusion is that the world is ruled by a Combine that takes the minds and hearts out of everybody and replaces them with electronic elements responsive to master suggestions. To escape the Combine he pretends to be deaf and dumb, and hence is allowed to hear everything that goes on in a big government sanitarium, evidently a veterans' hospital. His ward is ruled by a tyrannical nurse, Miss Rached, who wants to reduce everything to rules and system.

Into the ward comes Randle McMurphy, a big redhead who has simply feigned insanity to escape a term in the county workhouse. The book tells how McMurphy defies Miss Rached, how his rebellion puts new spirit into the patients, how the narrator gradually becomes sane by facing up to his difficulties, and how Miss Rached destroys McMurphy by shock treatments and finally a lobotomy. But the narrator by then is sane enough to escape (and in fact we see that there has been an element of sanity even in his delusion, if the delusion is taken metaphorically). There are two enormous scenes in the last part

---

* Mac was Cowley's moniker at Viking. [ed.]

of the novel: eleven loonies, a doctor, and a whore on a sea-going salmon boat—that's one scene—and a big drunken party in the ward at night, with two whores this time and cocktails made with cough medicine that is eighty percent alcohol and ten percent codeine.

The faults of the novel, as I said, are obvious. The author can't spell. Sometimes the narrator, Chief Bromden, talks out of character, when the author wants to preach. The end of the story is false when Bromden kills the wreck of McMurphy and then escapes. If we are to believe that Bromden is really sane enough now to live outside the asylum, he shouldn't commit a murder. Some of Bromden's delusions are overdone: gratuitous dirt and horror. The manuscript would be improved by cutting. But it has enormous vitality and I think the youngsters are going to read and enjoy it.

This is the second novel by Ken Kesey that I've read. For the first he received a Saxton Fellowship on the basis of the early chapters, but Harper turned down the finished manuscript—and was right to turn it down; the book was full of powerful scenes, but became sentimental and lost its story line. In this second book the story line is never lost. Kesey—for biographical details—is an Oregon roughneck who went to the University of Oregon on a football fellowship. While there he took a course in radio script writing, for a gut. The instructor was so impressed by the imaginative power of his writing (though he couldn't spell) that he told Kesey to apply for a Stanford Creative Writing Fellowship, which he was awarded. That was three years ago. Since leaving Stanford Kesey has supported himself by working as an attendant in a loony bin. He's tough, sentimental, and inventive-experimental in matters of conduct—I could tell you about his diabolical punches made with dry ice, alcohol, and lime juice, so that the mixture boils and fumes as the ice melts, or about his experiments with hallucinogenic mushrooms. He'll probably end by corrupting the whole Stanford group of writers, among whom he's a leader. I'm sure, though, that he's going to be heard from and that he'll write many books.

Mac

490 Oregon Avenue,
Palo Alto, Calif.,
[Winter] 1961.

[to Mr. John Ervin, Director, U. Minnesota Press]
Dear Mr. Ervin,

. . . My current interest is Emerson. I've been giving an Emerson-Whitman seminar here at Stanford, and some time in the next couple of years I'd like to write about him. My tentative idea is that Emerson's central problem was how *he* could become a great writer, given the prevailing situation in American letters, given his ministerial training, and given—the most important point—his sense of personal coldness and low vitality *except at moments*. The solution he found was to cultivate those moments intensively, yield himself to his inspirations, set each of them down in his "bank account" (the journals), and then compose them into modified sermons, or lectures, a new art form. The ontology and epistemology presented in those lectures can't any longer be accepted, but the precepts he offers are a wonderful and *practical* course of action *for writers*. Also he does write like a New England angel. . . .

490 Oregon Avenue,
Palo Alto,
California
February 22, 1961.

[to Kenneth Burke]
Dear Kenneth,

Your letter: Intimations of Mortality from Recollections of Early Second Childhood. . . .

Forty-two years, Jesus Christ, I think of them and of the years still to come. I never forget that you and I were pretty obscure persons until we were fifty years old. I had an instinct or impulse or urge or drive, all the words are unsatisfactory, *not* to become a celebrity, but that was partly a conscious decision too. I'd seen too many talents ruined by an early success: what a price they pay for it in this country! I know you had that same instinct, and suspect that you made the same conscious decision, or series of little choices. Jesus X, ability isn't so widely distributed in our field that we both couldn't have been successful early by doing something only a little different from what we did. I feel now that the decisions were sound, though we were running the risk of bucket-kicking prematurely. Having survived into our sixties, things are a little easier and I'm no longer afraid of being well known or earning money—the big problem now is that with somewhat declining vigor (I'm speaking of mine not yours)—with, for me, somewhat increasing deafness, and sleepiness in the afternoons, and a less sharp eye for other people's conduct—I still have to create or put together a body of work while there is still time . . . And the great advantage—this time for you as well as me—is precisely that we *were* obscure, that the vast fickle public didn't get tired of us, that now we have the experience and part of the freshness too . . .

As ever,
Malcolm

PART FIVE

On Writers and Writing

EDITOR'S NOTE

Cowley had a singularly simple definition of the writer. As he put it bluntly, a writer is someone who has readers. Although Cowley's sense of the requisite genius for the making of true literature led him to claim that writers of the first water grew to have a mythic awareness of their projects, his everyday sense of writing—and I might add editing—was far more practical. Cowley took the practice of writing on that level as a craft rather than an art. For him, the "artistic" dimension of a writer's work came from the genius of the writer, not his or her routine of setting words to paper.

Cowley's ability and willingness to separate the two allowed him to speak comfortably of "the writer's trade," the day-to-day effort of what a poet once called "putting well into words," and the business that surrounds it. Thus in among his literary assessments of writers in his writing for *The New Republic* and other journals, there were estimations of both the state and conditions of writing. Frequently columns he wrote in *The New Republic* and elsewhere bore titles like "What the Young Poets Are Saying," "Publishing Today," and "How Writers Write."

In the early fifties Cowley reworked some of these pieces and added many others to produce a fascinating contemporary document of the scene of American writing entitled *The Literary Situation* (1954). Long out of print—the book's estimation of the hustle of fifties publishing and its unswerving search for the new provides its own reasons for its short life—*The Literary Situation* holds some curiously cogent estimations of writers' lives and publishers' problems that make sense even now. The effort as a whole could be termed one of "literary sociology" and deserves to be read entire. One section of it, though, about 100 pages, is entitled "A Natural History of the American Writer," and is a sometimes tongue-in-cheek, sometimes telling examen of the demography and "sociological habit patterns" (to use a jargon-laden phrase Cowley mocked) of American writers at mid-century.

A brief selection from it called "The Writer's Working Day" demonstrates the Thurber-like side of its overall tone. Phones ring, duties must be met, and if one good sentence emerges, it's been a productive day. Reading it now one notes how little has changed in thirty-five years of the domestic life of the writer. Though gender roles may differ, the telephone still rings with all its annoyances.

In "How Writers Write," a selection from Cowley's 1958 introduction to the first collection of *Paris Review* interviews to appear in book form, he plumbs the statements of a range of writers from Truman Capote to Georges Simenon (with Frank O'Connor, Thornton Wilder, and William Styron in between) to find a common level, namely, that most accomplished writers enjoy what they're doing, and, as Cowley often said of himself, that they "hate to write, but love to revise."

When Cowley's concerns focused on the practical nature of writing, they often focused on the nature of writers themselves. Cowley's oft-quoted statement, "no complete son-of-a-bitch ever wrote a good sentence," laid its stress on the word *complete*. To him, as he said once in an interview, there is a "Republic of Letters," a "very loose association" of writers and workers in the literary field "built on mutual respect" that holds to an unchartered system of ethics "in which people can be unethical and even criminal by laws of citizenship, and yet obey the laws" of this group.

"Artists who succeed," Cowley notes in his piece "Rebels, Artists, and Scoundrels," are "strong characters, which is something different from saying they are saintly. Some of them—most of them?—do scandalous and even scoundrelly things." They hold to a sensibility that is at once full of self-centeredness and self-abnegation. Their interest is not necessarily in art-for-its-own-sake (as Cowley demonstrates taking us through the lives of Hemingway, Frost, and even Proust), but in both masking and presenting a life involved with the making of art.

What ultimately keeps writers from being complete sons-of-bitches is a loyalty to good work. "The real capital of an author," Cowley once noted, is his or her ability to state "when I say something I mean it. I don't want you to *accept* what I say, but I want you to understand it and give me credit for being honest about it."

At a time in the late sixties and early seventies, almost every product of American writing seemed to be anti—anti-hero, anti-novel, anti-story—Cowley, at least on the surface, belied his support of a new generation of writers he had already heralded (among them Kerouac and Kesey) by writing "A Defense of Storytelling." This piece, borrowing frequently from the work of Kenneth Burke and extolling the virtues of narrative fiction, was viewed as reactionary in its time (1971), but by today's light appears as a strange herald of the writings of Ann Beattie, Raymond Carver, and Richard Ford among others, writers who I think Cowley would acknowledge as contributors to the ongoing tradition of American writing. (I doubt very much that Cowley would ever claim that John Barth or Robert Coover, for example, writers who are alluded to in the essay, were ever outside an American literary mainstream. His effort, as usual, was to try to build a larger circle that could bring them in.)

In this piece Cowley presents a lasting definition of what makes a story a story: "Something happens as a result of which something is changed." Like his definition of the writer it is both blunt and simple and has the elements of hindsight and prescription.

His concerns with writing brought Cowley in the fifties and sixties to teach the subject at various universities. In an era in advance of MFA programs in writing, he doubted openly if writing could be taught. "All a teacher of writing, like a good editor, can do," I can remember him saying, "is prevent a good student from writing poorly." "How Writing Might Be Taught" is a previously unpublished reworking of Cowley's Hopwood Lecture at the University of Michigan in 1957 (the lecture itself was published under the title "The Beginning Writer and the University," by the University of Michigan Press). It both reflects on his own experiences as a fledgling writer and anticipates his 1960 work at Stanford in a now legendary writing class that counted among its members then completely unheralded writers such as Ken Kesey, Peter Beagle, Larry McMurtry, James D. Houston, C. J. Koch, and

Gurney Norman (and included writers from previous Cowley classes at Stanford such as Tillie Olsen and Ernest J. Gaines).

Still, given that it is as a critic of writing Cowley is best known, his "Adventures of a Book Reviewer," Cowley's afterword to a collection of his writings from *The New Republic* in the thirties, ("Think Back on Us . . ." edited by Henry Dan Piper) tells us a great deal more than imagination might permit about how a reviewer works on a day-to-day basis. Here we're given to see, sometimes humorously, what it's like to be a voice of literature and be on deadline at the same time. Cowley's statement, "the relatively short book review was my art form for many years; it became my blank-verse meditation, my sonnet sequence, my letter to distant friends, my private journal," was balanced by his own realistic view, an addendum which too many hack reviewers and self-important academics seem to ignore: "I did not fall into the illusion that it was a major form; no, it was dependent for its subject matter on the existence of novels or plays or poems worth writing about."

Regardless, the amblings and trials of an out-of-city writer well prior to the time of modems and fax machines which now dominate New York publishing is an adventure story in itself.

Following this chronicle is a brief summation ("On Criticism: The Many-Windowed House") in Cowley's own words of his view of the role of the critic. It is an elegant self-estimation and a credo all at once. Far more than any piece in this section it explains, at least generally, how Cowley might look at such disparate writers as Hawthorne, Willa Cather, John Dos Passos, William Faulkner, or John Cheever with the same steady eye. As he writes of the critic's role in the piece, he says:

> I believe the first of his functions is to select works of art worth writing about, with special emphasis on works that are new, not much discussed, or widely misunderstood. . . . His second function is to describe or analyze or reinterpret the chosen works as a basis for judgments which can sometimes merely be implied. In practice his problem may be to explain why he enjoys a particular book, and perhaps to find new reasons for enjoying it, so as to deepen his readers' capacity for appreciation."

In a published interview, Cowley, speaking from his study, said of his criticism,

> You know, when I was writing weekly reviews for "The New Republic"—in this room, by the way—I could never finish them on time, or rather the time I *set* myself to finish them was always the time to catch the last mail train into New York. I've told that story. I could have finished them much sooner, you know, if I didn't argue with myself about what word to use in a certain place. But nevertheless I would always keep on to the very last minute. Now, was that work wasted? I don't think it was wasted. I think it wasn't wasted because I made the job harder for other people. When they start out they think the job is easy, and it is, but then they find out how hard it is and they set standards which other people have to work hard to meet. . . ."

I take for Cowley's valedictory piece in this volume an estimation of the effort of memoir writing and autobiography entitled "Looking for the Essential Me." It was an occasional piece, given originally as a lecture at a PEN meeting held at New York University in 1984, where Cowley shared the dais with his son, Robert. The subject was memoir writing, and Cowley took it as an exploration of autobiography. I chose it purposely to echo the beginning piece of this volume, itself a posing of the question, "who was I?" I trust by reading this section after examining the whole of the book the reader will have, in Cowley's words, at least the rudiments of an answer.

THE WRITER'S WORKING DAY

(from *The Literary Situation*)

It may be as short as fifteen minutes and as long as fifteen hours or more. The fifteen-minute day was that of Francis Parkman when he was writing *The Conspiracy of Pontiac*; he suffered from a nervous affliction that kept him from working longer. In fifteen minutes he could write six lines, on the average, but the lines were *written* and didn't have to be changed. The working day of fifteen hours or more is that of magazine writers meeting a deadline or novelists making corrections just before a manuscript goes to the printer. Hemingway worked on the printer's draft of *For Whom the Bell Tolls* from Miami to New York, sweating over the pages in a Pullman drawing-room where the air conditioning was out of order. Later, in New York, he rewrote the galley proofs in ninety-six consecutive hours, during which he didn't leave his room at the Hotel Barclay. But the first draft of the novel had been written on an easier daily schedule; he started after an early breakfast and stopped before lunch—though sometimes, if a chapter was going well, the lunch might be delayed until the middle of the afternoon. As a general rule the more disciplined writers—Hemingway is one of them—have the shorter working days; they spend from two to four hours at their desks, then try to forget the book until next morning, trusting that their subconscious minds will carry it ahead while the writers are busy with other activities. Undisciplined writers often spend long days in and out of their studies. They hardly ever stop thinking about their work and never get much of it done, except in bursts.

The working day is often the working night. That schedule has the great advantage of providing freedom from interruptions: there aren't any more visitors or door-to-door salesmen, the children have been put to bed, the telephone doesn't ring. Night is favorable to certain types of writing, to flights of fancy and also to miserable hack work that is hard to do by day, when the writer's critical sense is livelier. Young writers who have to support themselves by other occupations have no choice but to work at night. I know a young novelist who runs a second-hand bookstore that opens at noon and closes at nine in the evening. He goes home, eats a late dinner, and writes until five. His schedule doesn't leave enough time for sleep, and I doubt that he will be able to continue it after he is forty.

Middle-aged writers usually work in the morning, although there are many exceptions to the rule. One exception was Amy Lowell, who rose at three in the afternoon and started working after midnight. She liked to have guests for dinner, distinguished foreign men of letters or bright innocent Harvard students, but she sent them away from her big house in Brookline at five minutes after twelve, just in time to catch the last streetcar that rumbled down Boylston Street. Then she sat in a deep leather armchair before the fireplace, with her feet on a stool, a blotting pad in her lap, and a collection of finely sharpened pencils on a narrow table, and worked until dawn. The interlined manuscripts were left in the hall to be copied by her two secretaries, who weren't allowed to use erasers and had to destroy every typewritten page on which there was a mistake. It was a schedule that required, among other things, a great deal of mental vigor and a household of trained servants. Most writers after the age of forty find that they haven't any longer enough energy to work effectively at night. They have their best ideas early in the morning, when they are also best able to criticize the ideas, and the older the writers are, the earlier most of them go to work. I know two distinguished men in their sixties who regularly start writing at six in the morning.

Let us picture the working day of a somewhat younger and more typical writer; he might be forty years old and he lives in the country with his wife. The day is one of those when he is starting work on a "piece"—which is anything short intended for magazine publication—or on a new chapter of a longer work. After sitting for half an hour over a second cup of breakfast coffee he goes upstairs to his study. There he takes the typewriter out of its case, puts in a sheet of paper, and writes a first sentence that he has been thinking about all week. But the next sentence isn't clear in his mind and he

On Writers and Writing

starts pacing from window to window like a caged animal. He is tempted to escape into the garden, which is getting weedy; perhaps he could think more clearly with a hoe in his hand. Resisting the temptation, he suddenly thinks of another sentence. He is at the typewriter when he hears the telephone ring and hopes the call is for his wife, who answers it—but no, New York is calling person-to-person for the writer. New York turns out to be a buzz of confused conversation, a wait, and then a clear voice saying, "I'm sorry, Miss Maybank has stepped out of the office. We'll have to call you back."

His wife drives off to the village to do the shopping. Watching her go, but not really seeing her, the writer thinks of another sentence and rushes upstairs to set it down. He reads over what he has written, tears the sheet out of the typewriter, and does a revised version of the three sentences; then he goes back to pacing from window to window. He wonders who Miss Maybank is and what she wants him to do. The telephone rings and he goes downstairs, calling out to the empty house, "I'll take it, dear." It is somebody from the school board with a question for his wife. He says, "Just a minute, I'll call her," then remembers she is in the village. He goes to the kitchen, finds that there is some cold coffee in a pot, and puts it on a burner. The telephone rings again and this time, after another wait, Miss Maybank introduces herself. She is a fact-checker for a magazine and wants to know the source of a quotation that he has used in a forthcoming article. He runs upstairs, goes through his papers, and finds the quotation. Miss Maybank starts to thank him at length, but there is an acrid smell from the kitchen and he has to hang up; the coffee has boiled over. While he is cleaning the stove his wife appears with an armful of groceries, and they get into an argument about the mess he always makes. He goes upstairs, still muttering, and finds that he can write another sentence, but it will be the last that morning.

The mail has come, and he reads it after lunch. It includes a manuscript by an unknown author who begs him to recommend it to a publisher and thanks him profusely in advance, but doesn't enclose postage. There are galley proofs of two novels that their publishers hope he will like and say a few kind words about, to print on the jacket. An almost total stranger wants to be sponsored for a Guggenheim fellowship. The writer has saved one envelope for the last, because it looks as if there might be a check in it, but what he finds is an appeal for funds. He reflects that every established writer is regarded as a sort of unpaid service bureau for the literature industry. Why not incorporate himself and ask for tax exemption as a charitable organization? Unfortunately he has no organization, not even a secretary to take care of his correspondence. He remembers Oscar Wilde and his remark that he had known scores of young men who came up to London and ruined themselves by answering letters. Nevertheless he composes a rather testy letter to the author of the manuscript, asking him please to send return postage. Then, feeling too drowsy to stay indoors, he goes out to work in the garden. Late in the afternoon, while he is hoeing a row of beans, another sentence occurs to him. He goes back to the typewriter and works fast for twenty minutes, with the words coming easily, but then his wife calls upstairs to remind him that George and Betty are coming for dinner and he'd better get dressed and be ready to mix the cocktails, of which he will drink too many.

Next morning he starts by reading over what he has written. "This won't do at all," he says aloud as he drops the two sheets into the wastebasket; then he plucks them out again and lays them aside for reference. This day, and the two or three that follow, there are fewer interruptions, but now the writer would almost welcome them; his new obstacle is a torpid and recalcitrant mind. He tries to provoke it into activity by lying on the couch in his study and looking fixedly at a point on the ceiling. Thoughts occur to him, but they all seem unpersuasive or unusable. He paces the floor while the typewriter stares at him with its forty-two round keys like so many accusing eyes. "You damn father symbol," he says to it. He escapes the typewriter by working in the garden until he lapses into a state of brute exhaustion. Next day he takes a long walk on a dull road, hoping to hear the right words repeated by an inner voice, in time to his footsteps, but the words aren't right or writable. His appetite is poor, his sleep broken, his temper so bad that his wife keeps out of his way. He begins to worry about paying the bills, with no money coming in and wonders whether he shouldn't consult a psychoanalyst. But we are talking about a professional writer, not one of the symptomatic artists who might be Dr. Bergler's* patients. The professional has obligations to fulfill or a deadline to meet, and he usually ends by meeting it.

Gradually and in part subconsciously the story has been taking shape in his mind as he walked and worried. One afternoon he is surprised to find himself typing away at it. He eats dinner with an abstracted air, replying briefly to his wife's remarks, then goes back to his study. If he is working on a magazine piece he is likely to finish a first draft of it that night, while the conception is fresh in his mind. He seldom retains a clear picture of the hours when he is actually writing; all he remembers afterward is that the typewriter kept up a nervous clatter, with intervals of silence when he walked the floor between paragraphs, and that he filled a big wastebasket with discarded pages. Once when he came back to the room after getting a drink of water he found it foul-smelling and hazy with smoke. Most writers smoke too much when they are working, not so much for the taste of tobacco as for the need to have something in their mouths; those who stop smoking are likely to chew gum or pencils or kitchen matches.** This particular writer has filled a big bowl with pipe ashes, and when he finishes the piece at three o'clock his mouth feels as if he tried to swallow a boiling infusion of bitterweed. Words and phrases keep echoing in his mind; some he decides to change tomorrow, but others are so completely right that they give him a sense of elation. There is a gray light in the window before he falls asleep.

Tomorrow—or rather this afternoon—he will revise what he has written, an easier operation that he usually enjoys; then he will send it to the magazine just in time for the issue that is going to press. The next day he will go fishing, with a good conscience, and the morning after he will start his struggle to write another piece. Magazine writers are like sprinters, always in severe training to run short races; they live in brief cycles of depression and elation. Book writers are like cross-country runners, jogging along at a steady gait. After the first struggle to get started they can work on their projects for a

* A psychiatrist prominent at the time (1954), whose writings about the failures of artists Cowley mocked earlier in the piece. [ed.]
** A friend of mine signed a contract for a second book, but hasn't written it. "Every time I start to work on it," he says, "I think of all the cigarettes I'll have to smoke before it's finished." [M.C.]

few hours each day, week after week, always knowing that they will start each morning where they left off the night before—unless, or until, they are stopped midway in the book by some new problem that demands another period of silent wrestling with their minds; then they are off again at the steady trot that many continue to the end—though often they find themselves sprinting in the last desperate half-mile.

[1954]

HOW WRITERS WRITE
(excerpts)

There would seem to be four stages in the composition of a story. First comes the germ of the story, then a period of more or less conscious meditation, then the first draft, and finally the revision, which may be simply "pencil work," as John O'Hara calls it—that is, minor changes in wording—or may lead to writing several drafts and what amounts to a new work.

The germ of a story is something seen or heard, or heard about, or suddenly remembered; it may be a remark casually dropped at the dinner table (as in the case of Henry James's story, *The Spoils of Poynton*), or again it may be the look on a stranger's face. Almost always it is a new and simple element introduced into an existing situation or mood; something that expresses the mood in one sharp detail; something that serves as a focal point for a hitherto disorganized mass of remembered material in the author's mind. James describes it as "the precious particle . . . the stray suggestion, the wandering word, the vague echo, at a touch of which the novelist's imagination winces as at the prick of some sharp point," and he adds that "its virtue is all in its needle-like quality, the power to penetrate as finely as possible."

In the case of one story by the late Joyce Cary, the "precious particle" was the wrinkles on a young woman's forehead. He had seen her on the little boat that goes around Manhattan Island, "a girl of about thirty," he says, "wearing a shabby skirt. She was enjoying herself. A nice expression, with a wrinkled forehead, a good many wrinkles. I said to my friend, 'I could write about that girl . . .'" but then he forgot her. Three weeks later, in San Francisco, Cary woke up at four in the morning with a story in his head—a purely English story with an English heroine. When he came to revise the story he kept wondering, "Why all these wrinkles? That's the third time they come in. And I suddenly realized," he says, "that my English heroine was the girl on the Manhattan boat.

Somehow she had gone down into my subconscious, and came up again with a full-sized story."

The woman with the wrinkled forehead could hardly have served as the germ of anything by Frank O'Connor, for his imagination is auditory, not visual. "If you're the sort of person," he says, "that meets a girl in the street and instantly notices the color of her eyes and of her hair and the sort of dress she's wearing, then you're not in the least like me. . . . I have terribly sensitive hearing and I'm terribly aware of voices." Often his stories develop from a remark he has overheard. That may also be the case with Dorothy Parker, who says, "I haven't got a visual mind. I hear things." Faulkner does have a visual mind, and he says that *The Sound and the Fury* "began with a mental picture. I didn't realize at the time it was symbolical. The picture was of the muddy seat of a little girl's drawers in a pear tree, where she could see through a window where her grandmother's funeral was taking place and report what was happening to her brothers on the ground below. By the time I explained who they were and what they were doing and how her pants got muddy, I realized it would be impossible to get all of it into a short story and it would have to be a book." At other times the precious particle is something the author has read—preferably a book of memoirs or history or travel, one that lies outside his own field of writing. Robert Penn Warren says, "I always remember the date, the place, the room, the road, when I first was struck. For instance, *World Enough and Time*. Katherine Anne Porter and I were both in the Library of Congress as fellows. We were in the same pew, had offices next to each other. She came in one day with an old pamphlet, the trial of Beauchamp for killing Colonel Sharp. She said, 'Well, Red, you better read this.' There it was. I read it in five minutes. But I was six years making the book. Any book I write starts with a flash, but takes a long time to shape up."

The book or story shapes up—assumes its own specific form, that is—during a process of meditation that is the second stage in composition. Angus Wilson calls it "the gestatory period" and says that it is "very important to me. That's when I'm persuading myself of the truth of what I want to say, and I don't think I could persuade my readers unless I'd persuaded myself first." The period may last for years, as with Warren's novels (and most of Henry James's), or it may last exactly two days, as in the extraordinary case of Georges Simenon. "As soon as I have the beginning," Simenon explains, "I can't bear it very long. . . . And two days later I begin writing." The meditation may be, or seem to be, wholly conscious. The writer asks himself questions—"What should the characters do at this point? How can I build to a climax?"—and answers them in various fashions before choosing the final answers. Or most of the process, including all the early steps, may be carried on without the writer's volition. He wakes before daybreak with the whole story in his head, as Joyce Cary did in San Francisco, and hastily writes it down. Or again—and I think most frequently—the meditation is a mixture of conscious and unconscious elements, as if a cry from the depths of sleep were being heard and revised by the waking mind.

Often the meditation continues while the writer is engaged in other occupations: gardening, driving his wife to town (as Walter Mitty did), or going out to dinner. "I never quite know when I'm not writing," says James Thurber. "Sometimes my wife comes up to me at a dinner party and says, 'Dammit, Thurber, stop writing.' She usually catches me in the middle of a paragraph. Or my daughter will look up from the dinner table and ask, 'Is he sick?' 'No,' my wife says, 'he's writing.' I have to do it that way on account of my eyes." When Thurber had better vision, he used to do his meditating at the typewriter, as many other writers do. Nelson Algren, for example, finds his plots simply by writing page after page, night after night. "I always figured," he says, "the only way I could finish a book and get a plot was just to keep making it longer until something happens."

The first draft of a story is often written at top speed; probably that is the best way to write it. Dorothy Canfield Fisher, who is not among the authors interviewed, once compared the writing of a first draft with skiing down a steep slope that she wasn't sure she was clever enough to manage. "Sitting at my desk one morning," she says, "I 'pushed off' and with a tingle of not altogether pleasurable excitement and alarm, felt myself 'going.' I 'went' almost as precipitately as skis go down a long white slope, scribbling as rapidly as my pencil could go, indicating whole words with a dash and a jiggle, filling page after page with scrawls." Frank O'Connor explains the need for haste in his own case. "Get black on white," he says, "used to be Maupassant's advice—that's what I always do. I don't give a hoot what the writing's like, I write any sort of rubbish which will cover the main outlines of the story, then I can begin to see it." There are other writers, however, who work ahead laboriously, revising as they go. William Styron says, "I seem to have some neurotic need to perfect each paragraph—each sentence, even—as I go along." Dorothy Parker reports that it takes her six months to do a story: "I think it out and then write it sentence by sentence—no first draft. I can't write five words but that I change seven."

O'Connor doesn't start changing words until the first draft is finished, but then he rewrites, so he says, "endlessly, endlessly, endlessly." There is no stage of composition at which these authors differ more from one another than in this final stage of preparing a manuscript for the printer. Even that isn't a final stage for O'Connor. "I keep on rewriting," he says, "and after it's published, and then after it's published in book form, I usually rewrite it again. I've rewritten versions of most of my early stories, and one of these days, God help, I'll publish these as well." Françoise Sagan, on the other hand, spends "very little" time in revision. Simenon spends exactly three days in revising each of his short novels. Most of that time is devoted to tracking down and crossing out literary touches—"adjectives, adverbs, and every word which is there just to make an effect. Every sentence which is there just for the sentence. You know, you have a beautiful sentence—cut it." Joyce Cary was another deletionist. Many of the passages he crossed out of his first drafts were those dealing explicitly with ideas. "I work over the whole book," he says, "and cut out anything that does not belong to the emotional development, the texture of feeling." Thurber revises his stories by rewriting them from the beginning, time and again. "A story I've been working on," he says, ". . . was written fifteen complete times. There must have been close to two hundred and forty thousand words in all the manuscripts put together, and I must have spent two thousand hours working at it. Yet the finished story can't be more than twenty thousand words." That would make it about the longest piece of fiction he has written. Men like Thurber and O'Connor, who rewrite "endlessly, endlessly," find it hard to face the interminable prospect of writing a full-length novel.

For short-story writers the four stages of composition are usually distinct, and there may even be a fifth, or rather a first, stage. Before seizing upon the germ of a story, the writer may find himself in a state of "generally intensified emotional sensitivity . . . when events that usually pass unnoticed suddenly move you deeply, when a sunset lifts you to exaltation, when a squeaking door throws you into a fit of exasperation, when a clear look of trust in a child's eyes moves you to tears." I am quoting again from Dorothy Canfield Fisher, who "cannot conceive," she says, "of any creative fiction written from any other beginning." There is not much doubt, in any case, that the germ is precious largely because it serves to crystallize a prior state of feeling. Then comes the brooding or meditation, then the rapidly written first draft, then the slow revision; for the story writer everything is likely to happen in more or less its proper order. For the novelist, however, the stages are often confused. The meditation may have to be repeated for each new episode. The revision of one chapter may precede or follow the first draft of the next.

That is not the only difference between writing a short story and writing a novel. Reading the interviews together, I was confirmed in an old belief that the two forms are separate and that mere length is not their distinguishing feature. A long short story—say of forty thousand words—is not likely to be written by the same person. Among the authors interviewed, the division that goes deepest is not between older and younger writers, or men and women writers, or French and English writers; it is the division between those who think in terms of the short story and those who are essentially novelists.

Truman Capote might stand for those who think in terms of the short story, since he tells us that his "more unswerving ambitions still revolve around this form." A moment later he says, "I invariably have the illusion that the whole play of a story, its start and middle and finish, occur in my mind simultaneously—that I'm seeing it in one flash." He likes to know the end of a story before writing the first word of it. Indeed, he doesn't start writing until he has brooded over the story long enough to exhaust his emotional response to the material. "I seem to remember reading," he says, "that Dickens, as he wrote, choked with laughter over his own humor and dripped tears all over the page when one of his characters died. My own theory is that the writer should have considered his wit and dried his tears long, long before setting out to evoke similar reactions in a reader." The reactions of the reader, not of the writer, are Capote's principal concern.

For contrast take the interview with Simenon, who is a true novelist even if his separate works, written and revised in about two weeks, are not much longer than some short stories. Each of them starts in the same fashion. "It is almost a geo-metrical problem," he says. "I have such a man, such a woman, in such surroundings. What can happen to them to oblige them to go to their limit? That's the question. It will be sometimes a very simple incident, anything which will change their lives. Then I write my novel chapter by chapter." Before setting to work Simenon has scrawled a few notes on a big manila envelope. The interviewer asks whether these are an outline of the action. "No, no," Simenon answers. ". . . On the envelope I put only the names of the characters, their ages, their families. I know nothing whatever about the events which will occur later. Otherwise"—and I can't help putting the statement in italics—*"it would not be interesting to me."*

Unlike Capote, who says that he is physically incapable of writing anything he doesn't think will be paid for (though I take it that payment is, for him, merely a necessary token of public admiration), Simenon would "certainly," he says, con-tinue writing novels if they were never published. But he wouldn't bother to write them if he knew what the end of each novel would be, for then *it would not be interesting*. He discovers his fable not in one flash, but chapter by chapter, as if he were telling a continued story to himself. "On the eve of the first day," he says, "I know what will happen in the first chapter. Then day after day, chapter after chapter, I find what comes later. After I have started a novel I write a chapter each day, without ever missing a day. Because it is a strain, I have to keep pace with the novel. If, for example, I am ill for forty-eight hours I have to throw away the previous chapters. And I never return to that novel." Like Dickens he lets himself be moved, even shattered, by what he is writing. "All the day," he says, "I am one of my characters"—always the one who is driven to his limit. "I feel what he feels. . . . And it's almost unbearable after five or six days. That is one of the reasons why my novels are so short; after eleven days I can't—it's impossible. I have to— It's physical. I am too tired."

Nobody else writes in quite the same fashion as Simenon. He carries a certain attitude toward fiction to the furthest point that it can be carried by anyone who writes books to be published and read. But the attitude in itself is not unusual, and in fact it is shared to some extent by all the true novelists who explain their methods in this book. Not one of them starts by making a scene-by-scene outline, as Henry James did before writing each of his later novels. James had discovered what he called the "divine principle of the Scenario" after writing several unsuccessful plays, and in essence the principle, or method, seems to be dramatistic rather than novelistic. The dramatist, like the short-story writer, has to know where he is going and how he will get there, scene by scene, whereas all the novelists interviewed by *The Paris Review* are accustomed to making voyages of exploration with only the roughest of maps. Mauriac says, "There is a point of departure, and there are some characters. It often happens that the first characters don't go any further and, on the other hand, vaguer, more inconsistent characters show new possibilities as the story goes on and assume a place we hadn't foreseen." Françoise Sagan says that she has to start writing to have ideas. In the beginning she has "a character, or a few characters, and perhaps an idea for a few of the scenes up to the middle of the book, but it all changes in the writing. For me writing is a question of finding a certain rhythm." (One thinks of Simenon and his feeling that he has to keep pace with the novel.) "My work," says Moravia, ". . . is not prepared beforehand in any way. I might add, too, that when I'm not working I don't think of my work at all." Forster does lay plans for his work, but they are subject to change. "The novelist," he says, "should, I think, always settle when he starts what is going to happen, what his major event is to be. He may alter this event as he approaches it, indeed he probably will, indeed he probably had better, or the novel becomes tied up and tight. But the sense of a solid mass ahead, a mountain round or over which or through which the story must go, is most valuable and, for the novels I've tried to write, essential. . . . When I began *A Passage to India* I knew that something important happened in the Malabar Caves, and that it would have a central place in the novel—but I didn't know what it would be."

Most novelists, one might generalize on this evidence, are

like the chiefs of exploring expeditions. They know who their companions are (and keep learning more about them); they know what sort of territory they will have to traverse on the following day or week; they know the general object of the expedition, the mountain they are trying to reach, the river of which they are trying to discover the source. But they don't know exactly what their route will be, or what adventures they will meet along the way, or how their companions will act when pushed to the limit. They don't even know whether the continent they are trying to map exists in space or only within themselves. "I think that if a map has the urge to be an artist," Simenon muses, "it is because he needs to find himself. Every writer tries to find himself through his characters, through all his writing." He is speaking for the novelist in particular. Short-story writers come back from their briefer explorations to brood over the meaning of their discoveries; then they perfect the stories for an audience. The short story is an *exposition;* the novel is often and perhaps at its best an *inquisition* into the unknown depths of the novelist's mind.

Apparently the hardest problem for almost any writer, whatever his medium, is getting to work in the morning (or in the afternoon, if he is a late riser like Styron, or even at night). Thornton Wilder says, "Many writers have told me that they have built up mnemonic devices to start them off on each day's writing task. Hemingway once told me he sharpened twenty pencils; Willa Cather that she read a passage from the Bible—not from piety, she was quick to add, but to get in touch with fine prose; she also regretted that she had formed this habit, for the prose rhythms of 1611 were not those she was in search of. My springboard has always been long walks." Those long walks alone are a fairly common device; Thomas Wolfe would sometimes roam through the streets of Brooklyn all night. Reading the Bible before writing is a much less common practice, and, in spite of Cather's disclaimer, I suspect that it did involve a touch of piety. Dependent for success on forces partly beyond his control, an author may try to propitiate the unknown powers. I knew one novelist, an agnostic, who said he often got down on his knees and started the working day with prayer.

The usual working day is three or four hours. Whether these authors write with pencils, with a pen, or at a typewriter—

and some do all three in the course of completing a manu-script—an important point seems to be that they all work with their hands; the only exception is Thurber in his sixties. I have often heard it said by psychiatrists that writers belong to the "oral type." The truth seems to be that most of them are manual types. Words are not merely sounds for them, but magical designs that their hands make on paper. "I always think of writing as a physical thing," Nelson Algren says. "I am an artisan," Simenon explains. "I need to work with my hands. I would like to carve my novel in a piece of wood." Hemingway used to have the feeling that his fingers did much of his thinking for him. After an automobile accident in Montana, when the doctors said he might lose the use of his right arm, he was afraid he would have to stop writing. Thurber used to have the sense of thinking with his fingers on the keyboard of a typewriter. When they were working together on their play *The Male Animal*, Elliott Nugent used to say to him, "Well, Thurber, we've got our problem, we've got all these people in the living room. What are we going to do with them?" Thurber would answer that he didn't know and couldn't tell until he'd sat down at the typewriter and found out. After his vision became too weak for the typewriter, he wrote very little for a number of years (using black crayon on yellow paper, about twenty scrawled words to the page); then painfully he taught himself to compose stories in his head and dictate them to a stenographer.

Dictation, for most authors, is a craft which, if acquired at all, is learned rather late in life—and I think with a sense of jumping over one step in the process of composition. Instead of giving dictation, many writers seem to themselves to be taking it. Mauriac says, "During a creative period I write every day; a novel should not be interrupted. When I cease to be carried along, when I no longer feel as though I were taking down dictation, I stop." Listening as they do to an inner voice that speaks or falls silent as if by caprice, many writers from the beginning have personified the voice as a benign or evil spirit. For Hawthorne it was evil or at least frightening. "The Devil himself always seems to get into my inkstand," he said in a letter to his publisher, "and I can only exorcise him by pensful at a time." For Kipling the Daemon that lived in his pen was tyrannical but well-meaning. "When your Daemon is in charge," he said, "do not try to think consciously. Drift, wait, and obey."

Objects on the writing table, which is the altar of the Daemon, are sometimes chosen with the same religious care as if they were chalices and patens. Kipling said, "For my ink I demanded the blackest, and had I been in my Father's house, as once I was, would have kept an ink-boy to grind me Indian-ink. All 'blue-blacks' were an abomination to my Daemon. . . . My writing-blocks were built for me to an unchanged pattern of large, off-white, blue sheets, of which I was most wasteful." Often we hear of taboos that must be observed—even by Angus Wilson, although he is as coolly rational as any fiction writer who ever set pen to paper (the pen in his case is medium and the paper is, by preference, a grammar-school exercise book). "Fiction writing is a kind of magic," Wilson says, "and I don't care to talk about a novel I'm doing because if I communicate the magic spell, even in an abbreviated form, it loses its force for me." One of the interviewed authors—only one, but I suspect there are others like him—makes a boast of his being superstitious. "I will not tolerate the presence of yellow roses," Capote says—"which is sad because they're my favorite flower. I can't allow three cigarette butts in the same ashtray. Won't travel on a plane with two nuns. Won't begin or end anything on a Friday. It's endless, the things I can't and won't. But I derive some curious comfort from these primitive concepts." Perhaps they are not only comforting but of practical service in helping him to weave his incantations. I can't help thinking of the drunk who always carried a ventilated satchel. "What's in it?" said his neighbor on a bus. "Just a mongoose. To kill snakes." The neighbor peered into the satchel and said, "There's nothing in it. That's an imaginary mongoose." The drunk said, "What about the snakes?"

At a summer conference on the novel, at Harvard, one of the invited speakers gave a rather portentous address on the Responsibilities of the Novelist. Frank O'Connor, on the platform, found himself giggling at each new solemnity. After the address he walked to the lectern and said, "All right, if there are any of my students here I'd like them to remember that writing is fun." On that point most of these authors would agree. "I have always found writing pleasant," Forster says, "and don't understand what people mean by 'throes of creation.' " "I write simply to amuse myself," says Moravia. Angus Wilson "started writing as a hobby." Thurber tells us that the act of writing "is either something the writer dreads or something he actually likes, and I actually like it. Even rewriting's fun." At another point he says, "When I'm not writing, as my wife knows, I'm miserable."

The professional writers who dread writing, as many do, are usually those whose critical sense is not only strong but unsleeping, so that it won't allow them to do even a first draft at top speed. They are in most cases the "bleeders" who write one sentence at a time, and can't write it until the sentence before has been revised. William Styron, one of the bleeders, is asked if he enjoys writing. "I certainly don't," he says. "I get a fine warm feeling when I'm doing well, but that pleasure is pretty much negated by the pain of getting started each day. Let's face it, writing is hell." But a moment later he says without any sense of contradiction, "I find that I'm simply the happiest, the placidist, *when* I'm writing . . . it's the only time that I feel completely self-possessed, even when the writing itself is not going too well." Not writing is the genuine hell for Styron and others in his predicament; writing is at worst a purgatory.

Whatever the original impulse that drives them to write—self-expression, self-discovery, self-aggrandizement, or the pain of not writing—most authors with a body of work behind them end by developing new purposes. Simenon, for example, would like to create the pure novel, without description, exposition, or argument: a book that will do only what a novel can do. "In a pure novel," he says, "you wouldn't take sixty pages to describe the South or Arizona or some country in Europe. Just the drama with only what is absolutely part of this drama . . . almost a translation of the laws of tragedy into the novel. I think the novel is the tragedy of our day." Critics have always advised him to write a *big* novel, one with twenty or thirty characters. His answer is, "I will never write a big novel. My big novel is the mosaic of all my small novels."

At this point Simenon suggests still another purpose, or dream, that is shared by almost all the writers who were interviewed. They want to write the new book, climb the new mountain, which they hope will be the highest of all, but still they regard it as only one conquest in a chain of mountains. The whole chain, the shelf of books, the Collected Works, is their ultimate goal. Moravia says, "In the works of every writer with any body of work to show for his effort, you will find recurrent themes. I view the novel, a single novel as well as a writer's entire corpus, as a musical composition in which the characters are themes." Faulkner says, "With *Soldier's Pay* I found out that writing was fun. But I found out afterward that not only each book had to have a design, but the whole output or sum of a writer's work had to have a design." Graham Greene says, in *The Lost Childhood*, "A ruling passion gives to a shelf of books the unity of a system." Each of these novelists wants to produce not a random succession of books, like discrete events for critics to study one by one, without reference to earlier or later events, but a complete system unified by his ruling passion, a system of words on paper that is also a world of living persons created in his likeness by the author. This dream must have had a beginning quite early in the author's life; perhaps it goes back to what Thornton Wilder calls "the Nero in the bassinet," the child wanting to be omnipotent in a world he has made for himself; but later it is elaborated with all the wisdom and fire and patient workmanship that the grown man can bring to bear on it. Particle after particle of the living self is transferred into the creation, until at last it is an external world that corresponds to the inner world and has the power of outlasting the author's life.

I suspect that some such dream is shared by many authors, but among those interviewed it is Faulkner who has come closest to achieving it, and he is also the author who reveals it most candidly. "Beginning with *Sartoris*," he says, "I discovered that my own little postage stamp of native soil was worth writing about and that I would never live long enough to exhaust it, and that by sublimating the actual into the apocryphal I would have complete liberty to use whatever talent I might have to its absolute top. It opened up a mine of other people, so I created a cosmos of my own. I can move these people around like God, not only in space but in time." And then he says, looking back on his work as if on the seventh day, "I like to think of the world I created as being a kind of keystone in the universe; that, small as that keystone is, if it were ever taken away the universe itself would collapse. My last book will be the Doomsday Book, the Golden Book, of Yoknapatawpha County. Then I shall break the pencil and I'll have to stop."

[1958]

REBELS, ARTISTS, AND SCOUNDRELS
(excerpts)

Some friends were arguing about whether there is any correlation between character and art. The conclusion they reported to me later is that there is no correlation: a scoundrel can produce a masterpiece and so can a saint. I brooded over that statement. Isn't it much too simple and isn't there more to be said?

That a saint can produce a masterpiece I know from having read St. John of the Cross. I haven't met any saints in the literary world of today and yesterday, but I have met some truly good men and women (Van Wyck Brooks, Marianne Moore, and Heywood Broun among others). I have met my share of scoundrels in that same world. For instance there was Henri the dancer, who liked to boast that there wasn't a man in New York he hadn't lied to, stolen from, or sodomized—"Maybe you're the exception," he conceded disarmingly. Henri went on to Berlin, which, under the Weimar Republic, was a happy setting for scoundrels and for artists too. When he died suddenly, the whole artistic community attended his funeral. Also I remember Lancelot the poet—that isn't his name—who supported himself for almost a year by collecting funds for his friend Erica to have an abortion (she wasn't pregnant). One morning we left him and Erica sleeping in our apartment while we went to our respective offices. They were gone when we came back and there was a gap in our bookshelves: Sandburg, Sappho, Shaw, Shelley, Sophocles, Spenser, and Swinburne were missing. Both Henri and Lancelot were charming and rather gifted persons, scoundrels with a touch of roguery, but I note that neither of them produced a masterpiece.

Perhaps my hesitation in the argument is due to the blunt word "scoundrel." Max Perkins of Scribners, an upright editor, used to tell his colleagues, "The trouble with American

writing today is that there aren't enough rascals." He might
have been defending his young friend Thomas Wolfe, who
was in truth something of a rogue (as Max would learn to his
cost, but without losing his affection for Wolfe). Both "rogue"
and "rascal" are words often used with an undertone of play-
ful or even admiring disapproval. There is no such undertone
in the use of "scoundrel," which my big old Webster's defines
as "a mean, worthless fellow; a rascal; a villain; a man without
honor or virtue." The suggestion here is of barefaced fraud
and swindling. Real scoundrelism is a career in itself, like
writing or painting, and it would take a man or woman of
unflagging genius to succeed in both professions.

Artists who succeed are strong characters, which is something different from saying they are saintly. Some of them—
most of them?—do scandalous and even scoundrelly things,
as we keep learning from new biographies of famous writers;
all their secret sins are being put on display. Ranged as it
were in museum cases, the sins have lost their scarlet radiance.
"So it's true that Byron committed incest," we say without
wagging our heads. "After all, Lady Augusta was only his
half-sister." That his adored Maid of Athens was really a boy
seems rather less shocking than the fact that John Ruskin died
a virgin. And George Sand: should we condemn her for taking
many lovers, including a woman, or merely for having treated
them badly? The 1960s have wrought so much confusion in
our moral standards that we try not to pass judgment.

One learns in the course of years that artists and writers,
as a tribal group, have certain defects of character. To be
quite simple, they drink too much; all the older ones drink
except the reformed alcoholics. The younger ones drink less,
but most of them smoke reefers or pop pills in the effort to
stimulate their imaginations. Their sexual drives are probably
stronger than those of the population as a whole and their
inhibitions are weaker; I am far from being the first to suspect
that there is a connection between literature and libido. They
may or may not be loyal husbands or wives—though I have
known artists' marriages that lasted for fifty years of complete
fidelity—and they are often neglectful parents. They may be
the best of neighbors, at any rate the most amusing, but they
are seldom loyal adherents of a government or a party, as the
Communists were pained to discover in the 1930s. Financially
the younger ones are not very responsible—how could they

be?—and sometimes they wreck the furniture of rented houses.

Is there any psychological or professional basis for this pattern of conduct? Perhaps there is; perhaps artists are more inclined than others to be egocentric and hence unfeeling in their personal relations. They need strong egos to do good work. It may be that their working habits, if nothing else, often lead them into a manic-depressive cycle. During the manic phase they write or paint furiously, but then the words and visions stop coming and they fall into a depressed phase of guilt and self-questioning. A special weakness of imaginative novelists and poets is that they often project fantasies with themselves as heroes. Some of them boast and lie, to put it bluntly, and by so doing they create immense difficulties for their biographers (as I have noted in the case of Erskine Caldwell, while mentioning several other names). That doesn't make them scoundrels. A scoundrel also boasts and lies, but he does it for profit, in the course of a swindle. There is something innocent, I find, in the stories that many imaginative writers tell about themselves; something connected with the quality of the image they project and hence ultimately with their work.

"An artist is a creature driven by demons," Faulkner said in a famous interview. ". . . He is completely amoral in that he will rob, borrow, beg, or steal from anybody and everybody to get the work done. . . . He has no peace till then. Everything goes by the board: honor, pride, decency, security, happiness, all, to get the book written. If a writer has to rob his mother, he will not hesitate; the 'Ode on a Grecian Urn' is worth any number of old ladies." Here as in other instances Faulkner was romanticizing his public image, for he ended, in fact, as a dutiful son and a responsible member of the community. He spent the first thirty years of his life piling up debts and the last thirty years paying them back to the last penny and the last returned favor. The writing of more than one book had been postponed while he slaved in Hollywood to support his family. Moreover, he was mistaken in what he said about the complete amorality of artists in general. Many of them beg and a few of them steal, but the good ones try—not always successfully—to live and work by a harsh code that the public fails to recognize because, at many points, it runs counter to ordinary moral judgments.

Thus, I have heard more than one poet condemned for being a good citizen, on the ground that by living respectably he was putting blinders on his imagination. As for family responsibilities, "One has no business to have any children," we read in Henry James's "The Lesson of the Master." "I mean, of course," the Master explains to a new disciple, "if one wants to do anything good." Children, he says, are "an incentive to damnation." James's version of the code was too uncompromising for most artists to accept, but still one hears echoes of his judgments. When a gifted novelist fell short of his mark, one of his rivals explained to me why he had failed: it was the result of his having stayed married to a saintly woman. "Why didn't he leave her," the other novelist said, "as soon as he found out that she was interfering with his work?" In the artist's code of morals, "work" is always a verb in the imperative mood, even when it seems to be a noun. A merely human relationship should be broken off if it keeps one from working.

On the other hand—to choose an example from the past—Hawthorne is thought to have shown moral courage when he refrained from working because he felt that his mind had lost its temper and its fine edge. "I have an instinct," he said in a letter to his publisher, "that I had better keep quiet. Perhaps I shall have a new spirit of vigor if I wait quietly for it; perhaps not." Shortly before writing the letter, Hawthorne had lost his little fortune through entrusting it to a friend. He wanted to provide for his family. That shouldn't have been an insoluble problem, since he had already earned his reputation and since any new novel of his, good or bad, would have had a wide sale. Lately he had started three different novels and the last start had been promising; he had only to continue as best he could and publish the result. But he stopped, feeling that however profitable the result might be and however much it might help his wife and children, it would not be up to his own standard of excellence. That was an artist's decision, for which he is respected by other artists.

Then what shall we say about the very different example of Anthony Trollope? Week in, week out, in the midst of other exacting duties, he produced forty pages of fiction, even when the week was spent in stage coaches or at sea. "As I journeyed across France to Marseilles," he says in his *Autobiography,* "and made thence a terribly rough voyage to Alexandria, I wrote my allotted number of pages every day. On this occasion more than once I left my paper on the cabin table, rushing away to be sick in the privacy of my state-room. It was February, and the weather was terrible, but still I did my work." He does not say whether it was good work or whether it had the taste of bile; quite simply it was work performed on schedule. Yet Trollope as well as Hawthorne is now admired by other writers (after a period of hesitation, it is true) and is felt to have carried out a moral choice.

There is no real conflict in this judgment about the two men. Both Hawthorne and Trollope were devoted to their craft, to their vocation, and were willing to make sacrifices for it—in one case a financial and family sacrifice, in the other a sacrifice of comfort. Therefore both were observing the artist's particular code of morality.

Not often formulated, sometimes jeered at for being irrelevant or elitist (as in the 1960s), but still enforced by famous examples, this code can be reduced to a very few commandments that persist today in the depths of an artist's mind.

First, he must believe in the importance of art, as well as the all-importance in his own life of the particular art to which he is devoted, whether this be fiction, poetry, painting, sculpture, or music. "O art, art," Henry James wrote in his notebook, "what difficulties are like thine, and, at the same time, what consolation and encouragements, also, are like thine? Without this, for me, the world would be, indeed, a howling wilderness."

Second, he must believe in his own talent, something deep in himself and apart from his daily life, yet having a universal validity. He must try by any means whatever to unearth this buried talent, with the conviction that, if fully expressed in works, it will be treasured by future generations. In a sense he is competing for a share in the future against every other artist in his field, with the chance of success ten thousand to one against him.

Third, he must honestly express his own vision of the world and his own personality, including his derelictions. Hawthorne, the least confessional of our great writers, said near the end of *The Scarlet Letter,* as if appending a moral to the story, "Be true! Be true! Show freely to the world, if not your worst, yet some trait by which the worst may be inferred!"

In the chapter about Conrad Aiken, another devoted artist, I quote his statement that the real business of the poet was "consciously or unconsciously to give the lowdown on himself, and through himself on humanity." I also quoted from a stern letter he had sent me after reading some of my poems. "But you?" he said, "what do you think or feel which is secretly you? shamefully you? intoxicatingly you? drunkenly or soberly or lyrically you? This doesn't come out?" He accused me—I hope wrongly, but in accordance with the artist's code—of having "avoided the final business of self-betrayal."

Fourth—to continue this rather seldom solemn list of commandments—the true artist must produce grandly, to the limit of his powers. Here again one can quote from James's notebooks. "I have my head, thank God, full of visions," he wrote for his own eyes in February 1895, a month after the catastrophic failure of his play *Guy Domville.* "Ah, just to let one's self go—at last; to surrender one's self to what through all the long years one has (quite heroically, I think) hoped for and waited for—the mere potential, and relative, increase of *quantity* in the material act—act of application and production. One has prayed and hoped and waited, in a word, to be able to work *more.* And now, toward the end, it seems, within its limits, to have come. That is all I ask. Nothing else in the world." At the mere thought of producing *more,* James felt himself to be a happy and virtuous person.

Conversely, when an author produces less, he is oppressed by guilt at having violated this fourth commandment. He may hesitate, however, before going to a psychiatrist for confession and absolution. To mention one example, Scott Fitzgerald wrote long letters to various psychiatrists who had been treating his wife Zelda. Some of them recommended that Scott should also be treated. We learn from one of his biographers, Andrew Turnbull, that "Fitzgerald balked at psychotherapy for himself, partly from pride . . . and partly from the artist's instinctive distrust of having his inner workings tampered with. He was afraid that psychiatric treatment might make him a reasoning, analytic person rather than a feeling one, and he instanced several novelists who had been psychoanalyzed and had written nothing but trash ever since." Like many other writers he regarded his neuroses, drinking included, as part of his literary equipment; perhaps that is another of the tribal weaknesses. As Louise Bogan said in her poem "Several Voices Out of a Cloud,"

Come, drunks and drug-takers; come, perverts unnerved!
Receive the laurel, given, though late, on merit; to whom
and whenever deserved.
Parochial punks, trimmers, nice people, joiners true-blue,
Get the hell out of the way of the laurel. It's deathless.
And it isn't for you.

The fifth and last commandment has to do with the deathless laurel. It is that the work of art should be so fashioned as to have an organic shape and a life of its own, derived from but apart from the life of its maker and capable of outlasting it. Only the work provides the artist's claim on the future, his hope of heaven, and it is worth almost any sacrifice of earthly comfort. Proust said at the end of *Time Recaptured,* "Let us allow our body to disintegrate, since each fresh particle that breaks off, now luminous and decipherable, comes and adds itself to our work to complete it at the cost of suffering superfluous to others more gifted and to make it more and more substantial as emotions gradually chip away our life." For Proust, and I suspect for others as well, every true artist is a sculptor chipping away at his own flesh, turning it to stone, and leaving behind him a lasting effigy.

I have said that these five commandments, this pentalogue, have seldom been formulated, but that they persist in the depths of an artist's mind. They inculcate a sense of duty that sometimes, at moments of stress, bursts forth with moral vehemence. "*A mighty will,* there is nothing but that!" James wrote in his notebook. "The integrity of one's will, purpose, faith!" Fitzgerald harangued one of Zelda's psychiatrists about the integrity that makes one writer better than another. "To have something to say," he lectured, "is a question of sleepless nights and worry and endless ratiocination of a subject—of endless trying to dig out the essential truth, the essential justice. As a first premise you have to develop a conscience and if on top of that you have talent so much the better. But if you have the talent without the conscience, you are just one of many thousand journalists."

Will, conscience, probity: the solemn words keep recurring when artists are speaking about themselves and forget to be ironical. "A writer should be of as great probity and honesty as a priest of God," Hemingway said in his introduction to *Men at War*. "He is either honest or not, as a woman is either chaste or not, and after one piece of dishonest writing he is never the same again." Later he said to me, "If you once do something shitty it spoils everything else you do, like the one bad apple in the barrel." We have learned from the record that Hemingway did many shitty or scoundrelly things, perhaps more of them than any other famous American writer except Robert Frost, our other great example of a man who produced masterpieces in spite of moral failings (or partly because of them, who knows?). Most of Hemingway's derelictions were caused by his raging desire to be first in everything. Many of them took the form of attacks with stiletto or bludgeon on persons who had helped him—Sherwood Anderson, Ford Madox Ford, Fitzgerald, Gertrude Stein—as if he were trying to obliterate the notion that he had ever accepted help. His image as an omnicompetent hero had to be preserved at any cost to his friends. As a writer, however, Hemingway tried hard to observe those five commandments, including the adjuration to give the lowdown on himself (as note "The Snows of Kilimanjaro").

Frost too was bent on being first, though not in everything; he merely wanted to be first in public esteem as a poet and a sage. He too made ruthless and sometimes childish attacks on anyone who seemed to threaten his primacy. In reviewing Lawrance Thompson's biography of Frost, James Dickey said of him, "No one who reads this book will ever again believe in the Frost Story, the Frost myth, which includes the premises that Frost the man was kindly, forbearing, energetic, hardworking, goodneighborly, or anything but the small-minded, vindictive, ill-tempered, egotistic, cruel, and unforgiving man he was until the world designed to accept at face value his estimate of himself." Bernard DeVoto, who had worshiped him, put all that in simpler words. "You're a good poet," he said after Frost had carried jealousy to the point of setting fire to a fistful of papers in order to disrupt a poetry reading by his rival Archibald MacLeish—"You're a good poet, Robert, but you're a bad man."

Frost agreed with him in a letter to DeVoto that tried and failed to effect a reconciliation, "Look out for me," he said. ". . . I'm telling you something in a self conscious moment that may throw light on every page of my writing for what it is worth. I mean I am a bad bad man." No less than Hemingway, however, he observed those five commandments in his work, which was sometimes foolish—when he tried to be a pundit—but was never fraudulent. He spoke in his true voice. In his work he was the opposite of a scoundrel.

One feature of the artist's code is that it preaches a curious mixture of extreme self-centeredness with something close to self-abnegation. The ideal artist, according to the code, is completely absorbed in himself, or rather in the task of producing something out of himself, but he forgets himself in the task, often to the point of deliberately incurring hardship, illness, or public ridicule. A more disturbing feature of the pentalogue is that it is dangerously incomplete. Unlike the Decalogue, it is not a guide to one's daily conduct as a spouse, a parent, or a neighbor. It does not guard the artist against the seven deadly sins, except possibly sloth; for the rest he can be proud, covetous, lustful, angry, gluttonous, and bursting with envy. The code even leads him into temptation with regard to some lesser sins or defects of character, as notably selfishness, vanity, neglect of one's family, and the abuse of stimulants or depressants in the hope of releasing one's imagination. Nevertheless it *is* a moral code and one that some great artists have followed with saintlike dedication; one thinks of Flaubert, James, Mallarmé, Joyce, Thomas Mann, and of a few others, including some who literally sacrificed their lives to their work. Art has its own hagiography and its Book of Martyrs.

Marcel Proust is clearly one of the martyrs. He died at fifty, having surrendered what should have been his remaining years on earth in order to bring his novel as near as possible to completion. Living alone, except for the family housekeeper; gaunt, wasted, unshaven; barely sustaining himself on beer and ices (he had them brought round from the Ritz); refusing other nourishment because someone had foolishly told him that the brain functions best on an empty stomach, he worked night after night on his enormous manuscript. In his last months, when he took to writing in bed because he no longer had strength enough to sit at a table, the work went very slowly. One night at three o'clock he made the old housekeeper sit beside him and—now that he was too weak to hold a pencil—dictated to her for a long time. "Celeste," he said at last, "I think what I've made you take down is very good. I shall stop now. I can't go on." He died the following afternoon.

Proust was a social climber, a shameless careerist, and an invert who loved nobody after his mother died; for others his strongest feeling was jealousy. Still, there is no question about his deliberate self-martyrdom; and one can think of many others who lived and died as victims to their art. In some cases such as those of Fitzgerald, Hart Crane, and Dylan Thomas, the victimage resulted from their persisting in a course of conduct which they recognized as self-destructive, but which they thought essential to the production of masterpieces. One might call some of them rogues, but they were clearly not scoundrels or sons-of-bitches.

And so, by a long detour, we come back to the original question, whether character and art are correlated. The answer is that they are, but in a complicated fashion. Masterpieces can be produced by saints of art or of the church; they can be produced by rascals or crazies or even, at times, by accident; but I refuse to think that they can be produced by genuine scoundrels, "men without honor or virtue." The artist, no matter what his sins may be, is bent on giving himself away; the scoundrel has no choice but to hide himself as best he can. In the end he cannot help revealing his scoundrelism— not so much in his subject matter or in what he seems to be saying about it, as rather in the shape and sound, the color and rhythm of his words. False, false, the reader unconsciously feels, closing the book. Once I made in my journal a statement that needs to be qualified, but that still holds a general truth. "No complete son-of-a-bitch," I said, "ever wrote a good sentence."

[1978]

A DEFENSE OF STORYTELLING
(excerpts)

The present disparagement of storytelling is directed against a very ancient art, perhaps the most ancient of all. When our remote ancestors gathered round the fire in a cave, some of them looked for walls on which to draw pictures of the animals they hoped to kill—such pictures survive in the caves of Lascaux and Altamira—but I like to think that even earlier, by generations and millenniums, the cavemen or their predecessors listened while someone told hunting stories, broken at rhythmic intervals by incantations for success and by the praise of tribal heroes. There were also priests among the cavemen, we have reason to surmise, and they must have found words to picture the beginnings of this pleasant earth and of the wholly admirable tribe to which they belonged. Those words must have taken the form of myths, that is, essentially, of stories.

All this would accord with a fundamental operation of thought, to be distinguished from conceptual thinking. Conceptually, we say that one thing is so *because* another thing is so *because* still another thing is so. We observe a phenomenon, then look for its cause inductively, then for the cause of that cause, until we reach the first or highest Cause. Or, reversing the process, we start with a general principle and reason deductively to particular results, all of which exist timelessly in a world of essences. But since we live in a world of time that is filled with events, we are less moved by conceptual thinking than by a storyteller who says, "This happened . . . and *then* this happened . . . and *afterward* this happened," as if each event were the direct cause of the one following it.

Post hoc, ergo propter hoc is a logical fallacy, but it is also an essential form of human thought, embodied in the mythology of every culture. A myth might be defined as a doctrine presented in terms of successive events; in other words, as

doctrine transformed into story. To borrow a phrase from
Kenneth Burke, a myth is the temporization of essence. A
familiar example is the biblical myth of Creation:

> In the beginning God created the heaven and the earth.
> And the earth was without form, and void; and darkness was
> upon the face of the deep. And the Spirit of God moved upon
> the face of the waters.
> And God said, Let there be light, and there was light.
> And God saw the light, that it was good, and God divided
> the light from the darkness.
> And God called the light Day, and the darkness he called
> Night. And the evening and the morning were the first day.

Here is the creation of the world in terms of story, in terms
of events that follow one another in sequence. Here, too, the
events are combined with a *naming* that forms part of the
narrative process—"And God called the light Day"—as well
as with a phrase about the evening and the morning that will
be repeated to mark elapsed time, in the same way that poets
use rhymes and refrains:

> And God called the firmament Heaven. And the evening and
> the morning were the second day.

> And the earth brought forth grass, and herb yielding seed
> after his kind, and the tree yielding fruit, whose seed was in
> itself, after his kind: and God saw that it was good.
> And the evening and the morning were the third day.

And so to the seventh day, when "God ended his work
which he had made; and he rested on the seventh day from
all his work which he had made." In Kenneth Burke's illuminating comment on the first three chapters of Genesis (see
The Rhetoric of Religion, 1961), he sets forth the doctrines
implicit in the story they tell. These, as he explains at length,
include Original Sin, Redemption, and the coming of a Redeemer. At this point, a process is being reversed: Just as
essence had been temporized into myth or story, so myth can
be conceptualized into timeless doctrine, with the *post hoc* of
narrative transformed into the *propter hoc* of logical relation.
It is indeed a question which came first, the doctrine or the
story.

I have been talking about the story in very ancient times,

but I do not mean to imply that it belongs to the past or will ever become "obsolete." In one important respect it seems peculiarly suited to modern society. Narrative deals with a sequence of events, that is, with a becoming, with a process rather than a pattern, and process thinking is an essential trait of the modern mind. Living as we do in unstable situations, we try to recognize the forces of change: How fast are they moving and in which directions? What seems obsolete in the light of such questions is the image thinking and pattern thinking of many contemporary authors. They might all be disciples of Zeno the Eleatic as they try, in effect, to demonstrate once again that Achilles could never overtake the tortoise and that an arrow is motionless at every instant of its flight. Because they present the world as a spatial concept, a stasis instead of a process, they offer misleading pictures of the world in which we live.

It seems to me that the real adventure for writers of each new generation lies in a different field. Instead of pasting snapshots into albums, they might look hard for new stories and new ways of telling them. They would then be helping to create the myths of what is always, and for each of them, a new age.

The function of the story in itself and the challenge it offers to the writer's inventiveness have usually been neglected by critics. Even novelists, when they write about their art, are likely to disparage the narrative element—as E. M. Forster does in *Aspects of the Novel* (1927), where he says that the story is a "low atavistic form," on which a good writer should rely as little as possible, his merit depending rather on what he has to say about the narrated events. As for professional critics, when they praise a novel it is usually—and for three centuries has almost always been—by describing it as something else than a novel: for example, as an object lesson in manners or morals, a much-needed sermon, a sweeping social panorama, a portrait gallery, a searching inquiry into the human psyche, an allegory, or a re-creation of the Orestes myth. Of course it can be any of those things or others, including a clinical report, if that is what the author was truly impelled to write; but unless it also tells a story, it ceases to be a novel.

Because critics do not often concern themselves with narrative as a challenging art in itself, they have reached no agreement on the terms used to describe its various features: one man's "theme" is another man's "subject" and still another's "ground-situation." Even the key word "story" has several different meanings. Forster defines it as "a narrative of events arranged in their time sequence," thus including all sorts of factual reports, but apparently excluding fictions in which the time sequence is fragmented or in which the author works backward toward the hidden meaning of some event in the past. A lesser English novelist, Margaret Kennedy, offers what seems to me a more accurate definition. In her useful but neglected book *The Outlaws on Parnassus* (1960), she says that a story is "a pattern of events so narrated as to evoke an intended response." That has the advantage of bringing in the reader or listener, without whose hoped-for response the story would not be told; but still her definition leaves us wondering about the difference between a story properly speaking and, let us say, the newspaper account of a disaster by land or sea.

As a basis for that distinction, I might suggest that the story proper, if it is complete, will include four elements. A *person* (or group of persons) is involved in a *situation* and performs an *act* (or series of acts, or merely undergoes an experience) as a result of which *something is changed*.* Person, situation, action, something changed: all four elements are present in a complete story, but of course they assume a diversity of forms. Instead of being a person, the protagonist may be a wild animal, or a tame one like Black Beauty, or a big fish, or anything else personified—even a storm or a forest fire, as in two of George R. Stewart's novels; even a spermatazoon moving with thousands of others toward union with an ovum, as in John Barth's brief and memorable "Night Journey." The situation may lie in the future, or in some imaginary world (I am not arguing here for realism); or again it may lie in the past and the present action may include a search for its true meaning; one example is Faulkner's *Absalom, Absalom!* The action may be simple or extremely complicated. Often it results from a decision by the central character, but in natur-

---

* A similar statement of the elements, not in a story, but in a drama, was offered by Francis Ferguson in his *Idea of a Theatre* (1949). I am especially indebted to his emphasis on the "something is changed." [M.C.]

alistic novels its course is determined by natural laws, not by persons. These merely suffer the effects of natural laws, with the result in many cases that nature (or society) becomes the real protagonist.

As for the fourth element, the "something changed" that makes the action irreversible, it is often hard to recognize. In novels of sensibility such as those by Virginia Woolf and in stories such as those by Sherwood Anderson and his army of successors, there may be little change—or none whatever— in the objective situation; but the protagonist, who is most often a woman or an adolescent boy or girl, will have achieved a higher degree of self-awareness. It is this change in the protagonist during a moment of insight—an "epiphany," to use Joyce's word—that transforms a random series of impressions into a story. The device was used so often in the 1950s that it became one of the idols to be smashed in the 1960s.

I feel that the "something changed" is the most important of the four elements. Since it results from an interplay of the other three, it unites them into a single action marked off in time and set apart from the confusion of daily life. Here I am thinking of Aristotle, who said that stories "should be based on a single action, one that is a complete whole in itself, with a beginning, middle, and end, so as to enable the work to produce its own proper pleasure with all the organic unity of a living creature." I have to concede, however, that there are many true stories from which the fourth element is omitted, and wisely so, if it is present by implication. Person, situation, and action have all been so vividly presented that the author feels no need to tell his readers how the story ended; they can picture the change for themselves. I think of an early Hemingway story, "Cat in the Rain." It starts with a young American couple spending a rainy day in their hotel room on the Italian Riviera. The husband is sprawled on the bed reading a book. The wife looks out across the empty square and sees a cat trying to shelter itself under an iron table. "I'm going to get that kitty," she says. The husband goes on reading. The wife ventures into the rain after greeting the hotelkeeper, who sends a maid after her with an umbrella. She finds the iron table, but the cat has disappeared. Back in their room, the young wife says, "I wanted it so much. I wanted that poor kitty. It isn't any fun to be a poor kitty out in the rain." The husband goes on reading. There is a knock at the door and the maid appears, this time with a big tortoise-shell cat in her arms. "Excuse me," she says, "but the padrone asked me to bring this for the signora." End of the story. Apparently nothing has changed, but the reader knows that the wife is a kitten in the rain and feels that she may some day seek refuge with the hotelkeeper or someone else of the same big, paternal sort. The first Mrs. Hemingway was to do so in her second marriage, thus reinforcing one's feeling that good stories have a predictive quality.

There is another fairly numerous group of stories in which the point seems to be made that nothing has changed in reality; the end circles back to the beginning. A beggar is invited into a wealthy merchant's house; he is bathed, given rich clothes to wear, and ushered into a feast at which he is guest of honor. He drinks too much, insults his host, falls asleep, and wakes in the street dressed in his familiar rags. Stories like these, older than *The Arabian Nights*, faintly echo the myth of eternal recurrence. In other forms of the myth, a hero spends a season in hell or paradise, then reappears among his own people. But he is never the same hero as he was before he entered the earth, just as the beggar carried out of the rich merchant's house is the same only in outward appearance as he was before he entered it. Something has changed for him.

There is still another group of stories—if we call them stories—in which the author's purpose is to present a wholly typical day in the life of some character, usually one with a low degree of self-awareness. An example is "Mr. Reginald Peacock's Day," by Katherine Mansfield. I had forgotten Mr. Peacock and have absolutely no desire to reread the account of his day, but I might quote the clear summary that Edith Mirrielees gives in her book *Story Writing* (1947).

> The very point of the story [she says] is our certainty that the day before and the day after exhibit Mr. Peacock exactly as does the day described. Whether it is Mr. Peacock's response to his wife's waking him . . . or his singing in his bath; whether it is the Duke's addressing him as "Peacock"—"quite as if he were one of themselves"—or the titled music pupil leaving her violets in his vase, the happening effects neither a change in, nor an added revelation of, Mr. Peacock's attitudes and emotions, nor does it show him meeting any crisis. The purpose of each is to

display one foible, which same foible any hour of his life except
a sleeping one would display with equal fidelity.

A feature that irritates me in such a narrative is the tone
of condescension announced in the title. The "Mr.," standing
before Reginald Peacock—in itself an emblematic name—is
a nudge from the author warning us that we are not to identify
ourselves with this person, but instead to thank God that our
days are more varied than his and that something unexpected
will happen to us tomorrow. But let us forget Mr. Reginald
Peacock, who represents the weaker side of Katherine Mansfield's great talent, the sniffing attitude of revulsion into which
she was always in danger of falling. Let us think about slice-
of-life narratives in general and ask a simple question: Are
they stories properly speaking? Whether they deal with peasants or people in the slums or middle-class snobs like Mr.
Peacock, don't they belong to a type best described as fic-
tionalized sociology? Being fiction they have less authority
than reports by genuine sociologists. Lacking an essential element, a something changed, they afford less pleasure to the
reader than a story in which the action is a complete whole
in itself. The true story is an organized period of time, much
as a sculpture is organized three-dimensional space. Time, as
we learn again at every moment, is irreversible. The quality
of any moment in life, or in a good story, depends on the
moments that preceded it in irreversible sequence. It is true
that slice-of-life narratives usually deal with given periods of
time, an hour, a day, a week, but since they do not embody
changes in quality, they are not organized in time; they are
merely sliced out of it.

I consulted a list of best sellers for the year 1976 that appeared in *The Times Book Review*; it was confined to hard-
bound fiction and nonfiction sold in bookstores. What
impressed me about the annual list, which includes sales figures, was the immensely greater popularity of nonfiction. The
ten best-selling novels had a total sale (as reported by their
publishers, sometimes with a little optimism) of 1,605,174
copies. This was to be compared with 3,390,717 copies, or
more than twice as many, for the ten leading nonfiction titles.
Among these "general" books, five were in the broad field
of self-knowledge or self-improvement. The other five were

"subject books," and they included *Roots*, by Alex Haley, which is truly a nonfiction novel and which, after its success on television, promised to be among the most widely read books of the decade. But all five had a strong narrative element and presented their factual material as "a pattern of events so narrated as to evoke an intended response."

That phrase, as may be remembered, is Margaret Kennedy's definition of a story, and I said that it had the advantage of bringing in the reader or listener and his response. The listener is always present, if only in the storyteller's imagination or on the subconscious level of his mind; if not for the listener, why should the story be *told*? One might answer that children tell stories to themselves, but at such times the child plays a double role: he is both the teller and the listener, the artist and his audience, and if the listening side of him gets bored, the story is never finished. As for adult storytellers, they are not compulsive talkers or writers bent merely on expressing themselves and having their say. They don't say, they tell or render or, to be more accurate, they use the medium of words to show us persons acting or being acted upon, while arranging the acts in a sequence calculated to grasp and reward our attention. Form, Kenneth Burke said long ago in *Counter-Statement* (1931), is "the psychology of the audience. Or, seen from another angle, form is the creation of an appetite in the mind of an auditor and the adequate satisfying of that appetite." The revolt against form and "stories" is, in one of its aspects, an effort to abolish the audience.

When the story ends something has changed, as I emphasized, and the change is for better or worse. It follows that in the broad sense every story is a fable with a moral concealed, sometimes deeply, in the texture of events. That concealed moral transforms the *post hoc* of narrative into the *propter hoc* of conceptual thought. Usually the good or prudent characters are rewarded after a fashion, if only in their hearts, and the wicked are somehow punished. Often, however, the process is reversed, with the good punished by malign forces or simply by accident, in which case the storyteller implies that there is no justice or reason in this chaotic world. That too is a sort of moral, or anti-moral, and one that may express his inmost feelings with force and brilliance. Kurt Vonnegut, to mention one of the "black" novelists, was twenty-two years old and a prisoner of war in Dresden when the city was destroyed by a firestorm in which 135,000 persons lost their lives. With other surviving prisoners he was detailed to gather and burn the corpses, which he remembers as those of "babies, old people, zoo animals, and thousands upon thousands of rabid Nazis, of course." It was an experience that confirmed his atheism and shaped his future novels. Joseph Heller, another "black" writer, was a lieutenant in the Air Force; he didn't bomb Dresden, but he had his fill of a murderous bureaucracy. Most readers, however, live out their relatively peaceful lives without being sentenced to death by the Air Force, or by Hitler or Stalin. They would rather not accept the anti-moral, even when they bear in mind the crimes and follies of the years since 1914.

They also feel uncomfortable about a story in which the heroine is killed by accident when, for example, she steps in front of a bus. Accidents, they feel with Aristotle, should be placed at the beginning of a story, not at the end. No matter how sophisticated they may be, they still prefer a pattern or sequence of events that implies some general scheme of rewards and punishments. Shaped as I was by the confident years before the Great War, I confess to sharing, with reservations, that innocent preference. I also confess to feeling that life is the ultimate source of all fictions, even the most fantastic, and that, in its blundering, dilatory, often secret way, it provides an infinite number of fables, renewed in substance and form for each new generation.

[1978]

HOW WRITING MIGHT BE TAUGHT

For some years after World War II, it seemed that almost everyone in the new generation, and many older people as well, dreamed of becoming a professional writer. Thousands of aspirants attended the summer writers' conferences then being held all over the country. Many other thousands displayed their American faith in formal education by enrolling in universities that offered advanced courses in creative writing. It was a time when departments of English flourished as never before (and never since, as younger professors often complain). Even small colleges had their writers in residence, not to mention their tenured or visiting professors who had published several novels or books of poems. To the world of professional writers, those colleges offered a new economic resource, one that took the place, if on a less affluent scale, of Hollywood in the 1930s.

I too was on the staff of several writers' conferences. I also did a good deal of knockabout teaching and lecturing, most often at Stanford, though never for more than an academic quarter or at most a semester. I used to joke with friends about our playing the role of wandering scholars and poets in the Middle Ages. Though I liked meeting young writers and even liked teaching, which seemed to me easier than writing, I conscientiously refused to serve for longer periods after finding that I couldn't teach and write at the same time. During a semester at Michigan in 1957, I was asked to give the annual Hopwood Address, and I chose to speak on the very old question whether and how the profession of writing could be taught in a university. It seems to me that my remarks, here slightly revised, still have a practical value.

I.

Today there is no generally available form of apprenticeship, no clearly marked path for qualified beginners that will lead them into the writing profession. That wasn't always the case in American writing. We can see in retrospect that during the nineteenth century there were two such paths, each of them followed by many young men with literary ambitions. I have mentioned those paths in an earlier book, *The Literary Situation*, but I make no apology for repeating myself, because the facts are necessary as a background for what I want to say. One of the paths led through a divinity school, usually Harvard, and later through the pastorate of a small church, most often Unitarian. The young minister would write sermons, polish and publish some of them, then write for general magazines or book publishers, and finally he would resign his pastorate. Writers trained as clergymen had the great advantage of a flowing style acquired in the pulpit; for most of them the words came easily. They had the disadvantage that the style was intended to impress a congregation instead of being directed to the hearts and minds of individuals.

The other path appears to have held more promise for writers proper as opposed to moral teachers. It was the one that started in a printing shop, usually in the composing room of a weekly newspaper. After leaving school at fourteen or fifteen, the apprentice man of letters was employed there as a copy boy or printer's devil; then he would be taught how to read proof and how to set type by hand. It was the most practical sort of training, for at worst or least the apprentice would learn the rules of grammar, punctuation, and spelling— which are becoming an esoteric knowledge—and at best he would learn another lesson as well. By handling a type metal alphabet, he would learn that words have body and weight as well as sound; he would acquire an almost tactile sense of language; and he would also learn that big words and oratorical turns of phrase wasted his time, like that of readers.

The first truly effective American prose writer, Benjamin Franklin, was a printer, just as the second, Jonathan Edwards, was a clergyman. In the nineteenth century those who followed Ben Franklin's path were, among others, Whitman, Howells, Bret Harte, Mark Twain, and Lafcadio Hearn, all of whom set type at some stage in their early careers and each of whom learned to write fluent and accurate English. After setting type for a newspaper, they each wrote stories for it. The best of their stories were reprinted so widely that magazine editors began asking for their work, then book publishers, and they were launched on their literary careers—sometimes without quite knowing how it had happened.

After 1890 most of the newspaper composing rooms were unionized and no longer offered casual employment to schoolboys serving their literary apprenticeships. The new path to recognition led through the city room of a big-town newspaper, where the miserably underpaid staff kept changing and there were always jobs for ambitious young men. If they survived the first few years—as not all of them did in those hard-drinking days—young writers learned to get their facts, put them in proper sequence, and also learned a great deal about the tough underbelly of American life. Except for Stephen Crane and H. L. Mencken, not many of them acquired the devout feeling for words that was shown by earlier writers who had worked in printing shops. Dreiser, Huneker, Harold Frederic, Jack Reed, and David Graham Phillips—in fact most of the new writers who appeared between 1890 and 1915—got their start as cub reporters.

In a new age the situation has changed again. Newspaper work has ceased to be a poorly paid apprenticeship for other professions, including authorship, and has become a rewarding career in itself. On-the-job training for writers is something that still exists in a few places, but the places are hard to find. Most of the beginners go to college and many of them continue into graduate schools, where they are exposed to the best formal education that the country has offered. Unfortunately, if they still want to be writers, not critics or teachers, it isn't always or often the best education for the careers they have in mind.

This general tendency in the field of writing—I mean the decline of apprenticeship, with our educational system coming forward to supply the professional training on all levels no longer provided by masters and employers—is one that extends into all fields of American life. More and more of our high schools are being transformed into trade schools, offering a maximum of shop practice with only a seasoning dash of book learning. The demand for professional training has forced our universities to expand far beyond the original four faculties of theology, law, medicine, and the liberal arts. Engineering first, then agriculture, forestry, schoolteaching, nursing, advertising, selling, management of all types, household economics, getting married, having babies: almost every human activity has become a subject for university instruction, often at the postgraduate level. For the artistic and literary professions there are many famous schools or departments of architecture, journalism, music, design in all its branches, and the drama. A similar development is taking place in the field of writing, but here the professional training has neither been carried so far nor organized in such a systematic manner as in other fields. Indeed, the popularity of courses in advanced writing is a fairly recent development.

So far as I have been able to learn, the first writing course for students who seriously planned to become men of letters was given at Harvard in the 1890s by Lewis E. Gates. To judge by his students, who included a number of brilliant poets and novelists, he must have been a gifted teacher. Frank Norris's first novel, *Vandover and the Brute*, was one of those written in Gates's course. A few years later the same sort of instruction was being given at Michigan by Fred Newton Scott, who was Avery Hopwood's admired professor and was thus indirectly the cause of the Hopwood Awards.

After Gates died in 1903, his place at Harvard was taken by two other famous teachers: the scholarly Dean Briggs, whose deeply wrinkled face bore a look of sympathy and saintliness; and C. T. Copeland—"Copey," as everybody called him—who was more of an actor than a saint or a scholar, but who had an eye for details and an ear that quickly distinguished good from awkward prose. At conferences he used to sit back in his armchair like a pale-bronze Buddha and listen while we read our themes aloud; then he would dictate a comment for the student to write. I remember two of these. Once when I had described the swirling dust in a Pittsburgh street he asked, "Don't you remember the smell of dried horse dung? Why didn't you put that in?" And once when I read him a sententious editorial written for *The Harvard Advocate*, in which one wondered how the country knew who . . . he shook his bald head with a shifting highlight on it from the afternoon sun and groaned, "Malcolm, when are you going to stop using those knew-whoings and one-wonderings?" I stopped that afternoon.

In the first two decades of this century, Harvard was a seedbed and plant nursery of American authorship. Almost all the writers who were there in any of the years from 1905 to 1920 took either Copey's course or Dean Briggs's course, or both of them. The only exceptions were the thirteen dramatic writers—Baker's Dozen—admitted each year to George Pierce Baker's English 47 Workshop. In that period when all Americans worshiped success, and especially early success, an event of the year 1907 gave special prestige to the 47 Workshop as if this had been sprinkled with gold dust, some of which rubbed off on the other advanced writing courses. The event was the long Broadway run of Edward Sheldon's play, *Salvation Nell,* which had been written in English 47 while Sheldon was still an undergraduate. Later Eugene O'Neill was a still more famous product of the course.

In 1925 Baker moved his 47 Workshop to Yale, where a flourishing school of the drama was built around it. In 1931 the University of Michigan, which had retained a lively interest in writing courses, was enabled to broaden its program and award substantial prizes as a result of the Hopwood bequest. Soon universities all over the country were trying to attract young writers by offering courses in advanced or, as it is usually miscalled, creative writing. Excellent programs were being conducted at some of the smaller colleges, including Kenyon, Bennington, and Hollins. Larger universities were more or less expected to have writers' workshops. At Stanford the writing program had its own generous endowment and was able to offer fellowships. At Iowa there was a postgraduate school of writing that conferred a master's degree, with the student submitting a novel or a book of poems as his magisterial thesis.*

Most of the present courses everywhere are conducted by able and hardworking teachers. Most of the students—of

* Writing twenty years later I should also have mentioned Syracuse, with a school of writing conceived more or less on the Iowa pattern (but smaller and with more emphasis on poetry); San Francisco State, with a succession of well-known writers on the faculty; and the Writing Division of the School of the Arts at Columbia. This last offered a two-year Master of Fine Arts program and was proud of the record made by its graduates. [M.C.]

course not all of them—are willing to work seriously and aren't taking the courses just for credit. Many of the former students have made names for themselves, as one can see by reading a list of the former Hopwood Awards. If the courses accomplish less than the teachers hope for them, perhaps that results from a misconception of what they might properly undertake.

Often the misconception is embodied in the name of the course: Creative Writing, Creating the Novel, Creating the Short Story, or even Creating the Fifteen-Minute Script. I doubt that any instructor, however earnest or inspired, can teach any group of students, however talented, to create anything whatever. He cannot give them experience of the world, or a desire to communicate the experience, or do more for their power of invention than merely to encourage it, if the power already exists. What he can properly teach the students, or expose them to the opportunity of learning, are the rules and practices to be deduced from other people's writing, the standards of the writing profession, and the known resources of language as a medium. He cannot teach the *art* of writing, since that is unteachable by definition; it is something a fortunate student will learn for himself.

Partly because of a false emphasis on the art rather than the craft, some writing programs become suffused with an atmosphere of artiness, of waiting for inspirations that don't always come—and when they do come, the student has not enough of the craft to embody them in the necessary words. Other teachers, trying to be more realistic, avoid this emphasis and like to say that they could never teach their students how to write—"But at least," they add, "we can teach them how to read." So the so-called workshop in creative writing is transformed into an exercise in critical analysis, very useful to most students, but not necessarily serving as a prologue or apprenticeship to their own work. Sometimes it has the opposite effect of developing their critical sense to the point at which they can't write at all, or can write nothing but explications for the literary quarterlies.

I think there is another kind of writing program that might be offered, beginning at the undergraduate level. In a completely dogmatic and rather impractical fashion, with no attention to administrative problems or interdepartmental rivalries, I should like to suggest what such a program might be.

2.

Its purpose would be to teach the skills that are needed by every professional writer. It would be concerned with working habits, with problems of structure and style, and with methods that writers in the past have found for solving them—not forgetting that new writers might try to find new methods better suited to their personalities. In other words, the program would not be creational or expressional or inspirational or analytical or therapeutic, but, I hope in the strict sense of the word, professional—like the best of the programs that have long been offered in architecture, the drama, and musical composition.

It would be open to juniors and seniors, with an optional third year for graduate students. For juniors and seniors it would require at least as many hours of credit as the present honors program in English literature. In the postgraduate year it would be designed to occupy the whole, or almost the whole, of the student's time. In most cases there would be no second postgraduate year, since the student should then be ready to learn new lessons from practical experience in writing. One thing he should never be encouraged to do is to travel from one university to another, taking more and more writing courses, supporting himself with fellowships and never getting his work published—until at last, like a student I used to know, he gets married and finds a post at some community college as an instructor in creative writing.

The instructors in the program I have in mind would be men and women with a passion for teaching younger persons how to write, and with the hope that they will some day find and encourage a young writer of high enough stature to justify their teaching. Whether they should be professional writers themselves is a question that hasn't really been settled. Many or most of the famous instructors today are writers who manage to combine their professional careers with college instruction. I might mention among others Archibald MacLeish at Harvard, Robert Penn Warren at Yale, Mark Van Doren at Columbia, R. P. Blackmur at Princeton, John Crowe Ransom at Kenyon, Allen Tate at Minnesota, Hudson Strode at Alabama, Mark Schorer and George R. Stewart at Berkeley, Theodore Roethke at the University of Washington, Wallace

Stegner at Stanford, and Allan Seager at this university.* All these have published several books, and whatever they tell their students has the weight of experience behind it.

On the other hand, most of the famous instructors of the past were not professional writers, and here I am thinking of men and women like Gates, Copeland, Briggs, Edith Mirrielees of Stanford, and Fred Newton Scott. The greatest writing teacher of our age was not a writer, or connected with any university, but he had a passion for good storytelling and the passion was communicated to others. He was a publisher's editor, the late Maxwell E. Perkins, who was the friend of Hemingway and Fitzgerald, the spiritual father of Thomas Wolfe, and the adviser of many capable if less distinguished authors. It should be noted, and not incidentally, that Perkins and the older instructors I have mentioned could write very well when they were called upon to write or forced themselves to do so. That ability should be required of every instructor in a writing program. There are many English professors, respected in the academic world, who should be disqualified as teachers of writing by the first paragraph, even the first sentence, of any critical study they may have contributed to *The PMLA Quarterly*.

A requirement for students in the program is that they should have distinguished themselves in whatever writing courses they have taken during their first two years of college work. They need not have distinguished themselves in other courses because the sad fact is that future novelists and dramatists, unlike future critics and some poets, aren't always the brightest students in courses outside their own field. Every student in the program should have proved himself capable of writing clear sentences and well-constructed paragraphs. One reason for that requirement is that instructors shouldn't

* The names are of the year 1957. Twenty years later all those distinguished men were dead or had retired from teaching. There were possibly not so many writers-in-residence as there had been as late as 1970, owing to the reduced budgets of English faculties. Still, the relation between the literary world and the academic world was closer than ever, so close, in fact, that it was affecting the history of American literature. Signs of inbreeding had begun to appear. Among the productive novelists attached to faculties were John Barth, Saul Bellow, Vance Bourjaily, Kay Boyle, George P. Elliott, John Gardner, Mark Harris, John Hawkes, and Hortense Calisher, to mention only a few, and I shan't even try to list the poets, critics, and biographers who were tenured professors. [M.C.]

have to bother with such fundamentals, but there is the additional reason that future men of letters are more likely to reveal themselves by their passion for getting the words right than by their wealth of material. Eventually they will be judged by what they say, but their early promise depends more on how they say it.

I should hope that the program would be difficult enough to frighten away the mere yearners and tender spirits and seekers for help in unfolding their personalities. It is the difficult programs that attract the best students—and if the program I have in mind proved difficult and fruitful enough, it might attract good students from all parts of the country.

It would include three or four subjects that are not usually taught in universities, even the largest. For example, it could begin with what might be called—even if we don't like the term—an indoctrination course on the history of the writing profession. Entirely too much attention is being paid to the faults and delinquencies of famous writers, with the result that people have formed a false picture of the profession as a refuge for the weak, the abnormal, the self-indulgent, and the self-destructive. Not only the public but young writers too are being encouraged to forget that writing is a profession with its own difficult standards of conduct, with its high virtues and with sins like dishonesty and self-deception that are regarded as sins against the Holy Ghost. Writing has its saints and heroes—like Keats and Flaubert, who is sometimes a dangerous model; like Trollope as antidote to Flaubert; like Tolstoy, James, Conrad, and Thomas Mann—and their lives might be studied as models of courage for the new generation.

There would also be a course in the creative process, or simply in the mechanics of finding a subject, developing it in words, and putting the words on paper. The course would include such topics as how to observe a scene, how to remember it, how to visualize, how to meditate on a subject in the manner of Hawthorne and Henry James, how to write first drafts, and finally how to revise what one has written. But there would be other topics too: how to take notes or not to take them, how to make outlines and scenarios, when to write and where, and how long every day. Most of those questions have a different practical answer for each writer, and the answers have to be found by experiment. Accordingly there might be such practical exercises as writing at different times of the day (including midnight and six o'clock in the morning), writing alone, writing in the company of friends, and writing in a room full of strangers. Every student should practice different methods of putting words on paper—with pen or pencil, with a typewriter, and by dictation—so as to learn the essential lesson that writing goes on in the head and that putting down the words is chiefly a process of transcription.

Again there might be a course in translating from a foreign language, simply because translation is a most effective means of learning the spirit and resources of one's own language. There is no better way of acquiring a prose style, except possibly the writing of verse. Such a course might be given in the English Department, or better in the writing program, by an instructor familiar with at least three foreign languages, though each of the students would have to know only one of these. The emphasis of the course would not be on an accurate rendering of the original, though a reasonable degree of fidelity would be expected, but rather on the quality of the translation as English prose.

The core of the writing program would consist of four courses, each lasting a semester and all required of undergraduates who specialize in the field. They would be courses in writing stories, in writing short plays, in writing nonfiction, and in writing verse. I say "verse" because it would be unreasonable to expect students with a primary talent for fictional or nonfictional prose to write anything that might properly be called poetry. But there is no reason why they shouldn't learn to write verse, according to the traditional rules of English prosody as well as some recent adaptations of the rules, or why they shouldn't be called upon to produce, for example, Elizabethan blank verse, Spenserian stanzas, rhymed quatrains in iambic tetrameter, eighteenth-century heroic couplets, modern syllabic verse, and Petrarchan sonnets. Scott Fitzgerald said in a letter to his daughter, who wanted to write, "The only thing that will help you is poetry, which is the most concentrated form of style." In another letter he said, "I don't think anyone can write succinct prose unless they have at least tried and failed to write a good iambic pentameter sonnet."

I think the course in writing verse would come first among the four writing courses because, in the history of literature, verse comes before prose. Then would come writing short plays, to get an ear for dialogue and a sense of construction; writing stories, a practice that includes the other skills; and writing nonfiction, which comes last because good nonfiction involves the use of fictional techniques. In all the courses there would be a similar emphasis, not on self-expression, but on the methods and conventions of the given medium. The student should learn the rules before breaking them, so as not to break them through awkwardness or inadvertence. Most of the exercises would be on assigned topics or problems. Only in the postgraduate year would the student go to work on a longer project of his own choosing: a novel, a collection of stories, a full-length play, a "subject book" (the term that publishers use for many types of nonfiction), or a book of poems.

I am not thinking here of the future critics, who would require a different sort of preparation, more in the conventional field of English and foreign literature. Still, they might be required to take at least two of the writing courses, and perhaps all four of them, so as to gain some firsthand knowledge of the problems faced by other writers. A good deal of present-day criticism has gone up in the air, as if in an untethered balloon. It is impressive and ingenious, but it doesn't always make sense to those who have undergone the drudgery of writing a novel or a play. Taking courses like those I suggest might give young critics a sharper sense of reality.

As for courses outside the writing field that students in the program might take as undergraduates, there should be more than a little individual choice and diversity. Writers are primarily men of words, and it is not a bad idea for the apprentice to learn as many words or signs as possible in as many languages as possible—not only French, German, Spanish, or Latin, but the special languages of the sciences, or philosophy, or mathematics—if he has any talent in that direction—and perhaps even the barbarous language of sociology. Writers have to deal with human beings alone and in social groups, and it is a good idea for the apprentice to learn something about history, psychology, anthropology, mythology, and human relations. There should be a close cooperation, with exchange of courses, between the writing program and the departments of speech and journalism. Perhaps it is better for the writing student to know a little about many fields outside his own than to learn a great deal about one field. In particular it is dangerous for him to specialize—as many young writers have been doing—in contemporary literature and the close analysis of texts. He should read a great deal of contemporary literature, in college and afterward, but he should read it for himself, to find what he really thinks about it and not what critics have agreed that he should find.

Remember that I am thinking about students who want to become professional writers, not about those who want to become teachers or merely to acquire a general education. Every professional writer is at least a double personality: he is at the same time a compulsive speaker, at least under his voice, and a severe listener to his own speech; a creature of instinct or emotion and a cold reasoner; a creator—to use the proud word—and a critic. In great writers those two sides of the literary personality are both developed to the utmost possible degree. In little writers and failed writers they are out of balance—usually because the critical side is too weak, but sometimes for the opposite reason, because it has developed too far and too fast in relation to the imaginative side. The sort of training that is best for a future critic or teacher—the sort now given in our best universities—is often dangerous for an apprentice writer. If he spends too much time on the close analysis of texts or the tracking down of symbols, especially in modern texts, the critical side of him ceases to be a listener, making its comments in an undertone; the voice of the critic becomes louder, firmer, more admonitory, and perhaps the other voice, that of instinct or emotion, may be frightened back into the depths of the mind.

3.

There is a traditional way of teaching advanced writing courses, one that goes back to Gates's course at Harvard in the 1890s. The class is small, usually consisting of ten to fifteen students. It meets once a week for a two-hour session, and sometimes there is a second meeting as well. At each meeting one of the students reads his latest story—or a short play, or a chapter from a novel he may be working on—then the other students make their comments and perhaps offer suggestions for improving his work. In addition the instructor has a conference with each of the students, usually one every two weeks.

I have met writing instructors, including two or three very good ones, who prefer not to meet their students as a group and who work with them only in the private conferences. Those instructors say that class meetings lead to an unhealthy sort of rivalry. They say that a student who reads his work in class is likely to become painfully self-conscious. They also say that the other students are sometimes too harsh in their comments, having adopted this fashion of asserting their own superiority, and at other times are entirely too gentle, because they will have to read in their turns and hope to be treated with equal kindness.

In spite of these valid observations and the difficulties they reveal, I believe that the traditional method of teaching advanced writing courses is still the best—though always with the proviso that each instructor must find his own most effective way. It would seem to me, however, that the class meetings are as important as the private conferences, and that a combination of the two is best for the instructor because it ends by saving his time. Most of the advice he has to offer can be utilized by all his students and might as well be addressed to them as a group. Then, in the private conferences, he can deal with finer points of structure and style. But class meetings are desirable for the students too, because they can learn at least as much from one another as from the instructor, and sometimes they learn much more. Reading their work aloud teaches them to judge its effect on an audience. They learn whether the points they tried to make are being understood, and whether their own words are awkward to pronounce. The test of good prose is reading it aloud.

As for the competitive spirit that appears when each of the students waits for his own work to be jeered at or praised, it can lead to a morbid sort of jealousy, but it can also lead to harder work and better craftsmanship. There is no reason to make a secret of the fact that writing is a highly competitive profession, and that every writer is jealous in some degree of every other writer whom he suspects of being more facile or inventive or held in higher esteem than himself. This is especially true of writers belonging to the same age group and regarding themselves as jockeys in the same race. But the literary mind has another aspect too, and writers as a group are somewhat more willing to help one another and quicker to recognize talent than members of most other professions, feeling as the best of them do that sacrifices are owed to their art. Beginners in the profession might as well be exposed to this mixture of jealousy and generosity at a very early stage in their careers, so as to inure themselves to praise and blame like Indian boys learning to undergo cold and hunger. Then the young writers may be better prepared for the ordeal of having their first books treated as masterpieces, or dismissed in a few contemptuous words, or simply overlooked.

The spirit of competition will always appear in a writing class, but the spirit of cooperation might well be encouraged. One possible though difficult way to encourage it is to have the class, or members of the class, embark on some common undertaking. The project method has been applied with great success in schools of architecture, where teams of students are often formed in the graduating class and each team is given some big architectural problem to solve. Since the days when George Pierce Baker was teaching at Harvard, the project method has also been applied in schools of the drama, where many students work together on the production of a play that one of them wrote and all of them criticized. There is no reason why a similar method might not be applied in a writing workshop.

Any one of a number of common projects might be undertaken by an advanced writing class, or by chosen members of the class. For example, the project might be the preparation of a book-length manuscript containing the best stories produced by the class, or the best essays or poems. If there were funds available and if the manuscript was good enough, it might be published. At Stanford the best stories from the top writing class have been chosen each year by vote of the class and issued as a book by the Stanford University Press.* That gave the class pride in itself as a group and a definite goal toward which to work.

A less ambitious project for a writing class—and less expensive for the university than publishing a book with a problematical sale—is for the class to issue, during the year, two

---

* I haven't seen that annual publication for many years; perhaps it was abandoned as being costly; but I can testify to the good effects of earlier volumes. At Syracuse, also with an effective writing program, the annual volume is *Syracuse Poems*. [M.C.]

or three numbers of a magazine containing the best work of its members in all fields. The class would not only write the magazine but would act as a board of editors to select material and suggest desirable revisions; and members of the class would be assigned to act as copyeditors and proofreaders. The magazine wouldn't be sold, so as not to compete with independent periodicals, including those issued by under-graduates, but it might be distributed free to bigger magazines and publishing houses. Not only would it offer practical ex-perience to students in a writing program, but it would serve as a showcase for their work and perhaps as a first step toward wider publication.

And what would be the end result of such a program, for students who took part in it?

The directors of the program could not promise to make them great writers or popular writers. For that they would need inborn or inbred qualities that no course of professional training could supply. They would have to possess what Thomas Wolfe called "the foremost quality of the artist, with-out which he is lost: the ability to get out of his own life the power to live and work by, to derive from his own experi-ence—as the fruit of all his seeing, feeling, living, joy and bitter anguish—the palpable and living substance of his art." Beyond that they would have to possess obstinate patience and energy, combined with more than the usual degree of critical judgment. But if they did not possess this rare com-bination of talents—a combination that does not always reveal itself at an early age—the talents would not be wasted, as they often are today, for want of practice and for ignorance of the fundamental writing skills.

For others in the program who proved to have critical judg-ment but lacked the imaginative force and persistence that good writers require, another prospect might be opened. As crowded as the writing profession seems to be at certain levels, there are hundreds and thousands of modest but necessary and sometimes remunerative places in the profession that are not being properly filled for want of younger men and women with the necessary training. I am thinking of places like those of story editors, copy editors, scenario and script writers, feature writers, business and technical writers, translators (the best of them are now receiving some of the credit they earned long ago), revisers of manuscripts, collaborators (sometimes known as ghosts), play doctors, and book reviewers—a whole collection of honest literary trades that are now being practiced either cynically, for shudders and laughs, or else, in many cases, with a painful degree of ignorance and ineptitude. They should be practiced with competence and integrity, not only for the sake of the literary profession and the public, but also for the sake of literature as an art—because high standards in all the literary crafts are the foundation from which great works can rise like towers against the sky.

[1957, revised 1977]

ADVENTURES OF A BOOK REVIEWER

When reading the manuscript of this book,* I remembered how I had written these pieces and a hundred others like them. "Pieces" will do for want of a better word: some of them are essays, some are reports, some are editorial pontifications, but more are unabashed book reviews—and why not? The relatively short book review was my art form for many years; it became my blank-verse meditation, my sonnet sequence, my letter to distant friends, my private journal. I did not fall into the illusion that it was a major form; no, it was dependent for its subject matter on the existence of novels or plays or poems worth writing about. Nevertheless it was *my* form: and for years I neglected my obligations to family and friends in order to get the review written. As writers tend to do with any form imposed on them by accident, I poured into it as much as possible of my adventures among events and opinions.

The accident that imposed the form was a change in my status on *The New Republic*. I had been doing a good deal of editorial work, besides running the book department since 1930, the year when Edmund Wilson decided to become a roving reporter. I had also been writing articles and reviews for the paper when there was time, but that wasn't every week; I never learned how to dash them off. Then in the autumn of 1934 Bruce Bliven and George Soule, my senior colleagues, decided that I should do less editing and more writing. They proposed that I should contribute a weekly book review and that, to have more time for it, I should spend only Tuesdays, Wednesdays and Thursdays in the office.

From that autumn the review gave a definite rhythm to my week. It started—not the week but the review—on Thursday afternoon as a vacancy at the beginning of the book section, all the rest of which was in galley proof. I knew what book I

* *Think Back on Us . . .* , edited by Henry Dan Piper. [ed.]

was going to discuss, but often I hadn't read beyond the first chapter.

"How much space will you need for your piece?" Betty Huling would ask me as she pasted up the galleys. Betty was in charge of make-up and copy editing.

"Oh—one page and five lines," I would answer with a false air of decision. (Or again, if I hoped there might be more to say, the answer would be, "One page and exactly a column on the next.") Then I would go back to dictating letters, another chore that was left to the last moment. In my three days at the office I never had time for everything.

FRIDAY. It was my day for reading the book, that is, for being confronted in solitude with a new personality and a subject matter that might be totally unfamiliar. What should I, what could I say about them? A general reviewer is supposed to have been endowed at birth with challenging opinions on every topic, but the good fairies had neglected me. Instead of starting with opinions, I had nothing but a pretty wide range of interests and a few presuppositions: as notably that literature is a part of life, not subordinate to other parts, such as politics and economics, but intimately affected by them and sometimes affecting them in turn. All the parts were interwoven, I believed, in the web of history. That was a serviceable belief, but only as a background for opinions about the book at hand. Those I must find by going deeper into the book and into myself. What was the author really saying, as opposed to what he intended and appeared to say? What light did he cast on the drama of our times? What did I truly think about him? It seems to me now that I was writing not so much to express my opinions as to discover what they were.

Parenthetically. That search for opinions, consistent ones if possible, goes a long way toward explaining the popularity of Marxism in the 1930's, particularly among reviewers, commentators and foreign correspondents. The secure world of their childhood had fallen apart. They were looking for a scheme of values, a direction, a skeleton key that would unlock almost any sort of political or literary situation (and help them to write a cogent page). Marxism, in a more or less rudimentary form, was the key that many of them found. Uncompromisingly materialistic as it purported to be, it served the same unifying purpose for writers of the depression years that Emerson's uncompromising idealism had served for New England rebels of an earlier time. Emerson wrote in 1837, ". . . let me see every trifle bristling with the polarity that ranges it instantly on an eternal law . . . and the world lies no longer a dull miscellany and lumber-room, but has form and order; there is no trifle, there is no puzzle, but one design unites and animates the farthest pinnacle and the lowest trench." Writers of the depression years also believed in an all-pervasive design and in a law of universal polarity which they called the class struggle. Adopting that "long view," as it was called, I wrote in 1934 an essay called "Art Tomorrow," reprinted in this volume.

> Two housewives [I said] gossiping on the back porch about their husbands' jobs and the price of groceries, a small merchant bankrupt in the next block, a love affair broken off, a mortgage foreclosed, a manufacturer's rise to power—all these incidents take their place in a historical pattern that is also illuminated by revolts in Spain, a new factory in the Urals, an obscure battle in the interior of China. Values exist again, after an age in which they seemed to be lost; good and evil are embodied in men who struggle.

I did not realize that I was being less Marxian than Emersonian—though without Emerson's poetic force; or again that my companions of the 1930's would be more bitterly disillusioned than the rashest of his disciples at Brook Farm. Close parenthesis.

SATURDAY. In the rhythm of the week, that was the day when I confidently expected that the review would write itself. I set to work in the morning, then found again that nothing wrote itself, not even the first sentence. After staring at the typewriter, which had assumed a hostile face, I would go back to the book, reading parts of it more attentively and taking pages of notes that there would never be space to use. In the afternoon I would go for a long walk. After the first mile I found my opinions taking shape in words, as if tramped out of clay, and on happier Saturdays I might come back with a first sentence and even an outline of what I hoped to write.

SUNDAY. In the end that became my day for writing, simply because the review had to reach the Steinberg Press in Brooklyn by ten o'clock on Monday morning; otherwise I might have spent another week on it. I started early, in the deluded hope that I might be finished by late afternoon; then for once we could go out for dinner and the movies. But there was always something to add or delete, something to rephrase, and the result was that I worked late into the night. Why did I make everything hard for myself? One reason, I suspect, was that I had been trained as a poet, not a journalist, and that I instinctively tried to combine the qualities of sound journalistic prose with those of a poem or a short story. That is, I tried to make an accurate report that would place the book in our momently changing world, but at the same time I hoped that the report would have strength in itself to outlast the moment. I wanted it to stand as a balanced structure, fashioned with an economy of materials, a richness of internal relations, a beginning that set the tone, and a cadenced march to an inevitable conclusion. The problem, I found, was largely one of sequence. Each statement had to follow another logically—for I was presenting an argument—but there also had to be an associative or temporal connection between them, as in a poem. Somehow I had to unite "then" and "therefore," the *post hoc* of narration and the *propter hoc* of exposition, if I wanted to produce a reasoned criticism that could be read like a story.

Of course I did not often succeed in reconciling those contradictory purposes, but I would keep trying through the night, while facing the additional demands of space and time. Space was the easier to meet of those two inexorable conditions. When I said off-handedly on Thursday afternoon, "One page and five lines," or, "One page and a column on the next," I had issued a challenge to myself and, in effect, had given a form to the review, as if I had undertaken to write the fourteen lines of a sonnet or the twenty-eight of a ballade. On Friday and Saturday I was haunted by that vacancy of precise dimensions: how could it ever be filled? By Sunday, however, I had always assembled too many notes, and the problem became one of selection. It seems to me now, in memory, that I solved the problem by omitting my best paragraphs; usually these are the easiest to omit because they are more personal or general and less essential to the immediate argument. As for revising to an exact number of lines, that became a simple matter as soon as I learned to set the margins of my typewriter to the average character count of a *New Republic* column. Betty Huling told me that I never went wrong by more than a line.

Time was a more difficult requirement. My stubborn habit of revision, combined with what seems to me an invincible sluggishness of spirit, kept me working into the early morning hours. I would glance at my watch to make sure there was still time to catch the last mail train for New York, then write another version of the final paragraph. Always it threatened to become either briefly dogmatic or wordily sententious; one or the other of those faults was hard to avoid when I was filling exactly ten lines at three in the morning. Sometimes I saw the full moon setting from my study window, and in summer I might still be at my desk when the room was brightened with dawn.

That was after we moved to the country in 1936. Earlier reviews had been written in a variety of places: our Greenwich Village apartment (till we found that my typing disturbed the baby and vice versa); a room in the Hotel Chelsea, where the walls are thick; at Yaddo, the artists' colony in Saratoga Springs; or in the very old Riverton Inn, thirty miles from Hartford. I became a virtuoso in mail trains and post-office schedules. There was a train from Saratoga at two in the morning; from Hartford at three (I nearly missed that one after a dash over icy roads); from South Norwalk at four (but that was a forty-five mile drive); then at last I discovered that I could give my special-delivery envelope to the mail clerk on the six-o'clock train from Pawling, New York, only ten miles from our house. Once I missed the train at Pawling and raced it twenty miles down the line, till I caught up with it at Croton Falls. Once I nearly didn't get home. It was a lovely June morning alive with birds, and the train was half an hour late. On the drive back I began to fall asleep. That had happened before, and I had parked by the roadside and taken a brief nap. This time I was so close to home that I thought I could hold out. "It's only a mile," I said to myself, biting my lip hard. "I can keep awake . . . awake." Suddenly I woke and found the car on a bank twenty feet above the highway with its left front wheel in the air. I wrenched at the steering wheel, saved the car from falling, and bumped my way along the bank till it sloped over rock ledges to the level of the road.

Thanks to the postal service, which must have been more reliable in the depression years, the review always reached the Steinberg Press before the Monday-morning deadline. Betty Huling was there to read it, and she turned it over to the linotyper without changing a word (though sometimes she ventured a comma). Nobody else saw the review until copies of *The New Republic* were delivered to the office on Wednesday morning. Often Bruce Bliven and George Soule must have been dismayed by what they read, but as gentlemanly colleagues they never complained and never suggested that I might show them the manuscript before sending it to the printer. In effect I was speaking for myself, on my own responsibility, to what had become my own circle of readers. It was an extraordinary privilege for which, if I could have afforded the gesture, I would gladly have paid *The New Republic* instead of accepting a salary.

I like to think that the personal tone of these reviews and reports—with the extra hours that went into each of them and the accumulation of notes that could not be used, but that still became implicit in what I said—has given them a certain durability. Perhaps, by making things harder for myself, I also made them harder for other reviewers and thereby contributed a little toward raising the standards of the profession. As for the subject matter of the pieces, they deal with past events and with an assortment of authors among whom some are lastingly famous, but others are out of fashion; they express judgments that in some cases are embarrassingly simple and far from those I would express today; but I think they have their value as part of the historical record. To keep the record straight, I made no changes in the text beyond striking out some adjectives, adverbs and conjunctions, of which there were too many, and omitting two or three of those questionable last paragraphs. The opinions stand as dredged from my mind on Fridays and Saturdays; the judgments stand as revised on those long-ago Sunday midnights. They tell the story of how a rather unsophisticated young man, endowed by accident with a degree of independence, confronted the social and literary issues of the depression years, and how he gradually learned that they were a great deal more complicated than they had seemed in the beginning. Perhaps the young man's story might stand for that of many others.

[1967]

ON CRITICISM:
THE MANY-WINDOWED HOUSE
(excerpts)

First of all I believe that a definition of criticism should be as simple and short as possible. Mightn't it be enough to say that *criticism is writing that deals with works of art?* Any narrower definition would restrict the liberty of the critic and might also restrict his usefulness.

I believe that criticism should be approached as one of the literary arts. The word "literary" implies that it should be written in the language of English literature and not—as a great deal of recent criticism has been written—in some variety of philosophical or medical or social-scientific jargon. When a critic's language is awkward, involved, and pedantic, we are entitled to question his ability to recognize good prose. As for the word "arts," it implies that criticism is not a science based on exact measurement. If it is going to be persuasive, however, it had better include a great deal of objectively verifiable information.

I do not believe that it is one of the major literary arts. The major arts are poetry, fiction, drama, and also nonfictional or documentary writing so long as this last is a field for exercise of the interpretive imagination. Without those arts, literary criticism would cease to exist for want of subject matter. Therefore a critic cannot afford to be arrogant. He is dealing in most cases with better works that he has proved his capability of writing.

I believe that the first of his functions is to select works of art worth writing about, with special emphasis on works that are new, not much discussed, or widely misunderstood. Incidentally this task has been neglected by academic critics, most of whom prefer to write about works already regarded as canonical. His second function is to describe or analyze or reinterpret the chosen works as a basis for judgments which can sometimes be merely implied. In practice his problem may be to explain why he enjoys a particular book, and perhaps to find new reasons for enjoying it, so as to deepen his readers' capacity for appreciation.

In practice, again, I always start and end with the text itself, and am willing to accept the notion of the textual or integral critics that the principal value of a work lies in the complexity and unity of its internal relations. But I also try to start with a sort of innocence, that is, with a lack of preconceptions about what I might or might not discover. To preserve the innocence, I prefer not to read the so-called secondary or critical sources until my own discoveries, if any, have been made.

What I read after the text itself are other texts by the same author. It is a mistake to approach each work as if it were an absolutely separate production, a unique artifact, the last and single relic of a buried civilization. Why not approach it as the author does? It seems to me that any author of magnitude has his eye on something larger than the individual story or poem or novel. He wants each of these to be as good as possible, and self-subsistent, but he also wants it to serve as a chapter or aspect of the larger work that is his lifetime production, his *oeuvre*. This larger work is also part of the critic's subject matter.

In this fashion the author's biography comes into the picture, and so do his notebooks and letters. They aren't part of the text to be criticized, but often they help us to find in it what we might otherwise have missed, and they serve as a warning against indulging in fantasies about the text or deforming it into a Gothic fable of love, death, and homoeroticism.* We should read not to impose our meanings on a work, but to see what we can find.

Innocence is the keynote, and ignorance that tries to become knowledge by asking questions of many sorts. There are internal questions of structure and style and imagery to which the answers are vastly revealing, but there are also questions about the external relations of a work of art. Whom was it written for? Is the author a spokesman for some particular region or group or social class (as Dreiser, to give one instance, spoke for the new men of the Middle West)? Is he trying to invest some new background with the dignity of legend? What is the implied moral of his fable? If he has

* A reference to Leslie Fiedler's work, mentioned previously in the essay. [ed.]

written several books, have they always implied the same moral? (Here I am calling to mind the simple fact that authors change, and that critics are wrong when they speak of "Hawthorne" or "Whitman" as if each name stood for a single and permanent aggregate of qualities. "Which Hawthorne?" I like to ask them, and "Whitman at what period of his career?")

One might also ask whether every book an author has written is a proper subject for certain elaborate methods of criticism, including symbolic analysis. Sometimes details from an author's life might help us to decide. We know, for example, that Melville spent about a year on *Moby Dick* and that he rewrote the book from a lost early version concerned chiefly with the whaling industry. We also know that he wrote *Pierre* in about six weeks while on the edge of a nervous breakdown. That of course is biographical knowledge, but aren't we justified in using it? Aren't critics losing their sense of proportion when they discuss both books, the masterpiece and the nightmare, in the same elaborate terms, especially if those terms make the nightmare seem more important than the masterpiece? Aren't they wrong to look for the same sort of symbols in *Pierre* that Joyce put into *Finnegans Wake*, on which we know that he slaved for almost twenty years?

Innocence is the keynote, but not innocence that refrains from learning about an author's life on the ground that such knowledge would destroy the purity of one's critical method. A truly innocent search might lead us into studies of the society in which an author lived, if they were necessary to explain his meaning. Or again, remembering as we should that a novel or a poem is not merely a structure of words but also a device for producing a certain effect on an audience, as if it were a motionless machine for creating perpetual motion—remembering this, we might try to find the nature of the particular audience for which it was written. That would be deviating into the sociological or affective fallacy, but still it might be a useful and stimulating piece of, yes, critical research.

I believe, in short, that criticism is a house with many windows.

[1970]

LOOKING FOR THE ESSENTIAL ME

In the general field of what might be called memoiristic literature the distinction between nonfiction and fiction is sometimes hard to maintain. Both the autobiographer and the
autobiographical novelist are trying to impose a shape on
events related in sequence; they both tell stories. They both
have as material their personal experience and acquired
knowledge—in other words, their memories. The difference
is that the novelist feels free to combine memories from different sources and even to recount events that never took
place. The memoirist is more humble in his acceptance of
"what happened" as a guide to what he should write. Perhaps
he feels that life itself is the source of all good stories and
that his central problem is one of recognition and interpretation rather than invention.

There are times, however, when the difference between
the fictional and nonfictional memoirs seems to be chiefly a
matter of pronouns. The true memoirist says "I" or "we";
the novelist more often says "he" or "she," and when he does
speak in the first person, he is usually presenting the thoughts
of an imagined character. But generalities about pronouns
are riddled with exceptions. Two of the best American autobiographies—*Ushant* by Conrad Aiken and *The Education
of Henry Adams*—are narratives in the third person; Aiken
refers to himself as "D" (or Demarest) while Adams is always
"he."

Are there other fictional elements in these two exemplary
memoirs? In rereading *The Education* one cannot fail to observe that important episodes in Adams's life—as notably his
marriage—are totally omitted from the narrative. His account
of each event is "the truth" so far as he can render it, but he
has made a selection among true events in order to give the
book a novelistic form. It can indeed be read as a novel—a
better one, incidentally, than Dreiser's purported novel *The
"Genius,"* which was also the work of an author looking

back at his career and trying to capture the essence of what happened.

The specific qualities of memoiristic books, whether or not they purport to be novels, largely depend on the period in life at which they were written. Often they are a product of youth, written before the author had accumulated enough experience to speak with authority. A few such books have a vividness and immediacy that might have been lost if he had waited a few years; a famous example is *The Sun Also Rises*, published when Hemingway was 27. John Glassco's *Memoirs of Montparnasse* was mostly written before the author was 21, although it wasn't published until long afterward. It should be read at last and recognized as the most dramatic of the many narratives dealing with Paris in the 1920's. But those two books are exceptions to a general rule, namely, that most memoirs are written too soon. They appear (or don't appear) as first novels that might all bear the same title: *The Education of* (supply the author's name). Usually the story they tell is that of his progress from being a mere twerp to becoming an oaf.

Memoirs written in middle life deserve, and are likely to find, more readers, since the author has by then accumulated a richer store of memories. He may choose among them after reflection or he may simply probe into his unconscious: Whatever lives there vividly will be what he needs, and perhaps what the world needs. The middle-aged author may also have achieved a higher degree of self-awareness, and this is one of the standards, perhaps the central standard, by which memoirs should be judged. At the same time he retains enough animal vitality to work hard and long at his chosen task.

Animal vitality is one of the gifts that an old man may find he has lost. I have to make this observation when speaking of memoirs written in age, a subject close to my present concerns. I have been a memoirist almost from the beginning; even my first book of poems, *Blue Juniata*, was a memoir of sorts. My first prose book, *Exile's Return*, started out as a personal memoir, though later, in the course of writing and revision, it became something close to a collective novel about the members of my literary age group. I wish now that I could write again with the same confident ease.

Having continued to work in the field at intervals for half

a century, I find that the aged man or woman writing memoirs is burdened with special handicaps, among which the mere lack of energy is not the greatest. A worse affliction is that some of his memories are not as sharp or richly detailed as they were when he was a mere septuagenarian. But the details can be recaptured if one perseveres; there are letters and daybooks to consult and tunes that run in one's head, each suggesting a mood of yesteryear. Meanwhile one finds that the older memoirist has a few real and surpassing advantages over his younger rivals. Perhaps the greatest of them is that he knows exactly what he wants to do, which is to shovel aside the rubbish that has accumulated over the years and to find beneath it his—or her—real shape and story.

In the course of my own search through and under memories, I have looked for what Kenneth Burke, my oldest friend, used to call watershed moments, that is, the scenes or episodes after which one's thoughts flow in a different direction. One of those moments occurred when I was 14 years old. I stood alone on the east bank of the Mississippi at Quincy, Ill., where my grandmother lived. The river was a mile wide and from bank to bank its current moved past me solidly, relentlessly. A hundred yards from shore a water-soaked log bobbed up and down while being carried onward. The scene haunted me, I didn't know why, and later I dreamed about it. In the dream I had become that water-soaked log, but somehow the log had eyes to observe what happened on the bank as it was carried along. Still later, much later, I came to feel that I had found a guiding metaphor. The river was history and we were all involved in it as objects on its relentlessly moving surface. It would never turn back. Our only freedom was to become more conscious of the spectacle as it unrolled.

That was an underlying perception, and there were others. My father was a religious man, a Swedenborgian with an utter faith in the wisdom of Divine Providence; for him, everything that happened was part of God's plan. I accepted the faith for a time, as children do, then gradually abandoned it. In part and instinctively I replaced it with another faith, this time in nature or life or the human community, I wasn't sure what to call it. Whatever its character, there was some force outside ourselves that would take charge of things in its secret and dilatory fashion. It was no use being vastly ambitious for one's person. If there were capabilities inside us, they would come out over the years and people would recognize them: "We pass for what we are," Emerson said. If there was little inside, we had better accept the situation and live with it.

Not so long ago, as one comes to reckon time, I used to hear college students asking, "Who am I?" They were genuinely distressed in those days about the question of their personal identities. I listened to them with sympathy, but also with a measure of disdain. "When I was your age," I wanted to tell them, and didn't, "I knew damned well who I was." Now I am not so certain. Since I am 85, the question comes back to me, if in a slightly different form: "Who *was* I?" and the answer isn't always what I expected. As late as 1930 I had regarded myself as one representative of a new generation in American letters, one person among many, and otherwise as a young man without special qualities. I was not a leader, not an exhorter, not an actor in the great events of our time, but chiefly an observer and recorder. I listened and remembered without trying to enforce my opinions on others. There is the possibility, however, that I was a more uncommon character than I suspected at the time. I was to write of myself in the foreword to a recent book, *The Dream of the Golden Mountains*:

"And that author, that observer who is trying to be candid about himself, what sort of person was he in 1930? If one looks back at him he seems to be less typical, even of his own age group, than he once fancied himself to be. He was still a country boy after spending most of his life in cities; he had a farmer's blunt hands. 'Look at the hands if you get a chance,' that man of elegant letters John Peale Bishop wrote to his Princeton friend Edmund Wilson. 'The plowboy of the western world who has been to Paris.' The plowboy admitted that he was awkward, credulous, either rash or exuberant at moments, and usually persistent (or would you call it stubborn?). He never forgot that he came of people without pretensions, not quite members of the respectable middle class. He was slow of speech and had a farmer's large silences, though he was not slow-witted; people were fooled sometimes. He mentally revised his words, often until the moment had passed to utter them. Perhaps one might call him a wordsmith essentially, working at his forge and anvil, devoted to the craft of hammering his thoughts into what he hoped would be lasting shapes."

That was Malcolm Cowley in 1930, so far as his character can be reconstructed from memory and, where memory fails, from written records supplemented by the impressions of surviving friends. I welcome him back. To search for one's past is a fascinating occupation and one that may be appropriate to the older memoirist; it is among the privileges that partly compensate for his handicaps. In earlier years he had been too busy living among others to think much about himself, but now at last he has an opportunity, if not always the time, to discover the shape of his life. He has the perspective of years, in which crucial events continue to stand out, while much that is trivial fades into the background. He may have acquired the useful feeling that he has lived in history.

All these are advantages enjoyed by the older memoirist, if he can make the most of them. Also he is free to write with perfect candor, remembering, as he should at every moment, that he has nothing to lose by telling the truth. He feels that every human life is a drama, brief or prolonged, commonplace or astounding, and different in detail from every other human life. The difference, however, is not complete. If the outlines of the drama have been laid bare, if the protagonist has truly depicted himself, then others will recognize their own features in the portrait. Every man, every woman, is not only a person but also a representative of the age in which he has lived. An old man can cite that principle as an ultimate justification for seeking a shape in his own life.

And so I continue the search. Erect in an armchair or sprawled on a couch, I try to read the book of my days. It was set in type long ago by an apprentice, with errors great and small. Later it was left outdoors to be sunned on and rained on. Many of the words are blurred. Whole pages, whole chapters have been torn from the binding and mislaid. I strain to reconstruct those chapters, often finding that I would prefer to forget them, but still I persevere. This occupation carried on in silence, not even my eyes moving as I turn an imaginary page, absorbs me more than the reading of any published book. When I come to the last chapter, what shall I have found—a drama, an essay, a novel, or even a sequence of novels? In any case I shall have read a story in still unwritten words, a story that is long, apparently confused, but that still has a beginning, middle and end ordained by nature or biology. I shall have discovered or unveiled a shape in time. I shall have revealed to myself a person who is possibly the real Me. What if it should prove to be only a bag stuffed with straw and having painted-on features instead of a face? In that case it will still serve to frighten away the blackbirds from my secret garden.

[1984]

A BRIEF BIBLIOGRAPHY OF
CRITICAL WRITINGS ON
MALCOLM COWLEY

Bak, Hans, *Malcolm Cowley, The Formative Years, 1898–1930*. Nijmegen, The Netherlands: Katholieke Universiteit, 1988. (*A critical biography running more than 800 pages, the most comprehensive so far. A second volume is expected.*)

Butts, William and Yolanda, eds., *Horns of Plenty: Malcolm Cowley and His Generation* (an ongoing quarterly begun in 1988). 2041 West Farragut Avenue, Chicago, Illinois 60625. (*A wide-ranging source of Cowley ephemera, related studies, and anecdotal pieces.*)

Core, George, "Malcolm Cowley 1898–," in *American Writers,* Supplement II, Part 1. New York: Scribners, 1981. (*One of the best brief studies of Cowley's life and work available, an elegant piece.*)

Eisenberg, Diane U., *Malcolm Cowley, A Checklist of His Writings, 1916–1973*. Carbondale: Southern Illinois University Press, 1975. (*A nearly exhaustive bibliography; invaluable for research.*)

Herendeen, Warren, and Donald J. Parker, eds., *The Visionary Company, A Magazine of the Twenties,* Special Malcolm Cowley Issue, Summer 1987, v. 2 #2, v. 3 #1. Dobbs Ferry, New York: Mercy College. (*Contains many fine critical and anecdotal pieces, as well as an important update of the Eisenberg bibliography.*)

Kempf, James Michael, *The Early Career of Malcolm Cowley, A Humanist Among the Moderns*. Baton Rouge: Louisiana State University Press, 1985. (*A ground-breaking study of lasting value, quite readable.*)

Piper, Henry Dan, introductions to "Think Back on Us . . . ," and "A Many-Windowed House." Carbondale: Southern Illinois University Press, 1967 and 1970, respectively.

(*Broad-ranging and lively; among the first critical esti-mations of Cowley's work.*)

Revell, Peter, "Malcolm Cowley," in "American Poets, 1880–1945, Second Series," *Dictionary of Literary Biography,* v. 48. Detroit: Gale Research Company, 1983. (*A general biographical study focusing on Cowley's poetry.*)

Simpson, Lewis, "Malcolm Cowley and the American Writer," *Sewanee Review* 84 (Spring 1976). (*A detailed examination focusing on the theme of exile in Cowley's criticism, memoirs, and poetry; an estimable piece.*)

Young, Thomas Daniel, ed., *Conversations with Malcolm Cowley.* Jackson: University of Mississippi Press, 1986. (*Contains many significant pieces, among them the* Paris Review *interview and Cowley's interview with the FBI.*)

INDEX